FOR MALICE

AND

MERCY

A World War II Novel

FOR MALICE AND MERCY
A World War II Novel

By Gary W. Toyn

American
Legacy
Media

Published by American Legacy Media - AmericanLegacyMedia.com

This is a work of fiction. Names, characters, places, and incidents are a product of the author's imagination, or are represented fictitiously for literary effect. Any references to actual businesses, entities, events, or locales, is unintentional and without malice. With the exception of public figures, all characters depicted herein are fictional, despite some that may appear to resemble actual persons, living or dead, and such similarities are entirely unintentional and coincidental. The opinions expressed are those of the characters and should not be construed as the author's.

Cover design: Kim Alexander, Interior design: Sue Thurber

Softcover ISBN : 978-0-9818489-7-6
ISBN Kindle format: 978-0-9818489-8-3
ISBN EPUB format: 978-0-9818489-9-0
ISBN Audiobook format: 978-1-7364576-0-3

Library of Congress Cataloging-in-Publication Data

Names: Toyn, Gary W., 1961- author.
Title: For malice and mercy : a World War II novel / by Gary W. Toyn.
Description: Clinton : American Legacy Media, 2021. | Includes
  bibliographical references. | Summary: "A meticulously researched World
  War II family saga inspired by actual events, about a German-American
  family from Utah. The parents are targeted as Nazi sympathizers, sent to
  an internment camp then forcefully deported to Germany as pawns in FDRs
  top-secret prisoner swap with the Third Reich. When their son's B-17 is
  shot down over Germany, his ability to speak fluent German helps him
  evade capture. When the Gestapo is on his trail, he's pursued as a spy
  and faces certain death if they can catch him. His life depends on the
  daring plan of two unlikely collaborators. The family must endure the
  unthinkable if they hope to be reunited"-- Provided by publisher.
Identifiers: LCCN 2021000314 (print) | LCCN 2021000315 (ebook) | ISBN
  9780981848976 (paperback) | ISBN 9780981848983 (kindle edition) | ISBN
  9780981848990 (epub)
Subjects: LCSH: World War, 1939-1945--Fiction. | German Americans--Fiction.
  | GSAFD: Historical fiction. | Spy stories.
Classification: LCC PS3620.O987 F67 2021 (print) | LCC PS3620.O987
  (ebook) | DDC 813/.6--dc23
LC record available at https://lccn.loc.gov/2021000314
LC ebook record available at https://lccn.loc.gov/2021000315

Printed in the United States of America
2 4 6 8 10 9 7 5 3 1

Dedicated to:
Danita, My eternal companion and dearest friend
and
My goodly parents,
Robert E. and Joy W. Toyn

CHAPTER 1

June 3, 1939, 9:30 a.m.
Huntsville, Utah

Hank Meyer walked with purpose across his dew-soaked front yard, passing by his kitchen window. He waved at his sister Ella and her best friend Billie Russell. They looked on in curiosity. Hank smiled as he chatted with the boy they didn't recognize. The girls' eyes were glued on the new young man as he walked behind Hank through the front door. Hank cleared his throat and announced, "Hey everyone, this is Chester Bailey. He just moved into the old Johnson home."

Ella and Billie gave him an admiring giggle. Chester's broad shoulders were a clear indication he was not afraid of hard, physical work. Scruffy around the edges, he was all farm boy. He stood at least six feet tall, a few inches taller than Hank, but both were similar in their athletic build. Chester wore faded denim overalls, a snug fit over his solid frame. His piercing green eyes contrasted with his unkempt, sun-bleached hair. Ella nudged Billie and whispered, "Stop staring."

"This is Ella, and this is Billie," Hank pointed, then watched as Chester looked first at Ella, then back at Billie. Ella's dark hair outlined her round face and rich, brown eyes. Her plump frame was in stark contrast to Billie's build, which was long and lean. Her blonde hair was pulled into a tight ponytail, and her bright blue eyes glowed against her tanned complexion.

"So you must be Ella," Chester pointed with confidence. "You look like your brother."

"That's me." She ventured a half-hearted wave, her face turning pink.

"And this is Billie. But don't call her Virginia," Hank teased. "She hates her real name." Billie shot him a glower and he ignored it, just like he had the countless other times she had shot him a nasty look.

Ella tilted her head toward her friend, "Billie lives in that house over there." Ella motioned westward, then pointed out the kitchen window. "Her grandma lives next door in that house to the east."

"I just stay here in the middle house to save time," Billie said with a shrug. Chester laughed, and Billie grinned back at him with delight.

"Her mom and dad are sort of like humanitarians," Ella explained. "They go around giving away food and stuff to people who are down on their luck. Billie stays at her grandma's house while they're gone and she gets to use her mom's car whenever she likes. How would that be?" Ella teased, not trying to hide her envy.

Just then, Hank and Ella's parents entered the room and smiled at the group. Hank pointed at Chester with an open hand "Mama and Papa, this is Chester Bailey." They both dipped their heads to acknowledge the new visitor in their home.

Chester offered his hand, and they both gave it a polite shake. "It's a pleasure to meet you Mr. and Mrs. Meyer."

"They were both born in Germany," Hank explained. "They joined the Church there and then came here to be with the Saints in Utah."

"That's interesting," Chester nodded. "How long have you lived here?"

"Many years now," Papa looked up at the ceiling for an answer. "Over twenty years now for me. For Mama, a little less than that. But ve are both proud to be Americans! Ve love it here."

Chester grinned at hearing Papa's distinct German accent.

"Just so you know, Chester," Hank added, "you may hear us speak German among ourselves at home, but we all speak English too."

Chester gave a curious but interested grin.

"So, Chester," Papa asked, "vere are you coming from?"

"Logan, Utah, sir," he replied.

"Vat brings you to Huntsville?"

"Well, sir…" Chester scratched his arm as he thought. "My dad needed more land to graze his sheep. We made an offer on the Johnson's property, and they threw in that old house to sweeten the deal, so we just decided to move up here and fix it up."

Papa grinned and was about to ask another question when Billie interrupted.

"What year in school are you?" She flipped her ponytail over her shoulder, a flirtatious smile spread across her face.

"I'll be a junior next year." He looked at Hank with a grin.

"Oh!" Billie's eyes opened wide. "You'll be going to Weber High School with me and Ella. We're both juniors."

"Yup, I guess so," Chester answered.

And Hank will be just starting at Weber High, as a little ol' freshman," Billie added.

Hank gave a slight shake of his head, but he had no comeback.

"Did you play any sports at your old school?" Billie asked, a clear challenge in her voice.

Hank jumped in, not about to let Billie dominate the conversation.

"Chester is a great pitcher. It's too bad he didn't grow up here. We could have won a game or two."

"Our school has lost every game for the last twenty years. Even Lou Gehrig couldn't have helped us win a game," Billie declared and everyone chuckled.

Chester eyed Billie and asked, "So you must be the girl baseball player Hank told me about."

"Maybe. What did he tell you?"

"Oh, that you can play about as good as any boy. Maybe better."

"Hank said that about me?" She looked at Hank with a raised eyebrow. "Well at least he admits that I'm better than he is. It's about time."

Hank looked at her in mild protest, but knew better than to start another argument.

"So," Chester looked at Billie. "I hear there's a pick-up game at the park in a half hour. You wanna come play?"

"Absolutely," Billie replied. "Let me get my mitt."

Hank watched her dash to the door toward her house, then after a few steps she stopped, hung her shoulders, and returned to say, "I forgot." Her voice dripped with embarrassment. "Charlie Wangsguard has my mitt, and he's at work tonight."

Hank looked at the ceiling, knowing Billie was stretching the truth.

Ella looked at Hank, sensing a confrontation brewing. "Hank, don't you have an extra glove somewhere for Billie?"

"Yeah." Hank let out a exasperate sigh. "Let me go find it." Billie smiled with relief as she followed Hank up to his room.

As they reached the top of the stairs, Hank confronted Billie. "Why didn't you just tell him you always borrow a mitt from Charlie Wangsguard?"

"I didn't lie," Billie protested. "I always use Charlie's extra mitt. And he has it."

Hank rolled his eyes as he knelt down in front of his messy closet. He rummaged through boxes of childhood memories and keepsakes he had accumulated over the years.

"It's got to be in here somewhere," Hank complained. Digging beneath old coats and wrinkled shirts, he uncovered a dusty leather suitcase and tossed it aside.

"I know I saw it in here a few months ago," he mumbled to himself. The treasure hunt seemed to go on forever.

"Hank, they're waiting. We haven't got all day," Billie complained.

"There it is!" Hank smiled as he retrieved the mitt and slapped it a few times on his hand to shake away the dust.

"Great." Billie took the glove and tried it on for size. "It'll do for now. It shouldn't take me too long to break it in again." She twisted and tugged on the mitt's leather to loosen it up.

As Hank threw his clothes back into his closet, Billie noticed the bright label attached to the handle of the leather suitcase.

"Aw, how cute," she gushed. "Look at little Hank's handwriting. In crayon, no less."

Hank smiled at his eleven-year-old penmanship, which carefully spelled the word *Deutschland* on the luggage tag.

"Are these your keepsakes from your trip to Germany?"

"Yeah." Hank loosened the belt buckles on the suitcase. Carefully, he opened the lid to reveal the valuable souvenirs he had safeguarded for the last five years.

"What is that?" Billie's eyes bulged as Hank's hand hovered over a brown shirt with a black and red armband emblazoned with a swastika.

"That's my uniform for the Hitler Youth. They gave it to me." He removed the long-sleeved shirt and a pair of lederhosen and held them up for inspection. Billie caressed the uniform as though it was a museum artifact.

"Wow. It's so tiny. Look how small you were," Billie laughed. "That shirt wouldn't even fit over your shoulder," she teased.

Hank held up the shirt to his neck and chuckled, "Maybe if I try, I can still fit in it?" They both laughed as the small uniform was dwarfed by Hank's chest and arms that strained the fabric of his well-worn shirt.

"How did you get all this stuff?" Billie raised one eyebrow.

"I was eleven years old. I don't remember too much anymore, but I do remember that two older boys showed up at our scout meeting and said," Hank paused and then spoke in perfect German, "You are now part of the Hitler Youth Organization. Seig Heil!" Hank smiled, raising his hand in a mock Nazi salute, then laughed. "To me, it was all just fun and games, going camping, doing drills, singing songs."

"That was the worst summer ever for me because I didn't know what to do while you and Ella were gone," Billie laughed at herself.

Hank removed a souvenir black and white photo of Hitler, and Billie shook her head.

"Isn't that the German guy they talk about all the time?" she asked.

"Yes. Adolf Hitler," Hank replied, tossing the photo aside.

"Why did you keep that?" A dark, bitter tone laced Billie's voice.

"I don't know. Just did. They gave each of us a few of these photos and told us to hang them up in our room or wherever we could. At the time I didn't know who he was. Someday they may be valuable. Who knows?"

"What else is in there?" Billie reached to the bottom of the suitcase for a large, folded piece of red cloth, a dark black stripe visible along one edge. "What is that?"

"What do you think it is?"

"Is it a flag?" Billie's eyes were wide in disbelief.

"Yeah, but don't take it out. I don't want to fold it up again."

"Th...that's..." Billie stuttered. "That's a real Nazi flag? How'd you get it?"

"My *Opa*," Hank paused, figuring she didn't know what *Opa* meant. "My Grandpa ripped it down from a light pole near his house and asked me if I wanted it to show my friends. He told me to hide it while we were in Germany, and I just put it in my suitcase."

"Why on earth would you want to keep that?"

"I don't know. At the time I thought it was a fun souvenir to bring home and show off, I guess."

"Don't you think it's a little spooky to have a Nazi flag?"

"Well…I never thought about it until now," Hank hesitated. "Mama and Papa still don't know I have all this stuff, and I just forgot about it. But Mama would be furious."

"Well, look at you," Billie teased. "Strait-laced Hank Meyer is keeping secrets from his mommy. I won't tell a soul."

Hank looked at her with skepticism, then heard someone coming up the stairs. He slammed the suitcase closed and stashed it under his mountain of dirty clothes.

A knock came on the door frame. "Are you coming?" Ella asked. "Chester's feeling pretty awkward down there explaining to Mama and Papa about raising sheep. You need to go rescue him," she laughed.

Hank took one last look at his closet, making sure his suitcase was still hidden.

CHAPTER 2

June 3, 1939 – 11:00 a.m.
Huntsville, Utah

The baseball diamond at Huntsville Town Park was about a quarter mile away. As they walked, Hank pointed to the sky as a small airplane flew overhead and shouted, "J-3 Piper Cub!"

"Yep, sure is," Billie answered with a little frustration in her voice. She scanned the horizons for more aircraft, scowling at Hank's smug face.

When they arrived at the park, a group of six boys were playing catch.

"It's about time you guys got here," one of them called out. "What took you so long?"

Hank stuffed his fingers into his glove. "Shut up, George. Just be glad we're here."

Chester put on his glove and began playing three-way catch with Hank and Billie.

Ella sat on the grass as she watched the players throw the ball to each other.

Chester looked at Hank and asked, "So, how do you play with only nine players?"

"We play work-ups," Hank explained.

"What's that?"

"We rotate positions with every at-bat. After you bat, you go to right field, and you work your way up until it's your turn to bat again."

"After you bat, you go to right field, then center field, left field, and so on?"

"You got it." Hank rubbed his thumb over the seam of a ball. "You rotate after each at-bat."

"Okay," Chester nodded. "Do you run the bases?"

"When you get a hit, you run. And you run as far as you can make it on your turn. If you get a home run, you bat again. If you make it to third base then your turn is over and you go to right field."

"Home run or nothing?"

"Yep."

Hank watched a familiar visitor approach him from behind the backstop. He smiled at the burly sixteen-year-old, who was making his annual visit from Cedar City in southern Utah. Hank had to look up to him a bit more this year, and Bob waved.

"What have you been eating, Bob?"

Bob roared with laughter, tossing the ball back to another player as they warmed up.

"Let's get started," Hank called out. "We're wasting time."

Chester approached and whispered to Hank, tilting his head toward Bob. "Who's that guy?"

"He comes around every summer for a while. He's the best power hitter I've ever seen," Hank smiled. "Last year he hit a ball so hard it bounced out of the park and into that hayfield over there." Hank pointed southward to a far-off field.

Each player took a turn. Hank hit a double; Chester hit a high foul ball that took forever to come down, and one of the boys made a spectacular catch. Chester clapped his hands in frustration and headed out to take his place in right field.

As Bob came to bat, Billie was playing catcher behind the plate. Bob settled in at the plate. Kicking up a dust cloud between pitches, he watched two pitches go by, waiting for just the right pitch. The pitcher drew his arm back and released. Bob's eyes widened as a fastball whizzed toward him. He swung hard and sent the ball screaming skyward.

"Uh-oh," Billie watched the ball go flying after Bob's monster swing.

The ball sailed high, long, and over the centerfielder's head.

"Home run!" Bob flipped the bat end over end with flare. "Another home run!"

Bob lumbered around the bases, thinking the ball was long gone. He didn't notice how fast the centerfielder had chased down the ball.

"Home run for Bob," he spouted as he rounded second base. His arms raised in victory as he plodded toward third base. The other boys began to yell frantically, "Get him! Get him!"

As Bob rounded third base, he peered over his shoulder. To his amazement, the ball was in play, and he watched wide-eyed as the cutoff man sent the ball flying toward Billie. She was guarding home plate, her mitt positioned in front of her. With a pop, the ball settled into her mitt.

"We got 'im! We got 'im!" the outfielder shouted.

The play wasn't even close. Billie caught the ball a full second ahead of Bob, and he instantly knew he was going to be tagged out. He lowered his shoulder and barreled toward Billie.

"Don't drop the ball," she whispered to herself.

Seeing the inevitable crash, every player held his breath waiting for the collision. Billie would not back down. She stepped one foot behind her and leaned onto her back foot to brace for impact, her mitt tucked near her chest with both hands, clenching the ball. She tagged him in the arm and tried to get out of his way, but he leaned into her, wanting to make her to drop the ball. Billie let out an audible grunt as the force of the collision sent her flying. She landed several feet behind home plate and Bob stepped toward her to admire the results of his effort. He smiled at the sight of Billie sprawled out on the ground. Putting his hands on his hips, he glared at her. "You dumb girl. You knew I was going to plow you over."

The other boys gasped as Billie lay motionless on the ground. They rushed to see if she was hurt. Hank figured she was probably dead, or at least knocked out cold. As the dust cleared, Billie stirred. She strained to stand and pull herself to her knees. With a groan, she wobbled to her feet and paused to gain her balance.

As she steadied herself, she lifted her arm above her head, the ball secured in her mitt. With as much disdain as she could muster, she drew herself up and looked Bob in the face. "How's that for a dumb girl?" She hurled the ball at his chest and it bounced to the ground.

Bob gave her a look of disgust and turned away. Just as he turned his back on her, Billie's knees began to buckle. Still feeling the effect of the collision, she stumbled. Hank reached out to help her, but she brushed him away. She collapsed in a dusty cloud.

Bob roared with laughter as she lay there motionless. Chester jumped in Bob's face and shouted, "Why'd you do that? What were you thinking?"

Undeterred, Bob reached out with his long, pudgy arms and pushed Chester back.

"That's how you play the game. If she wants to play with the men, she's gotta take it like one."

Chester shouted back, his face turning red. "If it was me or any other guy, you would have taken the out. This is a pickup game. There ain't no umps. No trophies. Who're you trying to impress, you jerk?"

Bob squared his shoulders, broadening his chest. "And you're trying to impress your girlfriend here, acting like such a tough guy, aren't you?"

Hank rushed over and pointed his finger inches away from Bob's face "Just go away. You're not only a bully but you're a coward, too. Pickin' on people smaller than you."

The other boys on the team joined in, yelling, "Go back to Cedar City," and, "Go away if you're going to play like that."

Bob gave them a dismissive wave and turned his back to walk away. He mounted his bicycle and rode away in a huff.

Billie made it to her feet. When they turned to look at her, she fixed her eyes on Hank and snarled, "Knock it off! He did what any one of you would have done, especially if I wasn't a girl." She grabbed the ball and readied herself to throw it to the pitcher. "Let's just play. It's my turn to bat!"

CHAPTER 3
August 14, 1939
Huntsville, Utah

To everyone else in Huntsville, Wilhem Meyer was just "Whiskey Will," the town drunk. To Hank and Ella, he was Uncle Willy. Each week during the summer, they visited him to deliver groceries.

"Uncle Willy?" Hank called out as he opened the rickety plywood door to Willy's little shed. The run-down shack measured only fifteen feet square, perched just a stone's throw from the banks of Pineview Reservoir. Hank wrinkled his nose as he walked in. It reeked of booze, tobacco, and stale fish.

Willy caught a lot of fish. He had a knack for it. Sometimes he couldn't eat all the fish he caught before they spoiled, and they would sit in his house for days until he was sober enough to throw them out.

Willy was collecting wood in a thicket of trees about fifty feet away. When he heard Hank's voice, he hurried toward them. As he drew near, he greeted them with a broad smile. Speaking English with a thick German accent and still a little hung-over, he exclaimed, "Vell look who ze cat dragged een." In a boisterous laugh, he spoke in German, "Good morning Gisella and Heinrich."

"Please don't call me Heinrich," Hank complained in German. "You know I hate that name."

Willy winked at Ella with a mischievous grin, and said in German, "What about you Gisella? Should I stop calling you by your German name?"

"Ella will do just fine," she replied in kind, knowing Willy struggled to converse in English.

Hank cleared off some papers and dirty coffee cups from the cluttered countertop and set down a loaf of fresh bread his mama had baked. Ella also left a half-dozen eggs on the countertop. Hank looked for a place to set a bottle of milk he had milked from their cow the night before. Throughout the night, a thick layer of yellowish cream had risen to the top while it sat in their icebox.

Hank and Ella didn't mind visiting Willy, but they preferred him to be a bit more sober. Marta sent food to Willy each week to make sure he had something nutritious to eat. He didn't buy much bread and milk on his own. More often than not, he spent his meager income on cheap booze and tobacco.

Willy smiled. "Tell your Mama I appreciate her sending me the food. I'm surprised your papa lets her do it."

"We love doing it, Willy." Ella shook her head. "And my papa loves you, too."

Willy looked down and mumbled, "That'll be the day." He looked up and blurted, "Who wants to go fishing with me?"

Ella looked at Hank out of the corner of her eye to see if he was up to it. Hank raised his eyebrows and shrugged his shoulders. "Sure, why not?"

Uncle Willy jumped up to reach for his spare fishing rods, pushing one toward Hank and another toward Ella. "Let's go catch some fish." He gave them an impish grin.

The mid-morning summer sun dazzled on the surface of the lake, and Ella lifted her hand to eyes to avert the glare. Hank unbuttoned his shirt as the summer heat intensified.

Willy rushed to his favorite spot, an outcropping with a quick drop-off where the fish were prone to hide. Ella was first to thread her nightcrawler onto the hook and throw her line in. Hank was just a few moments behind her. On Hank's first cast, his fishing pole bent almost to the water. "I've got a big one!" he exclaimed.

He reeled it in and held up a massive brown carp. His excitement turned to disgust.

"Blechh!" Hank wrinkled his nose in disgust.

"That thing is huge!" Willy let out a boisterous laugh. "It's almost as big as you!"

Hank dragged it onto the shore and set to removing the hook. The carp's slimy skin slid out of his hands as it flopped in the dirt.

"Oh, you stupid fish," Hank yelled, "hold still!"

Willie and Ella laughed at Hank while the fish jerked. Hank twisted the hook from its mouth and the fish made a pitiful gurgling noise, startling Hank. When at last he dislodged the hook, he held the fish high above his head with both hands and slammed it on the rocks. The helpless fish flopped around on the ground. Hank picked it up and smashed it on the rocks a few more times for good measure. After a moment, it stopped twitching. He lifted the carp by the mouth, making sure he had a decent grip on it.

"Here you go fish; here's breakfast," Hank said, and he swung the heavy fish with all his might, hurling it into the water.

Just as Hank let go of the fish, Willy yelled in protest, watching as the fish flew through the air. "No! What are you doing?"

Hank looked dumbfounded.

"You can eat carp. Don't be crazy."

Ella reeled in her line and shook her head in disgust.

"It's a trash fish," Hank argued. "Everyone knows that."

"No, not if you know what you're doing."

Hank gave him a glower, but Willy persisted. "I'm serious. I know the secret to cooking up a good carp," he whispered, as if someone might be listening to steal his recipe.

Using his hands to paint a picture, he whispered, "First you gut the carp, and make sure you take off the head. Sometimes they get too long to cook in an oven. Then, you sprinkle some salt and pepper all over the entire fish. Now get a board about the size of the fish; any kind of board will work, but cedar or pine works best. Once you've warmed up your oven to about three hundred fifty degrees, you cook it on the board for about an hour. I like to cover it with tin foil. Then, after its done cooking," Willy raised his finger as if to give Hank a serious warning, "it's going be hot, so be very careful." He raised his eyebrow giving a long, dramatic pause. "Tip the fish off the board straight into the garbage. Now, eat the board!" Willy roared with laughter, doubling over as if he had just told the world's funniest joke.

Ella and Hank had heard the joke more than they cared to admit, but they laughed at Willy because he couldn't stop laughing. The harder Willy laughed, the more they giggled. Willy spent the next ten minutes trying to catch his breath. Each time he threw his line back into the water, he laughed out loud. Hank smiled at Willy as his lips retold the joke to himself again in his mind.

As the excitement of fishing died down, they sat on the shore without saying a word. The silence grew awkward, and Willy didn't want them to become bored and give up. He asked Ella a question he knew she would answer. "So, what do you think about all that's going on in Germany?"

Ella perked up. She was quite conversant in current affairs and had a strong opinion about the country she visited a few years earlier. "I wouldn't be surprised if Hitler starts a war with Poland before too long. It's a real mess over there."

"Oh?"

"He's already annexed Austria. He invaded Czechoslovakia, and now Poland is next," Ella said with confidence. Willy's increasing lack of focus left him unable to follow everything Ella was saying.

"I didn't know you were such an expert on social studies." Willy gave her an encouraging grin.

"Ever since we got back from Germany, she reads everything about it," Hank chimed in.

"I'm worried about *Oma* living there," Ella interrupted. "Why shouldn't I learn as much as I can?"

Willy cut in before Hank could argue. "Ella, that's nice to be thinking of your *Oma* like that. Especially since your *Opa* died."

Ella tipped her head to Willy, then shot an impatient glare at Hank.

"What do you hear from her?" Willy lifted the end of his pole a bit after feeling a slight tug.

"Not much." Ella reeled in her fishing line as she spoke. "We haven't gotten a letter from her in months. In her last letter, she said she's afraid because they declared Mormons to be 'enemies of the state.'"

"You should see the missionary tract she sent us," Hank piped up. "It's a brochure that talks about how the Mormons and the Nazis have a lot in common, like how both the Mormons and the Nazis avoid alcohol and tobacco."

"Papa couldn't believe it when he saw it," Ella said. "He couldn't believe the church leaders would allow the Mormon name to be alongside the Nazi swastika."

"We saw it with our own eyes," Hank said.

"My papa thought it was blasphemous. He said we shouldn't be…"

"I was interested in what you were saying until you brought your papa in to it," Willy muttered.

Hank turned to Willy. "Why don't you like my papa?"

Willy rubbed his scruffy beard. "What does it matter why I don't like him? Your papa doesn't like me."

"I've never heard him say that." Hank looked into Willy's eyes. "In fact, he's always stood up for you."

Willy exhaled. The air whistled through his teeth.

"He stood up for me? Has your father ever told you the real reason why we haven't spoken in years?" His words dripped with disdain.

Ella and Hank looked at each other. "Yes, he has."

"Have you ever considered that he hasn't told you everything?" Willy jerked his line back to check the bait on the hook. Seeing his bait gone, he let out an impatient groan.

"Why don't you tell us," Ella shot back.

He hurried to re-bait his hook and tossed it in the water.

"What does he say is the reason we don't talk?"

"He just says you haven't liked each other since you moved out of the house."

Willy paused a moment. "I guess he's kind of right. But there's a bit more to it than that."

"We moved to America when I was eleven. Your papa was about fifteen. My mama and papa, who would be your *Oma* and *Opa* Meyer, came here to 'Zion,'" his words were drenched with scorn, while his arms motioned to imply the whole state of Utah.

"They expected everything to be great once they got here, but after about three years, they decided it wasn't everything they had hoped for and decided to move back to Germany. We boys wanted to stay here. When Mama and Papa couldn't convince us to go back, they agreed to go back to just visit Germany so they could see their parents. We were to stay here and take care of the farm and the house."

Ella stared at the calm surface of the lake; her line bobbed back and forth. Hank rested his elbow on his knee, watching his uncle's face.

"From what we heard, somehow they both caught some strange sickness on the ship and they died. That left me and your papa by ourselves to take care of the house and the farm. That's a big responsibility for two teenagers. Once everything had settled, your papa thought he was in charge of me. I didn't need anyone to take care of me, and we just kept arguing until I finally decided to move out. I went and lived in a sheepherder's cabin up in the mountains." Willy pointed to the southern hills above Huntsville. "That's where I learned to hunt and fish and take care of myself. But your papa kept begging me to come help him at harvest time or to help him fix the house. Things like that. It wasn't fair that he lived in the house and I didn't live there, and I didn't want to work for free. Eventually, we stopped talking. When I turned eighteen, I joined the Army and went to serve in the Great War. When I came back afterwards, I wasn't about to live by his stupid rules, so I left for good, and I've never gone back."

"I don't get it," Ella said. "You're mad at Papa because of what?"

"He thinks he's my boss. Well he isn't. And he thinks he can tell me what to do, well…"

"I'm pretty sure he just wants to be your brother and have you over for dinner every once in a while, things like that."

"Ya, that's what he *says*," Willy snapped back, "but once that happens, then he'll start telling me what to do. Then he'll tell me 'Stop smoking, Willy,' or 'Stop drinking, Willy…' well, I don't need him preaching to me."

"Maybe you shouldn't smoke and drink," Hank blurted. Ella nudged Hank's shoulder.

Willy gave exasperated look in Hank's direction. "You're just like your papa, aren't you, Hank? Trying to shove religion down my throat."

Hank stood, saying nothing for an awkward moment. "I guess we're going to go now."

CHAPTER 4
May 16, 1940
Huntsville, Utah

Ella, Billie, and Chester graduated from Weber High School at the end of May. The tradition in Huntsville was to celebrate the first full day of summer with a pick-up game of baseball at the park. Billie waived to Ella as she sat with the small crowd who gathered for the annual ritual. Billie joined Hank and Chester, along with the usual group of players, plus last year's graduates, like Charlie Wangsguard, Bud Jensen, Harry Stallings, and Richard Shaw. Within minutes they had selected teams and began to play. For almost two hours they played, until, one by one, the players left to take a break from the heat, or just to go to work.

As the teams fell apart, with people walking off the field to go their separate ways, Billie dropped her mitt on the ground and let out a sigh of exhaustion. "I'm pooped." She smiled at Charlie, and he remembered he wanted to make an announcement.

"Hey guys." Charlie's high-pitched voice was grating, and everyone turned to listen. "I just finished my pilot training program, and now I have my pilot's license! I need to get in as many hours as I can so I can earn a higher rating. Does anyone want to go on an airplane ride with me tomorrow afternoon?"

Billie had known Charlie since elementary school. He was on the scrawny side, at least when compared to Hank and Chester, and his nervous twitch and bad complexion didn't inspire a lot of confidence. But finishing the demanding flight training course counted for something, at least in the eyes of Billie and Hank. Both had talked about their dream of flying an airplane someday. Since Charlie was, well, Charlie, nobody ventured a word, unwilling to trust their lives to his too-recently-acquired piloting skills.

"You want one of us to be your first guinea pig, er uh, passenger?" Hank joked. "No thanks."

"No, I'm kinda busy cleaning my bedroom. So, sorry," said Chester.

"I'll go with you," Billie blurted.

Heads jerked around to see if she was serious. They were only a bit surprised by the look of determination on her face.

"I've always wanted to fly. Let's do it!" she added with forced bravado.

"Great!" Charlie smiled. "I figured you'd be the first one to go. These guys are just chicken."

"We've seen how you drive," Chester blurted out, and everyone let out a raucous laugh.

"Too late for you. Billie's gonna go," Charlie shot back at Chester. He looked at Billie and asked, "Can you be at the airport tomorrow afternoon?

"Sure. What time?"

"Be there at three. I've got to do some paperwork and buy the fuel. I think I'll have enough for about a half hour. But you'll be able to see plenty in that much time."

"Plenty, like the undertaker." Chester covered his mouth in a mock whisper.

Billie gave a nervous smile, already feeling a tinge of regret. Chester and Hank were laughing with each other, ignoring her, but she narrowed her eyes, set her shoulders, and said, "See you tomorrow, Charlie."

———◈◇◈———

Billie drove her mother's car to the Ogden Airport. As she approached, she noticed Charlie checking on a plane. Cautiously, she waited to see if he noticed her. She took her time parking and at long last, pulled into the slot. She gripped the wheel and hesitated to turn the car off, fighting the temptation to drive back home. She got out of the car and walked toward Charlie. The closer she got, the more her stomach twisted in knots. She shook her head, irritated with herself. She caught a glance of the small, single engine Piper Cub.

"Hi, Billie! You ready?" Charlie wiped his hands and smiled at her.

"As ready as I'll ever be. Let's hope you can get this little plane airborne," Billie teased, trying to hide her anxiety. If any of her baseball buddies found out she had chickened out, they would never let her live it down. Still, she strained to think of an excuse to bow out gracefully. At the last possible moment, she pulled herself into the cockpit next to Charlie.

"Just unbuckle the strap in an emergency." He demonstrated how the quick release latch worked.

"The plane's got a whole bunch of safety features; I'm sure we'll be fine," Charlie said. "Are you going to be okay?"

Billie couldn't hide her fear now but gave a quick nod as she clung to the handle on her seat.

"You can get out if you want."

"No, just go," she demanded.

After a bit more explanation about flight safety, he asked again "Are you sure you're okay?"

Billie narrowed her eyes and shot Charlie an impatient look but said nothing. Charlie knew her well enough to know he had better get going. The plane roared to life, and he let it idle while the engine warmed up. Once it was ready, he released the brake, and the plane inched forward. Heading into a stiff, western breeze, the small plane bumped and bounced while it taxied down the short runway. Through Charlie's headphones, Billie overheard the voice of the tower clearing him for takeoff.

Billie clutched a handle on the side of the fuselage, her knuckles turning white. Her other hand clung to a knob attached to her seat. At this point, she didn't care if Charlie knew that she was terrified. Her feet pushed hard on the floorboard, her eyes almost as big as saucers.

Slowly, the plane picked up speed, jostling both in their seats. Billie's jaw clenched, and her pulse raced. Nausea leapt from her gut and she fought the urge to empty her stomach. Clenching her eyes shut, she tightened her grip and breathed until the urge passed. As the plane lifted off the ground, it jerked and dropped. Billie's stomach jumped, and she shouted, "Are you trying to kill us?"

Charlie smiled and patted her arm, and Billie was too sick to recoil from his touch.

"No, you'll be okay. It will smooth out here in just a second." Within a minute, they were five hundred feet in the air, and the leaps and lurches stopped. With an audible sigh of relief, Billie beamed, feeling at long last the plane had settled in.

She opened her eyes and savored the thrill of flight as the plane continued its climb to a thousand feet. She looked out the window. The Great Salt Lake spread below them. Its vast shimmering water glowed of turquoise and green, dominating the view below.

"The lake is huge!" she exclaimed. "I didn't know it was so big."

Charlie banked left, then nosed the plane upward, lifting higher and higher to clear the mountains east of Ogden.

"Do you want to fly over Huntsville?"

"Sure!" Billie smiled as she sat up to get a better view, a little more confident that she would indeed survive the experience. The plane leaned to the left, and she was eye-level with the tops of the rugged mountains, still capped with snow. After a few minutes, Ogden Valley and Pineview Reservoir appeared below them. Billie looked on in awe at the sight of the beautiful reservoir nestled into the steep mountain terrain.

Minutes later, Charlie dropped the plane over the main concentration of homes in the town. Billie spotted her grandmother's home, the Meyer's, and all the other homes in her neighborhood.

"It looks so different from up here," she said. "I can barely recognize it. It's so small."

Before she knew it, Charlie was headed east and back toward the airport.

"I just love it up here. I don't want it to end."

"I know. It's amazing isn't it? Now you know why everyone wants to learn to fly."

"I wish I could take the CPT course, but they don't accept girls."

"I know. It's too bad. You'd make a good pilot," Charlie said.

Billie stared out the window, drinking in the view, pained at the thought that this could very well be her only chance to fly. As they drew nearer to the airport, Billie's eyebrows furrowed.

The landing was a little bumpy, but otherwise didn't bother Billie one bit. The plane taxied to a hardstand and Charlie shut down the engine.

"Well?" he asked. "Did you like it?"

"I loved it!" Billie exclaimed. "I don't care how I do it, I want to learn how to fly."

As she climbed from the plane, a bright red banner caught her eye as it hung from a nearby building. Big black letters declared, *Andrews's Flying Service, Anyone Can Earn a Pilot's License... Ask Us How*!

"Do you know anything about this?" she pointed to the sign.

"Yes, that's where I got my flight training. Art's a great guy. Go talk to him."

"Okay. What have I got to lose?" she replied with some wavering in her voice.

Chapter 4-Note 1: Against fierce political and military opposition, President Roosevelt created the Civilian Pilots Training Program (CPT). The champion of the CPT was Ogden native Robert H. Hinckley, who headed Roosevelt's Civil Aeronautics Authority, the precursor to the FAA. Hinckley wanted to prepare America for any potential military conflict, and he launched a nationwide effort to find, qualify, and train young men as pilots. Army officials were dubious that any civilian program could adequately train pilots for the rigors of flying military aircraft. Regardless, the CPT proved it value, working in conjunction with thousands of colleges and universities around the country. Because of Hinckley's influence, Weber College was among the very first to successfully maintain a CPT program, despite its small size (less than 2,000 students). The government paid for seventy-two hours of formal ground school instruction, followed by forty hours of in-flight instruction.

CHAPTER 5
May 27, 1940
Ogden, Utah

Billie walked with long, confident strides toward the hangar. She would find out for herself if they really meant that *anyone* could be a pilot.

The brick surface of the building held dusty windows, and the door hinge creaked in protest when Billie pushed it open to step inside. The hangar spread above and around her like a cavern; its two massive doors revealing the bright blue sky. A small room with a door marked "Office" filled one far corner. Loud, ambient sounds of mechanical workings and voices obscured her footsteps, as men leaned into the inner workings of Piper Cubs, talking over each other's shoulders. She made her way to the office and peeked inside a window with tattered curtains hung by a thread from a bent curtain rod.

She pushed the door open. A desk scattered with papers and coffee cups faced her, another doorway behind it. She listened for a few moments until she heard rustling in a back room. She knocked on the door with a loud rap.

"Anyone here?"

Seconds later, a pimple-faced teenager appeared in the doorway. With a high-pitched voice he said, "Hi there… how can I…" His voice trailed off to a mumble as he stared at Billie. "You're a girl."

Billie hesitated and replied with a counterfeit smile, "Thank you for noticing. I'm sometimes mistaken for a half-back."

The boy was slow to understand but knew enough to realize she was making a joke at his expense. He managed a half-laugh through his nose, then stood speechless and slack-jawed.

"Is there anyone here who can help me?" she asked.

Just then, an older man wearing a leather jacket walked through the door. At first glance, he looked to be fifty or sixty years old. But as he drew near, Billie could see he was much younger. With dark, sun-beaten skin and graying hair, his long and wiry frame towered above the younger man. He walked with a slight limp, favoring his left knee. His gentle, kind eyes were bluish-gray, their brightness stood in stunning contrast to his tanned, leathery face.

He looked at Billie with a spark of recognition in his eyes and smiled. "Are you the girl they sent out to help me with my bookkeeping?"

Her pulse quickened, but she narrowed her eyes and cleared her throat. "It all depends on what kind of bookkeeping you're talking about."

He gestured to the pile of papers on his desk with a sweep of his arm, shaking his head in exasperation. "I'm just so behind that I need someone to keep track of everything in our logbook and make a deposit each night."

"Sounds simple enough," Billie replied.

"Great!" the man said. "Can you be here for about two or three hours a day, three or four days a week? Will that work for you?"

Billie paused to think it through. Should she make such a commitment? She had no business experience but had taken half a year of bookkeeping in high school. *How hard could it be?*

"Okay. I'm your gal." She couldn't hide her nervous smile. "When do I start?"

"Let's start with introductions. I'm Art Andrews; this is my son David."

"I'm Billie Russell."

"So," Art said. "Where're you from? Where'd you grow up?"

"I grew up in Huntsville. My dad is Frank Russell. He worked making guns for John Browning. He retired a few years ago."

"Oh yeah, I know your family. Your parents are doing a lot of good, from what I hear. Not all people with money have big hearts like your dad and mom."

Billie's palms began to sweat. If he knew about her parents, how soon would he discover her lie?

"Yes, sir," Billie admitted. "I hardly ever see them. But that's fine with me. I'm more or less on my own. I live with my grandma up in Huntsville, but I often stay at our other house up on Ogden's east bench," Billie pointed toward the towering mountains to the east.

"Well it's great to meet you," Art said. "I'm the owner. We're glad you're here. I'm just surprised you got here so fast. Do you have much bookkeeping experience?"

Billie blushed and replied quickly, "Enough that I can do what you need."

"Come on back and I'll show you. I hope you can start next week."

He escorted Billie past the counter into dark and gloomy room. The light fixture dangled from the ceiling in a metal hood painted drab green. Only one of the two light bulbs flickered against the surrounding dingy darkness. The half-drawn curtains allowed a sliver of sunlight inside the room. Billie shuddered. She would have to fix it or be miserable.

"Do you always work in the dark?" she asked.

Art shrugged. "I guess we just got used to it. You can open the curtains if you like. As you can tell, we can also use some help cleaning up a bit. I hope you don't mind doing some manual labor?"

"Absolutely no problem at all. I'll get this place looking spic and span," Billie put her hands on her hips and surveyed the room up and down.

"Great!" Art smiled. "Oh, and the agency said they would talk to you about your hourly pay rate. Are you okay with that rate?" he asked.

"I don't know a thing," Billie replied honestly. "What did you have in mind?"

Art thought for a moment, then said, "Make me an offer."

Billie looked at him, searching his eyes for any clue for how to respond. Then it came to her in a flash. "I'll give you a choice," she stated with a hint of coyness. "I'll take ten cents more per hour than the agency quoted you, or you can pay me with flying lessons until I can earn an advanced license."

"Deal!" Art said. "I'll do you one better. I'll take you up on your offer for flying lessons, then if you do your job, work hard, and study hard, I'll give you a five cent per hour raise once you pass your basic exam, and five cents more after that when you pass your commercial rating. If you get your instructor's rating, then we can talk about a much bigger raise. I'm desperate for more instructors."

"I can live with that," Billie fought to suppress her excitement. "When's my first lesson?"

"We can start next Wednesday, but I need you here on Monday to show you around, if that's okay?"

"Yep," Billie exclaimed with confidence. "I'll be here."

"But you have to know, Billie, I can only help you with your flight time. You'll have to go to ground school to get your license."

"Oh?" Billie raised her eyebrow, afraid her plan would fall apart now as it grew more complicated.

"Yes, it's an eight-week course that meets three times a week at Weber College. The next class starts Monday night. I'll get you in contact with Merlon Stephenson, the faculty director of the aviation course, and see if there's room for you. Last I heard, he had twenty-eight boys enrolled in his next course, but he can take a total of thirty."

A grin spread across her face as she and Art shook hands on it.

Billie noticed a few welcome changes when she arrived for work at four o'clock that next Monday. Art had cleaned and organized a desk for her. New curtains were drawn wide open, and two new light bulbs shone brightly in the still dust-covered light fixture.

"Once you get settled, I need to talk to you," Art said matter-of-factly.

Billie set her purse on her chair, nervous. "Is there something wrong?" She was going to be fired for lying about being a bookkeeper. She knew it.

"It's about your ground school," Art admitted. Billie's tense shoulders relaxed.

"Merlon Stephenson doesn't have any room in his class. He has to accept full-time students first, and if there's room, he can take part-time and then non-students. He doesn't have room for you this time around but might when the next class starts in eight weeks."

Billie looked past him as she thought about what to do.

"However," Art continued, "you could sit in on the class tonight if you wanted to. It won't cost you anything."

Even if she waited for eight more weeks, there was no guarantee she would get in on the next class.

"I think I'll go sit in on the class tonight," she said. "It won't hurt; I was planning to go anyway."

"That's my girl," Art said. "I think it will help you a ton once we get you up in the air a few times."

She sat at the desk. He turned to leave but stopped in the doorway and looked over his shoulder. "Oh, just so you know, I can give you your first lesson on Wednesday, but you'll need to be here an hour earlier, at three o'clock. Can you do that?"

"No problem. I'll be here." Billie felt a surge of adrenaline.

"I'm sure I can teach you what you need to know. Just make sure you listen closely and do exactly what I tell you. And that goes for whenever you're flying, too… do exactly what I tell you."

"Yes sir," Billie replied. "And thank you for the opportunity," she added in all sincerity.

At five o'clock, Billie grabbed her purse and dashed for her car. She sped toward the middle of town and within minutes, spotted a place to park near the Weber College campus. She wasn't familiar with the campus and didn't know her way around. Luckily, she spotted a young man carrying some books, and she stopped him.

"Excuse me, can you show me where the…" she paused to look at her notes. "I don't know how to pronounce it." She showed her notes to the boy.

"That's the Moench Building."

"I was going to say it differently. 'Moench' rhymes with *launch*?"

"Yeah, and it's that three-story building straight ahead," he said, staring at Billie.

Billie felt an instant sensation of revulsion as the young man gawked at her. With biting sarcasm she replied, "Thanks, I think."

"Any time," he answered with a toothy smile.

Tall trees with large leafy boughs surrounded the building, with a manicured courtyard at its center. Stepping inside the large lobby, Billie was confronted with a massive marble staircase leading to classrooms both upstairs and down. She followed two other boys heading down the stairs, guessing they were going to the same class.

The old, Corinthian-style building had a placard saying it was dedicated in 1892 and, by the looks of it, had seen better days. Billie crinkled her nose in disgust at the odor of caustic chemicals emanating from the chemistry lab below. She peeked through the crack between the door and hinge to see who was in the classroom. She noticed two familiar boys from high school, relieved that she wasn't in a room full of strangers.

After a long day of classes, the room had a distinct smell of men's body odor and formaldehyde. Billie fought off the urge to gag. She took a seat just as the teacher walked into the room. His tall and imposing frame dominated the lectern, but his booming voice portrayed a surprising cheerfulness as he called the class to attention.

"Let's get started," he announced. "My name is Merlon Stephenson. This is the ground school instruction course sponsored by the Civil Aeronautics Authority. If you haven't done so already, you need to pay the cashier fourteen dollars and fifty cents for this class. We are required to give you at least seventy-two hours of class instruction. We will cover aviation regulations, history, meteorology, navigation, parachutes, plane instruments, flight theory, and mechanics. If you miss a class without talking to me, you will lose your place. Your only option will be to wait until the next class that starts eight weeks from now. Is that understood?"

The students mumbled their agreement, and Stephenson repeated a bit louder, "Is that understood?"

"Yes sir," the roar of voices thundered, echoing through the classroom and spilling into the hallway.

Stephenson bounded up to the platform and stepped around a podium to the chalkboard, reaching for a piece of chalk. "Let's get started."

As Stephenson spoke, Billie scribbled down everything he said. She copied the board filled with his diagrams and notes, never tiring of taking it all in. Before she realized it, it was nine o'clock, and class was over. She sat in her seat while most of the students filed out of the room. With apprehension in her step, she approached Mr. Stephenson.

"I was told by Art Andrews that I could sit in on this class. I hope that's okay?"

"No!" his words jumped from his mouth with emphasis. "You cannot sit in on this class."

Billie took a step back.

Merlon winked and then smiled. "I didn't mean to startle you. I was joking. I've had a young man cancel because of a family emergency. Instead of trying to recruit another student, I'm willing to offer you the seat, if you can pay by tomorrow."

"I sure can!" Billie shot back. "I'll take care of it in the morning, first thing."

Merlon gave her a warm smile. "Art called me this afternoon. He's got high hopes for you."

"Oh really," Billie cocked her head in curiosity. "Why is that?"

"If all goes as planned, you'll be ahead of everyone because you'll have most of the flight-time you'll need by the time the class ends. Art hopes you can then pass the written test to earn your license," he said.

Billie grinned with delight.

As she drove home, her mind raced as she wondered whether to tell her grandmother about her new adventure. Her parents would be thrilled, but her grandma, not so much. Billie's parents were not expected to return for several weeks. Rather than risk having her grandmother put a stop to everything, she decided to tell her only about her new job at the airport. What her grandma didn't know wouldn't hurt her.

CHAPTER 6
October 1, 1941
Huntsville, Utah

———————————

The door of Grandma Russell's house flew open and Billie dashed across the yard to the Meyer's back door. It was left open to let the afternoon breeze cool the house. Ella sat at the table gazing out the kitchen window. Her books and notes lay open, pen resting idly in her hand. The flurry of motion caught her eye. As Billie ran into the kitchen, her shoes pounded the floor, her cheeks flushed red from exertion.

"Ella!" She exhaled breathlessly. "You won't believe it!"

Papa and Hank walked into the kitchen just as Billie walked in the back door. Papa joked as Billie closed the door. "Knocking is old-fashioned; just valk in."

"Don't mind if I do," Billie shot back, smiling.

Hank ignored Billie and took an apple from the bowl on the kitchen table. He sat in a chair as he took a bite, appearing not to listen in on the conversation.

"What's going on?" Ella asked with eagerness in her voice.

"Ella! You won't believe it. My father just got us four tickets to go to see Glenn Miller and his Orchestra at the White City Ballroom. Tonight!"

"You're joking. Those tickets have been sold out for months."

"I know. I don't know how Dad did it. I've already talked to Chester, and he can go, so do you want to come?"

"Not if I have to go alone. That's embarrassing." Ella recoiled at the thought.

"Ella. This is Glenn Miller, for heaven's sake. Just come," Billie pleaded.

"You may feel comfortable going alone, but…" Ella's voice trailed off.

Billie leaned one arm on the counter and scratched her head with the other hand. "Okay, who can we get to be your date? In an hour?" Then she slapped her hand on the table.

"Why don't you just go with Hank?" Billie looked at Hank with a threat in her eyes.

Hank sunk in his chair, trying to hide from Billie's penetrating stare.

Ella tilted her head in thought. "That's not a bad idea. That way I won't walk in alone, and if anyone recognizes us, we'll just say we had tickets that we didn't want to go to waste."

Hank cringed, trying to hide himself. "Oh, no! Count me out."

"Oh, please come, Hank," Ella begged. "It's the Glenn Miller Band, and they may never come to Ogden again!"

Hank crossed his arms, saying nothing.

"I can't go alone," Ella said. "How embarrassing would that be?"

"And who in his right mind would go dancing with his sister?"

"You don't have to dance with me," Ella argued. "Just walk in with me."

Hank looked at the floor. He appeared to be deep in thought but didn't reply. Billie watched as Hank's mind churned away for a rational response. She waited, keeping her intense stare leveled on him as she leaned back against the table.

"You've always said you wanted to see Glenn Miller! Come on, Hank!" Ella blurted.

Hank protested, but it lacked conviction. "Nope. I've got homework."

Papa spoke up in protest, his deep voice penetrated all of them. "Hank, I sink you haf some different reason. Vat's going on?"

"Nothing. I really do have homework," Hank said, avoiding his papa's scrutiny.

"But you luf Glenn Meeller. So is it about homevork, or is it your pride?"

Hank shuffled his feet uncomfortably and was about to speak when Billie stepped closer to him. She whispered, "Hank, please. Your sister wants to go, and the only thing stopping her from going is you. This is a chance of a lifetime. What do you say? Be a sport and go with us."

Hank paused, uncomfortable as all eyes were on him. Not wanting to contradict his father. "Okay. Just to get you guys off my back. But promise me you and Chester won't start arguing again on the way home. You always do that after a dance, and it drives me nuts."

"We don't argue every time after a dance," Billie protested. "Sometimes you're just so annoying..." Ella jabbed Billie in the ribs. Billie nodded and gave Hank a phony smile.

"Be ready at seven sharp. Chester will pick us up," Billie insisted. "Don't be late."

As Chester drove his Chrysler sedan through the winding roads of Ogden Canyon, Billie, Hank, and Ella chatted with each other during the forty-five-minute drive to Ogden.

"How many people do you think they'll cram into White City Ballroom?" Chester asked anyone who would listen.

"At least five thousand." Hank spoke with authority. "They say it can hold that many. That's why they call it Utah's largest ballroom."

"What's the most they've had in there?" he asked.

"At least that many for Jimmy Dorsey. The same for Duke Ellington. It was packed," Billie replied.

Chester smiled, and their excited banter continued until they arrived. After parking a few blocks from the venue, Billie and Chester rushed toward the front door. Hank and Ella lagged behind.

The ticket line forming at the door was abuzz with excitement. Couples smiled and laughed as they waited to get in. Some strained to see inside the door, wondering what was holding up the line. Billie stopped in her tracks. "Look at the sign." She pointed to a small hand-written sign attached to one of the doors.

Chester read it under his breath. "No one under eighteen will be admitted. Oh, no!" He scanned the entryway, anywhere, for a solution. "I hope Hank doesn't see that. He'll spill the beans that he's only seventeen."

"Are they checking anyone for identification?" Billie asked.

Chester peered over the shoulder of the tall man in front of them toward the entrance, watching as guests were ushered in. "It doesn't look like it. Maybe they just didn't want teenagers to try to sneak in?"

"Just don't let Hank see the sign. He'll go on for days about how he didn't want to break the rules," Billie whispered to Chester, and he agreed.

He looked around and noticed the other door didn't have the same sign. "How about you go and block his view of the sign. I'll guide Ella and Hank toward the other door."

"Do you think it will work?"

"There's enough chaos that I think we'll be fine. You go in."

As the crowd outside waited their turn to enter, Chester watched, biting his lip until Hank and Ella approached the line.

"Come on over to this door; the line is moving faster," Chester suggested.

One by one, they moved toward the ticket taker. Billie was up ahead turning her back to them, hoping Hank wouldn't recognize her as she positioned herself to block the sign.

"Where did Billie go?" Ella asked.

Chester shrugged. "She jumped the line to go the bathroom," he lied, then tipped his head in the direction of the restroom.

Inch by inch, they approached the door, and Chester handed the man their three tickets. He looked at each one carefully, assessing the age of Ella, Chester, and then Hank. Chester held his breath. With an approving nod, the man ripped up their tickets and let them enter. Chester waited until they were a few steps away from the man before letting out an audible sigh.

They picked up their pace and stepped through the double doors, Billie joining them on the other side. As they entered the ballroom, a dull roar came from the mass of people inside. A wall of music exploded from the bandstand. Chester turned to Billie with a mischievous grin, "Let's go give 'em a show, Billie, shall we?" They took each other by the hand and Chester shouted to Hank just before they disappeared into a sea of dancers. "We'll meet you right here when it's over, okay?" Hank smiled, put two fingers to his eyebrow and saluted.

"That's him," Ella shrieked with delight. "That's Glenn Miller!"

She smiled as Hank stood on his toes. "It sure is!" he said, beaming with excitement. Hank shoved his hands deep in his front pockets, his arms stiff as he moved through the crowd, Ella close behind him. With trepidation, he walked around the perimeter of the dance floor, trying to avoid eye contact with everyone. People stood shoulder-to-shoulder. Most couples tried to stake out a small spot they could call their own. As the tide of people filled the massive dance floor, many couples gave up hope of dancing and just stood on the sidelines to watch the band-leader, his trombone glistening in the bright lights.

When the band played just a note or two of a familiar song, the crowd cheered. Like a swarm of bees the crowd flew to their feet, buzzing around the dance floor for songs like "American Patrol" and "Chattanooga Choo Choo."

Hank and Ella looked at each other in amazement at the gigantic crowd that filled the ballroom beyond capacity. Both were getting knocked and bounced around like bumper cars, but the music filled their ears, and they tapped their feet, grinning. Between songs, Ella picked her way through the brief gaps of stillness, moving closer to the stage. Hank followed closely, but someone shouted his name.

"Hank? Hank …is that you?"

He looked around to see his high-school friend, Muriel Davis.

"Hi Muriel!" Hank yelled over the din. "Funny seeing you here. Have you been stepped on or crushed yet?"

She laughed and replied, "No. Not yet. But isn't this a killer-diller? I've never seen so many people in here before, but it's Glenn Miller. Can you believe he's really here? In Ogden, Utah?"

"I know," Hank said. "We're just lucky to be here. My sister and I found out we had tickets this afternoon. She couldn't get a date, so she brought me along," he offered sheepishly, pointing to Ella standing near a column about ten feet away.

Muriel's eyes widened with excitement, "Well if you're both here without a date, let me introduce your sister to my cousin, Tom. They'd make a great couple." She pointed toward the crowd, where the people on the dance floor hopped with excitement.

Hank narrowed his eyes at Muriel and asked, "Have you met my sister before?"

"Sure, I knew her from school. She's two years older than we are, right?"

"And she's very shy, and really…" he trailed off.

Muriel looked at Hank, dipping her head waiting for him to finish.

"Speak up," she shouted over the clamor. "I can't hear you."

Hank cleared his throat. "She's been more and more self-conscious lately about her weight." Hank looked at the floor. "I just don't want her to get hurt, you understand?"

Hank searched Muriel's face looking for some indication that she understood what he meant.

"Hank, how long have I known you?" Muriel raised an eyebrow and gazed into Hank's eyes.

"Forever," he smiled.

"I know who she is. I wouldn't suggest they meet up unless I thought they would hit it off."

"So, he's not going to hurt her, is he?"

"He's an angel," she said. "They'll have a great time. All I've got to do is find him in the crowd. I know he's in there somewhere."

Hank watched with a helpless grin as Muriel stood on her toes, scanning the crowd for her cousin. Waving as she spotted him, Hank felt her grab his hand and pull him in Tom's general direction through a sea of bouncing couples. They barged past couple after couple, shouting apologies, "excuse me" and "pardon me," several times until she could reach out for Tom's hand.

Hank watched Muriel snatch Tom's hand. He jumped, startled.

"Come with me, Tom," Muriel said. "I want you to meet someone." With Tom in one hand and Hank in the other, she dragged them in Ella's direction. She was leaning against a pillar, lost in the music.

Muriel stopped in front of Ella. Hearing someone shouting her name, Ella straightened, her eyes widening as she looked at the nice young man who stood in front of her.

Hank could see Ella admiring Tom's broad-shoulders. He had a solid, yet thin build, not quite six feet tall, with dark wavy hair receding a bit around his temples. His rugged chin outlined a handsome face. Even Hank noticed the kindness in his eyes that deepened when he smiled.

Hank strained to hear Muriel as she leaned over to Tom and almost had to shout over the din. "This is my high school friend, Hank Meyer, and his sister, Ella. They're here just like we are." She covered her mouth, faking a whisper, "None of us have real dates, but we wanted to see Glenn Miller. So, we won't tell anyone that we came with family, will we?"

Hank laughed, and said, "Your secret is safe." Tom tipped his head to Hank and offered his hand. Both gave each other a firm grip and replied simultaneously, "Pleasure to meet you."

Hank stepped aside and pulled Ella into the circle. Tom extended his hand to Ella and have her a good-natured shake. "How nice to meet you, Ella. Where you from?"

"Huntsville," Hank and Ella answered in unison. The song ended, and after the cheers erupted and subsided, the voices of their small group felt loud in the sudden silence.

"Wow." Tom's eyes widened. "I love it up in the Valley." This brought a nervous, yet kind smile from Ella. Hank watched his sister's face blush. He grinned at seeing her flirt with him.

"I didn't think I would dance at all tonight," Tom admitted.

"Me either," Ella said. "I'd love to, if you're up to it?"

From the stage came the sound of snapping fingers, the opening rhythm of "Little Brown Jug" filling the air. The crowd roared with approval. Hank watched as Tom and Ella found an opening on the dance floor. Within minutes they were swinging and twirling each other as if they'd been dance partners for years.

"I suppose they'll be just fine." Muriel looked at Hank and smiled.

"I guess so."

Hank reached out his hand to Muriel. "Would you like to dance?"

"I thought you'd never ask." Muriel gave him a bright smile.

He took her hand and they slipped into a small opening, joining the music.

After the show ended, Hank and Muriel thanked each other and stepped outside into the cool air, waiting for Tom and Ella. Hank spotted them as they sauntered out of the large double doors. Ella's flushed face glowed as she clung to Tom's arm, chattering away.

"Looks like you two had fun." Hank tipped his head and pointed to their clasped hands.

"We sure did," Ella glowed. "We had a grand time, didn't we?" She tilted her chin, catching his gaze in hers.

Tom smiled and agreed, "Your sister's a great dancer."

Hank shot him an approving glance, then announced, "Well folks, I'm sorry to put the brakes on you little love-birds, but we have a bit of a drive to make it home." Hank smiled and teased.

Tom winked at Ella. "I'll call you tomorrow."

They gave each other a quick hug and Ella thanked him.

"I had the time of my life," she whispered, glowing with affection. "We'll talk soon."

As Tom and Muriel walked away, Hank turned to Ella and said, "What was all that about? You act like newlyweds."

Ella said nothing, but gave him a coy smile, shrugged, and nodded in agreement.

"He's gentle and polite, a voracious reader, handsome as the devil, and he's not a bad dancer," Ella responded analytically, as if she was reviewing one of her library books. "Not quite the dancers that you and Chester are," she added. "But not bad at all."

Hank knew his sister well enough to recognize her tone. Exhilaration bubbled beneath the surface of her cool composure, struggling to show itself. She couldn't catch her breath, and a smile kept breaking through despite her conscious efforts to stifle it.

"There you are!" an indignant voice called out. "We've been looking all over for you."

Running footsteps approached them, Chester breaking into view with Billie clinging to his hand.

"Did you dance at least once, or did you just stand on the sides and watch?" Chester asked in a mocking tone.

"I danced with Muriel Davis all night, if it's any of your business," Hank shot back.

"And you left your sister all by herself?"

"Ask her," he tipped his head at Ella. "I assure you she wasn't a wallflower."

"Ella, did you meet someone?" Billie asked with excitement.

"Yes! And he's a dream!" she blurted, and then they both screamed and laughed like schoolgirls. Billie threw her arm around Ella's shoulder as they walked to the car. "Tell me everything," she said. "I want to know every juicy detail."

Chester started the car, and Billie sat in the front seat. Ella and Hank were in the back. Billie put her arm on the back of the bench seat and lifted her knee to better see Ella's face.

"He's twenty-one, did a year at Weber College, and then went to California to get his pilot's license!"

Billie covered her mouth, eyes wide with excitement. "You're kidding, right?"

"Nope. He's a lieutenant in the Army Air Corps, and he's going to learn how to fly pursuit airplanes," Ella added. "Then they'll make him a captain, or something like that."

Billie shook her head, saying under her breath, "What a dream that would be, to fly pursuit planes."

"He's waiting for his orders, and he'll be gone in a month or so. And get this. He loves to read. He loves books as much as I do!" Ella burst with such glee that Chester rolled his eyes and snickered.

Chester drove in silence, listening to them chat, gasp, and giggle all the way home. Hank interjected a question now and then, more out of curiosity than anything else. This was his sister's first and only romantic interest, at least the first he'd ever known about. The glow in her eyes and breathless way she spoke of all the details showed a new side of her.

As Chester stopped the car, Hank thanked him for the ride and shut his door.

Billie held Ella close in one last hug. "I'm so happy for you," she whispered.

Hank watched Ella let go of her embrace, and for the first time, saw a look of fear in Ella's eyes.

Biting her lip Ella blurted, "What if he never calls me again? What if..."

Billie interrupted. "Oh stop trying to over-analyze everything, Ella. He'll call you back for heaven's sake. I promise," Billie assured her. "Now go to bed and have sweet dreams."

Ella wanted to believe her. She looked to Hank for some reassurance, and Hank tipped his head toward Billie and admitted, "She's right. You're overthinking it. Again."

Hank could see Ella was playing out the heartbreaking scenario in her head.

"It was a great night, Ella. Don't spoil it by assuming the worse thing is going to happen." Hank tried to put his arm around her and guide her toward their front door. Ella pushed him away.

Chapter 6-Note 1: The White City Ballroom" in Ogden, Utah had a reputation as one of America's largest and most beautiful ballrooms. Opened in 1922, it was incredibly lavish, even for its day, with massive and opulent chandeliers and many other expensive accouterments. It could accommodate a capacity crowd of 5,000 people, attracting dancers from several surrounding states. (It is not to be confused with Chicago's "White City Ballroom," notorious for its whites-only policy.) During its heyday, most of the big-name bands made at least one visit here. While it's doubtful that Glenn Miller and his Orchestra came to Ogden in 1941 because of their recording and filming schedule, it is well-documented that other big groups, like Tommy Dorsey, Gene Krupa, and Benny Goodman, did visit Ogden during this era.

CHAPTER 7
Sunday, December 7, 1941
Huntsville, Utah

Ella and Hank chatted in German at the kitchen table, dressed and ready to go to church. They giggled as Karl and Marta walked in, their tired, aimless gazes looking around the kitchen. Ella asked, "What time did you get home last night, Mama?"

"Not as late as we thought we'd be," Marta answered, reaching into the icebox. "I think we got in about two in the morning." She poured herself a glass of milk and asked, "Do you want a glass, Papa?" Ella watched as her papa nodded.

Ella kept an eye on her father as he tiptoed barefoot onto his back porch to inspect his frozen and muddy shoes. He crouched to examine them, rubbing his ears as the crisp morning air nipped at them. As he lifted his shoes, she giggled again as frozen mud dripped from the soles.

"You must have come home last night during that downpour," Hank said. Papa nodded, too tired to respond. He then stumbled back to the house and into a chair at the kitchen table, catching himself as he sat down. He rubbed his stubbly chin, then rested it in his hand as he propped his elbow on the table. Ella giggled again at seeing her frazzled father.

"What happened? I thought this German social club thing was supposed to last all night?" Ella asked.

"We thought so too," Papa said as he scratched his head. "It started out well with some great food and folk dancing. We even sang some old songs we haven't heard since we were children."

"Then…?" Ella's voice trailed up.

"Then two Nazis got up and took over the meeting. They went on and on. Nobody dared tell them to sit down, so, we just left."

"Nazis? In Salt Lake City?" Ella shot him a confused look. "What were they doing there?"

"Oh," Papa said, waving his hand as if brushing it away, "they were trying to recruit for their little club. Many people ended up walking out like we did." He grimaced, stroking his throat in disbelief. "I don't know how anyone could buy into what they're selling."

"But a few stayed to listen," Mama added.

"So you drove an hour-and-a-half both ways, and didn't stay much longer than an hour or so?"

Karl and Marta looked at each other, contemplating the wasted evening.

Ella looked at Hank and smiled. "We both have to be at the church for a youth meeting at ten. Maybe we'll see you at Sunday School at eleven?" Hank asked, a tease in his tone.

"We'll be there," Mama smiled. "We may be half-dressed, but we'll be there," she chuckled.

The bright, sunlit morning was brisk and perfect. The thin layer of frozen rain was finally melting from the ground as the sun appeared over the eastern mountains. Shortly after noon, the members of the Huntsville Ward emerged from the old rock church after Sunday School.

Hank stretched his back as he walked out of the building. Ella kept pace with Hank's quick steps.

"I'm tired of meetings," Hank looked ahead, not expecting Ella to respond. They were about ten minutes ahead of their parents, who moved slow anyway but often lingered a little longer to chat. Hank and Ella said nothing as they strolled toward home, breathing in the crisp December air.

Hank looked over his shoulder at the sound of an automobile speeding towards them. He pulled Ella aside off the path, turning to watch the approaching car. As the tires screeched to a stop in front of them, Chester leaned out the window, a look of terror on his face. "The Japanese just bombed Hawaii. We're at war!"

Hank looked at Chester with skepticism.

"Oh stop it, Chester," Ella scolded Chester. "That's nothing to joke about."

"I'm not joking. It's all over the news. Jump in. I'll take you home, and you can hear it for yourself."

As soon as they folded themselves into the car, Chester sped off, and the car bounced over the road.

"I can't believe it. I just can't believe it," Chester looked up, shaking his head. "We're actually being attacked. Our country is under attack."

"Are you sure you heard it right?" Hank asked. "Maybe it's just a false alarm."

"No sir. My mom got a call from her sister in Ogden and she heard it on KSL radio, so it's no joke."

Hank's heart raced. If this was true, everything was going to change. With great anxiety, they rushed into the house and turned on the radio. The signal from station KLO in Ogden was scratchy and faint.

"So to repeat," the announcer said, "the Japanese have attacked Pearl Harbor in Honolulu, Hawaii. The attack started at about seven-fifty-five this morning Hawaii Time. We're waiting for further details from Washington, and we'll pass along whatever we learn. This is not a drill. We are at war," the announcer finished breathlessly.

Hank switched off the radio. "Then it's true. We really are going to war."

"Definitely. No two ways about it."

Hank's heart dropped as the reality of Chester's words hit him. "Are you going to join?"

"Darn right I am," he replied.

"I doubt my papa would let me. Not until I'm eighteen." Hank felt a growing anger toward his father's obstinacy.

"I'm going to sign up tomorrow," Chester announced with pride. "And I wanna fight. No way I'm going to sit behind a desk or take some other boring job. I'm going to put a rifle to good use."

Ella shook her head at Chester's bravado. "Why not be a mechanic or something like that so you'll have a skill you can use when the war is over?"

"No way! After what they've done to us? I'm going to join the Marines and kill those dirty Japs."

Hank and Ella's faces cringed at hearing Chester talk with such ugly words. It wasn't like him.

The next day, Ella and Billie, along with all the other students, arrived at Weber College only to learn administrators had cancelled all classes due to the national emergency. The student body gathered in the auditorium to hear a special radio announcement from President Roosevelt. Finding a row near the front, Ella pointed to some seats where they sat waiting for the special broadcast to begin.

The scratchy hiss of the amplified radio signal gave way to an announcer's voice, and the clamor of students grew instantly silent.

"Senators and representatives, I have the distinguished honor of presenting the President of the United States."

The Senate floor erupted in applause and cheers, sprinkled with whoops and hollers. The constant applause sounded more like a hiss that lasted for almost a minute, finally fading away as the voice of President Roosevelt began firmly:

"Mr. Vice President, and Mr. Speaker, and Members of the Senate and House of Representatives. Yesterday, December 7, 1941—a date which will live in infamy—the United States of America was suddenly and deliberately attacked by naval and air forces of the Empire of Japan.

The United States was at peace with that nation and, at the solicitation of Japan, was still in conversation with its Government and its Emperor looking toward the maintenance of peace in the Pacific. Indeed, one hour after Japanese air squadrons had commenced bombing in the American Island of Oahu, the Japanese Ambassador to the United States and his colleague delivered to our Secretary of State a formal reply to a recent American message. And while this reply stated that it seemed useless to continue the existing diplomatic negotiations, it contained no threat or hint of war or of armed attack."

Both Ella and Billie paid close attention, drinking up every word as students nearby shook their heads in anger and disbelief. The speech continued, and the hushed audience gave way to a range of emotions.

"Those stupid Japs lied to us!" one of the students shouted when the radio went silent for a moment. Ella readjusted herself in her seat, then looked over her shoulder to see who was so upset.

"You can't trust those Japs; they're sneaky!" another shouted.

The broadcast continued. After the commentators resumed regular programming, the college president, Henry Aldous Dixon, stood to speak to the assembled crowd.

"Students, what you have just heard might well be a defining moment in your life. This is a historic day that you will tell your children and grandchildren about. I would like to have everyone join for a brief, silent prayer for those who died yesterday, and for the future of our country."

Somber silence filled the room, a sniffle here and there echoing as students bowed their heads. After a few moments, President Dixon stood again. "Thank you everyone. I don't think I need to remind you boys that if you're not already talking to your draft board, you should be."

Dixon cleared his throat. "I also hope that everyone will resolve today to do your part..." he paused, tears welling up in his eyes, "...to protect this wonderful country of ours. This struggle will not be easy, but we have no choice but to fight or become subject to these tyrants. May the Lord bless each one of you as you do your part."

As President Dixon dismissed everyone, the students filtered out of the auditorium. Ella and Billie sat in silence next to each other. Ella fought back tears. She looked at Billie who stared at the auditorium curtains, seeming to be lost in thought.

"I'm afraid for these boys, Billie." Ella's voice cracked. "Chester, Hank, and all the guys we know. They're all going to leave sooner or later."

Billie raised her eyebrows and gave a nod of agreement. Ella watched as she stood to walk toward the door of the auditorium. Ella followed a few steps behind, watching as Billie shuffled out the door. After leaving the warmth of the building, Billie buttoned up her coat in the chilly air. Ella caught up to her and asked softly, "Are you okay?"

Billie shrugged a bit. "It's just a lot to take in. There's so much that can go wrong."

A breeze stirred, bringing a sudden chill. Ella pulled her coat tighter, fastening the buttons. "We can only try our best, and let God take care of everything."

Billie smirked and rolled her eyes. "What if Japan wins? What if God doesn't take care of us?"

"Of course He'll take care of us," Ella protested. "Why wouldn't He?"

"Maybe because our country has gone off the deep end," she used her fingers to make quotes in the air, "and He's decided we don't deserve to win?"

Ella furrowed her brow, then slowed as Billie stopped to look at her. "I heard them say on the news that Germany could declare war on us any day now. How on earth can we win against both Japan and Germany?"

The thought of not winning, not succeeding despite everything it would cost them, sank like a punch into Ella's gut.

"I don't know. I guess we'll just have to figure it out," Ella replied, only half believing it herself.

"Everything we know could change." Billie stared as Ella's shoulders sagged under the weight of what she already felt. Billie looked with steeled eyes at Ella, making sure she understood her point.

"You really think it's that likely we'll lose?" Ella asked.

Billie nodded, and continued walking.

"You're scaring me, Billie," Ella's voice cracked. "What if you're right? What if we have to fight Japan and Germany, and we're just not ready for it?"

Hearing the panic in Ella's voice, Billie knew she had gone too far. "Don't get all worked up, Ella. The news guys were just wondering if it would happen. Trust me, we won't go to war against Germany."

Chapter 7-Note 1: One of Hitler's biggest tactical blunders was declaring war on the United States on December 11, 1941. If he had waited, as he was advised, then America would have launched all of its efforts toward Japan, making the war in Europe a secondary priority. Churchill was thrilled that Hitler declared war on the United States, as he feared a preoccupied Roosevelt would have otherwise sent even fewer resources to help Great Britain. It also gave the United States a reason to support Great Britain and the Allies without incurring public opposition, as the din of pacifist voices was still potent just before Pearl Harbor and the German declaration of war. Hitler's bravado had committed Germany to continue fighting their battle of attrition against Russia, while also having to fight an emboldened Great Britain on a new western front. Hitler stupidly abrogated control of the timing of when the United States joined the European fight. If he had waited, he could have focused all his efforts on defeating Russia. Once Russia was defeated, then he would have had more resources to commit to defeating Great Britain.

CHAPTER 8
December 21, 1941
Huntsville, Utah

Hank practiced the speech in his head for what seemed like the hundredth time. The words rang with confidence. Maybe he could convince his father to let him enlist after all. Every conversation had ended the same way, but maybe this time, with Chester and all his friends already enlisted, his father would understand. The nine months until his eighteenth birthday were going to be the longest nine months of his life.

Before dinner that evening, Papa sat alone at the kitchen table, a newspaper spread out before him. Hank slid into a chair next to him, thinking of the best German words in his head.

"Papa, can we talk for a moment?"

Papa glanced up at the sound of Hank's quiet but determined voice and agreed.

"I know you've said before that you won't sign the papers so I can enlist, but…"

"Hank," Papa replied with a stern voice, "that discussion is over. I will not…"

"But just listen to me for one minute," Hank insisted. "I've spent a lot of time thinking this through, so at least hear me out."

Papa took a breath, folded his arms and leaned back in his chair to listen.

"I know you don't want me enlisting one second before I have to, and I understand that. But the longer I wait, the more likely it is that I'm going to be a foot soldier. I really want to join the Air Corps, but I've heard that everyone enlisting is going in either the Air Corps or the Navy. By the time I'm eighteen, the only spots left will be in the infantry."

Papa gave a quick nod, but the stern look clouding his face did not change.

Hank continued, "Papa, you know I've always wanted to be a pilot. This may be my only chance."

Hank waited a long time for his papa to answer, watching to see any sign of change behind his eyes.

43

At last, Papa cleared his throat. "Hank, I understand your concerns, but you have to realize that I'm not trying to punish you, I'm trying to protect you. I've seen what war did to Uncle Willy, and I just don't see any need to rush into it."

"But let's face it," Hank said. "The war isn't going to end within a year or two. There's really no way I can avoid being in the military. You're just delaying the inevitable, and then if I have to be a foot soldier carrying a gun, I'll be in greater danger."

"I can see you really want this, but I've also got to think about all you do at home. How would I manage if I have to take over all your chores? I rely on you for so much around here. It would be a real hardship for your mama and me."

Hank looked away from his papa. He hadn't considered what his leaving would do to them. "I understand it wouldn't be easy on you and Mama, but one way or another, I'm going to be leaving. It's going to happen sooner or later," he said. "Maybe it's time we sell some of the cattle? Or get rid of the milk cow?"

Papa face turned red in protest. "We live on the money we get from the milk cow and the beef cattle. We would never be able to make ends meet."

"What are you going to tell the draft board, Papa?" Hank snapped, slamming his hands on the table. "That I can't be drafted because I have chores to do?"

"I hear they make hardship cases for farmers needing help to keep their farms going."

"Are you going to ask the draft board to exempt me from serving?"

"Maybe." Papa exhaled deeply, mustering his self-control, his eyes growing colder. "I just may do that."

Hank stood abruptly and shoved his chair back. He left the room with clenched fists, shaking his head, unable to speak.

The Meyers' house was filled with the smells of *lebkuchen* and other traditional German Christmas treats. Ella helped her mother string up pine cones and other decorations.

The day before Tom was scheduled to come home, Ella called Tom's mother to finalize their holiday plans.

"Hi, Myrtle. What's the word about Tom? What time does he get in?"

"I'm sorry to break the bad news to you, but Tom just called and said his holiday leave was cancelled at the last minute."

Ella's heart sank. "Oh no, you're joking!"

"I wish I were. Apparently, everyone at Muroc Air Base has to stay there for Christmas because of some special operation. He couldn't say much else other than that."

Ella sat on a kitchen chair, choking back a cry rising in her throat.

"Is there any chance he can come home after Christmas?" Ella already knew the answer, but it was the only thing she could say without crying.

"No," Myrtle answered in a drawn-out voice. "He said all furloughs were cancelled. He didn't know when he was going be able to come home. I'm so sorry."

"I'm sorry for you, too." Ella couldn't hide her disappointment. "I know his little brothers and sisters all miss him."

"Yes, they do," Myrtle said, "but they'll be fine. You're more than welcome to come down on Christmas Eve. We're having a turkey," she boasted.

"Oh, that's nice. Thanks for the invitation, but my family likes to have a stuffed goose, and my mama is making some other traditional German foods we haven't had in a while. This is a big year for us, so she's going all out."

"Oh," Myrtle replied, "that makes sense. Has Hank already enlisted?"

"No, not yet. His eighteenth birthday isn't until next September, and my papa won't sign the papers."

"That's your father's choice. But I'll bet Hank isn't too happy about it."

"You have no idea the tension it causes. It's like walking on eggshells sometimes," Ella admitted. "But either way, who knows what Christmas will be like next year. This could very well be our last Christmas together, you know?"

"Maybe you can drop by and see the kids before you go back to school in January?"

"Maybe so," she said, already knowing she wouldn't have the time. "I'll let you know."

CHAPTER 9
January 15, 1942
Huntsville, Utah

Billie's car skidded on the snow into her grandmother's driveway. She jumped from the car and ran through a trail in the snow across the Meyer's yard. As Billie burst through the back door, Ella looked up from her studies at the kitchen table.

"Ella, you won't believe who called me today!" Billie giggled with excitement.

"Who?" Ella's eyes widened.

"Jackie," Billie paused for effect. "Jackie Cochran."

Ella furrowed her eyebrows in confusion. "You mean that famous pilot who pals around with Amelia Earhart?"

Hank's voice shouted from the other room. "She holds all the speed records!"

"That's the one!" Billie said.

"She asked me if I had my instructor's rating and had logged two hundred hours, and I told her I did. Then she said she was looking for qualified women pilots to ferry military planes from the factories to bases around the country."

"Are you going to do it?"

"What do you think? I'd be out of my mind if I didn't. I have to be officially selected first, but Jackie said I have all the qualifications!"

Ella stood, opening her arms to give Billie a hug. "Congratulations! You deserve it after all your hard work."

"So, my boss wants me to find my replacement at work to take over the bookkeeping, and I suggested that you could do it, no sweat."

Ella shook her head. "There's no way I could swing going to class, keeping up on my clinicals, studying for my tests, *and* holding down a job on top of it. No possible way."

Billie looked at Ella with confusion. "Oh come on. You could use the money to pay for school."

Ella contemplated Billie's argument. "I don't know, Billie. I just don't..."

"I'll do it."

They turned to see Hank standing in the kitchen doorway, leaning against the frame.

Billie whispered to Ella, grimacing. "Not Hank. No, not…"

"Why not?" asked Ella. "Hank is much better at numbers than I am. He'd do great, and you know it."

Hank walked into the kitchen. "I really need a job to pay for the truck I'm going to buy from Mr. Wangsguard," Hank explained. "He said I could make payments until I could get enough money to buy it outright."

"No, no, no, no, *NO!*" Billie stamped her foot. "You and me working together at the same place? Absolutely not!"

"Oh, come on, Billie," Ella pleaded. "You're a professional, aren't you? You can be professional and get along with Hank for a few hours a day, couldn't you?"

Billie looked into Ella's eyes, squinting in rage. "That's not fair, and you know it."

"What's not fair?" Ella responded with an innocent smile.

"You know darn well what I'm talking about," Billie interrupted. "Don't look at me with those cherubic eyes."

"So Billie, are you a professional? Or would you throw a temper tantrum."

Billie took a deep breath and looked up at the ceiling. An awkward silence hung in the air. Hank stood with his hands in his pockets, and Billie was annoyed as Hank and Ella stood silently, exchanging glances while they waited.

"Oh, alright!" Billie let out an exasperated sigh, then turned to Hank and answered in a soft tone. "His name is Art Andrews. You can go talk to him, but don't tell him you know me."

"Oh, come on now, Billie," Ella protested. "He's got to be able to say he was referred by you."

"Okay, you can tell him you just met me, and that you overheard a conversation about the job." Billie crossed her arms and looked at Ella. "That's the truth."

Ella stared at Billie blinking a few times.

"Fine," Billie said. "Say whatever you want. I'm a professional. If I can handle working with Hank, I can handle anything."

Hank cracked a nervous smile, but said, "Thanks, Billie." If only he could be sure she wouldn't sabotage his application.

Chapter 10
February 1, 1942
Ogden, Utah,

On Hank's fourth day on the job, a short man in a well-pressed business suit walked through the door at Art Andrews's Flying School. His hair was slicked back and he carried a black briefcase. Hank looked up from his desk and greeted him with a smile.

"My name is Special Agent Johansen. I'm with the Federal Bureau of Investigation." He reached for his wallet and revealed his FBI badge to Hank.

"I'm looking for Heinrich Meyer."

The way the man pronounced his name sent an icy chill up Hank's neck.

"I'm Hank Meyer."

"You prefer Hank, I take it?"

"Yes," Hank said. "Only people who don't know me call me Heinrich. Or my enemies." Hank tried to stifle a nervous laugh.

"I need to ask you a few questions. I understand you're a new employee?" Johansen snapped open his briefcase and pulled out a notepad and pen.

Hank nodded his head to agree.

"All new employees working for a defense-related business must go through an extensive background check as a matter of national security. Have you got a few minutes?"

Hank relaxed his shoulders. "Yes sir."

"Your parents are from Germany, is that right?" He flipped to a clean page and waited, pen tip resting on the paper.

"Yes," Hank answered, trying to hide a frown flickering across his face.

"And you were born here in the United States?"

"Yes."

"Are your parents naturalized citizens or resident aliens?"

Hank tilted his head. "I don't know what that means."

"I understand you traveled to Germany in 1935. I assume you traveled on a U.S. passport?"

"My mother did, but I didn't need to have one," Hank responded.

"So, your mother and, I assume, your father, are both naturalized citizens. That means they went before a judge somewhere and were given a certificate of citizenship."

"Oh. Yes. I've seen that certificate before."

"Can you tell me about that trip to Germany?"

"I was eleven years old," Hank said, shrugging. "I don't remember a whole lot, other than we went to see my *Oma* and *Opa*."

"Oh, so I assume you speak German?" Johansen glanced up.

"My mother tried to teach us German growing up. I still know some of it." The fib slid more easily off his tongue than he'd have ever thought himself capable.

"But I understand your mother doesn't speak English?"

"Sure she does!" Hank insisted. "She speaks English all the time. She just prefers to speak German at home."

The man scribbled away. A knot formed in Hank's throat.

The door opened and Art stepped into the lobby, seeming to stop in surprise. He glanced from the stranger to Hank and back again, a frown tightening his brow.

"Can I help you?" Art asked.

The man again reached for his wallet and showed Art his FBI badge.

"My name is Special Agent Johansen. I'm with the FBI. We're required to do a background check on all new airport employees, as a matter of national security," he said.

"I'm Art Andrews, I own this business, and Hank here is a fine young man. I can vouch for him and for his family too."

Johansen again wrote in his notebook, then asked Hank, "What have your parents told you about Germany and Adolf Hitler?"

Hank shot Art an apprehensive glance, then cleared his throat. "They say that Germany is far different than the Germany they grew up in," Hank said. "Hitler has ruined Germany."

Johansen smiled slightly, writing his notes, and underlining some words several times.

Hank took a deep breath and blurted, "Am I under suspicion because my parents were born in Germany?"

"Everyone is under suspicion right now. We are finding Jap and Nazi spies all over the place, but especially in defense-related businesses, so we can't be too careful now, can we?"

"I guess not, sir."

Johansen countered with a smug grin, "If you or your family sympathize with an enemy government, we'll find out. We don't take very kindly to Nazi spies or Nazi sympathizers around here."

Anger swelled inside Hank, and under the desk he clenched and unclenched his fists, breathing slowly to calm himself.

"But if you're a loyal American, like this man says you are, you'll have nothing to fear." Johansen tucked his notebook into his briefcase and said, "Thank you for your time. Good day." He turned away quickly and let himself out.

When the door clicked shut, Art muttered, "Jerk."

"What was that all about?" Hank asked. "Have all your employees had to go through a background check?"

"No, but you're the first person I've hired since the war started," Art said. "I hope we don't have to do this every time we hire someone."

"He made it sound like everyone needed a background check if you work here," Hank said.

For the rest of his shift, Hank replayed the conversation in his mind. Anxiety gnawed at him through the end of the day. As he opened the door to go home, he glanced around the hangar. The empty space still pressed at him, as he couldn't shake the feeling of being watched. He dashed to his truck without looking back. The truck rumbled to life, and all the way home Hank wondered if he had made a mistake. Had he somehow put his family at risk? He needed to get home to talk to Ella.

When Hank walked through the back door into the kitchen, Ella was at her usual place at the table, doing her homework. Hank didn't bother to take off his coat. He sank into a seat across from Ella, unleashing a river of words as he recounted everything. Ella listened, covering her mouth in surprise.

"How did the FBI know so much about our family?" she asked.

"I have no idea."

"That's strange." Ella's brow lowered, deep in thought. "And frightening, too. Don't say anything to Mama or Papa. It would worry them."

"I thought about that a lot," Hank said. "Don't you think they need to know?"

She pursed her lips in thought, then said, "Let's sit on it for a few days and see if something else comes up. If the FBI is talking to our neighbors, then someone will tell us about it."

"Okay," Hank said. "We'll give it a couple days. But I sure hope the whole thing blows over soon. This is unnerving."

CHAPTER 11
March 15, 1942
Ogden, Utah

After finals were over for the winter quarter, Weber College was poised for the full brunt of the war. Enrollment for the spring quarter was half that of winter quarter because so many boys had enlisted in the service.

The evening of March 15, family and friends of recent enlistees—most of them Weber College students—arrived at the Union Pacific train station in Ogden. Over two hundred family and community members had gathered to show their support for fifty-one Ogden-area boys who had enlisted to serve.

Chester was a little disappointed when he first learned he wasn't going to be in the Marines like he had wanted. Instead, he was assigned to the Navy. While he still wanted to carry a rifle, being on a big ship with a chance to shoot one of their massive guns soon filled him with excitement. It didn't matter; he just wanted to make a real contribution.

Although Chester wasn't a student at Weber College, his family and friends were among the crowd of local citizens there for the big send-off. The college marching band played patriotic songs, energetic notes from John Phillip Sousa marches ringing out over the crowd.

Chester's parents and family gathered around him. Hank and Ella stood nearby.

When he saw Ella, Chester glanced around. "Where's Billie?" he shouted over the band.

"I don't know. She told me she was coming."

"Do you think she just forgot?" Chester asked.

"No. We talked about it last night."

"Maybe she couldn't get away from work."

"Maybe," Ella replied with trepidation, "but she's usually off by now, so I don't know. Haven't you and Billie spent nearly every night together this past week?"

"All except last night," he smiled. "We've had a great time together this week."

"I just don't know where she is. I hope she'll be here soon."

The music ended, and a voice called out over the hum of the crowd. As people around them hushed, they looked up to college president Henry Dixon, who stood at a podium, waiting for silence. "Can I have your attention, please?" he shouted.

The rumbling of conversations grew quiet.

"Thank you all for coming out to give these boys a proper send-off," Dixon said. "Can I get all the enlistees to come line up in front of me?" he asked.

The enlistees came to the front, all dressed in suits and ties. The audience erupted in applause and cheers as they assembled in a line, a few casting shy smiles to the ground. Chester beamed at Hank.

"You know I call you boys, but you are making the decisions of men. You are choosing to do your duty and serve your country as men."

The audience was silent.

"Each one of you, I hope you never forget that we love you. You are representatives of Weber College, this community, and the ideals we all believe in, such as honesty, integrity, liberty, and freedom. You will be fighting for these and many other important principles."

He stopped to clear his throat. "I hope you will always look back on this day. Look around and take a mental picture of your family and friends nearby, but also of the entire community, who have come to show their love and support for you. Don't ever forget this day. You are special men with a special purpose. May heaven's choicest blessing be upon each of you, and may you all return one day, having accomplished this critical mission. Now I know our time is short, and your train is due to leave in a few minutes…"

He paused again, gathering his emotions. "For all you Weber College students and alumni and anyone else who would care to join us, will you please sing with me one last time, our beloved school hymn, 'Purple and White'?"

In a reverent tone, the band played as almost everyone in the crowd began singing in unison.

Proudly waving o're ole Weber, an Ensign of truth and right.
I'll honored be if true to thee and dare to do the right.

As the band played, a path emerged in the crowd from the enlistees to the waiting train. The boys made their way down the path, shaking hands with people they passed and embracing family members one final time. A few stopped, choking back sobs or wiping their eyes.

Chester hung back at the end of the line, chin held high as he scanned the crowd for Billie's face. Disappointment settled heavy on his shoulders as he neared the last steps to the gate. At the last minute, he turned to find his family, Hank, and Ella, and gave one last wave before disappearing into the train.

"Sometimes that girl makes me so angry," Ella muttered under her breath. "I just wish for once she would treat a guy with respect."

Hank raised his eyebrows in agreement. Being a no-show to say goodbye to Chester was probably the worst he had seen from her.

The whistle blew, and the train lurched forward.

Chester looked out the window of the train, disappointment written on his face. He was leaving home for an uncertain future, and the girl of his dreams didn't show up to say goodbye.

The train went forward with a creak of its wheels, and as it cleared the station, the snowcapped mountains came into view, towering majestically over Ogden. A figure stood on the edge of the parking lot. As the train picked up speed, all the passengers looked out their windows in curiosity at the lone figure, her arm raised in a long, slow wave. Chester's heart leapt as the train whooshed by her distinctive athletic form, waving slowly and wiping tears from her face.

Chapter 12
March 24, 1942
Ogden, Utah

One afternoon at work, Hank approached Art. Taking deep breaths to draw up his courage, he squared his shoulders and asked softly, "Uh, Art?" Hank looked at his feet. "Can I ask you a quick question?"

"Sure Hank, what's up?"

"I've always wanted to learn to fly, and the more I've worked here and been around pilots, airplanes, and everything, I really want to learn how to fly more than ever."

"That's great Hank!"

"I was wondering if you could work out a deal with me so I can earn my license, like you did with Billie? You know, trade work hours for flight time?"

Art tilted his head, looking over Hank with a thoughtful gaze.

"Hank, I'd love to, but the timing couldn't be worse. Right now, I'm not in charge anymore; the Army is making most of the decisions. I can't bypass their system because they've claimed all of my planes and instructors for the foreseeable future. Even if I could squeeze in some flight time, you'd still need to finish ground school before I couldn't schedule any flight instruction, and the waiting list is a mile long. But if you're serious, I'd get your name on the list and we'll see what happens."

Hank looked deep in thought, fidgeting with his shirt button.

"I'm sorry, son." Art put his hand on Hank's shoulder. "I think you'll just have to bide your time. You'll get your turn soon enough. Just be patient."

Hank could do nothing but accept Art's answer. It made sense, but his life was still on hold. The months had crawled by. Something had to give.

That next Sunday after church, Billie walked through the Meyer's front door and asked, "Where's Ella?"

"She's upstairs in her room," Marta replied. Billie headed straight for the stairs, but Marta stopped her and asked, "Goot to see you, Billie. Has your letter come yet?"

The look on Billie's face said it all, but she replied, "Not yet."

"Maybe it vill come dis veek," Marta added.

"I hope so," Billie said. "I've never wanted anything as much as I want this."

"If God sinks it is best for you, zen it vill happen," Marta said. "You must trust Him in zese matters."

She sounded just like Hank. His constant references to God and faith were just echoes of his mother. But somehow, when Marta spoke of her faith with a warm smile and kindness in her eyes, a calm came over Billie. She flinched at the words but relaxed, nowhere near as bristled with defensiveness as when it felt like Hank was pushing religion down her throat.

"It's hard to have faith sometimes," Billie said. "I wish I could believe like you."

"You vill, Billie." Marta smiled and said, "But you get vat you vant when you verk hard enough."

Billie walked up the stairs and knocked on Ella's door. "It's me." Without hesitating, she opened the door.

Ella gasped and covered herself. "Wait just a second!" she demanded. "Oh, it's just you."

"Just me?" Billie retorted with sarcasm.

Ella rushed to get dressed while Billie paced back and forth, searching for the right words to start the conversation.

Ella didn't wait. "Where've you been this whole week?"

"Just busy, I guess."

"Too busy to show up to see Chester off?"

Billie hung her head. "I just don't like sappy goodbyes."

"So, you spend all week with him, build up his hopes that you two are serious," Ella scolded, "then just when he's the most vulnerable and he's getting on the train, you're a no-show?"

Billie didn't reply.

"How could you do that to him? He was heartbroken."

Billie snapped her chin up. "I'm not his property. I don't belong to him."

"You go out almost every night for a week, and you don't think you've sent him a message?"

"I didn't want to make a scene."

"Couldn't you at least be a friend and show your support? Say 'good luck' and 'take care'?" Ella asked.

"I told you, we enjoyed being with each other, but is it really a surprise that he likes me a lot more than I like him?"

"So why would you lead him on like that?"

"He's fun to be with."

Ella crossed her arms and pierced her with a dark gaze. "Be serious. Your on-again-off-again romance over the past few years has been nothing more than a relationship of convenience for you."

"What does that mean?" Billie asked.

"Well you have to admit, Chester is nice to look at, he's fun, and watch out when both of you get on the dance floor."

Billie looked at Ella and smiled. "There's no doubt people like to watch us dance together."

"But you just use him when you're in the mood. Otherwise, he's in the way," Ella voice was almost to a shout and shaking with frustration.

"I think Chester is a nice boy, most of the time. Sometimes, well…" Billie trailed off.

"But deep inside," Ella spoke softly, "You've always thought you could do better, right?"

Billie looked out the window and fidgeted with her coat buttons.

"You want someone who's a bit more cultured, more sophisticated, and more interested in the things you like, right? Like airplanes and seeing the world. Chester is just so…rural, so small-town. Right?" The sharpness of Ella's accusing tone made Billie shoot her a glare.

"What's wrong with wanting a guy whose hands aren't cracked from milking cows in the dead of winter, or whose fingernails aren't caked with dirt and… heaven knows what else is in there?" Billie shuddered. "Is that too much to ask?"

Ella shook her head in exasperation as silence filled the room.

"Okay. So, what's really on your mind?" Ella asked, changing the subject. "Did you hear back from Jackie Cochran?"

"No!" Billie replied, her face revealing her panicked desperation. "Time is running out. They were supposed to send a letter two weeks ago."

"What if it's just not the right time?" Ella asked.

"That's what I'm afraid of—that all I'm ever destined to do in my life is get married and have babies. That's not what I want."

"You know what?" Ella asked. "I'll bet I know you better than almost anyone, including your mom. And I know you want to do this more than anything because it's a chance to make your mark. To show the world what you're made of. To prove that you are truly one-of-a-kind."

Billie agreed with a nod.

"And it would certainly help to rub shoulders with people like Jackie Cochran," Ella said.

"You're absolutely right. It's not so much that I want to be famous, but I'd take it if it happened," she laughed. "Maybe I would be a good representative for the church. I could show the world that Utah women aren't so weird after all."

Ella coughed and laughed at Billie. "You? An example to the world of what Utah women are all about?"

"What's so funny?" Billie protested.

Ella snickered. But seeing Billie's face turn red, she forced herself to stop laughing. "I'm sorry Billie. It just struck me as funny. You've spent most of your life trying to prove you aren't like Utah women. But I didn't mean to laugh at you."

Billie stood taller. "I may not be a Bible-thumping know-it-all like you, but that doesn't mean normal people wouldn't think I was a good ambassador for people from Utah," Billie declared.

"I didn't say that. What I meant was, if you're not trying to be that person now, what makes you think you'd do it if you were famous?" Ella asked.

"How dare you judge me, Ella," Billie shouted. "You don't know how normal people outside of Utah look at us. Especially at Mormon women. Why couldn't I be the woman to change that?" Billie looked at Ella with disdain.

"Because you aren't the typical Mormon girl," Ella thought to herself, but feared that response was not likely to deescalate the conversation. Ella stood in silence, shaking her head at a loss for words.

"That's it? That's all you have to say?" Billie demanded.

"Calm down, Billie," Ella pleaded. "I don't know what to say."

"Maybe an apology? Something like 'I'm sorry, Billie. I didn't mean to imply that you weren't a good girl'?" Billie spat. "I *am* a good girl and despite what you think, I haven't done anything that I am ashamed of. You may think I'm some floozy or an alcoholic, but I don't do ninety-nine percent of the things you think I do."

Ella looked on, surprised by Billie's selective memory. Ella had endured Billie's frequent complaints about church youth leaders who warned against "passionate kissing" and "petting," and how it can lead to serious sins. Billie often admitted those rules were stupid. But now wasn't the time for Ella to remind her.

Billie's anger was reaching unfamiliar levels. The passion under her rage revealed a deep hurt behind her eyes.

"I'm sorry. I didn't mean to hurt your feelings, Billie." Ella looked upward, knowing she was in trouble.

Billie put her hands on her hips and leaned down into Ella's face. "You just don't get it, do you? You don't realize that I'm the normal one. It's you and everyone else living in this 'Utah cocoon' who are the weird ones."

"All I said Billie, was that if you're going to hold yourself up as an example of Utah womanhood, don't you think…"

Billie pounded her foot on the floor, hot tears brimming in her eyes. "I'm finished with this conversation." She stomped out of the room and slammed Ella's door. She bounded down the stairs and out the front door, mumbling to herself as she crossed the yard and swung open the front door to her grandmother's house.

"Billie, is that you?" her grandmother called. Billie didn't reply but stormed to her room.

At six the next morning, Billie tiptoed into the kitchen, but as she entered the room, a light flared to life on the kitchen table where her grandmother sat, her patient gaze stopping Billie in her tracks. "What's got you all tied up in a bundle?"

"Nothing," Billie replied.

"Was it something Hank said to you again?" Grandma asked.

"No, and I'm in a hurry. I'm late for work," she replied with a cold tone.

"Are you sure there's nothing I can do?"

"It's nothing, please, Grandma."

Billie had emptied her closet and draped her clothing over the sofa. Three pairs of shoes rested on top of it all.

"It looks like you're going to be gone for a while. Where are you going that you need all your clothes?" she asked Billie with caution in her voice.

"It's just easier for me to stay at our house in Ogden, and I'm going out tomorrow night with some college friends." Billie reached her arm under all the clothes resting on the back of the sofa. With a slight grunt she lifted them and held them in her arms.

"I don't think I'll be here for the next few weeks. We're really busy at work, and I promised Art I would work a few weekends to try to catch up."

"I see," her grandmother said. "When will I see you next?"

Billie shrugged her shoulders but didn't want to commit to a specific day. "I'll let you know. I've really got to go."

Billie gave her a quick kiss on the cheek and rushed out the door.

As she drove away, the confrontation from the night before kept surfacing in her mind, playing over itself, each of Ella's accusing words echoing louder each time. The longer she drove through the steep curves of Ogden Canyon, the angrier she became.

She arrived at the airport, parked the car, and took deep breaths to calm herself. She was here to work. No one should know she was upset.

After a long and exhausting day, Billie was glad she didn't have to drive back to Huntsville and had the much shorter trip to her parents' house instead. She didn't dare get her hopes up that the letter from Jackie Cochran would be there. Without thinking she shifted into park, turned off her car and rushed to open the mailbox. She jerked it open and pulled out an envelope. Smiling broadly, she instantly recognized the name of Mrs. Jacqueline Cochran in the upper corner, along with a Washington, D. C. postmark that added a look of officialness to it all.

Billie shrieked in anticipation and ripped open the letter. She scanned it in vain to find any indication that she was accepted. Instead, she caught the word "regretfully," and her heart sank. She was stunned. She re-read the letter, hoping she could find some good news, but there was none.

Dear Miss Russell,

It was nice speaking with you about our effort to build the first squadron of women pilots to ferry new planes to military bases throughout the country.

Regretfully, the military officials have determined that the minimum number of flight hours required for this assignment will be 500 hours.

Given your impressive flying career at such a young age, I anticipate you will be hearing from us in the future when you have the required number of hours.

Sincerely,
Jackie

Billie shuffled into the house. As she shut the door, weeks of pent-up emotions flowed from her eyes. In complete frustration, she dropped to the floor.

Chapter 12-Note 1: Born in 1906, Jackie Cochran was a celebrity prior to the outbreak of WWII. In 1935, she was the first woman to enter the famous Bendix Transcontinental Air Race. In 1938, she won the race and became world-renowned. She was friends with Amelia Earhart and other famous women pilots. Jackie was also a successful business executive, owning Cochran Cosmetics until she sold it in 1963, and was the first woman to break the sound barrier. She was inducted into the International Aerospace Hall of Fame in 1965 and, in 1971, the U.S. Aviation Hall of Fame.

CHAPTER 13
April 2, 1942
Huntsville, Utah

Like it was any other night in early spring, the Meyers' house was silent after dark. The entire town of Huntsville was buried in a sleepy quietness. Seven inches of heavy, compressed snow had fallen throughout the night, blanketing the landscape.

Hank was startled awake at three in the morning; a deep rumble disturbed the frozen stillness. The sound shuddered to a stop, echoing through the silence into his room. He rose from his bed to look out the window, but only an empty patch of white stared back at him. He heard Ella stir in the adjacent room.

"Did you hear that, Ella?" he said in a whisper just loud enough for her to hear through her open door.

"Yeah," Ella answered in full voice, not afraid to wake everyone else.

Hank jumped from his bed and rushed into Ella's room. She held her breath as they both tried to listen more closely. From Ella's room on the other side of the house, Hank peered out her window, studying the road in front of their house. His sleep-filled eyes opened wide. Human shadows approached the house. Within seconds he could see a group of people walking in their yard. As they drew closer, their feet made a crunching sound in the snow beneath them. When Hank heard their muffled voices, he rushed back to his own room to look down from the window. He could see the shadows of three men standing on the front sidewalk. He strained in the darkness to make out their faces.

"What's that noise?" Papa jumped from his feather blanket and rushed to the window. Hank dashed into his parents' room to see his papa flinging open the curtains, revealing a crowd of men standing knee-deep in snow in front of his porch.

"What's going on?" he said under his breath.

"What is it, Karl?" Marta mumbled.

"I don't know. There are some men in our yard."

The window panes rattled as someone pounded on the front door. "FBI! Open the door!"

Marta screamed as she jumped up in bed, instinctively covering her torso with her pillow.

Karl said nothing, but his anger boiled with each incessant pound on the front door.

"Karl?" Marta asked, "What's going on? Who is it?"

A loud voice yelled from the front porch. "Open up! This is the FBI."

As Hank stared out the window, Karl grabbed his robe from the bedpost, fumbling in the darkness to put it on. He stepped into his slippers and stumbled from his bedroom. "Just stay there," he ordered his wife.

The pounding continued. "Hurry up!" the voice from outside demanded.

Karl walked down the stairs, one hand holding the rail. Hank and Ella followed close behind, but, at a sign from their papa, they stood locked in place at the top of the stairs. Karl turned on the light in the living room and was in no hurry to unlatch the lock. The instant he cracked the door open, a strong hand pushed it open, sending Karl stumbling to the floor as a team of men burst through.

"Vat's going on?" Karl shouted in English. "Who are you? You haf no right to barge into my home!"

Two men dragged him to his feet, pinning his arms behind his back. "You must be Karl Meyer?"

Karl struggled, and the agent twisted his arm tighter against him.

Hank and Ella looked on as Marta emerged from her room. They all stood at the top of the stairs, dumbfounded at the scene unfolding in their living room below.

"Vat is going on here?" Marta called out, her voice shaking.

Another agent's head jerked up to look at her. He dashed up the stairs and grabbed Marta's arm and demanded, "Come with me."

He dragged her down the stairs in only her nightgown and slippers. She cried out. "Stop it! Vat are you doing?"

"Shut up," the man said, slapping her on the cheek. He thrust his weight into her shoulder, pressing her against the wall. Unabashed, he frisked her everywhere for weapons, caring little about where he touched her. When he was finished, he shoved her to the floor.

She grunted with pain. "Stop, please. I'll do vatever you ask. But please, stop!"

"You're coming with me," the agent barked.

Ella's throat tightened at the silver glint of handcuffs in the dim living room light.

Hank rushed down the stairs. "Stop it! You have no right! You can't just barge in like this!"

Another man rushed up from behind Hank and grabbed his shoulder, spinning him around. He jabbed his finger in Hank's face and said, "You shut your mouth you little Nazi or I'll shut it for you!"

Karl sucked in air through gasps of pain as the two agents lifted him to his feet. They cinched his hands behind him tight enough to make him grimace. The last agent stepped forward, his fedora and woolen coat dusted with snow. He pointed at Hank and said, "I'll give you thirty seconds to get their coats. Starting now!"

Hank jumped, anger rising in his eyes. He dashed into the kitchen to retrieve his parents' coats. His hands fumbled and he dropped them. He scooped them back up and stormed into the room, throwing the bundle of wool and leather at the agent.

The man's face turned red. "You're lucky we're only here for your parents. But I have half a mind to take you and your sister too, and let headquarters sort it out later."

Hank gave the man a defiant stare.

"Unfortunately, you're both working for the war effort, and to make matters worse, you were born here." His words dripped with derision.

"Where are you taking my parents?" Hank demanded. "What are you charging them with?"

"Your parents are being detained under the Alien Enemies Act and are suspected of collaborating with German intelligence. They are being taken in for questioning."

Hank stuttered, a stream of questions gushing out. "What? How? German intelligence? That's crazy!" He wrung his hands. "They would do no such thing. That's ludicrous."

But the man motioned to his agents. "Go find the evidence. Search upstairs."

Six men dashed up the stairs. Within seconds, Hank cringed at the sounds of dressers and closets being flung open and men rummaging and shuffling upstairs. The crash of glass echoed throughout the house. Ella looked at Hank with terror in her eyes.

A thought pierced through Hank's anger, dread swelling up inside him. The sudden memory of the suitcase brimming with his Hitler Youth Uniform and other Nazi memorabilia flashed like a burn. His closet. Hank's face flushed and his heart thudded in his chest. Without thinking, he rushed up the stairs into his room and shouted, "You have no right to destroy our property!" he demanded. "Get out!"

The two FBI agents looked up in surprise, then smiled at each other. "There must be something in here he doesn't want us to see," one added in a mocking tone. The man stood considerably taller than Hank, and his arms extended beyond the sleeve of his coat, exposing hairy hands and fingers. With spite in his eyes, he reached toward Hank's German cuckoo clock on the wall, slamming it to the floor. Hank was powerless to protect his German keepsake, and watched it shatter into pieces. The agent looked at Hank with a mocking smile. "You have something to say about that?"

Hank was incredulous. He rolled his shoulders as if his own clothing made him uncomfortable. A wave of fury welled up, and he took a half step toward the man, his hands clenched tight.

"You threatening a federal agent, little man? Go ahead. Take your best shot," the agent taunted.

Hank looked away with rage still burning in his eyes. His glance stopped on his closet, and at that instant he realized his mistake, jerking his head away.

"Look in the closet," the agent told the other.

The men yanked his closet doors open. They threw coats and clothing in every direction. Hank watched in terror as they peeled away layers of his belongings. The man stopped to inspect a binder with pictures from Hank's childhood. Finding nothing incriminating, he threw it aside.

Heart pounding in his chest, Hank stepped out of the room. In his parents' room across the hall, two other men fumbled through books and papers and set some of them aside. Hank turned back around. An agent lifted his hidden suitcase from the bottom of the closet.

"What does it say on the label?" the tall man asked the other. The other man tried to pronounce it but mumbled.

"Deutschland," Hank called out without hesitation. "It says Deutschland. It means Germany. I wrote it when I was eleven years old when I visited there with my mother and sister. Do you want me to show you what's inside?" he asked with contempt.

The man gave a nod. "Sure. Go ahead."

Hank unbuckled the belt, opened the case to reveal his uniform.

"I got this when the Nazis took over a scout meeting I attended. They gave each of us one of these Hitler Youth uniforms." He pushed aside the photos of Hitler and the agent snatched them up to inspect them. Hank dug the folded flag from the bottom of the case and threw it at the agent. "My grandfather tore this down from a streetlight. He gave it to me and I brought it home to show my friends. My mama and papa don't know I have it."

The large man grabbed the flag from Hank and unfurled it. "Will you look at that? A genuine Nazi flag," his voiced raised with astonishment. "You ever seen one of those before?" he asked the other.

"Nope, never seen a real one like this."

"I don't know about you, but I think we've got enough."

Dutifully, they stuffed the items back into the suitcase and buckled the belt.

"Those are all *my* personal belongings. My parents know nothing about them," Hank pleaded.

"You're sure about that? Your parents didn't know anything?" The agent raised an eyebrow. "We'll leave that up to the judge."

The men began filing downstairs, clinging to a handful of books and Hank's old leather suitcase.

"We found more than enough evidence," one man announced, shooting a satisfied smile at the man in the fedora. The remainder of the men came stomping down the stairs behind him. The man in charge gave Karl a shove, guiding him toward the front door.

"That was easier than I thought," he smirked.

Marta was lifted to her feet, and Ella rushed to pick up Marta's coat from the floor and wrapped it around her mother. Hank also jumped up, placing the coat around his papa's shoulders. An agent pushed

Karl out the door and down the snow-covered pathway, caring little that Karl's coat was about to fall off.

Hank and Ella stepped to the door to watch what they were doing to their papa. Car exhaust puffed from two black sedans idling in the snowy driveway. One of the doors opened and the men thrust Karl into the back seat. Once his feet were inside, the door slammed shut. The car started to back out of the driveway.

As the car drove away with Karl in it, Marta was being pulled off the front porch. She landed on her knees, and as rough hands gripped her and pulled her to her feet, she felt icy snow inside her slippers. Two men pushed her from behind. With her hands cuffed in front of her she lost her balance on the slippery sidewalk. She reached down into the snowbank to regain her footing. Careful not to fall, she neared the second black car and a mysterious man opened the car door. From behind, she was shoved towards the door opening and her foot slipped. As she fell, her head slammed into the car door frame and she gave a loud cry.

"Stop it," she begged. "You're hurting me."

"Then keep your head up."

He hefted her small frame and tossed her inside the open door. She landed in a heap on the back seat. Groaning, she struggled to sit up, and she reached for the coat that had slipped off her shoulders; it obstructed the door from closing. The man shoved the coat inside and slammed the door shut. Another man standing behind the car tapped the trunk twice. "Okay, we're clear back here."

As the vehicle began to pull away, Hank reached to draw Ella closer to him. They both watched as their mama looked at them with tearful eyes, too shocked to utter a sound.

Hank's face blanched with anger; a pained expression written on his face.

"How can they do this?" Ella whispered. "It's not right."

Within seconds, the entire caravan of cars drove off into the darkness, picking up speed and fishtailing on the snow-covered roads. Soon, only their taillights remained in a cloud of snow before everything melted into blackness.

CHAPTER 14
April 2, 1942
Huntsville, Utah

Dawn broke only a few hours after their parents were taken away. Ella and Hank sat stiff and numb, half asleep on the sofa. The emptiness of the house settled over them with an overwhelming loneliness. As the sun brightened the room, Ella watched as Hank stood from the sofa, then knelt to retrieve a book that had tumbled to the bottom of the stairs. With somber resignation, she also stood to stretch her arms and legs. She also reached down to pick up a broken clock, some porcelain figurines, and other precious keepsakes, all scattered in pieces, thanks to the careless federal agents.

Knowing they needed to eat something to sustain themselves, they each made themselves two slices of toast for a quick breakfast. As they sat at the kitchen table, a soft knock came from the front door. Ella's heart raced as panic rushed over her. The glint of a badge and stern gazes flashed through her mind. She glanced at Hank, knowing he was thinking the same thing. She stood slowly, crossing the room and calming her racing heart, telling herself the knock was too soft to be a threat. Hank jumped in front of her to open the door.

With great caution he cracked the door open, Grandma Russell smiled back at him. He exhaled with relief, opened the door, and invited her inside.

"I had the strangest dream last night," she laughed. "I dreamt you had an all-night party and people were coming from everywhere. It was the craziest thing…"

"It wasn't a dream," Ella interrupted, the tears pooling in the corner of her eyes. She stepped aside to let Grandma sit on the sofa, turning her face away.

Grandma looked at Hank, her eyes tightened with concern. Ella swallowed and said, "The FBI came last night."

"Where are your parents?" She glanced around the kitchen.

"They were arrested," Ella said. Hearing it aloud for the first time made her chest tighten. "For being spies."

Grandma stood, gulping back disbelief. "I thought I heard a commotion, but apparently I was sound asleep. So what happened?"

Ella recalled the events, emphasizing the cruelness of the ordeal. Hank listened from the kitchen doorway, nodding in agreement with Ella's description.

"We've got to help you find them," Grandma insisted. "We can't just sit here doing nothing. How can I help?"

"We don't know yet," Ella said. "We're still cleaning up."

"Do you have any idea about where they may have taken them?"

"No idea whatsoever," Ella replied. "They said nothing except that they were suspected as spies."

Grandma shook her head in disapproval, but recognition dawned in her eyes. "I wonder if this had anything to do with the FBI agent who came knocking on our door a couple weeks ago? He asked both me and Billie if we had seen any Japs or Nazi people lurking about. Or if we knew anyone who may be sympathetic to the enemy. They asked me about both of you and your parents, but nothing that would be cause for concern. That was basically all they said. I don't know what they asked Billie, but I'm sure she wouldn't say anything bad. You're her second family for heaven's sake." Ella gave a nod in recognition.

Hank cleared his throat. "I'm glad you said something about them coming to talk to you," Hank said. "They were probably stalking us for weeks."

The telephone rang and Ella answered.

"Hi, darlin'," Tom answered in a cheery voice. "I made it!"

Ella exhaled as she said, "Oh, hi, Tom."

"That's the best you can do? An 'Oh, hi, Tom?' We've got three whole weeks together. Aren't you excited?" he asked with a flirt in his voice.

How could she tell him? She took a few deep breaths, taking far longer a pause than she meant, but she finally said, "It's been a horrible few hours. You won't believe it."

"Horrible in what way?" he asked. "What happened?" She explained the details of what occurred just a few hours earlier, but now it seemed a lifetime ago.

"That's awful. That's simply unbelievable. Are you all right?"

Ella tried to say more, but her voice tightened and all she could get out was a squeak.

"I'll come over right away," he said. "Let's figure out where they are. They can't be too far away, right?"

Despite Tom's plans to go dancing or hiking or driving to visit Temple Square in Salt Lake City with Ella, every spare moment of his leave was spent following up at police stations and federal offices looking for answers. The FBI said nothing. They wouldn't even confirm that they were in Huntsville anytime in the past month. Local police officers, the sheriff, and other government officials also said nothing. After a week of hitting one roadblock after another, Tom decided to work his military connections to try to get some answers.

One of his friends from high school was stationed in an Army Intelligence unit at Fort Douglas in Salt Lake City. He and Ella made the hour-long drive and parked in front of a bustling office that housed hundreds of workers. Tom opened the car door to help Ella out, and she walked beside him toward the front door. She reached out to hold his hand, but his long strides and intense, focused gaze made her pull back. She had never seen Tom like this, and even though it made her smile, a tinge of fear made her hesitate.

Tom led them through the entrance, glancing around for directions to the Office of Army Intelligence. Down a long, sterile hall with a shiny, polished tile floor, Tom found the office and approached a young woman at a desk near the doorway.

"I'm Captain Davis. I need to speak to Major George Hale about a sensitive matter."

"He's not available."

"How do I make arrangements to speak with him? Today. It's urgent."

The woman looked at Tom and Ella. Tom watched Ella lift her chin with determination. The woman gave an audible sigh and said, "Wait here."

"Thank you, ma'am." Once the receptionist turned her back and walked into a back office, Tom smiled at Ella. Tom gestured to a chair, and Ella sat down. She glanced around at the walls, the desk, the floor, folding her hands in her lap, which seemed to calm her nervousness. The minutes crawled by.

An office door down the hall opened, and a lieutenant emerged. When he saw Tom, he saluted. Tom smiled and returned the salute.

"How can I help you, Captain?" the lieutenant asked respectfully.

"I have information relating to a pair of German-Americans that are currently being held for questioning. I must speak to Major Hale now."

Tom stood tall, adding nothing else.

Sensing Tom's confidence, the lieutenant nodded. "Okay. I guess you can explain the details to the Major. I'll set you up for three this afternoon. That's his only open slot. Will that work?"

"We'll make it work," Tom replied, and thanked him. Tom turned and motioned for Ella to follow him. As they left the building, they could do nothing but sit and wait a few hours for their meeting.

"What do you think he can do?" Ella asked.

"I'm not sure," Tom said. "It just doesn't make sense that no one knows where they are. I hope he's willing to give me a clue of their whereabouts."

"Will he get in trouble?"

"Oh, he's not going to do anything that would risk his career. We'll press as hard as we can because we've really got nothing to lose."

Just before three o'clock, Ella and Tom entered the office and waited to be called.

"The major will see you now," a receptionist announced with a smile. Tom gave Ella a surprised glance at the receptionist's cheerfulness, and Ella shrugged with a slight smile.

Tom walked into the major's office and saluted. With a broad smile Major Hale recognized Tom "Why if that isn't Tom Davis. How the heck are you?"

"I'm not doing so well, George." Tom's face was all business. "I've got a serious problem, and I need your help."

"Okay. How can I help?" His reply was amiable.

"Right now, I'm attached to the 81st Fighter Group at Muroc Army Airfield in California," Tom said. "I'm on furlough before heading overseas, and I need your help in finding some American citizens of German descent who are being held by the U.S. government. How do I find out where they are being held?"

"Why is it any concern of yours?"

"This is Ella Meyer; she's my girlfriend, and these people are her parents," he said, putting an arm around her shoulder. "And all the evidence is they are being denied their constitutional rights."

"What makes you think their rights are being denied?" the major asked.

"They have had no contact with their family since they were detained on April 2. That's just not right. No one knows of their whereabouts."

When the major stared back with an impassive look, Tom didn't blink. Ella watched Tom as his face darkened, and she could hear the restraint he used not to raise his voice. "We haven't been told why they were arrested, or what, if any, charges they are being held on."

The major spoke, "We are at war, Tom. Enemy spies are everywhere. We have to take extraordinary measures to protect ourselves."

"I understand the risks," Tom replied, "but regardless of the threat, our country operates under the rule of law. I know of no law that allows for American citizens to be arrested without charge and held without the right to see an attorney, or that denies them the ability to communicate with their family."

The major furrowed his eyebrow as he looked at Tom, saying nothing.

"I can assure you that these people, these American citizens, are completely innocent of anything other than speaking German," Tom said. "The feds are holding two naturalized U.S. citizens and denying them due process. We are fighting to protect the world from the abuse of power and to defend the rights of all people, not just the powerful." Tom glanced over to Ella as she stared at the major.

"I can't give you sensitive information about an FBI case, Tom." The major's statement had a finality to it.

"I just need to know where they're being held," Tom countered. "I'm not asking you to break regulations or do anything illegal. I just need to know where they are. That's all. Nothing more."

Major Hale exhaled and replied with resignation, "Okay, what are their names?"

"Karl Meyer and Marta Meyer."

"Where do they live?" Major Hale continued.

"Huntsville, Utah," Tom said.

The major took some notes on his notepad and said, "I'll have someone get on it. It may take me a few days."

"A few days?" Tom protested. "I have to report back to my unit at the end of the week."

"Hey, this is the army. You should know by now that we do things in their proper order. If I can get that information, then great. If I can share that information with you," he paused for effect, "even better."

The major wrote down Tom's contact information and shook his hand.

"I can't thank you enough," Tom said, relaxing into a smile. "I appreciate your taking the time to hear me out."

The day before Tom was to report back for duty in California, he received a call from Major Hale at Fort Douglas.

"They are being held in the Salt Lake County Jail, along with several other enemy aliens."

Tom jotted it down in a notepad.

"But Tom," the major said, "they are not permitted to have visitors."

Tom frowned. "But sir—"

"You cannot go visit them; do you understand?"

"I promise you I will not visit them."

Tom thanked him and hung up.

"Operator?" he shouted.

He asked to be connected with Weber College, and the secretary tracked down Ella within minutes.

"What happened, Tom?" Ella asked.

"I just got a call from Major Hale." He spoke with a deliberate pace, listening to her reaction.

"And…"

"Your parents are being held in the Salt Lake County Jail."

"That's odd. Why there?"

"Major Hale didn't say, but apparently that's where the FBI is holding other enemy aliens."

"Did he say we could go see them?"

"He made me promise that I wouldn't go visit them," Tom said, a sly grin spreading across his face. "But I didn't promise anything for you."

"Maybe we can start by writing them a letter."

Tom thought for a moment and responded, "He didn't say we couldn't write a letter. Why not give it a try?"

When Hank called the jail and asked for an address to mail a letter to his parents, the jailer claimed they had no prisoners by that name. He hung up the phone with a frustrated slam and told Ella and Tom.

"They refuse to acknowledge they're even there."

Tom crossed his arms, deep in thought. "We need a lawyer."

Ella looked up in surprise. "Where are we going to get a lawyer?"

"There's one who lives in my neighborhood in Ogden," Tom said, "Frank Loveland. I'm sure I can arrange something with him."

Tom made another call. As news of the Meyer's situation had become known throughout the community, Frank Loveland agreed to take on their case without charge.

In Loveland's office, Tom and Ella sat across from his large, oak desk. Loveland was attentive as Ella explained the situation. After jotting down a few notes, he looked at Ella and Hank and offered as much encouragement as he dared. "My guess is we'll need to submit a writ of habeas corpus," Loveland said.

"What's that?" Tom asked.

"It's a legal process that requires a jailer or warden to give a valid reason why a prisoner is being held."

"Great, why don't we just do that now?"

Loveland had a ready answer. "I've already looked into it. There is no evidence of any legal trial or hearing. In the legal system, your parents don't exist."

Ella gave Tom a puzzled look.

"Without evidence that they are being held somewhere in a judge's jurisdiction, there is technically no violation of due process."

"So, what are our options?" Ella asked.

"We can force them to admit they exist," Loveland shrugged. "We really have nothing to lose."

Ella gave a nod of approval.

"I'll prepare the legal document threatening an order of habeas corpus if there are prisoners being held without charges."

"What will that do?" Ella asked.

"Not too much, more than likely. If they want to keep them hidden, they have ways of keeping them hidden."

"So what's the point?"

"If you show the writ to the jailer, you may be able to scare them into admitting your parents are being held there. But you have to go in with confidence," Loveland explained. "You can't overstate your position, and you have to remind them that they can be held personally liable."

"So you think our only option is to confront the jailer?" Tom asked.

"At this point, I do," Loveland said. "You don't have much to go on, but if you can bluff your way into getting some information, you really have nothing to lose, unless they want to arrest you for disrupting the peace or something silly like that."

"They can do that?" Ella asked.

"They can do whatever they want. They have a lot of resources, too, if they want to act above the law. It's your choice if you want to take the risk."

Tom looked at Ella, and she shrugged her shoulders. "I'll take Hank. He wants to help in some way. We should be okay," Ella said. "If I'm not back by tomorrow night, you'll have to come bail me out." Her laugh was a bit too loud, revealing her fear she might not come back.

In the parking lot of the Salt Lake County Jail, Hank and Ella pulled their car into a parking stall and turned off the car. Inhaling deeply, they shared a look, bracing for the worst. They walked in silently, approaching the jailer's desk.

The bald, round-faced jailer filled the entire chair, even spilling over in some places. He barked, "Visiting hours aren't until later today; you'll have to come back."

"Are you the jailer of record here?" Ella asked with confidence in her voice.

"No. He's here, but he can't be bothered right now."

"If you are under his authority, then I need to notify you that you are holding two prisoners here without a formal charge. We are here to protect their rights to due process. We intend to hold all jail personnel legally and personally responsible if they provide untrue or misleading information."

Ella produced a large envelope, the documents prepared by Mr. Loveland, tucked inside. She handed it to the jailer, and said, "Under Article one, Section nine of the U.S. constitution, as it pertains to *habeas corpus*, you can be held personally responsible if you are deceptive about holding prisoners without charge, and do not confirm their presence here. Their names are Karl Meyer and Marta Meyer. Are they here?"

Hank watched Ella square her shoulders and look the jailer in the eye. This was a side of Ella he hadn't seen before. When the guard glanced away with an unsettled look in his eyes, Hank smiled.

The guard slapped her papers on his desk. "Wait here." He walked over to an intercom and pushed a black button. It made an angry buzzing noise and after hearing a faint reply, the guard half whispered into the speaker. "Do we have Karl Meyer or Marta Meyer here?"

There was a long pause. The voice was soft and distorted, and Ella stepped closer to eavesdrop.

"It depends on who's asking," a deep male voice replied.

The nervous jailer looked over his shoulder. Ella turned away from the conversation, straining to hear, but pretending to be gazing out the window.

The man on the intercom whispered clear enough for Ella to hear. "If it's anyone but the feds, tell them there's no one here by that name."

Ella whipped around. "Then they are here!"

The jailer jumped away from the intercom, his face turning red.

Ella pounded the desk. "I heard what he said! If it's anyone but the Feds, they're not here. So they *are* being held here without charge and without legal counsel. You can't deny it."

The man cleared his throat, took a deep breath, and walked back to the counter. "I am not authorized to provide information about any federal prisoners that may or may not be held here. You must contact the Salt Lake County Attorney if you have further questions."

"We heard what you said. We know they are here!" Hank leveled his gaze at the man. "You will be held accountable for lying."

Another officer rushed into the room from an office behind a wall. This man was much larger than the first, nearly filling the doorway, his broad chest and thick arms even more intimidating.

He stared at Ella and commanded in a menacing voice, "We are not authorized to provide information about any federal prisoners that may or may not be held here. You must contact the Salt Lake County Attorney if you have further questions, do you understand me?" His voice more forceful and terrifying.

Ella didn't blink and shot him a cold stare. "What is your name and badge number?"

The first jailer threw up his hands, eyes bulging as he turned on Ella. "Listen to me little miss know-it-all. You don't scare me with all your legal huffing and puffing. I told you what you need to do. Now you take our chubby little fanny somewhere else, or I'll arrest you and your boyfriend here for impeding the duty of a uniformed officer."

Hank curled his hands into tight fists, shaking with anger. "Don't you dare touch her," he said. "We caught you lying. You are a poor excuse for an officer of the law. You will be sorry you lied to us. You will be sorry. Mark my word."

"Are you threatening a police officer?"

"You've lied to us, and now you insult my sister? You are about as stupid as they come, aren't you?"

Ella grabbed Hank by the shoulder and spun him around, pushing him toward the door. She could feel him resisting, turning back to say more, but Ella dug her grip into his arm. "Just walk away," she demanded. "He's taunting you so you'll do something stupid."

"There you go. Be a good little boy and run away to your mommy," the officer snickered.

"Ignore him, Hank," Ella demanded in his ear. "Don't let him control you."

Hank took a deep breath and turned back to the officers.

Both officials folded their arms and stared at Hank with haughty smiles.

"We will see that both of you are held personally responsible. You are not above the law," he spat at the two officers before taking Ella's hand and stepping toward the door.

Ella followed behind, staring at the floor unable to respond. She didn't see Hank look over his shoulder one last time. The first jailer taunted Hank, extending the back of his hand with a "run along child" gesture.

Hank boiled inside with anger, but he turned and walked out the door. Once they were through the door, Hank took a shuddering breath and dropped his shoulders. As they returned to their car, Ella's eyes brimmed with tears and she couldn't speak without her voice trembling.

"How humiliating; how demeaning."

"You were pretty impressive back there," Hank smiled at Ella. "You had that guy scared for a minute. You got him good, and he knows it."

Ella looked up at Hank and shook her head. "And who was that back there mouthing off to a policeman? Where did that come from?" she asked with an anxious smile.

Hank grinned, rubbing the back of his neck with a tense exhale. "It didn't change anything," he admitted. "They still won't acknowledge Mama and Papa are in there."

"Maybe not, but now they know their secret is out." Ella squinted her eyes as she mulled over the situation. "We know they are in there, and they know we know it."

"What if they come after us now?"

"They're not coming after us," Ella reassured. "But at least we learned where they are, for sure. That's more information than we've been able to get in a week, right?"

"I guess. But now what?"

"Now we need to get a judge to order that habeas corpus thing," Ella said. "That way we can get the legal ball rolling."

They sat in silence for the drive back to the lawyer's office. When they were allowed in, Mr. Loveland looked up as Hank said, "Salt Lake County Jail wouldn't let us see them."

Mr. Loveland listened as they explained everything, jotting a few notes here and there. When they finished, he set his pen on his desk. "I guess we have no choice but to file the necessary papers for the writ of habeas corpus," he said with clear resignation in his voice. "I'm sorry, but it may take several days. I'll have to sort it all out, but I will file the motion as soon as I can."

"We appreciate your help," Ella said.

"It's just so frustrating that they can get away with this," Hank complained.

"It happens," Loveland answered without hesitation. "But I hope not too often. I'd hate to think that everyone would act like this. It'll take me about two days to write up the documents. I'll submit them, and when I hear something, I'll be in touch."

They waited four days and heard nothing. The phone sat silent in the hall, and dread began to fill them again.

A week passed. Ella and Hank met at Mr. Loveland's office again.

"I'm glad you stopped by," Mr. Loveland said. "Just this morning I received a call from the judge, and he was not happy."

Ella's heart sank.

"Our attempt at forcing the federal government to act didn't work," he said, shoulders slumped with resignation as he met their gazes. "But what's unusual is that the judge personally called me to explain what happened, and why he couldn't do anything about it."

"What happened this time?" Hank grumbled.

"We can verify that your parents were at the Salt Lake County Jail yesterday. But by the time the judge's order arrived at the end of the day, your parents had been moved to somewhere outside of Salt Lake County, possibly outside Utah."

"You've got to be kidding me!" Hank protested.

"How can they do that?" Ella buried her face in her hands, voice strained trying to keep back tears. "How can they do whatever they want and get away with it?"

"It does seem that way." Loveland's face had a look of resignation.

"So why can't the judge's order force them to cooperate?" Hank asked.

"The only way an order of habeas corpus is valid is if the prisoners are within the jurisdiction of the court that issues it. They knew what they were doing," Loveland said. "Somehow the Feds caught wind of the order and had your parents moved. Unfortunately, you'll have to find them again and start over. I'm sorry."

"Thanks Mr. Loveland. We appreciate all you've done." Ella hung her head as they turned to leave the office.

"I wish I could have done more. But frankly, this is out of my league. You'll need to hire an expert with experience in working the Federal System," Loveland apologized.

Hank was preoccupied in thought as he drove home.

"Hank," Ella interrupted his reverie. "We're running out of money."

He drummed his fingers on the steering wheel.

"And we can't keep neglecting the farm. The house payment…"

"I know."

"What do we do?" She watched his dark expression, shadowed in the pale moonlight, and feared his answer.

He let out a strained exhale and paused. "We wait, I guess."

Ella gave a blank stare into the darkness.

"I'm sorry. I don't know what else to do."

"I know," Ella mumbled. "We just don't have any more leads."

Hank and Ella had been so preoccupied trying to find their parents and following up on leads, that they attended church in whatever community they found themselves. Throughout Utah, churches were in every community, and the services were all similar.

At the end of April, they were finally able to attend their own church in Huntsville. As they approached the building's doors, instead of a warm greeting, most members averted eye contact. Hank led Ella by the arm to a pew in the back, and they sat as their mother had taught them as children, hands folded in their laps.

An elderly lady and her husband came up behind Ella and Hank, saying loudly, "The government doesn't arrest people unless they have a darn good reason."

Hank looked over his shoulder, meeting the woman's disdainful gaze with his own.

Another woman marched up to their seat, surprise written on her face. "How did you get out of jail? I thought they arrested your whole family?"

"No," Hank snapped impatiently, "just Mama and Papa."

She walked away, shaking her head.

Ella hid her face as she wiped tears from her eyes. "What is wrong with these people? Don't they know we've done nothing wrong?"

Hank frowned and looked away blinking fast. He turned to Ella. "What's going on here? A month ago, these people were our neighbors and friends."

"They're treating us like traitors," Ella whispered.

Throughout the service, Hank watched as heads would turn discreetly, children and adults alike, to steal a glimpse of them as they sat at the back of the congregation. Hank kept his head down, preoccupied by this unfamiliar feeling of being unwelcome in the church he loved. He stared at the cover of a hymnal, then turned as Ella wiped her nose with her handkerchief, tears pooling in her eyes.

Chapter 14-Note 1: The details of Karl and Marta's apprehension in this chapter and others are based on the journals and sworn statements of numerous German Americans written after World War II. Most were apprehended and detained without charge and had their property searched and seized without warrant. Almost all trials and sentencing occurred without due process. Suspects were often apprehended based on uncorroborated, hearsay evidence gathered by federal intelligence agencies. German suspects had their homes raided and ransacked. Fathers, mothers, (and at times both parents) were arrested and simply jailed without concern for underage children who were left to fend for themselves; some children were eventually placed in orphanages. See The German American Internee Coalition, P.O. Box 714, New London, NH. http://GAIC.info/

Chapter 14-Note 2: German and Japanese Americans were repeated victims of the government's practice of using shell-game tactics to avoid writs of habeas corpus. One such account comes from the personal experience of Doris Berg Nye. Her German American family lived in Hawaii at the outbreak of war. Her father was held without charge, along with thirteen other Americans of German and Italian descent. When attorneys for these detainees produced a writ of habeas corpus, without warning, these detainees were put on a ship and sent to an internment camp in Sparta, Wisconsin (Camp McCoy). When their attorneys learned of their whereabouts in Wisconsin, they filed new writs of habeas corpus. The judge denied the writ on the basis that the prisoners were no longer in that jurisdiction. The detainees had been suddenly loaded onto trains and sent to Angel Island, in San Francisco Bay. See The German American Internee Coalition, P.O. Box 714, New London, NH. http://GAIC.info/berg-story

Chapter 14-Note 3: The Salt Lake County Jail was used to hold 13 enemy aliens in 1942, including German, Italian, and Japanese citizens. The portrayal of unprofessional behavior by these police officers is purely fictional and is in no way intended to depict a typical jail or other law enforcement agency, especially those of the Salt Lake County Jail. It is used to illustrate the types of legal obstacles German American families faced during this very chaotic episode in American history.

Doris Berg Nye. "Internment and Abandonment." *America's Invisible Gulag: A Biography of German American Internment & Exclusion in World War II: Memory & History. The Freedom of Information Times* online, accessed December 1, 2020, *www.foitimes.com/internment/Berg2.htm.*

CHAPTER 15
May 12, 1942
Salt Lake City, Utah

Karl stirred in the darkness, waking as he heard a sound, the clanking of the metal door opening. Harsh light spilled over him, and he shut his eyes tight. The jailer bellowed, and it echoed in his small cell.

"Get up. You're being moved."

"Vere are you taking me?" he asked, still groggy from sleep.

"Tooele. Now get moving."

"Vy am I going vay out there?" he asked. The jailer didn't answer.

After a small breakfast, they cuffed his hands in front of him and shackled his ankles. He stumbled along in a line of prisoners from the jail to two waiting trucks. One by one, they climbed into the back, the tarp over the truck protecting them from the sun. As the guards pushed Karl into the truck, he glanced at the other truck and saw Marta, her hands cuffed in front of her. His heart sank at seeing a guard manhandle her.

Karl settled into his position in the bed of the truck. The engine whined as it shifted gears and picked up speed.

"Do not speak to each other," one of the guards said. "There are severe punishments for anyone who speaks."

The truck rumbled on for over an hour. Karl grew stiff and sore, his mind drifting to Marta. When they pulled to a stop, a guard took Karl to a cramped cell with a bed and a stool.

"Stay here until we're ready to have someone talk to you," the guard demanded.

Footsteps shuffled in the hall, and a guard passed his cell escorting another prisoner. The prisoner's face was angled, dark hair hanging around it. But Karl caught her gaze. Marta's thin, gaunt face brightened, and he flinched at the sight of her eyes, how hollow and dark they were. He stepped forward to reach out for her but remembered himself and gave a stiff glance at the guard. The door of his cell slammed shut, and his guard walked away, the keys clanging on his belt. Marta had given him a quick, warm smile, and the fears rising in his throat calmed, if only a little.

After waiting almost an hour, a small, thin man entered Marta's cell. He had a small, graying mustache and wore a dark suit. "Tell me about your trip to Germany in 1935. Why did you go for an entire summer?" He scanned her with his narrow-set eyes, face stern and cold as stone.

She swallowed, unsure of her English. She concentrated to rid her words of her unmistakable German accent. "To see my parents."

"And you brought back Nazi reading materials to give away when you returned?"

"No," she said. "I vanted Karl to see how bad it vas in Germany."

"So you bring back a Nazi flag and a few pictures of Adolf Hitler because your husband needed all those copies?"

"A Nazi flag?" Marta asked. "I don't haf a Nazi flag."

He reached into a pocket and slapped a photograph in her lap. She leaned forward to peer at it in the dim light. She drew in a sharp gasp. The black and white photograph showed the unmistakable image of Hank's suitcase.

"I know about ze Hitler Youth uniform," she admitted. "They gave it to Hank ven he vas eleven. But I haf no idea about ze flag."

"It was hidden in the same suitcase," the man eye's narrowed to just slits.

Marta shook her head in exasperation. "My children brought back many souvenirs."

He grabbed the photograph and stuffed it back into his pocket, sneering at her.

"And you are Mormon?"

"Yes."

"You brought back materials to convince your Mormon friends that Hitler was a respectable man? We found a pamphlet that compares the Nazis and the Mormons, and how much they have in common."

"No," Marta winced. "My mother sent zat flyer to me. It's written in German. How could I use it to influence my friends if it's not in English?"

The man hesitated, thinking of a comeback.

"Why would your neighbors think you are a Nazi sympathizer?"

"My neighbors did not say zat about us."

"Then how did a neighbor know about the Nazi flag and where to find it?"

"Vat neighbor?"

He gave a coy smile. "Well," he hesitated. "She claims to be a friend of your daughter. I'll just leave it at that."

Marta gasped.

"Impossible." Marta sneered at the man in contempt. "Billie wouldn't say vee ver Nazis."

He didn't reply.

"She vouldn't say dat. You're lying."

"Oh, we've spoken to all your neighbors. They tell us some interesting stories about you and your family."

Marta adjusted herself on her bed, a shudder running through her.

"We know you prefer to speak German rather than English."

Marta looked at the floor and thought of her answer. "I vanted my children to be able to speak to zeir *Oma* and *Opa*."

"We know you and your husband like to attend the Nazi meetings in Salt Lake City under the guise of attending a German Social Club." His smug smile was unnerving.

She looked up again, eyes filling with fear.

He smirked again and then laughed "You know what I am talking about, don't you? Don't deny that you attended that Nazi event in Salt Lake City."

"Ve didn't know ze Nazis vould be zer."

"How many times did you go?"

"Just zat vun time only."

"And you know that Nazi sympathizers run that club?"

"No! It vas only going to be German food and music."

"So you long to be back in Germany again, huh?"

"No. Not until ze police here started acting like Nazis," she stared at him without emotion.

He looked at Marta with disdain and spat, "I don't believe you. You lie, just like all Nazis. You are a conniving, up-to-no-good Nazi, and if it was up to me, I'd ship you back to Germany tonight." The man stood and closed the cell door behind him.

A week after arriving at the Tooele jail, Karl and Marta were taken back to Salt Lake City Jail, where they were photographed, fingerprinted, and given an alien registration number. Officially, they were designated "alien enemies," and their status as naturalized U.S. citizens was revoked.

On May 21, they were escorted to a makeshift courtroom inside the jail. Both were shackled at their ankles, but for the first time since their arrest, they were allowed to sit a few feet away from each other. A man in a baggy gray suit sat at a table across from them. He read a prepared statement: "Karl Heinrich Meyer and Marta Hildebrandt Meyer, you are both here because the evidence shows you are sympathizers to an enemy of the United States of America. You must answer the questions asked of you. If you are uncooperative, your detention could be extended much longer. Do you understand?"

Karl and Marta both answered in a whisper, "Yes."

He looked at Marta and asked, "Do any of the items on the table belong to you?"

"The pamphlet, yes," she replied. "But not ze flags and other tings."

"Silence!" The judge snapped. "You will only answer the question. Do not give an explanation or try to defend yourself. You may be given that opportunity later."

"Do you deny that these items were in your home?"

Marta whispered, "No."

He turned to Karl and said, "Do you deny that these items were in your home?"

"No."

"Did you do anything to remove or destroy these items that were in your home?"

Karl seemed defeated and gave a slight shake of his head.

"For the record, the defendant indicated his answer is 'no'."

"Did you make an effort to remove the Nazi flag or the photograph of Adolf Hitler from your home?"

"I've not seen zat flag before, but ze photos and ze uniform..." Karl dropped his gaze. "Zey belong to my son."

The judge deepened his scowl, then scribbled a note on a notepad. "I think we have enough evidence. I'll have my ruling sent to each of you by the end of the week. Until then, you will be sent to the Santa Anita Assembly Center until further notice."

Karl tensed, eyes filling with fury. "You said ve could defend ourselfs. How can you rule before ve defend ourselfs?"

"Ve are American citizens!" Marta cried. "Vy are you treating us like ze enemy? I luf America!" The guard thrust the end of his weapon toward her ribs but stopped shy of touching her.

"Quiet down," he spat.

"Ze Germany I knew as a child...is no more," she said, tears running over her tired, worn face. "I'm an American, I luf Amer..." She gave a sharp cry as the guard shoved the butt of his rifle into her ribs. Karl jumped to his feet, but the guard grabbed his shoulders and shoved him back into his seat.

"You sit your butt down or the same will happen to you," he said.

Karl wrenched himself out of the guard's grasp, rage filling him with strength and bursting over. He shoved the guard out of his way and rushed to Marta's side. Two other guards lunged at him and pulled him to the ground.

"Karl!" Marta cried, "Karl don't."

Two more guards leapt on top of Karl. He struggled, breathing fast, but one twisted his arm far behind his back. Karl cried out in pain and stopped struggling.

"Stop. Stop. I'll do vat you vant. Please don't break my arm."

Still breathing heavily, he lay still on the floor. The guards waited until every ounce of resistance had melted away. Two guards then lifted Karl off the ground and slammed him to the floor again, crushing his chest and knocking the wind out of him.

Karl panicked to catch his breath. They ignored his plea for help, and they readjusted their weight to keep him from breathing, pressing him into the floor without mercy.

"Please get off," Karl coughed. "I can't breathe!"

He glanced up for Marta, but her shaky silhouette was distorted, the darkness closing in around him. Karl's strength was leaving him. His mind was a blur, but he could sense a guard pushing his knee into Karl's hip. Having no strength to resist, Karl felt the guard roll him onto his back. With one last burst of energy, he opened his eyes to see Marta, her face buried in her hands, shaking, quivering.

Karl drifted in and out of consciousness, and he didn't know how long he was gone. Taking a few shallow breaths he tried to force his eyes open. His head bobbed and his eyes fluttered as he struggled to focus. In the dim light he searched for his dear Marta, but she was gone.

Chapter 15-Note 1: Santa Anita Assembly Center was one of fifteen makeshift concentration camps created in the western United States to temporarily incarcerate 92,000 enemy aliens until more permanent internment camps could be constructed. The inmates were mostly Japanese Americans from Southern California, but it also held German Americans and other naturalized citizens who descended from countries allied with the Axis powers. Construction of the camp began in March of 1942, and in addition to the horse stalls, another 500 barracks were constructed in the parking lots. An estimated 18,000 internees were locked up behind barbed wire fences and large towers guarding the perimeter. Over 200 soldiers were assigned to guard this facility until all the prisoners were transferred to permanent internment locations throughout the west. Santa Anita Assembly Center was closed October 27, 1942. "U.S. Army. Final Report: Japanese Evacuation from the West Coast, 1942" (Washington, D.C.: GPO, 1943).

CHAPTER 16

July 4, 1942
Huntsville, Utah

Hank and Ella sat at the kitchen table, pages of the newspaper divided between them. Ella scanned snippets of every section while Hank bent over the sports, drinking in every word. The sun beamed through the window across their shoulders, and Ella's summer school textbooks leaned against each other in their place on the shelf, untouched that day.

"Listen to this, Hank." Ella lifted a page to read. "Since this is the first Independence Day celebration since the attack on Pearl Harbor, President Roosevelt has admonished all Americans to keep working, and avoid taking the day off. The Post Office, along with the War, Navy, and State Departments are ordered to work today. President Roosevelt set the example by scheduling a full day's work. Did you know that?"

Hank's head popped up. "Know what?" he asked.

"That the post office and federal buildings are all working today?"

"Yes," Hank said. "They wanted us to stay open, but Art refused."

Ella laughed. She finished reading the paper and asked, "Are you going down to the park for the celebration?"

"Probably not," Hank replied, running his finger over the baseball box scores. "I'd rather not take a chance that some old lady is going to call me a Nazi. What about you?"

"I guess it wouldn't be the same, not without..." Hank glanced up when she didn't finish. She flashed a smile and said, "Besides, I have a day off and I'm planning to take a long nap."

"Me too," Hank smiled. "And I won't feel guilty one bit. But wouldn't it be nice to have one of Mama's apple pies right now? It's the Fourth of July for heaven's sake."

Ella smiled as a wave of nostalgia swept over her. She nodded in agreement.

Hank rested his chin in his hand and gazed out the window. Across the way, Grandma Russell trudged out to her mailbox, stuffing a few envelopes inside and flipping the flag up.

He looked at the clock. "Guess I better check the mail. I'll be right back."

He walked barefoot to the mailbox and waved at Grandma Russell. She smiled and waved back. The sun-soaked ground burned his feet. Rushing, he reached inside the mailbox and found a handful of mail, the box stuffed full after a few days of neglect. Hurrying back to the cool grass, he shuffled through the pile, consisting of bills and other correspondence. One postcard caught his eye. He tucked the pile under his arm and examined it with care. Its nondescript details were addressed to "Ella and Hank Meyer, Huntsville, Utah."

The return address sent his heart racing.

Santa Anita Assembly Center, California
Wartime Civil Control Administration
Arcadia, California

The form letter had his mother's distinctive handwriting in the space left for them to print their names:

Karl Meyer and Marta Meyer are being detained at Santa Anita Assembly Center, California. This lawful detention is in response to Federal laws enacted to prevent seditious acts committed by enemy aliens during a state of war.

Only direct relatives may visit, providing a visitor pass is issued beforehand. Visiting hours are from 2–4 p.m. daily and are limited to one hour-long visit per month. To apply for a visitor pass, enter at the Baldwin Avenue gate during business hours.

"That's it?" Hank laughed. He turned the postcard over to see if there was anything else. He drew in a deep breath, excitement bursting through him, and let out a hearty cheer.

He ran to the front door, stumbling into Ella.

"What's the matter?" she asked.

"We got a postcard from Mama and Papa. They're in California!" Hank held the postcard high in his hand, waving it back and forth.

He handed it to Ella. She mumbled as she read the words "lawful detention" and laughed, wiping a tear from her eye.

"They're alive," Ella exclaimed through her tears. "They'll even let us go visit them. Should we go?" she blurted.

Hank shrugged his shoulders. "I'd have to get off work somehow. But what if we get all the way there and they won't let us see them?"

Ella scrunched her face in thought.

"Let's see what Mama and Papa say. Maybe they'll know if it's worth it for us to make the trip."

"I guess we could write a letter."

"Regardless, I'm so glad we found them," Ella said. "I was starting to wonder if we'd ever hear from them again."

"Me too," Hank said. "It's an answer to our prayers." He flipped the postcard over again.

"Where's Santa Anita?"

Ella answered, "I think it's near Los Angeles."

Hank reached into a drawer and handed Ella a pen. She took some paper from her notes. Hank sat at the table watching her write. Sitting deep in thought, her hands hovered over the page. "There is so much I want to tell them; I don't know where to start.

"Do you want me to start?" Hank smiled, knowing Ella would object.

"I'll start the letter," Ella insisted. "You can add whatever you want at the end. Okay?"

Within a half hour Hank had watched Ella write three entire pages full of news and updates. She explained that the animals were well cared for and the farm was running well, but that milk and cream sales were sporadic because they weren't home very often due to work. She asked what they should do about feeding the cows over the winter. Should they buy hay or just sell the cattle before the snow started to fly?

Her pen flew fast, ink filling the page. She paused before asking the heaviest question, the one that made her hand tremble.

"Should I ask if it's worth the risk for us come visit them?" Ella's kind eyes looked at Hank, calculating the pros of cons.

"You can ask. They'll tell us what they think," Hank added.

Ella handed Hank the letter, and he added a short note of his love and appreciation. He placed a five-dollar bill inside. Ella addressed the envelope, then placed a purple, three-cent stamp at the corner and sealed it.

"Let's hope they get it," she said.

Sunday morning, Hank stood in front of the bathroom mirror, fixing his tie for church. Footsteps pounded up the stairs, and Ella leaned into the bathroom doorway.

"Listen to this, Hank." She cleared her throat. "Thirty-nine persons of Japanese ancestry, including two enemy aliens, were held in the Utah County jail after a state highway patrolmen and agents of the Federal Bureau of Investigation arrested them for violating military curfew regulations."

"Can you believe that?" she asked. "They're rounding up the Japanese, too."

She looked down at the paper again and read: "Jay C. Siener, a special agent in charge of the FBI said the group passed through the Utah County smelter military zone at eleven-thirty last night as they were returning to their homes after a church picnic. Persons of Japanese ancestry are forbidden to enter such zones between eight p.m. and six a.m."

Hank listened as he frowned into the mirror, adjusting the knot in his necktie.

"I guess we're pretty lucky that we're not with Mama and Papa," Ella added.

"Would they arrest us even if we're natural-born American citizens?" Hank asked. "They wouldn't take us, would they?"

"You never know," Ella said. "But let's be careful about where we go and what we do in public. Especially after eight o'clock at night."

She folded the paper and said, "I've been thinking, Hank. Going to California would be too big a risk. If anyone stopped us, they could lock us up and not think twice about it."

Hank turned away from the mirror, disappointment written on his face. "You're probably right," he sighed. "It's like we're prisoners in our own country."

Chapter 17
August 17, 1942
Santa Anita, California

The Santa Anita raceway was about thirteen miles northeast of downtown Los Angeles. The Wartime Civil Control Administration leased the site from its owners, converting its thousands of horse stalls into living quarters for internees.

Upon arrival in early June, Karl and Marta had been given a small room in the barracks. At first it seemed like a blessing not to live in a converted horse stall. But the Southern California heat pounded the corrugated steel roofs, absorbing the sun's energy, and radiating the repressive heat back into each room.

The day they arrived, Karl and Marta stood in line to receive their utensils for mealtime. Both were handed a plate, cup, fork, and spoon, all made of tin. "These are all you get, so be very careful with them that they don't get lost or stolen. You will not get a replacement," the guard barked.

Inside the mess hall, the meal tables had been intended for children, on loan from the local school. The tables were portable and could be stored away if they needed to use the mess hall for other purposes. Inmates would fold and unfold themselves to get in and out of the undersized benches. While most of the Japanese prisoners had no problems with the table, Karl and the other, taller inmates weren't so fortunate. At six-feet tall, Karl needed to sit at the far end or else he couldn't stretch his legs.

The next morning, they learned about the showers. Just a hundred and fifty showers were available for an ever-increasing population of prisoners. With almost eighteen-thousand Japanese and German prisoners, the shower-to-inmate ratio was one for every thirty prisoners. Marta waited an hour to take a shower. Not only were there a limited number of showers, but they were also all out in the open, providing no privacy.

After sending the postcard to Ella and Hank a few days after they arrived, all they could do was wait for a letter from home. As each letter required the review of a censor, it would often take a month or so to get it. The long, tedious days were hard to distinguish, but on a sweltering afternoon in mid-August, the postal officer called out "Meyer." Marta's heart skipped. She hadn't had good news for so long, her hands trembled as she struggled to open the letter. At the sight of Ella's and Hank's handwriting, her throat tightened and her eyes pooled with tears. The first page explained all their efforts to find them. The end of the letter read:

It is such a relief to hear from you. We can't tell you how worried we've been.

What can you tell us about where you are and why are they holding you? We have so many questions. We would love to know more so we can help you.

Hank and I are doing fine. We take care of the animals. The crops are doing well and we expect a normal harvest in the fall. Hank milks Berta both in the morning and night. I try to help with the other chores. So far, it's going smoothly.

Hank graduated the first week of June, and he is still working at the airport, doing Billie's old bookkeeping job. Billie is now a flight trainer. School is going well for me. We're both keeping very busy.

Hank was told by the draft board that they would give him a hardship deferral on his enlistment until we can figure out when they will let you come home. He was so looking forward to enlisting on his birthday September 11, but that will have to wait.

We're also not sure what you want us to do with the cattle. We'll probably have to buy some hay for winter. We're not sure what you would want to happen. Do we spend the money on hay or sell the cattle?

We miss you terribly, and we're doing everything we can to get you out of there. We are trying our best. We want to come to visit you, but do you think it's worth the risk? Either way, remember that we love you and will always love you.

Love,
Ella and Hank

Marta walked with a bounce in her step back to her barracks. Sitting on the bed, she read the letter to Karl.

"You can tell Ella is trying to cheer us up," Marta said. "I miss them so much." Marta wiped her eyes, but turned to re-reading the letter, savoring each word from home.

Karl leaned back and closed his eyes, listening.

"You know," Marta muttered, "before this letter, home felt like a distant memory, almost like a place that never existed." She gave a soft exhale as relief washed over her.

"Like a cruel joke your mind played on you," Karl added.

"But I'm holding a paper that just a few weeks ago was held by my children. I feel like I've woken from a bad dream! I actually have hope that I'll see my family again. Don't you feel it too?"

"Yes, Marta," Karl replied with caution in his voice. "Of course I do. But I still see no hope of getting out of here any time soon. Who knows how long it will be?"

Marta snatched up a scrap of paper to respond to Ella.

Chapter 17-Note 1: For purposes of demonstrating the callous nature of how internees were held, the Santa Anita facility was used as an example of the deplorable conditions that existed. However, no evidence exists that German enemy aliens were held in large numbers at Santa Anita Detention Center. Most were held at the Tuna Canyon Detention Station in Tujunga, California.

"Tuna Canyon (detention facility)." Densho Encyclopedia online, accessed June 6, 2021, http://encyclopedia.densho.org/Tuna_Canyon_(detention_facility).

CHAPTER 18
September 2, 1942
Huntsville, Utah

Back in Huntsville, a hint of fall colored the mountains, the upper peaks tinted with red, orange, and gold. Bright patches of green on the hills had faded to brown, scorched after a long, sweltering summer. College classes were back in session, and the sun dipped below the western hills just after seven o'clock. With the long twilight, the Ogden valley glowed until darkness blanketed the basin each night.

Hank worked full time at the airport now, as the growth of Andrews's Flight School had exploded because of the wartime demand for trained pilots. Hank was an integral part of the operation, managing the office, bookkeeping, keeping student flight time records, and submitting all logs and other paperwork to the federal government.

Both Ella and Hank woke at five-thirty each morning. By six o'clock Ella had breakfast ready, and Hank had already milked Berta, their beloved cow, and finished getting ready for work. Hank would drop Ella off for her seven-thirty class at Weber College before making it to work by eight o'clock.

After work one day in mid-September, Hank and Ella drove home together, chatting about the day's events. Arriving at home, Ella stepped out of the car and reached into the mailbox. She glanced through the mail, stopping to study one of the envelopes. "It's a letter from Mama and Papa," she cried. "A real letter!"

Hank turned off the car to listen. Ella sat in her seat with the car door open. Her mother's handwriting covered the page, some areas blocked with black ink. "It's been censored," she said, shaking her head. She read the legible parts out loud:

> Your father and I believe you should sell the cattle at the end
> of the summer, or whenever you can get the best price. There
> is no reason to buy hay for the winter because you probably
> won't break even if you do. Pay bills with whatever money you

get, and if you can put some into savings, do it. I hope we'll have some left when we return.

If you can find a way, keep Berta for as long as you can. She will be hard to replace. We get a small amount of money from her milk, butter, and cheese to help us make ends meet during the winter.

We're happy that Hank received a hardship deferment from the draft board. It's an answer to our prayers; we're hoping he will stay home for the duration of the war.

We would love to see both of you, but because of the risks we've heard about, we don't think it is a good idea to come visit us. You must trust us on this. We wish we could say more.

With our deepest love,
Mama and Papa

Ella nodded in approval. "There you have it. We can sell the cattle. That's such a relief."

"At least we don't have to worry about them over the winter," Hank added. "But even after we sell the cattle, I don't know how long we can do this."

"How long we can do what?"

"Pay all these bills."

"After we sell the cattle, shouldn't we have enough to get by until I graduate and get a nursing job?"

"No, because you'll only be a first-year nurse. You'll make less than I do."

"It's better than nothing."

"And you won't finish your first year until next June. We'll be broke if we have to wait that long," Hank protested.

"Your paycheck will help," she countered.

"I make just forty-five dollars a month; we still have to eat, you know," Hank countered.

Ella shook her head in frustration, "What do you suggest we do?"

Hank paused, choosing his words. "I know Mama and Papa won't like it, but it'd be a lot easier for both of us if the Army was paying me a hundred bucks or so a month."

Ella was torn between wanting Hank to be home with her and wanting to keep the family homestead from going into foreclosure. She looked at Hank earnestly, and said, "I'd hate to see you go, but we may not have a choice."

Hank looked at her with surprise. This is the first time she had been open to the prospect of him going into the service.

"The guy at the draft board said my deferment will end in November, so I can enlist if I want to. He'll leave it up to me."

"It's up to you, Hank. The truth is, I don't see how we'll make it until next summer with what we're both making now."

"I hear all the guys on bomber crews are automatically ranked up to staff sergeant. They make a hundred-fifty bucks a month." Hank couldn't hide his anticipation.

"What are the chances of that?"

"I'd have to be accepted into the Air Corps, and then be accepted into aerial gunnery school."

"Good luck with just getting into the Army Air Corps. They're not letting enlistees pick their branch of the service anymore."

"I heard that, too," Hank admitted with disappointment. "Too many boys are enlisting in the Navy, and they don't have enough foot soldiers."

"Maybe you'll get lucky. Who knows?" Ella replied. "So, I guess we'll know more in November?"

"Yeah," he answered. "And we should have enough to make it until January or February, if we sell the cattle. What are you going to do with Berta if I go?" Hank asked. "Is Mr. Wangsguard still willing to take her?"

"That's what he said. Whenever we're ready. And he also said he'd give her back to us whenever you or Papa get back." Ella gave a nod of approval.

"I'd love to give her to him now. Maybe I'd have time to go to ground school."

"What's the point if you can enlist in a month or so?"

Hank pursed his lips and exhaled in dejection.

"I know you've always wanted to get your pilot's license," Ella tried to console Hank, "but without her milk to sell, we'll never make enough money to get by."

"I know," Hank stared at his feet, "but if I hadn't had to come home every night to milk the cow, just think about how many flight hours I could have racked up already."

Ella had no reply. Hank shoulders slumped, and he walked dejectedly up the stairs to his room.

CHAPTER 19

October 15, 1942
Huntsville, Utah

Fall was in full swing. The mountains exploded with bright colors of amber and orange. By mid-October, the nights were now cold and were expected to get still colder with each passing week.

Billie studied her day's assignments, staring at a clipboard and double checking each student's readiness for the day's training flight.

"Hey, Billie," Hank called as he walked into the hangar. "I have some letters for you from your grandma's house. She gave these to me a couple days, ago but I forgot to give them to you."

"Thanks a lot, Hank," Billie rolled her eyes. "I hope there's nothing important in there."

"I saw one letter that looks important." She watched with anticipation as he fished into his bag and handed her a stack of envelopes.

As Billie thumbed through the letters, Hank watched her with mild interest. He exchanged a glance with her student, a freckle-nosed boy that not only appeared nervous about his first flight lesson, but even more terrified of her.

Her eyes widened with excitement and she stopped to tear open an envelope. Her hands fumbled as she unfolded the paper. She read, devouring every word. "Listen to this Hank:

"Dear Billie,

You have been identified as a qualified pilot and instructor, possessing important aviation skills needed for the war effort. You are hereby invited to accept a position with the Women's Flying Training Detachment under the command of the United States Army Air Forces.

This new civilian organization will consist entirely of women pilots who will provide important flight-related services. Your objective will be to relieve male pilots assigned to domestic ferrying tasks and other training assignments and permit them to fulfill combat assignments overseas.

If you accept this invitation, you must travel at your own expense to Houston, Texas no later than Tuesday, November 13, 1942. We must receive your acceptance of this offer by Friday, October 30.

Please be advised that upon arrival, all trainees must pass a comprehensive physical examination prior to being accepted into the program.

We have included a document providing specific instructions about this program. Additional information may be obtained by contacting this office.

Sincerely, Jacqueline "Jackie" Cochran.
Director, Women's Flying Training Detachment"

Billie raised her fists and shouted, "Yes! Yes! Yes!" Her volume startled her student and a couple of mechanics working on a plane nearby. Her arms wrapped around Hank, giving him a tight squeeze. He was startled by her sudden closeness. His arms were glued to his sides, and Billie couldn't see his smile, or how he tilted his head a bit to enjoy the smell of her perfume and the scent of her hair. She let go, and he hid his disappointment behind a smile.

Billie looked at the letter again and smiled at Hank. "I've got until the end of this week to let Jackie know that I accept her offer. Hank, do you think I should send a telegram or just make a long-distance call?"

Hank raised both hands, palms up. "It's up to you. How much are you willing to pay?"

"Oh, to heck with it. I'll pay for a telegram. Can you send it for me?" she asked.

"I can figure it out. Just tell me what you want it to say."

"Great! But first, I've got to tell Art," she said. "Where is he?"

"He just went out on a training flight," Hank said.

"Of all the luck." Billie shot him a playful grin. "Oh well. He'll find out sooner or later. When you see him, let him know I'm looking for him. But don't say anything. I want to tell him."

"Okay." Hank smiled as Billie danced out the door, dragging her student by the jacket sleeve.

An hour later, Art came into the office and Billie startled him with an exuberant "Guess what, Art?" Her excitement spilled over like a child on Christmas; her face brightening in a huge grin.

"You're quitting to join a troupe of lady barnstormers?"

She blinked. "Wait…? What did you say?"

"Never mind. Tell me your good news," Art smiled, admiring his attempt at humor.

"I got a letter from Jackie Cochran. This time she wants me to join an all-women flying detachment. I report on November thirteenth." Billie handed the letter to Art.

He skimmed the letter, nodding his head with approval. "So you only have a few weeks to find your replacement. You better get hoppin'," he insisted sternly, but with a wink.

"I'll get right on it," she replied.

"Well, congratulations," Art reached out his hand to shake hers. "I'm surprised you've lasted here as long as you did."

"I thought I'd be stuck here forever," she answered without thinking, before clapping a hand to her head. "I didn't mean it like that." He shrugged with a smile, so she continued, "So, what are you going to do to replace me?"

"Don't know right now, but we'll figure it out," Art laughed. "I'm almost late for my next lesson. We can talk later."

Billie wore a smile throughout the day, telling anyone who would listen that she had been selected to join an elite group of women pilots. But with each person she spoke to, she ached more and more to share it with Ella. How many months had it been since she had stormed out of her grandmother's house or since she and Ella had a heart-to-heart talk? How many months since she'd even been up to Huntsville? As the day wore on, and her excitement mixed with this melancholy, she realized she had been longing to talk to Ella for a long time.

Billie followed Hank home, dashing up her grandmother's porch and slipping in through the door. When her grandmother looked up from making her dinner, Billie caught her breath, and her eyes filled with tears. She bent down and hugged her grandma, lingering to show her how much she loved her.

Billie glanced up through the window across the space between their houses, spying Ella in the kitchen. "I'm so sorry, Grandma, but I'm in huge rush and I can't talk right now; I have to talk to Ella, and then I've got go back to Ogden tonight."

"Oh, come now, why don't you stay here?" her grandmother said with pleading in her voice. "Your room is still the same as you left it."

"I know, Grandma," Billie said, "but I've got everything I need for work in Ogden. I promise to visit more often." The words burned as they left her mouth. The truth gave her a hollow feeling that she hoped her grandmother didn't sense.

She squeezed her grandmother's hand, then dashed to the Meyers' house.

Stepping up to the front porch felt different this time. An uncomfortable feeling hung over her as she glanced around. Even without seeing them, the house felt emptier without Karl and Marta. So much had changed since her outburst.

She took a deep breath. As she opened the door with caution, she knocked a few times, saying "Knock knock…anybody home?"

Hank peeked around the corner from the kitchen as Billie closed the door to the living room. He smiled and said, "Ella, Billie's here to see you!"

"Really? Wow. Be there in a sec," she called out.

Billie gave an awkward gaze around the living room, then sat on the sofa. Not long ago she would have marched right up to Ella's room. But things were different now. Just then, Ella bounded down the stairs and threw her arms around Billie.

Billie smiled, but looked at the wall, returning her hug with apprehension.

"I'm so glad to see you," Ella said, giving her a last squeeze before letting her go.

"How have you been, Ella? What's the latest between you and Tom?" Billie asked.

"I get a letter from him almost every week, unless he's traveling somewhere," Ella gestured to a world map hanging on the wall, dotted with pins where, Billie presumed, Tom's letters had come from. "Then I get two letters the next week," Ella laughed.

"Where is he now?" Billie glanced over the map.

"He gave me a cryptic clue in a letter. From what I can piece together, he's probably going to end up somewhere in Africa," Ella replied. "He's in England now. Or at least that's where he was scheduled to go first." She looked down at her hands, fidgeting with her fingers.

"Sounds pretty scary to me," Billie replied.

"I guess it is," Ella said with a shrug. "I try not to think about it too much. There's not a whole lot I can do anyway." She settled herself on the couch. "So, I hear you have some news?"

"I'm so excited," Billie said. "You have always been the first one to hear my big news. I couldn't wait to tell you. What did Hank tell you?"

"Only that you wanted to talk to me," Ella replied in all honesty. "He didn't say why."

Billie handed Ella the letter from Jackie Cochran. Ella smiled at the name at the bottom of the letter.

"Can you believe it?"

"I can believe it," Ella said. "I think what you do is amazing."

The two discussed the letter and the Women's Flight Training Detachment. Billie explained the program for twenty minutes, then asked Ella directly, "I want your honest opinion. What do you think?"

"I think it sounds like a great opportunity. I know how much you respect Jackie Cochran. You'll be doing something important for the war effort, and it looks like this opportunity may be better than the first one she talked to you about. Right?"

"You were right about waiting," Billie affirmed with a nod. "I don't think they really had the program all worked out when they first contacted me. But now it looks like they've got Army brass behind it," Billie said.

"When do you go?"

"I have to be in Houston on November thirteenth, so I don't have a whole lot of time," Billie smiled.

"Let's make sure we do a lot together before you leave. We have some time to make up," Ella said. "It's... it's been a long time for us to be mad at each other."

Billie forced a smile as a tear dripped from the corner of her eye.

"I know." Billie hung her head. "It's my fault. I'm sorry I was so bull-headed."

Ella wrapped her arm around Billie and leaned her head on her shoulder. Billie heaved a sigh of relief, letting much of her regret and shame melt away.

CHAPTER 20
November 11, 1942
Ogden, Utah

As everyone crowded around Billie, the reality of what was happening filled her more with terror than excitement. Ella and Hank had joined Grandma Russell at the Ogden train station to say goodbye. Art pulled up in a truck with a handful of mechanics, and Billie could only smile as everyone surrounded her.

Art handed her a small package wrapped in an old, tattered newspaper. "A going away gift," he said.

"Well it's clear your wife didn't wrap this, Art!"

Art raised an eyebrow. "Just open it."

She peeled off the paper and lifted a hardbound book entitled *High, Wide and Frightened*, a memoir by Louise Thaden.

"Oh, thank you! I've always wanted to read this book."

"You can start reading on the train."

"I guess I'll have plenty of time, won't I?" Billie answered.

"You know who she is, right?" Art tilted his head.

"Who doesn't?" Billie said. "She's held most every flying record there ever was for distance, speed, and endurance."

"But did you know she also retired from flying to raise a family?" Art paused, gesturing with his hands as he searched for the words. "I see a lot of her in you, Billie." Art choked back the tears. "Louise was a true aviation pioneer, and she said something I totally agree with: 'Women are innately better pilots than men.' You are a testament to that."

He reached out to embrace her, and she stepped in to give him a tight hug. Both wiped away tears as they separated. Art stepped back and, one by one, Billie shook hands and chatted a moment with the other instructors and mechanics. As the small crowd dispersed, Billie reached over to Art and playfully punched his arm.

"Thanks for teaching me everything I know. I couldn't have had a better teacher."

Art cleared his throat, and his eyes twinkled at her. "I saw something in you when you first came in and faked your way into a job as my bookkeeper."

"You knew all along?" Billie's eyes widened.

"I knew the next day when the real bookkeeper showed up with the correct paperwork," he smiled.

"Why didn't you ever say anything? I worried for months you would fire me because I wasn't a real bookkeeper."

"I had my reasons." Art gave a wry smile. "My instincts were right about you. You are an amazing pilot, and I know you will go far, if you work hard and don't take shortcuts."

Art's mouth twitched as he fought tears. Looking at Hank, then back at Billie, his voice squeaked, "I've… I've gotta run. We'll see you around." He stepped back a few steps, giving a quick glance at Billie, then turned in a hurry to make his getaway.

Hank's hands were in his pockets, as he stood by, just looking at her.

"It's been really…" he paused, "It's been great getting to work with you. Even though we didn't see each other that often," Hank stammered. "You'll be missed, and not just because you're a great instructor."

"Aww Hank, that's so nice of you to say," Billie replied with a warm smile. "I have to admit, I'm surprised at how well we got along. You're not so bad after all."

Hank blushed and dipped his head.

"So, what are your plans? Are you going to enlist soon?" Billie's eyes looked deeply into Hank's eyes. His heart leapt with delight.

"They gave me a hardship deferment because my parents are gone, but that ends next week," Hank replied. "Art doesn't know that yet. I want to know for sure it will work out before I tell him I'm going to quit."

"Well Hank Meyer! Sneaking around and keeping secrets from the boss." Billie hit Hank's shoulder playfully.

"I know. I feel awful, but if I tell him, he'll fret over it and make everyone miserable in the process," Hank admitted with unusual confidence.

"Yeah, he would."

As Hank looked at Billie, a rush of energy surged through his chest. The knots in his stomach twisted tighter, and he opened his mouth but didn't know what to say to her.

Billie looked at him, her eyes misty. "You're a good man, Hank. I'm sorry for how I've treated you all these years. You deserved better from me."

"Just remember me when you're famous and on the cover of *LIFE* magazine." He gave her a hopeful grin.

Billie laughed, then reached out both arms and gave Hank a quick, awkward embrace. She drew back right away, a nervous smile tugging at her lips.

"You deserve to be there with all the other talented pilots." Hank added with a kind and soft voice. "Don't you ever forget it."

"Thank you, Hank," Billie blinked back a tear. "That means a lot to me."

"Take care of yourself," he pled. "Please."

"I will."

She felt a tap on her arm and turned to find her grandma.

"Remember who you are," she added as she hugged Billie. "Don't be afraid to stand up for what is right."

"Yes, Grandma." Billie didn't meet her grandmother's gaze as she reached in for a hug.

Ella stepped forward and embraced Billie. "We'll keep an eye out for your name in the newspapers."

"You'll be looking for a long time." Billie gave a quick laugh.

"You never know," Ella said. "You're going to be with some pretty famous people, making history. I'm excited for you."

"I don't want to get my hopes up," Billie said. "With my luck, I won't pass my physical, or I'll wash out the first day."

"You'll do just fine. Just go in there with confidence. And do as your grandma says…remember who you are," Ella said.

"Yes, Grandma," Billie said, rolling her eyes.

Billie picked up her suitcase, breathed deeply, and waved. She put on a broad smile to hide the terror rising in the pit of her stomach. Squaring her shoulders, she stepped up to the train car, paused to get one last look at the people she loved and disappeared.

CHAPTER 21
November 13, 1942
Fort Douglas: Salt Lake City, Utah

With his pickup truck spitting and steaming during the hour-long drive from Huntsville, Hank ambled his way onto Fort Douglas in Salt Lake City. He parked his truck and made his way toward a large, sandstone brick building that housed the military enlistment offices of the Army, Navy, and Marines. Inside, a group of military men in sharply pressed uniforms milled about.

As Hank approached the desk, a broad-shouldered junior officer looked up. "How would you like to serve your country today, young man?"

"I would like to enlist in the Army Air Corps."

"You know you can't enlist in a specific branch anymore, right? There's a chance you can still get assigned to the Air Corps, but it's all up to Uncle Sam."

"I wanted to enlist, rather than be drafted. Can you help me with that?"

"Are you eighteen years of age or older?"

"Yes, sir," Hank smiled. "My birthday was in September." Hank produced a copy of his birth certificate. The officer glanced at it.

"Great. Have you registered with the Selective Service?"

"Yes," Hank replied. "But I had a hardship deferment for a couple months. That's expired now."

"Have you been in contact with your local draft board?"

"Yes, sir. They know I'm coming here today."

"Good." The officer shuffled through some papers on his desk. "We get one or two openings every now and then for the Air Corps, but they're pushing us to fill the ranks of the infantry, so I can't guarantee anything. You'll also need to pass our aptitude tests."

"And if I do well, will I have a better chance of enlisting in the Air Corps?"

"We'll just have to wait and see, but if you do well, it will improve your chances," he replied with a smile.

An hour later, with the aptitude test already behind him, and still catching his breath from the physical assessments, Hank stood at attention in a roomful of almost thirty other enlistees. An Army major stood before the row of young men, looking them over before speaking.

"Gentlemen, thank you for coming in to serve your country by enlisting today. Is everyone ready to take your oath?"

"Yes, sir!" Hank shouted along with everyone else.

The major smiled and cleared his throat quickly, saying, "Please raise your right hand and repeat after me: I, state your name."

The young men raised their voices in a cacophony of their names, then, sentence-by-sentence, they repeated the oath:

"…do solemnly swear that I will support and defend the Constitution of the United States against all enemies, foreign and domestic; that I will bear true faith and allegiance to the same; that I take this obligation freely, without any mental reservation or purpose of evasion; and that I will well and faithfully discharge the duties of the office on which I am about to enter. So help me God."

The words echoed through Hank's head, filling him with a strange, robust feeling. As he caught glances from the young men around him, he knew they felt it too.

"Congratulations, gentlemen. You're officially enlisted. May I wish each of you the best of luck and encourage you to work hard and train hard because your country needs you, and millions of others around the world are looking to you to bring an end to this war. May God bless each and every one of you."

"In a few weeks you'll be notified as to where and when to report for duty. Any questions?" He paused. "If not, then you're all dismissed."

Hank drove home, anxiety building at the thought of having to join the infantry. Images of him running over open ground with a gun over his shoulder, bullets slicing through the air, dark skies overhead, and panic all around him wouldn't leave his thoughts for the drive home. There had to be a way he could avoid it.

CHAPTER 22
November 14, 1942
Houston, Texas

Billie arrived among a group of twenty-eight women at Houston's Municipal Airport for training. Each carried a small suitcase and a purse, and a woman in civilian attire led them to a room where they stood, waiting for instruction.

At the back of the room, Billie leaned against the wall, arms crossed, trying to calm herself in spite of the fluttery feeling in her chest.

"Where you from?" A voice next to her spoke. A tall blonde smiled at Billie.

"Utah," Billie said. "How about you?"

"Hawaii. My name is Betty. Glad to meet you." She offered her hand, which Billie shook with enthusiasm.

"Isn't this amazing? I hear we're the 'guinea pig' class for the Woofteddies."

"Woofteddies?" Billie smiled with curiosity.

"Yeah, W.F.T.D., the Woofteddies."

"Oh, I get it," Billie laughed.

"They said we're going to be the first American women ever to fly military planes."

"If they ever let us near an airplane." Billie tried to hide her mocking tone.

Just then, the woman made an announcement.

"Ladies, there's a bus waiting outside to take us to our classroom. I'll meet you out there." She turned on her heel and marched out the door.

One by one, each woman stepped onto the bus and found a seat. Some were stoic; others chatted with ease. In ten minutes, the bus pulled to a stop at the end of the runway. The women gave each other puzzled looks. The bus driver twisted around in his seat, and with an apologetic tone announced, "This is the end of the road, ladies. I'm sorry but I'm not authorized to take you any further. Your classroom is in that small building over there." He pointed to a shack about a half-mile away.

"You'll have to walk the rest of the way, ladies. I'm so sorry."

Billie caught snatches of the words, "that far?" and "in heels?" from the women around her as they grumbled under their breaths. Billie stepped off the bus into the sunlight, walking with shoulders squared and her head held high. They trudged over the pavement, and in a few minutes, reached the building at the far end of the runway.

An instructor greeted them in a kind, yet professional tone. "Ladies, please come in. We have a special visitor waiting for you."

They gave each other curious looks as they entered the tiny, worn shack. The room was arranged with desks and chairs like a typical classroom. At the front, a woman stood with her hands clasped behind her back. A woman behind Billie whispered, "It's Jackie Cochran."

Gasps of recognition floated through the crowd as they filed in. Jackie shook hands with every pilot. When they settled in their seats, she gave a warm smile before clearing her throat to speak.

"I'm so glad to meet all of you, and I'm sure we'll be seeing plenty of each other in the coming weeks and months. Could I ask each of you to introduce yourself and give a brief overview of your flying experience, how many hours you've logged, and where you're from?"

Billie listened as the women stated their names. Eleanor Morgan, Betty Blake, Byrd Howell, and Marjorie Deacon were names she remembered. They hailed from cities large and small, from all over the country. Some had over a thousand hours of flight time. When it was Billie's turn, she shuffled her feet and her voice trembled as she spoke. "My name is Billie Russell. I'm from Ogden, Utah. I've been an instructor for almost a year now and have a little over five hundred hours." Her voice felt small, and she coughed to clear her throat.

Jackie looked at Billie with a kind smile. "I'm thrilled to have all of you here. But before we go much further," she said with a note of caution in her voice, "I'd like to read a portion of a letter General Hap Arnold received from the Pentagon. It was not meant for me to see. He passed it on to give me an idea of what we're up against."

Every woman seemed to hold their breath; eyes fixed on her.

She looked at the letter closely, scanned down the paper, and added, "Here's what the War Department thinks of you and the Women's Flight Training Detachment. Quote: 'We know we need to give these women an opportunity to fly, but we do not think they will ever be able to fly military aircraft. Get rid of them as soon as possible.'"

A gasp erupted from many of the women, who covered their mouths with astonishment.

"I don't want to frighten you." Jackie beckoned with her hands to calm them down. "But you need to know that they expect us to fail. I've handpicked each of you because I need women with stamina and strength for the first class of trainees. If you don't cut it, this whole plan will go down the toilet."

Jackie was silent for a moment to let it sink in. "We have an important job to do. So, get ready because it all starts now."

The girls applauded, and a few cheers filled the room.

"This," Jackie gestured to the shack around them, "this lovely little place will be our home for all ground instruction. They've promised to bring us a portable toilet, but until then, the closest ladies' room is in that hanger over there." She pointed out a small window to a two-story building at least a half-a-mile away. "We'll have to make do. They would like nothing better than to have us quit because of these conditions. The nearest food is in the main terminal almost a mile away. Make sure you pack a few snacks and some drinks."

Jackie motioned for them to follow her as she headed out the back door of the building. Passing a large flagpole where the sound of the rope slapped against the pole in the breeze, Jackie pointed to several airplanes lined up in the distance.

"I'm not sure you can see them from here, but if you look really close you might see our aircraft."

They gathered behind Jackie on the pavement. Billie could make out the olive drab color and big white star on the side of the fuselage of a few Piper Cubs.

"The military brass, all the way up the chain of command, don't think you're capable of flying those planes," Jackie said. "But after a few days of ground school review, you'll start. I want to warn you about something else. To get an idea of your flying skills, they've given us whatever aircraft they could slap together, like those Cubs."

Many of the girls looked at each other with disappointment.

"Each aircraft has a military instructor assigned to it. Show these lieutenants the respect they deserve. But just so you know, they have been given orders to," she paused to draw quotations marks in the air, "teach you how to fly."

The girls erupted with laughter, looking at each other and shaking their heads in disbelief.

"Now you know and I know that your entire flying career has been in the cockpit of civilian aircraft. These young men, bless their hearts, are trained military pilots, and I'm guessing they have never flown a civilian plane. So, they're coming into this assignment with a chip on their shoulder already, because they think flying civilian aircraft is a step backwards. They will be looking for excuses to fail you."

"I'm not saying you should take any unnecessary risks because any mishap would shut us down in a heartbeat. But I chose each one of you for your skill and professionalism. I have the utmost confidence that you can show these young lieutenants a thing or two about flying. Is that understood?" she asked.

"Yes, ma'am!" Their reply rang out in unison.

"When the time comes, I want you to get out there and show them what you're made of."

Billie soon learned that, as a paramilitary group run by a civilian contractor, the Woofteddies weren't restricted by the same rules of conduct as men with full military status. After a long day's work, the women would be free to do whatever they wished. In an initial briefing, though, they also learned they had no military benefits. No health care, no uniforms. At the end, the instructor gave them the details everyone was most concerned about—their pay.

"You will each be given a base pay of a hundred and fifty dollars per month," she explained.

Billie and the others nodded with approval, despite each of them taking a significant pay cut from an instructor's salary.

"You will also be given an additional twenty dollars a month for housing and five dollars and thirty cents a week for food and mess hall." The instructor looked over her notes and added. "We discussed this at length with Jackie, and even though the Army won't give us a uniform allowance, we'd like to make sure we look like a military unit. We want each of you to buy your own uniform. Please get a few pair of khaki slacks, several white blouses, and a regulation garrison cap. A typical officer will wear a garrison cap as part of their Class A uniform, but for the Woofteddies, it's going to be your primary headgear when you're on the ground. That means you wear it when you march or whenever you're seen in public, you got that? No exceptions. We always wear our garrison cap."

On the first day of flying, the girls all agreed the first pilot would be Theresa James. She had earned her pilot's license in 1934 and had amassed over two thousand hours. While those qualifications alone were impressive enough, the group also selected her to be first because she had earned her secondary instructor's rating in an Advanced Aerobatic and Inverted Flying course.

Standing with his hands on his hips, the lieutenant assigned to the Stinson asked, loud enough for the entire Woofteddy class to hear, "Can you really fly this thing?" The instructor was unaware of her experience.

Theresa spoke in a soft, yet firm tone "Do you really want to see?"

"Sure, show me what you got," he scoffed.

As Theresa got her airplane into position for takeoff, the tower gave her the go ahead. Feigning caution, she made a perfect takeoff. When she reached about fifty feet off the ground, she inverted the plane and flew the length of the runway upside-down.

The Woofteddies cheered as Theresa showed her skills.

"Look at her go!" Billie called out in glee.

The nose of the little Stinson turned up, shooting straight up until it reached a thousand feet. Losing its momentum upward, the plane slowed to a stop. It hung in the air, balanced, as everyone held their breath. Then it fell earthward and the nose rolled toward the ground. As the plane picked up speed, Theresa jerked the controls into a tailspin, then another, and another. A few hundred feet before hitting the ground, she pulled the nose of the plane up. Using the momentum of the fall, she completed a series of quick, jerking spins. Billie and the other girls giggled and clapped with delight.

After positioning the plane into the wind, Theresa set up for her landing. She approached the runway, and the wheel kissed the ground in a perfect landing.

The Woofteddies cheered as the plane came to a stop. The door of the plane flew open, and the lieutenant stumbled out and collapsed in a heap on the ground. Shaking, he staggered to his feet, fighting to regain his balance. "I'm never flying with these crazy women again." He dusted himself off and marched past the group, muttering under his breath.

Billie smirked to herself.

The next woman clapped her hands and rushed up to the plane for her turn.

The commanding officer held out his arms. "Listen up, girls!" he barked, disdain oozing from his lips. "When you are on this base, remember that I, for one, do not believe you belong here. In fact, I resent your presence." His face bloomed red with anger. "You may think that little stunt was pretty cute, but it was dangerous. One more show of stupidity like that and I will have this program shut down faster than any of you can say 'washed out,' is that understood?"

"Yes sir!" The women looked ahead and nodded, speaking in near-unison, but as the commander turned away, Billie wasn't the only one who covered her mouth to stifle her laughter.

Chapter 22-Note 1: For the purposes of maintaining the flow and interest of the story, Billie was included in the guinea pig class of WFTDs at age 19, although the official minimum age was 21.

Chapter 22-Note 2: While appalling by today's standards, the letter from the Pentagon stating, "Get rid of them as soon as possible," has been reported in the memoirs of several WASP pilots. This account (as portrayed here by Jackie Cochran reading a letter given to her by General Hap Arnold) was reported by Ginny (Virginia) Hill Wood (WFTD Graduate W-43-4), in her book, *Boots, Bikes and Bombers,* Karen Brewster (ed.), (University of Alaska Press. 2012, 176).

Chapter 22- Note 3: Theresa James was indeed a well-qualified pilot, a "barnstormer" with stunt flight experience. Upon arriving for training, she had 2,254 hours in the cockpit. The story in this chapter about the WASP pilot's stunt flight on her initial qualifying run comes from a later WFTD graduate, Dorothy Kocher Olsen (WFTD graduate W-43-4).

Dorothy Kocher Olsen, *oral history, Texas Women's University,* as quoted by Sarah Byrn Rickman in *WASP of the Ferry Command,* (University of North Texas Press, 2016), [68].

CHAPTER 23

December 15, 1942
Santa Anita, California

Karl and Marta huddled together, shivering in the thin-walled room of their barracks. "It's ten days until Christmas." Marta's voice was soft and low as she leaned her head against Karl's shoulder. "I thought it was always summer in California."

"Utah will have snow by now," Karl mumbled.

Their door rattled with a harsh knocking. A camp official entered, not waiting to be admitted.

"You will be leaving this camp in a few days for an internment camp in Texas," he declared without emotion.

"For what reason?" Marta frowned.

"This place is only a temporary stopover. We've intended all along to send all of you to a long-term place until the cases are resolved."

Marta looked at Karl with concern. "I guess we're not going home anytime soon."

"I suggest you write a letter to your family about the move. We'll forward any letters we receive to your new place." He closed the door to their barracks and walked away.

"Maybe this is good news." Karl looked at Marta with some trepidation.

"Let's hope so," Marta replied.

On one hand, the new camp might provide better facilities, including a warmer room and a little more privacy; they were both tired of using public toilets and showers. On the other hand, it would be harder for their family to visit them in Texas. But that didn't really matter; it wasn't practical or safe for their children to visit anyway.

On December 17, Karl and Marta, along with a handful of other German internees, were called together for a briefing. A tall, lanky guard approached the group. They waited for him to speak as he casually picked food from his front teeth. Digging with his tongue, his lip bulged until he was satisfied.

"You'll be leaving today to go to a new camp called Crystal City." He glanced at his notes and then back at their faces. "It's in Texas, and it will take you a few days to get there."

The internees shared looks of both fear and anticipation.

"It's a brand-new camp, still under construction, so you'll have to put up some dust when you get there," he said. "But from what I hear, you'll have better conditions there—your own cottages and showers."

Karl held Marta's hand, squeezing it gently.

"We'll give you a half hour to get packed and be back here. If you're late, you'll stay here. It's your choice."

None of them were late. The group was herded into a converted cattle truck and taken to a nearby train station. After two full days of sitting and sleeping on the passenger seats, Karl, Marta, and the other internees stepped off the train onto the sunburned Texas landscape.

They entered the gates of Crystal City, dust hanging in the air around them from the constant flurry of construction men scurrying about and vehicles rumbling past. Guards escorted them to a collection of roped-off buildings and cottages. Uniformed members of the U.S. Border Patrol stood guard, backed by half-finished fencing and towers.

The Meyer's first stop was the camp surveillance division, where employees examined their baggage and paperwork. Afterwards, they were taken to the mess hall where all internees received their meals until they were assigned a cottage with cooking facilities.

Internees were given a small subsistence allowance of small, coin-like tokens to buy groceries, meat, and other food items from a general store. The number of tokens they received was based on the size of the household, as outlined by the Geneva Convention. They were also given an allotment of cooking utensils, furniture, bedding, clothing, and other necessities.

The Internal Relations Division assigned Karl and Marta to their quarters. Unlike cottages reserved for families with children, they did not have the luxury of a toilet in their home. They had to walk a few steps to use a public toilet and shower. Still, it was a world of difference compared to Santa Anita.

CHAPTER 24
December 20, 1942
Huntsville, Utah

The fresh snow obscured the trail from the house to the barn. Hank opened the gate and pulled the cord on the dim light hanging from a nail on the ceiling. The anxious cow paced as she bobbed her head a few times, stamping her foot and demanding relief.

"There you go, Berta," he mumbled under his breath and reached toward her mouth with a handful of hay. She licked his hand, scooping up the hay with her wet, coarse tongue.

"Well, Berta," Hank added as if he expected a reply, "it looks like we've found you a new home." He positioned a small stool on the ground and caressed her coat as he sat to begin milking her.

"I'm taking you over to Mr. Wangsguard tonight, and he'll take care of you from now on—or at least until Mama and Papa come back." The milk made a swooshing sound as it hit the pail.

A sound caught his ear. He stopped, listening for it again. Footsteps? He leaned over to see around Berta.

"Who's there?" He heard no answer. He held the milk bucket still. "Anyone there?"

Holding his breath to listen, Hank was still for a moment but heard nothing. It must have been his imagination, he thought. He returned to milking, the milk coming in steady white streams and frothing in his pail.

"I hope they take good care of you Bert..."

A shadow crossed over him.

"Do you always have heart-to-heart conversations with your cow?"

"Chester!" Hank's eyes widened with excitement. He lifted the pail from beneath Berta and set it a safe distance away, then rushed around the fence and shook Chester's hand.

"How you been...how long have you...when did you...I can't believe..."

"Whoa buddy, slow down there. I'm not going anywhere," Chester roared with laughter.

"When did you get home?"

"I just got in tonight. I'm on a quick furlough for Christmas. I have to go back the day after tomorrow."

Hank looked up and down at Chester's uniform, straining to make out the features in the dark.

"What are you doing wearing a Marine uniform? I thought you were in the Navy."

"I am in the Navy, but I'm a corpsman attached to the Marines. I get to wear both uniforms."

"How does that work?" Hank gave him a puzzled look.

"The Navy supplies the Marines with their medical corps. I trained with the Marines before we went to Guadalcanal."

"Oh, wow! I heard about Guadalcanal. Sounds like it was pretty rough going." Hank stopped talking and noticed Berta fighting the rope attached to her bridle. "She's not too happy right now, but I'm almost done milking her, Chester. Hang on for a few minutes while I finish."

Chester nodded and followed Hank into the shed. Hank rubbed Berta's nose and she snorted in appreciation. "So, tell me about Guadalcanal."

"Oh," Chester's expression seemed distant. "Maybe some other time, okay?" He cleared his throat and paused to think what to say next. Hank noticed Chester seemed a bit more subdued than he remembered, but he couldn't be sure.

"So, did I hear you right?" Chester gave him an awkward smile. "This is the last time you'll have to milk her?"

"Yeah," Hank answered with a little sadness in his voice. "It's a bittersweet goodbye."

Chester didn't seem to hear Hank's response. "I heard about your parents. That's a rotten deal if you ask me."

"That's why I'm giving Berta to Mr. Wangsguard until it all gets straightened out."

"I'll bet it'll be a relief not to milk her twice a day."

Hank considered Chester's comment with great care before replying. "You know, after all this time milking her night and morning, I think I'll miss her," Hank laughed. "Me and Berta have been through a lot over the years." He sat on the stool next to the cow, reaching for her udder to milk. In his excitement, he pulled harder than usual.

Berta stamped her back leg and almost kicked over the milk pail. "Whoa, Berta. I'm sorry. Didn't mean to hurt you,"

"Why is ol' man Wangsguard taking her now? Where are you going?"

"You probably wouldn't know, but my deferment expired and I enlisted. I'm just waiting for my orders."

"Well I'll be darned," Chester laughed. "I thought you had to be on a deferment until your mom and dad got back."

"Nope. I begged them to let me enlist because we need the money to pay the bills."

"Wow. That's great."

"I'm hoping I can get in the Army Air Corps, but from what I hear, my chances are pretty slim."

"I've heard that too." Chester looked down, not wanting to disappoint Hank. "So, tell me more about your parents. When do you think they'll come back?"

"Don't know for sure. Whenever they get this whole mess straightened up. But they'll be back. They live for this little homestead."

"Have you heard from them? Where are they?"

"Some internment camp for Germans and Japs." Hank's voice trailed off, not wanting to admit his souvenirs had played a role leading to their detention. That story was just too painful to talk about.

"I hope they can come home soon," Chester offered with clear sadness in his voice. "It's just a shame what the government is doing to them."

Hank finished milking the cow and stood, patting Berta one final time as he leaned into her. "Now you should feel better until they milk you in the morning,"

They followed Hank's earlier footsteps in the snow back to the house. Once they entered the warm living room, Ella exclaimed in surprise, "Well, Chester Bailey! What on earth are you doing here?"

"Just checking up on you two. My parents have my schedule planned out to the minute, with family parties and get-togethers." He looked down at the floor and hesitated. His responses seemed to require a great amount of mental effort. Hank and Ella glanced at each other with a look of confusion but said nothing.

"I wish I could stay longer, but I told my folks I'd be right back. They understood that I had to come and say hello to you two."

"Oh, Chester, that's so nice of you. It's too bad Billie's not here. You heard about her, didn't you?"

"Yes," he answered. "She wrote me a long letter. She sounds really excited to be flying military planes. And who can blame her?"

"I'm glad she's writing you," Ella smiled with relief. "I can tell in her letters she's thrilled to be there with all the other women pilots."

They chatted for a few minutes until Chester looked at his Navy-issued watch. "I'm sorry, but I've gotta run. It's really nice to see both of you. Maybe next time I come back we can go dancing or get a cone at Farr's?"

"Sounds great," Hank smiled, reaching out to grasp Chester's hand. "Let's do it."

Ella stepped up and gave Chester a friendly embrace. "You take care Chester, okay?"

Hank and Ella watched Chester as he stepped toward his car, careful not to slip in the slick snow.

"Do you think he looks okay?" Hank asked.

"No. Something's not right. He seemed a little off, but I can't put a finger on it."

"He's just not that fun-loving type of guy we've always known," Hank answered.

"Maybe he's got a lot on his mind?"

"I asked him about Guadalcanal, and he didn't want to talk about it."

Ella closed the door. "I sure hope he's okay."

By Christmas time, Hank's induction letter was overdue. Every day that it didn't come, Ella was relieved. She stole a glance at her brother, raising her hopes he would still be home for Christmas.

The day before Christmas Eve, Ella received a package in the mail from Tom. She opened it to find a crescent-shaped, cobalt-blue glass perfume bottle. In elegant script, the label read *Soir de Paris*. While Ella wasn't known to wear perfume much, she was thrilled at Tom's thoughtfulness. She unfolded a sheet of paper and began reading a letter.

My Dearest Ella,

I got your letter a few days ago. Oh how it makes me happy to see your letters! You'll never know how much I rely on them to keep me going.

The rain here in England makes everything dismal and depressing. It also makes flying a challenge sometimes. We have to make regular training flights to keep our skills up.

I hope you like the perfume I bought you. I hear it's very popular. At least that's what the girl at the fancy department store told me. I've tried to pack it well, so it won't break. If it did break, I hope the mailman enjoyed the pretty smelling box he delivered to you.

You asked about church. I attend a church about an hour away. I can't go as often as I would like because I am often working. But the Brits are good people, and I have learned to love them for their courage and faith.

I can't say much else, but I want you to know that I won't be able to write to you for a long time. As soon as I am able to write, believe me I will write you a big, long letter and let you know what I'm up to.

Love, Tom

Ella sniffed the perfume and clutched the letter to her chest. How had he been able to send the package? He had been expected to go to the front sometime in early December. She dug around in the box and found a receipt from a British perfumery dated November 9, 1942, stuck between the flaps in the bottom. Either he had made the purchase long before he left, or he was still in England. But given that his almost daily letters stopped in late November, she figured he asked someone to send the package in early December to make sure it arrived in time for Christmas.

Ella did her best to decorate the house for the holidays, but it just wasn't the same as when Mama decorated. Every year her mother set up a miniature German village near the Christmas tree. The tiny ceramic houses were lit up with candles inside and glowed like a quaint village nestled in the mountains. Ella arranged the pieces near the tree, lost in her thoughts. An idea came to her.

She gave Hank a playful grin. "You know what, Hank? Since Christmas is all about family, and since our only family nearby is Uncle Willy, what do you think about inviting him to join us for Christmas Eve dinner tomorrow night?"

"I don't know. Do you think he'd be sober enough?"

"We can tell him he has to be sober. So do you think he'd come?"

"With Papa not here, maybe he'll come this time."

"Let's go ask him." Hank lifted his coat from the hook behind the door. "Do you want to come with me?"

"He won't say no to me." She smiled as she pushed her arms into the sleeves of her coat and tugged on her hat. "I'm his favorite niece."

They trekked through the snow along the banks of Pineview Reservoir. Willy's shack came into view, isolated and small. Smoke billowed from the makeshift chimney and cords of cut firewood sat in piles around the place.

Willy heard them coming and opened his door to greet them in German. "What on earth are you two doing out here, making me open the door and lose all my heat?"

"We wanted to invite you over for Christmas Eve dinner tomorrow night." Ella gave an encouraging smile as she looked at his weather-beaten face and overgrown beard. "We haven't seen you since Mama and Papa left, and we thought you might like to come over."

Willy blinked and rubbed his chin.

"Oh, come on. Spend Christmas Eve with us," Hank added in encouragement.

Willy raised his eyebrows in curiosity, crossing his arms against the cold.

"And if you want to use our tub, you can fill it up with some nice hot water and just relax!"

"Oh, that's awfully tempting," Willy smiled.

"I'll even come pick you up. How about five o'clock?"

Willy put out his hand. "It's a deal. I'll be ready at five o'clock."

"Now Willy, all we ask is that we get to be with you when you're at your best," Ella asked with a firm, yet kind smile. "Please?"

"I promise. I'll be stone-cold sober."

After soaking for an hour in the hot bathtub, Willy emerged from the bathroom with his hair combed back and his beard still dripping.

"Papa's denim jeans seem to fit perfectly," Hank complimented Willy.

"I really like this flannel shirt," Willy said. "It's nice and warm and feels great. Willy looked around the living room, admiring the Christmas decorations. "This is the best Christmas Eve ever. Reminds me of when I was a child." Willie smiled gratefully at Ella.

Willy asked, "How's your mama holding up? Is she doing okay?"

Ella beamed at Willy's kindness. "That's very nice of you to ask. Both of them are doing as good as can be expected, barbed wire considered."

Willy gave a nervous nod as Ella turned away. He caught a glimpse of a tear glistening in her eye.

"It sure smells nice. What's cooking?"

Ella motioned for him to sit down at the table. "Red cabbage, potato dumplings, and a stuffed chicken."

"Apple and sausage dressing?" Willie asked with unveiled enthusiasm.

"Of course," Ella smiled. "Traditional. Just like my mama makes."

Over dinner they reminisced about their Christmas celebrations of the past. Willy also shared his memories of family traditions. Eventually, the conversation led to Hank's looming departure to boot camp.

"You know, I was in the Army in the Great War." Willy looked down at his plate.

"Yeah," Hank said. "My papa said you were a hero."

"Your papa said that?"

"He also told us you came back a completely different man."

"I did come back changed. Before I left, I was a good little Mormon boy," he joked. "But it's a long story."

"We've got all night," Hank said. "Please tell us."

"No, I don't think so." Willy's opposition was waning.

"I really want to hear it." Hank sat back in his chair.

"Leave him alone, Hank," Ella chided. "He doesn't want to talk about it."

"Oh, come on," Hank begged.

Willy squinted and shot Hank an intense glare. "It doesn't have a happy ending."

"That's okay. Please, tell me. I really want to know," Hank insisted. "I've heard bits and pieces of this story, and I'd like to hear it from you."

Willy held his glass up to his eye and looked down at the drops of milk left. He made a figure eight motion with his glass, whirling the residue in the bottom. "Well." He waited for the right words to come. "A few years after I came to the United States, your papa and I had our falling out, so I joined the U.S. Army and went to fight for my new country. Sadly, I had to fight against my old country. I fought against friends that I grew up with. When the Army found out that I spoke fluent German and knew my way around, they sent me to espionage school. They told me I was going to learn how to be a spy."

"Go on," Hank said, looking at Willie and seemed to be hanging on his every word.

"My superiors taught me to be a German junior officer, and I learned everything I could about the German military. They quizzed me and tested me on everything. It turned out to be very dangerous work because whenever the Germans expose a spy, they usually torture him to death."

Hank gave a quick nod as though he understood.

"If they catch an American soldier out of uniform or without his dog tags, that's it. You're dead."

"Why would that matter?" Hank gave a dubious look.

"It means you're trying to hide, and only spies need to hide."

"It must have been terrifying."

"Yes, it was, but I ended up being a pretty good spy."

Hank glanced at his sister with a look of curiosity. She seemed as interested as Hank.

"After finally infiltrating into Germany…" he paused and put the back of his hand to his mouth as if to whisper. "But that's a story for another day. Anyway, I quickly made friends with many Germans who were pretty high up. I was invited to their big, fancy parties where they would spare no expense on food, wine, and imported liquor. You name it. Sooner or later, after they'd loosen up a bit, they would tell me things like battle plans and troop movements, things they should never be talking about. One day I was at a party and one of the officers walked up to me and said, 'Aren't you Wilhem Meyer?' He recognized me as a schoolmate from where I grew up. He kept looking at me, and I knew he was looking at me like I was his friend. I almost panicked."

Hank sat up in his chair and leaned toward Willy.

"So, this guy approaches me again," Willy explained, "and he says, 'You look exactly like Wilhelm Meyer from Karlsruhe.' I said, 'No, and I have no idea what you're talking about.' Then he said, 'and don't you have an older brother named Karl?'"

Willy's lips pressed together in a slight grimace. "When I said 'no', he grew even more suspicious. He said to me, 'They went to America after they joined the Mormon church. You look and act just like him.' Well, I was scared to death, and I had to find a way to convince him that I wasn't who he thought I was. Then the guy said to me something like, 'well, if you're not Wilhem, then you're not a Mormon, so let's drink a toast to the Kaiser.' He handed me a glass of schnapps. I said 'sure!' and I took a drink. I had never tasted alcohol. But if I didn't drink it, I would have given myself away and been killed."

Willy eyes were alight with rare emotion and clarity. "Somehow, he knew that Mormons don't drink or smoke. I had to take a drink just to convince him that I wasn't Wilhelm, and it worked, at least for a little while. Unfortunately, I had to be around this man for several weeks. He always looked at me with suspicion and often tried to trip me up with trick questions. It was terrifying, and the stress started to eat at me. I almost cracked. I was a mess because I couldn't let my guard down."

Ella blurted out, "What did you do?"

"I tried another tactic. I lit up a cigarette in front of him. After about week or so of smoking in front of him, he finally stopped bothering me. Fortunately, I got reassigned to another place. After that, I went back to England to wait for my next assignment, and before long, the war ended. But I credit smoking and drinking for saving my life."

"Why didn't you quit drinking and smoking when you came home?"

"It's not that easy to do, Hank. Besides, I had seen too much war and I wasn't thinking straight. I saw people die in horrible ways. I saw the Germans force young girls to deliver ammunition to the front lines. Those poor girls were killed in ways I will never get out of my mind."

Ella winced, looking down at her empty plate.

"Drinking helped me forget about all those bad things. Smoking helped me relax when I got too wound up to think straight." Willy took a deep breath, "So, yes, your papa was right. I came back a completely different man. I tried to stop drinking and smoking. I've tried hundreds of times, but I just can't."

"Maybe that's why I don't like cigarettes. They make me sad when I think of you," Hank blurted.

"Do me a favor. Promise me you will never drink or smoke—even if it kills you. I sometimes wish they had killed me because I've felt like a prisoner ever since."

Willy looked at Ella, her elbows were planted on the table. Her palms pressed into her cheeks. She sat up in her chair and looked at Hank. "Can you believe that Hank? What an amazing story."

"The reason I told that story," Willie continued, "was because you're about to go off to join the Army. I can bet you a dollar to a doughnut they're going to ask you to be a spy. Once they find out you speak German and you're smart, they'll do everything they can to get you to do it. Don't do it. Don't let them do that to you. They won't care if it turns you into a crazy man like it did me, as long as they get the information they want; you're nothing but another body they can throw against the enemy."

A quiet tension lingered in the air. Willy turned a troubled look at Hank to make he had gotten the message.

"Promise me you won't let them do that to you. Okay?" Willie searched Hank's eyes for an answer.

"Okay, Uncle Willy," Hank smiled. "I promise. If they come and ask me to be a spy, I'll tell them no, my uncle told me I couldn't."

Ella and Willy chuckled, but Willy pointed at Hank. "I'm serious now."

"I know you are, and I appreciate your advice."

Hank stood to stretch his legs, moving to the kitchen out of sight. He rubbed his forehead, releasing pent-up emotions.

Ella cleared the dishes from the table. When all the dishes were finished, she announced, "We have a special gift for you, Uncle Willy." She reached under the Christmas tree for a small, colorful package. "Here. This is for you." Willy reached and smiled as he accepted the gift.

"Oh, Ella," Willy beamed. "You really shouldn't have. I don't have anything for you two."

"You know that's not why we did it, Uncle Willy." Ella's voice was rich with emotion. "We love you, so Merry Christmas."

Willy unwrapped the small package with care, beaming at the sight of a new pair of knitted socks and a pair of thick gloves.

"I hope you like them. Maybe it will help you stay warm," Ella said.

Willy smiled, stepping in to give Hank and Ella a quick embrace. "I really appreciate you both. It's very nice of you."

Willy watched as Ella reached again under the tree to retrieve four envelopes. Both Hank and Ella had received letters from their mama and papa. Willy watched with a satisfied smile while they read their letters. The only sound he could hear was a few sniffles from Ella and the occasional pop and hiss from the fireplace.

Late on Christmas Eve, Marta and Karl had little to celebrate. They exchanged Christmas cards handmade from paper and string and anything they could find.

Karl brought out a small brown paper package that Ella had sent to them. They had agreed not to open it until Christmas. Only the camp security officers knew what it contained.

Karl gave the package to Marta, asking her to open it for both of them. She peeled open the wrapping.

"Oh my, Karl! Oh my!"

From a small box, she lifted her personal copy of the scriptures. Karl hadn't seen that look on her face for a long time. A jolt of bittersweet joy shot through him.

"I've cherished these since I left Germany as a young girl." She caressed the gold engraved letters, *Das Buch Mormon*.

Karl reached inside and pulled out his own set of scriptures. The *Heilige Bibel* and English *Book of Mormon*. He cracked open the spine to pages full of underlines and countless markings and notes in the margins.

"It's like being reunited with a long, lost friend."

The construction did not let up even for the holiday. With all the people hurrying around during the day, it seemed no one cared that it was Christmas. No one had time to celebrate. It was clear that many more people were expected to come to Crystal City. Karl and Marta's only question was how long they would be forced to stay there.

The day after Christmas, Ella went to the mailbox to collect the mail. She came running into the house calling excitedly, "Hank! You got your letter! You got your letter! Hurry up and come open it!"

Hank bounded down the stairs, and Ella handed him the letter.

"This is it," he smiled as he inspected it.

"Come on. Open it."

"What if I have to be a dog-face soldier?"

"You won't find out unless you open it."

Hank tore open the envelope and read a form letter, mumbling a few words, saying under his breath,

"The President of the United States…" He muttered a few more words until he got to the important part. He cleared his throat and read aloud: "You are hereby notified of your selection for training and service in the Army Air Forces." He smiled at Ella, then turned to finish reading the letter. "You will report to the Ogden Union Pacific Station at 6:45 a.m. on Saturday 9 January, 1943 for transportation to Keesler Field in Gulfport, Mississippi."

Hank looked up at Ella and exhaled in a flood of relief.

"I get to fly!" Hank declared through a huge grin. "Maybe I'll get to fly in one of those gigantic bombers after all."

CHAPTER 25

January 4, 1943
Huntsville, Utah

The bitter cold wasn't uncommon for a January morning in Huntsville. Winter had settled hard in the Ogden Valley. Pineview Reservoir froze solid with at least a foot of ice. Some nights the temperature dipped to fifteen degrees below zero.

Ella and Hank were finishing breakfast and reviewing the unopened mail from the previous few days.

"Is that a letter from Tom?" Hank asked.

"No." Ella shook her head in disappointment.

"When's the last time you heard from him?"

"I've had just one letter since I got his Christmas package. He said he couldn't write for a while, so I'm not really expecting anything."

"Where do you think he is?"

"All I know is what I hear from the news." Ella cleaned off the dishes from the table and put them in the sink.

"Do you think he's part of the invasion in Africa we've been hearing about?" Hank asked, but when her eyes shifted over to the map on the wall, he regretted it.

"More than likely, but I just don't know. It's so stressful to think that he's over there being shot at. I just can't let myself think about it too much or I…" Ella stopped to think, then pointed her finger to her temple. "You know what? I forgot to tell you we got a letter from Mama and Papa yesterday. They're at a new camp in Texas."

Hank looked up from his pile of mail.

"She said it's a brand-new place that's larger. She wrote down some of the details but the censors crossed them out. There are over a hundred Germans there now, and it's designed for families with children, so they have a school and a playground and everything."

"They're locking up children now?"

"No, these are families who want to stay together. They're letting wives and children come so they don't have to be separated," Ella explained.

"Maybe we should volunteer to become internees?" Hank joked. Ella gave him a scowl.

"Mama said it's much better than the other place in California. They're living in a new cottage all by themselves."

"That is better," Hank smiled. "But what to do with those pesky armed guards."

Ella ignored his sarcasm. "It's called Crystal City. It's out in the middle of Texas somewhere. I'll put their new address in your book. Please make sure you send them a letter once you get to Mississippi."

Hank answered with a small nod.

Hank's final days at work were uneventful. He trained his replacement, a bright and studious college student named Joy. She had learned bookkeeping from her father, who owned the old Exclusive Pharmacy downtown. Because she was such a fast learner, Art told Hank to take Thursday and Friday off to get ready to go. "Go spend time with Ella. Go be with your friends," Art encouraged.

"I didn't expect to say goodbye so soon."

"We're going to miss you, Hank." Art shook Hank's hand. "I've always felt bad that I couldn't help you get your pilot's license. But I'm sure glad you got into the Air Corps."

"Me too. I sure hope I don't get stuck in a desk job. I want to fly."

"My guess is you can be just about anything you want. A navigator. A bombardier. A gunner."

"I hope so," Hank smiled. "I just want to be in an airplane. That's all."

Art looked at Hank and paused.

"For your sake, I hope so son. You've got what it takes, and if you test well, you'll help yourself a lot. But just remember, sometimes the folks in the Army make some pretty dumb decisions. Just be ready for anything."

During the next two days, Hank and Ella were with each other at every opportunity. Ella got out of class a little early each day to spend time with him. They used the time together to splurge at Hank's favorite places, like *Ross and Jack's* for a burger and spuds and *Farr's Ice Cream* for a large cone.

Friday evening was their last night together. Using their final meat ration before the end of the month, Hank watched as Ella prepared a near flawless reproduction of Mama's *wienerschnitzel* recipe.

After dinner, Hank went to take the garbage outside, struggling against the door.

"What's the matter?" Ella teased.

"I don't know. I think the door is frozen shut." Hank pulled on the door until it squealed opened. "I can't believe how cold it is out there." Hank stepped over to the thermometer and called out. "Ella, come and look at this. It's already minus twenty, and it's only eight o'clock."

"What time do you have to be at the train station?" she asked.

"Six-thirty."

"I'm not so sure we're going to be able to get the car started in this cold. What happens if you don't make your train?"

"I can be arrested for being AWOL," Hank said. "I have to be there on time. They won't take any excuses."

Ella tapped her fingers on the table as she thought. "We could put blankets over the engine. Papa used to do that when it got cold."

"Yeah, but it didn't always work. If we want to make sure she'll start, we'll have to take turns throughout the night to get up and start the car, especially if it's already twenty below," Hank explained.

Hank bundled up in his coat, gloves, boots, and scarf, and hurried over the beaten path to their 1935 Chrysler sedan. The cold had already gripped the battery, and it was slow to turn over.

"Oh, come on, you stupid car," Hank complained to himself as he stepped on the gas. It fired up at last, and he breathed a sigh of relief. He let it idle for several minutes then turned it off. Taking a blanket from the trunk, he popped open the hood and unfolded the blanket over the engine. After closing the hood, he scurried inside to get warm.

Each hour, they took turns bundling up, starting the car, and letting it idle for a while. At midnight, Hank felt Ella push on his shoulder. "It's your turn."

Hour after hour, they took their turns venturing out in the frigid cold to start the car.

At four-thirty in the morning, Hank walked back into the house and into the kitchen to check the thermometer. "Thirty-one below," he mumbled to himself. He had left the car running, as they planned to leave in about an hour. With the slick roads, they needed at least an hour to make it to Ogden with a few minutes to spare before his train left at six-thirty. Hank dropped himself down onto the sofa next to Ella, still bundled up and asleep from taking her turn an hour earlier.

Something inside Hank's head woke him up. He had somehow turned off the alarm clock on the end table.

"Ella! Wake up! It's twenty minutes to six. I'm going to miss my train!"

He flipped on the light and found Ella awaking from a deep sleep.

"I'm sorry," she mumbled. "I couldn't drag myself up those stairs and must have dozed off here."

Scrambling to get dressed, Hank gathered all of his belongings and both of them dashed out the door into the idling car.

"How're we doing on gas?" Ella asked.

"Maybe a half a tank. We should be okay."

A steady snow was falling, making each perilous twist and turn in the road even more treacherous than usual.

"Be careful, Hank," Ella demanded. "I'd rather have you court-martialed than dead."

Hank gripped the wheel tighter, his knuckles white as he muttered to himself.

After years of driving Ogden Canyon's winding roads and steep curves, Hank knew to take advantage of the light traffic on Saturday morning. When he could, he'd straighten out the turns if no other cars were coming. Hank smiled at Ella, pressing her foot to the floor and holding on tight as Hank sped through the steep canyon. "Please slow down, Hank."

131

Hank checked his watch and pressed on, unwilling to let up until he could get to the train station.

"Hank!" Ella screamed. The car fish-tailed as Hank over-corrected to avoid an oncoming car.

"I've got it. Calm down." Hank's wide eyes contradicted his words. "We'll be okay." He slowed down to right himself, then picked up speed again. Hank glanced over at Ella, her lips whispering a prayer as she clung to the door handle.

The thirty-minute ride seemed like a lifetime, but at last they emerged from the mouth of the canyon.

"There," Hank said with a smile. "That wasn't so bad, now was it?"

Ella slapped Hank on the arm.

"I thought I was going to die."

Hank peeked at his watch. "It's six-twenty. I've still got a chance to make it."

"We've made it this far. Please don't kill us in the final few miles, Hank. Please," she begged. Hank ignored Ella's plea and accelerated the car, speeding through Ogden's abandoned, snow-packed streets.

He looked again at his watch and said, "I think I'm going to make it. I've got four minutes."

Hank ran a stop sign, then another.

Ella screamed, "Stop it, Hank! It's not worth getting us both killed."

"We'll be okay. There's nobody on the streets. Not even the cops are up this early."

Ella dipped her head into her hands. With each hard bump her hands jerked away from her face.

"We're going to make it. My watch is a few minutes fast. If I'm lucky, I think I can still make it."

Hank pulled up to the train station and skidded against the curb. The overhead announcer made a final call for Hank's train.

"See, I told you my watch is a little bit fast. I've got a minute to spare," he laughed. He reached in the back seat to grab his suitcase.

As he slammed the door shut, Ella looked at Hank with tears in her eyes. "Aren't you going to say goodbye?"

Hank's smile fell when he saw his sister's worn face and trembling shoulders.

"I love you, Hank," Ella said, voice cracking. Hank pulled her next to him with his strong arms.

"I love you, sis," he forced a smile. "You take care of yourself and don't work too hard. Everything is going to work out just as it's supposed to."

Hank watched as Ella took a deep breath. "I'm sorry there aren't more people here to see you off." Her voice squeaked as she spoke.

"It's early." Hank gave Ella a playful smile. "I'm not too worried about it. Besides, we're not the most popular people in town right now."

"Please…be…careful." She eked out each word slow and clear. "We need you to come home."

She buried her head in Hank's arms.

"I will," he mumbled.

Suddenly, she pushed him away.

"You'd better get going," her voice was firm and clear. "You'll miss your train."

Hank smiled, then turned and ran through the huge double doors leading to his train. He rushed past a train official, stepped up to the train, and watched Ella vanish in the darkness.

Ella waved as the whistle blew. Within seconds the train began inching away from the station. As Ella looked on, a flood of emotions rushed through her. Her brother was on that train. He was the final connection to her family. She had never felt so isolated and alone. Despite how much she wanted to cry, she was spent. She was too tired to do much of anything but get back in the car and drive home.

Ella drove home though the canyon. The snow had let up, making the roads only a little less treacherous. After a still-harrowing drive home, she pulled into her driveway. She dragged herself inside the house and removed her coat. Something was different. A new and overpowering loneliness hit her as she realized this house was now her responsibility.

Before she headed to her room to sleep, she went to a drawer in the kitchen and removed a small rectangular piece of material about the size of an envelope. She had sewn it just for this moment. A blue American star was sewn on a white background, bordered with two red vertical bars on each side. Gold fringe decorated the bottom. She hung it in the front window, then turned back to an empty house. Millions of other households throughout the country had hung a blue star in their windows. Now, she could do it too.

CHAPTER 26
March 24, 1943
Crystal City, Texas

The Crystal City internment camp exploded with growth, from the number of internees to the size and scope of the facilities. Although construction hummed along at a furious pace, the facilities were still unfinished when new internees kept arriving.

"We got another group of Germans today," Karl announced to Marta while she sat at her table, writing letters to Ella and Hank.

"We also saw a few more Japanese, too. I heard one of the security officers say that this new group brought the camp population to well over five hundred. There are three hundred seventy-five Germans now, and almost a hundred and fifty Japanese."

"Where are they putting them all?"

"I don't know. They keep telling us that they're going to move all the Germans somewhere else, but then they squeeze in more Germans," Karl replied. "Luckily the German families are getting the cottages with the toilets. I don't think they have cottages with bathrooms over on the Japanese side. At least not yet."

Marta agreed and added, "I also heard they've completely given up the idea for Crystal City to be all Japanese. That was the original plan, but there are just too many Germans. They're even bringing in Germans from South America who speak Spanish."

"That doesn't make any sense. Why would America be rounding up Germans from other countries?"

Marta shook her head in confusion. "Why are they doing any of this?"

Just then, they heard a brisk knock on their door. Marta opened the door with trepidation.

"Hi, Helga," she smiled, "come in."

Helga Fischer was a round, rosy-cheeked woman who wore her hair pulled back in a tight bun. She was an acquaintance from Santa Anita, a socialite of sorts, and they didn't have too much in common. Still, they were cordial.

"You know Mr. O'Rourke, right? The camp director?" she asked.

They both gave a quick nod.

"So far, I've seen no reason to dislike him."

"I can't say I have either," Karl said.

"He wants a better system of addressing our complaints and grievances. But because so many people complain to him or ask him for help, he'd like a German representative to speak on behalf of all Germans. I would like to nominate you, Karl," she said. "Would you be willing?"

Karl drew back. "Why me? There are plenty of others who really like being in charge."

"That's what I'm afraid of," she explained. "I don't want a zealot in charge. You know who I mean, right?"

"We know who you mean," Marta added. "Some of those Nazi fanatics would be unbearable."

"You're much more level-headed and will represent all Germans best," she added smiling at Karl.

"Okay, I'll do it if you think it's for the best," Karl said with hesitation.

"Great, I'll let Mr. O'Rourke know."

Karl shrugged and grinned at Marta as she walked out.

"It would be good for you." Marta nudged him in the ribs and smiled.

Two weeks went by, and no spokesman had been named. Everyone knew about the delay and had a theory about a power struggle happening behind the scenes.

One morning, as Marta and Karl walked home from the showers, Helga stopped them.

"This is what I heard," she explained, gesturing with her hands. "A man named Heinz Schmidt arrived from Ellis Island and has at least twenty members of his family and friends with him. When they learned that the camp spokesman appointee was not decided yet, they demanded that Schmidt be selected. A few days later, a man named Horst Müller came in from Camp Forrest in Tennessee. He also has a large number of family and friends and they wanted *him* to be spokesman." Helga shook her head in exasperation.

"So, Horst Müller's group threatened mutiny if Müller wasn't chosen. The next day, the Schmidt delegation got wind of what the Müllers were doing, and they threatened mutiny if Schmidt wasn't selected."

"So what's going to happen now?" Marta asked.

"I think O'Rourke is going to get you and the other two leaders together and try to hash things out. So, don't be surprised if he invites you to his office," she said with a chuckle. "It's such a mess."

Two days later, Karl sat in O'Rourke's office with Müller and Schmidt.

The camp director explained his dilemma, hands folded in front of him on his desk. Since O'Rourke didn't speak German, the three were forced to speak English.

"Since I can't get you Germans to agree on a single spokesman, I will ask the three of you to work together."

"Okay." Karl shrugged his shoulders.

Müller's face twisted into sour contempt. "Ve vill only vork with you ven our living conditions are improved."

O'Rourke furrowed his brow.

"The Swiss protectorate has visited and reviewed conditions here. They have found we are in compliance with the Geneva Convention," he snapped.

Schmidt didn't reply, tilting his head back and gazing at O'Rourke in defiance.

"We need to solve the problem we're having with the irrigation pool now," O'Rourke explained. "If we leave the water in this pond it will grow algae. If that happens, the pond will need to be drained, and you will not have irrigation water for the duration of the summer. We are proposing to drain it now and line it with concrete so we can have water for gardens during the summer. We will pay for the concrete and other materials, but we need your laborers to make it happen."

"Vill our laborers be paid?" Karl asked.

"Yes, ten cents per hour, as usual," O'Rourke replied.

Schmidt hesitated, on the verge of losing his temper. "I vill discuss your proposal vit the laborers and get back to you vit an answer."

Not to be outdone, Müller looked at O'Rourke, his nostrils flared. "Vy should we participate in any project that does not directly benefit the German population?"

"It does. You can use the water to irrigate your gardens."

"Could ve use it for a community pool?" Karl's friendly tone angered both Müller and Schmidt.

O'Rourke thought a moment about Karl's question. "I don't see why not."

Karl turned to Müller and retorted in German, "There's your direct benefit. Let's do it."

Müller lifted his nose at Karl, choosing not to respond to Karl and instead addressed O'Rourke, "I vill gif you an answer in five days."

"I will give you twenty-four hours, and if I don't hear from you, I will proceed on Karl's acceptance of my proposal," O'Rourke demanded.

Müller sneered at Karl and said, "*Volksverraeter.*" Both he and Schmidt stormed out of O'Rourke's office.

"I guess I am a traitor for vanting a swimming pool," Karl said.

O'Rourke exhaled sharply in exasperation. Karl smiled, stood and walked out scratching his head.

Upon arriving back at his cottage, Karl explained to Marta what had happened. "I guess I'm not a very good negotiator," Karl told Marta. "But I see nothing wrong with providing laborers who get paid and ending up with a pool that everyone can enjoy."

Karl went from door to door explaining O'Rourke's proposal and asking what the other German prisoners thought. He watched as the idea filled many eyes with excitement, and hopeful questions and rumors floated throughout the community.

When Karl knocked on the door of one of the newest cottages, he didn't hear an answer. He turned to move on, but from inside came a rustling sound. The door creaked open and Karl could see only the face of the man who answered in German.

"What do you want?" the man scowled.

"My name is Karl Meyer, and I am asking my fellow Germans what they think about fixing the irrigation pond—"

"Yes, *Herr* Meyer, I've been waiting to speak with you."

Karl was startled at the menacing tone lacing the man's voice.

The man waved him in and said, "Sit right here."

Karl stepped with caution over the threshold, leaving the door open behind him.

"My name is Otto Koch; I am a friend of Horst Müller. Sit down."

"No, I'm fine," Karl responded.

"Sit down now, Meyer." The door slammed behind him, and three large men emerged from the shadows. Two men with similar features, barrel chests, and small bellies hanging over their belts, shoved him down into a chair. Karl guessed they were brothers. The stockier of the two held him down. A third man, younger and muscular, looked at him through thick eyebrows, crossing his arms over his chest. His dark green coat could have been owned by a soldier.

"You have been going from house to house, haven't you?" Koch asked, malice in his voice, "To undermine Mr. Müller and promote the propaganda of the camp director."

"Propaganda?" Karl replied, "What propaganda?"

"You know what I'm talking about. You and the camp director are trying to force Germans to work on projects that only help the Japanese."

Karl exhaled and ran his fingers through his hair. His mouth gaped open, but nothing came out.

"You're joking," he stammered.

"This is not a joke Mr. Meyer. You are the traitor Mr. Müller warned me about. You want to be the German spokesman so you can do the bidding of the camp director. We will not tolerate a rogue like you, who seeks personal favors at the expense of his fellow Germans."

Koch gave a subtle nod, and in an instant, the two short men grasped Karl's arms and lifted him from his chair. The largest man reached back and with all the power he could muster, punched his fist into Karl's stomach.

Karl grunted in pain, and his head began to spin. The room went dark. Flashes of light scattered across his eyes as his vision cleared. The man stood over him, his fist clenched, ready to strike again. Karl's knees buckled, and he fell on all fours, panting between groans of pain.

"That is what happens when someone betrays the German people," Koch hissed. "There's plenty in store for those of you who act so selfishly."

Karl eyed the door, but he had no strength to run. His abdomen throbbed with pain.

"And if you report this incident to anyone, I *will* hear about it," Koch said, "then you will see how we deal with collaborators."

Karl tried to stand but lost his balance. He took a deep breath and waited a moment before trying again. When enough strength returned to stand, he wobbled to the door and opened it only as wide as needed to squeeze himself out the door. He heard the men laughing as he limped away.

Karl stumbled across the compound and into his cottage. Faltering, he dropped to the floor.

"What happened, Karl?" Marta sprang up from the table, knocking her chair aside with a clatter.

"Müller's thugs said I was a traitor because I was collaborating with O'Rourke."

She knelt beside him, bringing a hand to her mouth. He lifted himself to his knees and mumbled through the pain in his ribs. Marta bit her lip as she helped him to the bed.

"This has gone too far. I'm not going to stand for this bullying." Angry tears rolled down Marta's face. "We're going to O'Rourke and filing a complaint. If we have to, I'll file a complaint with the Red Cross."

Chapter 26-Note 1: This episode of having three spokesmen was described in camp director O'Rourke's final report. From his description, it is clear his well-intentioned attempts to allow the Germans to govern themselves through democratic rule was no match for these avowed national socialists who knew how to abuse the democratic process as a means of seizing power. He stated,

"Upon arrival of the Ellis Island contingent in Crystal City, it developed that two individuals were vying for the spokesmanship, and with the arrival of the remaining family members from Camp Forrest, a few days later, (because of) their desire for representation, this office agreed to a tri-head speakership; so for several weeks (this) officer in charge (O'Rourke) daily conversed, explained, and negotiated with these three individuals. It was soon apparent, however, that the transaction was literally going around in circles, since the three spokesmen could themselves not agree on any issues of importance. The German group was then instructed to elect one individual to serve as spokesman, and unfortunately, the person chosen (a man by the name of Karl Kolb, was one of the three previously mentioned) was an individual thoroughly sold on his own importance and with the deep-seated Nazi philosophy which proved detrimental to the peace, harmony and welfare of the German group in this camp. His theory was that of a strict dictatorship, with not only every internee subject to his whims and fancies, but every action of his administration subject to his approval. Life was soon miserable for most Germans in the camp."

J.L. O'Rourke, "Historical Narrative of the Crystal City Internment Camp, September 9, 1945." Record Group No. 85, *Immigration and Naturalization Service Crystal City Internment Camp*, File 217/021.

CHAPTER 27
March 1, 1943
Keesler Field, Mississippi

During Hank's first week of basic training at Keesler Field, he and all the other new enlistees were required to take a series of aptitude tests. Hank's test scores qualified him for just about any type of training he wanted. He chose Aircraft and Engine school.

A few weeks into that three-month long training, his duty officer took him aside.

"Hank, there's an OSS officer here who wants to talk to you."

"OSS?" Hank furrowed his brow. "Why?"

"He wouldn't say, but he's here now and you have to come with me."

He escorted Hank into a small room where an intimidating, handsome officer stood waiting for him. The man scowled at Hank, looking him up and down—assessing Hank as an adversary would size up a would-be foe.

"Please shut the door behind you," he ordered Hank's escort.

Hank's pulse raced and a bead of sweat ran down his neck. *Did this have something to do with my parents? Am I going to be sent to a detention camp?*

"My name is Captain Dietrich. I'm with the Office of Strategic Services," he declared with authority and paused. "And you are Heinrich Meyer?"

Hank stiffened. "My name is Hank Meyer. Only my enemies call me Heinrich. I've never, ever used that name. My school records and my military ID say I am Hank Meyer." Hank pulled out his dog tags and held them up. Captain Dietrich kept his gaze on Hank's face, looking straight into his eyes.

"Your birth certificate says your name is Heinrich."

In defiance, Hank crossed his arms in front of his chest and narrowed his eyes.

Dietrich lifted his chin and smiled, leaning back against his desk. He picked up a pencil and twirled it between his fingers, watching as Hank waited for him to speak.

"You are among a handful of Americans who are very skilled in the German language. We also know you have no discernible accent."

Hank took a deep breath and stated quietly, "I am not interested in espionage, if that's what you're here for."

"You are quite astute, aren't you?" Dietrich smirked.

"Save your breath. I will never volunteer to join the OSS, and even if I am ordered to do so, I would rather spend the rest of the war in Leavenworth."

"I can arrange to have you court-martialed and sent to Leavenworth for disobeying a direct order from a superior officer."

Hank shrugged his shoulders and cocked his head to one side, narrowing his eyes. Dietrich blinked slowly and cleared his throat.

"Maybe I'll have you arrested as a Nazi sympathizer. Maybe you're afraid you'll become a turn-coat like your 'mama and papa.'"

Hank wanted to step toward Dietrich's desk, but he hesitated. His fist curled into a ball, but he thought better of threatening a superior officer. He took several deep breaths through his nose. "My mother and father are proud, American citizens. They have the papers to prove it. But because they speak with a German accent, some idiot thinks they're Nazi sympathizers. Well, you know and *I* know my parents are being held on false charges."

"Your neighbor friend told us about what you were hiding. She said you had a Nazi flag and pictures of Adolf Hitler," Dietrich shot back.

"*My* neighbor friend? Who was that?" Hank frowned. "Was it Billie?"

A small smirk crept across Dietrich's face.

Hank's heart fluttered in his chest as dread formed a knot in his stomach. "It had to be Billie, right? She's the only person who had ever seen my souvenirs. Not even my mama knew about them."

Dietrich's unwavering stare told Hank what he needed to know, but he couldn't be angry with her. How could she ever have known her innocent comment would lead to his parents arrest and detention?

"Those were my things," Hank said. "I got them when we visited my grandparents. I was eleven years old, but no one thought or cared to ask me or my sister who those things belonged to. No one wanted to know why those things were in *my* room. They just assumed my mom and dad were Nazis and locked them up. No charges, no lawyers, and no trial, just like they do in Nazi Germany." Hank took a few deep breaths as he looked Dietrich with contempt.

"If you are a good American, then it's your duty to go where you are needed most."

"Uncle Sam has already invested a ton of money to train me for a critical mission with an air crew. Our job is key to winning the war. I'll be far more valuable on an air crew than I would being a spy."

Dietrich looked at his watch. He looked down his nose at Hank.

"Sir, am I being given a direct order to join the OSS?"

Dietrich looked at his feet and tapped his pencil against his knee. After a few moments of silence, Dietrich admitted, "I cannot give you a direct order, but I can sure make your life miserable."

Hank knew it was an empty threat. He wanted to smile from ear to ear. Instead, he looked at Dietrich without emotion. "Request permission to be dismissed, sir."

Dietrich hesitated, then swore under his breath as he called Hank's duty officer waiting outside.

"Come and get this worthless piece of…"

Hank stood tall, gave Dietrich a snappy salute, and walked out of the room. As the door closed behind him, his knees started to buckle. He looked at his duty officer, drew in a deep breath, and raised his arms in victory. With a bounce in his step, Hank returned to his aircraft training.

CHAPTER 28
March 2, 1943
Houston, Texas

Major Farmer, the commanding officer over the WFTD, made a surprise visit to the women's classroom while they were all studying for a navigation exam. He cleared his throat with gusto to get their attention.

The girls looked at each other with concern. As she turned to Betty who was sitting next to her, Billie said, "Uh-oh, this looks like trouble. What's this all about? Do you think they're going to cancel the program?"

"Shhh!" Betty scolded. "Just listen."

The major waited for the chatter to stop.

"I'd like to announce a change to this Woofteddy program that you may find interesting."

Billie looked around the room, noticing she wasn't the only one with a look of concern.

"The Pentagon will soon be making a few changes with the command structure, and you're all about to get a new name. You'll no longer be Woofteddies," he admitted with a smile.

"Jackie Cochran's Woofteddies and Nancy Love's Women's Auxiliary Ferry Squadron will be officially merged into a single organization called the Women Airforce Service Pilots." He scratched his head and smiled. "I guess that will make you all WASPs." Billie laughed as she realized the acronym. "You'll hear more about it later, but I wanted to give you the good news."

A collective sigh of relief surged through the room.

"I'd also like to congratulate you on your training. I know you weren't too happy with me when we bumped up your physical training routine. But I'm happy to see your progress. I'm pleased with what you are accomplishing. I am here to let you know that for those of you who complete your training, you will receive your wings on April 24, just a few weeks away."

The room erupted with cheers.

After her graduation ceremony, Billie chose to be assigned to the Ferry Command in Long Beach, California. Most of the aircraft manufacturers, from the maker of the B-17 to the famous P-51 pursuit fighter, were based in the Los Angeles area. If Billie wanted a chance to fly any of these aircraft, her best chance was to be right there in Long Beach.

She traveled with Betty and a group of five other WASPs to California. Arriving with jitters and glances of uncertainty between them, they disembarked from the plane. They found their way to the control room, and stifled their laughing and chatting as they walked in. Billie looked for the officer in charge and found him. He looked back with suspicion as his gaze flickered over their group.

"What are you doing here?"

Billie glanced at Betty with a confused look, but neither said a word.

The officer turned to his staff and mumbled a few curse words, intentionally audible even under his breath. He ran his hands through his hair, heaving a harsh exhale before turning back to the group of women pilots. Billie stepped up, and after clearing her throat, shot him a smile that should have melted any man's demeanor. "I have orders here Major, uh," she paused, peering at his crossed arms covering his name tag.

"Stevens!" he barked.

"Stevens," she stood straighter. "Major Stevens, my apologies. I have orders here from General Hap Arnold, indicating our assignment to this ferry command." She held out the papers.

"Let me see that," Major Stevens grumbled. He ripped the orders from her hand and scanned the page. Billie smirked as his eyes bulged, settling on General Arnold's signature at the bottom. "Do you want to see my identification?" Billie held out her hand, offering him her ID.

"No, keep it in your pocket, missy." He turned to a lieutenant sitting at a desk and commanded, "Don't just stand there. Get these little girls a place to stay until we can find a place on base."

The lieutenant sat up in his seat and reached for the telephone. Billie overheard the words "hotel, a few nights." He glanced over to their group.

"Six." When he hung up, he handed a note to a captain, who approached the women and said, "I have three rooms for you ladies at the Riviera Hotel in Long Beach."

Billie stared at the captain with raised eyebrows, the corner of her mouth lifting in a smile.

"'Home of the Admirals,' huh?"

He waved away her comment with a grunt and replied, "I'll have a driver take you there, but you'll need to take a cab back here tomorrow. Just come in here and see me in the morning and I'll have it all straightened out."

"Thank you, Captain," Billie said. "We appreciate *your* kindness."

The captain stiffened, giving a quick glance to his commanding officer and pointing to a junior officer as he headed for the doorway. "The lieutenant will escort you to the car."

Dusk began to fall as they drove along Ocean Boulevard, the view of the ocean to their right shimmering with the last of the daylight. The boulevard hustled and bustled with thousands of people.

Squished between two other girls, Billie leaned over Betty to peer out the window at the neon lights to their left as their car inched along through bumper-to-bumper traffic.

The driver pointed out the green, steeply pitched roof of their hotel coming into view among the other buildings. As they drew closer, Billie's eyes widened as the magnificent hotel came into full view. "Will you look at that? It's huge!"

The hotel's white, French Gothic architecture towered above them at sixteen stories. At the apex was a turret-like tower commandeered by the Navy as a lookout for enemy ships.

The driver began to slow in front of the hotel, but before the car came to a complete stop, the passenger door opened. A tall, thin man in a bellhop uniform bent down with a warm smile.

"Welcome to the Hotel Riviera. Allow me to take your bags."

Before Billie could protest, he had taken her luggage and placed in into his cart. She scrambled out of the car with the other girls, and by the time she had thanked the cab driver and given him a tip, the bellhop was already twenty feet ahead of her, entering through the stunning gold and glass hotel doors.

When she caught up with him at the check-in desk, he said cheerfully, "Here you go ma'am. Y'all take care now." He smiled as she collected her bags from him. He stood smiling, as though waiting for something. Billie reached into her pocket and handed him two quarters.

"Thank you," she said.

"Thank you, ma'am. That's very kind of you." He gave a polite smile, and Billie wondered if she had tipped him enough.

After checking into their room, Billie and Betty rushed to change into their bathing suits and head straight for the beach, just a few steps from the hotel. For most of the night they sat on the sea wall, digging holes in the sand with their bare feet and watching the ocean until they couldn't keep their eyes open.

"Can you believe it?" Betty said, leaning back on her palms and admiring the ocean.

"Believe what?"

"We're sitting on a beach and getting paid to fly airplanes."

"And we haven't ferried one plane yet," Billie laughed.

"Yes, but we're trained to fly real military airplanes, even though all those bigwigs thought we were going to wash out. We did better than anybody ever thought we could." Betty stretched her long body out on the towel beneath her.

Billie breathed in the delicious sea breeze and watched the sun about to set.

"Have you ever seen anything so pretty?" Billie beamed as she scanned the horizon.

"As a matter of fact, I have. In Hawaii, we get these gorgeous sunsets all the time."

"We get our share of wonderful sunsets in Utah, too. Especially when the sun dips below the mountains in the west and reflects on the snow-covered mountains in the east. We see this magical glow of pink and blue. It's amazing."

"Who do you miss most back home?"

Billie thought for a moment, then said, "My best friend, Ella. We've known each other since we were five. She keeps me on my toes. She's like a mother, always trying to tell me what to do." Billie giggled as she thought. "But I miss talking to my best friend. Do you know what I mean?"

"Oh, yes," Betty replied quietly.

"I also miss dancing with my friend Chester. That boy could dance," Billie smiled as she shook her head "And he is really nice to look at, if you know what I'm saying."

"Is he your boyfriend?"

"Yes and no. We dated a lot. But he could drive me crazy sometimes," Billie chuckled. "I really miss him now." Billie gazed off into the horizon beyond the sparkling blue water. "He's off in the Pacific somewhere. The last I heard he was a medical corpsman somewhere with the Marines."

"Oh, heavens." Betty squinted as she grimaced. "That's some rough duty there. I hope he's okay."

"He'll take care of himself. He'll be okay," Billie said, drawing something in the sand with her toes before scribbling it out.

The next morning, their cab arrived and took them to the airport. As the women stood erect, chins high inside the command center, the captain greeted them with an all-business smile.

"Ladies, we're unable to find housing for you just yet, and it's not going to happen for a few days."

"So that means we stay at the Riviera?" Billie asked.

"Yes, until further notice. And we have no work assignments yet until we get it all straightened out." Arriving at their hotel, and after wasting the day away, Billie and Betty dressed up and went to spend the evening at the Pacific Coast club, next to the hotel.

As they entered the big, double doors, familiar band music triggered a huge grin on Billie's face. The club was filled with hundreds of officers and junior officers, but most were Navy men wearing their summer white dress uniforms. Betty struck up a conversation with an officer at a table nearby, and Billie wandered away, bouncing on the balls of her feet, tapping her fingers on her side in time to the music. She scanned the room for a partner.

The maître de approached Billie and escorted her to the bar to wait for a table. Billie said nothing and stepped up to a barstool. Avoiding eye contact with the bartender, she swung around with her back to the bar and watched the handful of couples dancing to Benny Goodman's "Jersey Bounce."

"This dance band is amazing," she shouted, but the band drowned out her voice. "They sure know how to swing." She bounced her head along to the music. She had never been to a dance club like this, but she marveled at how well the band played the popular big band songs by Tommy Dorsey, Benny Goodman, and Glenn Miller. When the band started playing, "I've got a Gal in Kalamazoo," couples grabbed each other by the hand and jumped onto the dance floor. From the corner of her eye, Billie caught someone approaching. She turned to smile at a stocky, well-built Navy lieutenant.

"Care to dance?" He offered her his arm.

"Sure," Billie smiled, and he led her onto the dance floor.

She couldn't find her footing initially, and his dancing was a little clumsy, but soon the music synced their movements, and they danced until Billie's heart raced, and she had to catch her breath. When the music stopped, they returned to the bar.

"My name is Jack," he said with a slight southern drawl as they walked to their table. "What's yours?"

"Billie!" she held out her hand.

"It's a pleasure. Mind if we move over to that table? It's a bit more comfortable." She nodded and followed. He held her chair as she sat, and they talked over the din of music and crowd noise.

"What brings you to Long Beach?"

Billie hesitated. What should she tell him? Did she have anything to gain by being modest? "I'm a pilot, a WASP. And what about you?"

"I'm waiting to head overseas to help build new Navy installations." He tilted his head and gave her a curious look, "What's a WASP?" His eyebrows raised in curiosity.

"Women's Airforce Service Pilots. We ferry military airplanes around the country."

"Wow, that's a pretty swell job. How'd you get to do that?"

"I've been a pilot for a few years. I was an instructor when Jackie Cochran called me."

His eyes widened.

"Jackie Cochran. That's amazing."

She grinned.

"So where are you from?" Jack grabbed a few nuts from the bowl at the center of the table and tossed them into his mouth.

She knew the question had to come sooner or later. She didn't know how to talk about Utah without talking about religion. She shrugged, "I'm from a small town in Utah. You've probably never heard of it."

"Try me."

"Huntsville, Utah."

"You're right," he smiled with a sheepish grin. "Never heard of it."

Billie smiled, her eyebrows arched with curiosity.

"But I have heard of Huntsville, Alabama. I'm from Birmingham. Ever heard of that?"

"I sure have," Billie took a few peanuts herself. "Aren't you about a hundred and fifty miles west of Atlanta?"

"Sheesh, how'd you know?" he asked.

"I'm a pilot. We have to know geography."

"I'm impressed."

Just then, a waitress walked by, and Jack hailed her over and whispered in her ear. She nodded politely and walked away. Minutes later, she returned and set two drinks on the table.

Billie reminded herself of the promise she'd made with Ella as teenagers to never drink alcohol. But that was long ago, and this young man had already spent money on her.

"This one's for you," he gave a kind smile. "I hope you like it. It's one my mother always said was a proper drink for a lady."

Billie's face flushed as she assessed the drink in front of her. Her mind raced with a thousand conflicting notions. It's better to accept his kindness and not make a scene, she told herself. Then the voice of Grandma Russell echoed in her mind, warning her that some men would use alcohol to do something "immoral." She envisioned Ella shaking her head in disappointment. "What is it?" Her nose wrinkled. "It looks like green medicine."

Billie lifted the drink to her nose to smell it and was surprised by how delicious it smelled.

"It's a grasshopper," he explained with enthusiasm. "It's kind of minty and chocolaty. Just give it a sip. I promise you'll love it."

Chapter 29

May 1, 1943
Keesler Field, Mississippi

After five months of intensive basic training and aircraft school, Hank jumped at the first chance to attend Flexible Aerial Gunnery school. If he could finish gunnery school, it not only meant he was guaranteed the rank and pay of a sergeant, but it also meant he would likely be assigned to a heavy bomber.

The first week of April, he boarded a train in Gulfport, headed for Kingman, Arizona, the home of the recently constructed Flexible Aerial Gunnery school.

The Army paid twenty dollars for basic fare, which meant a single seat in a drafty coach car. Hank splurged and spent an additional nine dollars and seventy-five cents for a roomette and five dollars more for an upper berth.

When Hank boarded the train, he weaved his way through cars packed full of servicemen and civilians, nodding politely and clutching the handle of his suitcase until he found his roomette. He drew in a deep breath, smiled, and set his baggage down to wait.

Large enough to sleep three people, the compartment's furnishings filled the room with a comfortable amount of space left over. Two seats faced each other with a table between them, and large windows showcased the passing landscape. The upper bunk swung down from the ceiling, but when Hank reached for the latch to bring it down, it held fast and didn't budge with his tugging. He'd have to find the porter to unlock it.

Hank grabbed a pillow and tucked it behind him as he leaned against the window. Pulling a chair close, he propped up his feet, crossing his ankles as he opened his copy of C. S. Lewis's *The Screwtape Letters*. As he thumbed through to find his place, the name inscribed in the cover caught his eye. Would he be back someday to return the book to the USO in Gulfport who had loaned it to him? Thoughts like these ran through his head as the train rumbled away and he started to read.

Four tiresome and uncomfortable days later, Hank stepped off the train in Kingman and arrived at the base just as the sun sank below the horizon.

A small group of trainees had assembled in the growing darkness, and after glancing around, Hank joined their group and listened to the quartermaster calling out instructions.

"I will give each of you a mattress and bedding. Take it with you to the barracks down the hill," he pointed. "Just follow that path."

"How long is the path?" Hank asked.

"You'll see it. It's not far." The sergeant appeared annoyed.

Apparently, Hank's definition of "not far" and this cranky staff sergeant's definition were quite different. He dropped his mattress and bed pack twice on the darkened trail during the thirty-minute jaunt. The barracks stood in dark and empty silence until someone flipped the lights on. Hank threw his mattress onto the closest cot and put his bed together.

Row after row of bunks lined the long, green barracks. At the end of the building was the latrine; twelve open toilets without stalls and twelve open shower heads.

"I guess there's no such thing as privacy in the Army," Hank muttered to the man next to him.

"You'll get used to it," the man shrugged.

"Yeah, but that doesn't mean I'll like it."

They heard the rumble of an automobile engine as it approached, stopping just outside the barracks before going quiet. The door opened with a bang. The staff sergeant who entered walked with a tall posture, his spit-shined shoes tapping the floor, the buttons of his crisp, ironed shirt gleaming in the light of the barracks.

"Ten hut!"

All of the men jumped to their feet and stood at attention, although some were shirtless. Two men were in the latrine, and after a brief moment's delay, they stepped out and stood at attention, holding their pants at their waists.

"Lights out at 2200 hours. Calisthenics at 0530. Breakfast at 0630. We'll start with classroom instruction for a few days, then move to live ammunition training. When it's time to check out your guns and ammunition, you must have all your equipment checked out before classes start promptly at 0730. Is that understood?"

A collective "Yes, sir" rang through the barracks.

"Very well. At ease, gentlemen. Welcome to Kingman Army Airfield." He looked over the men briefly and turned around to walk out of the barracks. Within seconds, the vehicle started again and the engine noise faded as it drove off.

"Who was that?" Hank asked, not expecting an answer.

"*What* was that?" Someone else bellowed sarcastically.

That ended up being the only orientation they received. In the morning, they began a whirlwind of intense gunnery training that lasted for the next six weeks.

After graduation from gunnery school, all trainees were required to sign for their combat training pack before they could leave the base. It included a leather, fleece-lined helmet with goggles, oxygen mask and cylinder, winter gloves, the coveted A-2 bomber jacket (a leather jacket lined with fleece), a Mae West life preserver, and a parachute with a harness.

As Hank finished checking out of Kingman Army Airfield, he glanced over his orders to learn that his next assignment was at Pyote Army Airfield.

"Where's that?" he asked under his breath, not really caring if anyone else heard him. He opened a map from his pocket and ran his finger over the names of training bases until he found Pyote Army Airforce Base. Then it dawned him, "Oh, Rattlesnake Field," he mumbled. He'd heard about this B-17 training base located in a forsaken place called Pyote, Texas. It was an isolated training base about two hundred miles east of El Paso and about forty miles due south of the Texas panhandle and the New Mexico border.

Hank measured the distance from Pyote to Crystal City with his finger; more than three hundred miles. Could he make it work? Could he visit his parents? He'd be going overseas soon, and then he wouldn't see them until…he wouldn't dare make a guess. But his orders gave him only five days to arrive at Pyote, no later than Monday, June 21. His shoulders slumped as he put the thought aside. He purchased a ticket from Kingman to Pyote with no detours or connections.

Watching the Texas countryside pass by him, his loneliness and longing intensified his desire to see his parents. He wondered what it would take to go see them. Would they let him visit, or would they send him away? Contemplating such matters were too heartbreaking to dwell on. He pulled out his copy of *The Screwtape Letters* to help him clear his mind.

CHAPTER 30
September 10, 1943
Crystal City, Texas

A dreary gloominess hung over the camp's German internees. The Immigration and Naturalization Service officials were also troubled by the underhanded dealings of Horst Müller, the duly elected German spokesman. Karl's bruises had healed, but he walked the camp with a wary eye, avoiding confrontation with Müller's men. Karl looked for signs of assault on other people, but if they had been attacked, their injuries were concealed under their sleeves or collars, or perhaps they hid a limp when they walked. Nobody dared breathe a word against Müller.

For weeks, all was quiet, and Karl started to relax a bit.

Then Müller went on the offensive.

The morning of September 15, Karl and Marta made their morning walk to the store. Up ahead, a commotion from Müller's gang got everyone's attention. Karl halted and reached for Marta's hand. They watched with a sickening feeling as Müller's men pulled down the American flag.

"Karl!" Marta gasped. He tightened his grip, speechless.

The men whooped and hollered as they threw the flag on the ground and stomped on it.

"They're putting up a Nazi flag," Marta whispered.

Karl's stomach twisted. He glanced around for the guards, but before they could notice anything, Müller's men had raised a Nazi flag to the top and lifted their voices to sing the German national anthem, *Horst Wessel Lied.*

Raise the flag! The ranks tightly closed!
The SA marches with calm, steady step.

"Hey, take that flag down!" a guard shouted.

Germans clustered together around the flagpole to keep the guard from approaching. With more and more Germans joining them, their song grew louder.

Clear the streets for the brown battalions,
Clear the streets for the storm division!
Millions are looking upon the swastika full of hope,
The day of freedom and of bread dawns!"

A guard pushed his way past the rowdy Germans, reaching to retrieve the American flag from under the protesters' feet. Another guard grabbed the rope of the flagpole and ripped down the Nazi flag. The crowd cried out in anger.

Müller stepped up. "You can't do zis. Ve haf our rights." He gestured with wide, charismatic sweeps of his arms as he wailed, "Dis is against ze rules of ze Geneva Convention. We have a right to fly ze flag of our country."

"Not in my country," the guard replied. "Neither you nor any of your Nazi gangsters will fly that flag anywhere on American soil."

"So be it." Müller tightened his fists at his side. As he turned away, Karl caught a shadow of a smile on his face.

That day Müller filed an official complaint with the Swiss government, the designated liaison for German prisoners being held in the United States. Within days, he filed another, then another—every complaint requiring official inquiry, occupying officials' time and resources.

After a month, O'Rourke wrote a letter to summon Karl and Marta to his office. A guard escorted them from their home under the cover of darkness. As they walked, they looked over their shoulders, hoping they wouldn't be seen.

Karl held Marta's hand, giving it a soft, reassuring squeeze.

"Do you think they're going to transfer us again?" Karl whispered.

"I doubt it," Marta said. "They wouldn't tell us ahead of time, especially the director. They'd just tell us to start packing."

"Do you think we're in trouble for something?" Karl suggested.

"Just calm down. He'll tell us in a minute." Marta couldn't hide her impatience.

"Are you sure you remember how to speak English?" Karl teased, trying to change the mood. Marta looked back and gave him a sarcastic nod.

They approached the main gate of the inner compound where O'Rourke's office was located—a small building in plain view of everyone.

"Come in, come in." O'Rourke gave them a pleasant smile as he closed the door behind them. "Have a seat, please." He sat, relaxed on the front of his desk, just a few feet in front of the Meyers, and his smile was kind and reassuring.

"I apologize for calling you here at this late hour, but I wanted to keep our meeting a secret from the other internees for reasons I'll explain in a minute."

Karl looked at Marta nervously, then gave O'Rourke a questioning look.

O'Rourke said, "This summer has been particularly hard on you, on all the Germans, for that matter. I think we both know who is primarily responsible for that."

Karl and Marta spoke in unison, "Horst Müller."

O'Rourke smiled and nodded. "Several months ago, you made me aware that you had been assaulted, and I greatly appreciate that. I apologize that I've been unable to give you any justice as yet, but my hands have been tied by international rules governing prisoners of war and their right to obtain a redress of grievances. But I've had enough. You've had enough. And I'm sure most of the Germans in here have had enough. I'm about to pull the trigger on something, but I want to run it by you first. It might be risky."

Karl stiffened, giving anxious glances to Marta.

O'Rourke reached back to his desk and handed Karl a draft memorandum.

"Each time Müller makes an official complaint, I have to prepare an official response and send it to both the Swiss Protectorate and the International Red Cross, explaining our side of the alleged mistreatment at Crystal City. We know Müller's objective is to cause chaos and confusion, and he hopes to wear us down. Up until now, that plan has worked," he admitted. "I see no immediate solution other than to have him removed and sent to another camp." He gestured to the letter in Karl's hands. "This letter describes the discord among the German population," O'Rourke explained, "and why Müller and his agitators have been able to wreak havoc here. It also explains why he needs to be removed. Now keep in mind, the people at the INS know all about his tactics; this letter is really aimed at Müller and his followers. Go ahead and read it carefully."

Karl held the paper next to him so both he and Marta could read it.

Memorandum

To: Henry B. Hazard, Immigration and Naturalization Service
From: J.L. O'Rourke, Director Crystal City Internee Camp
Date: September 10, 1943
Subject: Request to transfer Horst Müller

In the spirit of complying with the Geneva Convention stipulations, we have promoted democratic self-government among the internees here at Crystal City. We have encouraged both the German and Japanese populations to select their own spokesman, someone who can speak on behalf of their fellow countrymen.

As you are aware, the Japanese were quick to designate a spokesman through a popular vote. While their style of self-governing may seem a little strange to Americans, it seems to be working for them, with few exceptions.

Unfortunately, for the Germans, citizen-led self-government has been a disaster. For some, they see democracy as an American ideal and are uninterested in imitating the form of government promoted by Americans.

To further complicate matters, our offer of self-rule has been exploited by an individual seeking dominance. Using intimidation and threats against other internees to influence the election, Horst Müller was selected in April as spokesman of the German contingent. From the outset of his tenure, he has sabotaged all efforts at establishing a good-faith relationship of cooperation with camp leadership.

Müller is thoroughly sold on his own importance, compounded by a deep-seated Nazi philosophy. His involvement as spokesman has proved detrimental to the peace, harmony, and welfare of the Germans in this camp. He has tried to follow his Führer's practice of strict dictatorship. He demands that all internees seek his permission before accepting work positions. He has meted out punishment to those not giving the "Heil Hitler!" salute. He instigated a work-stoppage on several camp projects to the detriment of other Germans, who were denied wages and who lost the benefits of the construction projects that were intended for their use.

We have recently learned that Müller's supporters have assaulted at least one German detainee who challenged his authority. This person courageously came forth to report the assault and is willing to testify in this regard. Doing so brings great personal risk and would require that we exercise the utmost caution to protect him from retribution, should he be asked to testify in this matter.

Unfortunately, we believe there are many others who have been assaulted, or who have been threatened with assault; but they have not come forward.

Because of these and many other damaging actions that occurred with Müller serving as German spokesman, we intend to remove Mr. Müller from his position, declare him *persona non grata* in Crystal City, and request that he be immediately transferred to the camp in Algiers, Louisiana.

Any questions or concerns can be directed to me.

JLO

Karl watched Marta's eyes as she finished reading, then they looked up at O'Rourke.

"So, what do you think?" O'Rourke asked. "I intend to send this to the INS, but I wanted you to know first."

"Vy?" Karl asked.

"Do you know if there are others who were assaulted? If so, that may help protect you. If you were the only one, then it's likely they can identify you as the informant."

Karl knitted his brow in thought. "I… No, I don't know. I have not asked anyvone."

"We're confident that German spies are embedded within the INS," O'Rourke explained. "So, if you were the only one to report the assault, or if you told anyone else, I'm afraid that others may blame you for having Müller transferred out of here."

"It's been months. I don't remember vat I said. I don't sink so, but I'm not sure." Karl's voice was almost a whisper.

"If I have no one to testify against him, I'm afraid it may greatly complicate my request to have him transferred," O'Rourke said.

Marta set the letter gently on O'Rourke's desk. "Karl, if zere is a chance that sending zis letter will bring about his transfer, do you sink it's vorth the risk?"

Karl whispered. "I sink so. But I'm a target if I agree, at least until he's gone." He looked at O'Rourke and asked, "How long vill it take to get him transferred?"

O'Rourke hesitated, but said, "It could take weeks or even months."

"Months?"

"I really have no idea how long this process will take." O'Rourke gave a regretful smile. "But I need to be up front with you. If I don't get it started now, we'll never get rid of him. This entire situation is already out of control."

"Do I haf to talk to someone at the INS?"

O'Rourke gave a slow, thoughtful nod. "Maybe. But I'll discourage them. If they insist, I'll make sure we conduct the interview somewhere off-site. Would that work?" O'Rourke asked.

Karl sat motionless. He was being asked to trust the U.S. government to protect him. A glance at Marta showed she, too, didn't know what to think of his proposal. Marta was usually so confident, so sure. She was the one he looked to for inspiration and support. It was clear she was fed up with all of it.

"Vit all due respect, vy should I trust you to protect me?" Karl blurted.

O'Rourke drew back in astonishment.

"Because, Mr. Meyer, we're the Americans. We're the good guys. We operate in good faith and earn the trust we deserve. Have I given you any reason not to trust me?"

"You can't be serious?" Karl laughed.

"Ve are here. The very reason ve are here is vy we can't trust you. Ve haven't been given vun single reason to trust anyvun from ze U.S. government."

O'Rourke shuffled in his seat but pushed on.

"Haven't I been kind and respectful? Haven't I shown you that I really want what's best for you, even under these circumstances?"

Marta leaned forward, gripping the arms of her chair as she glared at O'Rourke.

"You are living a fantasy if you believe zat," she spat. He flinched, his jaw dropping at this uncharacteristic outburst from Karl's composed, level-headed wife.

"I haf eighteen months of reasons to distrust you and efry single government person in zis country. Ve haf been ripped from our home and locked up visout charges." Marta stared down O'Rourke. "You sink you deserve to be trusted? After all ve haf been through? I sink ve deserve to be treated like Americans. *Zen* maybe I beleef you if you say 'ze Americans are ze goot guys.'"

The words shot from her mouth. Karl watched with wide eyes, feeling each word seethe with loathing. He reached out to her arm to comfort her, and she stopped herself from saying more. Silence hung like a cloud over the room. Karl looked at Marta, and her breathing finally slowed.

O'Rourke looked at his shoes then confessed, "I'm sure I'll never understand fully what you've been through. And I don't think I can give you many logical reasons to trust me. All I can do is ask that you trust me to do the right thing. If you don't want me to notify them that you're willing to testify against Müller," O'Rourke laced his fingers together and put them on his lap, giving a small shrug, "then I promise I won't say a word."

Karl and Marta stared at the memorandum again. What more could be said? They sat in anxious silence, swallowing more anger.

"We've really got no choice," Karl whispered in German to Marta. "Either way we lose, but if we can help get rid of him somehow, it makes sense to do something."

Marta took Karl's hand and shrugged.

Karl winked at her, then looked up at O'Rourke and said, "Ve'll do it."

"Are you sure?" he asked.

Karl looked at Marta and he gave an approving nod.

O'Rourke smiled. "I promise you won't regret it."

"But," Karl said, "please don't let any of Germans see that ve talk."

"I understand. I'll correspond with you via the mail, okay?"

They walked out of his office, looking in both directions, hoping not to be seen.

Marta put her hand in Karl's and apologized in German, "I'm sorry for blowing up back there. I hope I didn't cause more problems."

Karl gave her hand three squeezes. It was their secret code.

One quick squeeze for each word, *I love you.*

Chapter 30-Note 1: The German delegation's success at Crystal City mirrors the plan used to bring about Hitler's "election." In Germany, the Nazis successfully used an intense propaganda campaign in tandem with widespread ballot fraud, using the threat of violence and election manipulation to gain power. Although the official Nazi assertion was that 98.9 percent of the population voted for Hitler, the facts show the election was clearly a manifestation of economic self-interest and less about embracing antisemitism, or Hitler himself. For a significant number of Germans, the national socialists were a safer economic choice, given the increasing threat of communism, which many thought was a more dangerous threat.

CHAPTER 31
September 14, 1943
Dalhart, Texas

"How did summer happen without us?" Hank asked as he packed his duffel bag. He stood next to Captain Bud Sterner, the skipper of their B-17 Flying Fortress. Sterner was a civil engineering graduate from Southern Methodist University in Dallas. He was a fatherly guy who loved to give advice about everything from relationships to how to change a flat tire. With thinning hair and a bald spot on the crown of his head, he looked much older than his twenty-seven years.

"I don't know. It seems like it was years ago that we met in Pyote, but we've only known each other for a few months," Sterner laughed.

They, along with the rest of their combat crew, were back together after first being assembled as a crew in Pyote's "Rattlesnake Field." Their training lasted through June and most of July before they were transferred to Dalhart, Texas for advanced aerial combat training.

Sterner's crew consisted of a co-pilot, Second Lieutenant Henry Harris; a bombardier, First Lieutenant Melvin Connors; a navigator, Robert Donny and an engineer, George Howell, both technical sergeants.

Staff Sergeant Bill "Woody" Wood, trained Hank as the assistant radio operator. He was a good man, but Hank wished he wouldn't smoke as much as he did. Hank was eager to learn about the radio equipment and had only rudimentary training on how to operate it. Woody, however, was learning himself, so Hank had to squeeze in time to practice whenever he could.

At the aft of the plane, Hank's fellow waist gunner was a tough-talking kid from the barrios of Southern California, Ray Montoya. Hank and Ray were cordial but had so little in common they rarely just sat and chatted in their free time.

Al Barsauskas, the skinny, five-foot tall Lithuanian immigrant, was a perfect fit in the ball turret position. His unfortunate lack of confidence in his English skills meant he didn't talk much to anyone. But Hank liked him and encouraged him to speak up more often. Hank especially enjoyed Al's adventurous stories of emigrating from Kaunas to a Lithuanian neighborhood in Chicago.

Their tail gunner, Staff Sergeant Howard Lowe, spoke so fast and with such strong Bronx inflections that Hank lost every other word he said. The kid's cocky attitude didn't make it easy to listen to him, either.

Hank asked Sterner a question as he tucked items into his bag, stopping to smile. "Do you remember when we first climbed into a B-17?"

"Ya, but I also remember our first flight. It was on July Fourth," Sterner replied. "How could I ever forget? You couldn't stop puking." He laughed, shoulders shaking in his hysteria.

Hank gave an awkward grin.

"Almost every time we hit turbulence. We could count on you losing your lunch whenever we hit a bump," Sterner said, wiping the corners of his eyes.

"Yeah," Hank said, his flat tone a stark contrast to the way Sterner's words wheezed through his laugh. "Wasn't that fun?"

"I wondered if you were going to wash out because of it. But eventually you got used to the turbulence, and you've been okay since," Sterner said. "But boy, you were the pukiest person I've ever met and that includes my sisters!"

During those first few months of training, each crewman had been given his assigned responsibilities on the plane. Hank was first penciled in for the tail gunner position at the rear of the plane, but when he tried to squeeze into the small space, his shoulders were too wide.

"Looks like you're a waist gunner," Sterner had declared with authority. At the end of their eight weeks of training, Hank and the crew had daily practice in air-to-air combat or long-range, high-altitude bombing situations. Some of these flights lasted twelve hours, all in sub-zero temperatures.

"Do you think we're ready for the real thing?" Hank asked Sterner. Sterner didn't reply, but Hank knew the answer. Their training was exhausting but inadequate. And although they had passed their final test to graduate, Hank searched the eyes of his fellow crew members when he passed them in the hall or listened to their voices when they spoke about their first assignment. Something was missing, and it mirrored his own lack of confidence. Just the thought of flying through flak or being the target of a German fighter plane's attack sent fear tingling through his fingers.

The European theater was likely their next step. They had an eight-day furlough until they reported to Scott Field, Illinois. Once there, they would receive their overseas call. As a B-17 crew, it was likely they would end up in England, but some were headed to the Pacific. Hank's mind wandered over Europe, following the borders of France and Germany, winding through the German towns where, somewhere, his *Oma*'s house nestled in the countryside. Would she be safe for long?

He ignored the persistent thoughts bouncing around in his head. Thinking about his *Oma* was wasted effort right now. He turned his attention back to Sterner.

"Where you headed for your furlough, Skipper?"

"Plano, Texas—about four-hundred miles from here." He noted Hank's blank look. "It's just north of Dallas."

"Oh, that'll be nice," Hank replied as he lifted one of his shirts to his nose, sniffed it deeply, and then stuffed it into his duffel bag. "It shouldn't take you too long to get there. I'm thinking about going to Utah, but it'll probably take me two or three days to get there, and I don't know how long it'll take to get from Utah to Illinois," Hank said, giving a weary shrug. "So I don't know if it's worth it, but there's a bus leaving for the railroad station right now. I've got to see if they can get me out of Dalhart this morning. See you in a week." He slung his bag over his shoulder.

Sterner waved goodbye.

Hank ran across the street just as the doors of the bus slid closed. He waved frantically and pounded his fists on the side until he caught the attention of the driver. The bus stopped, and he burst through the doors before it sped forward. Breathlessly, he stood holding the overhead handle, balancing his duffel bag at his feet.

The dumpy, two-story Dalhart train station stood on the outskirts of the small, unremarkable Texas town. A southbound train had just arrived, causing a Texas-sized dust cloud to envelop the passengers who waited to board. Hank avoided the dust storm in the ticket line, rushing to get to the window.

"Is there any way to get me to Ogden, Utah and then go from Ogden to Scott Field, Illinois in a week? I have until the twenty-first of September to report for duty."

The ticket agent's tired face wrinkled in thought, but he added without hesitation, "Probably not."

Hank looked at him with confusion.

"Son, I don't see how to get you to Utah for any length of time, because you'll spend a few hours there, then have to turn right around and get back on a train."

Would it make Ella lonelier if he could only see her for a couple of hours? Maybe he could see his mama and papa instead. More than likely, she would want it that way anyway.

"Alright, then can you get me down to Dilley, Texas for a day or so, and then get me to Illinois by the twenty-first?"

"You mean down by the Mexican border?"

"Yes, I have some friends down there. If I can get to San Antonio, I think I can take the Missouri Pacific line to Dilley. I can get where I need to go from there," Hank explained.

"Are you traveling on military orders or will you pay a regular civilian fare?"

"Civilian fare to Dilley, but I'll have orders to get to Scott Field," Hank replied.

"Can I see your orders?" Hank handed him his papers. He looked at Hank with a tired smile, then inspected his papers. After a few minutes, he tapped a handful of papers on the table, organizing them into a neat stack before giving them back to Hank.

"Okay, this ticket will get you to San Antonio and then to Dilley. That train leaves…" he looked at the clock on the table in front of him, "in about an hour."

He gave Hank another ticket.

"This is your ticket to St. Louis. You'll have long stops in Dallas, Texarkana, Little Rock, and Memphis before arriving in St. Louis on the night of the twentieth. Let's hope you don't have any long delays."

"Let's hope," Hank agreed.

"When you get to St Louis, there's a shuttle bus that'll get you out to Scott Field. Just show up in uniform and it's free. Your total fare is forty-four dollars and fifty cents."

Hank reached into his pocket and handed him a five-dollar bill and two crisp twenty-dollar bills.

"Thank you, sir," he said politely, before taking a seat on the empty platform to wait.

CHAPTER 32

September 15, 1943
San Antonio, Texas

As Hank sat in the dining car waiting for the train to come to a stop at the San Antonio train station, his mind raced with questions. Every possible scenario played out in his mind. Would the local authorities let him in the internee camp? Would he even be able to see his parents? If so, for how long?

Hank had dressed in his uniform, hoping it would arouse fewer suspicions about why he was traveling to a restricted area. But in the stifling humidity, he second guessed that decision. Sweat oozed down the small of his back as he stepped off the train into a sea of men in uniform.

Hundreds of soldiers scurried about the station, destined for any one of the local military installations: Fort Sam Houston, Lackland, Brooks, Kelly, Duncan, or Randolph fields.

Hank retrieved his duffel bag and walked inside the small, unadorned train station. It had no other services except a little snack bar. The stout little Hispanic woman had not closed her shop yet, and she had a few stale sandwiches. He went to pay for a sandwich, but she pushed all she had toward him. "You can have them." She waved with the back of her hand. "I was going to throw them out anyway."

He thanked her three times for good measure and found a bench to enjoy his free meal.

The overhead announcer made a muffled final call for Laredo. Hank ran to the platform moments before the train made its first powerful lunge forward.

"Does this train stop in Gardendale?" he asked the conductor, presenting his ticket.

"Yes, sir, it does. It's the next stop after Dilley in about…" he took out his pocket watch and glanced at it, "ninety minutes."

"Do you know if there's a train from Gardendale to Crystal City? Apparently, the schedule isn't published."

"That's because most of the people going out there don't have a return ticket." He raised an eyebrow.

"I have official business out there." Hank's eyes narrowed, revealing his discomfort with the white lie. "Luckily, I'm not staying long. So, what's the best way there?"

"You're better off catching a bus," the conductor said.

"There's a bus station across the street from the train depot. Check with them."

Hank was the only passenger to get off the train in Gardendale. It gave him a sinking feeling as the click-clack of the caboose grew fainter. The oppressive heat had already taken a toll on his stamina. He glanced around for shade as the Texas sun beat down on him.

The small, wooden train station had seen better days. Not a single passenger lingered on the platform, and from the lack of benches, Hank figured it didn't have many. Only one employee could be seen inside the information booth, fanning herself behind the jail-like bars. She stared at Hank with a glower that deepened the closer he came.

Hank asked in soft voice, "When's the next train to Crystal City?"

She blinked twice, looking at him coldly, and said, "For passengers? Three days. For freight, every day."

"What's the best way to get there from here?" Hank asked.

"You're better off going back to Dilley and catching a bus," she said, with a little more kindness in her voice.

"And how would you suggest I do that?"

"Hoof it. Just start walkin.' It's about ten miles, but you're in uniform; you shouldn't have a problem hitchin' a ride."

Hank balanced his duffel bag on the dusty ground and loosened his collar and necktie. After crossing the small, two-lane road heading north, he walked for five minutes in the stifling heat. A truck rumbled by him, but when he turned to wave it to a stop, the driver ignored him. It sped on, throwing dust in Hank's eyes. He wiped his brow, still searching for shade, a tree, anything. The town of Gardendale itself was not much more than a propped-up sign on the side of the road, and not a sound was heard but the buzzing of insects in the blazing Texas summer.

At last, another truck rumbled along the road. Hank held out his thumb.

This time, it worked.

"Where you goin', soldier?" the Hispanic man in a cowboy hat asked with a welcoming smile.

"I'm headed back to Dilley."

"Hop in, I can take you to Dilley," the man said.

"That would be terrific," Hank lifted his duffel bag into the bed of the truck. "I sure do appreciate it."

"What on earth are you doing in Gardendale?" he asked with a laugh in his voice. "There's nothing there but dust."

"I figured that much out," Hank replied. "I'm trying to get to Crystal City and I heard there was train service from Gardendale."

"Hah. You'll wait a long time for a passenger train."

Hank was beginning to understand why the passenger train schedule wasn't published, and why he couldn't buy tickets all the way to Crystal City.

"You're in luck," the driver continued. "I'm going to Crystal City this afternoon, but I have to stop in Dilley. If you don't mind waitin' for about an hour, I can take you all the way there."

"That would be swell," Hank replied, and he settled in for the fifteen-minute drive.

"So, what do you know about that detention camp out there?" Hank asked to break up the silence.

"Only that they got a bunch of Japs and Nazis," he replied, narrowing his eyes. "They're always hirin' people, and they pay pretty well. But it's too hard to live anywhere else but just outside the camp. I turned down a few jobs 'cause it's just not worth the drive."

"Is there a hotel in Crystal City, or someplace I can stay for the night?"

"Yes, but they're all full of government and military people. Why aren't you staying inside the compound? You're goin' there for duty, aren't you?"

"I'm just not sure they've made all the arrangements." Hank wondered if he could hear the lie in his voice.

"I don't think there's a hotel room available, but if you go to the gas station, I know a guy there, and he can tell you who's takin' in boarders for a night or two."

The stop in Dilley took little more than fifteen minutes, and they were on their way to Crystal City by way of Big Wells and Brundage. The man chatted with Hank about rationing, Roosevelt, and the successes the Japanese were having in the Pacific. Before long they pulled into the gas station, and Hank glanced at his watch. The hour had passed without his noticing.

Hank jumped down from the truck, taking in the sight of the lonely gas station. An engine roared in the repair bay, its loud grumbling and fumes mixing with the summer heat. A small red ice chest with "Drink Coca-Cola, ice cold" displayed in dirtied white letters sat by the door of the office.

Hank reached into his pocket. The owner approached him, wiping oil and dirt from his hands with a rag.

"Take one. It's free for servicemen like you," he offered with a gleam in his eyes.

As the driver got out of the truck, he called, "This young man needs a place to stay for a night or two. Anyone in town takin' in boarders that you know of?"

"Millie Eskelson usually takes 'em. Y'all know where she lives, right?" he replied.

The driver tilted his head. "Not quite sure."

"Keep headin' on this road 'til you get to Crockett street and turn right at Seventh avenue. It's the only house out there."

Hank reached out to shake the driver's hand, thanking him with a smile. He grabbed his duffel bag from the truck and slung it over his shoulder. With a wave to the driver and the gas station owner, he set off into the late afternoon Texas sun.

Hank paused outside, lingering back to take a closer look at the house, if you could call it a house. The roof angled down the sides like a barn, and the door frame was splintered in places with white paint chipping. Two broken windows faced the road. A big-eared hound dog rose when Hank crept closer, his chain clinking as his nose pointed up with each loud bay. The dog thumped his heavy tail, but Hank stood fast, looking from the dog to the door and pursing his lips in uncertainty.

The door opened and a woman in a sleeveless smock yelled, "Rex, shut up and stop yer... oh, hi!" She flashed Hank a toothless grin, kneeling down to stroke the dog's head. "His bark's bigger'n his bite. He won't hurt ya. You needin' a place to stay?"

"Yes, ma'am," he said. "How much do you charge?"

"Five dollars a night and I feed ya breakfast... how 'bout that?"

"Do you mind if I see the room first?" Hank asked.

"Sure thing, honey. Come on in. I'm Millie."

"Pleased to meet you, ma'am."

Hank leaned his duffel bag on the side of the house and ducked through her doorway. They walked through a dingy entryway and came into a darkened kitchen where something simmered on the stove.

"Follow me; I've got a room here and a bathroom next to it," Millie said.

She led him into a small bedroom. The floor sagged beneath Hank's weight. He looked down to find a hand-made rug covering an ancient hardwood floor. Millie pulled a string in the center of the ceiling to illuminate a single light bulb. The bed in the corner looked clean and tidy, and the window let in a slight breeze.

"This'll do just great," Hank grinned as they headed back outside.

"Come and go as you please. I'll know it's you. No need to knock. Ya got that?"

Hank gave a nod of agreement.

"I could tell right off you were a good, wholesome American boy." Millie held the door open for Hank to grab his duffel bag.

"I get Japs here ever' so often, and I just tell 'em I ain't got no room," she admitted. "Ya never know 'bout those Nips."

Hank averted his gaze, instead reaching his hand out for the dog to sniff.

"And I can tell you about those sneaky Germans, too. I can spot them from a mile away. They got shifty eyes and such, and I don't let 'em stay here neither."

"Do you get many of those?" Hank asked.

"Sometimes." Her tone grew hushed. "I feel sorry for some of them 'cuz the one's they got locked up in that camp I hear are gonna be traded for American prisoners the Nazis are holdin'."

His heart raced. Through the sound of blood rushing in his ears, he said, "How do you know that?"

"Oh, I have my ways," Millie laughed. "I have my ways."

"Are there many visitors at the camp?"

"Oh yeah," she added with enthusiasm. "They come a lot, but they only allow visitors in the afternoons, so you have to get a visit approved in the mornings. Some people don't know that and they waste a lot of time."

He drew a deep breath, shaky and uncertain. Maybe he would be able to see his folks after all.

"So what brings you here?" Millie asked. "You on some secret mission?"

"No ma'am," Hank replied. "I'm here to take care of some routine business. I'll know tomorrow if I need a place to stay tomorrow night. I'll let you know."

"That'd be fine," Millie replied.

Hank enjoyed a fine dinner of roast chicken with potatoes and went to bed. He sat on the edge of his bed, watching the world turn from daylight to dusk as the moon rose in the sky. Laying back, Hank laced his fingers and cradled his head. The breeze off the Gulf encouraged him to open the window wider to freshen the room.

An hour after dark, a bright glow still reflected off his walls. Hank sat up, leaning forward to peer out of the window. Powerful, sweeping searchlights shined against the night, beaming from the guard towers at the camp. An awful feeling burned in his gut as he pictured gun-toting guards and the ten-foot barbed-wire fence trapping his parents inside. The injustice of it all made him angry and anxious. With the mesmerizing, bouncing lights reflecting off the walls in Hank's room that needed a paint job, he drifted off to sleep.

CHAPTER 33
September 15, 1943
Crystal City, Texas

The next morning, Millie offered Hank some coffee and toast. Hank waved the coffee away with a smile and a "no thank-you," picking up the piece of toast as he headed out.

As Hank approached the hefty wooden gate of the camp's main entrance, its looming size sent a chill through him. The morning air wafting from the Japanese compound smelled of rice and cooking fish. A handful of German teens chatted as they strolled toward the doors of Federal High School, not far from the main gate. As Hank stopped at the gate, a border patrol guard looked at Hank's uniform and stood straighter in recognition of his rank.

"How can I help you, sir?"

"I need to be directed to the office where I can make an appointment to see a detainee."

The man's jaw tensed, and his eyes narrowed. "Unless you are here to interrogate a prisoner, only immediate family is permitted to visit with detainees."

"And where is it that "immediate family" make those arrangements?"

"I'll need to see some identification."

Hank reached into his back pocket and pulled out his wallet. He held out his military identification to the guard, who leaned forward to see. He cocked his head a bit as he stared at Hank, then again back at the card.

"You've only been in the Army for six months and you're already a sergeant. How is that possible?"

"I graduated from Flexible Aerial Gunnery School and just finished combat training with a B-17 crew. I'm headed to Scott Field for my overseas call," Hank explained, "and I have traveled a long way to visit my parents. If you don't mind, I need to make an appointment to see them."

With the palm of his right hand, the guard pointed to the administration building. "You will need to be escorted, sir. Please wait here."

He gestured for Hank to walk in front of him, laying his hand on his holster. Hank looked away with a roll of his eyes, marching through the gate to the office building. The next guard used his rifle to point to a room. Hank opened the door and went inside. "How can I help you?" A petite woman with a clipboard under one arm greeted him.

"I understand I need to make a request to visit two detainees this afternoon," Hank replied.

"Okay," she said, wrinkling up her nose. "Are you with the OSS? Is this an interview for an ongoing investigation?"

"No ma'am."

"We can only allow direct family members to visit detainees. Are you a direct family member of a detainee?"

"Yes ma'am," Hank replied.

"Okay." She cleared her throat. "Visiting hours here are limited to one hour per month per visitor. Your request will need to be approved by the camp director. Please complete this form and we will inform you if it is approved."

Hank took the clipboard from her and used the attached pencil to fill out his answers. Within minutes, he handed it back. "How will you inform me?"

"We usually deal with these matters by mail," she said. "We don't get many visitors, but I will see what we need to do to get your request approved sometime this morning."

"I'm happy to wait here." Hank grabbed a chair from an unoccupied desk, planting it in the center of the room. He sat with his legs crossed and folded his arms.

She took a deep breath. "Oh my. Well then, that will have to do for now, won't it?"

The time seemed to drag. Office workers scurried about, passing his door every now and then and giving Hank curious looks. It was clear he had disrupted their rhythm, and they weren't sure what to make of this good-looking young man in uniform. Hank now understood why so few people came to visit. Not everyone would be willing to make such an arduous trip without the assurance they would see their loved ones. He adjusted his seat and lifted his chin, watching with mild interest at the parade of workers passing by to get a glimpse of him.

About an hour later, the young lady returned, leading a tall man in a white shirt and tie. He held out his hand. "You must be Sergeant Meyer?"

Hank stood and gave him a firm handshake, stretching out the stiffness in his legs and back. "Yes sir. Hank Meyer, USAA."

"It's a pleasure to meet you. I'm J.L. O'Rourke. I'm the director here at Crystal City. You are the son of Karl and Marta Meyer, is that right?"

"Yes, sir. Do you know them?"

"Yes, I do indeed," O'Rourke replied, a warm eagerness brightening his eyes. "I have a lot of respect for both of them."

Hank looked at him with skepticism. "That's, uh, nice to hear. I think my parents are both worthy of much respect."

"I'm approving your request for this afternoon. Our visiting hours are from four to five. Just come through the main gate, and they'll escort you to our secure visitor's hut."

"Okay," Hank's mouth hung open wanting to say more, but he couldn't make the words come out.

O'Rourke patted Hank's back, steering him toward the door. Hank balked and summoned the courage to say, "Can you tell me what I can and can't do when we visit?"

"Yes, I sure can," O'Rourke smiled. "You'll be required to have an armed guard in the room at all times. You will sit across a table with a barrier, and above all, you will not be able to touch or otherwise be close enough to pass contraband or documents between each other."

"Is there anything I can give them, like books or letters?"

O'Rourke cleared his throat, and said, "We suggest you mail it. Everything must go through our censors."

Hank looked up at the sky disapprovingly, frustrated with the bureaucracy of his own country. He left the compound and walked back to Millie's to wait until four o'clock. He perched on the edge of his bed, leaning his elbows forward on his knees as he lost himself in thought, relieved that he was just a few hours from seeing his parents. A grin spread over his face.

———◈———

After lunch, a knock sounded on the Meyer's door. A German detain-ee-turned-office-worker delivered the official notification. Marta opened the door and was handed a paper.

"We... *we* have a visitor?" Marta whispered. "But who...?"

Karl came up, leaning a hand gently on her shoulder. The woman pointed to the form and asked, "Do you know this person?"

"Hank?" Marta breathed. "He's here? Right now?"

Marta looked into the German woman's eyes. A hint of a smile flickered behind her blue eyes.

"Yes," she answered without emotion. "You must meet him in the administration building between four and five. I suggest you arrive early."

Marta staggered back, reaching for a chair. Could it be she was going to actually see her son...after eighteen nightmarish months? Or was it only more of the nightmare? Could it be true?

"Come to the administration building and tell them you have a visitor. They will show you where to go." The corner of her mouth tugged up in a faint smile, and she turned to leave.

At half past three Marta dressed in a special dress she had made at the sewing project building. She had been saving it for the day she was released, but this visit from Hank was almost as good. "Can we please go over now?" she begged Karl. "I can't sit here knowing our son is just beyond that wire fence."

"He's not going anywhere, my dear." Karl held her hands.

At three forty-five they left their cottage. After Karl showed their paperwork, the guards escorted them into a victory hut with two tables. A barrier stood between the tables, and a large window with a ledge let in the late afternoon sunlight.

Muffled voices came through the wall, and Marta sat in her seat, wringing her handkerchief in her hands as she listened. Looking through the small window, she held her breath as the door opened. At first, the young man in the army uniform didn't look like their son. His large, muscular arms filled every inch of his coat, his neatly pressed Army uniform fitting his frame well. But it was Hank's smile. Karl dropped his head to his hands, letting out a muffled sob.

Marta struggled to breathe, but she exhaled quickly saying, "My boy!"

Hank walked in front of the guard. He stepped around a barrier and then entered the room where he caught his first glimpse of his mama, then his papa. Hank wiped away tears with the back of his hand. As he stared at both of them, he flinched. His mother's face was gaunt and haggard. His father was thin and pale, but their smiles beamed at him from their drained and weary faces.

Hank smiled back at his mama as she watched him cross the room to sit. He tucked his hat under his arm and adjusted his brown tie to make sure it was tucked inside the second button on his shirt.

"Sit there," the guard barked. "Do not reach over the barrier or pass anything beyond that barrier, or your visit will immediately come to an end. Is that understood?"

"Yes, sir." Hank's determined voice echoed off the hard tile floor.

"Just so you know, we will speak German," Hank announced. He looked away from his parents and gave the guard a pointed stare.

"I don't care," he replied.

Hank shrugged and found his mama's gaze again. "Hi, Mama," he waved, forcing a grin.

"You're all grown up," Mama whispered. She cleared her throat and said, "I can't believe how good you look. You look like a man."

"How are you holding up?" Hank asked. "Both of you have lost weight; I can see it in your faces."

They gave a nod of acknowledgment. "It's been a rough year or so."

"Ella told me some thugs beat you up. What happened? Did you tell someone?"

"We've told those who need to know," Papa replied. "But justice is in short supply around here."

"So, tell me about it."

Papa drew in a breath through his teeth with a glance at the guard. "Can we talk about it later?" Seeing Hank's concerned frown, he said, "We want to know what's going on at home. We get so few letters and so little news. We have so many questions."

"Fire away," Hank said.

"First off, how did you get here, Hank? Why didn't you tell us you were coming?"

Hank explained his furlough and how he didn't have time to see Ella.

"I can accept that we're your second choice," Papa added with a smile.

"So, do you need money or clothes or food?" Hank asked. "What can I help with?"

"No, we don't need any money." Papa reached into the front pocket of his trousers and pulled out a few green and red coins that resembled poker chips. "Each week they give us tokens like these to purchase the food we need, and we can cook our meals inside our small cottage," he explained. "We can work for ten cents an hour and get more camp money. Both Mama and I work in the laundry room."

"They also let us plant a garden outside the gate," Marta chimed in.

"Most of the garden workers are Japanese," Karl added. "I signed up to help, and because so few Germans want to garden, I'm the only German out there. I'll get paid for that job as well as being able to keep some of the fresh vegetables we plant."

"You've always had a knack for growing a garden in the toughest conditions," Hank said.

"We get to buy clothing or material and other things we need. And they regularly deliver milk and ice to our door. It's quite convenient."

Hank raised his eyebrow with surprise. "So why are you both looking so thin? It looks like you aren't eating well."

"We're eating enough. Maybe we're not bulking up like you," Papa chided. "What do you weigh now, a hundred-ninety or two-hundred pounds? You look great. I've never seen your arms so big."

"No, I'm about one-eighty-five," Hank admitted. "It's all those push-ups and sit-ups they make us do. And of course, I can have just about all the food I can eat. What about you? Are you getting enough eggs and meat to eat?"

"Oh yes. In fact some of the guards and other workers complain that we eat better than they do because they have to use ration cards, and we don't have to," Mama explained. "Many workers eat in the cafeteria because they get more to eat here."

"Of course, they can come and go as they please and don't have roll call three times a day at gunpoint." Papa tipped his head in the direction of the guard, who sat in the windowsill, yawning, his rifle leaning against the wall.

Hank stared at the guard and smiled. The prolonged silence startled the guard, and he awoke.

"We even have a German butcher who makes sausages using traditional German recipes. It's very tasty," Mama added. "And there's a barber shop, a beauty shop, a hobby shop, and even a sewing room, which I used to make this dress," Mama said with pride.

"It's lovely, Mama."

"What about church? Are there any other Mormons here?"

"Not that we know about," Papa said. "But we've enjoyed going to a Lutheran service. They are very kind to us."

Mama agreed and said, "The truth is, Hank, you can help us the most if you could get us some reading materials from church. Maybe a book by James Talmage?"

"Do you think the censors will allow it?" Hank asked.

Papa rolled his eyes and smirked. "Who knows? I never know what is approved or not."

"I'll let Ella know, and she'll send what you need that day." Hank replied, then asked, "What has Ella told you about Tom?"

"All she's said is that he's in England training other pilots. She figures he'll be a part of the invasion of Europe, whenever that happens. Ella says he's probably stuck there for the duration of the war," Papa explained.

"You know Ella passed her LPN test, right?" Hank asked.

"Yes," Papa replied.

"She's working at the Dee Hospital, and you'll be glad to know we're keeping up with the house payments," Hank said. "Berta is with the Wangsguard's until you get back. We sold the beef cattle, but you know about that, right?"

Papa's eyes showed his disappointment. "Yes, I know. You had no choice."

With the windows closed, the air in the room had grown stagnant. Hank loosened his tie and the collar on his shirt and stood to remove his jacket.

"What kind of things have you been doing?" Mama asked.

Hank paused. "You know I'm flying in a B-17, right?"

"Doesn't that mean you'll be going to Europe?" Papa asked.

Hank shrugged. "I'm not supposed to say, but most likely."

"What has your training been like?"

"A lot of high-altitude flying, Papa. We have to wear oxygen masks once we reach ten thousand feet, or else we get sick," Hank trailed off. "The cold is the worst thing. I never thought I would hate to fly, but it's miserable when it's so cold."

"What's your job?"

"I'm a waist gunner. That means I operate a .50 caliber machine gun to protect the left side of the aircraft. There are guns on the front, back, top, and anywhere else they can fit a gun. They wanted me to be a tail gunner but I wouldn't fit, so they made me a waist gunner."

"Is that good?" Mama asked, her face drawn in concern.

"Yeah. The tail gunner is one of the most dangerous positions in the plane. At least, that's what I've heard," Hank replied.

"What kind of people do you work with?" Mama asked.

"My skipper is a guy from Dallas. He's a good egg. I like him," Hank said. "They're all swell guys, but they smoke a lot," Hank laughed.

"Every time we land, the first thing they do is jump out of the plane and light up. All of 'em! I'm the only one that doesn't smoke," Hank chuckled. "But I'm getting used to it, and I've learned not to complain!"

Papa grunted, rubbing his chin. "Have you met any other Mormons?"

"Nope. Not yet." Hank looked down at his shoes. "It seems hardly anybody is religious, or they're too scared to talk about it if they are."

"We know what *that's* like," Mama gave a tentative smile.

"So when do you go overseas? Papa asked. "What's next for you?" Hank could hear the anxiety in his papa's voice.

"That's where I'm headed next. They told us we're all ready for aerial combat, so off we go to war."

"You don't sound very confident." Papa looked at Mama, seeing if she agreed.

179

"I think it's because we don't think we're ready," Hank said. "Ready for combat, I mean."

"Don't they give you enough combat training?" Hank felt an accusation in his papa's question.

"We've practiced shooting at moving targets; we've practiced parachute jumps; we've flown for twelve and thirteen hours straight. We've had months of training, but I still don't feel I'm anywhere close to being ready for combat. None of us do, really. And it's not that I'm chicken or anything, but I just don't think we know what we're doing," Hank admitted.

From outside their building, a chorus of shouting reverberated against the walls. The guard stood and peered out the window.

Hank stood too, giving a curious glance at his parents. "What's that all about?"

"I don't know," Papa replied with a dismissive wave of his hand. "It's probably some of the troublemakers and hoodlums we have here. They make it miserable for everyone."

A handful of armed guards ran past the window. Hank watched, wide-eyed, and within seconds more guards were swarming into an area just out of view of their room.

The guard gave a nervous look and watched the door anxiously, but no one came. The voices became more strident and angrier.

"We've had problems with some of the more zealous Nazis," Papa said.

"They put up the Nazi flag and make trouble for anyone who disagrees with them. It's a real mess."

"I had no idea they allowed that in a place like this," Hank replied.

Bouncing on the balls of his feet with anticipation, the guard finally pointed a finger at Karl and Marta, saying, "Don't do anything stupid. I'll be back in just a second." He then darted out of the room with his gun at the ready.

Hank looked at his parents. A strange silence hovered over the room, despite the ruckus outside. Hank glanced at the door, waiting for the guard, listening for anything. He heard nothing, not even an echo of voices from office workers talking outside their door.

After a long silence, Hank said, "I know they won't allow me to hug you, but I'm going to do it anyway." He jumped to his feet and reached both arms out to embrace his father.

"Thanks for being such a great father. I hope someday to be like you, Papa."

Hank squeezed his eyes shut against the tears. Papa held Hank tightly, rubbing his back in silence.

When he turned to his mother, she wiped the tears from Hank's face and whispered, "Everything will be okay, *Liebchen*, don't ever forget that." She wrapped her arms around Hank's neck and held him close. Despite feeling her bones protruding from her shoulders and arms, he was already feeling nostalgic for the next time he could hug her. He knew the memory of this embrace would be held in a special place in his mind because he knew the next one may not happen again for a long, long time.

A rustling outside the room made Hank draw back from his mama. He collapsed into his seat. As the guard entered the room, Hank noticed the surprised look on his face at seeing everyone sitting right where he had last seen them.

Hank looked on, unable to hide his elation for having been able to steal an embrace without getting his parents in trouble. He could see the same look of joy in their eyes too.

At the end of the hour, just as the guard was about to end the visit, Hank stood, "I guess this is 'goodbye' for now. I'll be praying for you. Please write often so I know what's going on. I worry about you two all the time."

"We worry about you, too, Hank," Mama added in a hushed voice.

"I love you. Someday soon we'll be together again, and I'll be able to give you a hug legally," Hank winked, then gave a mischievous grin. His parents smiled back and waved as they left the room.

His parents disappeared from view, and the door closed behind them. As the door closed, Hank lost his smile. He felt emptier than ever before. A wave of grief washed the cheerfulness out of him.

Hank hurried to leave the camp. In the span of only a few hours, everything he once thought he knew about America had been turned upside down. Justice, fairness, law and order meant nothing anymore.

Random thoughts kept bouncing around in his head. *How can I fight for America when my country does such horrible things to good people? Maybe I should just give up my citizenship in protest? Maybe I should go AWOL from the Air Corps? Then again, how could I walk away from my friends that I've trained with all this time? And what about the greater threat to* Oma *and other Germans?*

The clank of the main gate closing behind him startled Hank back to the present. Thinking about his parent's deplorable condition made him physically ill, and he resisted a powerful urge to empty his stomach. His parents deserved better, much better.

His shoulders slumped and his feet shuffled toward Millie Eskelson's house a quarter mile away. Quietly, he let himself in, unannounced.

"Hank, is that you?" she called out from the kitchen.

He hated to be rude, but he closed the door behind him without answering.

Chapter 33-Note 1: Personal accounts of people visiting internees at Crystal City are few. Due to the logistics and onerous rules, relatively few family members were willing to visit their families while interred. Camp officials kept a detailed dossier on every internee, so any visits required pre-approval before visiting friends and relatives were approved. All visits required surveillance, but near the end of the war, a few college students and even soldiers on furlough were allowed to stay with their parents.

Chapter 33-Note 2: According to camp director James O'Rourke's rather sanitized final report, he describes the policy for internees having contact with the outside world

"The internees have been permitted contact with friends and relatives outside of internment through general correspondence and personal visitation. Although several policies of visitation have been in effect during operation of the camp, the present regulation requires all visits be conducted under surveillance. A visitation building was erected near the main compound gate to accommodate internees and their visitors."

J.L. O'Rourke, "Historical Narrative of the Crystal City Internment Camp, September 9, 1945." Record Group No. 85, *Immigration and Naturalization Service Crystal City Internment Camp*, File 217/021, pp 14–15.

CHAPTER 34
September 19, 1943
Fort Worth, Texas

"Here. Let me light that for you." A junior Navy officer in the passenger seat next to Billie leaned toward her, popping open his lighter.

"Thanks." She took a quick puff, exhaled, and sat back. The whirring of the plane's engines roared as they gained altitude. As he put the lighter away into his shirt pocket, his wedding ring sparkled in the bright sunlight glaring through the window.

"What brings you to Fort Worth?" He looked ahead as he thumbed through a copy of *Stars and Stripes* newspaper.

"I'm a pilot," Billie beamed with pride. "I fly planes for the Army."

"So that's how you can afford to fly. The Army is paying for it?"

"Yeah," Billie smiled. "I'm a WASP pilot. Do you know what that is?"

"I think I read about you gals in *LIFE Magazine*. Aren't you part of some airplane taxi service?"

"Close enough," Billie laughed. "We fly airplanes from the factory to a location where they can be shipped overseas."

"That sounds exciting. You must spend a lot of time flying."

"I just dropped off my twenty-fifth BT-13 over in Enid."

"Wow, twenty-five trips to Oklahoma. You sure live the glamorous life," he smirked.

"Not all of them were to Enid, just most of them," she laughed.

"So, are you going back for another?"

"Probably, but I'll know when I pick up my orders. Sometimes I don't even have time to run home and change clothes. They just keep us hopping," Billie explained. "So, what about you? Where you headed?"

"To see my wife and baby girl. I have a ten-day furlough before I head to the Pacific." His voice trailed off. They talked for a few more minutes, then he turned away. For the remainder of the five-hour flight, he didn't say another word.

Billie wished they could have kept talking, anything to distract herself from having to think, even if it appeared as though she was flirting with a married man. She shuffled through pages of magazines, getting lost in thought as she stared out the window until they landed in Los Angeles.

An hour later, Billie stepped into the Long Beach Operations Center, but no new orders awaited her.

"Your orders are on hold," the operations officer explained. "All WASP pilots have a special meeting with Nancy Love first thing tomorrow morning."

"Nancy Love?" Billie asked. "Why is she here?"

"She called a special meeting for every WASP pilot. Enjoy your day off," he said.

"I will," Billie answered with a smile. "Maybe now I can do the laundry that I've been ignoring for the past few weeks."

Love's unusual call for a closed-door meeting started the rumor mill whirling. Some said it was the end of the WASPs; others said the WASPs would start making overseas flights. Each rumor seemed to have a sliver of believability, which made the tension mount until the meeting began.

Love closed the door to the small room; she was the last to enter. A hush fell on the twelve WASP pilots. "Ladies, you know of the challenges we face being pilots in a man's Army. I'm sure each of you have been insulted or accosted in some way because of what you do."

Billie crossed her arms, exchanging a glance with Betty. Others around the room nodded, some revealing grim smiles and others tightening their jaws with resentment.

"Now, what I'm about to say must stay in this room. Do I have your word?" Love asked.

"Yes, ma'am," echoed through the small room.

"I want you to listen carefully because what I'm about to tell you may save your life." Smiles vanished, and they held their breath.

"Our mission is largely driven by the goal of relieving men from the domestic job of ferrying aircraft so they can fill combat positions overseas. But we've discovered some unintended consequences you need to know about."

"First, many of the men who now ferry aircraft do not qualify to fly overseas, especially in aerial combat. In those cases, these men must be assigned to infantry units. Understandably, they are not too happy about that prospect."

"Second, some of the ground support crews are made up of men who washed out of pilot's school, and it's like pouring lemon juice on a paper cut when they see you taxi in. If you start bossing them around or talking down to them, believe me, you are asking for trouble."

Billie had heard about other WASP pilots who were careless and made enemies of a ground crew.

Love continued, "As pilots, we've all grown accustomed to working among men, and I don't have to tell any of you that a man's ego is rather fragile. God gave us women enough sense to know we shouldn't mess with it. But no matter how hard we try to get along, or be agreeable, there are still too many men who just hate the fact that you're flying army airplanes. Some men are refusing to service WASP planes. We even had an entire squadron of tow target pilots demand to be transferred after they heard WASP pilots were coming to learn how to tow targets."

It was nothing Billie or anyone else hadn't heard before.

"If this is all we had to put up with, I wouldn't be here," Love admitted. "But we believe you need to be aware of these issues. So, please, when you check out a new plane, be careful. Don't rush through your inspections and routine checks. The older planes they give us tend to be the least maintained. Even new planes are often missing parts or have some other defect."

Betty leaned over to Billie and said, "Remember that BT-13 where the canopy wouldn't latch?"

Billie raised her eyebrows, nodding as the incident flashed through her mind.

"Please, ladies. If you don't feel safe, or you are concerned about maintenance or the integrity of a plane, don't fly it, and let me know.

Love cleared her throat and looked down before lifting her eyes to scan the room. "The next thing I need to tell you is the most important," she paused. "Now this is classified, so remember, this information does not leave this room. Is that clear?"

Everyone nodded.

"We learned the other day that a disgruntled ground worker, a washed-out pilot as a matter-of-fact, has been accused of removing or loosening bolts from the control stick of a WASP's airplane, just before she was about to fly."

Billie's throat tightened. Beside her, Betty stiffened.

"Luckily, the pilot spotted the problem before she got up to speed, but had she missed it, the plane would have been uncontrollable. The whole matter is under investigation. Now I know that's a really scary thought, and there's no need for you to worry too much because we believe this was just an isolated incident. But I'm telling you to be extra cautious. Keep an eye out for anything suspicious. Be extra kind to the ground crews. Don't show off or boss them around."

Love again looked down at the floor for a moment to collect her thoughts. "Here's my dilemma. On one hand, if word should ever get out that just one of you WASP pilots was at risk because of sabotage, and that somehow Jackie or I were ignoring the risk, we could be shut down overnight. The newspapers would have a hey-day about the scandalous Army brass not protecting you poor, defenseless women."

A scornful huff escaped Billie's lips.

"But on the other hand, I don't want to put any of you at risk of facing one iota of unnecessary danger. If I thought this was a system-wide problem, I would shut this program down in a second and go to the newspapers myself. But I'm going to leave it up to each of you to decide if you want to keep flying, or if you want to call it quits. If that's the case, just do it. There's no embarrassment or shame in that. Any one of you can call me or write me and say, 'I'm done.' You can do it tomorrow, in a week, or a month from now. All you have to do is tell me you want out of the program, and I'll take care of it, no questions asked. Agreed?"

Billie didn't want to meet the gazes of the other women because she knew who would be tempted to leave and who would stay no matter what.

"There are some men who will stop at nothing to keep themselves from going into combat and that means putting you at risk. There are others who will do anything to keep you from doing a job they wish they were doing. And some men are just threatened by you because you're doing a 'man's job'," she teased. The atmosphere of the room softened a little with chuckles.

"In all seriousness, please be careful. Let's not forget Cornelia Fort and the six other girls who have given their lives doing what we're asked to do. Our job is dangerous enough, and we can't let our guard down. Is that understood?"

"Yes, ma'am." The again-subdued voices of the WASP pilots echoed through the room.

"Okay," Nancy finished. "That is all. Dismissed."

Anxious yet determined, Billie rubbed her hands as she searched her memory of the countless ferry flights she had completed. She had experienced her fair share of engine or mechanical problems, but nothing she hadn't been able to handle. She turned to Betty and asked, "Have you ever thought it was sabotage?"

"No. Not really." Betty frowned and smoothed a strand of hair behind her ear. "But I wasn't really thinking about it at the time," she was deep in thought. "I'm trying recall each flight where I've had some kind of problem, and now I'm kind of spooked."

"Me too!" Billie whispered. "There's a part of me wondering if it's all worth it. With all the guff we have to take from these guys who would stoop to anything, how am I not going to look at them as if they're trying to kill me?"

"Don't you think that's what some of those bigwigs at the Pentagon want... to scare us so we'll all just go away?" Betty asked.

"Yeah, probably so." Billie stood and put on her garrison cap.

"But I don't want to die at the hands of some idiot who's supposed to be on my team."

Chapter 34-note: A number of pilots reported accidents cause by sabotage. Mary Ellen Keil was nearly killed when her flight controls came loose upon takeoff. Leona Golbinec survived an emergency landing when her controls mysteriously stopped working, and Lorraine Zillner bailed out of her plane because the rudder cable had been cut. These weren't just isolated incidences either. At Camp Davis in North Carolina, eleven female pilots made forced landings, more than at any other base. In all suspicious cases, sabotage was spoken of frequently but rarely investigated and never officially recognized. No one was ever arrested or otherwise brought to justice for the suspicious events and deaths associated with sabotage.

Lois K. Merry. *Women Military Pilots of World War II: A History with Biographies of American, British, Russian and German Aviators* (McFarland, 2010); Helena Page Schrader. *Sisters in Arms: The Women Who Flew in World War II* (Pen and Sword, 2006).

CHAPTER 35
September 20, 1943
St. Louis, Missouri

As the train slowed to a stop in St. Louis, a blur of vibrant fall colors flashed outside Hank's window. He had left Crystal City in plenty of time to make it to Scott Field a day before he was to report. He stepped off the platform and wandered aimlessly through the autumn town, breathing the humid air and noticing how it was so unlike Huntsville. Soon tiring of sightseeing, he got in line for the shuttle bus to the airfield.

After finally checking in and finding his barracks, Hank collapsed on his bunk—real sleep in a real bed, at last. He stretched out and closed his eyes, giving in to exhaustion. Unfortunately, chatter and bustle from the barracks woke him every hour. In the morning, he rose from a fitful night's sleep.

The next morning, Hank waited at the parade field for his crew. As they assembled in a group at the corner of the field, Hank gave a tentative smile. Sterner and all the boys shook hands and slapped each other's backs, but behind the wide-mouthed grins and shouts of hello, something haunted their eyes. With a pang of grief, Hank saw himself reflected in the distracted way they looked at the ground or didn't hear what someone was saying. A week spent with their families reminded them of what they were leaving behind. The short time apart seemed to dull everyone's focus. Once they made their way to the auditorium for their first briefing, Hank knew nothing would be the same.

"You look like a happy man. How was your trip home?" Captain Sterner asked.

"Okay," Hank lied. "Nothing out of the ordinary. What about you?"

Sterner looked down with a smile. "I kind of got engaged."

"That was fast!" Hank stood wide-eyed.

"I know. I know. But knowing I was going overseas got me to thinking. It's time to quit browsin' and get to makin' a purchase," Sterner laughed. "I thought I'd never get married, but there's just nobody like my girl back home, so I bought her a ring, and we're going to get married as soon as I get back."

He dug out his wallet, thumbed through the contents, and with a proud smile, held out a photograph.

"She's beautiful, Captain." Hank leaned over to Connors and said, "Look at Skipper's fiancée."

Connors grabbed the picture and exclaimed, "Holy mackerel! Get a load of the dish Sterner's engaged to."

The crew huddled around to look, giving Sterner grins and congratulations. Sterner turned red, but his eyes twinkled as he snatched the photo, put it back in his wallet, and stuffed the wallet in his back pocket.

Inside the briefing room, three dim lights illuminated a small podium and microphone. Two American flags stood on either side of the stage. Nine other crews gathered in clumps around the room, their chatter creating a dull roar while they waited for the duty officer to arrive. They talked for a few minutes about each other's girlfriends, until a colonel entered the room.

"Ten hut."

With a snap of their heels, the men stood at attention.

"At ease," he said. "Take your seats and listen up."

They settled into their chairs.

"You are here because each of you has proven yourself competent in your respective disciplines. Uncle Sam has invested a lot of money getting you qualified to defend this country and go on the offensive against a formidable enemy."

As Hank scanned the room, the faces of men from different ethnicities listened with focused gazes. He was probably the most German looking of them all, with his fair hair and light blue eyes.

"Each one of you has volunteered to fly with the best flying force in the world. It's a dangerous and deadly mission we're asking you to accomplish, but it's the only way we are going to win this war. We have to be tough. We have to be aggressive. We have to be ruthless in our quest to conquer our enemies."

"As you know, any of you could quit right now. You can just give-up, slink away at any time, and be given a non-flying assignment. That's your choice. But if you stay, then tomorrow you will embark on the greatest adventure of your life. An adventure so fantastic, your children and grandchildren will talk about your accomplishments with teary eyes and swelled hearts for what you will have done. Starting tomorrow, you will accomplish the crowning achievement of your life. You will look back on these events with great fondness, for never will you have worked so hard to achieve a goal so important."

A lump in Hank's throat grew larger as the colonel struggled to gain his composure. The room fell completely silent. The colonel choked up briefly and paused.

"I will also look back on this day and say I had a chance to rub shoulders with you. I got to look you in the eye and watch as you bravely took on this dangerous, yet vitally important assignment. From the bottom of my heart and with all sincerity, I want you to know that I am thankful to you, and I want you to know that your country thanks you."

He cleared his throat, and his voice became much more businesslike.

"Tomorrow, each crew will report to the main hangar. There you will be assigned to a new B-17G."

A small roar of excitement erupted among the men. Hank glanced at his captain with a grin, leaning in to murmur, "This is worth it to even see one of those, right?"

"These planes are direct from the main Boeing factory. You will notice a few important modifications from the F-model that you trained on," he explained. "Most notable, the heaters."

The audience roared with approval. They had all trained in refurbished models that had seen better days, and none were equipped with functional heating systems.

"You'll also notice a new, remotely operated chin turret with dual, .50-caliber machine guns. Also, you won't know by looking, but inside the wings are the new 'Tokyo Tanks,' giving you an extra thousand gallons of fuel, give or take. There is also added power from the turbo chargers installed to compensate for extra armor.

"You will be required to test these airplanes, put them through their paces, and get them ready for a transoceanic flight. Each pilot will receive his orders with a general idea of your destination once you've completed the testing of your airplanes and finished all training specific to this model.

190

"Now, let me just say a word about the latest practice of naming your airplane. Some of you have already made plans to have some scantily clad beauty painted on the nose of your new B-17. Let me encourage you to remember that the enemy will use every opportunity to use the name of your plane for propaganda purposes. Don't get carried away and do something stupid. That's all I'll really say about it."

Hank laughed. This was the first officer he'd ever met who campaigned for restraint in naming their planes. Some crews had painted nude models on their planes, and the Germans accused the Americans of being degenerates. Hank didn't disagree in this case.

"Now, one final thing. You will all be issued new flight clothing, including a pair of electrically heated long-johns that I'm sure you'll come to appreciate. Each of you will also be issued a new Colt .45 automatic pistol. You are required to pass a weapons training class and a shooting test to prove your proficiency with your new weapon."

"Best of luck to all of you. You're dismissed."

Excitement hung palpable in the room abuzz with chatter and questions. Hank exchanged grins with his crew, the light in their eyes eclipsing some of the dimness he had seen earlier.

The next morning, the crew waited at the hangar for Sterner to emerge from the quartermaster's office and tell them which plane was theirs.

"Well boys, I just signed my life away for y'all," he announced in an exaggerated Texas accent. He held up a small piece of paper and waved it around for effect.

"They made me put my John Hancock on this here receipt saying I take full responsibility for this brand, spankin' new B-17, and I'm now on the hook for two-hundred fifty-thousand dollars, due and payable to Uncle Sam if anything happens to it."

Sterner threw the receipt at Harris and said, "You guys better take care of this lovely new piece of American ingenuity, or my 'you-know-what' is on the line to the tune of a quarter million dollars."

Hank took the receipt, the captain's signature fluttering in the wind as he turned it over to look. He scanned it for the serial number: 43-01108.

"Look for tail number ending in one-zero-eight."

The crewmen took off in all directions. Within minutes, Sergeant Marker hollered, "Here it is."

The anxious crew approached their plane. Its polished metal and new paint gleamed in the early morning sunlight. Rows of perfectly aligned rivets outlined the plane's contours. The wings, the fuselage, the engines were all fitted and mounted, each without blemish. Hank breathed in deep the smell of fresh paint, lubricants, and fuel. It was a smell only a crewman could love.

"What are we going to name her, Captain?" Montoya asked.

"Yeah, it's really up to you, since you're the skipper," Marker said.

"I know a guy who can paint real good," Connors said. "He could even paint a nice rendition of that pretty little thing you're engaged to, no problem."

"Yeah, Captain." Montoya's eyes lit up with mischief. "What's her name?"

"I'm not telling you her name," Sterner replied. "I didn't want you to know for this very reason. I will not have a painting of my half-naked fiancée plastered on the nose of this B-17."

"Oh, come on, Captain," Montoya pleaded. "Everybody's doing it. Haven't you seen some of the women they've painted on these airplanes? Hubba hubba."

"Absolutely not. I've thought a lot about it," Sterner said. "I wanted to pick a name that represented America, but also one that has a connection to my home and family. We're going to call her *Plano's Pride*."

The crewmen looked at each other and didn't say anything.

Hank said, "That's not bad. I kind of like it."

"I'll grow to like that," Connors mumbled.

"I'd rather have a nice girl," Montoya complained to Barsauskas, "Don't you think so Al? Wouldn't a nice, sexy girl be better than dumb ol' *Plano's Pride*?"

Barsauskas ignored him.

One by one they climbed up through the bottom hatch and into the aircraft. They peered around corners and into every nook and cranny.

"Okay boys, it's time to stop gawking and start working. We've got a lot to do," Sterner barked.

Each man had been issued a checklist of items he needed to complete. The navigator and radiomen both had long, extensive lists of equipment and instruments to test, calibrate, and re-test.

For the next ten days, the crew took a crash course on their new airplane. Sterner and Harris were in the classroom, learning the specifics of the B-17G. Hank and Woody went to a special class for radio operators. All navigators, engineers, and bombardiers took special classes for their positions, too. Each crewman also had to spend time at the shooting range learning to fire his Colt .45.

On October 1, Sterner and Harris, along with the other crewmen, finalized their pre-flight checks for the first flight in their new bird. Sterner fired up the B-17, and the engines thundered to life. After checking various systems and instruments for almost a half hour, Sterner called over the inter-phone for the crew to prepare for taxi and takeoff. At the end of the runway, they awaited their turn to be cleared for takeoff.

When the tower gave the go-ahead, the powerful new Wright "Cyclone" turbo supercharged engines sprang to life, vaulting the aircraft forward. Within seconds, the plane reached ninety miles per hour and with great ease, leapt airborne. Minutes later, they were at eighteen hundred feet. The crew busied themselves testing their equipment and instruments, flipping knobs and switches, and calling through the static of their inter-phone and radios.

After an hour of flying at twelve thousand feet, they cruised over the brilliant fall colors of the Missouri flatlands. Hank squeezed himself into the cockpit to admire the view.

"I can't believe how different she is from that tired bird we trained on," Hank observed to Sterner and Harris, who were sitting in the first and second seats.

"Sure is a big difference in power and lift, and we haven't really tested these engines yet," Sterner replied. "We're doing slow-time now, but later on we'll test them at higher power settings and see how they do."

After six hours in the air, the plane glided back onto the field. The crew wore smiles, and the warm glow of the afternoon sun lit up their faces. In the roar and thrust of *Plano's Pride's* engines, the spirit of the crew had awakened again. They had found themselves.

Early on the morning of October sixth, Sterner returned from a pilot's briefing with their orders for an overseas destination.

"We leave today, but I can't tell you where we're headed until after we're airborne," Sterner laughed.

"Oh, come off it, Captain. Tell us where we're going," Hank complained, with similar mutters coming from the rest of the crew.

Sterner glanced over his shoulder, then leaned in close. "We're going to Great Britain," he announced with a playful smile.

"Oh that's just swell," Montoya sneered. "That part we know."

"That's all I can tell you," Sterner shot back.

"Yeah, but where?"

"We'll find out, won't we? So, don't worry about it; we'll have plenty of time to find out. Let's just get ready to go."

Within a few short hours, the crew had packed their belongings in their duffel bags and checked out of their quarters. On their way to the hangar, Hank and the other enlisted crewmen met at the Post Exchange. Hank roamed the shelves, snatching up chocolate bars. As the war progressed, sweets had become hard to find due to sugar rationing. He heard the situation was even worse in England. With Hank's sweet tooth, it was worth paying the extra cost of twenty-five cents each.

"What kind of chocolate do you want?" Captain Sterner looked at Hank as he hovered over the selection of chocolate bars.

"Beggars can't be choosers," Hank shot back. "I don't care what brand it is, as long as it's chocolate."

"You sure you don't want any of those silk stockings for the British ladies?" Sterner teased. "You better hurry over and get a few before they're all gone."

Hank gave Sterner a blank stare.

"You know what you can do for me, Hank?" Captain Sterner's tone dropped, a serious look shadowing his face. "They'll only let me buy three cartons of smokes. And since you don't smoke, would you go buy your three cartons for me? I'll give you the money."

A surge of anxiety swept over Hank. Buy cigarettes? He'd never so much as touched a carton, but could he disappoint Sterner?

"Uh, I guess," Hank replied sheepishly.

"Now Hank, are you sure it's not going to go against your church rules or anything?" Sterner asked. "Seriously, don't do it if it's going to cause you any moral conflict."

Hank smiled and answered, "I'll be okay. They're not for me. But I've never bought 'em before so this is a first for me."

"I'll give you a few packs of smokes if that will make you happy?"

Hank laughed out loud, "No, thank you!"

"So, you have to get the Lucky Strikes or the Chesterfields," Sterner whispered. "Don't let them give you any other brand, and if you have a choice, get the Lucky Strikes."

"Okay, I'll do my best."

Hank gulped as he stepped toward the cigarette counter and fought his way through the swarm of men elbowing their way to the front. He disappeared into the sea of men. After twenty minutes, Hank finally emerged.

"Here you go, Skipper. Three cartons of Lucky Strikes."

Sterner beamed as Hank handed the cigarettes to him. The look on Hank's face made Sterner smile. "I don't think they're going to poison you just by handling them."

"I know," Hank replied, his face red with embarrassment. "It's my problem, not yours."

By noon, *Plano's Pride* was "wheels up" and headed for Syracuse, New York for their first overnight stop. The flight was uneventful. The crew watched the New England autumn surge past them from 11,000 feet like a sea of gold.

At their next stop, Presque Isle Army Airfield, Maine, they stayed a few days to weatherize the B-17 for the long, high-altitude flight over a frozen and deadly wilderness.

The morning of October 10, a storm delayed their departure for another day.

The next morning, Sterner still didn't know when or where they would stop for refueling. The weather circumstances changed hourly. Sterner and all the other B-17 skippers were waiting to get out, but had been ordered to make plans to stay another night. With a potential break in the weather possible, Sterner had strict orders to check with the operations center each hour. His crew had to be ready to leave within one hour.

At four-thirty that morning, an urgent message awoke his dozing crew: "Must be ready to have wheels up within the hour."

As they stumbled into the flight operations center, Sterner barked, "Our orders are to depart at five-fifteen a.m. Let's get through these pre-flight checks quickly, but I'd rather be late than dead, so be thorough."

By the time they had taxied to position and waited for the green light from the tower, it was five-thirty-three.

After reaching a cruising altitude of five thousand feet, Hank rubbed his hands against the cold, breathing on them to warm them. Snow squalls whitened the sky in the distance. Sterner announced over the inter-phone, "Nice job everyone, getting us airborne on such short notice. We're making a course for Bluie West One. We're still waiting for a weather update, since we couldn't get one before we took off. Let's just hope the weather holds, at least until we land in Greenland."

Bluie West One, a small airport for refueling American bombers on their way to Europe, was in a remote fishing village in Narsarsuaq. Hank nudged Barsauskas as they chatted, "Greenland, huh? Good thing we're prepared for the cold."

Sterner climbed to eight thousand feet and settled in for the remainder of this five-hour flight. They all watched with growing fear stirring in them as a brewing storm whipped the ocean into mountainous whitecaps. It would be impossible to survive ditching the plane into an ocean like that. Sterner put the plane on autopilot and got up to stretch his legs. He stopped as he walked past Hank, who was sitting at his waist gun position.

"How you doing, Hank? You holding up?"

"I'm doing well, sir. I'd rather not deal with the turbulence, but I'm not getting sick like I used to," Hank chuckled.

"Remind me again," Sterner said, rubbing his chin. "Didn't you say you're from a small town, way up in the mountains?"

Hank looked up and smiled. "Yes. Utah."

"Is it just me or are all Mormons as happy as you?" His tone held nothing insincere.

"Oh, I doubt we're all happy," Hank blushed. "We have our share of problems and do our best to get through them, just like everyone else."

"Yeah, but you seem to be pretty even-keeled. You take everything in stride, and you always seem to have a smile. Is that because of your religion?"

"Who knows?" Hank shrugged.

"I know you're not married, but how many wives does your father have?"

"One," Hank replied in exasperation. "I hear this all the time, but you get kicked out of the church if you have more than one wife."

"Oh, is that right?" Sterner looked surprised.

"Yeah. About fifty years ago they stopped it." Hank look at his feet, embarrassed that he had to correct his skipper.

"I'll be darned." He looked at Hank with a curious smile. "I guess there's a lot I don't know about your religion. I know I've never seen you drink coffee, or smoke, or drink. And don't you have your own Bible?"

"We have the Book of Mormon. It's a companion to the Bible. We believe in both," Hank explained with a smile.

"I guess we'll have to sit down some day, and you'll have to explain it all to me." Sterner looked at his watch. "But right now, I've got to get us to Greenland."

"Yes, sir," Hank replied. "That's a very fine idea."

Sterner slapped Hank's knee as he walked back to the cockpit.

As Sterner passed Howell's position, Howell said, "Thank goodness for a tailwind. At this rate we'll make it there about forty minutes ahead of schedule."

The weather cooperated for the next two hours, the plane's steady flight becoming as familiar as the cold around them. But about a hundred nautical miles from the Greenland coast, the snow swirled in violent gusts, rocking the plane. Hank jolted against the side of the plane in the sudden turbulence and grabbed onto a handhold to steady himself. Below, the churning sea became obscured under the driving snow.

"Let's climb," Sterner said over the inter-phone. "Let's see if we can get above this." Effortlessly, the thirty-six thousand pound "Flying Fortress" climbed higher and higher, but the snow grew more intense. Sterner climbed still higher. *Plano's Pride* jerked and shuddered in the storm's rage. They reached eleven thousand feet. A light-headed feeling filled Hank's ears, and he drew in deep gasps for air.

"Captain, shouldn't we be using oxygen?" he asked on the inter-phone.

"Yes, Sergeant Meyer. Thanks for the reminder. Hey y'all, if you're not already using O-2," he said, "get it on now."

From the strain in Sterner's voice, things had to be tense in the cockpit, but Hank couldn't see anything from his waist gunner's position. He stepped into the radio room where Woody was focused on flipping switches and pressing his earpiece to his ear, listening with an intense scowl, and waiting for any clear signal on the radio.

"What's the latest on the weather?" Hank asked. "Heard anything?"

"Nope, but it doesn't look good. I'm getting a lot of radio fade, so it's hard to be absolutely sure. But from what I can tell, even if we turned back to Goosebay or Gander, they're all socked in."

"What about Bluie West One?"

"Still too early to tell, but it's lookin' kinda iffy, as of now."

Hank listened for a while as the conversation jumped back and forth on the inter-phone. Sterner reported he was climbing to eighteen thousand feet in hopes of finding relief from the turbulence. Minutes later, Hank glanced toward the cockpit. The pilots, navigator, and engineer were all huddled together, conferring about what to do. Hank stepped past the bomb bay to eavesdrop on the conversation. But even with his headphones on, their soft, controlled voices were buried under the sound of the roaring engines.

Marker, in the navigator's seat said, "At the briefing yesterday, they warned us about the difficulty of navigating to and landing at Bluie West One."

"Okay. What did they say?" Sterner asked.

"When we approach the coast of Greenland, we need to look for three fjords that are all practically identical. We have to be absolutely sure we enter the right one, or else we head into a dead end and have to make evasive maneuvers. We cannot make a mistake."

"So, what happens if we can't get a visual on those fjords?" Sterner asked in his microphone.

Marker didn't reply. Hank listened intently, pressing his headphone to his ear to make sure he heard every word of the conversation.

Sterner replied with strained bravado, "I guess we'll just have to make sure we hit the right fjord the first time."

As the final thirty minutes ticked by before their approach to Bluie West One, Sterner asked Woody for an update on the weather forecast.

"Can't hear much of anything from Greenland or back in Goosebay or Gander," he replied. "I'm trying, but everything just fades away."

Sterner turned to Connors. "Should we descend and take our chances on finding the correct fjord? What if we miscalculate and find a massive mountain in our way? If we turn back to Goosebay or try to make an unscheduled landing back on the Canadian coast, it's unlikely that weather conditions will allow us land, if we can even find a landing strip."

"It's a tough call, Skipper," Connors replied.

Sterner made his decision and announced. "Plot a course for Iceland. Marker, you and Howell figure out if we can make it to Keflavik."

Moments later Howell replied, "Captain, it's another nine hundred miles, sir. We're getting a nice tailwind now, so that will help with fuel. If we decide to turn around and go back to Newfoundland or Goosebay, we'd be headed into a pretty stiff headwind and I doubt we'd have any place to land. I'd have to calculate it for sure, but we're close to our point of no return."

They neared the Greenland coast, the turbulence now almost knocking Hank's head against the bulkhead. He sat with his arms held out to steady himself, closing his eyes.

"Well Howell," Sterner barked. "What's our fuel consumption looking like? Can we make it to Iceland or not?"

"Yes, sir we can, but not by much," Howell replied. "We should have begun our descent a few minutes ago for Bluie West One."

After a pause, Sterner said, "What do you think? Should we just keep going on to Iceland?"

Marker protested. "What if they're socked in there too?"

"We know that everything in Greenland is weathered in, and we can't go back," Sterner said, "so if we can't land here, I say we take our chances in Iceland."

"It's your call, Skipper," Harris replied, "but I think you're right. We have more choices to land in Iceland than here in Greenland. With the help of this tailwind, it should extend our range enough for us to make it there. If we're lucky, we'll have the fuel to find a place to put us down."

"I just need to get above or below this turbulence. It's killing me," Sterner replied.

Static crackled over the inter-phone, and Sterner's voice broke through.

"Boys, listen up for a minute. All the airports in Greenland are socked in. We could turn around and find a base in Canada, but we doubt there's a place to land there, either. We've decided to head straight to Meeks Field in Keflavik, but that will take another five hours. So, bundle up and keep your O-2 on. We're going to climb a bit higher to see if we can get out of this turbulence."

"Sir..." Hank blurted through the inter-phone. He cleared his throat and calmed his voice before continuing. "What about the risks of being at high altitude for so long?"

"I'm aware of the risks, Meyer. I have no choice. I'm taking us to twenty-five thousand feet."

Hank sucked in a breath through his teeth, giving an exasperated look at Woody. He'd heard too many stories about the bends, and how nitrogen bubbles formed in the tissues at just eighteen thousand feet. Already he gulped in deep breaths of air through his mask, and even in his battery-heated undergarments and wool coat, hat, and gloves, the cold pierced deep into his bones. The condensation of his breath fogged his mask and clogged it with ice crystals that he had to tap away every few minutes.

At twenty-five thousand feet, the plane still trembled and jerked with turbulence. As they climbed still higher and higher, the cabin grew darker. Hank pulled off his mask and wiped it off with his sleeve. He did this again and again, and each time the ice was denser and the pain of the air grabbing at his lungs was more uncomfortable with the intensifying cold.

Finally, a soft, steady beam of light broke into the cabin, and as they rose above the clouds, the plane's trembling relaxed to a slight shudder and then disappeared. Sunlight spread out around them, reassuring and soothing, everything visible as far as the eye could see. Over the roar of the engine, a voice strained, calling Hank's name. He pulled off his earpiece and mask to listen.

"Hey, Meyer," Montoya shouted.

"My inter-phone connection keeps going in and out. What's the skipper up to?"

"He's trying to get above the turbulence," Hank bellowed over the roar of the engines.

"By the looks of the sunshine we're above it, but how high are we?"

"The last altitude he called out was just over twenty-five thousand feet."

"I can hardly move. It's so cold." Montoya rubbed his hands and legs.

"It's either the cold or the turbulence. Take your pick," Hank barked.

"Have you heard what the temperature is outside?"

Hank held up a finger, signaling to wait as he pressed his earpiece into his ear. After a moment, Connors reported the air temperature. "Minus fifty-four," Hank called out. "At this temp, even the insulated fuel tanks can freeze."

"I can't feel my hands or feet," Montoya said, slapping his chest. "I think I'd rather have the turbulence."

Sterner's voice crackled through the inter-phone. "Boys, you've got to keep moving. You're going to get frostbitten if you sit down for very long. Keep rubbing your hands, fingers, and toes. Just keep moving."

Hank fit his headphone back on and put the mask over his face, listening to the conversation in the cockpit.

"How's our fuel looking, Howell?" Sterner asked.

"I think we're still okay. We lost our tailwind about an hour ago, so I'll have to recalculate it."

"Let me know," Sterner said.

A heaviness draped over Hank's limbs like a blanket, his eyes and head becoming thicker with sleep. He bounced on the balls of his feet, rubbed his legs, swung his arms back and forth—anything to stay awake, anything to stay warm.

Howell called out, "Hey Skipper, it looks like we'll be fine on fuel for the remaining two hundred miles until we arrive in Iceland, and we'll have some to spare, as long as we can land in Keflavik."

"Great news," Sterner said. "Now all we've got to do is cut through the pea soup down below."

"I just heard a weather report from Patterson Field in Iceland, and it looks like the storm breaks about a hundred miles offshore. We should have no problems landing," Woody chimed in from the radio room.

"Even better news," Sterner replied. "How soon can we start our descent? The quicker we can get acclimated to the lower altitudes, the better we'll all feel."

"We'll have a much harder time navigating in that storm," Howell warned. "And we'll probably have a very bumpy ride if we descend now."

"I agree," Marker said. "It's still pretty rough down there."

"I want to see if it's tolerable. I'm going to get down into it again and see if we can manage," Sterner said. "Hang on boys; it's going to get a little rough again."

The nose of the aircraft dipped slightly, and the plane began its downward path. Storm clouds enveloped them in darkness. As Sterner continued to head down into the raging storm, the turbulence intensified.

"As much as I hate the cold, Captain," Marker said. "I'd rather not have to deal with this turbulence for another hour and a half."

Sterner endured the turbulence for another few minutes, then said, "It's too bad we can't get any lower, but I think you're right."

The plane nosed upward as he lifted the plane again above the clouds. The sun returned and the buffeting from the turbulence subsided. But the cold also returned, and for the next hour the crew moved as much in their cramped spaces as they possibly could.

The crew made their final preparations to land at Meeks Field in Keflavik. The storm cleared as they neared the coast, and Sterner descended to five-thousand feet to begin their approach.

"At last…" Hank exhaled, taking his gloves off and rubbing the numbness from his hands. "It's finally warming up a bit."

Woody gave Hank a thumbs-up sign and called out another weather report.

"The skies are cloudy in Keflavik, but visibility is ten miles," he paused for dramatic effect, "instead of a few hundred feet."

Sterner had clearance for his final descent. Moments later, they had landed safely and taxied to a hardstand with two other B-17s.

One by one, the crew climbed down from the plane. Sterner walked around to inspect it, and everyone but Hank lit up a cigarette.

"That was a flight I'd rather forget," Marker admitted as he puffed fiercely. "I can't believe how sore I am. I feel like I've gone fifteen rounds with Sugar Ray Robinson."

"I'm feeling kinda dizzy myself," Hank muttered, rubbing his temples. "Maybe I caught a cold up in that ice box."

A Deuce-and-a-Half rolled up, and the crew took final drags on their cigarettes before they smashed the butts into the ground. One by one, they pulled themselves up into the back of the truck. It rumbled forward for several minutes, stopping at a small terminal and the Operations Center.

The driver hollered, "The Operations Center is straight ahead; enlisted men's quarters are in that Quonset hut; officer quarters are next door. We don't have a mess hall, but there are C-rations in your quarters if you're hungry."

"Harris and I have to take care of some business in here," Sterner said, pointing to the Operations Center. "You guys go get a bunk, and we'll catch up with you later."

A truck waited to take them to their quarters. When Hank lifted himself into the back of the truck, a wave of nausea washed over him. The voices around him dimmed, and he lowered himself to a seat. He slumped over, gripping the sides of his temples with a groan.

"Hank," Woody called out. "Wake up, Meyer! You okay?"

"I'm okay," Hank muttered, but he couldn't move. His eyes glazed over, then fluttered closed.

Hank heard someone yell, "Get the skipper. Hank just collapsed."

Hank could feel himself slip down to the floor. He was alert just enough to hear someone else shout, "Call an ambulance!"

Moments passed that seemed like an hour. Hank opened his eyes to see Sterner crouched next to him. "Hang on, Hank."

Hank could open his mouth, but a shaking numbness closed it again.

"He's breathing, but it's irregular," Sterner said.

Sirens blared, growing louder as they approached. Hank opened his eyes as he watched blurry figures move around him. White uniformed medics bent over him, putting their hands under his body. "Okay, on the count of three. One. Two. Three."

Hank felt the sensation of being lifted into the air. Unable to open his eyes, he could still hear the muffled conversations going on around him. The medics set him roughly on the stretcher, the pain of it jolting through Hank's body and he winced.

"What happened?" An unfamiliar voice asked close to Hank's ear. The hands that belonged to the voice started strapping Hank into the stretcher.

Woody blurted, "We were waiting in the truck, and he just slumped over and dropped like a rock."

Hank heard an older man's authoritative voice ask, "Are you guys the crew from that B-17 that just landed?"

"Yes," Sterner replied.

"Any chance you guys were flying at high altitude for any length of time?"

Hank wanted to reply, but nothing came out of his mouth. Woody chimed in, saying, "Yes, for about four hours."

The medic yanked the last of the straps down, a new urgency in his movements and in his voice.

"I don't care if you're all feeling okay now. Every single one of you needs to get to the infirmary now. This guy's probably got the bends and could die if we don't get him help. Any one of you guys could be next. Get in. We'll make room for all of you."

Hank grew more alert at the commotion. He lifted his head, and through the blur saw his fellow crewmen squeezing into any available space inside the ambulance. He felt the acceleration of the vehicle as it sped away to the far side of the base.

Hours passed. Hank looked at the blurry hands of the clock on the wall and could make out it was just after midnight. He gazed around the room, recognizing everyone in his crew resting in a cot. Hank winced, still feeling dizzy and having numbness in his hands. But he most disliked his aching joints and sore muscles. His discomfort continued as he woke on the hour, still wearing an oxygen mask. The others were forced to share the remaining four oxygen masks among them. All of them spent the night in uncomfortable cots, getting little or no sleep. It didn't help that a nurse and two orderlies had to keep checking their vital signs throughout the night.

By morning, Hank could see that most of his crew were feeling better.

"You feeling any better?" Harris asked Hank.

"Yeah, a little," he replied without conviction. "But my head is killing me."

By daybreak, most of the men were out of danger. Hank watched with envy as the others stretched their stiff limbs and walked out of the infirmary, glancing back at Hank and Woody.

At the end of the second day, Hank could sit up and answer questions, but was in no condition to fly. Fortunately, a severe snowstorm blanketed Iceland, shutting down the airports for two days and giving everyone some much-needed time to recover.

At last, the storm broke, leaving a blanket of deep snow that muffled the noise of airplane engines nearby. Hank and Woody, still pale and drawn, were relieved to escape the infirmary and join the rest of the crew getting *Plano's Pride* ready for flight again.

After several hours in flight, Sterner got up to stretch his legs.

"You still don't look well, Hank," Sterner quipped. "How's your dizziness?"

"That's not so bad anymore, but my joints still ache and my head just pounds," Hank said. "I'll be okay once we land in England."

"We'll be landing in Ireland in a little over an hour. If we need to stay overnight, we will. I don't think Woody is quite back to normal either."

Hank protested, his eyes pleading with Sterner. "Neither of us want to hold the crew up. Let's just get to England."

Sterner disagreed. "We'll get you both checked out in Ireland, and if the doc says you don't fly, then we don't fly. We'll stay however long it takes to get you both back to feeling a hundred percent."

"I promise Captain, I'll be okay. It's only two or so hours from Ireland. I can make it. Please don't make us all stay overnight."

"That's up to the doctor." Sterner turned away to head back to the cockpit, finality in his voice and authority in his steps. "I'm not taking any chances."

Chapter 35-Note 1: Hundreds of fresh, barely trained aircrews were forced to ferry their planes across the northern Atlantic in what was known as Operation Bolero, the code name for the program created to deliver combat aircraft into the European theater. The entire ferrying operation was not without its controversy. U.S. military officials decided against following the British method of assigning trained ferrying crews to shuttle aircraft over the dangerous North Atlantic. Instead, radiomen who could barely make sense of the flood of dots and dashes they received, navigators with only a cursory understanding of their equipment, and pilots who had logged fewer than a hundred hours, were forced to adapt quickly to the treacherous conditions. The controversial policy put American airmen in danger, as officials considered a 10 percent accident rate as acceptable. By the end of the first phase of the secret "Bolero movement" in late August 1943, 164 P-38s, 119 B-17s, and 103 C-47s had crossed to England by the North Atlantic ferry route. In total, 920 planes left North America destined for Europe. Of that, 882 successfully arrived. Of the 38 planes that failed to reach their destination, twenty-nine were considered "wrecked," and nine were "lost", reflecting a 5.2 percent loss rate. These numbers do not reflect the replacement airplanes sent in the post-Bolero movement but are given here to show the uncommon resiliency and resourcefulness of these young pilots and crews who achieved their mission despite having insufficient training and experience.

Chapter 35-Note 2: The account of *Plano's Pride* making the 2,100-mile trans-Atlantic crossing from Presque Isle, Maine to Iceland is within the 3,750-mile range of the B-17G, although it was uncommon.

"The Army Air Forces in World War II." W.F. Craven and J.L. Cate (eds.). *ibiblio.org*, accessed January 5, 2021. https://www.ibiblio.org/hyperwar/AAF/I/AAF-I-17.html#page645.

CHAPTER 36
October 1, 1943
Crystal City, Texas

At the end of each day, O'Rourke drove his Studebaker through the streets of Crystal City, assessing how the detainees were getting along, observing the progress of various construction projects, and trying to mingle with the internees.

Most Germans turned away when they heard his Studebaker rumbling up the path, but the Japanese gave him respectful smiles. The Japanese teens liked his good nature. Many would serenade him with songs like "Don't Fence Me In." Some would change the words to popular songs, singing "Crystal City choo choo, won't you choo choo me home." O'Rourke smiled at being the butt of their humor.

By mid-November, the INS still hadn't confirmed the transfer of Horst Müller to the camp in Algiers, Louisiana. O'Rourke noted on his nightly drives that a darker kind of fear shadowed many of the Germans. They watched over their shoulders, shielded each other from Müller's henchmen, and shuddered at his grandstanding tactics to distract the Americans. While O'Rourke looked for signs of abuse, just the threat of violence seemed to be enough to achieve the desired outcome—fear and obedience.

O'Rourke enlisted the help of German laborers on his irrigation reservoir project. Although Müller's men often came to glower at the German laborers, after months of work it was at long last completed. The new pool measured two-hundred fifty feet wide, with three diving platforms and a shallow area for children. Almost everyone in the camp, Japanese and Germans alike, seemed proud of their joint accomplishment.

One night in early December, Marta walked home from her laundry job, looking up at the cool, clear sky and watching her breath fog in the air. As she passed the bulletin board, a scrap of paper fluttered in the wind, catching her attention. She stopped to smooth it down and read.

Her heart raced. Could it be? She read it again, then ran home.

"Karl!" She burst through the door. "Did you hear?"

He stood reaching out his arms. "Marta, what's wrong?"

"Horst Müller is out of power."

"What?"

She laughed, clasping her hands together. "O'Rourke officially declared him *persona non-grata,* and he's no longer the German spokesman," she said. "There's going to be an election for the new spokesman! Can you believe that?"

Karl hadn't seen her this happy since Hank's visit. He smiled but looked down in thought at the floor.

"Be careful not to get too excited," he said. "That announcement is probably just the opening gambit."

"Oh Karl!" She threw her hands in the air. "Why must you be a killjoy? Why can't I have this moment of happiness? I get so little of it here."

"I'm sorry, my dear, but I can't believe this is the last we'll hear of Müller." Karl's words were drenched in loathing. "He's not going to give up power just like that."

Marta shook her head, but a laugh of relief bubbled up in her throat. She scurried to the small corner pantry and pulled things from the cupboard. She set butter, a tin of flour, and a small jar of cinnamon on the table.

Karl stood behind her, looking over her shoulder. "What are you doing?"

"Celebrating. I'm making *Franzbrötchen.*"

"You haven't made that in years." Karl sniffed, the scent of cinnamon eliciting so, so many memories.

After pulling her creation from the oven, they sat and enjoyed it, holding hands and reminiscing about Utah and Germany. With every bite, they savored the cinnamon and buttery puff pastry on their tongues, chatting throughout the evening. Karl said nothing more about Müller.

The next morning, however, a new bulletin confirmed Karl's suspicion.

By order of the Camp Director,

With the recent dismissal of the German spokesman, the camp governing body expected a new spokesman to be elected through a democratic process. However, it has come to our attention that, according to the Geneva Convention, prisoners are "authorized to appoint representatives to represent them before the military authorities and the protecting Powers." As such, according to the current bylaws drawn up by the German delegation, the outgoing spokesman retains the right to select a replacement.

Consequently, the outgoing spokesman has selected Heinz Schmidt as the new German spokesman, and an election will not be held as previously announced.

James O'Rourke
Camp Director

Just minutes after the bulletin was posted, many Germans voiced their anger, but did so looking over their shoulders, fearing that one of Schmidt or Müller's friends was listening. Marta didn't care anymore. She shouted, "This is completely unfair. What about our rights?"

Karl tried to cover Marta's mouth. "Keep your voice down, my dear. Any one of these people could be one of Müller's friends."

"No!" Marta demanded. "I will not be bullied."

Karl leaned into her ear and whispered, "Please, let's just see if anything changes."

Marta shook her head in protest and walked with Karl back to their cottage. She stewed over the situation and couldn't sleep. Over the next few days, it was clear who was still calling the shots for the Germans. Although Müller was stripped of his role as official spokesman, he and his supporters continued to use threats and intimidation to retain power, albeit behind the scenes.

"Karl," Marta announced one day after breakfast, her arms sunk up to her elbows in sudsy dishwater. "I'm taking matters into my own hands."

"How are you going to do that?"

"There has to be a way to restore justice. I can't be the only one who feels like this." She shot him a smoldering glower while she scrubbed a pot, her mind elsewhere. "Doesn't anyone else care about this anymore?"

"Of course we all want you to be safe. I care about this as much as you do."

She wiped her forehead with her wrist, still clinging to a dish towel. "I know. But I think if there were more of us, if we banded together... we're all just so afraid..."

"How will you find more of us?"

She looked around, as if searching the room for an idea. "I'll ask my sewing group. I can talk to other women at the laundry. There has to be more of us than we think there are."

Karl smiled. "I have full faith that you, of all people, could find them," he said. "But be careful—there are also more of Müller's men than we think there are."

Later that day, Marta asked her group of friends, "What do you think about Schmidt as spokesman?"

"I'm angry," one of her friends replied through clenched teeth holding pins, bent over a piece of mending. "But I don't know what choice we have except to live with it." Others nodded in agreement.

Marta slapped her hands on the table with conviction. The others were startled and looked up.

"We do what Müller says because we fear there aren't enough of us who oppose him. What if," she said, holding their gazes, "we took a straw poll to see what everyone thinks should happen about selecting the new spokesman?"

"How would you do that without Müller's people finding out and putting an end to it?" another woman asked.

Marta thought for a moment. "Why don't we estimate what a vote would be? There's about eight hundred Germans in the camp, right? And among all of us here, we know just about everyone. I know people you don't. You know people I don't. Don't you think we can get a pretty good idea about what everyone thinks?"

Nodding their consent, the group of eight women gathered around the sewing table. With paper and pencil in hand, Marta kept notes as they began their tally. Systematically, starting from the cottages closest to the gate, they went family by family, cottage by cottage, and made their best guess how each German internee would vote.

They lived in too close proximity to each other not to know something of each other's political leanings. In some households, the name of Hitler was spoken with great pride. In some it was just a whisper, and in some it was heard with derision. They knew some internees only supported whomever they were told to.

After an hour, their tally indicated a clear winner. They estimated roughly one hundred fifty Germans would vote for Schmidt. More than six hundred would vote against him. Seventy-five remained unknown, but Marta laid down the pencil with a satisfied smile.

"Those results are quite compelling," she said. "Now we need a plan to get the word out."

"Why don't we put an article in the camp newsletter," someone suggested. "Let's just tell people of our informal poll?"

"What's that going to accomplish? So, they know we took a poll. They're still in power," a woman spoke up.

"But don't you see," Marta said, "much of their power comes from a vocal minority. We have to put doubt in their minds about their base of support. What we need," she looked around, then reached for a stack of paper and a pen, "is a well-written letter."

"Inga was a professor of literature at Heidelberg University," someone said, speaking unsure of herself at first, her voice gathering enthusiasm. "I'm sure if anyone could craft the perfect letter..."

Marta's eyes brightened. "Inga?" she started.

Inga held out her hands for the paper. "I would love to, but I don't want a byline," she smiled.

On October 10, the next issue of the camp newsletter *Das Lager* appeared on the bulletin board. Marta snatched it up, scanning the contents for their anonymous article. Within an hour, the German camp buzzed with words from Inga's unsigned letter. The letter's final plea for a vote passed between them, growing louder every time Marta heard it.

Schmidt's supporters tore down every copy of the newsletter, but the damage was done. Müller and Schmidt demanded the editor rescind the "inaccurate" article. Caving to the pressure, the editor apologized, but the German community rose up in indignation.

Marta refused to put up with their strong-arm tactics.

"They're not going to get away with this, Karl!" Marta demanded, hands curling into fists. "We cannot live in fear, and I am not going to allow this to continue."

Karl moved out of her way as she shouldered past him, and he watched her sit at the kitchen table scribbling out an impassioned letter. "The INS needs to know about this," she said. "I'm writing to the director in Washington."

Within minutes, she called out to Karl. "Listen to this and tell me what you think," she insisted.

To: The Honorable Henry B. Hazard
Director, Immigration and Naturalization Service
Washington, D.C.

Dear Mr. Hazard

My name is Marta Meyer. I am a naturalized United States citizen. My home was in Huntsville, Utah, but my husband and I are detained as enemy aliens at Crystal City.

As you are aware, James O'Rourke, the Crystal City Camp Director, removed Horst Müller as the German spokesman because of his unwillingness to work with camp administrators and because he used terroristic tactics to force obedience from the German population here. After he was declared *persona non grata*, Müller retained the right to select his successor and consequently appointed a man who is little more than an imitation dictator, who rules with the same kind of threats and intimidation. The vast majority of Germans want to vote for a new spokesman, but we fear retribution from both the former and current spokesman.

We request your intervention to help the German detainees who wish to vote for a new German spokesman. Without your help, we will remain threatened with violence for wanting to exercise our right of self-government.

Sincerely,
Marta Meyer

"Are you sure you want to send this?" Karl asked.

"Yes. Just like it is."

"What about calling him an imitation dictator? Are you sure you want to say that?"

"Yes," Marta asserted. "Am I being untruthful or exaggerating anything?"

"No, but O'Rourke will worry about this letter getting back to Schmidt or Müller."

"I think O'Rourke is overly cautious. He even admitted he had no hard evidence that a spy existed at the INS," Marta replied.

"But what if he is right?" Karl asked. "What if there is a spy among his people?"

Marta took his hand and said, "I am tired of being afraid of these tyrants. I am tired of sneaking around, whispering among ourselves for fear of being overheard. Where has it gotten us? Nowhere... and we're still miserable. Someone has to stand up to them. Somebody has to speak up and encourage others to speak up. If everyone slinks away in fear, then we're playing right into their hands. If we speak up and expose them as weak and unpopular, they'll lose their power. They get power from our silence, and I refuse to be silent anymore. If I die in here, trying to stand up to these little dictators, at least I won't die a coward."

Karl took a deep breath. "I'm afraid for you because they've attacked me and nothing has happened to them. What's to stop them from attacking you?"

"I don't care. I'm not going to back down."

He stood, wrapped his arms around her and embraced her.

"Then we're in this together," he whispered.

She folded the letter with care, inserted it in the envelope, and wrote out the address and her return address. Hand-in-hand, they walked to the camp post office. Marta dropped the letter in and closed the door of the mailbox. It echoed with a thud.

CHAPTER 37
Saturday October 9, 1943
Ogden, Utah

Ella walked side-by-side with Virginia Kerr, a fellow nurse, as they ended their long Saturday shift at Dee Hospital. Ella and Virginia had known each other since nursing school.

"Are you okay, Ella?" Virginia asked.

Ella rubbed the back of her neck, aches and stress from school and long days of work visible in her tired eyes. "I'm doing fine," she smiled.

"Your uniform just hangs on you." Virginia was being kind but couldn't hide her concern. "You're losing so much weight; you're beginning to scare me."

Ella waved it off. "Oh, I just forget to eat sometimes."

"How much have you lost?" Virginia's eyebrows raised.

"I don't know for sure. Maybe thirty pounds since Hank left. It's mostly because I'm not cooking as much, so I'm not eating all that heavy German food Hank loved."

"I worry about you, Ella, but you're sure looking good, if that matters to you."

"I haven't been purposefully trying to lose weight. It just happened that way." Ella smiled as she tugged on her white nurses' uniform, her baggy clothes hanging on her shrinking frame.

"Did I hear you were asked on a date by one of the patients tonight?" Virginia teased.

Ella's face turned red. "How did you hear about that?"

She gave Ella a wry smile. "Oh, word gets around."

"I told him no; we're not allowed to date our patients," Ella stated with a mock tone of professionalism. "But he sure was cute," she added, holding her hand over her mouth and stifling a giggle.

Ella and Virginia had reached the employee entrance of the hospital.

"Be safe going home," Virginia said.

"I will. You too," Ella replied as she opened her car door and jumped in. In the late-night darkness of the parking lot, the stress of too many long days weighed heavy on her mind. Preoccupied with her thoughts, she fumbled for her keys. After a brief search, she found them in her purse and started her car. As she pulled out of the parking lot, she breathed out through her lips to regain her composure. She had forty-five minutes to clear her mind, before she would arrive home. There, her thoughts would be crowded out by the emptiness and loneliness of her house.

Maybe when she got home, she'd find a letter from Tom waiting for her. He had returned to England after the Allies drove the Germans out of Africa in May. He wrote every other day, which was not enough for Ella. Letters, fragile paper communication, were her only lifeline connecting her to Tom, her parents, Hank... her thoughts were drawn to those she loved. *How were her parents handling the Texas heat in Crystal City? Where was Hank now, or Billie? Did any of them worry as much as she did?*

Her car rumbled into her driveway after midnight; the sound of her engine and the gravel crunching under her tires were the only sounds breaking the stillness of the night. She got out and shut the door, careful not to wake the neighbors.

She approached her house in the dark, looking down at her feet, lost in thought. As she unlocked the door and grabbed the doorknob, her fingers touched something sticky. With a gasp, she snatched her hand away and looked up. The door glistened in an odd color in the dark, and the smell of fresh paint hit her nostrils. She ran back to her car, hopped in, and turned on the headlights, illuminating her front porch.

A huge red swastika covered the wooden siding of the house, stretching from the top of the door frame to the porch floor. Sloppy red paint splattered the windows, drying fast but still gleaming with freshness. A paintbrush lay in the far corner, tossed aside in haste.

Ella screamed.

The site of the ugly Nazi symbol made her nauseated. It was a clear threat meant to intimidate her. Mustering her courage, she stepped out of her car, closing the door with care. As she approached her porch, she couldn't control her trembling hands as they covered her mouth in shock.

"Who would do this?" Agony filled her voice, her words soft and strained. Looking around, numb and dizzy, her gaze caught something else through the blur of tears. A bottle full of liquid rested in the far corner of the porch, a rag stuffed inside glinted in the pale moonlight.

She walked over, wiping her eyes, and knelt to find a dark bottle. A rag stuck out of the top, flopping over the side. The unmistakable odor of gasoline struck the back of her throat, and she almost gagged.

Footsteps pattered up the driveway behind her. Ella jumped in terror, only to find Grandma Russell rushing to her side and breathing fast. Her night-gowned silhouette stood out against the yellow glow of her porch light across the way, wisps of her gray hair sticking out of her braid.

"Ella! What happened?"

Ella stood back, putting her hands on her hips. "Just look," she whispered through clenched teeth. Grandma rounded the corner, holding to the porch railing as the jagged lines, red like blood, came into her view. Ella bit back another sob. Anger boiled deep inside, clambering to the surface. She turned away from the sight, looked up at the night sky, and drew in a sharp, shuddering breath.

"Why can't they just leave us alone? We didn't do anything wrong."

"It's okay, honey. It's okay." Grandma Russell reached for her hand. "Don't go inside your house yet. We don't know if someone or something is still inside."

Ella's eyes widened, realizing the threat may still be nearby.

"Come with me to my house so I can call the sheriff." Together they walked across the yard. Inside her kitchen, Grandma reached for the telephone on the wall. She clicked the receiver up and down, shouting into the phone. "Operator. Operator. Hello. I need the sheriff."

Ella sank down into a kitchen chair, her face in her hands. She watched as Grandma Russell picked up her telephone receiver and tapped the lever quickly to get the attention of the operator.

"Hello. Get me the police," Grandma said. Ella could hear the loud clicks as a muffled voice answered.

"Is this the Weber County Sheriff?" Grandma asked, listening for confirmation.

Grandma cleared her throat. "Some hooligan painted a big read Nazi swastika on the front porch of the Meyers' house here in Huntsville. And they left a Molotov cocktail on the porch."

Grandma listened, her brow knitted in frustration. She looked at Ella as she held the receiver closer to her ear. "Okay. When could you send someone out?"

After waiting for a few moments, Ella jumped as Grandma shouted. "No, the house isn't abandoned. It was just the parents who were taken away. Their daughter still lives here, and she hasn't done anything wrong. I live next door, and I am terrified."

Finishing her conversation with the dispatcher, Grandma slammed the phone on the hook and turned to Ella. "They're on the way. They'll be here as soon as they can."

Ella could tell something was wrong, but Grandma looked out the window to change the subject. "I'm going out to turn off the lights on your car."

Ella followed her outside and watched from the porch. When Grandma returned, they sat on Ella's front steps. Grandma put an arm around Ella's shoulder, and they waited.

After waiting for a half hour or so, Ella looked at her watch and complained, "What's taking them so long?"

Grandma took a deep breath, "When I told them it was at your house..."

"Oh," Ella said.

"They said they're really busy tonight, so they'll get here when they can."

Ella shook her head. "I'm not surprised. Everyone thinks we're Nazis and that we have this coming to us."

After another half-hour wait, the lights of the sheriff's car flashed from the other side of Pineview reservoir, reflecting off the tall, leafless cottonwood trees that lined the streets. The car pulled into the Meyer's driveway. After a long pause, the door opened and the sheriff's deputy stepped out, ambling up to Ella's porch. Ella turned to Grandma "I've never seen him before. Is he new?"

Grandma shook her head. "I have no idea, he must be."

The officer rubbed his chin as he scanned his flashlight over the house, the bushes and trees that surrounded their home, then back to the house again.

Ella waited, growing more impatient with each slow, deliberate step he made.

Finally he spoke, to no one in particular, "Do you have any idea who would do this?"

"I haven't the foggiest," Ella answered with unmasked annoyance.

The officer stepped up on the Meyer's porch and looked around.

"That's a Molotov cocktail." He picked it up, swirling the liquid under his nose.

Ella rolled her eyes and looked at Grandma. "This guy is brilliant." Grandma stifled a laugh.

"Gasoline, all right. It looks like they were scared off by something. You're pretty lucky," he added with a hint of disappointment. "It could have been a lot worse."

Ella and Grandma followed him as he pointed his flashlight at the ground just off the porch. He noticed a footprint, then another. His pace quickened as he followed the trail around the house, but it disappeared.

"It looks like they're gone. Not much I can do now."

Ella tried to catch up but couldn't because he was walking too fast. She barked at him. "Would you please check my house? Maybe someone is inside."

The officer huffed, looking over his shoulder impatiently, then spat, "There ain't nobody inside. They're long gone. You'll be just fine."

"What's the matter with you?" Ella screamed. "Somebody committed a crime here. Aren't you going to do anything about it?"

"I don't have time to investigate every incident of vandalism. Especially when it's…" He stopped and cleared his throat. "There's nobody in the house. They ran away scared."

"You're absolutely sure about that?" Grandma asked, glaring.

"Yeah. Pretty sure. You'll be okay." The sheriff walked back to his car.

"Will you do anything for us?" Ella called after him.

Exasperated, Grandma said, "I'll go look around if he won't."

The sheriff kept walking but looked over his shoulder and laughed.

Grandma kicked the dried leaves from her slippers and approached the door, straining her eyes though the door window to see if anyone was inside. Ella held her breath as Grandma opened the back door and inspected the kitchen before flipping on the light switch. Through the window Ella watched Grandma as she looked around, walking with caution from one room to the next room. Ella could follow her movement as Grandma turned on the light in each empty room. Grandma came to the top of the stairs and hollered back to Ella. "Nothing looks out of place, Ella. I think it's safe now."

Ella stepped in the house, wide-eyed as she assessed the kitchen and living room. Grandma came down the stairs, unlocked the front door, and switched on the porch light.

"Come and have a seat Ella, there's nobody else in here."

Ella flopped onto the living room sofa.

"I just don't have the emotional energy to deal with this." Ella heaved a bitter sigh.

"I know, dear. I wouldn't expect anyone to."

A knock came at the door. "Who could that be at this hour?" Grandma looked at Ella with dread.

Ella jumped, ran to the window, and peeked through the crack in the curtain.

"Oh, it's the bishop." Ella exhaled with relief.

Grandma opened the door. "Hi, Bishop Renstrom. Come on in."

He passed through the door, glancing at the paint dripping from the door frame. "I saw the police lights so I thought I'd see what was going on." He turned to offer Ella a look of sympathy. "I can't imagine who would do such a thing. Is there anything I can do to help?"

Grandma breathed a loud moan. "Oh, that sheriff was useless, but there's nothing you can do about that, Bishop. Ella is going to sleep at my house tonight, and we'll figure out where we go from there."

"I'm so sad that you have to go through this," he added. "I hope it was no one from this valley that did this."

"The only people who know what happened to us are from this valley," Ella gave a cynical look. "Who else would do it?"

The Bishop pursed his lips and looked down at his hands. Ella waited, but he didn't answer her question. At last he looked up and said, "I will see what I can do to get this taken care of. Go get some sleep, Ella."

Grandma thanked him, reaching for Ella's hand as she locked the door, then led her outside, across their lawns and into her house. She closed the door behind her and made sure it was locked. Ella sat on a rocking chair as Grandma tucked a fresh sheet and blanket into the sofa. "There you go hon'. Sorry I've got Billie's room such a mess. But this is all ready for you."

"Thanks, Grandma. This will be fine. I appreciate you being there for me." Ella felt relief from being off her feet. She pulled the sheet and blanket up to her neck. Grandma smiled, turned out the lights, and climbed the stairs. Ella felt all alone, and the loneliness kept her awake for at least an hour. Maybe more. She slept fitfully, awakened easily by any strange noise. She tossed and turned, bolting up at every sound, until fatigue overtook her and she fell into a deep sleep.

She awoke to a clanging sound. Sitting up in the bright morning light, Ella reached to open the curtain, glancing outside. The mid-morning sunlight blazed through the window, and Ella had to shield her eyes against its brightness. Outside her house, she saw a dozen men busily working to clean things up. They carried brushes and paint cans, leaning ladders against the roof and calling out to each other. From this window she couldn't see the front of her house, but she watched as the men hurried about, laughing and teasing each other, clothes spattered with fresh paint, hustling as they focused on their work.

Ella rushed to get dressed and pull on her shoes. She stepped out into the cool morning air and crossed the yard to the front of her house. They had scrubbed with steel wool up and down the walls, scraping away the red paint to expose the wooden slats beneath. Fresh paint came next, in smooth strokes covering the walls. One man glanced over his shoulder and gave Ella a smile. She stood with her hands by her side, mouth open in astonishment.

In less time than Ella believed possible, they finished and scooped up all their tools. The men left with brief nods at Ella, and she kept opening her mouth to thank them, but nothing came out. Grandma Russell joined her, and they inspected the paint job. "They put on a quick coat of paint to cover it up, but they'll come back on Monday and put a finish coat on to hide it completely," Grandma explained. "If you look really close, you can still see it."

A hint of a pink swastika peeked through the white paint, but Ella grinned with relief.

The men climbed in their truck, and as the engine rumbled to life, she turned. "Thank you," she called. "I... thank you."

They waved as they drove off.

"How long have they been here?"

"About an hour or so, I'm guessing," Grandma replied.

"I can't believe I didn't hear them. I must have been sound asleep," Ella admitted.

"Let's go inside," Grandma Russell said. "I've got breakfast just about ready for you."

As Grandma piled food on Ella's plate, she sat her down at the kitchen table to discuss Ella's options.

"You know you're more than welcome to stay here with me," Grandma explained. "But I've already talked with Jane and Frank, and they said you can stay in Billie's room at their place in Ogden. They're not home most of the time, and you'll be on your own a lot, but at least you'll be closer to school and work."

"But I've got so much to do here," Ella cried. "I've got all those tomatoes to put up and all those cucumbers to pickle. This is my home. I want to stay in *my home!*"

"It's not safe for you here, Ella. Especially if whoever did this is still out there."

"But…" Ella's lip quivered as hot tears filled her eyes. "I just don't know what to do."

"You don't have to decide right now," she said, putting a firm hand on her arm.

"If I moved away to Ogden, I would be a coward…"

"No, of course not…"

"I would be admitting that they beat me—that I just gave up."

Grandma's jaw was set firm in a scowl. "That's not true."

Ella drew in a deep breath.

"Think about what it will be like if every time you came home, you have to wonder if it it's safe to go into your house."

Ella shook her head again in disappointment. Then her chin snapped up and her eyes brightened with an idea.

"What if we let my Uncle Willy live here?" She turned to see a look of questioning hope in Grandma Russell's tired eyes.

221

"Are you sure?" said Grandma, eyebrows raised. "He's not always alert, if you know what I mean."

Ella agreed with a nod.

"If they throw another Molotov cocktail into the house, Willy may never know what happened."

Ella looked at Grandma with curiosity and asked, "What would it take to move everything out of our house and put it in storage somewhere?"

Grandma pushed herself from the couch with an unintentional grunt. "Let's go look around your place first before we decide."

They crossed the yard and went upstairs. With trepidation, Ella pushed open the door to her parent's room and let Grandma walk in. Ella halted behind her, feeling the draft from the room within. She hadn't stepped in, hadn't so much as opened the door since that night. Grandma bounded in, hands on her hips and surveying the room as Ella trailed behind her. The bedclothes still lay in a rumpled mess, coated in dust, as were the dresser, the nightstand, and the windowsill. Grandma threw open the closet, seeing dust had settled onto the shoulders of the shirts and coats and into the creases and folds of their clothes. She inspected their trinkets, their wall hangings, and the sentimental knick-knacks.

"There's several decades of accumulated belongings in here," Ella commented. "It may take quite a bit of packing. It's a little overwhelming. Let's go look at Hank's room."

Hank's room was clean, as he had packed up most of his belongings and stacked them in a neat pile in the closet. "This won't take much," Ella added. "And my room will take a day, but I'll take care of my things."

"So, that leaves the downstairs furniture and the kitchen. That's going to take some time to get done."

"I have a few orderly friends from the hospital who are big and strong. They would help me get things moved out, if I can get it packed first. It wouldn't take more than half a day or so."

Grandma smiled and put her hand on Ella's shoulder. "Just get yourself packed for now and stay in Ogden. I'll see what I can do to work things out."

Anxiety gnawed away at the pit of her stomach, and she didn't want to think about it anymore. She looked at the clock.

"I'd like to go to church. Do you think we'll have time?"

"Oh sure, I'll be ready in a jiffy. We'll be a little late, but not by much."

Ella rushed to get dressed then dashed out to Grandma's car. As they pulled into the church lot, the voice of the congregation swelled from within the church, reaching out to them with the hymn, "We Are All Enlisted 'Til the Conflict is O'er."

Ella hurried in under the cover of voices singing, keeping her head low. She grabbed a seat at the back of the chapel, yet not before catching Bishop Renstrom's kind smile as he sat on the podium. After a prayer and administration of the sacrament, the bishop stood at the pulpit, gripping the sides of the podium as he gathered his composure. At last, he looked up and met the eyes of the congregation.

"Before our assigned speaker, I'd like to say a brief word about something that happened last night. Some of you may be aware that a violent and hateful act occurred at the home of one of our members." His voice thickened with tears, and he cleared his throat before continuing.

"A part of me hopes the culprit isn't among us. It would truly grieve me to think that any of our fellow neighbors could do such a thing, simply because of someone's heritage. But another part of me hopes they are here." He lowered a stern gaze on the congregation, and some gave each other uncomfortable glances. "That they may hear me condemn this act of bigotry in no uncertain terms. God condemns all acts of bigotry and hate. This is not how a Christian behaves. Christ taught us to love others, even our enemies. And what makes this act so appalling is that the family who was victimized is not our enemy, but our neighbor. How could such a thing happen among friends? I know some may say we're at war. But even war is no excuse. We can't let our yearning for peace justify our hatred for any of God's children. We cannot resort to the same kind of narrow-mindedness that started this war in the first place. I don't know yet what is going to happen with this family, but I suspect they will need our help. I'm hoping you will be willing to provide Christ-like service and do your part to assist them during this very difficult time."

The bishop sat back in his seat, and in the echo of his words the people looked at each other, stunned. Ella sank in her seat, willing herself to be smaller, or invisible, or forgotten. The assigned speaker took the pulpit, but Ella heard none of his words.

Near the end of the meeting, Ella turned to Grandma Russell and said, "I'm going to walk home."

Grandma gave Ella an understanding smile. Ella stood and tip-toed toward the door. Bishop Renstrom raised his hand to wave, motioning for her to stay, but his movement prompted the speaker to stop and look on in confusion. The congregation glanced at the bishop, then turned to stare at Ella. Her face flushed red and her heart pounded with embarrassment. She quietly slipped out of the chapel, heading home as fast as her legs would take her.

CHAPTER 38
October 15, 1943
RAF Nutt's Corner, Ireland

Upon landing at the Royal Air Force base in Nutt's Corner, Ireland, the crew completed the hours of processing necessary for all soldiers and airmen upon arriving in the European theater. The doctor also cleared Hank and Woody to fly by late afternoon.

They were all eager to know the new air base they would call home. Captain Sterner had to wait until they were airborne to tell them.

Plano's Pride taxied into position and made a picture-perfect take-off. After settling into their cruising altitude, Sterner called over the interphone. "Gentlemen we're headed to a base called R.A.F. Thurleigh. It's pronounced thurl-eye, not thurl-ee. I was warned that we better pronounce it right. It's a brand-new base about sixty miles north of London." He looked out the side window as he continued speaking. "We're assigned to the 306th Bomb Group where they have about seventy or so B-17s. That's about all I know."

Hank crossed his arms, relieved at knowing what base they were being assigned to. But with hundreds of Royal Air bases dotting the British landscape, no one knew where it was or what to expect. As they flew over the English countryside, the skies were clear and visibility extended for at least a hundred miles. Or so it seemed.

"How you feeling, Hank?" Montoya asked as they both enjoyed the view.

"I'll be okay," Hank muttered. "These stupid headaches are annoying, but I'm feeling much better than yesterday."

After a rough landing and a quick taxi to a hardstand, Sterner shut down the engines. As he turned to exit the cockpit, over his shoulder he caught movement out the window. People trickled in from all directions, flowing into a crowd that collected into a group outside their plane. A blend of uniforms and stained coveralls gathered, young and old, some standing alone, all of them gazing up at *Plano's Pride* with an emotion none of them could figure out.

"What's with the welcoming committee?" Sterner crossed his arms, looking on in curiosity.

As the engines quieted to a murmur and the crew began to remove their headgear, Hank stood to stretch. The gathering crowd caught his attention out the window. He put his hands on his hips and grinned. "Hey guys, look at all these people coming to see us."

As they crawled out of the plane one by one, they looked with amusement at the small group of people approaching. British civilian workers smiled, extending grease-stained, machinery-worn hands and smiling with wide, welcoming eyes. One man offered his outstretched hand, and Hank smiled as he shook it.

"Welcome to the war, blokes," declared a scruffy looking Brit with a broad, toothless grin.

One man stood under the shadow of the plane, craning his neck and running his gaze over its shimmering newness.

"Isn't she a sight for sore eyes," he said. "She's a crackin' beauty!"

Hank had never heard an Englishman speak before, but he liked the sound of it.

More people began to speak, peppering Sterner's crew with questions. The crowd buzzed with conversation, keen interest written on the faces of the welcomers and pride in the voices of the crew as they told their stories.

A truck arrived and a handful of American servicemen jumped out. They gave quick nods to Sterner's men, circling the plane and touching the skin of the new B-17G. But as Hank watched, he saw an emptiness in their expressions, something distant, that reminded him of the look in his own crews' eyes when they returned from their families. But this was darker, a hollow look under the smiles. They seemed to be forcing themselves to admire the plane and the new people it brought with it. They didn't ask questions of Sterner or his men. They didn't say much at all.

After watching for a moment, one of the British crewmen turned to Hank. "We've heard about these new G-model Forts. But this one's the first we've seen."

"Yeah, we feel like movie stars with all you fans coming to see us." Hank gave a nervous grin.

"Aww, they don't care about us," Connors quipped. "They just came to see the plane."

"Either way, we're glad to finally be here," Sterner added.

The British crewman's grim face hinted of grief and sadness. "Any good news helps us get our minds off everything that happened yesterday."

"What happened?" Hank asked.

The man raised a wary look at Hank, but meeting his gaze, his face softened. "We lost ten Fortresses yesterday."

A tremor ran down Hank's spine as the meaning of what the man was saying sank in.

"That's a hundred blokes what's not comin' back."

Hank swallowed. "Did you say you lost ten B-17s in one day?"

"Aye," he said. "We sent out fifteen Forts and just five came back. It was a sad, sad day for the 306th."

The man turned on his heel and walked away, and Hank watched the way his posture and stride seemed shadowed by something. Now he understood what it was.

After getting their duffel bags and other belongs, the crew of *Plano's Pride* loaded into two trucks and drove to their new barracks. As they approached, a parade of airmen hauled bedding on their shoulders, their faces stern and somber. Some carried duffel bags and other belongings in each hand, stacking everything outside the supply office. Hank moved out of the path of one airman, the backpack slung over the man's shoulder brushing Hank's arm as he passed. Hank figured it was a fallen serviceman's belongings. It was placed with care on a pile of other belongings where it would be inventoried and shipped back home to the serviceman's family. Hank recognized the look on the faces of his crew. They were trying to hide their anxiety, just like he was.

Their first days at Thurleigh were shadowed in gloom and discouragement. Reminders of the missing airmen and the lethal business they were all engaged in confronted them at every turn.

One day, when Hank tucked in the corners of his sheets, a piece of paper slipped out from under his mattress and drifted to the floor. He picked up the black-and-white photo carefully, holding the corner between two fingers. Two young children, their round faces streaked with dirt, played in a yard surrounded by trees. He reached around the mattress, patting its corners and edges until he felt another one, this time tucked into a torn seam. A picture of a curvaceous girl looking over her shoulder stared into Hank's eyes. Flipping the photo over, Hank found a short message in small, delicate penmanship that read, *To my darling husband Jay.* He stacked the photo with the other, though he was tempted to put them back in the mattress; after all, they didn't belong to him.

He walked to the supply officer, holding them in front of him like a lit match. He didn't look at them again.

"I found these photos in my bunk. I think they were…." He cleared his throat.

The supply officer reached out for the photos. "Thanks. I'll see if we can find who these belong to."

Hank shoved his hands in his pockets, now unsure what to do.

The supply officer waited for a moment, then slipped the photos into an envelope that he put on his desk. "Thank you for bringing them to me."

At the end of the first week, Hank struck up a conversation with Melvin Rodgers, a ball turret gunner who participated in the deadly October 14 attack. Melvin was an "Okie" from Tulsa and with a hesitant voice, spoke about the mission.

"It just happened so fast," he said. "We dropped our bombs and from out of nowhere came a swarm of *Messerschmitts*. They started picking us off one at a time. We got shot up pretty bad, but we were in the middle of the formation, so we were able to fight them off long enough to get away."

As Hank listened, a question that had been simmering in the back of his mind for weeks now voiced itself. "Melvin," Hank asked. "How many missions have you flown?"

"That was my ninth."

"What are the chances that a crew can actually complete twenty-five missions and go home?"

Melvin scoffed, his eyes turning to steel. "I ain't seen not one crew come anywheres close to completing fifteen, let alone twenty-five. It's the pot o' gold at the end of the rainbow."

"Why do you think the odds are so bad?"

"We're doing a dangerous job. What do you expect?" Melvin asked.

"From what I learned at gunnery school—"

"Gunnery school?" Melvin slapped his knee. "You think this is anything like gunnery school?"

Hank frowned. "I was told that if you just practice hard and learn to do your job well, you've got a fighting chance of coming home in one piece."

Melvin laughed. "You hafta forget everything you learned in the States. It ain't gonna do you no good here."

"What do you mean?" Hank shot him a confused glare. "Are you saying the stuff they taught us is a lie?"

"Most of those guys in the States aren't experienced gunners anyway. You just pay attention to the training the Brits give you here. They've been at it a lot longer than we have, and if you do what they tell you, it'll give you the best chance of surviving."

The next day, Captain Sterner gathered his crew together to share more unsettling news from the commanding officer of his bomb squadron.

"I was told I need to go back to school to learn how to fly again," he said, with a half laugh. "Apparently, they can teach us things that we didn't learn very well back in Texas—especially how to fly with a weighted-down plane for hours on end. So, we're all going back to school. That also means each of you will be learning more about aerial gunnery and new tactics and techniques."

Hank wasn't surprised, but the other crewmen looked disappointed at first; then it all made sense. Any additional training they could get before they were thrown into battle, anything that gave them a better chance, they were eager to latch on to.

"Also, I'm sorry to tell you that they are removing the cabin heating system from our plane."

A simultaneous groan came from everyone.

"It seems our friends at Boeing did a great job engineering an efficient heater, but the fluid inside the system is highly flammable. We've lost a few planes because of it, so it came from the top to take 'em all out."

Hank imagined he could already feel the frigid cold seeping into his fingers and toes. Then Sterner added, "If you recall, it didn't work so well on our long flight to Iceland, and we didn't have heaters in our old bird back in Texas. So, don't worry. We've lived without it before. We can live without it now."

"You got any other great news for us?" Montoya said. "Do we have to fly in our skivvies now?"

A few men gave him a courtesy laugh, but Sterner's hard face told them he was in no mood for sarcasm.

Chapter 38-Note 1: Thurleigh was the home of the 306th Bomb Group. The entire bomb group arrived in September of 1942 and eventually had a full contingent of seventy-two B-17s. After a long period of training and retrofitting their aircraft with more armor, they began bombing enemy strongholds in France in November and December of 1942. On January 27, 1943, the 306th attacked the docks of Wilhelmshaven. This attack marked the first American assault on German soil for any branch of service during the war. It was a point of great pride for the 306th to be the first to attack the Nazis. Although the success at Wilhelmshaven was an important milestone in the 306th's illustrious history, unfortunately, so too was the sobering loss of one hundred crewmen on a single day, October 14, 1943.

CHAPTER 39

December 3, 1943
Palm Springs, California

In late November, Billie arrived at Palm Springs Army Airfield for Pursuit Flight Transition School. This intense, four-week course started December 1, and if she completed the course, she would be qualified to fly four of the army's best fighter planes: the P-47 Thunderbolt, P-39 Airacobra, P-40 Warhawk, and the P-51 Mustang.

She had plenty to do before class started.

Billie shared a room with Betty in a two-by-four barracks. Betty won the toss and chose the bottom bunk.

Dorothy Scott and Helen Richards shared the bunks on the other side of the room. Both were among the original twenty-eight women that made up the Women's Auxiliary Ferry Squadron, or WAFS, the predecessors of the Woofteddies. Billie watched them as they unpacked their things and settled in, wondering what it had been like for them in the WAFS, thinking it might have been her if she hadn't been rejected.

Both Dorothy and Helen had logged over fourteen hundred hours of flying before joining the WAFS and were considered superstars of American women pilots. Billie unfolded her uniform as they finished arranging their side of the room.

Dorothy turned, saw Billie looking, and smiled. Billie brightened and grinned back, feeling relief as the brief connection eased away the knot of envy and intimidation forming inside.

Despite the notoriety of some of the pilots, they all had to live in austere conditions, with no inside plumbing or hot water. Like everyone else, they endured the outside toilets and cold showers. But even with their meager accommodations, whenever Billie exchanged glances with Dorothy or Helen or Betty, the thrill in their smile was contagious. She knew she didn't want to be anywhere else in the world.

Only eight of the forty-three students were women, but Nancy Love and General Turner gave explicit instructions to the staff: all students were to be treated alike.

Half the women pilots, Billie and her roommates, were assigned to Flight A and the other to Flight B. Billie's half did their flight training in the morning, then switched places after lunch and spent the afternoon in classroom instruction.

As they arrived on the flight line, their instructor, Captain George Norbert, greeted them with a kind smile, then explained how he had piloted a P-39 and had earned all his points in Africa. Billie liked his modest attitude and generous demeanor.

"Here's how this is going to work," he explained. "We will spend about a week training on each of these four pursuit planes, starting with the P-47 and the P-39. The next week will be the P-40, and that should leave us a few more days to spend training on the P-51."

P-51. A thrill shot through Billie's whole body.

"But first, we're going to spend a couple days in these modified BC-1s." Captain Norbert pointed to a row of AT-6 Texans. "Now, I know they look like any other Texan you've flown before," he said, "except we've modified the rear seat to simulate the cockpit of a P-47."

"For the first couple of flights, an instructor will be at the stick, while you get used to the new instruments. Then we'll let you take the stick and get used to the controls yourself. Later in the week, we'll have you up in the 'Bolt, and you're on your way from there."

"Hey, look. It's Nancy Love." Betty nudged Billie in the ribs.

"I wonder why she's here?" Billie stood on her toes to see over someone's hat.

"She's probably checking on us," Billie said.

"Maybe she's here to see for herself that her WASP pilots are actually training on pursuit planes. She's been promoting the idea for so long; it's about time it all came together," Betty replied.

"Wasn't she good friends with Helen and Dorothy?" Billie asked.

"They were in the WAFS together. Maybe she's really here to see Dorothy or Helen be the first to fly!" Betty joked. "But I'm sure she wants to make sure none of us are cheated out of a chance to fly these planes."

The weather couldn't have been better on their first day of training at the stick. Visibility stretched clear and bright for miles in every direction. When Nancy arrived on the flight line, Dorothy was in the rear cockpit of the BC-1. Her instructor, Bob Snider, another pilot Nancy knew, sat in the front cockpit.

Nancy chatted with Helen, Betty, and Billie, watching just a quarter mile from the runway, close enough that the heat from Dorothy's plane rolled over them with each landing she made. They strained to make conversation as five other planes buzzed overhead, shouting louder as they circled closer.

Nancy watched as Dorothy put her BC-1 through its paces, smiling with pride at her flawless maneuvers.

"For as long as I've known Dorothy, she's been a great pilot," Nancy yelled. "I can hardly wait to see her at the stick of a P-51. If they'd let her, she could fight as well as any man out there."

For fifteen minutes, Dorothy guided her plane through the sky, effortless as a bird.

Dorothy got into position for her final approach, reaching her gliding altitude. A P-39 zoomed above her from behind, closing the distance between them.

"Oh no," Nancy said. "That P-39 thinks he's cleared to land, and he doesn't see Dorothy."

Nancy and the other WASPs held their breath.

"Come on tower, you've gotta call 'em off!" Nancy shouted.

The P-39 dropped into a descent, Dorothy's plane just below him. Billie's heart raced.

"Call him off!" Nancy screamed. "Call him off!"

The two planes drew closer together, occupying the same small piece of the sky. They made one shadow on the ground below. Billie winced, almost turning away. Helpless, she and Betty watched the P-39 accelerate into its final descent, with Dorothy still in his blind spot below him.

The explosion reverberated throughout the airfield as the P-39 smashed into Dorothy's plane, severing its tail section. Both planes tumbled out of control, an array of burning pieces and scorched metal scattering in the sky. The P-39 crashed into the runway in a ball of fire. Dorothy's plane made a nosedive, heading straight for Nancy, Billie, Betty, and Helen. They shoved each other out of the way, Billie grabbing Betty's arm, and Nancy reaching for Helen as she let out a horrified cry.

Dorothy's plane hit a grassy mound, bursting into a raging fireball and scattering dirt and mud. A wave of heat rushed over Billie, and she looked over her shoulder. Dorothy's plane skidded toward them across the grass. In a cloud of smoke and dust, the burning plane came to an abrupt stop a mere hundred feet from where they stood.

They looked on unable to move, wanting desperately to dash into the wreckage of fire and smoke, but they were halted by the intensity of the flames and fumes. Sirens blared and far away there was shouting. Billie clutched her side, gasping.

As the fireball came to a stop, Dorothy's heartbreaking shrieks rang out from among the screeching metal. Her terror-filled screams pierced their ears. Somehow, they all knew her helpless cries would haunt them forever.

Chapter 39-Note 1: The description of Dorothy Scott's deadly crash is based on the existing historical record. The accident occurred on December 3, 1943 in Palm Springs, California. The official report attributes fifty-five percent of the blame to the "carelessness" of the male pilot, and forty-five percent to Dorothy Scott, citing her "carelessness" as an underlying cause. This, despite witness reports acknowledging that Dorothy was on her final approach in her BC-1 and could not have seen the approaching P-39. According to witness statements from pilots in the air who witnessed the accident, they heard no conversation between the tower and either plane. One pilot claims to have asked the tower to give a warning to both planes, but his request was ignored. The narrative also hints at absolving the male pilot of the P-39 because of the "position of the sun, and the banking attitude of the P-39." Subsequent to this accident, all pursuit training aircraft were painted yellow.

Report of Aircraft Accident No. 44-12-3-7, December 20, 1943, War Department, 21st Ferrying Group, Palm Springs, California.

CHAPTER 40

January 20, 1944
Crystal City, Texas

The open letter calling for a new spokesman in *Das Lager* caused an uproar among the Germans in Crystal City. Marta and her sewing friends waited for official word from camp officials about an election. If all went according to plan, perhaps, at long last, the horrible reign of Schmidt and Müller would come to an end.

"I told you, if we stand up to them, they'll start doing stupid things because they're afraid to lose power," Marta explained to her friends.

"I have never seen a grown man so terrified that he would lose a popular vote," one woman said. "It reminds me of elementary school." The room roared with laughter.

Müller and his family campaigned against the referendum, claiming it was just another example of American interference with the Germans' rights.

O'Rourke scheduled the election-day for January 27, 1944.

Camp employees officiated the voting in the community center. Schmidt insisted some of his own people observe the voting process, and O'Rourke allowed it with a dismissive wave of his hand.

O'Rourke's staff tallied the votes and looked at each other in shock. They recounted again, and again.

"It's a landslide for Schmidt," announced the clerk.

"That can't be," O'Rourke ran the back of his hand over his forehead in frustration. "Count them again."

"I've counted them three times," she replied.

As O'Rourke probed further into the entire process, he discovered a gap in the custody of the ballots. His staff had been sloppy, leaving them unattended. It was all the time Schmidt and Müller needed to replace the exact number of ballots with their own, forged ballots.

If he called for another election, Schmidt would accuse them of tampering with the results of an internal election. An international incident caused by such an outcry would be far worse for the Germans in Crystal City than anything else. O'Rourke had only circumstantial evidence of tampering anyway. But he couldn't declare Schmidt the winner. He did nothing, and the camp waited for days for an official report. None came.

Schmidt claimed his victory. "You won't certify election results you don't like, so you do nothing," he accused O'Rourke in his office. "Doesn't that make you a coward?"

O'Rourke sat at his desk, looking him in the eye until Schmidt left with a jeering laugh.

Schmidt asked Müller to pen an open letter for *Das Lager*. Schmidt handed the newsletter to every shop owner and hung it in every storefront where Germans congregated. Karl brought his copy home and read it to Marta.

She kneaded a roll of bread dough as she listened, flour scattered across the kitchen table.

> To All Loyal Germans:
>
> Traitors and collaborators are among us, and they work to divide and conquer us. They are agitators who wish to weaken our resolve. Our enemies must not be allowed to sow division among us.
>
> We call upon all Germans to be loyal to each other and to your fatherland. Be diligent to live up to the lofty ideals Germany is fighting for. As we work together, we can keep our community strong.
>
> Heinz Schmidt
> Spokesman of German Prisoners

Marta pounded her fist into her bread dough. "How did they get away with this? It doesn't make sense."

"I guess O'Rourke is simply no match for these Nazis," Karl replied.

"I'm not so sure it's O'Rourke. He is bound by the rules set by the Geneva Convention, but Schmidt can use the rules against him to get what he wants."

"How so?" Karl asked.

"O'Rourke has to answer to the Swiss about every single complaint, whether it's a lie or not. It keeps him preoccupied while Schmidt is free to do as he pleases. He can lie. Make up stories. Make threats. It's all part of the game. Müller started it and Schmidt has perfected it."

The next day, as Karl and Marta walked to the store, a friend of hers started to lift her hand in a wave, then drew back and turned away.

"Wasn't that Wilhelmine Gunther?" Marta asked.

"It looked like her," Karl yawned.

"Why didn't she say hello?" Marta asked with a little indignation.

"Maybe she didn't see you."

"Maybe." She tilted her head to the side.

A moment later, another friend turned away as they passed.

"Something is going on," Marta said, glancing around. "I just saw Gretyl Weitz duck into the butcher shop when she saw us."

"Are you sure?" Karl didn't want to believe Marta, but he sensed it too. When she spotted her friend Frida Hubert walking her way, she called out. "Frida. Do you know what's going on? What's the matter with everyone?"

Frida looked over her shoulder with a furtive glance. She put her hand by her mouth and spoke in a hushed voice. "Come over here for a minute so we're away from prying eyes." They stepped cautiously behind a building and she blurted. "I'm sorry Marta, but you both have a target on your backs. If we're seen talking to you or helping you, we will also become targets of Schmidt's henchmen."

"Why?" Marta cried.

"Schmidt has threatened retaliation against anyone who helps collaborators. If we help you, we will lose our jobs."

"They called us collaborators?"

"We all have to be very careful." With an apologetic look, she dashed away.

Karl spent much of the day trying to gather more information about their predicament. That night at dinner, he reported, "The people they consider traitors won't be able to purchase food at the store or eat in the cafeteria. We can't go to the barbershop, the butcher shop, or participate in any community events—that includes the sewing room for you. Anyone who helps us will also be labeled as a collaborator and will be treated as such."

"How are they going to follow through with this threat?" Marta said. "I'm not buying it. They don't have that much power."

"You don't think they can stop us from buying food at the store?"

"Not without a guard finding out or O'Rourke," she argued. "I just think it's another one of their empty threats."

"For safety's sake," Karl replied, "let's please keep a low profile."

"I'm not going to cower to those thugs and neither should you."

"Marta, it's dangerous." Karl reached for her hand. "Just do it for me?"

Marta turned her head away.

The next day as Marta walked across the compound, one of Schmidt's friends stepped in her path.

"Heil Hitler," he said, giving the Nazi salute.

Marta went around him.

"Heil Hitler!" his loud voice declared again. The man darted in front of her again and planted his feet.

She stopped.

"It is polite to salute and say 'Heil Hitler' in return, Frau Meyer. Aren't you going to be polite?"

As she tried to walk around him, the man stepped in front of her again, forcing her to stop and side-step around him. He laughed and again stepped in front of her, but she continued to step around him. Her face turned red as she stepped around him again.

He laughed and grabbed her upper arm. "Why are you being rude, Frau Meyer? Maybe you think you can be rude because you have the protection of the camp director?"

Marta pulled against his hold, but he gripped her arm tighter.

"Maybe it's because you want to be the spokesman."

He let her go with a shove and she stumbled, but found her footing and walked away. "Or maybe it's because you want to be an 'imitation dictator.'" The words flew from his mouth intending to cut deep.

Marta stopped short. He grabbed her again and pushed her against the side of a building, pinning her arms behind her. He moved in close, his face inches from hers, and spoke into her ear.

"So, you want to be an imitation dictator, do you?" She could hear the sneer in his voice. "You are not a very good spy. Your eyes betray you."

Marta's heart raced and she swallowed hard, fighting back tears. Shadows of passers-by floated on the wall, and she wanted to see, to know who to call out to. She couldn't move her head.

"You must listen to me, Mrs. Marta Hildebrandt Meyer. We know you were born in Bremen, lived in Hannover for a time, and moved back to Bremen before you joined the Mormon Church and came to America," he accused derisively. "There's a lot more we know about you; you cannot hide from us. Will you deny that you wrote a letter to the Immigration and Naturalization Service and are collaborating with the Americans?"

Marta shuddered at his touch. How did he know so much about her? Onlookers had stopped to see the confrontation. Distracted by the crowd, the man released his grip somewhat.

Marta pushed against the building, shoving her assailant away. "You are a spineless coward. You can easily stand there and threaten a hundred-pound woman, but when it comes to having any courage to stand for what's right and truthful, you skulk away. You don't know or care about what's right or what's wrong, do you? You have no principles, so you do the only thing you know…"

He cackled. "That's all you have for me, a lecture on morality? You are no match for us. You will not only regret insulting me, but you will also regret betraying your fellow Germans. Soon you will see how real Germans behave once they know you are the traitor." He stepped aside and let her pass by him.

Marta walked away, trembling. She went home to Karl, only regaining some sense of safety after she sat behind her locked door. After a few hours at home, she calmed down, mustering enough courage to visit the butcher shop to get sausages for dinner.

She waited her turn in line. "Hi, Otto, may I have two links of bratwurst?"

Otto looked at her with dread in his eyes. He didn't reply.

"They threatened you, didn't they, Otto?"

Otto glanced over his shoulder, his gaze running over the street, then gave a slight nod of his head, up and down.

"And," Marta dipped her head, inviting him to reply. "You cannot sell me anything. Is that what you were told?"

He nodded.

"And you would really appreciate it if I would leave and not come back?" she stated with sadness in her voice.

Otto couldn't hold his silence any longer and whispered, "I'm so sorry Marta, but they will turn on me. I will lose my job, and they will not let me work anywhere else."

"It's okay, Otto. I'm sorry to put you in this position," she said. "I will go now."

She slipped past two other customers, who looked through her as if she wasn't there.

At the grocery store, friends recognized her but averted their eyes until she passed, then a symphony of whispers echoed as she left.

At the sewing room, Marta walked in, only to see others stepping outside, like water around an island, isolating her from everyone else.

When Marta returned to her cottage, her sad eyes met Karl's. "I'm sorry. I totally underestimated them," she admitted. "I know you warned me, but I didn't think they were capable of this."

Karl listened to the desperation in her voice, wishing he hadn't been right.

"What happens when we run out of food, Karl? What are we going to do?" She hid her face in her hands in desperation. "And what will they do to us if they see us report this to O'Rourke?"

Karl put his hand on her shoulder trying to comfort her. "We may have no choice but to report it, but let's see how it goes with getting our friends to help us first."

"And what if that fails? What next?" Marta appeared defeated, then stood to look in her cupboard to see what few ingredients she had to make dinner.

Later that evening, Karl left their cottage to meet a friend who had agreed to smuggle food out of the cafeteria. At breakfast the next morning, Karl hid between two cottages, watching for his friend to appear from the dining hall. His eyes widened with relief as the man appeared, his hands in his coat pockets.

"Here are some potatoes and a couple sausages. I hope this helps you and Marta." With sympathy in his voice, the man handed Karl two napkins full of food.

"I can't thank you enough." Karl stuffed the food in a coat pocket.

The next day, two of Schmidt's guards were posted at the cafeteria doors. They waved at Karl with a malevolent smile. He walked home empty-handed.

Karl and Marta were already thin after a year of poor nutrition. After the second day without as much as a morsel of food, Marta told Karl she would go to get help from a Japanese friend.

"I'm going over to Mrs. Tamaguchi's place," she announced in a raspy voice.

"Do I know her?" Karl asked.

"We met at the pool a while back," Marta explained. "We talked for a while, and she has invited us over for dinner, but I've just never had the sense to go. I owe it to you to find a solution since I put us in this situation."

"You don't owe me anything, and you didn't put us in this situation. You are not responsible for what others do." Karl patted her hand.

"If I hadn't been so convinced we could stand up to these thugs, we wouldn't be starving now." She hung her head, trying not to cry.

"My dear, I'm going stay with you. I'm not going to let you go anywhere without me."

After sitting for a while to gain her composure, she looked up at Karl. "I'll be okay. It's not that far."

"I will not let you go out alone, not in the dark, and not without someone to lean on."

They walked slowly, hunched over each other, venturing toward the Japanese camp in the quiet and dimmed streets. Few people roamed about at this dark hour.

A car rumbled toward them. It was O'Rourke in his Studebaker on his nightly round. The car beamed its headlights on them, casting their shadows long and thin before them. Marta jumped out of the way, but the sudden movement sent her stumbling. Karl reached out, but she collapsed to the ground.

"Marta," he cried.

O'Rourke slammed on his brakes and jumped from his car to help her. "What happened?" he asked.

"I think she fainted. She hasn't eaten in a few days," Karl said, his mouth as dry as chalk and his voice raspy.

"A few days?" O'Rourke cried. "You don't look so well yourself, Karl. Why in heaven's name haven't you eaten?" he asked.

Karl knelt next to Marta, cradling her head in his lap. He answered quietly, "We are being punished."

O'Rourke cocked his head in frustration. "I'll have to deal with that later, but let's get her to the hospital. Can you help me get her into my car?"

Karl lifted under Marta's arms, and O'Rourke lifted her feet. They set her down with care into the back seat.

At the hospital, the Japanese doctor rushed to help her. He checked her eyes to see if Marta's pupils would dilate; they were slow to respond to the light. Pinching the skin on the back of her hand, he released it to see if the folded skin would return to its original position. When it didn't, he knew she was dehydrated. He pumped a blood pressure cuff on her bony arm, then pressed a stethoscope to her chest. Frowning at not hearing much, he moved it again to another spot. A look of alarm crossed his face and he shouted to the nurse, "Get an IV going now! I can't get her blood pressure!"

Chapter 40-Note 1: The overall events and circumstances in this chapter are based on historical reports gleaned from multiple sources. The historical narrative written by camp director James O'Rourke explained the untenable environment created by our characters Horst Müller and Heinz Schmidt (The real names were Karl Kolb and Heinrich Hasenburger, respectively). O'Rourke wrote: "(Kolb's) theory was that of a strict dictatorship, with not only every internee subject to his whims and fancies, but every action of (this) administration (was) subject to his approval. Life was soon miserable for most of the Germans in this camp."

Historical Narrative of the Crystal City Internment Camp, Written by J.L. O'Rourke, September 9, 1945. Source: Record Group No. 85, Immigration and Naturalization Service Crystal City Internment Camp, File 217/021, pp 14-15.

CHAPTER 41

January 23, 1944
RAF Thurleigh, Bedfordshire, England

Hank and his crew reported for breakfast at the usual time of 0430. Their first mission briefing started promptly at 0530. The squadron intelligence commander, Major Bairnsfather, called the crews to attention.

"Today's mission is to Kiel."

A few of the experienced men grumbled. The 306th had completed several missions to Kiel in the past year. It was a frequent target of both British nighttime and American daylight bombing missions. Since the war began, it had already been bombed more than fifty times.

"For the new crews who may not be aware, Kiel is located on the Baltic." He pointed to a spot on the map of Germany hanging on the wall behind him.

"It's home to Germany's U-boat submarine force, or as we call it, the 'Wolf Pack.' Typically it is among the most defended targets we encounter, with flak installations all along the way."

Several pilots nodded their heads. Everyone despised flak.

"We've inflicted major damage on Kiel in past missions. Unfortunately, as soon as we destroy their shipyards and submarine pens, the Germans are right back the next day, rebuilding them."

The major explained their plan for assembling the formation.

"Your path will take you to this point, almost to Hamburg, before making a new heading northwest toward Kiel. The initial point—IP—is here and, as usual, your navigation equipment will take over from there." Major Bairnsfather pointed to a location twenty miles southeast of Kiel. "You'll make a ninety degree turn here and set up for your bomb run."

Captain Sterner, Connors, and Harris were busy taking notes, scribbling down everything the major said.

"We anticipate that, flying at twenty-four thousand feet, you will arrive at the IP at 1230 hours, and the target at 1235 hours. You should arrive back at base by 1530 hours."

The crew spent the next hour or so making preparations, checking fuel, and testing equipment. The bombs were installed, and Hank helped make sure they were secured. Sterner started the engines and pulled the B-17 into his station at five minutes after eight. They taxied into position just as they were instructed at 0815 and took off on schedule at 0825.

After a successful takeoff and rendezvous with the main group, they spent several long hours trying to remain warm as they passed the time until their first turn toward the IP. Hank's stomach churned with anxiety. Sitting in silence with his oxygen mask secured to his face, he folded his arms against his chest and listened to the captain give instructions over the inter-phone. He tried to appear relaxed, lowering his shoulders, but the cold would tense him up every few seconds, and the knot in his stomach wouldn't go away.

When they approached the first turn, flak bursts boomed outside the plane. Puffs of black smoke dotted the sky. Fortunately, most of the flak was too far away to do any damage. Hank heard the slap of shrapnel hitting the plane. "Good thing those flak guns aren't any closer," he stated as he looked at Montoya. "Let's hope we don't get much of it going back."

"You just keep prayin' for all of us, okay Meyer?" Montoya smiled at Hank. Since they met at training in Pyote, Montoya had teased Hank whenever he said a prayer or left the light on in his bunk to read his Bible or *Book of Mormon*. Today, Montoya didn't tease at all.

Hank looked out his window and saw a handful of P-51s flying below them.

"See those Mustangs out there?" Hank said, smiling as he scanned the air in every direction. "Look at 'em. Aren't they a sight?"

Although the flak bursts were getting closer, only small fragments had hit their plane so far. The flight was going just as planned as they approached their target.

"IP just ahead," Harris called over the inter-phone. Hank took a deep breath.

After reaching the IP, Sterner could not take any evasive action. When the flak was thick, sometimes an aircraft would be shot up and burst into a ball of flames. They held their breath, suspended in the sky for three minutes while their secret Norden navigation equipment flew the plane.

Finally, Connors called out, "Bombs away! All bombs have jettisoned and cleared the airplane!"

Sterner grabbed the control stick and made a sharp forty-five degree turn to his left. Everyone grabbed something to hang onto as the plane dipped sideways.

On Montoya's side, flak hit the fuselage and wings. The patter grew louder as they approached the coastline.

"Captain," Woody called over the inter-phone, "I'm not sure, but I think engine number four is leaking oil."

Just then, they crossed the coastline and were flying over the water.

"Do you hear that?" Hank asked Montoya.

"Hear what?" he said

"The silence. No more flak. It's gone."

Montoya tilted his head to listen for any indication of more flak. He looked out his window and noticed the German coast land getting smaller.

"Now, let's hope we can avoid any fighter attacks."

Just before they passed over the tiny island of Gröde, Harris called over the inter-phone, "I'm losing oil pressure in number four engine."

Sterner looked out. Oil sprayed from the engine, but somehow it hadn't caught fire. "I'm feathering engine number four," Sterner called to Connors, the engineer. "Make adjustments to our power and try to keep us up with the main formation."

Sterner watched as the propeller blades were angled into the airstream and locked in place, hoping to reduce drag, but it wasn't enough.

"We're losing speed, Captain," Connors called. "We can't keep up with the formation."

Hank's stomach sank as the safety of the main formation slipped away.

Howie screamed over the inter-phone, "Bogey at six o'clock... about a thousand yards out."

"Keep your voice down on the inter-phone," Sterner reminded. "Stay calm and tell me what it is."

"I don't know. What *is* that?" Woody looked out with real curiosity.

"I don't know either. It's too big to be a *Messerschmidt*."

The crewman strained to get a better look, but the large German plane seemed out of place for an attack plane.

"Doesn't it look like a Junkers 88?" Montoya said.

"It sure does," Woody said. "It's a Ju88 dive bomber."

Woody adjusted his goggles to make sure he wasn't mistaken.

"Does that bomber really think he's going to attack us?" Howie asked with bated breath. Sterner looked over his shoulder to keep an eye on the attacking plane.

"He's coming around to attack," Woody called out.

Hank readjusted his headset and cocked his .50 caliber rifle.

From the ball turret, Barsauskas called out, "He's coming up from six o'clock!"

The Ju88 fired its guns at their crippled B-17.

Sterner called out to his co-pilot, "I'm headed down to that bank of clouds below us. Hold on!"

Hank felt the pull as the plane seemed to drop from the sky. Within seconds all the gunner crew were clinging to whatever they could grab to avoid being thrown to the floor.

The Junkers struggled to catch up, it was too slow. Sterner kept dropping, then settled in at four thousand feet. Miles of clouds draped them in a protective cover.

After a few tense moments, Howie took a deep breath and reported, "I think we lost him. I don't see him anywhere."

"Me either," Hank called.

"No sign of him from my side," Montoya said.

"Barsauskas?" Sterner asked. "Can you see anything from the bottom turret?"

"Nothing, Captain. I can't tell if he's in here looking for us or not."

"Keep an eye out."

After more than fifteen minutes with no sign of the Junkers, Sterner called out, "I'm going to head for the deck and see if we can't make it home below their radar." He nosed the plane downward, heading for a break in the clouds. Although he risked being spotted by an enemy plane, he needed to see the ocean to help them navigate their way home. They flew just twenty feet above the water. Sterner picked up a navigation signal from England and was able to fix his position and direction.

"Holy moly!" Woody said, "Will you look at all those ships!"

A convoy of unescorted merchant ships bobbed on the water below them. Hank felt Sterner lift the plane to a thousand feet to get a better view of the amazing scene below.

"There must be thirty ships there. Boy, what a submarine captain would do with all those ships in a nice, tidy, little row," Woody said.

They passed over the convoy, flying a safe distance away.

The Ju88 dropped from the clouds and unloaded a barrage of rounds but missed *Plano's Pride*. The German plane made a steep dive and sped past the B-17, drifting by to the right.

The Ju88 again slowed and set up its attack from two o'clock. Sterner increased his power and made a sharp turn into the attack trajectory of the '88. As hard as the German dive-bomber tried to get off another shot, it couldn't get its guns aligned to shoot at *Plano's Pride*.

"He can't get a shot off, Captain! Nice move," Woody added over the inter-phone.

"That was an amazing bit of flying, there, Skipper," Howie said.

Sterner's quick evasive maneuver exposed the Ju88 to the full, concentrated fire of Connors, Woody, and Montoya. They unloaded a barrage of .50 caliber bullets into it as it passed.

"I think I hit him," Montoya said, "but I'm not sure."

"He's coming around again," Howie said. "Yeah, it looks like you got him. One of his engines is smoking."

Sterner pulled hard and again swung their aircraft inside of the '88's flightpath, keeping the B-17's dead engine on the inside of the turn.

"He's still trying to get a bead on us," Hank said.

"Keep it up, Captain, you're keeping him on his toes."

Sterner dipped his wing to the right, and the B-17 still had enough power to make a hard, tight turn. The '88 couldn't bring its guns to bear and again was exposed to the gunners on the left side. Each man let loose a burst of bullets, hitting the '88 on its wings, engines, and fuselage. Now both of its engines bellowed smoke. The aircraft pulled up and began to limp away. Just before it disappeared into the clouds, the '88 fired two bright red and yellow flares—a distress signal to the convoy of ships below.

"That was quite a display of piloting there, Skipper," Harris said.

"Captain, that was amazing," Connors replied. "Just amazing."

Sterner pointed his crippled aircraft back down to the deck, lowering it back to just twenty feet above the water.

After two hours, *Plano's Pride* limped across the North Sea, finally arriving at RAF Thurleigh a full hour later than the main formation. Sterner had brought his crew and aircraft back home safely, with battle damage to the fuselage and flak damage to the engine.

"I think it's a miracle we survived," Hank announced boldly to his fellow crewmen. "I don't think any pilot, no matter how good he was, could have survived that encounter, especially on his first combat mission, without a little help from the man upstairs." A few of the crew nodded, but no one else replied.

As Hank inspected the plane after landing, hundreds of bullet holes scarred the outside of *Plano's Pride*. He knew they would be out of commission until the repairs were made. How long that would take was the biggest question.

Chapter 41- Note 1: This true account of a B-17 pilot outmaneuvering a Junkers 88 can be found in the 306th Bomb Group Mission Reports, Thurleigh, England, 13 December 1943. The report states:

"B-17 #782 fell out of formation due to engine trouble, and lost altitude to 13,000 feet, a Ju88 flew 3,000 feet below it, climbed to its altitude and attacked from 7 o'clock. The B-17 at once headed for the deck and its bad engine caught fire. With the enemy plane on its tail, it managed to get into clouds at 4,000 feet, continuing down until only twenty feet from the water near Amrum Island. Here the fire went out. Then the Ju88 jumped it again and attacked from the tail. Pulling around to the right and preparing to make another attack from 1 or 2 o'clock. Our pilot turned sharply into the attack, thus preventing the enemy fighter from bringing its guns to bear and compelling it to turn away from our plane. It then turned left and across our nose, when the bombardier and top-turret gunner each fired bursts and saw tracers going into him. The Ju88 then turned left again, going down our left side and in the opposite direction with engines smoking. The left waist gunner got in a good burst, then, as both engines burst into flames, two series of red-yellow flares were seen to come from the enemy fighter, and it then disappeared into the haze, only forty feet off the water. We claim this Ju88 destroyed (and is) the only claim on this mission."

Headquarters 306th Bombardment Group (H), Intelligence Report 13 Dec 1943, Major John A. Bairnsfather; Declassified per executive order 12356, Jan 8, 1991, pg 9

CHAPTER 42

February 3, 1944
RAF Thurleigh, Bedfordshire, England

Plano's Pride was repaired, and the crew completed two missions deep inside France and Germany. Each time they came home after a successful mission, Hank stepped out, drew a shaky breath, smiled, and gave the plane's bullet-riddled fuselage a firm pat.

As he sat for their morning briefing at 0445 hours, Hank let out an exhausted yawn and stretched his arms high in the air. Murmurs of sleepy conversation twisted throughout the room as more men found their seats. Major Bairnsfather entered, and they snapped to attention.

"At ease," he called. "Gentlemen, today's mission will not be a milk run."

A few men slumped their shoulders just the slightest, holding back disappointed sighs. The more milk runs, the faster they reached the magic number of twenty-five missions.

"The primary target will be Hannover," Bairnsfather said.

Hannover! A tremor shot through Hank.

He'd dreaded this moment, but hearing the name spoken aloud was still different. He couldn't remember much of Hannover; the trip they made that summer during his childhood was clouded by so many other memories. The name evoked images of riding the train there from Bremen with his *Oma* and *Opa*, seeing the opera house, and basking in the warm summer afternoons. But now Hannover was not just a town his *Oma* once called home for a few years. It was a mission—a target with a strategic manufacturing center, oil production facilities, and a railroad junction. He saw it all in his head, homes and people, soon to be lying mangled on the ground, burning from destructive forces he his crew had risked their lives to deliver.

Beside him, Montoya kept turning his head to look at Hank. Hank kept his eyes forward, waiting for the briefing to continue.

"If the weather won't cooperate, the secondary target will be the sub pens in Bremen."

Hank's heart stopped. He took a deep breath, but couldn't stop blinking, as his mind raced with an endless number of horrible scenarios.

"What's wrong with you, Hank?" Montoya whispered. "You look like you're going to puke."

Hank sat up in his chair and took another deep breath. "Nothing," he spat. "Leave me alone."

Hearing their whispers, Major Bairnsfather gave Hank and Montoya the evil eye. They quieted and he continued.

"We have a total of nineteen aircraft from the 306th Bomb Group. With the other bomb groups joining ours, we'll have a total of thirty-four aircraft."

Hank stood, deep in thought, his mind a million memories away. He left the briefing room praying over and over in his mind for bad weather to scrub this mission.

A few hours later, the drone of airplane engines buzzed over the North Sea. Hank watched the water below disappear under the soupy cloud cover. He pressed the inter-phone to his ear, focused on hearing any news about the weather. A faint, fearful voice in his head was telling him he would go to Bremen. He didn't want to believe it, but as the rest of the planes in the bomb group disappeared into the thick clouds, the whispers grew louder.

"Captain, it's looking pretty overcast at Hannover," Navigator Donny reported. "We'll see as we get closer."

"Roger. It's not looking good for our primary target, Donny. Can you make sure we're ready to head to our secondary target if needed?"

"Sure thing, Captain," Donny replied.

They drew nearer to Hannover, and it was clear the town was concealed in clouds, protected by horrible weather. As they approached Hannover, bursts of flak pummeled their B-17, sometimes a bright flash bursting through the dimness. Some of the lead planes were forced to drop out of the formation.

"They've called off Hannover. We're confirmed for the secondary target," Sterner called over the inter-phone.

Hank's stomach dropped. The plane dipped as it changed course for Bremen.

His mind raced in a continuous prayer for his *Oma*'s safety. If only there was a way to get word to her, to warn her. He contemplated the many scenarios of what would happen to him if he warned her, but he could not. Her safety occupied his thoughts until he heard the words: "Bombs away!"

Connor's abrupt command sent a shudder through Hank's body, bringing him back from his unsettled thoughts. They were already here. The bombs wobbled as they cleared the bomb bay doors. The plane's payload of twelve five-hundred-pound bombs vanished from sight. Moments later, Hank flinched as bright flashes revealed the bombs had struck the ground.

On other missions, Hank had learned to compartmentalize the reality of what he and his crew did. Today, his bombs fell on historic structures, landmarks, and people. He was keenly aware that these were real places and real people. These people called Bremen home, and the structures he was helping destroy would never be the same. For the first time, he felt complicit in an unseemly deed of dishonor. His hands were stained with the destruction of irreplaceable historic landmarks and countless lives.

"Two Me101s at five-thirty! They're coming straight for us!" Howie called out from his tail gunner position. The ball turret guns unleashed a barrage of .50 caliber bullets, hitting one enemy plane's right wing. Smoke billowed from the engine and it dipped away to hide in the clouds.

The second plane banked to the left side of their plane. Only Hank was in position to get a shot off. In spurts of three, he let fly a salvo of bullets. But it wasn't enough. The Me101 fired a rocket, and Hank felt helpless as its explosion rocked the underbelly of their plane.

Instinctively wincing, he looked out to inspect the damage. His eyes widened as he noticed a slight crack appear between the wing and fuselage. Or maybe it wasn't a crack. He couldn't be sure, but he couldn't leave his position to assess the damage, so he waited for Barsauskas to give a report. But Barsauskas was silent.

The Me101 began its turn to make another pass. The pilot unloaded a barrage of bullets at *Plano's Pride*, ripping into the left wing. Hank followed its path, angling his gun, but he wasn't in position to fire.

Then more bullets slammed through the fuselage. Montoya screamed, grabbing his leg in pain and falling to the floor.

Hank looked at him in horror.

"I'm coming," he shouted as he let go of his gun and jumped to Montoya's aid. He knelt next to Montoya to inspect his wound. The bullet had ripped away half of his calf, pulsating crimson blood oozed from the dangling flesh. Hank cringed as Montoya gasped through his teeth.

"Hold on," Hank said. "Let me see if I can stop the bleeding." Hank removed a dressing from a pocket and fumbled as he unwrapped it. He pushed the dressing hard onto the open wound, Montoya screamed in anguish. Hank covered the wound tightly, just below the knee, pulling tightly to create a tourniquet. Montoya fell unconscious.

Bullets ripped into the fuselage again. Hank dashed back to his waist gun, donned his headgear, and scanned the horizon, hoping to get a shot off at the enemy plane.

Montoya started to stir. Hank glanced at him but had to leave him alone.

"Damage report!" Sterner demanded on the inter-phone, "Barsauskas, can you see what happened?"

Barsauskas didn't answer. Hank replied, "That rocket burst right next to him, Captain. Maybe he's hurt."

"Montoya, check on Al," Sterner said.

"Montoya was hit too, sir, in the leg. It looks bad," Hank said. "Woody, can you see anything from up there?"

"It looks like the tank under the wing may be on fire. Number two is smoking but I can't see anything else from up here," Woody replied. "There may be a crack on the seam where the wing attaches to the fuselage, but I can't tell for sure."

Hank jumped to the right side of the aircraft and looked out the right waist gunner's window. "The whole panel is missing on both engines, Captain," Hank said. "Wait," he paused, "I can see it, sir! There's definitely a crack in the fuselage!"

Sterner didn't hesitate. "Prepare to abandon ship!" He flipped a switch for the alarm bell, and it gave out three short rings. He reduced airspeed and switched on the autopilot.

"Woody, send a distress signal from our exact position. Harris, call out the coordinates while Donny calculates our position."

"Fifty-two point eight-nine degrees north," he paused, "and eight-point four-two minutes east."

"Got it," Woody replied as he wrote them down.

"We're almost to Wildehausen."

Woody sent a distress signal using Donny's coordinates. He also sent a radio message stating they were about to ditch the plane near the city of Wildehausen, heading west toward Sögel.

Sterner flipped the switch on the pre-jump alarm bell with a long, annoying ring. The crew prepared to abandon ship.

"That crack is getting bigger," Woody called out. "It's not gonna hold much longer!"

Sterner announced, "Stand by to abandon ship!"

Montoya winced as he sat up, in pain as he reached for his parachute. Hank rushed to help him get it cinched up, but the blood on Hank's hand made the clasp slippery. He struggled to cinch it closed.

"Come on," Hank grunted. He heard the bell ring for half a second, then die out. "Was that the abandon ship order?" he asked. Nobody answered. Hank looked at Montoya as he tried to fasten the clasp.

"It's not gonna work," Montoya shouted in frustration. "Just go."

"I've almost got it," Hank said. With a loud exhale he secured Montoya's straps. "There. Now let's get you over to the door."

Hank lifted Montoya under his armpits, dragging him to the rear exit door, fighting to open it. As the door burst open, it ripped away and fell earthward. Cool air rushed in and filled the rear of the plane.

"Can you get out or do you need help?" Hank asked.

"I'm not going without you and Howie," Montoya said.

"I need to wait for the Captain's signal," Hank replied.

"I'm not waiting. Let's go now," Montoya shouted at Howie.

Howie gave a thumbs-up signal and rechecked his parachute to make sure he was cinched in tight.

Hank looked for the bail-out light to glow, but it remained dark.

"What's taking them so long?" Howie asked. "That wing is starting to go. We need to bail out now, or we'll never make it."

Howie found Montoya's pull-string and placed it in his hand. "Don't forget to wait a minute or so before you pull it."

"Ready? Go!" Hank shouted, and Montoya dropped from the plane. Howie followed seconds later, jumping headfirst. Hank strained to see their chutes, but with the clouds, he couldn't tell whether they had opened.

Hank exhaled as he waited for the captain to illuminate the bailout light. Losing patience, he stepped sideways so his broad shoulders could fit through the narrow passageway, dashing along the small ledge adjacent to the bomb bay.

"What's taking so long?" Hank complained aloud.

A quick glance at the empty cockpit revealed he was the last man out. Rushing back to his waist gun he glanced into the ball turret. Blood spattered the Plexiglas. He looked away, not wanting to see what was left of Barsauskas.

Hank was startled by a screeching sound that echoed through the plane. He sensed it was the wing being ripped away from the fuselage, the clamor of metal-on-metal screaming in protest. The plane's forward momentum decelerated, plunging to the right. Hank slammed to the floor. His head struck a sharp edge of the bulkhead, and the pain shot throughout his body. In a daze, he lifted his hand to his eyebrow and felt blood dripping into his eye.

The plane nosed downward into a slow spin. Rivets shrieked as the aircraft began to rip apart from the force of the slipstream. Hank sat several feet from the escape hatch, but the centrifugal force had pinned him to the floor. As the rate of spin increased, he was unable to inch his way closer to the gaping escape hatch now taunting him to bail out. Turbulence pummeled the hapless plane, rocking it back and forth as its downward spiral accelerated.

Hank gasped, aching to draw in a full breath. It felt like a horse was sitting on his chest, pinning him in this awkward position. As the plane continued spinning faster, the blood left his head and his vision narrowed. The sunlight grew blurry. A dark, hazy tunnel appeared before his eyes and moving images of his life flashed before him.

He saw images of his mama, papa, and Ella, at home enjoying a traditional German dinner. He saw himself as an eleven-year-old with his *Oma* Hildebrandt making bread during his visit to Germany. A new scene showed his school, teachers, friends, baseball games. Then he saw himself hauling hay and milking the cow. The images were in a tidy chronology, alternating one by one. Then the images stopped on Billie. Why Billie? He noticed her wry smile as she taunted him without mercy, her blonde hair pulled up in a bun to reveal her powerful yet elegant shoulders. Without warning, the newsreel in his mind ended; his consciousness dissolved to black.

The tunnel of darkness lifted. After a second that seemed like an hour, a brilliant light seemed to sear Hank's eyes. As he came to his senses, he recognized the light was the sun overhead. Harsh, cold air bit at his hands and nose. His face grew numb in the icy air. Why was he so cold? And why did the sun glare at him with such intensity?

As he squinted to get a better look, a piece of fuselage passed over him, its silhouette obscuring the sunlight. A flash of recognition hit him. That was *his* B-17. The frigid air at ten thousand feet was painful, yet he watched, horrified as his plane was disintegrating a quarter mile or so above him, pieces of it were being torn apart bit by bit. Somehow, Hank had been ejected, but the G-forces prolonged his blackout. His foggy mind fought to think straight. He gazed down again, now wide-eyed as the ground rushed toward him at a million miles a minute. He reached to find the ripcord of his parachute but remembered he must wait for the right moment. He had already free-fallen thousands of feet, and he was less of a target if he waited until the last possible moment. With each second, he recognized his life-or-death predicament.

The whooshing of air was deafening. The ground was hurtling ever faster toward him. Hundreds of feet from the ground, something, someone, grasped the ripcord and pulled. A loud crash roared above him as his gleaming white parachute burst open. The force of the chute's straps gouged under his arms. It felt like they were being ripped from their sockets.

Now swinging beneath his parachute, Hank looked over his shoulder, then back again in all directions, assessing the German countryside below him. A January thaw had melted the snow, revealing patches of dark brown forest. A stiff wind carried him in the opposite direction of what was left of the airplane. Hank noticed no paved roads, only a few narrow dirt trails used by local farmers.

He must find cover fast. A downed American bomber and crew was sure to draw attention from all directions. Less than a hundred feet above the ground, he surveyed the landscape, locating a good place to hide. The roofs of a few farmhouses dotted the landscape, too far away to be an immediate threat. In the opposite direction of the forest, frozen farmland stretched as far as he could see.

The tops of the trees in a thick wooded area drew closer. Hank recited his landing checklist. "Keep my knees bent, chin tucked, elbows tucked, protect my face and throat from the parachute risers."

Coming in fast, his legs clipped a tree, then his body slammed into the unforgiving, frozen landscape. He let out a loud groan. A sharp pain shot through his back and shoulder as he rolled, entangling him in the risers of his parachute. The canopy drifted gracefully into a tree.

Hank stood, his back still stinging. He grasped the cords of his parachute, tugging and yanking, but it remained stuck in the tree's branches, fluttering in the wind like a flag calling to the world. He sat on the ground and unlatched his parachute clasps. Scanning the horizon, he searched everywhere for movement of soldiers or farmers... anyone. As far as he could tell, he was still undetected.

Reaching up, he jumped to the first branch of the tree. With a little effort he lifted himself, climbing several more branches to reach a section of his canopy wedged between two branches. Struggling to balance himself on a limb, Hank tugged on the canopy. It wouldn't budge. He stepped out further, the branch shaking under his weight. He made one final tug, and his foot slipped out from under him. Air rushed past him. As his arms scraped against the tree, his flailing hands reached for something to grab, fumbling for anything to latch on to. With one arm he managed to cling to the webbing from his parachute risers, breaking his fall with a jerk. Hanging ten feet above the forest floor he inhaled quickly, catching his breath. Listening as the rattle of dead leaves calmed to a whisper, a ripping sound above him made him look up. The canopy tore in two and dropped him hard to the ground.

A shot of pain blasted through his ankle. He shouted impulsively, then slapped his hand over his mouth. His voice echoed through the trees, mocking him.

He had to go somewhere, anywhere but here. Still smarting from his twisted ankle, he stood, put his weight gingerly on his ankle, and then limped away the pain. He scurried to gather his canopy and harness and bundled them under his arms, looking around wide-eyed for a place to hide it.

In a space between trees a few yards away, a pile of rocks stood five feet tall. He gathered his parachute and limped over to it. He bent over to inspect it, finding it cold and wet from melted snow. The rocks were stacked together neatly, years of work of stones cleared from a farmer's field.

Feverishly, he grabbed a rock and dropped it off the pile. He looked over his shoulder in both directions, stopping to listen in case anyone was nearby. Hearing nothing, he continued, removing more rocks. A fierce-sounding dog barked in the distance. Hank froze. After that brief second of terror, he exhaled in relief and continued working.

Once the hole looked deep enough, he compressed his parachute and harness, squeezing it into the opening he had created. He placed rock after rock back in the hole, using great care to hide the bright whiteness of the parachute.

After placing the final few rocks onto the pile, Hank inspected it from all angles to see if any white still peeked through. Then he turned and headed deeper into the cover of the forest. With the cloud cover, he couldn't be sure which direction he was headed, but he hurried away, annoyed his ankle was still bothering him.

He hobbled deeper into the forest for half an hour, then stopped to rub his ankle. Finding a clump of underbrush, Hank sat to rest while he figured out where he was.

He pulled a cloth map from the lower leg of his flight-suit pocket. His escape kit contained a detailed rayon map of Germany and France with a darkened line indicating the preferred escape route. The kit also included a most valuable compass, seventeen thousand Reichsmarks and twenty-seven thousand francs, a hard chocolate candy bar, caffeine pills, water purifying pills, and a small hack-saw blade.

After inspecting the map closely, he scanned the forest for a familiar landmark or physical feature that would give him a clue where he was. A powerful rumble echoed through the trees, and he rose to his feet with caution, listening. Hank held his breath to make sure he could identify the source of the noise. After a moment, he recognized it was the sound of a train. Realizing he could see no landmarks or markers from within the depths of this thick forest, he tried to remember the last location Woody called out in the distress call.

"I'm pretty sure it starts with a 'w,' at least I think it did," he whispered to himself.

He looked on his map for cities that started with 'w.'

"It wasn't Winkelsett, and it wasn't Wardenburg," he muttered. He turned the map this way and that, searching for cities until he saw it.

Checking his compass, he tapped the spot with his finger and looked up with recognition.

"Wildehausen, that's it!" he whispered to himself.

But he still had to narrow down his precise location. He calculated their airspeed had been about a hundred-seventy miles per hour. Considering the map, the compass, the landscape, the train tracks and having drifted for several minutes, he realized he was about ten miles east of Wildehausen.

He rubbed his chin and looked around for any other landmarks to confirm his suspicion. The train tracks lay to the east of him and farmlands to the west. He murmured to himself as he scanned the map with his fingers, looking in the spaces between train tracks and open fields. That clump of trees could be his position. *Maybe it was that cluster of woods right there?* The shapes on his map met with familiar images in his mind, and suddenly, his eyes widened, startled with recognition.

He let out a brief shout of delight, then stopped himself. His mouth gaped open with exhilaration and he whispered to himself, "I'm only about twenty miles from my *Oma*'s house."

His mind raced through the new possibilities.

"Maybe I could stay with her?" he gave a slight head nod. *"Maybe she would hide me for the duration of the war?"*

His eyes grew wide with the possibilities. *"Maybe she would contact the resistance and help me escape back to England?"*

He looked at his map again to solve his most immediate problem; he needed to be in constant motion. He knew someone must be looking for him. With his ability to speak the language, he had a better shot than most to evade capture. But he had to find a place to disappear until long after dark.

He ran through the shallow creek to hide his scent from search dogs certain to be looking for him. Stopping at times to catch his breath, he continued to push eastward toward his *Oma*'s house, not knowing how far he still had to go.

Hank often pulled out his map to make sure he was taking the best route to remain concealed during the overcast day. The trees were thick and dense. He could stay hidden in some bushes or a thicket. Should he look for an abandoned building or maybe hide in a canal or culvert?

He searched his mind, trying to remember what his *Oma*'s house looked like, trying to recall any nearby landmarks or cities. He had only been eleven years old; it was all such a blur now. She lived at the end of a long dirt road. The only part of her mailing address he remembered was the town of Stuhr.

He found it near the small town of Brinkham, southeast of Bremen. Other memories began coming back. He and his friends would watch the train speeding by, near his *Oma*'s house.

Now that he had an idea of where he was going, he needed to disguise himself. His first thought was to get out of his uniform, or at least find an overcoat or something to change into. He stuffed his map back in the envelope and placed it in the side pocket of his jumpsuit. He stopped and listened for any noises, but the dense forest made it difficult to hear anything beyond a few hundred feet.

He said a quick prayer and weaved his way between the evergreen and leafless deciduous trees. He looked for a canal to hide in but found nothing. After thirty minutes, the rumble of a large truck coming his way grew louder. His heart pounded, and he dove into some nearby bushes, not sure how close he was to the road. The truck passed nearby going about thirty miles per hour, on a paved road heading north.

The engine noise faded away, and Hank looked in all directions before approaching the road.

He walked a few feet, then stopped to listen and repeated that process for several minutes until he could see the clearing and the road. Standing motionless, he retreated into the trees to take another look at his map.

According to his calculations, Hank needed to travel about thirteen kilometers, or about eight miles, before reaching Stuhr. If he walked due east for two kilometers, he should reach the edge of these woods and find the train tracks. He figured he could get there in about an hour.

Hank looked at his wristwatch. It was about three in the afternoon. At this time of year, the sun would set at around five o'clock. He had about two hours to make it to Stuhr. It should all work out if he was fast and didn't make any mistakes.

Taking a deep breath, Hank dashed toward a tree, then dropped to the ground, inching his way forward. Still hidden by underbrush, he noticed a one-lane road. To the south, the noise of many trucks worked their way down the lane toward him. He lay motionless as a convoy of military trucks rounded a corner and passed by him. The Wehrmacht logo marked the driver's side door. German soldiers looked out from under the canopy at the endless rows of trees passing by.

Hank's heart raced. These soldiers could be looking for survivors from his plane. If they stopped to search the woods, he had little hope of avoiding capture. A few moments later, the trucks had passed, unaware of his presence. Hank exhaled, oblivious he had been holding his breath.

He studied the surrounding forest for any more signs of movement along the road. Making sure he could defend himself, he reached for his pistol, then felt his leg for his knife, feeling a sense of comfort in having these defenses; but he wondered whether he could really do it, really kill someone.

He again looked in both directions, hunched forward, muscles taut. Ahead of him, on the other side of the road, were more dense trees as far as he could see. They would give him good cover, at least for now. With silence in both directions, he stepped from the cover of the forest onto the paved road, slowly, quietly, not daring to make the slightest crackle of a twig or rustle of a leaf. He dashed across the road, his sore ankle still dragging his shoe against the pavement. He winced at the pain but didn't stop until he could duck into the foliage on the other side.

Once in the trees, Hank stood upright to catch his breath. Seconds later, he continued moving.

For an hour he hiked, now in a northeasterly direction, weaving between trees and stepping lightly over the forest floor. He stopped at times to check his compass and consult his map, making corrections to his course. Small black dots on his map indicated every house or building, and he traced his path in the spaces between them to avoid any people.

As the sun went down and twilight set in, Hank heard another train coming toward him, but this time he could feel the rumble in his feet as it passed less than half a mile away. The engine chugged toward Bremen.

He got to the tracks just in time to watch the train rush by. The rails glimmered in the light of the train's headlight. The last car disappeared around the bend, smoke trailing behind it. Hank walked parallel to the tracks for about a kilometer, looking for a bridge or anything to give him a launching point from which to leap onto the next moving train.

Two kilometers to the east, his map indicated the tiny town of Kirchseelte, where the road wound through a handful of houses. Hank counted seven. If he decided to walk, he could pilfer something to eat from one of these homes, or find a coat to help him blend in. But if anyone stopped him and questioned him about traveling on foot, he'd need a story. He tried a few words under his breath, in German. The sounds came fluidly but to his own ear he feared an American accent would betray him. Would his accent be discernible?

He walked a little further and still found no bridge or overhanging branch to give him a good jumping place. Instead of walking to Kirchseelte, he wondered if he could cause a train to slow down long enough for him to leap on—but even that carried many risks. Without a foolproof plan, he decided to rest again under a thicket of bushes.

The darkness swallowed him in a blanket of safety, and he nestled in under the cover of the dense leaves. But as he closed his eyes, night scents found their way to him on the breeze—smoke and grease from trains huffing by, earthy forest smells beneath him, even the cold, sharp smell of winter air. He smelled the leather of his shoes and his own scent of his clothes. No dog would have any trouble finding him anywhere he went, unless he kept moving. But he couldn't walk all the way to Kirchseelte without being detected.

The sooner he could catch a train, the better.

He remained close to the tracks, listening for slow trains. Between the passing trains, he counted intervals of forty minutes, although it wasn't regular. The engines chugged away, speeding by the place where he hid as if they knew he was there.

By midnight, hunger gnawed at his stomach. The idea of eating brought to mind the faces of his crew members. Had they found shelter? Food? Were any of them alone, like him? He had to find them, had to bring them all back together.

Words from his training repeated in his head like a sermon from Sunday school: His first priority was to get himself to safety.

As he waited, the cold bit hard on his fingers and toes. Frigid conditions weren't unusual to him after flying at twenty thousand feet in an unheated B-17. Still, he rested fitfully, waking every few minutes to the sound of a tree branch cracking, the wind blowing the leaves, or the rustle of some tiny animal's feet scurrying about on the forest floor.

At last, Hank was almost sound asleep when he was startled awake by another noise, louder and heavier. He lifted his head, craning his neck to listen. Footsteps crunched leaves and twigs as someone ambled their way about the forest. In the darkness of this wooded area, any person walking here at night would likely be using a flashlight. But he scanned the darkness, and no beams of light reflected off the leaves or danced between the shadows. The steps drew closer, inching toward him, drawing closer by the minute. Hank reached for his Colt .45 and prepared to shoot.

The ground rumbled with the familiar sound of another train approaching. It rounded the bend, illuminating the trees around Hank. He lay still, turning to watch the oncoming train. In the bright circle of its headlight stood the silhouette of a large roe deer, foraging just a few feet from Hank's hiding place.

The deafening noise of the train grew louder, the roar of the engine thundering as it approached. The deer grazed slowly, delicately, unfazed. Hank eased himself up a little to see better. Two small nubs for antlers crowned its head. Remembering the times he'd hunted deer with his father in Utah, Hank figured it had to be one or two years old, and it was just fifteen feet or so away. Hank looked down at his pistol. It would be too late for this train, but maybe he could be ready for the next one.

He raised his gun, fixing his aim on the deer's broad shoulders. From the corner of his eye he watched as the train drew closer, wanting to muffle the sound of his gunfire with the roar of the train's engine. Hank drew in a breath to steady himself. Too loud—the deer lifted its slender neck, turning its head, and resting its gaze on Hank. He squeezed the trigger.

The deer stumbled and dropped to the ground.

Hank staggered up in the dark as the light and sound of the train faded. He approached where the deer had fallen, his Colt .45 ready in his hands. He stumbled about for a few minutes, then tripped over something in the darkness and fell hard to the ground.

He rolled to the side and sat up. He fumbled in the darkness, but found the deer's shoulder, then the neck where warm blood oozed from a wound. He wiped his hand off on its fur, but winced as his fingers grew sticky from the blood. He didn't have much time. Latching onto a back leg, He dragged the carcass toward the tracks, breathing heavy under the weight of it—it had to be two hundred pounds—stopping every half minute to catch his breath.

Before he could reach the tracks, he heard another train in the distance. The embankment stretched up before him, still a long way to the top. He clambered up, leaning forward to keep his balance on the steep incline. He lost his footing, and the deer slipped from his hands, still slick and sticky with blood. They both tumbled down the embankment, leaves and dirt sliding with them as they fell to the base of the slope.

Time was running out. If he slipped or fell again, he wouldn't make it up the embankment before the train passed. He knelt down, gripped the legs of the deer, and hoisted it over his shoulders. Hunched forward to keep his balance, he took one firm step after another, his legs burning. Halfway up the slope, he fixed his eyes on the tracks above, the rails just visible in the moonlight. The soft thud of each footstep drew him closer, until at last, he crested the top of the hill. He dropped the deer on the tracks, adjusting it to look like the previous train had hit it. The sound of the train grew louder and louder.

Hank scurried back to safety. He crouched out of sight in some shrubbery, catching his breath. The train should pass him just seconds before the engineer would notice the hazard on the track.

As it sped by, the engines were thundering. Hank wanted to close his eyes, wanted to pray that his plan would work. An eternity passed before the brakes squealed, and the train started to slow. He watched for a door to open on the side of a train car, but nothing appeared. The screech of the wheels grew louder, as if the whole train fought to stop itself before running over the deer. Despite the train slowing down some, it was still moving too fast for Hank to jump aboard. Then the front wheels thumped into the deer carcass, sending a shudder through the train as the engineer slowed slightly to investigate.

Hank sprinted with every ounce of remaining energy, exhaustion weighing him down between every breath. Within a foot or two of a flatbed car, he reached out, straining his arm forward as he ran still faster. A chain dangled from the car, rattling and shaking with the movement of the train. Hank grabbed at the chain until his hands latched onto it. The speed and strength of the train jerked him off balance, jostling him about. He tightened his grip and clenched his teeth.

The train's speed increased with a jolt, yanking Hank's arm. He cried out in pain. The chain started to slip from his hands. Gasping for breath, he lunged himself forward, throwing his elbows and chest onto the bed of the car. Using all the upper-body strength he could muster, he lifted one foot on the bed, but it slipped off. His feet dangled inches from the rushing wheels below. Somehow, he found one last ounce of strength to swing his leg around. It landed right atop the flatbed. For an instant, he stopped to catch his breath before finding the strength to pull the other leg up.

Hank started to roll back away from the edge, but his shoulder blade struck something hard and metal. Lifting his neck, he twisted around to peer into the darkness at the large shape, following its silhouette down to the floor. He knew from the rattle of chains that it was fastened to the bed of the car. He reached out and found thick tank treads. Focused so intently on the ground, he hadn't seen what the flatbed was carrying, but with his first glance upwards, he caught the outline of the tank's long barrel and realized what it was.

He scurried around to crawl under the belly of the tank. The bed of the car vibrated with the movement of the train and, lying still, he could finally feel his racing heartbeat. Hidden under the tank, he peered out at the passing landscape and watched for any landmarks or signs. The train engineer wasted no time to regain full speed.

The light of a train station twinkled in the distance. He knew the track made a sharp right turn after the town of Gross Mackenstedt. He reasoned this would be the best place to jump off to avoid being found.

A few moments later the train made a sharp right turn and passed through Kirchseelte, then it lumbered past the tiny hamlet of Burstel. After ten more minutes, the train approached Gross Mackenstedt, and to Hank's surprise, it started to slow down.

Dread settled in his stomach. Would they be checking for stow-aways? His stomach churned, and he fought the urge to vomit.

The train entered the brightly lit railyard at Gross Mackenstedt, and the hissing wheels lurched to a stop. Hank tucked himself under the tank as far as he could, but with the lights that beamed across the train and into every dark crevice, anyone who so much as glanced under the tank would see him.

As the rumble of the engine and squeal of the brakes died down, the voices of two shouting men filled the silence. The sound seemed to be coming from the front of the train, but Hank couldn't understand what they were saying. From the rear, he heard footsteps in the crushed stone ballast that supported the rails and ties.

Two men approached, walking without any sense of urgency. The beams from their flashlights bounced across the train in rhythm with their footsteps and conversation. They groused about their work and made snide remarks about their boss. If they were looking for a downed American crewman, they didn't seem too determined. Hank pushed that thought out of his mind, held his breath, and listened. They lingered by the bed with the tank, pausing to murmur complaints out of earshot of their boss. Hank could see them from only their waists down, watching as their arms hung by their sides and their flashlight beams dropped toward the ground. After an eternity of griping, one of them finally sighed and turned away. The other followed, passing Hank's hiding place without a second glance.

The train inched its way out of the railyard. When Hank was sure it was out of sight of the switchmen, he poked his head out from under the tank. The train began to pick up speed, and then made the sharp right turn he had been waiting for. He would have to jump now, or he would never make it. Hank crawled to the far edge of the train car. As he rose to his feet, he put his arms out to keep his balance. He inched forward, step by step, watching to place his foot on the coupling between his car and the trailing one. He wobbled, but once he stood with both feet on the coupling, bouncing and jostling with the movement of the train, he crouched low. He scanned the passing countryside to the left of the train, dark and empty of houses or barns. All the muscles in his body tensed, ready to spring. The wind roared passed his face. As the train drew near a patch of grass, he jumped.

The tall grass cushioned his landing, and he let his body roll with the momentum into a thicket of weeds. He waited, motionless, while the train passed, before poking his head up.

Clouds obscured the moon, its faint white glow just visible behind them. It was dark enough. Hank could keep moving without being seen. He stood, the grass rustling with his movements, and brushed dirt and leaves from his clothes. Beside the tracks, several yards away, a road wound through the land like a dark ribbon. This one was broader than the road he'd crossed before. It was a main highway for busy daytime traffic. It was empty and silent now, but even at this time of night he had to be careful. Hank spotted a ditch and crawled into it, hoping its path led underneath the road. The culvert was small, but not so small that he couldn't fit inside and crawl to the other side. He lifted his head to try to see the other end of the culvert across the street, but in the dark, everything blurred together and he couldn't tell whether the other end opened on the opposite side of the road. He lay still for a moment, glancing in both directions. All was silent. He dashed across the street and dove into some bushes.

Rolling over, he yanked his map and compass out of his pocket. Stuhr was northeast of his position. He searched around him, spying here and there for a lonely farmhouse on a distant ridge or hillside.

Nothing remarkable matched anything on his map. He folded it and exhaled with frustration. He had no choice but to trust his map to get him to his *Oma's* house. If it was accurate, she was just a kilometer away.

The temperature was dropping, and Hank realized he needed to find some place to stop for the night. He crawled through the grass alongside the road, until a dark opening in the ground caught his eye. The other end of the culvert lay hidden behind thick weeds. He stood, hunched in a crouch, and dashed over to it. Before jumping, he stopped. A glimmer of water and ice covered the bottom of the ditch, just a few inches deep, but he would regret spending the night in ice and water. Just the thought made his teeth chatter, and already he was rubbing his hands to keep them from getting numb as the night grew colder. He looked around again, and there, a little distance from where the road curved and dipped over a hill, stood a small farmhouse surrounded by trees. Near the house, but still a short distance away, the corner of a second roof stuck out from the trees, its dark angle visible like a sharp blade against the gray shadows of the sky. It had to be a barn or shed. If all was as quiet as it seemed, everyone had turned in for the night. He could hide there until morning.

Hank felt his way through the ditch, crouched over with his hands running alongside the bank beside him. Slowly, he trudged through the muddy ditch, following its length through the field until he came within fifty feet of the barn.

He smelled stale hay in the cold night air. In a corral close to the barn, two horses breathed softly, heads bent in sleep. Hank crawled out of the ditch, and crouching low, he dashed between the trees to the side of the barn. Stopping, his back to the barn's wall, he caught his breath before inching along to the barn door. He listened. The horses didn't stir. He gave a gentle push on the door, the old wood creaking and groaning under the slightest movement. Easing it open just enough for him to slip through, Hank peered through the opening. He ducked in and found himself inside a large, cavern-like building covered in loose hay. High above, moonlight streamed in from a small window, illuminating the scattered hay on the ground. As his eyes adjusted to the darkness, he found a ladder leading up to a loft filled with hay. Among the smell of hay and earth, the musty scent of feathers met his nose. Hens rustled somewhere in their nesting boxes, but he couldn't see them.

He climbed up to the loft and looked around for an escape route. The only way out was the same way he had entered. That was not ideal, but he had no alternative. Inside the barn, blackness shadowed every corner, but outside, the sky was already beginning to lighten from black to gray. With dawn approaching, he would have to stay until the sun went down again.

Hank settled on top of the hay on the far side of the loft, hoping he was out of view of the door. Exhausted and hungry, he fell asleep. He dozed at times but was awakened by the slightest sound. After an hour, he jolted awake. A dog barked just outside the barn. Hank lay still, listening. Soft sunlight filtered through gaps in the barn wallboards and knotholes in the wood, illuminating the dust around him. The dog's bark grew louder and more frantic, until an old man's voice shouted in German, "Milo, get over here."

Hank detected a Swiss accent in his words. The dog quieted for a moment but began barking again. The man's voice drew closer as he yelled at the dog. Hank buried himself deeper into the haystack. Through a small opening, he watched the barn door.

"I'm coming, Milo. Hold on. I'm coming."

The barn door swung open. Two shadows stretched across the floor in the morning sunlight. The dog bounded into the barn, thrusting his nose to the ground and running about, following a scent…Hank's.

Hank's heart was in his throat. He parted some hay to create a small tunnel to peek through, holding his breath. The old man tended to his chores but glanced up now and then with a frown at the dog's antics.

The man's tattered overalls and shabby coat hung about his thin frame as he moved about, in no hurry. The brim of his hat drooped over his eyes. Even the scarf tied around the dog's neck was faded and ragged. Hank remembered he needed to steal a coat or some clothes for a disguise. He swallowed, wondering if this was the right place to take something that didn't belong to him, no matter how desperate he was. For that matter, were any of the small farms or homes around here the right place?

Something moved near the wall just a few feet away, startling Hank. The outline of the man's arm reached for a pitchfork hanging on the wall.

Hank reached for his pistol on his leg, the feel of the cold metal at his fingertips bringing a sense of relief even as dread filled him. He didn't want to face that choice, not here. The dog leapt over to the man's side. Its whole body shuddered with each fierce bark.

"There's nothing in here, Milo. Just be quiet," the man said.

The farmer stuck his pitchfork into the hay, the sharp prongs slicing into the pile just inches from Hank's side. He lifted the fork and carried the load over to his horses, spreading the hay in the manger. The man's footsteps then carried him to the other side of the barn, and at each squawk of a chicken, Hank could count how many eggs he collected into his basket. He turned to the barn door and called for the dog to follow as he hung the pitchfork back in its place on the wall.

Hank kept still as the dog took one final lingering sniff in the air, then ran to catch up to the farmer. The man shut the door behind him.

After a few minutes, an odd squeaking sound rang out from the corral, muffled by the barn walls. Then came a splash of running water, its stream pounding into the metal bottom of the horse's trough. As he imagined the clear, cool water he realized how his dry tongue stuck to his mouth and his throat burned. Hank listened as the trough filled higher and higher, and from the sound of it, he guessed the farmer used a hand-driven well pump.

The noise stopped and the dog's bark receded as they walked back to the farmer's house. Hank breathed in deeply, letting go a big sigh of relief as he settled back into the hay. Within minutes, he fell into such a deep sleep, he didn't wake until afternoon.

As he awoke and looked around while he came to his senses, he scolded himself. He shouldn't have slept so soundly. He couldn't afford to be so careless if the *Gestapo* was on his trail—especially since the dog knew he was here, and the farmer wasn't sure if the dog was on to something.

Hank wiggled his way out of the hay and looked out from his perch into the cavernous barn. The bright daylight exposed a treasure trove of tools and other items he could use to his advantage. Hanging on the wall was a bridle, a saddle blanket, and saddle, along with a shovel and the pitchfork. In the corner near the door, a pair of coveralls, almost as shabby and faded as those the farmer had been wearing, dangled from a rusty nail on the wall. A coat lay slung over a wheelbarrow, covered in dust and hay. Hank took a deep breath, realizing his good fortune.

CHAPTER 43
February 4, 1944
Groß Markenstadt, Germany

Just before sundown, the farmer returned to the barn to feed the horses again. Hank had expected this and waited until he left before stirring. This time the dog didn't bark, but Hank couldn't help but notice the frown that darkened the man's withered face as he scanned the barn.

Hank unfolded his map one more time and held it close to his face in the waning light. He counted the number of roads and intersections he would have to navigate between here and *Oma*'s house, reciting their names to himself to burn them into his memory. Once he was on the road, he would need to walk like a local who knew these roads as well as he knew streets back in Huntsville. The names rolled around on his tongue with familiarity, but it had been so many years, and he had been so young. He may not recognize them by sight.

The map's legend had a bold statement highlighted in red: "Road classification not based on reconnaissance. Reliability uncertain." At the bottom, a grid with segments in red indicated the primary bomb target area. Hank spotted his exact location on the map, and then followed the roads and landmarks with his finger until he found a small square just outside the primary target area. His eyes widened with relief, and he recognized that the red line stopped just short of her house, like the edge of a scarlet shadow. She didn't even know she lived on the doorstep of something so dangerous.

Hank crawled out of the hay and climbed down the ladder, brushing bits of straw off his clothes. He tiptoed across the barn and lifted the overalls from the nail by the door. They were faded and worn, but just what he needed to blend in. He would carry the bridle and the saddle blanket and pretend to be a farmer looking for a horse that had escaped its corral. Unfolding the coat, he brushed off dust and cobwebs as loose bits of hay fluttered across the floor with each vigorous shake. Still limping from his sprained ankle, if someone stopped him and was close enough to notice his age, he could explain he had a war injury. In all, he was confident he had a plausible story for being on the road, on foot, after dark.

He stripped everything from his jumpsuit pockets, including the maps and compass, and zipped them into his bomber jacket pockets. He took off his shirt and dog tags, then rolled them up inside his jacket, compressing it as tightly as he could. Grabbing some twine nearby, he tied it all up and hid it inside the saddle blanket.

He was surprised the coveralls were a good fit over his clothes. The jacket was not. It draped over his shoulders, the sleeves hanging past his wrists. He wore only his thermal underwear beneath it, and was bound to be cold, but wearing his uniform was not an option.

He climbed back to the loft to wait until nightfall.

At about seven, it was pitch black outside. Hank climbed down the ladder; his limbs numb from lying so long. As feeling returned, pain from his injured ankle shot up his leg. He didn't need to fake a limp as he left the barn, clinging to the saddle blanket and bridle to keep them from making any noise. The moonlight was just peeking over the eastern horizon, its light a welcomed assistant. Maybe the light would be enough to help him to find his way around and recognize his *oma*'s neighborhood.

Glancing around in the darkness, he spotted the well pump. He tiptoed over and drew some water, careful to not make a sound. He took a long, delicious drink from the tip of the spout. He eased the handle up and down, holding his breath, listening for the dog each time it squeaked. After a few tense moments, he had drawn enough to gulp down several swallows. The cool liquid slid over his dry tongue and throat, refreshing and energizing. He wiped his mouth and continued to the edge of the barn.

Hank looked again for any signs of movement. Seeing nothing, he made a quick dash across the field. When he reached the road, he ducked low in the ditch, the same way he had come in and stopped to catch his breath.

The still winter night felt warm for the season. A distinctive ring encircled the moon, a sure sign of an approaching storm. If a storm was coming, he needed to get to *Oma*'s house before his boots would leave prints in the fresh-fallen snow.

He crawled up from the ditch, stumbling toward the road. He tucked the bundle under his left arm now, slinging the bridle over his right shoulder, the way he would if he were searching for a missing horse back home. Except for the rustle of wind in the grass or the distant howl of a train, the silence that filled the night around him could be the same silence on a cold night in Huntsville. If he closed his eyes, he could be wandering the roads near his home, helping Grandma Russell bring home a lost cow or horse. He followed the predetermined course in his head, remembering the map.

The first group of houses would be in the small town of Blocken, less than a mile away. Walking as fast as his injury would allow, he switched the blanket from one arm to another every few minutes.

Headlights swept the road ahead of him as a car rounded a curve. His heart pounded. He looked away from the car as it neared him, letting the bridle swing by his side and looking into the darkness around him with a searching gaze. Once it passed him, he took a deep breath.

As he approached the houses at Blocken, dogs erupted in angry barking. In one house, a light flickered brightly on the second floor. The curtains parted and a bare-chested man looked out the window. Seeing only Hank, the man snapped the curtains shut and the light went dark.

Going through Blocken was the easy part; the hardest part was ahead. For another half hour, he ambled by a long row of houses while several cars rumbled past him on the road. He still didn't recognize where he was and had yet to find a landmark because it was still too dark to see the landscape with any clarity. Hank had no choice but to keep walking.

After a few more minutes, a car approached from behind, this one slowing as it drew closer. Hank held his breath. He could dash into those bushes by the side of the road. But, no, it was too late now. He switched the bundle to his other hand again, making sure the bridle was visible in his right hand.

Hank kept walking as the car pulled up next to him. The passenger window slid down and a man called out, "Do you need some help?"

Hank looked up with a shrug and a smile.

"No, thank you. I'm fine." His German was as good as the man's. "I'm looking for my horse; he gets out of his corral somehow. I can usually find him up here visiting a little filly."

The man laughed. "Okay. Hope you find it." He drove away, unhurried.

Hank kept his eye on the car to see if it pulled over or turned around. After he watched it for a few nerve-racking moments, the car disappeared into the night.

Hank had counted five cross streets on the map before he had to turn right. The sixth road was ahead, and nearby he would find a dirt road, leading to his *oma*'s house. He hoped his map matched his memory of this neighborhood.

He now entered the most dangerous area on his route. To his left, twenty houses lined up side by side, facing the road. On the right, large tracts of open farmland yawned for miles to the west. If his map was right, his *oma*'s house should be somewhere out in the middle of those fields.

Hank turned right at the sixth intersection, his palms sweating despite the winter night. Nothing was familiar.

Somewhere, the dirt road to his *oma*'s house met this street, if he continued southeast. But after ten minutes, Hank wondered if he was lost, if he would search long into the night and still not find it. Worse yet, if he couldn't find her house, he'd have to find a place to sleep. In this populated area, his choices would be limited. His stomach growled, and every hour he'd been walking had weakened him more and more. He hadn't eaten since his last chocolate bar, two days ago.

One more intersection lay ahead, featuring a large rock barn with a single dim light that lit the street below. Hank rounded the corner, then stopped short. A car sat in the darkness, the headlights off, as if waiting for Hank. It was too late for Hank to retreat back into the shadow of the barn. He entered the quiet intersection, his heart racing.

He passed the car within a few feet of the bumper. Something urged him to look up, and when he did, he met the eyes of the driver who'd spoken to him earlier. Dread tightened around his chest, but he glanced away as if he didn't recognize the man. He kept walking

"Still haven't found your horse yet, huh?"

Hank turned around, jerking his head as if he was startled by the familiar voice.

"Oh, it's you again," he said. "Yeah, I usually find him in one of two places."

"That's a long way to walk. Are you sure you don't need any help?" The man poked his head out of the window, resting his arm on the side of the car and eying Hank up and down.

"If I don't find him up here, maybe I'll come back and you can take me home. How long will you be here?" Hank asked confidently.

The man blinked in surprise, tilting his head in thought. "Not too long, I hope. My wife is visiting her mama, though, so it could be all night."

"It looks like you need more help than I do," Hank added with a chuckle.

The man smiled back. "You're probably right."

Hank turned around, gazing into the darkness. He walked on, growing more anxious as he searched for the dirt road.

At last, he spied it. The outline of the house was familiar and unmistakable. A surge of energy burst through him and he picked up his pace. He was no more than a quarter mile from his *oma*'s house and the safety of being with family, not to mention having a bed, a warm bath, and some food and water.

Until now, he hadn't thought about her reaction. He had been a boy the last time they had seen each other. From the road, he could see a light in the living room, making the small house glow welcoming and warm.

Hank tip-toed up to the porch to peek inside the window. The porch slats shifted under his foot and he stumbled, catching himself without making any noise. If *Opa* were still alive, it would never have been left in a state of such disrepair.

Then it hit him like a punch to the gut. What if something had happened to his *oma*? What if she was dead? What if she wouldn't let him in? Letters between Germany and America had been cut off years ago. He had no way of knowing.

The curtains were drawn, but a small opening offered enough of a view that he could see inside. Soft music played on the radio, the crackle of static drifting between the symphony's notes. A small fire flickered in the fireplace. The silhouette of a chair sat in front of the glow of the fire. He only knew that some old lady was sitting there, probably reading a book. He didn't know if it was his *oma*. This woman's hair was much whiter than he remembered. He looked at the floorboards, second-guessing himself. *What if this isn't my oma?*

He would knock on the door and see who answered. If it wasn't his *oma*, he would ask for her. He stepped quietly to the front door, setting his saddle blanket and bridle on the porch. He took a deep breath and whispered to himself, "Well, here goes."

Hank knocked slow and soft. "Anyone home?"

Her voice answered after a long pause. "Coming, hold on one moment." The newspaper rustled briefly, then her soft steps approached the door. "Who is it?" she asked through the door.

"My name is Heinrich. Are you Frau Hildebrandt?"

He could hear her unlock the door and turn the handle.

Tears welled up in his eyes as the door opened with caution. This was an older woman, hunched over and wrinkled. She looked up at him from eyelids old and delicate as butterfly wings. Her white hair shone like snow in the moonlight, her thinning eyebrows just traces of white above her eyes. Her smile revealed several missing teeth.

But it was her. It was definitely her.

"Hello *Oma*, it's Hank!" he said, not daring to raise his voice above a whisper for fear his voice would crack.

She held her hands to her mouth, stepping back.

"Hank? Is that really you?"

"Yes, *Oma*."

Suddenly, a fierce look came into her eye. She lunged to grab his coat and tugged him hastily inside the house. Before she closed the door, she looked out into her yard in both directions.

"What are you doing here? You'll get us both killed!"

"I'm sorry *Oma*; I was hoping you could help me. You were my only hope."

"Who knows you're here? Who has seen you? Why are you dressed like that?"

"Calm down, *Oma*, nobody has seen me." Hank held up his hands, gesturing for her to be calm. "I was shot down two days ago, and I've been hiding in the woods. Last night I stayed in a hay barn in Gross Mackenstedt."

"But you can't stay here; they'll be looking for you. They'll send the *Gestapo*. They execute anyone who harbors the enemy," she grabbed him by the wrist, holding firmly. He drew back in alarm at the strength of her grip. She looked deep in his eyes. "*You* are the enemy."

She dropped his hand, but her words pierced his soul. Breathing fast, she paced the room, stopping in front of her chair. One hand was on her hip, and her other hand was running her fingers through her white hair.

"But *Oma*, I'm also your grandson."

She shook her head. "You don't know what they're capable of doing to you. Or to me."

"I think I have an idea. I've heard some pretty bad things."

As she looked up at him, her expression hollow, the weight of his own words sank into him. *What had I been thinking in coming here?*

"Did anyone see you? Did you talk to anyone?"

"Not really."

"What do you mean 'not really'?"

"Some guy stopped and asked if I needed help, and I told him I was looking for my horse. He just laughed and drove off."

"And that's all?"

"Uh," he paused. "I saw him again at the next corner—by that barn with the streetlight."

"You mean at the end of this road?" Her voice raised in pitch and she trembled.

"He was sitting in his car, waiting for his wife. He saw me and asked about my horse. I said I'd be back if I didn't find it, and he offered to give me a ride. That was it."

"Was he suspicious of you?"

"I don't think so. Is my German not good enough?"

"No, it's just fine. But I still can't believe you thought it was okay to come here. You can't stay here," she said, her arms locked by her side.

Hank stared at her, not believing what he was hearing. "Where do you want me to go? I barely survived being shot down. I landed about twenty miles from here. Where else would I go if my own grandmother was nearby? Or maybe I should just turn myself in to the nearest *Gestapo* agent and say, 'Here I am'?"

She took a deep breath in, then said, "No," exhaling in resignation.

"Come here," she motioned for him, reaching out to pull Hank to her breast and embrace him. "You have grown so much I didn't recognize you. You are such a handsome young man. Come here and let's get you out of that hideous coat and overalls."

"My shirt and coat are outside on the porch, wrapped inside that saddle blanket. Let me get it."

"No, no, I'll get it. You need to stay inside and away from the windows." She walked to the window and made sure the curtains were shut tight.

She opened the door, lifted the saddle blanket inside, and closed the door again. "Ewww, that thing stinks. It's not staying in my house."

"Okay, okay. Let me get my things out of it, and you can throw it outside on the back porch."

Once Hank had retrieved his bomber jacket with all his belongings, she grabbed the saddle blanket from him. She held it as far from her body as she could, opened the back door, and dropped it on her back porch. She clapped her hands, brushing away dirt and horsehair.

"*Oma*, have you got some bread or something I could eat?"

"Sure, son. Come in the kitchen and I'll get something for you."

She turned the light on in the kitchen, then turned off the living room lamp, glancing out her windows before returning to the kitchen. She sliced off a piece from a fresh loaf of bread and handed it to Hank, then reached inside her icebox and found him a block of soft cheese.

He took a bite of the cheese and broke off a chunk of bread and stuffed it in his mouth.

"Oh, I've missed bread and cheese like this," he mumbled around a mouthful of food. "You can't get anything this delicious in America."

She smiled, but her gaze roamed the room with anxiety. He knew her peaceful life in this little farmhouse had just been turned upside down. She would be overwhelmed. If only he could get her to understand they were safe from the *Gestapo*'s threat if she would just agree to help him.

He finished the bread and cheese within a moment, then asked, "Do you have anything I can drink?"

"Oh, of course. I'm sorry, I wasn't thinking." She stepped outside on her porch and reached for a bottle of milk. She said nothing as she poured him a glass of the warm milk.

He could see the wheels turning inside her head. He didn't anticipate that she would be so unhappy to see him. He thought she would welcome him with open arms and keep him hidden in her upstairs room until the war was over. It was all quite simple in his mind.

He gulped down the milk. "Thanks, *Oma*, that was great."

Her eyes softened. "I'm so sorry I'm only concerned about myself. I'm sure you've been through quite a bit."

Hank uncrossed his arms and smiled. He explained what had happened two days earlier when he was shot down, how he survived a free fall, and just before he hit the ground, something helped him open his parachute.

They sat at the kitchen table and talked. He told her everything that had happened since the war began, about Ella, about Tom, about school. He talked about himself, about Billie and her work as a pilot. He stopped for a breath, and she waited, her hands clasped in front of her on the table.

"And what about your mama and papa?" she asked. "How is the farm?"

"You haven't heard?" Hank ran his hands through his hair. "No, I guess you wouldn't know. The government arrested them as Nazi spies. They're in a prison camp in Texas." He couldn't say much more, not without choking up. He knew very little about them since arriving in England anyway.

She stared at the table in front of her. After a moment, she asked without looking up, "How... how are they doing?"

"As well as can be expected. They're getting what they need but are just disappointed and alone."

"So, they can do that in America? Just arrest you and throw you in jail without any charges? I thought that only happened here."

"Me too, *Oma*. People do strange things when they are threatened. That first year after Pearl Harbor was attacked, the war wasn't going too well for us. It looked like Japan and Germany were invincible. Somehow, all that stuff about rights and the law got pushed aside."

"The Jews have been the biggest targets here, but so has anyone who opposes Hitler. They are ruthless. That is really what killed your *Opa*," *Oma* replied.

"What?" Hank exclaimed. "The *Gestapo* killed him?"

"Not directly," she explained. "Just the constant threat of being jailed for some small infraction."

Oma reached into her apron pocket and pulled out her handkerchief. "Your *Opa* was such a good man. You remind me a lot of him. So brave." She smiled as she dabbed a tear from her eye. "But no one stands a chance against the *Gestapo*, and that's why I just don't know what to do with you here."

Hank watched her as her hands trembled, her face flush with terror.

"I can't lose both you *and Opa* to those terrible, vicious men."

277

"I'm sorry, *Oma*. I was desperate."

She reached over the table and put her soft, warm hand over Hank's.

"Oh, my son. I don't blame you. You did what you thought was best. I'm so glad to see you, and under any other circumstances I would be thrilled to have you here. But there are so many issues to consider."

"Other than your safety?" Hank asked with confusion. "What else?"

"Everything we Mormons do is monitored by the local *Gestapo* and other Nazi leaders. They send spies into our meetings to see if we're planning something subversive. We have always tried to show them our loyalty to our country. We've shown them our Articles of Faith and how we strive to be 'honest' and 'true,' and that we are willing to be 'subject to rulers,' and 'sustain the law.'" A sob choked her throat, stealing away her words. She dabbed the corner of her eyes again but could say no more.

After a moment, she cleared her throat, breathed deeply, and said, "So, what's going to happen to your Mama and Papa? Will they just stay in that camp until after the war?"

"Probably. I think the government doesn't really know how to let them go free without admitting they were wrong. I don't see a way for them to get out until the war is over."

"There's still a lot of war ahead of us," she admitted as she looked out the window again. "And it's looking like it may end up in a stalemate."

"It will be over sooner than you think, *Oma*. I've sat in on some pretty interesting briefings, and the invasion of France will happen soon—sometime this year, in fact. The *Luftwaffe* has been just about wiped out. The Germans surrendered in Russia at Stalingrad a year ago last February. Now we're in Italy making our way toward Germany. Plus, the Russians are making their advances from the east."

"Really?" She cocked her head in surprise. "We keep hearing about all our victories here and there, and how we've got the British and Americans on the run."

"Don't believe what they're telling you, and you can expect even more bombings here in Bremen, and Bremerhaven and Wilhelmshaven. It's inevitable."

"Oh, I've lived through those bombings. They're terrifying. And when an American is shot down and survives, they run to the police because the locals would probably kill them."

Hank eyes widened with recognition. "We've heard stories about Americans killed with pitchforks and shovels. That's why I was so happy I landed near a forest and could hide so quickly."

"There's nothing we can do to change things. You're here now. So, let's get you upstairs to bed, and we'll figure out what to do tomorrow. You know your way around up there, right?"

"Has anything changed?"

She laughed and said, "I think you and Ella were the last ones to sleep in those beds."

He hugged her and kissed her on the cheek. "I'm so sorry to put you through this."

As he walked up the stairs, she said, "Oh, and Hank, try not to turn the light on upstairs, okay? You understand, right?"

"No problem. I'm used to fumbling around in the dark."

When Hank's head hit the pillow, he was out and didn't wake up until the bright morning light shone in his eyes. He looked out the window to a beautiful, snow-covered countryside. Even with the snow, the daylight brought familiarity. The barns, the fields, everything was just how he remembered it.

The smell of sausage cooking drifted up from the kitchen. He got dressed and walked downstairs to investigate.

"That's a smell you never forget. Now I feel like a kid again."

She gave him as many eggs and sausages as he could eat, and he ate like he hadn't eaten in days. As he stood from the table, he held his stomach and laughed. *Oma* smiled at him.

Hank explored the living room, picking up old photographs here and there. She wiped her hands on a dish towel as she stood between the kitchen and living room.

"Um, Hank," she hesitated. "I wanted to let you know that my bishop is coming over."

"You're bishop? Really? Why?"

"Well, I just need to talk to him." She looked at the floor, avoiding eye contact. "I need some guidance about things, you know…" Her voice trailed off.

"Okay," Hank replied with doubt in his voice. "If you think that's the best thing to do. When is he coming over?"

"He said he'd be here at any time."

"That's nice of him to drop everything to come here for you." He turned back to inspect a photograph of his *opa*, from before Hank was born. He did see the resemblance his *oma* spoke of last night.

She cleared her throat. "Just so you're not surprised when you see him," her smile was strained. "He's a *Hauptmann* in the *Wehrmacht*."

He set the photo down, turning toward her. "Your bishop is an officer in the *Wehrmacht*?"

"Yes." She lowered her head. "It's because there's not many male members of the church around to fill priesthood offices, but he's been very kind to help out widows like me."

This contradicted everything he had supposed German officers to be. They were cruel, unfeeling, and incapable of showing compassion to anyone, especially an elderly widow.

A Nazi officer could never be a bishop.

"Lately, most congregations of the church have had to meet in homes. They even meet here on occasion. He travels around to a few houses each Sunday, if he can get away from his military duties, that is."

"Isn't a *Hauptmann* like being a captain in the American army?"

"Yes, something like that."

Hank nodded.

Within minutes, a knock on the door rang throughout the house. It sent a shock of panic through Hank. Breathing hard, he looked for a way to escape, but he stood still. Running away would upset her.

She looked at him with a strange look, something like longing, and something like regret. Tears pooled in the corners of her eyes.

"Just go into the kitchen and wait. I'm going to go outside and talk for a minute." She looked at Hank with a strained smile. "Just remember I love you. Okay?"

"I love you too." At the fear in her face, a stronger wave of panic washed over him.

He stepped into the kitchen and watched her close the front door behind her. Muffled voices conversed for a few moments, but he couldn't make out their words. Then without warning, there was nothing but silence. He closed his eyes to focus better on hearing what was going on outside, but the new fallen snow muted all sounds like a heavy blanket. Suddenly, a car door opened and closed a few seconds later. The engine revved, then sped away.

Adrenaline rushed through Hank's muscles. Would the back door provide a safe escape?

Before he could work out his escape plan, someone opened the front door and entered the house, kicking the snow from his boots. Hank peeked around the corner. The man's immaculate *Wehrmacht* uniform fit his tall, commanding frame to perfection. Flared breeches tucked into his glossy black boots. His stiff tunic flowed freely when he moved, and the black collar extended high on his neck. On his throat, a black iron cross medal covered the top button of his tunic.

"Hank. May I talk with you for a moment?" He spoke near-perfect English.

Hank emerged from the kitchen, peeking first around the corner.

"I am *Oberleutanant* Geissen. Your grandmother told me you were here."

"I thought you were her bishop." he said in German.

He replied in German, saying "*Hauptmann* Roterman you mean, the Mormon? He was unable to come."

Hank's heart raced. A tingling flushed throughout his body.

Where is my *oma*?" Hank asked, then he shouted at the door, "*Oma, Oma,* come back!"

"She is gone."

Hank's eyes widened with recognition.

"Where is my *oma*?" he asked in a panic, clenching his teeth.

Geissen bit back a smile but remained silent.

"Where did she go?" Hank said with pleading in his eyes.

Geissen tilted his head, watching Hank until he could comprehend the situation.

Hank clasped his head in his hands, staggering back in disbelief. "She set me up, didn't she? She knew you…"

"Your *oma* did her duty and chose not to be complicit in harboring an enemy fugitive."

"My own grandmother betrayed me?"

Geissen pointed to Hank's coat draped over his *oma*'s reading chair. "Is this your jacket?"

Hank ignored him. Geissen stepped around the room with his hands clasped behind his back like a man of authority, gazing at the photos on the wall with an air of scrutiny. Hank wanted to laugh in spite of everything. This man was trying too hard. Geissen stopped to inspect the family pictures and other knick-knacks on the end table. At last he turned around, lifting Hank's coat from the chair. He rubbed the lamb's wool between his gloved fingers.

"Very nice," he said. "You will need this where you're going."

Hank heard footsteps on the porch. The door burst open and two *Wehrmacht* soldiers pointed machine guns at him.

"Search him!" Geissen ordered.

Hank put his hands in the air.

Geissen rummaged through Hank's jacket and removed the Colt .45. "This will make a nice souvenir," he declared with a smirk.

Hank stood motionless as the soldiers felt his belt line and down his leg. They lifted the pant legs of his jumpsuit and removed his knife and escape kit, along with his maps and compass.

"You won't be needing these either," Giessen's voice dripping with self-satisfaction. He threw the jacket in Hank's face.

"*Herr* Meyer, you now belong to the Third Reich."

Chapter 43-Note 1: From 1942 and beyond, pro–Nazi President Anton Huck led the Western Germany Mission of the Church of Jesus Christ of Latter-day Saints. President Herbert Klopfer, another Nazi sympathizer, presided in the Eastern Germany mission for the duration of the war. Klopfer entered military service soon after the outbreak of hostilities. During the first few years of the war, Klopfer's military assignment kept him close to Berlin where he conducted church-related affairs both through his wife and other members. I wanted to create a character who would reflect the contradictions inherent to being both a leader in a Christian church and a functioning military leader within the Nazi government. The character of Hauptman and Bishop Roterman is a fictional incorporation of both Presidents' Huck and Klopfer.

Steve Carter. "Patriotism and Resistance, Brotherhood and Bombs: The Experience of the German Saints and World War II," *International Journal of Mormon Studies*, 5 (2012): 6–28.

CHAPTER 44
February 12, 1944
Crystal City, Texas

Marta remained in the hospital after her collapse. Karl sat by her side, supported her whenever she had enough strength to walk. He read to her every day. Her thin frame had begun to fill out and her cheeks, he thought, were almost rosy again. But he still wasn't ready for her to go back. They would find her again, and they would make their lives more miserable. If they beat Karl again, he wouldn't have the strength to protect her. Not out there.

Days passed and O'Rourke came to see them one afternoon, a large packet of papers tucked under his arm. Marta sat upright in a chair by the window and Karl held a book on his lap.

"Marta," O'Rourke smiled as he shook her hand. "You're looking much better."

"Yes," Marta said. "I'm back to vere I vas a few veeks ago."

Karl watched her confident smile. A few weeks ago, he thought. She was still not the same as a few years ago, or even a few months ago. He knew from the way Hank had looked at her, and from what happened long before Horst Müller had taken over the German sector of the camp.

O'Rourke slapped his knee as he sat down.

"That's just what I wanted to hear. And how about you, Karl?"

"Much better, sank you."

"You are both getting enough to eat, I hope. There haven't been any disruptions or problems with your stay here?" O'Rourke rubbed the back of his neck.

"No," Karl said, shifting in his chair. "Ve are glad you didn't make us go back to our place. I heard it vas ransacked. There is nothing for us to eat…"

"That's why we've kept you safe in here," O'Rourke interrupted.

"But for how long? You can't keep us here forever." Marta glanced at Karl, and his shoulders stiffened as he waited for O'Rourke's response.

"Uh, yeah," he said. "That's what I've come to talk to you about." O'Rourke looked at his feet.

Marta watched his face as he gathered his thoughts. Karl looked away, watching the sunlight and shadows on the windowsill.

"Both of you have been selected by the INS to be repatriated back to Germany. You will be leaving tonight."

"You're sending us to Germany?" Karl's words were drenched with incredulity.

Marta gripped the arms of her chair. "I don't vant to go back to Germany. Please tell me zis isn't true. Vy does it haf to be us?"

"It's out of my hands," O'Rourke replied without emotion. "The State Department has approved the final list of six hundred and fifty-seven Germans being deported. We have two trains leaving tonight. You both will be on the first train, and Horst Müller is going to another camp next week."

Karl sat in silence, looking at Marta. He could see her eyes boiling with rage. "Vy don't ve haf a choice in zis?"

"I can give you a choice." O'Rourke thumbed through his stack of papers, he looked up at Karl after he found one. "You can sign this involuntary repatriation form, acknowledging you are being repatriated against your will."

"Hand it to me." Marta's nostrils flared.

"But remember, anyone who signs this will likely be treated more harshly than those who sign this paper." He presented another form.

Marta took them both and laid them on her lap, looking from one to the other. Karl stepped over and read with her, resting a hand on her shoulder. She reached up and grasped his hand.

"The second form states you are voluntarily requesting repatriation. Voluntary repatriates, especially Germans, will receive preferential treatment by INS officials. Your baggage will bypass customs inspection, and each of you can carry up to one hundred dollars with you. If you sign the involuntary form, you can only take just sixty dollars total between you. Your bags will also be searched by customs, and any questionable items, like books," O'Rourke paused to catch both of their gazes, "can be confiscated."

"Zat's not a choice." Karl could feel the anger rising in his gut.

"I'm sorry, Karl. This has to happen tonight. This is coming from the highest levels of the government, even the President himself. My hands are tied."

Karl and Marta looked at O'Rourke with suspicion. "Vy vould Roosevelt care?"

"I don't really know, to be honest. But we will all find out pretty soon, I guess."

"But," Marta blurted. "Our rights as American citizens haf been completely ignored."

"I can't change the fact that you're considered enemy aliens. I don't make the laws. I just enforce them."

Marta tapped Karl's hand again, and he leaned down for her to speak in German, "It looks like we're going whether we like it or not. If our luggage has to go through customs…" she paused to watch his face. "I don't want to lose anything else, especially my scriptures."

"I've really got to know your answer. And I need to know now."

Karl shot O'Rourke a sharp glare. "Give us ze voluntary form."

O'Rourke smiled then handed him a pen. "I think you'll find you have more flexibility, too, once you arrive in Germany, such as where you stay or how you travel."

Shaking her head, Marta scoffed. "Ver are two Americans supposed to stay in Nazi Germany? As far as zey are concerned, ve are ze enemy. Zey will kill us."

"I don't think it will be as bad you think."

"Who else here knows zey are going tonight?"

"They are all being told right now, at a meeting in the theater. I'll have a guard escort you back to your place so you can pack your belongings while it's safe."

Walking back to the main part of the German section, the guard led them through the silent streets, stopping at their cottage. "I'll wait for you." He turned and stood guard. Marta thanked him, and Karl reached to open the door. Up close, Marta noticed a large patch of splintered wood where the door had been bashed a few times and forced open. The door was off its frame slightly. Karl grunted as he pushed it open and walked inside their cottage, surveying the mess. Marta covered her mouth, mumbling in German, "They've ruined everything!"

Clothes lay strewn about the floor, and the draft from the open door sent bits of paper flurrying across the room. Marta bent down and snatched up a few pieces from the floor. "No, no," Marta's voiced cracked. She smoothed out a crumpled page from her Bible, finding another torn piece of the thin paper and lining them up like a puzzle. "Why did they have to do this to my books?" She exhaled and shook her head. "I have to fix them."

"That will take too long, Marta."

She gathered more pages from the floor, sticking them into the books. Their corners protruded haphazardly, and she flipped through them to find the right order.

"We don't have time," Karl urged.

Hiding from Karl's glance, she wiped at the corner of her eyes. On the floor in front of him, Karl's scriptures lay open, face down. He knelt to pick them up, folding the book closed and smoothing a hand over the worn cover. "These seem to be okay." He stopped suddenly.

"Oh no!" Karl let out a groan.

"What?" Marta's eyes widened.

"Did they find our savings we had hidden?" He stood, inhaling a sharp, panicked breath. Marta had sewn their valuables into a special pillow. He thrust his books into her hands and pushed past her, hurrying to the bed. He dug around the rumpled sheets and disarrayed blankets, then reached under the bed. He pulled out the pillow and unbuttoned it, his hands shaking. Reaching in, he felt around for the small bag. When he found it, he emptied out money and Marta's wedding ring into his hand.

"It's all here." Karl was relieved. "They didn't find it."

He counted the money. "Okay. Good. It's all here. One hundred and seventy dollars. Hopefully, it's enough to get us to Bremen."

The guard cleared his throat as he stood waiting for them. Marta stood looking around the room, one hand on her hip, the other running her fingers through her thinning hair. Karl rushed to pick up the clothes from the floor, straightening them out before packing them in their trunk.

"I need to write Ella," Marta said, out of breath. She sat on the arm of a chair, grabbing pen and paper.

Dearest Ella,

Tonight, we were told that we are being sent back to Germany. We're going whether we like it or not. We know nothing more than that. We will write to you as soon as we can.

Please contact the Red Cross and see if you can notify *Oma* that we are coming to stay with her. We don't know when we will arrive.

Give Hank our love. We miss you all terribly and wish we didn't have to leave. Please be safe.

With love,
Mama and Papa

By evening, the special trains from the Missouri Pacific Railroad had pulled into the Crystal City railroad station adjacent to the camp. Each pulled two dining cars, two luggage cars, and twelve Pullman sleeper cars. Each sleeper accommodated thirty-six people, with twelve berths each in one of the three sections. Two people slept in the lower berth and one in the upper berth. Each section shared a drawing room.

Karl and Marta had packed a trunk, consisting of clothing, bedding, and a few keepsakes. They also had a small suitcase with only a change of clothes, their scriptures and toiletries. The trunk was loaded onto a luggage car and sealed until their train reached its final destination, still undisclosed. They carried their suitcase with them onto the train.

As they boarded, several familiar faces greeted them. Karl tipped his hat to a few men as he passed their seats. Marta followed, until someone touched her gently on the wrist. She looked down.

"I'm so glad you are okay," one of Marta's sewing friends said as she sat next to her husband. He was stowing a small piece of luggage under the seat in front of them.

Smiling dimly, Marta breathed an audible sigh of relief.

"I am no worse than the rest of us right now." Marta followed Karl to the next row of seats.

"We didn't know how to help you." She gave an awkward smile. "Especially because they threatened us if we did."

Marta shrugged.

"It was all so miserable, but I'm thrilled that we're going back to Germany. I didn't want to put up with Müller and Schmidt for one more day."

"I don't want to go back to Germany," Marta said.

"You would have rather stayed at Crystal City?"

"Germany is full of people like Müller and Schmidt." She couldn't hide her disdain. "But now it's out of the frying pan and into… you know what I'm saying?" The woman nodded then turned away.

Karl and Marta found their berthing room and were told to meet in the dining car for further instructions. When they returned, a crowd of German internees filled the dining car. Karl and Marta squeezed their way in, stepping by other faces they knew. A thin, middle-aged man with salt-and-pepper hair stood before the crowd, two other men standing beside him with their arms folded in front of them. He cleared his throat.

"My name is Special Agent George Williamson. I am with the State Department. This is Special Agent Mallo to my right, and Special Agent Mikorski to my left. We will be available to answer questions after we're finished."

He glanced down at a clipboard, shuffling his feet.

"Because of security demands, we cannot disclose our final destination or where we will be making stops. Please don't ask us. You are not permitted to exit the trains for any reason whatsoever. The guards also have strict instructions to prevent all communication with anyone except other passengers on this train."

"The train portion of this trip will last no more than four days. You will then board a ship destined for a port in Europe. They will provide more information once you board the ship, so please don't ask us about that portion of your trip."

Karl leaned over to Marta. "Did you ever think we would be going back to Germany?" His voice was soft, yet full of curiosity.

"Not like this."

After the announcements, the dining car emptied within seconds. Passengers retired to their berthing rooms. At a half-hour past midnight, the train inched forward. Marta took one last glance out the window at Crystal City. Despite the darkness, it was lit up as bright as day.

They watched the countryside fly by for three days and nights.

Marta had fallen asleep with her head on Karl's shoulder. She awoke, stretching stiffly, and mumbled, "Where are we now?"

"Just passed Atlanta. I can't imagine it can be much further." Karl's patience was wearing thin. "There's a port in Virginia or Washington. They could make us go to New York or even Boston. Who knows?"

"I can't wait to get off this stupid train." Marta was also growing impatient with the long train ride. "They said four days, and tomorrow is the fourth day. It can't be much longer."

The next morning at breakfast, conversations among passengers roared over the noise of the train. Marta ate out of boredom rather than hunger, rubbing her temple with her fingers. Karl watched as the door opened and Agent Mallo entered. He started to speak, but the din of voices and clinking silverware drowned out his words.

"Can I get your attention please?" he shouted. The noise died down as people sat back in their seats and turned toward him.

"This will be your final meal on this train. After breakfast, please prepare to exit the train. We'll arrive at Exchange Place Station in Jersey City, New Jersey at about ten this morning."

Karl's eyes brightened. "At least we don't have to go all the way to Boston."

Marta gave a rueful smile and looked with eagerness out the window.

Mallo continued his instructions. "All passengers must clear U.S. Customs. Please have your enemy alien cards available. Those who don't have them will be required to have a new one issued. There are no exceptions. If you have a voluntary repatriation form, present it to the customs official as you exit the train. You will be taken to a special room designated just for those coming from Crystal City. Please be patient while we try to get everyone processed. We have over thirteen hundred people on sixty train cars coming in from camps all over the country. We need to do this quickly so the ship can depart tonight."

Marta leaned over and whispered to Karl, "I had no idea they had rounded up so many Germans."

"There's got to be more than just our thirteen hundred," Karl said. "I hear they are also keeping a huge number of German families at Ellis Island."

As the Meyers stepped down from the train, a voice with a heavy Brooklyn accent called out, "If you have voluntary papers, go this way." He gestured to a small room in the station. Karl led Marta by the hand toward the door. Ahead of them, a family led their dog on a leash, its tail whirling and its nose sniffing the ground behind their heels. Another couple sat with a small dog between them.

Marta laughed, turning to Karl. Her eyes twinkled, but whether from mirth or tears he couldn't tell. "They let people bring their dogs? How does that work? Does the dog need a passport?"

Karl recognized most of the faces around the room from Crystal City. Marta pointed out others she knew. None were Müller's or Schmidt's henchmen, at least as far as she could tell.

After a short wait, all the detainees from this group were escorted to a room where they waited to board their ship. The Meyers joined a small group, where a guard with a warm smile and graying hair struck up a conversation in German.

"Did you know you'll be boarding a very famous ship?" he stated with a proud smile, lifting his chin. When no one answered, he continued, undeterred. "This is the *M.S. Gripsholm*. It has made over twenty mercy missions to exchange prisoners of war."

The line ahead of Karl and Marta continued its way forward. Marta smiled at the guard as they shuffled forward toward the gangplank. Another guard looked stone-faced as they passed, then smiled when Marta asked in English, "Can I ask you sumsing?"

"Depends," he replied with caution.

"Do you know our destination?"

"Europe, ma'am. That's all we can say."

"Do you know vich port?"

"All I know is she's going to Europe. Your guess is as good as mine." He turned away from her.

Marta whispered to Karl and shrugged, "It was worth a try."

After getting settled in their berth, they were instructed to go to the main deck for instructions. Marta looked at her watch. It was six-thirty in the morning. The ship pulled out into New York Harbor. A chilled breeze swirled across the deck, and cold ocean spray misted their clothes. From the deck of the *Gripsholm*, they watched the lights of downtown Manhattan fade as the dawn approached. She wondered how long the next portion of their journey would be.

"New York City sure is different since the last time I was here," Karl said, his palms resting on the railing of the deck. "It's amazing how much the skyline has changed in thirty years."

"The Empire State Building wasn't here when I first came. There are so many more buildings now." Marta's gaze swept over the countless skyscrapers filling the space between the earth and the sky. Manhattan rested like many narrow, square mountains against the horizon.

"Can you imagine the amount of money it takes to build just one of those skyscrapers?" Karl said. As the city dimmed from their view, they walked to the other side of the ship for one last look. The *Gripsholm* steamed past the Statue of Liberty.

"I remember," Marta looked at the statue, forcing a melancholy smile, "when I arrived in 1921. How I was so excited." Her voice broke. "I wept when I saw the torch. The brilliant gold leaf was shining in the sun. I was sure it was on fire."

"I'll never forget when I first laid eyes on her either." Karl's smile ran away from his face. "I looked at her and said, 'Thank you for giving me a chance to prove myself. I promise to work hard and be worthy to be called an American.' I've never forgotten that moment." He cleared his throat.

They stood against the rail quietly, and one by one, the other passengers did the same. No one said a word until the last of the ship slipped by the statue.

"Ironic, isn't it?" Marta gazed behind them as the city grew smaller and smaller. "We came to America to be with the Saints in Zion. We came for a chance to be with people who believed as we believed, to live the American dream in the land of freedom." She let out a sardonic laugh.

Karl put an arm around her shoulders, listening.

"And now," she stopped, biting back a cry that cracked her voice. "It feels like she let us down. I don't know that I'll ever want to return to America again." She turned her back and grasped Karl's hand, leading him away from the rail. They walked through the heavy metal door, down into the interior of the ship.

Chapter 44-Note 1: Documents from the State Department indicate a very thorough and well-orchestrated plan to deport German aliens from their various camps from around the United States. The express intent was to exchange these detainees for American prisoners being held by Germany. Most of the details in this chapter surrounding the process of deportation are true. They were gleaned from the "Instruction to Agents" document given to INS agents on February 9, 1945, for transfer of detainees from detention camps at Crystal City, Kennedy, Seagoville, Texas, and Ellis Island, New York. All detainees were endorsed by the German government before they were approved for deportation.

"Second *Gripsholm*, Spanish Photostat List to Instructions to Agents," (Box 176 – ARC2173219 Entry A1 1357. RG-59 *General Records of the State Department, Special War Problems Division, Subject Files. Declassified* NND917307) 1939–1945.

CHAPTER 45

February 7, 1944

Bremen, Germany

Inside the truck bed with no windows, every bump and pothole in the winding dirt road jostled Hank and sent pain ricocheting through his aching back and swollen ankle. Alone in the enclosed bed of the truck, he was still determined not to cry out in pain and let the guards hear him. He clenched his jaw, folded his arms and pretended to sleep. Within minutes of the ride, he had lost his sense of direction. When the truck rumbled to a halt, Hank sat up from the uncomfortable bench seat and caught his breath. The doors slammed and heavy footsteps crunched snow, all muffled by the stiff walls of the truck. As the door swung open, the blinding light hit his face. Hank held up a hand to shield his eyes as a guard jammed something into his ribs, cold, metal—the tip of a rifle. He shouted in German, "Get out now!"

Hank shrugged, blinking away the brightness until he could see all of the guard's face.

"Get out, now!" the guard demanded again and grabbed Hank's coat, pulling him down from the truck. Hank stumbled, breaking his fall with his hands as he landed in the snow, the raw cold burning his palms and fingers.

"Stupid American," the guard spat. Hank stood, and the guard grabbed his elbow and pulled him along as he started walking. Two other guards walked on either side, and Hank stole glances at their eyes when they weren't looking at him. One had to be as young as Hank, with a fresh face and broad shoulders. If Hank had grown up in Germany, he could just as easily have been his friend.

The guard nudged him in the ribs, and he picked up his pace again. They led him to a small gray building with weathered walls and a faded placard that read *Stadtgefängnis Bremen*. They opened the door and took him inside, where the jailer stood from his desk and peered at Hank with curious eyes. He spoke to the other guards in a hushed voice, glancing at Hank. "An American?"

The jailer nodded, then escorted Hank down a dark hall to a cell, speaking in his best English. He unlocked the cell, letting the door creak open on rusty hinges. The smell of urine hit the back of Hank's throat. The guard smiled apologetically. "Thees best vee haf."

Hank thanked him for his kindness, then ducked into the cell. The guard's footsteps pattered back down the hall. Dark walls enclosed Hank, with only thin light showing the outline of a tattered mattress, bits of straw poking out from its seams, and a threadbare blanket crumpled at the foot of the bed.

The door to the cell hung open, as innocent as the door to his home, his church, or any other door. Perhaps they were tempting him to escape, to have reason to shoot him. He stood still and listened. No other sounds, not the faintest of voices or the slightest drip of a faucet, could be heard. He could be all alone in this jail, but he couldn't be sure.

Frustrated, he ran his hands through his hair. German interrogation tactics could be brutal and unpredictable. He paced next to his bed, replaying what he could remember of the briefing he'd attended months ago. They could use anything from mind games to torture. As he turned back and forth in each tight corner of the small cell, he wondered what information they could torture out of him? What deep, dark secrets did he carry with him that they would find of value?

He muttered something to himself in German. Then he froze. They must never know he spoke the language and that he could understand them. He would lose his advantage if they knew, and if they did find out, he would be treated as a traitor.

Another thought darkened his mind and he scowled. It seemed his *oma* was just like them. How could he be sure they didn't already know everything about him? He lowered himself onto the bed, resting his forearms on his knees. Anger boiled in the pit of his stomach, and he realized the sickening feeling in his throat for the last half hour was less from the foul smells and more from a thought stabbing his subconscious like a needle. She had betrayed him. She was one of them.

He knew she had been scared, and maybe had never planned to side with them. *But didn't her actions in the moment show who she really was?* The more he thought about her, the angrier he became. *Was she more than just the sweet grandmother who wrote his mama letters and attended church every Sunday? Is this who she truly was underneath it all?*

He should pray for her. But after several false starts and angry outbursts, he quit trying. He kicked at the wadded blanket on the floor, sending a spray of dust and straw into the air. Even a long, thoughtful prayer would be over in a second. Anger kept him energized for hours, muting the pain in his sore back and ankle. And what good was a prayer if he couldn't find the words?

Maybe German words could express it better, he thought to himself with a scoff.

He sat for a long time, staring at the ceiling, replaying everything over in his mind. How her skittish gaze should have warned him something was wrong; how he missed his chance to get away.

Before he knew it, the guard returned, holding a tray of food. He stepped into the cell, setting the tray before Hank. A bowl of weak soup with a single cabbage leaf floating on its lukewarm surface. Next to it sat a small piece of black bread and a cup of dark liquid.

The guard pointed to the cup and said, "*Muckefuck*," lifting his nose in disgust. *Muckefuck* was a coffee alternative. Hank took the mug in his hands, sniffing into it. Dark and earthy scents of an herbal ersatz coffee concoction filled his nose, the aroma eliciting dim images of his *oma* pouring out a pot of this caffeine-free brew made from rice or peas, chicory, or even dandelion.

Hank sipped. "It's okay. Not bad."

The guard wrinkled his nose again, his lips turning up in a smile of amusement. He turned and left, the door hanging wide open as before. Hank nibbled on the bread but then put it aside and drank the coffee.

It wasn't long before Hank needed to pee, thanks to *Oma*'s big breakfast.

"Hello!" he called out. "I need to go to the bathroom."

After no answer, he stuck his head out, peering up and down the hallway. Not a shadow or flicker of movement came from around the corner where the guard's desk stood at the entrance. Hank shouted again, but the guard must have left his seat because no one answered. He took a cautious step out of his cell. "Hello?" It was now an urgent matter to find a bathroom. He looked around at the other cells, all empty, though how long they had been empty, he couldn't know. At last there came a shuffling sound, and then footsteps heading toward him.

He dashed back to his cell and stood in the doorway. "Hello? I need to use the bathroom!"

The guard came into view.

"You, toileten?" he asked.

Hank nodded.

"Kome thees vay," he said, waving at Hank to follow him. He led him to a heavy, rusted door. A small rectangular opening with thick iron bars set at eye level allowed the guard to see into the bathroom while he waited. Hank held his breath against the nauseating odor of fresh urine and feces. Fecal stains soiled the bowl and toilet seat. Hank finished, trying to avoid getting his hands on the walls or toilet. He yanked on the rusty faucet, but when all that came was a hollow creaking sound from pipes that probably hadn't worked in years, he wiped his hands on his pants and opened the door. The guard was gone. Hank returned to his cell and sat on his bed.

The sun began to set, and any trace of light in the room faded as the cold settled in. Hank shivered, curling up on the mattress, and pulling the ratted blanket over his shoulders. At least he still had his heated long johns. He could turn them on, but rather than waste the battery for this moderate level of cold, he wrapped the blanket tighter around himself. He drifted off to sleep.

When he woke to a pounding sound on the cell door, night darkness filled every crevice of the room, and a chill had wrapped around Hank's face and fingers, turning them numb and stiff. The guard banged again and Hank sat up.

"Vee go now," the guard said. In German, he mumbled, "The *Wehrmacht* is here to take you to Frankfurt." He closed the cell door, and it clicked shut. The guard stepped back from the door with a pointed glance at Hank's face. He folded his hands and peeked down the hall as soft footsteps approached.

Hank rubbed the sleep from his eyes and stretched his muscles to wake himself up. A tall figure came into view, and a pair of polished boots came to a stop in front of Hank's cell. The guard told Hank to stand up.

Hank rose to his feet, coming eye to eye with a German officer. A surprised look flickered through the officer's eyes when Hank met his gaze. He tilted his head with a curious smile curled his lips. "How does it feel being back in your German homeland?" He let the German words fall fluid and natural from his mouth, watching Hank's face. Hank understood every word. His chest tightened and his pulse raced. He steadied his breathing, then furrowed his brow in confusion. "I'm sorry, I don't understand you. Where are we going?"

The officer gave a faint scoff of disbelief and beckoned for the guard to open the cell. The guard scurried over, glancing from the officer to Hank and back again as he twisted the key in the lock and stood out of the way for Hank to pass.

The officer led Hank outside. Light snow fell from the darkened sky and delicate icy snowflakes drifted on his face. Flashlight beams scurried across his vision in the dark. As his eyes adjusted, he made out the outline of a large truck. The officer gestured for him to climb in. Hank grasped the edge of the truck bed for a handhold and pulled himself in. As he sat up, he looked around at four other men sitting on the wood benches. He met their gazes one by one, and as he searched with questioning eyes from prisoner to prisoner, he noted the American bomber jackets and insignias.

For an instant, he saw men from his crew: that twitch of the eyebrow; that pattern of freckles; or that hairline. But it wasn't them. Somehow these four seemed to be together, or maybe they were strangers to each other? Just by looking at their faces, Hank could tell they had all been through as much as his own crew. A dark, blood-stained bandage was wrapped around one man's head. Another held his arm just below the shoulder. A lump formed in Hank's throat as he thought of Montoya limping, if he could stand at all, perhaps leaning on the captain's shoulder. He thought of their dirt-streaked faces and bloody clothes, crawling through the forest to find each other, to find him. His breath started to tremble, and he looked down at his lap to avoid the prisoners' gazes. Had they even made it that far?

The officer grunted, "No talking." Hank didn't look up. "Absolutely no talking. Do you understand?"

He slammed the door and locked it. A crack of light shone through the window from the cab to the bed of the truck, open so the drivers would hear even the most hushed conversations.

The truck bounced them along for twenty minutes. When it stopped, a roaring echo of voices, distant and bustling, mingled with whistles and loud hisses of steam. Hank jumped out first, and the other prisoners tumbled after him, one giving an arm to the man with a broken shoulder. They still did not speak to Hank.

An ominous brick building appeared before them. A few lights glowed like ghostly lanterns, illuminating a dusty sign reading *Hauptbahnhof,* half-worn above the tall doorway. Hundreds of windows, most busted in with jagged glass sticking from the edges like angry teeth, left dark gaps in the building's surface. The guards led them inside, where people shuffled and scurried about in their hats and coats, clutching suitcases. Trains blared their whistles above the din of people, as passengers gathered at one of the platforms to await boarding.

Beside Hank, a guard muttered something to someone. Turning his chin, Hank spied a *Wehrmacht* uniform. He snatched up the word *Frankfurt,* but before he could listen for more, they shoved him forward. The *Wehrmacht* guard barked, *"Geh schneller!"*

The guards led the prisoners through the sea of bustling people, who parted like the Red Sea to let them through. The people kept their heads down, stealing only rare glances at the prisoners. With each rapid glance, Hank flinched, waiting for that spark of antagonism, but their eyes only held curiosity or nothing at all. War had been weighing on them far too long, and it had settled into their features in ways that might never be erased. The weariness in their steps carried them as much as their own feet did, through the station, to the platform, onto the train, and beyond. Hank glanced at his companions, and from their searching eyes, he knew they saw the same things. He smiled at an elderly woman and watched a hopeful glance flicker across her face before she tucked a strand of her white hair into her scarf and kept walking.

The guards halted them outside a small room, where they waited in silence. A man came up from behind them, passing close enough to brush shoulders with Hank. A long over-sized coat draped over his tall frame, but there at the end, where his sleeve hung by his side, he held his two fingers in a "V" shape. Hank held in a gasp as he watched the back of the man's head, but he didn't turn to acknowledge Hank.

Minutes later, the man walked by again, and Hank nudged the American prisoner standing next to him. "Watch this guy coming at us. Is he giving us the "V" for victory sign?"

The prisoner frowned, watching the man as he passed. Two fingers peeked from the cuff of his coat sleeve.

"Did you see that? Not all Germans are against us."

Hank could only catch a quick glance at his face, then the man disappeared into the sea of people.

A train pulled up to the nearest platform, and at the nudging and grumbling orders of the guards, the Americans boarded a passenger car. Other passengers glanced up but then turned their back to the window or returned to their newspapers. The door slid shut with a bang, and the guards left the prisoners to themselves. Hank settled into a seat. Frankfurt—it had to be at least five hours away.

At the Frankfurt terminal, four guards waited with machine guns strapped to their shoulders. Hank and his group waited, yawning and blinking the sleep out of their eyes. The man with the bloodied bandage on his head leaned back against a wall, releasing a shaky sigh. More prisoners arrived, all haggard and beaten; one hobbled along on crutches. Twenty in all gathered in the terminal. Hank found himself searching their faces for a glimpse of someone he knew, from *Plano's Pride*, from Thurleigh, from anywhere. A pang of loneliness struck him in the pit of his stomach. The same pain and loneliness echoed back in the eyes of the other prisoners, also searching for someone familiar.

"*Schneller,*" the guards shouted. "*Schneller!*" They herded the prisoners across the street and onto a tram, crowding them in with other passengers.

Hank watched dim shapes and distant lights in the darkness outside the tram's window. After two stops, it began to climb higher into the hills. Higher and higher they went until they reached the crest. Looking back, the lights of the Frankfurt main terminal glowed, small enough to be about ten miles away. They passed a lighted sign that welcomed them to the town of Oberursel.

The prisoners stepped off the tram, then trudged another ten minutes until they approached a brightly lit area. A long, one-story building stretched as far as Hank could see. Between the building and the prisoners, a pair of tall barbed-wire fences reached into the darkness on both sides, disappearing in the shadows. A heavy wooden gate broke the line of wire in front of the building.

They advanced along the path to the main gate. On the ground beside them, hundreds, maybe thousands of large rocks were painted white and arranged in neat rows and curves. Even in the dark, the letters they formed spelled, like a loud cry peeling through the emptiness, "Prisoner-of-War Camp." Hank glanced at the sky, still clouded over with the snowstorm. On clear nights, the perfect nights for missions, Allied bombers may see this and hesitate. Hank doubted it would make a difference.

The guards split up the officers from the enlisted men, sending each group in opposite directions. Hank was escorted into a long, narrow building with many rooms. They led him by numerous doors, each a precise distance from the others. At last, they opened a door, and he went in, ducking under the six-foot ceiling. Light from the corridor showed a blackened window with metal bars welded to its frame. Beneath the window sat a rusted electric heater. The bitter cold in the room told Hank the heater was only for show, not for his comfort.

The solid wood bed frame had seen better days. A blanket lay bunched up at the foot of the bed. The impression in the thin straw mattress and the wrinkles in the sheets looked as though someone had just left and might return any moment. Hank wondered what had become of its previous occupant, and then, shuddering, wondered what would become of him.

He searched the rest of the room. He could find no toilet, only a small bucket that reeked of human feces. The walls, smooth and cold under his touch, stood silent around him as though no one had been here for years, looking on with apathy at whatever happened inside them. His thumb found a small, round button located near the corner, but when he pushed it nothing happened. A prisoner call button, maddening because it was disconnected.

He sat on his bed as the guard shut the heavy wooden door with a clank. Another clunk rang out as the bar latched over the door, and keys jingled in the lock until silence washed over him.

The silence stretched out around him; how far, he couldn't know. For all he knew, he could be all alone in this sector, and that was just what they intended.

The realization drenched him in a cold panic. He was in solitary confinement.

Later that evening, a guard entered Hank's cell, bearing some soiled prisoner clothing.

"Undress," the guard demanded. "You must wear this instead."

He handed Hank a large pair of coveralls, stained and reeking of human sweat; he assumed it hadn't been washed recently, or ever, for that matter.

"We must search your clothes for items you are not allowed to have," the guard said. "After, you come vit me to toilet."

Hank lingered while he stripped out of his jumpsuit, his bomber jacket, and his cherished battery-heated thermal underwear. The cold bit at his skin. He shuddered as he lifted the coveralls to his shoulders and buttoned them.

"Now, you must do toilet business; you not go back before tomorrow."

Another guard escorted Hank to a room with several toilets and a washbasin. Hank finished his business and washed his hands, relieved for the water streaming from the faucet. He bent down to drink the water.

"*Nein. Nicht trink wasser. Nicht!*"

The guard lunged toward Hank and pushed him away from the flowing water, but Hank had gotten his fill. Water dripped from Hank's chin as the guard shoved him back to his cell.

He fell asleep again.

A few hours later, Hank awoke to his door opening. A man stood just outside, a Red Cross armband crimson against his brown clothes. He held a clipboard and introduced himself in broken English.

"You avake?" he asked.

"Not quite," Hank said. "What time is it?"

"Oh, that vill not matter," he said. "I am Herr Janneman. I am vit de International Red Cross. Ve complete ze form so your family knows you here."

He handed Hank the clipboard and a pencil. The form, titled "Arrival Report," bore the markings of the International Red Cross in Geneva, Switzerland. The form asked for information about his squadron, group, and command. It also asked for details about the date he was shot down and the names of his crew members. The Army had warned them about this tactic.

Hank was in no frame of mind to put up with the ploy. "I will only complete my name, rank, and serial number. That's it. No more."

"Oh. Thees only for the Red Cross. Ve not share vit German officials."

"Why do you need to know the names of my crew members or my tail number?"

"It is important to identify you," he mumbled.

"You have my serial number; that's all they need to identify me," Hank snapped back.

Hank scribbled his name, rank, and serial number on the form, in handwriting his fifth-grade penmanship teacher would have scowled upon. "There you go." He tossed the paper at the man.

"Thees is no good," the man said, kneeling down next to Hank's bed. "Your letters undt parcels from home cannot find you. Your family vill tink you are dead. Is that vat you vant?"

"I'll take my chances." Hank rolled over, turning his back to the man.

"Oh, I am sorry for you. You not understant. Thees important for you. Vat is wrong vit you?"

The pestering and insistence made Hank scowl, and he realized how cranky and tired he was. All he wanted was for the man to go away. After another minute of urging and pleading, the man stood without warning, shutting the door behind him. Hank fell back to sleep.

The door opened once more, the light flipping on as a German officer sauntered into the room. His voice, deep and strong as he introduced himself as *Hauptmann* Rimpel.

"So, I hear you are not doing very well, eh?" His perfect American English was crisp and clear as anyone's back in Utah. "Can you sit up on your bed and talk to me a minute, please?"

Hank thought to himself, *How could this man speak English so well?* Hank was curious but didn't want to look too impressed.

Hauptmann Rimpel said, "Would you like a cigarette?"

"No," Hank replied.

"I have Lucky Strikes, the American favorites. Here, go ahead. I'll light it for you."

"No. I don't smoke."

"I thought all Americans smoked cigarettes."

"I guess not," Hank replied with contempt.

"And why is it that you don't smoke?"

There was no sense in discussing his religious beliefs with this man, and his shoulders sagged as he realized that he didn't want to anyway. Not with anyone, not anymore. "Just never liked it, I guess."

"I'm impressed. Wouldn't it be nice if all young men were like you?"

The compliment sounded hollow in Hank's ears.

"You remind me of my son. He is a *Luftwaffe* pilot fighting in the east right now. He has a strong will, like you. Are your siblings as committed to not smoking as you are?"

Hank waited for him to keep digging.

"If I were your parents, I would be very worried about you. Worrying would just about kill me, if I didn't know whether my son was dead or alive."

"They will find out soon enough."

"I can tell you right now that your parents are at home, worried sick about you. They received a telegram from the secretary of war saying you are missing in action. You don't think that would concern them?"

Hank stifled a smile. "There's a lot you don't know about my family."

"Look, I know you are tired and hungry, and you're probably worried about your parents. I understand, and I would like to help you. But if we don't know how to reach your parents, we can't let them know you are here."

"As I said, there's a lot you don't know about my family."

"How so?"

"Look," Hank replied with growing impatience. "I am an American war prisoner. All I am required to give you is my name, rank, and serial number. So, don't sit there and act like you are some kind of benevolent fatherly figure. It's not going to work with me. You can stop asking me all these stupid questions because I will not answer them."

The officer looked at Hank and smiled, "Suit yourself." He turned off the light on his way out, like a parent putting a grumpy child to bed.

Hank rolled over in his bed. Something crawled on his back. He slapped at it until the crawling sensation stopped. Another bug tickled his shoulder, then another his neck. He stood and rubbed his back on the wall, wincing at the welts on his back, neck, and shoulders. If he tried to sleep anymore, the bed bugs in the straw mattress would eat him alive.

He sat on a small stool in the corner of the room, leaving the blanket. He shivered, rubbing his bare arms.

Without warning, the electric heater switched on. Warm air wrapped around him, comforting and easing the tension from his spine and every muscle. The heater blew hot air until sweat formed on Hank's forehead. He unbuttoned his coveralls, sweating furiously, and moved the chair as far from the heater as possible. He took off his coveralls and sat spread-eagled on the floor.

He knocked on the door and shouted, "It's too hot in here!"

The heater pumped for another fifteen minutes. Hank knelt near the crack under the door, struggling to breathe some cooler air. The concrete floor pressed against the pain in his ankle, his sore knees, and ribs, until he sucked in air through his teeth in agony. Then, just as the heater had turned on without warning, it rattled and turned off.

Cold swept over the room and Hank donned his coveralls again. Flipping over his mattress, he lay down, hoping he could fall asleep before the bed bugs bothered him again. But sleep didn't come, and wouldn't, thanks to his jailers. Every hour, almost on the hour, Hank's cell became sweltering hot. Hank would strip down, lie on his bed, and sweat until the heater stopped. Once it turned itself off, the cell would cool until Hank shivered in the winter air and his own sweat.

Hank knew it was morning when a guard entered to give him breakfast. It consisted of two thin slices of black bread, a teaspoon of gloopy jam, and a cup of ersatz coffee. The guard entered again for lunch with a measly cup of watery soup. For dinner, he received two slices of black bread laced with something gritty. He didn't want to know what was in it.

Hank had to request water from the guard, and after sweating so frequently, his mouth was sticky and dry. The guards only allowed Hank to drink a sip of water from the tap when he went on his daily visit to the latrine.

This combination of solitary confinement, dehydration, and lack of sleep took the intended toll on Hank's resolve.

Chapter 45-Note 1: Many Allied prisoners in Dulag Luft reported suffering from bedbugs and the use of alternating heat and cold to harass prisoners, all in direct violation of the Geneva Convention. These and many other tactics were used by the Germans to break down their prisoners psychologically. British officer Ken Fenton describes his first day in the "cooler" this way: "In the cooler, the prisoner was forced to strip completely, all possessions and clothing was taken away, leaving the prisoner naked in a small, paneled room with a single bed. They were then given an army uniform to wear (while) their clothes were searched."

"Capture and incarceration – Dulag Luft," Ken Fenton's War, https://kenfentonswar.com/dulag-luft, accessed January 3, 2021.

Chapter 45-Note 2: Hank's account as a war prisoner is based on the composite experiences of many Allied prisoners of war. I have relied heavily on the incredible personal account of POW Ray Matheny from American Fork, Utah. In his book, *Rite of Passage*, he tells the story of the German in the train station making the "V" sign for victory:

"A man wearing a suit and a fedora stood in an arched doorway staring at us. As we passed, he swung his arm draped with an overcoat towards us, revealing his right hand with which he was making the victory sign with two fingers upright. The coat cleverly shielded his right hand so that the guards who followed could not see it. A feeling of encouragement swept over me and some of the other men softly responded."

Ray Matheny. *Rite of Passage: A Teenager's Chronicle of Combat and Captivity in Nazi Germany* (American Legacy Media, 2012): [205].

CHAPTER 46
February 15, 1944
Ogden, Utah

Ella lost count of how many times she had called the Red Cross office in Ogden. Each time, they referred her to the state office, but she hung up, letting out a frustrated exhale through her teeth. Long-distance calls would have to wait until her next payday.

At last she gathered the money together and phoned their office.

"Utah Red Cross, how may I help you?" the women answered in a business-like tone.

"My name is Ella Meyer. I'm calling long distance, so I'm sorry about rushing through this, but I've been trying for the past few days to get the Red Cross to send an urgent message to Germany about two American prisoners of war."

"Are you wanting to communicate with an American being held in a German war prisoner camp?"

"No, I need to get a message to a German citizen, my grandmother," Ella explained. "My parents are being deported to Germany by the American government. They are being sent to Germany against their will. My grandmother lives there and needs to know they are coming because they have nowhere else to go."

"So, let me get this straight," she replied. "You want the Red Cross to send a message to your grandmother, a German citizen? And the people who are prisoners are actually Americans?"

"Well, sort of. They are no longer American citizens."

"Then they are German citizens?"

Ella lowered the phone as she frowned. Were they German citizens? "Well, technically, I suppose so."

"I'm sorry, but I don't think that qualifies as an emergency that concerns the American Red Cross. Since the United States has no diplomatic relations with Germany, you'll have to contact the Swiss consulate in New York."

"Look," Ella cried. "They are American civilians who have been stripped of their legal rights, and they are now refugees. The Red Cross helps refugees, right?"

"Yes, of course," she replied.

"Okay, then. My parents are refugees. They aren't Americans anymore, and they are being forced to live in Germany. But right now, they have no home and no country."

"I don't think international law recognizes deported enemy aliens as refugees, but I'll have to check on that."

"You've got to help me. I'm desperate! My grandmother lives near Bremen, which is bombed all the time. She could be forced to leave her home on a moment's notice, and she would never know that her daughter is trying to find her. Don't you see?"

"Miss, I am sorry. Truly I am, but I'll have to ask someone if we can do this. In the first place, I don't think the Germans will allow us to send a message like that. The Red Cross is committed to following the letter of the law in Germany; we have to be careful, or we won't be allowed to help."

"Can I give you my number so you can call me once you find out?" Ella asked.

"Yes. That would be helpful."

Ella gave her work and home telephone numbers. "Keep me informed, please," she said, slamming the phone on the hook.

She walked into her room and flopped onto her bed, covered her face, and screamed in her pillow. Her parents were in international limbo, and she could do nothing about it.

It was turning out to be a frustrating Saturday. Normally, this was her best day of the week—her day to catch up on her studies and clinical assignments. She also ran errands on Saturdays, and once all the errands were finished, sometimes she'd have time to just relax.

She wished she could go on a date or just chat with someone. Anytime she found herself alone, she thought of how she would describe her day in a letter to her parents, to Hank or Tom. Or Billie.

How long had it been since she'd communicated in any other way? And now, even letters would never reach the people she loved.

The Russell's had been home only once since she moved in, and that lasted just a few days. Since then, Ella had the house to herself. The large spacious living room was decorated with imported furniture from Europe. Thick Persian rugs covered the floors in the hallways and dining room, soft to walk on in her bare feet, especially on cold days. Although she could have chosen any of the five bedrooms, Billie convinced her to stay in her old room—mostly because of the queen-sized, four-poster bed. Ella had never slept so well as in that goose down comforter from Germany, and vowed she'd buy a feather bed once she had the money.

She sat on the bed for a few minutes, then gathered her shoes and purse to run a few errands. As she was about to leave the house, the telephone rang.

"Hi Ella, this is Myrtle Davis."

"Hi there, Myrtle. How are you? What's the latest from Tom? I got a letter from him Monday," Ella offered, sensing something wrong in Myrtle's tone.

"Tom's been in a terrible accident," Myrtle interrupted, her voice cracking.

Ella closed her eyes tight, shaking. "Please tell me he's okay," she begged, as if saying aloud would make it true.

"Yes, he is. At least, as far as we know, he's okay. We got a telegram delivered from the Red Cross. Let me read it to you: 'The International Red Cross reports that your son, Captain Thomas Davis, was injured in a training accident Monday, February 14, near RAF King's Cliffe, England. More details to follow'."

"This—this is all I know," Myrtle stammered. "I just got the telegram about ten minutes ago."

A million thoughts rushed through Ella's head. "They didn't tell you anything else?"

"That's all I know, dear. I wanted to tell you as soon as I found out. It hasn't been more than a few minutes since the Western Union boy left."

Ella answered softly, "Thank you for calling me."

"I'm so sorry to be the bearer of bad news, but all we can do now is wait and see," Myrtle said, and from the muffled, last few words, Ella imagined her dabbing her nose with a handkerchief. Myrtle had spent the last ten minutes choking back tears long enough to call.

"His letter to me on Monday said he was training other pilots and having the time of his life," Ella said. "He said he misses me, and he misses home. That's about all he said."

"I think you get a lot more letters than we do, so if you hear anything else, please let us know."

"I sure will. Let me know as soon as you hear anything."

Ella hung up the telephone and sat in the dining room chair. She rested her elbow on the table, burying her face in the crook of her arm. She rubbed her forearm mindlessly with her other hand.

After a while, she stood, took off her coat and hung it on the back of the chair in the dining room. Kicking off her boots near the door, she made her way to her room, shaking from disbelief and cold. She had never felt so helpless. Her head dropped onto her pillow. She lifted her feet and tucked them under the blanket draped over the foot of the bed.

Nausea boiled in her stomach. A tingling in her mouth warned her she needed to rush to a toilet, but as soon as the urge to vomit came, it vanished. She sank back into the pillows. A half hour passed, then an hour, but her mind wouldn't stop racing with all the dreadful scenarios. She didn't know when she drifted off into sleep.

The doorbell startled her awake. She sat up on the edge of her bed, arranging her hair. Leaning over she took a quick look in the dresser mirror. "Coming," she called with as much volume as her hoarse voice would allow.

She opened the door smiling but flinched at the sight of two men in military tunics. Small crosses pinned to one man's lapels glinted in the winter sun. The other man, an Army captain, stood by his side in solemn silence. His hands folded in front of him.

"Oh no," she said. "Not today. Please no," she begged.

"Are you Ella Meyer?" The chaplain asked, a kind warmth in his eyes and an understanding his voice.

Ella gave a reluctant nod. If only she could go away, disappear somehow.

"We went to Huntsville first, but were told you were here."

Ella's anxiety was exploding in her chest.

"I'm very sorry to inform you that your brother, Staff Sergeant Hank Meyer's plane was shot down over Germany on February third.

Ella gasped, covering her mouth.

"He is reported as missing in action."

He kept speaking, but his voice faded away. The other officer added a few more words, but it was all just noise to her. The Chaplain handed her a piece of paper, and through the ringing in her ears, she caught the word *telegram*. She let it slip from her hand, and it fell at their feet.

Ella looked past the two men on her porch, past the yard, and over the mountains surrounding the valley. She couldn't breathe.

The chaplain took her arm and helped her to the sofa in the living room. Ella shook her head, muttering and biting her lip as her vision blurred. Was she crying? She didn't know for sure if she were standing or sitting.

She didn't know how much time had passed before the chaplain spoke again, his voice reaching her through the fog. "Are you going to be okay? Is there anyone else here?"

Ella inhaled through her nose to clear her head. She picked up the telegram from the sofa next to her and ran her eyes over it several times until she could read the words. She looked at the chaplain. "There's no one but me. When will I know anything more?"

"As soon as the Red Cross is notified by the German government of his whereabouts, you'll be contacted immediately."

Ella stared at the Western Union logo on the telegram.

"Thank you for sitting with me. I'll be okay now."

The two officers stood, stated their regrets again, and saw themselves to the door. Ella lay down on the sofa and closed her eyes.

CHAPTER 47
February 16, 1944
Dulag Luft, Oberursel, Germany

The door latch clicked open and a light shone into Hank's eyes, bright as the sun. He shielded his eyes and squinted, but the room was still blurry. His dry eyes itched, and his tongue stuck to the roof of his mouth. Leaning forward, he started to stand, but fell back into a sitting position on his bed. He knew he was too weak to be steady on his feet.

A *Wehrmacht* officer strolled into his cell. He shouted in a proper British accent. "You will stand when a superior officer enters the room!"

Hank stood slowly, reaching out to the wall to steady himself.

"That is better. I am *Obertleutanant* Haussman, and you are Heinrich Meyer?"

"No."

"No? No, what? You are not Heinrich Meyer?"

"My name is Hank Meyer. I am a Staff Sergeant in the United States Army. My serial num…"

"Stop!" Haussman snapped. "I do not need to hear your stupid recital of name, rank, and serial number. I know most everything about you. Now if you want to get out of here, you need to help me fill in a few blanks."

Hank gave a blank stare, saying nothing.

"I know you are 'Hank' Meyer," he said, his first name coming out in a nasal American accent, like it disgusted him. "And I know you're from Ogden, Utah."

That's pretty close. How did he know? Hank thought and couldn't hide his look of surprise. Haussman snorted with laughter. "We have so many resources at our disposal. We have informants in your country clipping newspapers about every American airman. We intercept your radio communications, and we have a few other tricks up our sleeves."

Hank couldn't hide his contempt. His face sneered with loathing.

"We know you were a waist gunner on a B-17 named *Plano's Pride*, named after your captain's hometown of Plano, Texas. You were shot down near *Wildehausen,* and your plane crashed near Harspedt. You were the only survivor."

The words "only survivor" knocked the air out of him, like he'd been hit in the stomach with a baseball bat. His knees gave out. The only survivor? The captain, Montoya, everyone… No, the *Oberleutanant* had to be lying. Or was he?

"You were based in Thurleigh with the 306th Bomb Group. Your target on February 3 was Hannover, but your secondary target was Bremen. Your payload was twelve five hundred-pound bombs."

Hank couldn't disguise his astonishment.

"I am intrigued by you," Haussman said, raising an eyebrow. "You are a very bright boy. You were able to evade detection, nearly derail a train with the dead deer, and slept in a farmer's barn before you stole from him. Then you made it to your *oma*'s house in Stuhr without raising any suspicion." He paused and smiled. "You are very resourceful."

Hank gave a faint smile. The weariness in his eyes could not mask his surprise or his concern. And with every detail this Nazi recited about his mission, his crew, his crash, and everything else he said being true, perhaps he was not lying about his crewmates being dead.

"Your *oma* did a very brave thing, turning you over to the authorities. She has proven her loyalty to the *Führer* and will be rewarded accordingly."

Hank cringed. He mustered every effort to hide his repulsion but wasn't sure if Haussman was on to him. Whether the hatred or the exhaustion was too great—or both—he was too tired to care about it now.

The *Obertleutanant* curled his lip in contempt. *"Du kanst dich nicht vor uns verstecken. Du sprichst Deutsch."*

Hank didn't flinch but he raised his eyebrows to show he couldn't understand.

"Wenn du nicht länger eingesperrt sein willst, frag mich einfach auf Deutsch."

"Whatever you're saying, I can't understand a word," he said, but he wondered to himself if revealing his secret was worth leaving solitary confinement. All he had to do was ask permission in German.

"You are lying." His voice was peppered with loathing. "But I don't have time to waste on an enlisted man. You have nothing to lose from speaking German, you know. You may be treated better for it, when you go to the prison camp."

The *Obertleutanant's* words contradicted all the stories he'd heard about German-speaking Americans receiving harsher punishment. He stormed from the room and closed the door. Hank held his breath to listen to his conversation with the guard. "I need this bed for pilots, not enlisted crewmen. Give him one more day." Hank could hear each word with clarity.

Twenty-four more hours of solitary confinement. After seven days, he could endure one more.

"Geh raus, geh raus!" the German guard shouted as he threw Hank's clothes, long johns, and boots at his head. *"Geh schneller!"*

Hank, exhausted and dazed, snatched up the clothes. He fumbled with the sleeves of his shirt, "I'm going as fast as I can," he thought, but somehow, he subconsciously replied in German, *"Ich gehe so schnell ich kann."* The words weren't loud, but they were loud enough, and the guard narrowed his eyes. *"Was hast du gesagt?"*

"I'm going as fast as I can." Hank repeated in English.

The guard stepped closer, his eyes inches from Hank, asking him in German "What did you just say?"

Hank realized his mistake and tried to cover up. "What do you want from me?" he asked in English.

The guard gave a slight smirk, not knowing for sure, but suspecting Hank had understood German. As Hank finished dressing, he scolded himself for being careless when responding to German commands. He could only hope his secret wasn't blown. He glanced at the guard but couldn't be sure.

They left his room, the guard shouting, *"Geh raus, geh raus!"* By the lavatory, Hank stopped to use the toilet. After washing his hands, he took a big drink from the tap.

"Hör auf. Halt!"

Hank knew he was being commanded to stop, but he drank until the guard pushed him away. The water, metallic and bitter though it was, filled his body with energy. His vision cleared. He walked without holding on to the walls. The guard escorted him outside, where he shaded his eyes until they adjusted to the sunlight. The guard grabbed Hank's arm and pointed to a long barracks with beds as far as he could see.

"You are on your own until we transfer you somewhere else."

Prisoners surrounded him like a sea, leaking from every corner and streaming into the middle of the room. One prisoner rested on a cot, elbows behind his head "Find a bunk and claim it," he said.

Men of different ranks, both RAF and American forces, sat on the beds or passed between the rows of cots filling the barracks. In the sea of men's faces, he caught glimpses of familiar features. Other times he heard them speak in a regional dialect that seemed to flow in and out like the tide. Out of the corner of his eye, Hank would see a jawline or a profile that he could have sworn belonged to one of his crew. Would anyone here perhaps know if they had survived? He wondered, if he ever saw them again, would he recognize them? Already their faces were becoming blurred in his memory, leaving him feeling lonely. He found an empty bunk, settling down to rest and avoid the gazes of unfamiliar eyes all around him. Of all the seas to drown in, he never imagined this would be the cruelest.

CHAPTER 48
February 16, 1944
Ogden, Utah

Myrtle Davis had called Ella four times that morning before leaving for church. Ella didn't answer. After church, Myrtle drove to Ella's house to check on her. She rang the doorbell. Then she put her ear to the door. If Ella wasn't home, why was her car in the driveway?

"Ella, are you in there? Are you okay?"

A faint stirring, then slow footsteps sounded from within. The door latch clicked, then opened a few inches, and Ella peaked her nose out. She wiped a sleeve of her nightgown across her face, then recognized Myrtle, looking at her with eyes that screamed for help. She opened her lips, then closed them again, reaching up to smooth down her messy hair.

"Oh, my poor girl." Myrtle pushed her herself past Ella and put her arms on her shoulders. "Tell me what happened."

Ella pointed to a piece of paper flung on the floor near the front door.

Myrtle picked it up and read it.

"I'm so sorry, my dear." She drew Ella into her embrace and held her, stroking her back. "Have you told your parents?"

Ella pulled away to look into Myrtle's face. "My parents are being sent back to Germany."

Myrtle stepped back in surprise. "They're what?!"

Ella took a deep breath, "They being deported to Germany. Against their will."

"I can't believe that," Myrtle said. "Back to Germany? Why in heaven's name would the government do that?"

Elle shrugged, then covered her face with her hands.

"I don't think you should stay here alone. You're going to come home with me. I'll bet you haven't eaten in a while, right?"

Ella dipped her head, saying nothing.

"Go get dressed."

Ella stood still for a moment, before looking into Myrtle's eyes and whispering, "Thank you."

Myrtle followed her to her room and could see she was having a hard time deciding what to wear. She helped Ella to her closet and pointed to a dress. After a long pause, Ella pulled the dress off the hanger and pulled it over her head.

"Here's your sweater," Myrtle said. "It's a bit chilly out." Ella put one arm in her cardigan, then another. "Will these shoes and socks be okay?"

Ella nodded again. Myrtle put them beside Ella and watched as she put them on. Ella then stood and shuffled past her dresser mirror, stopping to run a brush through her hair. With each stroke, the brush snagged in her tangles. After a few attempts to smooth it, Ella set the brush precariously on the dresser and walked away from the mirror. The brush dropped to the floor. She looked down at it and shrugged as she left the room.

"Is that your coat?" Myrtle pointed to the coat draped over the back of the kitchen chair.

In slow motion Ella lifted the coat. Myrtle helped her put her arms in each sleeve. Ella looked back and whispered, "I don't think I could bear being alone today."

"I couldn't bear you being alone, either."

As they drove, Ella watched the neighborhood. She turned to watch the shadow of a bird as it flitted overhead, the corners of her mouth lifting. She smiled a little brighter at a group of children with ice skates slung over their shoulders. At last, the fresh air and company brightened her face, and Ella found words to say something louder than a whisper.

"It just all happened at once," she said. "It's like everyone I loved just…"

"I don't know how anyone could deal with all of that bad news, all at once."

Ella smiled faintly as she felt Myrtle's warm hand on her arm. She stared out the window, watching the way the sunlight glinted off the roofs of snow-covered houses.

"When did the telegram come?"

"It's all a blur, but I think around three or four, yesterday," Ella said. "The chaplain was very nice. He talked to me for a while, then I just stayed on the sofa all night."

Myrtle pulled into her driveway and turned off the ignition.

"Maybe it's a sign that I should just pack up and find a way to be with my parents in Germany. Maybe that's what God wants?" Ella knew how silly it sounded as soon as she said it.

"Sometimes things just happen, dear. There doesn't have to be some hidden message."

"But don't you think it's odd that I got all this bad news at once? You think maybe God is telling me something?"

"If anything, he's telling you that you're strong enough handle it all at once," she said, "even if *you* don't think you are."

"I just think it's too much for one person to handle," she said, wiping tears from her cheeks. "Do you think God punishing me?"

"Absolutely not, Ella!" Myrtle sat up in her seat. "God is not like that. But bad things happen to good people. It's really just as simple as that. Other than that, I just don't know what more to say without sounding patronizing."

Ella smiled and took a deep breath, "Can we go inside where it's warmer?"

Of course," Myrtle smiled. "Everyone will be excited to see you."

As Ella stepped through the back door, sounds of children echoed throughout the house. All eight of the Davis children came flooding into the room, shouting "Ella!" They crashed into her, and she forced a smile as she leaned over to give each one a hug.

"Make yourself at home. There's a roast in the oven, and we'll be ready in just a jiffy," Myrtle said.

"It smells heavenly," Ella said. "I've missed that wonderful smell."

Myrtle turned to her oldest daughter, Helen, and said, "Please set another place for Ella."

"Can I help with anything?" Ella asked Helen.

"No, but thanks. I think we're just waiting on the rolls."

"I love the smell of fresh-baked dinner rolls. They smell like my mama's rolls." She fell into a chair, overcome with the loss of those happier times.

After finding their seats, the family sat with hands folded as one of the children prayed to bless the meal, remembering Tom and all the other young men from this small community who were in harm's way. Ella ate the first good meal she'd had in a week. "It's so nice to sit around the table as a family." Ella's face brightened as she listened to the family's conversation.

These children were so much like their brother, and they even shared Tom's mannerisms. Everything about them made her smile with recognition, and she listened and laughed.

While Ella helped clear the table, the doorbell rang, and one of the children ran to answer the door.

"Mom, Dad, it's a Western Union boy again."

Ella's heart stopped. She watched as Myrtle took the telegram and closed the door. As she read the telegram to herself, she smiled and looked at Ella, "It's okay. Don't worry."

317

Ella heaved a sigh of relief.

Myrtle's spoke loudly so everyone could hear. "'Banged up with broken legs, back, and right arm. Stop. Will heal completely in time. Stop. Will write soon. Stop. Tell Ella I love her. Tom'."

The room was silent as they drank in the news.

A small child, with small fists and quick feet, danced over and hugged Myrtle's leg. She looked up at her mother with large eyes and said, "Will Tommy be okay?"

"Yes!" Myrtle replied. "It means Tommy will be just fine." She turned to Ella.

"Now that we know Tom will be okay, let's focus on your mama and papa. Maybe I can help you figure out a way to communicate with your *oma*."

"Do you think there's a way?"

"This old dog still knows a few tricks," Myrtle winked. "I'm not going to promise anything, but I think we can figure out something."

CHAPTER 49

February 23, 1944
Dulag Luft, Oberursel, Germany

The next seven days in *Dulag Luft*, Hank waited. Now, he was just another *Kriegie*—short for *Kriegsgefangener*—German for war prisoner. He would lie on his back in his bunk, staring above him, wondering where they'd send him next. When he saw a guard or officer, he'd follow them, asking questions and searching their faces for clues, for any sign that gave away what they would be doing with him. The officers turned away, waving him off and trudging away through the snow. None of the other prisoners had anything worthwhile to tell him either.

One day, as Hank wandered by a bulletin board, his own name caught his eye. He scanned the list of ten names that were to report at the gate at 0800. It still wasn't much, but maybe somebody would tell him something now.

The guards escorted the group of prisoners to the electric tram. After all the men were boarded, it ambled down the hill to the rail yards at *Frankfurt am Main*. Upon arrival, they waited at another transition point. All Hank knew was they'd be transported to one of the many prisoner-of-war camps somewhere throughout the *Reich*. But the guards still answered his questions with nothing more than silence or deep grunts. One told him to get in line to get new clothing. Hank frowned but joined the end of a line that shuffled forward to gather coats and shoes.

When his turn came, the guard motioned for him to hand over his bomber jacket. Hank peeled it off and the guard yanked it out of his hands.

"Pick a coat," the guard demanded, gesturing to a table where two American summer field jackets lay, limp and crumpled. Hank picked up the larger one, and while it pulled tight around his chest and shoulders, it would have to do.

The guard shoved a knitted hat and a pair of wooden shoes from Holland into Hank's arms. Hank slipped his feet into the shoes. They weren't the boots he wanted, but he shrugged in surprise at how well they fit his feet.

He followed the line of men shuffling into another, much larger room. A wall of cigarette smoke hit his face, filling his lungs, and he coughed, staggering back. Waving his hand to clear the air, he blinked the water from his eyes. Looking around, he saw hundreds of *Kriegies* milling about, leaning against the wall or draping over a chair, cigarettes dangling from their fingers. A haze of smoke drifted at eye level, and the prisoners glanced up at him without much interest. Hank stepped forward and found a seat, folding his hands in his lap. He watched the other passengers as their empty gazes flickered over him.

Darkness descended and, one by one, the last cigarette embers were stomped out on the concrete floor. Men huddled together as the cold filled the room. Hank leaned back and closed his eyes.

"Raus! Raus!" The chorus of guards' voices stirred Hank from his sleep. He sat up, blinking in the darkness. Around him, other men jumped up as guards prodded them to their feet.

"Get up, we're going!" one of guards shouted in English.

Hank joined a group of twenty other Allied prisoners as the guards herded them across the rail yard. The first gray light from the dawning sun revealed an old steam engine tugging a line of wooden boxcars stretching a quarter mile. From the splintered wood and rusty couplings, Hank wondered if the train was from the First World War. As the guard nudged him forward, he pulled himself up into an empty car. In the darkness, the smell of ammonia and sweat emanated from the walls and floor of the car. The odor wrapped around him as heavy as a blanket, and he choked. He stepped over gaps in the uneven floorboards, watching the early morning shadows dance across the railroad ties below. The whole car shook with each step as more *Kriegies* climbed in behind him.

In the corner, he saw a small, antique, wood-burning stove with a tin stovepipe jutting out from the back, reaching to the ceiling. Inside, the stove was cold and empty. The men settled themselves down along the bare walls and floor.

"What are we going to do if we have to pee?" someone asked. Hank wondered how long this stretch of the journey would be, and realized he needed the bathroom already.

No one dared answer. From the looks of it—and the smell—these boxcars were used to transport live cargo, both human and animal. Hank settled himself into a corner, happy to have a spot to lean against the wall.

Was this how Germany shamed Americans specifically, or was this how they treated all war prisoners? If the journey ahead was to be a long one, a dignified toilet was only common decency. But boxing up humans like beasts, with no windows and the floorboards damp with nauseating smells, couldn't be normal. These men were regular people, he told himself, decent Germans just like decent Americans. He thought it over and over again, but each time it sounded more like a hollow echo than a truth he could believe.

They waited in the stillness for hours. Hank watched the shadows beneath the train grow sharper as the sun rose, stretching over the frost-covered ground. Around him, men stirred and tried to move in the cramped space, the car trembling under their footsteps. In desperation, someone called out to the guards outside the car, asking for the bathroom. Others joined him, but the guards slid the door shut, and the train lurched forward. The car wobbled and bounced along the tracks, aggravating Hank's painful bladder. Other men grunted in discomfort.

After what seemed like a lifetime, the train came to a stop in the middle of a snow-covered field. Farmhouses dotted the edge of the field a quarter mile away, nestled between trees and fences.

"Raus! Raus!" the guards bellowed, pointing their guns at the prisoners. "Do your toilet business."

Stiff and sore, the prisoners crawled from the boxcar into the open field. They squatted in front of each other to defecate, not knowing when they would be given another chance. They hurried back through the snow, wrapping their arms around themselves against the cold. Inside the car, Hank found his spot again and settled down in the corner. This time a different POW plopped down next to him, offering him a kind nod and warm smile.

Hank gave him a courteous raise of his eyebrows, glancing at the man's bandage on his left hand, stained with dried blood and caked-on dirt.

"Feel better now?" he asked Hank.

The man's voice rang strange but comforting over the repetitive clacking of wheels on the tracks that had filled Hank's ears for hours. He grinned, "Was it that obvious I was in pain?"

"You weren't the only one looking pretty desperate."

"I guess this is how things are going to be from now on, as formal guests of the Nazi government," Hank said, wrinkling his nose.

"They need to learn a thing or two about hospitality," the man said.

"What happened there?" Hank pointed to his hand.

"Shrapnel, the day we went down."

"And they didn't change your dressing or look at it?"

"Someone looked at it and said, 'You're okay'…does that count?"

"Is it getting any better?"

"I think it's infected. It's swollen, and I can feel my fingers throbbing."

"Maybe when we get wherever we're going, there will be a doctor who can help," Hank replied.

"I'm not holding my breath. These Nazis couldn't care less about us."

Hank held out his hand. "I'm Hank." As the man took it in a firm grasp and gave it a shake, Hank said, "I probably shouldn't say too much, especially to someone I just met, but what the heck. They know everything about me anyway, so what does it matter? I'm from the 306th out of Thurleigh."

A spark of suspicion darkened the man's smile for a moment. But he shrugged. "I guess you're right. I'm Donald Carter," he said, pulling his hand away. "Call me Don. I'm with the 379th out of Kimbolten. We were practically neighbors."

Hank laughed. "We landed at Kimbolten once when we couldn't land at Thurleigh. Boy, that seems like years ago now."

"It all seems like a dream. I can barely remember my life back home, and what I can remember seems like a fantasy or something, ya' know?" Don nodded in recognition.

"So, where you from originally?"

"Oklahoma." Don's eyes widened as he spoke of home. "A small town called Mounds, 'bout twenty miles south of Tulsa. How about you?"

"Small town called Huntsville, Utah, east of Ogden."

"You must be Mormon."

"All my life. Are you religious?"

"My family is Church of Christ. Every Sunday, Bible study at nine-thirty, worship at ten-thirty."

Hank tilted his head back in a soft laugh. "Same here. Two meetings in the morning, and one in the afternoon for good measure."

"One more than I would like." Don looked down at the floor. "Isn't everybody a Mormon in Utah?"

"No, not quite. But a lot of us are. What's it like in Oklahoma?"

"There's a few Church of Christ congregations in Oklahoma. But mostly there's a ton of Baptists, Catholics, and Methodists."

Hank leaned forward. "You're about the first person I've met since joining the Army who's not afraid to talk about religion."

"It's an important part of my life," Don replied.

"Me too," Hank offered out of habit, but something in him cringed from the subject. Perhaps it had been too long since he'd been able to talk about it, or maybe he didn't want to talk about it anymore. He found himself saying, "Some of the guys think I'm eccentric, or maybe just plain odd. So, I don't talk about it too much, unless they ask."

They continued to talk about their families, home, their favorite movies, just about anything to keep their minds off where they were and where they were going. For the most part it worked, and when the conversation lulled into silence, one of them would pick it up with another question, and the other would know why he was doing it.

Several hours into their train ride, when the afternoon sun had warmed his back, Hank spied something in the shadows between the wood slats on the walls and floor. He bent down to take a look. He reached out to trace the small etching of a star. Words below it had been rubbed too thin to be legible.

"Look at this," Hank waved Don over. "Isn't that a Jewish Star of David?"

"That's what it looks like to me."

"I can't read the rest of it. Maybe it's in Hebrew? I don't know." Hank inspected it at closer range, but in the dim light and the shifting, rattling train car, he couldn't focus. "Why would that be there, tucked away in the corner of this boxcar?"

"You've heard the rumors that the Nazis have camps where they work Jews to death?"

"Yes." Hank glanced at Don. "But I doubt it's really as bad as some people make it out to be. Besides, if they were rounding up Jews like they say, don't you think it would be front-page news?"

"If the Germans treat us like cattle, why wouldn't they do the same to the Jews, or worse?"

Hank shrugged, hoping against the evidence that most German wouldn't condone such treatment.

At night, they slept in the cold, rickety train, huddling next to each other to stay warm. For three days, Don and Hank talked in soft tones in the corner, falling asleep and waking with questions that picked up where they had left off. At times, their train was forced to stop to make way for faster trains. About every six or seven hours, the men were allowed to get out of the boxcar to relieve themselves. Once, the guards tossed them small chunks of black bread to share. The prisoners devoured them, eager for anything to eat.

At the end of the third day, the train came to a slow, grinding halt. The guards opened the doors to an empty rail yard. The fresh, crisp air stirred in the darkness through the train car, clearing out the smell of humanity after their journey. Prisoners crawled to the door, but guards shoved them back to keep them inside. Guards detached the boxcars from the main engine, and the train struggled to get away.

"*Geh raus! Geh raus! Eile. Du musst jetzt gehen.*"

"Where are they taking us now?" Hank asked Don, who shrugged.

Hank jumped down from the boxcar, pain shooting through his aching limbs as his feet hit the ground. He stood behind a huddle of other prisoners and glanced at the trees surrounding the rail yard. Through the dense foliage, a shining silver thread of a river wound in the distance. But what river it was, he had no way of knowing. He searched the faces of other *Kriegies* for any sign of recognition. They shuffled their feet in the snow and shared glances as confused and curious as his own.

About twenty new guards arrived on the scene. These guards, older and less sharp than others, grunted and shoved the prisoners into a marching column. Hank fell into step behind someone, behind someone else, behind another man. Don slipped into place next to Hank, but they didn't speak while they marched out of the rail yard.

As they left the city limits, Hank looked behind him. A sign stood near the entrance, bearing the name *Krems* with a dark red line striking through the word. They marched through the little town and approached a busy road. Traffic slowed to a halt as guards stopped cars and pedestrians, who watched as the prisoners passed. Hank glanced at the faces of the people, their eyes drinking in the hundreds of Americans, their thousands of footprints darkening the snow that covered the ground.

Between someone's elbow and a guard's shoulder, Hank caught sight of something on a car. He glanced around for another, then found more and more. On the license plates of cars parked along the streets, Austrian tags marked most vehicles, with a few German ones here and there. He leaned over to Don and muttered, "We're in Austria."

"Really? How do you know?"

"The plates on the cars."

"We were on that train long enough to get to Africa," Don laughed.

Their march had been flat, but now a hill loomed before them. From the base, they marched upward through farm fields and into a large, wooded area. As they climbed, the column of men slowed, stopping to scoop handfuls of snow to wet their mouths, or to catch their breath and rest their legs. The guards kept pushing them, shouting German obscenities and vulgar words, Hank cringed, turning his chin away so guards and the prisoners couldn't see his face. He wondered if he would ever tell Don, or anyone, that he understood them.

At last, over the crest of the hill, a large clearing spread before them, and Don and Hank exchanged looks of relief.

"Do you think that's it?" Don asked. "It looks like it."

"I hope so. I don't know how much further I can go," Hank admitted between gasps of breath.

Billows of smoke rose to the sky, gray columns filling the winter white air. As the prisoners reached the top of the hill, the outline of a massive compound came into view, with almost uncountable rows of barracks. The sharp-cornered gray buildings stood in contrast to the clumps of trees around the compound with snow covering their branches and soft green needles stirring in the breeze. Tall fences lined the compound, mounted with wires and lights connected to guard towers that loomed above the place.

A sign above the wooden gateway read: *STALAG* XVII-B.

CHAPTER 50

February 26, 1944
Stalag 17-B, Krems-Gneixendorf, Austria

The columns of marching prisoners stopped at the gate, where a handful of American prisoners waited with forms and instructions. When Hank shuffled forward, stepping up to the gate, a prisoner waved him over and put a clipboard into his hands.

"*Vorname* means first name and *familienname*, is your last," he said, gesturing to the form. "Understand?"

Hank followed where he pointed, listening to his instructions with a curious look. "Okay."

"You have to remove your dog tags and replace them with German dog tags," the prisoner told him.

"Why?" Hank asked. "Why can't I keep both?"

"Don't ask questions. Get used to doing what you're told."

"Here, we have to take your identification picture," a voice with a distinct Austrian accent grunted as he tapped Hank on the shoulder. He held a chalkboard in one hand and a camera in the other. The man squinted as he inspected Hank's new tag, then wrote in chalk: *106445*. He thrust the board into Hank's hands.

"Under chin." The man insisted in broken English, pantomiming how Hank should hold the board under his chin. Hank looked stone-faced at the camera until the flashbulb burst.

The next room was the razor room. Hank recoiled as he felt someone shove him from behind into a barber's chair. Hank flinched as the razor raced over his head. He watched his light hair slip to the floor, in a pile of blonde, black, and brown hair belonging to the other prisoners. The barber grabbed Hank's arm and pulled him from the chair. Rubbing his head with his palm, Hank disliked the cold air on his bare skin. The feeling of his bumpy scalp dredged up memories of basic training when he'd first had his head shaved, so long ago.

In the next room, they gave each prisoner eating utensils: a thin-metal spoon, bowl, and mug.

"Be very careful with those," Hank's guide warned. "Replacements are hard to come by."

Hank and Don entered the final room where each of them was issued a threadbare blanket, made with assorted pieces of fabric haphazardly sewn together.

"From the looks of this, I'm guessing it was sewn by a third grader," Don joked.

Hank's guide folded his arms. "You are in barracks 17-A. We'll go there now and find your bed. It's the only barracks left with a few unoccupied beds. Follow me."

He led them past a group of men roaming the compound, who watched the new prisoners with expressions Hank couldn't identify. Sympathy? Jealousy? When he entered the barracks, he understood why their glances could have multiple meanings. The prison, full to bursting already, had been flooded with even more men; where would they fit all of them?

Row after row of bunk beds stacked three-high housed at least one-hundred fifty men. Maybe more. "Find a bunk and claim it. It's first come, first served around here," the guide warned.

Hank glanced at each bunk. As he passed, he looked for a pair of socks or a coat, anything that would indicate a current occupant. When he came to an empty bunk, he climbed to the top to find a thin mattress resting on wooden slats.

"I guess we'll take this, eh?" Hank glanced at Don for approval.

"Works for me," Don said. "I hear there are some barracks with three to a bed. We'll have to see how long it takes before someone else joins us."

Hank stood at the foot of his bed, looking around at his new home, rubbing his newly shaved head. He closed his eyes to shut out the crowded barracks. He yearned to go home, if only in his mind. Within seconds, his thoughts drifted over his yard and front porch, watching sunsets over the mountains, or Billie's kind smile the last time they saw each other.

Then a thought struck him with great intensity: he wasn't going anywhere. He was stuck here for the duration of the war, however long that would be—having nothing but time on his hands to think and worry and fret over every little thing. How long could he last in such a place? Don raised an eyebrow. "What's wrong?"

Hank swallowed, looking away. "I guess I just realized that I'm going to be here for a very long time."

Hank grabbed the rail of the top bunk and pulled himself up. Don joined him in the bunk.

Don gave a wry smile. "It's the price we pay for freedom, and apple pie and…"

"That's a joke," Hank interrupted. "Freedom is a matter of being on the right side of whoever is in power. Those in power dictate who is free."

Don dipped his head and looked at Hank with a puzzled look. "That's quite a cynical statement. Especially coming from you. You mind telling me what you mean by that?"

Hank looked away, afraid to explain the circumstances of his parents being in Crystal City and all that happened leading up to their internment.

"I just know that Americans are pretty quick to stomp all over the precious Constitution if it suits them. Look at how they rounded up all those Japanese in California. You heard about that, didn't you?"

Don nodded, but still looked at Hank with a raised eyebrow. "What does that have to do with you?"

"Let's just say I know some people who were put in jail simply because they were born in the wrong country." Hank's voice grew louder. "It's pretty hard to be loyal to a country that can treat people like that."

"And so now," Don added. "You're mad at America?"

"No, it's not that. It's just that things aren't always what they appear to be. I used to think that everything was either all bad or all good. I was taught there's a right and wrong to everything.

"Okay. I'm not sure I believe that, but go ahead."

Hank scratched the back of his head while he thought of what to say. "I've just always believed everything had a clear choice between right and wrong. I chose to join a B-17 crew. It was the right decision for many reasons but look what happened."

Don nodded again.

"I used to think that Germans were decent, upright people. Heck, my family comes from Germany, but look at how they're treating us. And don't get me started about my family. There's a bunch of other things that have come up that have just sent my mind spinning in all directions. I just don't know what to think anymore."

"Well…" Don had a ready answer. "…when that happens to me, I just turn to God."

He let the silence hang in the air for a moment waiting for Hank to agree with him. Hank hesitated, saying nothing.

"You've got your religion, Hank, right? Doesn't that help you when things don't make much sense?"

Hank released a long, heavy exhale. "I don't know anymore."

He'd never questioned his faith, but after being betrayed by his *oma* and her bishop, his faith was shaken to its core.

"It's a long story. Someday I'll tell you about it. I'm just glad you're here, though," he said. "Thanks for listening to all my griping."

Don laughed. "Don't mention it. Maybe someday you'll get it all figured out."

Early in the morning on the third day, a stillness hung over the barracks, broken only by Don's occasional rustling as they huddled to stay warm in their upper bunk. As Hank lay in that transitory state between sleep and wakefulness, listening to the steady breathing and occasional creaking of bunk boards around him, something odd happened. An apparition of Billie emerged in his mind and a sudden peace enveloped him. Her delicate blonde hair and piercing blue eyes glistened as she sat next to him on their sofa in his living room. She searched his eyes, smiling at him in a way she had never yet smiled at him. She was drinking in his affection. A surge of delight spread through him as he reached for her hand. But when he brushed her fingers, the image wavered like rippling water, then disappeared. He grasped for it, squeezing his eyes tight to bring it back.

He lay in his bed, his heart racing. What he saw had been so much more vivid than a dream, but could it have been a vision, a foretelling of what may come? He'd never experienced anything like it before.

He played the scene over and over in his imagination, tucking away the moment into his mind like a souvenir in a suitcase, carefully wrapping the image of her hair and smile with every breath as he fell back to sleep.

CHAPTER 51
February 26, 1944
Port of Lisbon, Portugal

Karl's and Marta's arduous overseas journey included a full week of storminess and rough waters. Sea sickness left much of the ship smelling like vomit. Most passengers smiled with relief as they arrived in Lisbon. At long last, they disembarked from the *Gripsholm* and straightway boarded a train.

Portuguese guards escorted them on their quiet journey from Lisbon to Madrid, Zaragoza, and Barcelona. Once they crossed the border into France, trouble began at their first stop in Perpignan.

"Why are we stopping?" Marta asked one of the guards.

"The French government has refused to supply us with fuel and food." He crossed his arms with a snarl.

"Is this our final stop on the train, then? Do we walk from here?"

"Probably not. The Germans are in charge here. They should help us. It will just take time to squeeze it out of the locals."

Marta turned away. Of course, the locals would be unwilling to give away any of their meager food rations to assist a train full of former German Americans. She wasn't sure she was willing to take it from them.

After a four-hour delay, the train began its trek again. "Finally," Karl added with a relieved grin. "It's about time."

Just after the train had reached full speed, one of the guards opened the door to the cabin with slices of bread and cheese for all the passengers.

"This is probably the last time we'll have food for you," he said. "The Swiss will be no different than the French, so you'll need it make it last for a few days."

After waiting for most of the night, the passengers watched the morning light illuminate the Swiss mountains surrounding Geneva. The train, at long last, had taken on enough fuel to make it to its last stop in the small border town of Kreuzlingen.

A tall, thin Swiss guard called all the internees to the dining cabin for a mandatory briefing. "You will need to pay close attention, as you must follow my instructions exactly," he commanded. "The Swiss government has agreed to act on behalf of the Americans. You will all be part of a prisoner exchange."

Karl grabbed Marta's hand. She tipped her head to acknowledge the guard, then whispered to Karl, "Pay attention."

"When this train stops in the train yard, another train from Germany will pull up next to us. A representative from the German government will come aboard and call out five names at a time. When you hear your name, gather your suitcase and step off the train, keeping to your right until you are directed to get aboard the train headed back to Germany."

Karl wrapped his fingers tighter around Marta's hand, and she knew what he was thinking. As if in answer, the guard said, "Don't worry if you are traveling with family and not everyone is called at the same time. You will all be called eventually. Don't worry about your other luggage and large trunks. They remain secured in the luggage car and will be attached to the German-bound train. That car will remain sealed until you arrive in Germany."

The Swiss guard bent down to look out the window, his fingers drumming out his impatience on his leg. "We will have to wait," he said. "The Germans are notoriously on their own schedule."

After almost two hours, the rumbling of an approaching train grew louder. The German train pulled alongside theirs and the windows aligned as the train inched to a stop. The passengers exchanged awkward glances across the space between the tracks.

Marta spoke to Karl under her breath. "They look like regular people, don't they? Were there men in uniform? Some of them looked pretty banged up."

"They must be relieved because they're one step closer to home," he said.

After a few minutes of silence, a German official stepped onto Karl and Marta's train and called five random names. One by one, each prisoner stepped off the train, walked around the end of the train and toward the German-bound train. Those on the German train did the same, crossing the tracks and boarding the American-bound train. The prisoners were never close enough to look or talk to each other.

Swiss guards stood by, watching the slow exchange. One German prisoner for one American. The names rolled off slowly. After an hour. Karl's and Marta's names were called together. Stepping off the train and onto the train tracks, they walked hand-in-hand while Karl clung to their single piece of luggage.

For hours, this process continued until seven-hundred-fifty Germany-bound passengers had boarded. More than six hundred American citizens were headed for freedom, and more were still boarding. These lucky passengers consisted of businessmen, friends of politicians, missionaries, and other Americans detained by the Germans.

As the last group of passengers waited to board the American-bound train, outside the car, two Swiss guards spoke with excitement to each other. Marta stepped closer, listening through a crack in the window. She heard a few words and phrases, then ducked back into her seat and whispered to Karl, "It sounds like there were over a hundred and fifty people from a place called Vittel, somewhere in France. You ever heard of it?" she asked.

Karl shook his head.

"I can't be a sure, but from what it sounds like, many of those exchange prisoners were Jews." Her voice quivered and she drew in a breath before continuing. "They seem pretty excited about saving these people from a place called Auschwitz. I couldn't quite follow everything they were saying. What do you think it means?" she asked.

"I have no idea." Karl shook his head.

Chapter 51-Note 1: Many of the events depicted in this chapter are based on actual events. The Swedish ship, *SS Gripsholm*, was chartered to sail from the United States with internees hailing from INS camps from across the country. German–American detainees were traded for Americans being held by the Nazis, in a one-for-one exchange. These exchanges occurred in two primary movements, one in February 1944, and a second in December 1944.

Chapter 51-Note 2: FDR's secret prisoner swap program recruited ethnic Germans from Latin America, intending to use these prisoners to free Americans being held by the Nazis. The U.S. put pressure on countries like Costa Rica, Panama, Honduras, and Columbia, among many others, to arrest and detain ethnic Germans living there. They convinced these governments to send the Germans to the U.S. where they were held without charge and subsequently deported. As depicted in this chapter, ethnic Germans were swapped for American businessmen, diplomats, Jews, and other VIPs being held by the Nazis. In addition to thousands of German Americans, records indicate 1,813 individuals from Latin America were deported against their will to Europe. According to General George C. Marshall in a memo dated 12 Dec 1942 to the Caribbean Defense Command, he admits the government's intentions for many German internees: "These interned nationals are to be used for exchange with interned American civilian nationals." Beginning in early 1942, over 4,000 German Latin Americans came to the U.S. and were held in American internment camps without the benefit of due process.

"Special War Problems Division: Subject Files, 1939-1954." Entry A1 1357, Boxes 116 and 120, Declassified April 2010.

Chapter 51-Note 3: The documentation regarding the prisoner exchange at Kreuzlingen confirms the exchange of 160 Jewish internees from the Vittel camp. The Vittel internment camp was established in German-held France in 1941, located in a resort in the Vosges Mountains near the German border. One of those prisoners was Mary Berg, her mother, father, and sister. These four American citizens held valid U.S. passports, but the German government capriciously refused to recognize their passports and threatened to ship them to Auschwitz. The Bergs were among the 160 exchanged at Kreuzlingen as depicted in this chapter. Of the prisoners who remained at Vittel afterwards, 250 were removed in May 1944, sent to Auschwitz, and gassed.

CHAPTER 52
March 3, 1944
Kreuzlingen, Germany

The northbound train chugged and jerked to gain speed, leaving Kreuzlingen with its cargo of prisoners from America. Karl and Marta stared out the window at the darkness it left behind and felt the strange emptiness they hadn't noticed before. The other train full of people would be going to the home Karl and Marta had left, to families they might not have seen since the war began. Marta wished she could send something with them or wish them well. Maybe give them a message for Ella, perhaps.

Journeying deeper inside Germany gave her an empty feeling. She was confused by her fleeting feelings of longing for their home in Crystal City. It didn't make any sense. Being in Crystal City, with all its political machinations, was oddly more appealing than stepping into the bullseye of the Allied offensive. She dismissed these odd thoughts as mere anxiety about the unknown circumstances they would face.

"At least we don't have to deal with grumpy Swiss officials anymore," Marta said.

"I think the Germans will be even grumpier," Karl replied.

They continued sitting by each other, holding hands, until the train pulled into the Ravensburg station just after midnight. They were told to retrieve their trunk from the luggage car and leave the train to wait somewhere else, even though it wasn't scheduled to depart until morning.

"Why can't we stay here in the train?" Karl asked, "It's not going anywhere."

The train official shot Karl a threatening stare. Marta nudged Karl not to argue.

They stepped off the train, gathering with the other prisoners in front of the German immigration office. Someone rattled the doorknob, but the locked door would remain shut until morning. Passengers slept on the chilled, hard concrete in the drafty railroad station, surrounded by their bulky trunks and suitcases.

Marta grabbed Karl's wrist to look at his watch. "Karl, it's six a.m. Look at the line for the immigration office. It's already twisted down the long corridor."

Karl helped Marta to her feet as she stretched the soreness from her limbs and grabbed their suitcase to get in line.

In typical German fashion, the immigration office windows opened just as the clock read eight. Officials started processing those waiting in line one by one. Most were Austrian and Swiss citizens seeking admittance to visit family. Karl and Marta handed their enemy alien cards to a thin, bony-faced woman. She raised her eyebrows and asked, "Is this all you have? American papers? This is unacceptable. I need papers in German telling me who you are."

Karl gave a helpless grimace and said, "This is all we have."

"Don't you have any other papers, like a passport or anything else showing your identity?"

"No," Karl said. "We were taken from our homes before we could collect any type of identification."

"What documents do you have to prove who you are?" she demanded.

"Other than this, it was all taken from us. We were deported against our will."

The women took some papers from a stack of forms and selected one.

"Go to that area over there to complete this form," she said. "This is for your liberty certificate. You must complete every question, or your application will be denied."

She pushed the papers at Karl. "Next."

The lengthy form asked for a history of their residence for the past fifteen years. It also asked about their genealogy, going back generations, seeking out any signs of Jewish blood. As with most Mormons, Karl and Marta knew the names of their families for at least four generations. They filled in the forms and reviewed each other's work before joining the line again to wait their turn.

After an hour, they approached the window, where a large man greeted them.

"Your paperwork, please."

Karl handed over their American identification and the form they had been asked to complete.

The man glanced over the new form, a frown darkening his face. "This is wrong. Why did you fill out this form? Who gave this to you?"

Karl's shoulders sagged a little. "A woman a few windows down."

He mumbled, then glanced at her with a look of disgust. He looked up at Karl with a pleasant smile. "Aren't you from that special train that arrived late last night?"

"Yes."

He reached for a clipboard and ran his finger down a long list of names. "Let me see, Meyer, Karl. Meyer, Marta. There you are. We have your information here. We know who you are. That stupid woman gave you the wrong instructions."

Karl flinched at the hostility in his tone. The man walked over to the woman and interrupted her, shouting obscenities and threatening to fire her. She left her window in tears. The man then returned and sat again, saying "She should know better. You are Germans sent here from America, right?"

"Yes, sir," Karl replied.

He grabbed a large rubber stamp and pounded it with vigor on several forms. He rolled a half-sheet of paper in a typewriter, positioned it, then entered the Meyers' information in the blanks. After a few anxious minutes, he handed each of them their identification papers. "We can only give you temporary German identification. This will expire in six months, and you will need to reapply for a permanent card. Do you understand?"

"Yes." Karl smiled as he reached for the papers.

"Thank you for your help," Marta added.

They turned away from the window.

"We're on our own now, I suppose," Karl said. "We'll need a train if we don't want to lug our things all the way to Bremen on foot."

"Who is going to want American money? We need to find a way to exchange our dollars for Reichsmarks."

They wandered down the street, drinking in the German shop names and street signs. On the corner, Karl nudged Marta toward a small café. He held the door for Marta. A husky, bright-eyed woman in her mid-thirties attended to customers at the cash register. Karl waited his turn and approached while Marta stood behind him. "Do you know where we can exchange some American money into Reichsmarks?"

Her eyes sparkled with excitement. "You have dollars? Ill exchange them and give you a better rate than you'll get anywhere else."

He pulled out his wallet, but she waved it away.

"No, not here. Put your wallet back. Are you crazy?"

"I'm sorry. I didn't know."

The woman frowned in confusion.

"We just arrived here," Karl offered an apologetic shrug.

"You," she said pointing to Marta. "Meet me in the toilet room. How much do you have to change?" she whispered.

"One hundred sixty dollars," Karl replied.

"Oh," she gasped. "I can't exchange that much. The official rate is two Reichsmarks to the dollar. I can give you three to one. That means I'll give you a hundred-twenty Reichsmarks for forty dollars. Will you do that?"

"What will I get from a bank?" Karl asked.

"Probably less than two-to-one, if you're lucky."

"It's so much of our money though."

"If you go to the bank, they'll ask a lot of questions." The woman's eyes narrowed. "But it's up to you."

"Just do it," Marta muttered next to him. "We can't do anything without money."

"Okay. We'll do it." Karl agreed with reluctance.

"You go over to that table. In about five minutes, I'll bring you something. In another five minutes, she can act like she's going to the toilet. Is that clear?"

Trying to appear as though nothing underhanded was about to happen, they sat at a table for two.

The cashier came over with two steaming mugs of foul-smelling coffee, placing them on the table as she said, "Here's your coffee. Would you like anything else?"

Karl smelled the coffee and watched as she walked back to her register.

The café was almost empty. A lone man sat at a table reading a newspaper. Marta watched the brim of the man's hat over the top of the newspaper as Karl fumbled in his coat pocket. He pulled out two twenty-dollar bills and put them in Marta's hand. She clenched the money in her fist and folded her arms, pulling her gaze away from the stranger at the other table.

Marta sniffed her coffee. "I can't understand how people can drink this stuff."

Karl wrinkled his nose in protest but sipped it without drawing attention to himself. After five minutes, the black liquid still filled their cups to the brim, Marta stood to look for the women's toilet.

After a moment, the cashier hurried in and locked the door behind her. She showed Marta the Reichsmarks. "Do you have the forty dollars?"

Marta opened her clenched fist and let her money fall into the women's hand.

The woman held it closer to her face. A smile curled her lips. "You must keep this a secret," she insisted. "The government punishes anyone who changes money. They use dollars to buy oil and materials on foreign markets. But they don't give us a fair rate."

The woman turned around and unlocked the door, then stopped all of a sudden and insisted, "You wait here for a few minutes before you come out again, okay?"

Marta agreed, and locked the door. After two minutes, she returned to sit with Karl.

"Did you get it?" he asked.

"Yes." She sank down into her chair.

"We need change to call your mother. Where should we get it?"

"Let's wait a few minutes and ask the cashier. She's our only real hope to get some coins for the pay phone."

Marta downed her coffee, hiding her grimace with every swallow. With her empty cup, she approached the cashier again, gesturing to her mug.

The woman smiled. "Ready for a refill?"

"If you please." Marta held it out to her and whispered. "Could you give us coins for the pay phone?"

"Sure, how much do you need?"

Quietly, Marta answered, "I'm not sure. I need to call my mother in Bremen."

"A three-minute call should be about three to four Reichsmarks."

"Then give me change for five, just to be safe."

Marta thanked her, and the cashier smiled back. Karl led the way as both of them walked out the café's door. Before the door closed behind them, Marta noticed the man reading the newspaper had stood and looked around. Holding Karl's hand, Marta glanced over her shoulder and saw the man picking up his pace to catch up to them. The door to the café flew open, and she pushed Karl into doorway of another business.

"Just wait here a minute." She held Karl's elbow. Her heart pounded as she watched the man's head hurry past the window. "I think that man from the café is following us."

After a few breathless moments they found the pay phone and stepped to the back of the line. Four other people were ahead of them. Marta fidgeted with her coat sleeves, her buttons, her ring. Karl squeezed her hand, but she drew in sharp anxious breaths. After a few nervous moments, Marta looked over her shoulder, then snapped her gaze back to Karl and pointed. "There he is."

Karl stiffened, turning to hide his face. He whispered to Marta, "Do you think he's with the *Gestapo*?"

Marta lowered her profile, but out of the corner of her eye spotted the man. "I don't know. He's looking in our direction, but I don't think he's seen us."

Marta poked her elbow into Karl's ribs. "Calm down. Everyone's looking at you. You look like a child with your hand in the cookie jar."

Karl took a deep breath and exhaled, struggling to stay in control of his emotions.

The woman ahead of them finished her conversation and hung up the phone, Marta pushed Karl to step forward, then took one final glance around the room. "I think he's gone?" Still unconvinced, Marta continued looking for him.

Karl turned to lift the earpiece from the cradle. Marta watched while Karl waited for the operator to answer. That instant, she recoiled as she felt a stranger tap her shoulder. She gasped in fear at seeing the man from the café.

"Oh, I'm sorry," he stepped back as she spun around. "I didn't mean to startle you."

Marta looked on in terror.

"I think you left your luggage in the café. Is this yours?"

Marta looked down, his hands clutching their suitcase. "Oh, I can't believe I did that. Yes, this is ours. Thank you for tracking us down. I can't thank you enough." Her pounding heart slowed, but the thought of losing all their belongings still clenched her chest with fear.

"It's my pleasure to help," he said. "Have a safe journey."

Karl handed the phone to Marta. She paused to catch her breath, then spoke into the mouthpiece.

"This is a station-to-station call please. The number is Stuhr 11-42-11, Hildebrandt residence."

The operator replied in a monotone voice. "One moment, please."

Marta looked up at Karl. "What if she's not there?"

He shrugged.

"I haven't spoken to my mama for ten years. What if she doesn't recognize my voice?"

The operator said, "Please deposit two Reichsmarks-seventy for three minutes."

Marta slipped the coins into the payphone, then waited for the operator to acknowledge. "One moment please."

"Who is calling, please?"

"Mrs. Marta Meyer."

A series of clicks and beeps sounded in Marta's ear before a voice, as familiar as her own, answered. "Hildebrandt residence."

Marta held her breath.

The operator said, "Please hold the line for a call from Mrs. Marta Meyer."

"My Marta is calling? How could that be?"

Another click. "Go ahead," the operator instructed.

"Hi, Mama." Tears pricked Marta's eyes.

"Oh, my Marta. How are you calling me from America?"

"It's a long story," she said, sniffing, "but I am in Ravensburg."

"Ravensburg! Why in heaven's name are you in Ravensburg? Is Karl okay? What about the children? What is going on?"

"Listen, Mama, I don't have much time to talk." She explained their arrest, detention, and transoceanic voyage. "Karl and I arrived in Ravensburg late last night. But we have no place to go. I was hoping we could live with you for a while."

"Of course, you can," she said. Her voice turned firm as she asked, "Do you have the proper papers?"

"Yes," Marta frowned. "Why would that even matter to you?"

"That, too, is a very long story that must wait until you get here. How long will that take?"

"I don't know, Mama. It's almost 700 kilometers from here, and I don't know what to expect, or even how we will get there."

"You must be very careful," her mother warned. "Avoid Frankfurt if you can. The trains are constantly attacked. And the rail lines are damaged almost everywhere."

"We will do our best to get there as soon as we can. Okay, Mama?"

Marta hung up the phone and stepped out of the phone booth. A man waiting in line brushed past her and grabbed the phone. Karl took Marta's elbow and led her away.

"What did she say?"

"She asked if we had papers. Why would she be so concerned about that?"

Karl scratched his chin. "Maybe she's renting out rooms to help supplement her income?"

"That doesn't sound like my mama."

"Let's go. The sooner we can there, the better."

They waited their turn at the ticket window. Karl stepped up to the agent with a forced smile and said, "Two tickets to Bremen, please."

CHAPTER 53

March 8, 1944
Stalag 17-B, Krems-Gneixendorf, Austria

Hank jumped up to a sitting position on his bed. He didn't know what a restful sleep felt like anymore—not until tonight, when he had fallen into deep sleep and then something startled him awake. Sleeping next to him, Don flinched at his sudden movement. The blanket they shared slipped, and Don grabbed it before it fell to the floor. Hank was breathing fast. He scanned the barracks in the darkness, expecting to see a commotion.

"What's wrong?" Don asked.

"I thought I heard gunfire." Hank was confused, still not fully awake. The subdued sounds of slumber filled the barracks. Everyone else still slept.

"You must have dreamt it. But thanks for waking me up."

"Sorry about that."

"Shut up you two," came an angry whisper from another bunk. "It's too early."

Hank lay back down, pulling the blanket over their shoulders. They had to sleep in their clothes every night, sharing each other's body heat. But even in his sleep, Hank could still feel Don trembling in the cold.

"I don't think my feet will ever warm up," Don said. "These boots just aren't doing the job."

"Too bad you didn't get a pair of these wooden, clog-like things; my feet stay warm all night and all day."

A loud "Shhhh" came from a man in the bunk below.

Hank laid back down and put his hands under his head.

Don whispered, "I don't think I've ever been this hungry. How do these guys get used to it?"

"I guess it takes time."

"What day do they bring the Red Cross parcels?" Don asked. "Is it Fridays?"

"Yeah. Tomorrow."

"These have been the longest four days of my life. And it's not just the cold and no food or seeing the poor Russians over there being treated like pigs. It's the hopeless grind with nothing to look forward to. Nothing. I don't think I'll ever get used to it."

"It will get better once you get something to eat."

Their hushed voices finally drifted back into a light sleep. An hour later, the 0600 reveille resounded throughout the camp. "We can go outside now without being shot." Hank was groggy as he mumbled. Don grunted in reply. Some men with work details tumbled out of bed and left the barracks for their daily jobs.

"Come on." Hank shook Don's shoulder as they shivered in the cold morning darkness. They stumbled outside to the washroom between the two barracks. For breakfast they were given a measly ladle of hot water. Some used it for coffee, if they had some from the Red Cross parcel. For most, breakfast wasn't worth the bother. Hank and Don held the hot water close to their faces and breathed in the warmth.

Two guards wandered by, and a bunkmate beneath Hank and Don shuddered, looking away from them. "Keep an eye out for those two," he warned.

"Why?" Hank asked.

"See that oversized oaf over there? That's *Stabsgefreiter* Schröder. He's gotta be at least seven feet tall; we call him 'Big Stoop'."

Hank glanced where the prisoner pointed and snickered. "He reminds me of that Chinese character in *Terry and the Pirates*."

"Be careful around him. Big Stoop has a sadistic streak a mile long," Hank's bunkmate said. "Stay out of his reach, 'cause he's been known to hit prisoners for no reason, other than he enjoys seeing them writhe on the ground in pain."

Big Stoop's arms hung by his side; his catcher's-mitt-sized hands curled into fists swinging with each step. "His hands are huge."

"A couple times he just blind-sided a prisoner and cold-cocked him in the ear. It ruptured the guy's eardrum, and while he thrashed in pain on the ground, Big Stoop stood over him laughing."

"That's horrible."

"But that's not the worst of it. Big Stoop's attacks are always encouraged by his partner." He pointed to a guard who looked to be about thirty years old, with pasty skin and sinister eyes set deep into his gaunt face. His uniform hung on him like a drape, giving him an unkempt, sickly look.

That guy is *Gefreiter* Sikkar, but we call him 'Sicko,' partly because of his sick sense of humor—he's always egging on Big Stoop—and because he looks like he's about to keel-over any day now."

"I can see how the name fits him so well," Don smiled.

"Whenever Big Stoop whacks someone, this guy's cackle gives me the creeps."

Hank watched the two guards and their slow, methodical pace. "I guess he seems a little scary, but is he really that much worse than Big Stoop?"

"Absolutely." The prisoner looked Hank in the eyes. "No one has ever witnessed Sicko actually hit anyone. He's more of a cheerleader than a brute. Stoop has a tendency toward violence, but Sikkar is more Machiavellian. He's corrupt and scheming. He'll do anything or say anything to get what he wants. Don't ever trust him."

Roll call sounded at 0800. After the prisoners had gathered and then dispersed again, Hank watched Big Stoop and Sikkar from the corner of his eye. After a moment, Sikkar nudged Big Stoop with his elbow and pointed to where Don and Hank stood. They marched over, and Sikkar tilted his head as he looked at Hank. He spoke in German. "Looks like we have some new guests at *Stalag* 17-B."

Big Stoop smiled menacingly, and Hank turned away. Big Stoop made a crude sexual comment about Don, and Sikkar laughed in a nasally, sickening cackle.

Hank flinched, disgust flashing across his face

Sikkar stepped around to stare Hank in the face. "What is your name?" He asked in very clear English.

"Staff Sergeant Meyer."

Sikkar reached into Hank's coat and pulled out his German dog tag. "Heinrich Meyer. Are you German?"

"I'm an American," Hank stood tall, his shoulders squared.

"Do you speak German?"

Other prisoners walking by stopped, hanging back just near enough to hear Hank's reply.

"No sir."

Sikkar nodded as he assessed Hank's facial expressions to see if he was lying.

Hank stiffened and smirked.

"I think you're lying," Sikkar spat.

"*Stabsgefreiter* Schröder," Sikkar accused in German. "I think this American pretty-boy needs to learn a lesson or two about respecting authority, don't you think?" Sikkar smirked, then let go a string of vile and offensive insults. Hank turned his face to stone, hoping his eyes didn't betray something he couldn't control. After a while, he shrugged.

Sikkar stepped back, crossing his arms. "I think I need to learn more about you and your history"

Hank looked past him.

Sikkar circled Hank, inspecting him like a side of beef. Returning to speak German, he said, "I think I need a special name for him. A fitting name for a German traitor."

For the first time, Hank wondered if any other prisoners in camp could understand what Sikkar said. He fought harder to keep his breathing steady.

"Yes," Sikkar continued in German, "A name that fits all traitors like." He looked at Hank menacingly. "I think I'll call you..." He lifted his chin in thought, a sneer curled his lip. "*Schweinehund.*"

Big Stoop roared with laughter.

"*Schweinehund!* That's a good one," Stoop said. "And he'll never know what it really means."

"Oh, but I think our traitor here understands it very well."

Hank's heart dropped. Sicko and Big Stoop turned away laughing with each other. Once they were gone and out of earshot, Don asked Hank, "What did he say?"

Hank knew the word *schweinehund* was among the most despicable thing a German could call someone. Hank looked at Don and shrugged. "No idea."

Chapter 53- Note 1: The term *schweinehund* is translated to English as simply pig-dog. Most Germans today consider it an archaic expletive, as it has now assumed much less offensive meaning in today's vernacular. But in a World War II context, it was considered among the most offensive of all German epithets.

Chapter 53-Note 2: "Big Stoop" was a guard in *Stalag* Luft IV and among the Allies was likely one of the most hated of all guards. According to POW Leslie Caplan, a medic, "He was about six feet, six inches tall, weighs about 180 or 190 pounds, and was approximately fifty years old. His most outstanding characteristic was his large hands, which seemed out of proportion to those of a normal person.

"Big Stoop" would cuff the men on the ears with an open hand sideways movement. This would cause pressure on the eardrums which sometimes punctured them. I treated some of the men whose eardrums had been ruptured by the cuffings administered by "Big Stoop."

"War Crimes Testimony of Dr. Leslie Caplan," *The Evacuation of Luft IV,* 31 December 1947.

CHAPTER 54
March 16, 1944
Near El Paso, Texas

Billie hovered five thousand feet over Texas. She had just refueled her P-51 in El Paso and was headed for an overnighter in Oklahoma City. Another five days would take her the three-thousand miles to Presque Isle, Maine.

Her right hand gripped the center stick, her left on the throttle. In the plane of her dreams, she cruised at three hundred sixty miles per hour, reveling in the smoothness of its speed, responsiveness, and maneuverability. Only a few hundred men could fly the P-51, and she was among just a handful of women who had ever gotten this far.

After she had "broken-in" a plane, putting it through its paces, she knew it was important to get the new engines running at high RPMs. This helped temper the engine and prepare it for the abuse it was bound to endure overseas. She'd floated over the country until she flew over the dull, quiet plains of Oklahoma or Texas where she could take it up to its maximum speed. Her left hand curled around the throttle, and she checked the skies around her. She pulled on the throttle, yelling out in exhilaration. Her plane burst through the sky, her speed cranking up to four hundred miles per hour. As a grin spread across her face, she startled herself with a strange thought: *If only Chester or Hank could see me now.* A dull calm washed over her. Not that it numbed the thrill of burning through the skies, but a peacefulness prompted a contented half-smile. With flare no one could see, she moved the throttle back and resumed her cruising speed.

As she approached Oklahoma City, she spoke to the tower in Fort Worth before switching her radio frequency to the Army Airways Communications System.

The voices of four other P-51 pilots came over the static of the radio, too far away to see but close enough for Billie to listen in. They tossed back and forth conversation about the weather, navigation, landing issues, or problems they'd encountered in other planes.

After several minutes, the dialogue made an awkward turn when one of the pilots told an explicit joke. The others laughed. Heat crawled up Billie's neck, and she gripped her center stick in anger. The pilots shared more jokes, snickering at details unsuitable for military officers and inappropriate for mixed company.

One pilot began, "Guys, here's another one…"

Billie pushed a button on her stick. "Hey fellas, knock it off with the dirty jokes."

The frequency wavered in near silence for a few long seconds. Muffled engine noises rumbled over the static.

"Did that sound like a woman?"

"It sure did, but it couldn't have been from the ground."

"Well how else would we hear a woman's voice on this frequency?"

Billie bit her lip, waiting in silence. At least the jokes had stopped.

"Are we sure it was a woman? Maybe it was a man with a high-pitched voice," he laughed.

Laughter erupted again. "Did you hear the one about…"

"Hey fellas, knock it off with the dirty jokes," Billie snapped. "I mean it."

"Who are you?" one of them demanded, "and why are you on a military frequency?"

"Because I'm flying a military plane."

This time the awkward silence hung as thick as storm clouds.

"So, it *is* a woman." The mix of astonishment, horror, and a hint of awe, in the man's voice made Billie smile.

She swallowed back her glee before she spoke. "I'm in a P-51B that I just picked up at the factory in Inglewood. It's a Razorback Merlin-powered Mustang, serial number 43-12161. Any questions?"

A long silence followed.

"I want to know who each of you are. I have half a mind to report you for this. This is not only an inappropriate conversation on a military radio frequency, but it's completely unbecoming of officers in the United States Army Air Corp." Their silence kept drawing a laugh from her, but she kept her voice stern, letting go of the button to giggle, imagining their gaping mouths and wide eyes.

"We're terribly sorry, ma'am," one of them said. "We didn't know women were flying military planes."

"I have over two thousand hours in a cockpit. I earned my wings as part of the Women's Airforce Service Pilots, and I finished pursuit school in Palm Springs. You'd better know we're up here."

"I had no idea. I am so sorry," he said. "If we had known, we'd never have talked like that in front of you."

"There's hundreds of us WASP pilots up here, listening in on this frequency, and we shouldn't have to listen to grown men talk like schoolboys."

"I'm sorry, too," another said.

"I apologize ma'am for tellin' such awful jokes," one said. "My mama taught me better'n that, and 'specially never to talk like that in front of a woman."

She muted her microphone and laughed aloud before she said, "Well then, I accept your apologies. But shouldn't we all just keep our conversations clean and professional?"

"Yes ma'am," they replied in chorus.

Billie spent a night in Oklahoma City and Columbus. Her next stop was in Providence before the final stop in Maine. After getting airborne in Columbus, she realized this was the first trip in a long time that had been uneventful. It was nice, but thinking about it might change her luck. She called to the tower for the latest weather conditions around her next destination in Buffalo.

"You picked a good day," the officer replied. "The weather is bitter cold up here today, but otherwise it's Ceiling and Visibility Unlimited your entire way!"

"I'll take CAVU any day."

For the next hour, the bright sunny sky gave her clear visibility as far as she could see. After crossing over Cleveland and heading toward Lake Erie, white clouds rose on the horizon in an odd formation that stretched from the ground to at least ten thousand feet. It seemed to be moving into her path.

She called the tower again. "I thought you said it was CAVU all the way."

"That's what our report says. Why?"

"I'm at about five thousand feet, and there's this enormous cumulonimbus formation directly ahead of me. It's unbelievable how big it is."

"Really?" he said. "It's not on our charts. Can you make your course around it?"

"Not now," she frowned. "I'm coming right into it, and I don't want to be delayed, so I'll just fly through it."

She had heard stories from pilots who encountered clouds of icy fog, especially over large bodies of water like Lake Erie, but it was unusual for clouds like this to extend this high.

She entered the cloud bank and darkness covered the cockpit. In a few minutes, her propeller glistened. Icy fog surrounded her as her plane pushed through the thickness of the cold air. It made her shiver.

She called in her observation to the tower in Buffalo. "Just thought I'd let you know that this huge cloud is fog. I'm getting an accumulation of ice on my wings and propeller. You may want to warn other pilots heading your way."

"Roger that," the tower called. "Good luck."

She could choose to fly through it, but the P-51 wasn't equipped for de-icing. No, she'd have to get above it, and she'd have to do it fast. The bright clear sky was somewhere above her. She just had to find it. She pushed the P-51 engine hard to climb in the oxygen-deprived air.

Black spots appeared before her eyes, and her feet began tingling with numbness. She couldn't understand why she couldn't think clearly or why her muscles weren't moving right. A few cups of coffee, she guessed, weren't quite enough to keep her awake after late nights of partying and early mornings for business.

Then it dawned on her. She was suffering from oxygen deprivation. A thought flashed through her mind to make a distress call to the tower. Instead, she reached for her oxygen mask, then remembered with fluttering panic in her chest that the hose from the oxygen regulator had a leak. She discovered it when she tested it before taking off, but figured it was not worth delaying her flight. She'd made a note on the repair log, assuming she didn't plan to fly high enough to worry about it.

The numbness and tingling moved into her hands. Before she knew it, her hands contracted into claw-like, clenched fists. The clear sky couldn't be much further.

She fought the urge to close her eyes. Darkness clouded her vision and her head swam with dizziness. She took in several deep breaths, but that didn't help. Everything slowed and darkened until only a small sliver of light glowed, far ahead.

Like hollow echoes, the voices of her family called out to her. She saw her parents, her grandma, Ella. Hank. Out of nowhere, a thought jumped into her head. *Ask God for help.* No, it was a waste of time, she told herself. But as fear clutched her heart, she cried out, "Oh God, please help me."

She reached for the control stick, but it was stiff and wouldn't budge. Using every ounce of energy she could gather, she pulled the throttle back with her forearm, struggling to draw the stick toward her. As the nose of the plane pulled up, her plane's forward momentum stalled. Without lift, she could feel the plane in a free fall, dropping slowly at first, then the powerful Merlin engines propelled her plane toward the ground. As the plane picked up more speed, the G-forces pushed her closer and closer to a blackout. With her vision obscured, Billie could only feel the plane in a hopeless, vertical dive. The engine whined as she plummeted.

Twelve-thousand feet.

Eleven-thousand five hundred feet.

Dizziness and tunnel vision clouded her mind, dulling the sense of danger like sound underwater. She could still hear it. She knew it was there. But it was so far away, the danger was more like a nightmare than reality.

Eleven-thousand feet.

The engine grew louder in her head, and clouds still blocked her view of the ground. The fuzzy altimeter dials whirred in a surreal motion.

Before long, she reached six-thousand feet. Using all her effort, she shook her head back and forth to keep from losing consciousness. Finally, her lungs sucked in oxygen. With so little in her stomach, vomit exploded in her mouth. She spat it out on the floor between her feet, sloshing it onto her boots. But she was startled awake now, blinking a few times to focus on the altimeter.

She grasped for the control stick, her claw-like hand fumbling. Using her wrists, she inched it toward her. The nose of the plane lifted slightly, but she would still smash into the ground if she didn't level up soon.

At three-thousand feet, with her mind at last clearing, she sensed the plane responding to her. With one last great effort, she coaxed the plane to level off.

As her oxygen intake increased, the black spots in her vision disappeared. While the cockpit controls still swam in a blur, she inhaled through her mouth to gulp in the precious oxygen. She leveled off at fifteen hundred feet, and the cockpit controls were coming more into focus. Her hands relaxed enough to grasp her entire hand around the stick and throttle.

Billie maintained her course eastward for another few minutes until she escaped the foggy cloud. Her hands and feet trembled as she breathed in deep through her mouth. Her flight instruments showed she was level.

I'm a fool. How could she be so sloppy with her pre-flight checklists to neglect her oxygen mask? She'd almost gotten herself killed. As a sense of calm settled into her bones, the recklessness of her life now surfaced in her mind. For once, it wasn't accompanied by Hank's self-righteous voice scraping against her ears, but she knew how wrong she was to live this way: parties, drinking, men. Sleeping with several different men who had since dumped her. To her, it only proved what she already knew about herself: she was unlovable. She had filled the emptiness with alcohol—first to help her sleep, then to just forget every stupid thing she had done. For not living up to what she had been taught by her parents and grandma. For inadvertently telling the FBI about Hank's Nazi memorabilia. How could she ever face Ella, or Karl and Marta, or even Hank ever again? And then on top of it all, she gave up on God, and when she faced certain death, she crawled right back to Him?

Despair rose in her gut. Usually, she could compartmentalize this internal battle of guilt-ridden voices and put them off for later. Today they echoed louder and louder. She chided herself for being a hypocrite. For turning to God only when she was desperate. Now, after all her failures in life, the words "shameless whore" echoed in her mind with as much violence as cast stones.

Shame was not a new feeling, pricking her conscience until it had burrowed its way into her deepest thoughts and dwelt there alongside her laughter, her hopes and dreams, her memories. In the disaster she'd just escaped, all of these conflicting emotions emerged, breaking the surface of her troubled mind.

She could find relief from all these tormenting thoughts. She could finish the job the fog cloud almost accomplished. Maybe for once, she could do this one thing right.

The power was in her hands. The lake rushed by below her. It would be so easy to make the pain in her heart go away. Tears welled up in her eyes and flowed down her cheeks, but she did nothing to wipe them away. She could end it all right now. The stick in her hand was so fragile, so easy to let go.

The surface of the water rippled in a silent breeze, like wind through the grasses near her Utah home. She envisioned her grandma's face as she was told of Billie's death. The thought made her gasp sharply, and she cried again.

After the war, she would hold her grandma's soft hands. She imagined seeing Ella again with her gentle and welcoming smile. Both of them were worth living for. She thought of Chester, the memories of fun they had always had together, invigorating her with a laugh. Then her thoughts turned to Hank. After all the guys she had encountered in the Army, she came to appreciate men like Hank. He wasn't so bad after all. In fact, she longed to be treated with the respect Hank had always shown her.

The water below her morphed into the greening fields of early spring. She, too, could evolve, even if it was a slow change, like the seasons. She would be the person her grandma always believed she could be and live up to her expectations. "Don't forget who you are. Be nice to other people, but don't forget to be nice to yourself."

Wiping tears from her eyes, she gave a sharp exhale between pursed lips. She glanced at her watch. She was only a few minutes behind schedule. If she hurried, she could make it there on time.

CHAPTER 55
March 11, 1944
Huntsville, Utah

Ella made the trip up Ogden Canyon to check on her house and visit with Grandma Russell. She kicked the snow off her feet as she walked into Grandma's cozy home. The fire in the fireplace popped and snapped.

"I can't believe how much of a difference living in Ogden is from living in Huntsville," Ella said. "It's spring in Ogden; the daffodils are blooming, and it's warm. I drive up here and it's still like the dead of winter. You have a foot of snow."

"I know. It's the price we pay to live in paradise," Grandma said. She stood at the sink, scrubbing a few dinner dishes. "How's school going, Ella?"

"Great! I can almost see the light at the end of the tunnel." Ella laughed at herself.

"Do you still love being a nurse, now that you're this far along in your program?"

"More than ever. My professor asked me if I had ever considered getting my doctorate and becoming a teacher. Can you imagine that?" Ella smiled.

"What a compliment that is. She must see a lot of potential in you."

"But a Ph.D. That's never crossed my mind."

"That's not a surprise at all, Ella—someone as talented as you."

Ella looked down, mulling over Grandma's confidence in her. For the first time, she was willing to consider she had the potential to get an advanced degree. Before now she couldn't allow herself to imagine such a thing.

"So how much school do you have before you finish?"

"I have one more quarter. I finished my clinical rotation at Dee Hospital, and I was just hired at Bushnell Hospital up in Brigham City. I need to work at least a year for the military since they paid for my education. I'll be taking care of our boys up there and doing what I've been trained to do. I am so excited."

"When do you start?"

"My finals are next week. Then I start the Monday after that. I'm going to work on-call whenever I can at the hospital because I don't want to lose my connection there. I'm hoping to get hired back after my military commitment is fulfilled." Ella propped her chin in her hands, leaning her elbows on the table as she stared out the window. Grandma moved around the kitchen, putting dishes away, seeming to be interested in Ella's chatter.

"Do you...do you ever hear anything from Billie?" Grandma wiped her hands with a dish cloth.

Ella's gaze wandered back into the kitchen as she sighed. "I was going to ask you the same question. I only hear from her every once in a while." She furrowed her eyebrows.

"I got a letter from her a few months ago," Grandma said. "But I rely on you and her parents to tell me the latest. She finished pursuit school, and now she's flying all types of fast planes. The Mustang something-or-other," Grandma smiled.

"It's a P-51 Mustang," Ella said. "I hear that she's hardly ever at her home in Long Beach because they have her flying all over the country. She'll go a week or two and never step foot in her apartment."

"Isn't that amazing," Grandma mused. "Well good for her. It sounds like she's having the time of her life."

"I'm not so sure she's having fun. In her last letter she had just broken up with another pilot she'd been dating for a while. She was pretty upset about it. She caught him cheating, apparently."

Grandma winced.

"I think she's pretty lousy at picking boyfriends, if you ask me." Ella folded her arms on the table and sighed.

"She should know better than to chase those wild boys who have only one thing on their mind." Grandma turned away.

"I think she's trying to be happy, but she's looking in all the wrong places." Ella watched Grandma's jaw, trying to catch her eye.

"Grandma," she offered with a bit of restraint. "Billie admitted... she drinks and smokes now."

At seeing the trembling in Grandma's shoulders, Ella hurried to say, "But, she said she doesn't like it anymore." She cleared her throat. "I think she wants help, but you know Billie; it's important for her to show how tough she is."

"Yes." Grandma was deep in thought. "I'm sure that's what is going through her mind." She sat next to Ella.

"I have to ask you, Ella, but I don't want to make things any worse for you. What have you heard about your mom and dad? Do you hear anything from Tom?"

Ella bit her lip, her gaze flickering over the wrinkles of worry creasing Grandma Russell's face before answering. "I haven't heard from my parents. The Red Cross would never agree to send a telegram to *Oma* in Germany. I guess she'll find out soon enough, if she's still living in the same place."

Grandma reached for her hand, the troubled look in her eyes softening as she listened to Ella.

"As for Tom, I was at his parents' when they got the telegram from him, saying he was okay. You heard about his accident, right?"

Grandma nodded.

"I've received a handful of letters from him since then, and he says he is on the mend. Sooner or later, they'll ship him stateside, but they haven't said when or where."

"Not even an estimate of when he may be leaving to come home?"

"Nope, they don't tell Tom a thing," Ella said. "But he's been good about writing me. He'll let me know when they're sending him home as soon as he knows."

Grasping Ella's fingers, Grandma said, "Dare I ask what you've heard about Hank?"

Ella scratched her chin, looking at the ceiling. "My understanding is when the Germans catch a prisoner of war, they let the Red Cross know, and the Red Cross sends a message to someone at the Pentagon. Then they send a telegram to the family."

Grandma read between the lines. If Ella hadn't heard from the Red Cross, with each passing day the chances that he'd been killed grew into something as undeniable as the war itself. But she still held out a glimmer of hope that he was a prisoner somewhere.

"How long since that first telegram?"

"Five weeks as of Thursday. But I just don't know how long I can expect to wait before they say he's presumed..." Ella looked away. "Waiting is the worst," she sighed. "And what about Chester? Have you heard from his parents?"

"The last I heard he was somewhere in the Pacific. They're thinking he was involved in the invasion of Guam, but they can't be sure," Grandma explained.

"Please let me know if you hear anything," Ella said. "I've written him a couple times, but I don't get anything back. I wonder if he's okay."

"I sure will, dear. You'll let me know if you hear anything from Billie, won't you? And I'm praying for you and your wonderful family."

Ella stood and gave Grandma Russell a hug.

"Well, I've got to check on the house, then get back to Ogden," Ella replied. "My Saturdays are about the only day I have a few hours to myself, and I wanted to see the house and make sure you're doing well. And, frankly, I just needed to reminisce a little about the good times."

"I'm so glad you came to see me. You be careful driving that canyon. There's black ice, so go slow."

"I know; I know," Ella said. "I've driven that canyon a million times. It's like riding a bike; you never forget."

Ella drove around the snowy streets of Huntsville, smiling at familiar houses and landmarks. She never imagined she would ever miss something as simple as this. But if it was this bad for her, after being away for only a short time, how much worse could the homesickness be for her parents, or Tom? Or Hank?

At the mouth of the canyon, the sun emerged, the snow was gone, and it was spring again. She rolled down the window and let the warm sun glow on her arm as the breeze stirred her hair.

She turned the last corner. An unfamiliar car parked in the driveway made her slow. It wasn't the Russell's car, or at least it didn't appear to be them. As she drew nearer, her heart dropped. A Western Union boy stood on her doorstep. She parked the car and jumped out to greet him.

"Can I help you?" she said. She bit back the terror ripping her apart inside.

"Yes," he answered with an official tone. "I'm looking for Ella Meyer."

"I'm Ella Meyer."

"This telegram is for you." He handed her the card bearing the familiar logo of Western Union.

Her hands shook, and she blinked back a tear.

The Secretary of War desires me to inform you that Staff Sergeant Hank Meyer is a prisoner of war of the German government, based on information received from the Provost General. Further information received will be furnished by the Provost Marshal General.

J A Ulio, the Adjutant General

Ella took a deep breath, crying out in relief. She looked heavenward with a grateful smile. Hank was alive. Hank is alive. But now a whole new set of concerns came to her mind. Was he injured? Was he being treated humanely? Had he been tortured?

After all she had been forced to endure, Ella couldn't help but assume the worst.

Chapter 55-Note 1: James Alexander Ulio, or J.A. Ulio, was promoted to Major General in March of 1942 and appointed as the United States Army's Adjutant General. His responsibilities included managing all personnel matters for more than ten million soldiers, overseeing promotions, awards, reassignments, and death notifications. As a result, his name appeared on over 250,000 telegrams notifying next of kin that a soldier had been killed or was missing in action. These telegrams made him an infamous figure during the war, as nobody wanted a telegram from J.A. Ulio. In addition to the death notifications, his name appears on tens of millions of other documents. No other person in the history of the United States is associated with more official documents than Ulio.

CHAPTER 56
March 3, 1944
Hannover, Germany

Karl and Marta avoided Frankfurt, journeying through Kassel and Göttingen and arriving at Hannover on the fourth day of their travels. There, they were informed of a delay that would last at least a few hours. They slipped inside a small café and took a corner table where they shared a small lunch and settled in for the wait.

Marta held a mug of ersatz coffee in her hands, her fingers interlaced around the cup with her elbows propped on the table. She sipped slowly and watched people in the streets as they stamped through the snow.

Karl pushed the dishes aside and unfolded his map, spreading it out on the table. "We're making fairly good time." He measured the distance with his fingers. "Maybe you should call your mother and let her know our progress?"

"It will keep her from worrying so much." Marta set down her coffee and counted out coins for the payphone.

They left the café quietly, though Marta caught a few questioning glances from others in the room, as well as from a few people they passed on the street as they headed back to the train station. At the payphone, she dropped the coins into the slot and twisted the stiff phone cord between her fingers, waiting for the line to connect.

Click. "Hello, Mama."

"Marta, where are you? Are you all right?" A thinness in her mother's voice made Marta purse her lips in concern before answering. Of course, she would be concerned, but why did she sound so anxious?

"Yes, we're doing fine. We're in Hannover."

"Hannover. That's wonderful. You're making it faster than I'd thought. Have you faced many delays?"

"A few, but we're feeling quite fortunate to have made it here so fast. We're hoping to be in Stuhr by tonight, if all goes well."

"Oh, that's wonderful! Thank you for calling."

"Mama," Marta blurted before she could hang up. "I-I... can't wait to see you." Anything to keep her mother on the line a little longer.

She closed her eyes, listening to the sound of her mother's voice. All the years in America, she hadn't wondered if she would ever hear that voice again.

"Okay, Marta. We'll talk tomorrow, I hope. Bye!" The line clicked, and only silence remained.

As Marta hung up the phone, the overhead speaker announced the impending departure of their train to Bremen. Karl and Marta lifted their trunk and set it next to the luggage car, then motioned to a pudgy, middle-aged steward that they were ready for him to take it. The man braced himself to heft it up onto the train. It swung up easily in his hands and landed next to the other luggage with a soft thud.

Karl and Marta found their seats in a passenger car and settled in for a three-hour ride to Bremen. As the train pulled away from the town, they could see the crumbing walls of homes and shops that lay in ruin. Many homes sat on the horizon like ghosts ushered in by the war. The people trudged along the ruins, with eyes glazed from distant memories of what their home was like before. Maybe, Marta thought, this was why some Germans gave her wondering looks that resonated with an expression she couldn't name. Did they somehow know they were from America? Were they looking at them with bitterness? Did they resent America, a country that killed and maimed and destroyed their homes and families? And now they had come here to live among them? Or was it shame that their homeland had nothing left? Maybe they were embarrassed hosts accepting guests into an unkempt house?

She leaned her head against the window and watched the broken world of her childhood rush by as the train picked up speed. "Oh, Karl," she looked at him with regret in her voice. "They've destroyed our opera house. It's gutted."

"It's a job that has to be done," he whispered so only she could hear. "Hank or one of his buddies could have dropped the bomb that did that."

Marta bit her lip. The Hannover Opera House she knew from her childhood was a landmark in so many people's memories. Now it was just a gutted shell of itself.

"Would you rather they shoot down those bombers? Our son could be in one of them."

An image of a plane in flames plummeting to the ground made her wince. She turned away from the window and rested her head on Karl's shoulder. He stroked her hair softly, looking over her head at the ruined town they left behind.

A few kilometers outside the city limits, the town's air raid siren blared faint and distant. Marta lifted her head to look at Karl. The train continued forward, negotiating a sharp turn.

The train's brakes screeched, the momentum flinging a few passengers from their seats into the aisles. Someone screamed and pointed out the window. An American plane bore down on the train, drawing closer every second. Passengers dove to the floor, covering their heads with their hands. Mothers clutched their children's wrists and pulled them down to the floor.

The P-47 roared as it attacked, strafing the train engine first, then each passenger car with its .50 caliber guns. Karl yanked Marta down, but not before she saw through the small window, the luggage car behind them bursting into flames.

Karl followed the sound of the plane as bullets ripped through the roof of their car, tearing apart a row of seats and sending wood and metal projectiles in all directions. An elderly woman let out a muffled groan, then dropped to the floor. Blood pooled beneath her stomach. The middle-aged man sitting next to her bent over to help her, covering his mouth with his hands. Karl grabbed Marta's hand and brought her out of their seat "We've got to get off the train. Now!"

The woman's blood spread, staining the floor of the train crimson. The man stifled sobs with his hands, squeezing his eyes shut. Marta reached for his shoulder, but before she could offer him any comfort, Karl pulled her away.

"Head for the door and don't stop running until we reach those trees," he said, pointing to a grove of trees about a hundred meters away. "Don't stop for anything, just get off before he makes another pass."

Hearing his instruction, passengers lunged for the doors, tugging them open and squeezing out. Some scraped and grasped at the windows, but the glass was sealed shut. Karl and Marta pushed through the tangle of frantic passengers, grabbing onto the door frame before they could be shoved away by people behind them.

"Jump now," Karl shouted. Marta leapt with him and both landed hard on the frozen ground. They stood quickly and dashed hand-in-hand-toward the trees. Marta stumbled, crying out in pain, but Karl lifted her up again. "Hurry," he encouraged through gritted teeth. "He's coming back."

Fire and smoke filled the air, the whine of the P-47 cutting through the haze. Passengers flooded away from the train, like the woman's pooling blood. The plane above them droned on.

"What's he waiting for?" Marta spat between gasps for breath.

"He's letting the passengers get off the train before he makes another strafing run," Karl said. The plane drifted upward, then looped around again heading toward the front of the train.

Marta looked back to the train and gave a sharp cry. A woman stumbled out of the train, clutching two newborns to her chest. Watching her run, Marta swallowed back hot tears of guilt. They'd been so selfish, so frantic to get off the train that they hadn't seen who they'd left behind. The woman lost her footing on a clump of frozen soil. She slammed into the ground with all her weight landing on a child. At her scream, Marta shot up and dashed over to help her. She knelt by the woman and rolled her over. "Let me take your children."

Karl ran up beside Marta. "Go, go!" he shouted. Karl reached under the woman's arms and lifted her to her feet, limping back to the trees. The babies screamed in Marta's arms, and she laid them back into the young mother's arms.

Breathing heavily, she looked at Marta. "Thank you," she panted. "Thank you from the bottom of my heart."

Marta reached and embraced her, one mother to the other, understanding the horror of what might have happened. She gave Marta a warm smile then turned away. Karl took Marta's hand and they stepped back into the canopy of the trees as the plane dove in for another attack.

The last man to escape the train, a rotund man with a large piece of luggage in each hand, struggled toward the trees. A bead of sweat rolled down his face with the effort. The wind from the plane rushing overhead blew over, and the man's fedora flew from his head.

"Leave it!" Karl shouted.

"Run, run!" A cacophony of shouts rang out from panicked passengers.

The plane made a dive toward the engine. Flashes of bullets erupted from the nose of the P-47. A burst of white steam and orange flames blasted in the air, the eruption lifting the hundred-ton locomotive off the ground. It jumped several meters off the track and landed, leaning on its side.

The plane made another sharp turn to set up for another attack to finish the job.

"What are you doing?" Marta shouted at the pilot with exasperation.

"He must not realize that he hit the main engine," Karl explained. The plane looped back from the rear and passed over the train, moving in closer as if inspecting the damage before making its escape.

From the rear of the train, shots exploded into the sky. One of the stewards had finally made his way back to the last train car where a loaded anti-aircraft gun sat ready for this type of aerial attack. The bright flashes of bullets discharged from the gun, making a direct hit on the P-47's engine. Bright amber flames erupted from the engine, a plume of smoke bursting skyward as the plane coughed and sputtered. The plane stalled, and the nose dipped toward the ground.

"Bail out!" Karl whispered.

Clasping her hands, Marta said, "Get out, get out!"

The crowd watched in anticipation as the plane smashed into the ground, cartwheeling as it erupted in a ball of fire.

Around the Meyers, people cheered.

Marta hid her head in Karl's chest as she wept.

One man turned a sharp glare on them, crossing his arms. "Whose side are you on?"

"That American pilot got what he deserved," another said. Others laughed, and Marta cringed away from them.

She and Karl slipped away from the crowd. A few yards from the train, he let her go and made her stay put while he crept close to the burning luggage car, tiptoeing as if any sudden noise would upset the flames. As he approached, the heat of the flames scorched his skin. He turned away to look at Marta with a small shake of his head.

Marta sniffed and wiped the tears from her eyes.

Karl then dashed into the passenger car, grabbing their small suit-case. When he climbed down and returned to Marta, she managed a small smile between biting her lip. Watching her force back her tears stung his heart. She had so much hope, so much courage. He wouldn't have made it this far without her. "I guess not all is lost," he said. He reached inside of his coat, turning out his pocket to reveal their remaining cash. "And we still have some money left, too."

The Meyers lagged behind the group of other passengers as they trekked through the cold back to the Hannover *Hauptbahnhof.* They spent the night in the cold, dank lobby of the Hannover train station, Karl stroking Marta's hair as she laid her head in his lap. When they would be able to leave for Bremen was anyone's guess.

Throughout the night, workers cleared the damaged train from the tracks. The next morning, weary passengers stood to stretch their sore muscles after spending the night on the cold, hard floor. Not long after sunup, a replacement train for passengers bound for Bremen rolled into the station. Their departure was announced for nine that morn-ing, but another air raid siren delayed their train.

"It's all right, though," Marta admitted with a yawn. "It's taken us a month to come this far; we can wait another hour."

They stopped for a few minutes in Bremen before going on to Brin-kum. As they passed familiar landmarks and houses of her childhood friends, memories flooded Marta's thoughts. Every fence and rooftop, every platform, and sign at the Brinkum *Bonhof,* though now tired and dingy from years of war, could have been photographed straight from her childhood.

She pointed out places where she had grown up, like the school and playground, and the public park where she and her parents would picnic in the summer.

Karl seemed enamored as he watched her face light up with sights as simple as a street corner, or a shop's sign. She asked in a hushed voice, as if not wanting to wake herself from a dream, "I wonder if the people here will remember me. Have I changed, Karl?"

Karl smiled. "Not at all."

The meander through Marta's memories finally brought them to the doorstep of her mother's house. Marta's hand shook as she reached for the door. Ten years. It had been more than ten years since she'd brought Hank and Ella here, ten years since she'd looked into her mother's eyes and held her hand.

The door was locked.

"Mama!" she called out, giving a gentle rap on the door with her knuckles. "We're here."

The door swung open.

"Mama," Marta choked. She threw her arms around her mother, feeling the thin frail shoulders through her embrace. "You're as beautiful as ever."

Her mother wrapped her arms around Marta, then pulled back to stare into her face. "I've been so worried about you."

She looked at Marta again, smiling with tears dripping from her eyes.

"I'm so happy to see you." Her eyebrows arched as she turned her head to search for more luggage. "Where is your trunk and other bags?"

"Our luggage burned up in a…" Marta swallowed. "This is all—oh, it's a long story? We're here now."

Oma sniffed and said, "Who's this?" She turned to Karl with a wry smile.

He stepped forward and hugged his mother-in-law.

"I've told you a lot about him in my letters over the past twenty years," Marta said. "But now you can finally meet him for yourself."

"Thank you for giving me an angel." Karl clasped *Oma*'s hand with great care. "She's that and everything else that's good in this world."

Oma smiled. "She has told me a lot of nice things about you, too."

She guided them inside and closed the door. "I want to hear about everything. But let me fix you something to eat, and we'll get you settled first."

After a small lunch, *Oma* set steaming mugs of ersatz coffee before them and settled in to hear their stories. The conversation continued for an hour as Karl and Marta explained their arrest and internment, the circumstances of their deportation, and how they ended up back in Germany. *Oma* listened with eyes that often wandered away. Karl watched as her chest sometimes heaved with a faint sigh, wistful in a way he couldn't quite figure out.

Marta chattered on. "Hank came to see us when we were in the Crystal City camp. We were just flabbergasted that anyone could make it to see us."

At the mention of Hank's name, *Oma* grabbed her mug and took a long sip, shielding her face. Marta glanced at her, then back at Karl.

"He was so worried about bombing Germany," Marta said. "He just couldn't get past that he could potentially drop a bomb on you. He hoped he never had to do that."

Oma's coffee cup came down a little too hard, sloshing the hot drink on the table. Her face turned pale as she reached for a towel to dab up the spill.

"Mama," Marta said, "are you all right?"

Oma's trembling lips flashed a pained smile, but she sighed and said, "I'm fine. I just didn't realize how much I miss my grandson."

Marta looked at Karl with curiosity as he drummed his fingers on the table. He looked back at her with narrowed eyes. For some reason, Marta's mother seemed to be guarded, or maybe it was just anxiety. Whatever the reason, it was unnerving.

Chapter 56-Note 1: The story of Karl and Marta's trip from Ravensburg to Bremen is based on true stories from German Americans repatriated to Germany against their will. One such account is of Mathias and Johanna Eiserloh, who wrote,

"On the final leg of their long trek across Germany, two U.S. planes strafed their train. The Eiserlohs and other passengers ran to the nearby woods. As the planes continued gunning the train, an anti-aircraft gun on the last train car was put into action and the family watched, with mixed emotions, as smoke filled the sky where two of the American planes were shot down."

"The Eiserloh Story," by Arthur D. Jacobs; https://www.foitimes.com/internment/Eiserloh.htm, Retrieved January 3, 2021

CHAPTER 57

April 17, 1944

Stalag 17-B, Krems-Gneixendorf, Austria

April in *Stalag* 17 was little warmer than the middle of January. By now, Hank and Don were more than just bunkmates; they had grown to be best friends. They shared their Red Cross parcels, and their valuable trade stash grew fast because Hank didn't smoke or drink coffee.

In early May, Don received a large parcel in a plain box from his parents. They took the package to an isolated corner of their barracks to open it.

"What do you think it is?" Hank asked.

"I have no idea, really." Don tore open the package. The rustling of paper went silent as he glimpsed what was inside. "I can't believe it."

"What is it?" Hank leaned over and saw the logo and an unopened box containing ten cartons, or one hundred packs, of the most sought-after cigarette brand in camp. Cartons stamped with the Lucky Strike logo filled the box, stacked together like bricks.

"I wrote a letter to the Lorillard Tobacco Company. I told them I was a prisoner and would like a few cartons of cigarettes," Don explained. "But didn't think they would send me an entire case."

"How on earth did this make it past the guards?" Hank asked. "It hasn't even been opened. It's completely sealed."

"I can't believe it."

"We've gotta hide this. Now," Hank insisted, in near panic. "There's a stool pigeon somewhere in this camp, and if the guards ever found out, they'd take every last one of those boxes."

After a quick glance to make sure it was clear, they rushed to their bunk and peeled off a few wood planks from the ceiling above it. Don stashed the cartons between the studs and replaced the slats and nails.

"Let's keep a few packs to bribe the guards. We may also need a few for haggling," Don smiled. "A few packs of these smokes means we're eating good tonight!"

Hank had a sheepish grin. "Cigarettes. Manna from heaven!"

———◆◇◆———

Hank grabbed the field jacket he'd been issued at Dulag Luft, pulling it over his arms. It billowed around his frame now, and he swung his shoulders freely. "I think my coat is getting a little big on me. What do you think?"

"Maybe," Don agreed off-handedly.

"When I got this coat, it was tight through the arms; now I've got plenty of room."

Hank lifted the coat around his arms, showing Don how loose it fit him. "See?"

"It's probably going to get worse, Hank," Don said.

"Maybe on Friday we'll get a double portion of Red Cross parcels. That'll help fatten me up," Hank joked.

"Don't count on it," Don laughed.

Friday was either the best day of the week or the worst. It was the day the Germans disbursed the Red Cross parcels to the prisoners. On a good day, the odor of cooking meats and other foods wafted through the camp. But having a complete parcel was the luck of the draw. The guards rifled through the packages and took whatever they wanted, leaving many *Kriegies* sorely disappointed.

When Hank and Don collected their parcels, Hank buzzed with excitement. "This is the first complete Red Cross parcel I've had in the six weeks we've been here."

"It's pretty crummy that the guards keep stealing our stuff," Don replied.

"Why do they always steal the D-bars?" Hank chuckled and added, "It's funny. When I first got to England, we called a D-bar 'Hitler's secret weapon.' Everybody hated them. They were bitter and tasted less like a chocolate bar and more like a boiled potato. Here, everybody fights over them."

"Okay, here's what we have." Hank pulled out one item at a time from the parcel, while Don made a list. "One can of Klim powdered milk; one package of sandwich cookies; a pound of oleo margarine; a half-pound of cubed sugar; a pack of K-ration biscuits; a can of coffee; two bars of soap; a can of peanut butter…"

"Oh, the peanut butter is a nice change from jam," Don commented, as if he were scrutinizing produce at the market and selecting his groceries.

"A twelve-ounce can of tuna; a six-ounce can of liver pâté; and a can of corned beef."

"Let's see…a package of prunes…"

"What? No raisins? I guess prunes are okay. I haven't been regular since we got here," Don joked.

"Five packs of smokes, Camels."

"Not quite Lucky Strikes, but they'll do."

"Okay. Some vitamin-C tablets; a can of vegetable soup concentrate; and two D-bars."

"How many D-bars do we have now?" Don asked.

"Six, including these. Remember we traded five for that bread knife," Hank said.

Don smiled with recognition. "I'm so glad we get our fair share of the bread now that we have a decent knife."

Fashioned out of part of a metal window frame, the knife's rounded tip gave it an innocent appearance, not at all weapon-like, in case the guards found it. It offered a clean slice into the dark, heavy bread that came just once or twice a week. The bread was laced with sawdust, which the Germans called *tree flour*, and sometimes contained black bugs or other additives. Prisoners ate it hungrily, stuffing the extra bits into their mouths with their fingertips. The man who cut the bread was allowed to scrape up the crumbs. That was his payment for cutting precise portions.

Cardboard boxes from Red Cross parcels were stored in the windows, insulating the pitiful single pane of glass. In Barracks 16A, some prisoners repurposed boxes for the "Cardboard Playhouse," constructing scenery, props, and stage items. They held concerts with their flimsy cut-outs and patched together plays from half-remembered stories.

Hank and Don finished their weekly inventory. Don left the barracks, and Hank headed toward the door to follow him. He closed it behind him. Someone tapped him on the arm.

Tech Sergeant Ted Ross, the Barrack's Chief, jerked his head in a gesture to follow him. "Hank," he hissed. "Come here a minute." He disappeared around the corner.

Hank glanced over his shoulder to see if anyone was watching them, then followed.

"Kurtenbach wants you to meet him in the White House in ten minutes."

"Kurtenbach wants to see me?" Hank whispered. "What for?"

"I wasn't told why, but I guess you'll find out soon enough," Ross said.

American camp leaders housed in Barracks 15A had nicknamed their place the "White House." As camp leader, Staff Sergeant Kenneth Kurtenbach had been a POW longer than anyone else there after he'd been shot down over France in December of 1942. Prisoners called him "The Man of Confidence." The Germans knew him as the ranking officer who had successfully organized more than four thousand American enlisted men into some semblance of military order. He assigned a barracks chief for each of the twenty-eight barracks. When he was allowed to arrange a meeting with the Camp *Kommendant, Oberst* Kuhn, he tried to negotiate better conditions on behalf of all the Americans.

Kurtenbach had final say on all breakout attempts. Those that ignored the line of authority faced internal discipline. In the end, Kurtenbach controlled all *Kriegie* efforts to "wage war behind the wire."

At the White House, a sentry approached Hank. "Who are you here to see?"

"Kurtenbach sent for me."

The sentry pointed to where a few bunks had been pushed aside to make room for a desk and chair. Hank approached with a salute. "Sergeant Kurtenbach? Staff Sergeant Hank Meyer, reporting for duty, sir."

"At ease. Why don't you step over here where we can talk privately?"

Hank sat on a bunk near the desk.

Kurtenbach lowered his voice. "We have it on good authority that you speak German."

Heart racing, Hank said, "Where did you hear that?"

"The OSS informed me that you declined an assignment in espionage, although you speak German with no discernible accent. Is this true?"

"Do they give you a dossier like that on all prisoners?"

"Not all, but a few," Kurtenbach replied. "This has strategic value, as long as no one else knows. You are *sure* no one else knows?"

"As far as I am aware," Hank said. "One of the guards may suspect something. He may be bluffing, but I'm not sure."

"Which guard are you talking about?"

"Sikkar."

"Stay away from him and Big Stoop. They are nothing but trouble. But otherwise, your knowledge of the language can be used to our advantage. Listen in on any conversation among the guards that you can. If you hear anything of value, report back to me, but don't blow your cover. Don't let anyone know you speak German. Not even your bunk mate, okay?"

"What if I get caught eavesdropping? Will I be punished?"

"You'll probably spend a day or so in the cooler."

Hank looked at the floor, mulling over the irony in being asked, once again, to use his German to be a spy.

"You don't have to do it if you don't want to."

"What kind of information are you looking for?"

"We want to know about transfers, troop movements, important cargo; whatever they talk about. Maybe they have a relative who is injured or on leave. Anything like that."

"And this will help the prisoners?" Hank looked him in the eye. "If I spy for you, you can use this to your advantage?"

Kurtenbach held his gaze. "Anything helps. But only if you want to do this."

Shrugging, Hank scratched his head. "Do you want me to just come here and tell you?"

"That will work for now, as long as it's not more than once or twice a week. Okay?"

Hank hid a flattered smile and left the White House, but as he made his way through the compound he wondered if agreeing to be a spy had been a mistake that would end his life. Entering his barracks, he fought the urge to look over his shoulder.

Chapter 57-Note 1: The account of a POW receiving a box of valuable cigarettes is taken from a true personal account written by POW Ray Matheny. In his book *Rite of Passage*, he tells how, despite tough German security, he was able to receive a box of Lucky Strike cigarettes.

"It did not take long for any newly-arrived prisoner to realize that cigarettes were money, the real currency system of the camp, and that it took a certain amount of money to survive. I promptly wrote home, asking for a whole parcel of Lucky Strike cigarettes, the most valuable currency of all. Somehow, my letter got home uncensored and my parents set about getting the order filled.

Later he described,

"I was greatly surprised to receive a parcel containing ten cartons of Lucky Strike cigarettes October 2, 1944. My parents had written the P. Lorillard Tobacco Company about my circumstance, and the company sent me the cigarettes. Somehow, this large package was not confiscated or pilfered by the Germans. It was like passing a bag of gold coins to a prisoner. Suddenly I was incredibly rich; I felt as if I were the wealthiest man in the Danube Valley. Cigarettes…could buy almost anything but freedom at Staling 17B."

Ray Matheny. *Rite of Passage: A Teenager's Chronicle of Combat and Captivity in Nazi Germany* (American Legacy Media, 2012): 244.

CHAPTER 58

April 23, 1944
Stuhr, Germany

The air-raid siren blared at three in the morning. Bleary-eyed, Karl, Marta, and *Oma* trudged downstairs to the crawl space to wait for the all-clear signal. While Americans attacked in the daytime, more often than not around noon, the British attacks came throughout the night, as unpredictable as nightmares.

"I wish I could sleep an entire week without waking up for an air-raid." Marta's light-hearted complaint drew a smile from Karl.

"If you sleep through one, then it's sure to be the one with your name on it," *Oma* retorted.

As they sat in the darkness, Marta looked to her mother and mused, "Do you ever wonder if Hank is on one of those planes?"

Oma didn't reply, but Marta noticed a calm in her eyes, and she didn't seem to mind talking about Hank as much as when they first came.

"There's no sense worrying about. It's out of our hands," Karl said.

"Do you ever wonder though?" Marta insisted.

The conversation died as the all-clear signal was given. They trudged back to their rooms for an hour's sleep, until the rooster woke them at sunrise.

Karl, and some days Marta, took over tending to *Oma*'s cow, her chickens, and to other needs on her farm. Marta would warn Karl to be careful as he ventured outside. She watched him sneak out before light and shut the curtains when he finally came back inside. The nearest house was at least half a mile away, but nosy neighbors might do anything. If the *Gestapo* arrested German citizens for no reason at all, Karl and Marta had little to keep them at bay. To be safe, when neighbors came to the door, Karl and Marta stayed out of sight.

On the last Sunday of April, Marta watched as her mother put on her best dress and did her hair.

Where are you going, all dressed up?" Marta smiled with admiration.

"It's my turn to host church today," When Marta's eyes widened. "Oh? So, people are coming over?

"Yes. You can't stay hidden forever. The bishop and some others already know you're living here, so you might as well join our meeting."

Bishop Roterman arrived to lead the meeting. Eight elderly women sat in a semi-circle in the living room. The congregants looked up from their hymnals to sneak a peek at their two visitors.

Roterman welcomed their newest members and gave a brief explanation of why they were there. After the administration of the sacrament, Roterman stood to conduct the remainder of the meeting.

He called Marta to speak first. Speaking in public made the pit of her stomach roil. She couldn't use her lack of confidence in English as an excuse here, like she did back home. This was her home now, and she had to change just like everyone else.

"I'm very nervous," she whispered, looking at her feet. "I don't like talking in church, but it's hard to say no to Bishop Roterman," she admitted with a slight grin.

"Karl and I were forced to come to Germany against our will. It's not that we don't love Germany. We do. The American government deported us because they thought we loved Germany too much."

As one woman returned Marta's gaze, Marta recognized the face of a friend's mother. The years had turned her hair white, but her smile was the same one that had encouraged Marta to go to America all those years ago.

"But although we love Germany, our home and family are in Utah. We were given papers showing that we are now German citizens, so here we will stay," she announced. "We've lost our home, and we'll miss our friends, but there's no use in being bitter. It's all behind us now." She cleared her throat and looked at her mama.

"I am grateful to my mama for letting us stay here. It's a good thing she had room for us because we had no other place to go." She wiped her nose with her handkerchief and swallowed back the lump in her throat.

"I've heard many stories about how you have suffered here. I know our suffering is no more painful than yours. I hope you will accept us as your friends and as fellow church members. We may have our hearts in two different places," she paused again, "but we feel there's a reason why we are here. Someday, we hope to figure it out."

As Marta sat in her seat, a woman reached over, patted Marta on the knee, and mouthed the words, "Welcome back."

Karl was asked to speak next. He stood, his knees shaking.

"As you know," he explained, "we are refugees without a country. The country where we raised our family doesn't welcome us anymore, and we are foreigners in the land of our upbringing. It's not clear yet whether your government...our government...will allow us to stay here undisturbed. We keep a very low profile and try not to bring attention to ourselves."

A surge of confidence made him draw a deep breath and raise his voice. "I beg of you, don't tell anyone that we are here. You never know who is listening, or what can happen."

The silence in the room was broken by the howling of the wind through the window cracks.

"On the train from Lisbon to Geneva, many of the other Germans coming from America had no place to go. Their families were already starving and suffering; they couldn't welcome them into their homes. Marta's mother has greeted us with open arms, and she has been able take care of us."

As the congregation stood to leave, Roterman took Karl and Marta aside. "You are wise to keep a very low profile; the *Gestapo* could be watching you. Be very, very careful."

"I keep busy with projects in the house," Karl said. "But I am a farmer. Working in the earth, the sun on my face... I can't stay indoors forever."

"I understand," agreed the bishop. "I think it's okay to work in your yard, but just be careful about riding the train, going shopping, things like that."

Marta replied. "I've wanted to go see some of the places I remember as a child, but I've stayed at home. We don't go shopping."

"I would add," Roterman said, looking at Karl. "Your being here is a huge blessing to your mother-in-law. She has worked very hard to keep this farm afloat. She is strong for her age. I've watched her dutifully milk her cow twice a day for years, even in the dead of winter. She's raised chickens and sold their eggs for all these years. She's even planted a huge garden and given away most of it to the neighbors."

Karl tilted his head. "I had no idea she was giving things away."

"Last year we were able to keep a few families fed over the winter with potatoes, turnips, and carrots from her garden. Your being here may turn out to be a Godsend not only for her, but for many people who will desperately need food this winter."

"Why do you say that?"

"I understand you have a gift for planting crops and getting the most out of them. We could really use your help."

Marta smiled with pride at hearing about her husband's reputation.

"I'm happy to help however I can."

Roterman put his hand on Karl's shoulder. "This winter could be a disaster, with or without the war. People will starve if we don't do something. We'll need as big a crop as you can produce."

"What about storage?" Karl rubbed his chin. "Should I build a root cellar..."

Roterman nodded. "Yes, that's a great idea. But starving people will do anything for food. Even pilfer. It would be wise to disguise it somehow, just to keep it safe."

Karl looked to the sky as he formed an idea of how to build a large root cellar. "Do you know where I can get seed potatoes and all the other things I need?" he asked. "For a plot this big..."

"How soon will you need them?"

"In a few weeks," Karl answered. "Maybe a month, but that's pushing it."

"I'll see what I can do. But I can't make any promises."

CHAPTER 59
June 6, 1944
Ogden, Utah

Ella worked an on-call, overnight shift on the maternity ward at the Dee Hospital in Ogden. Tonight, she had three patients to care for, all in different stages of labor. But Ella often cared for twenty patients at a time at Bushnell General Military Hospital, so this promised to be an easy shift.

Two hours into her shift, she left a patient's room, closing the door softly behind her. An orderly ran past, yelling to the staff in the hallway.

"Turn on the radio, quick. The invasion has started!"

Nurses and orderlies gathered at the nurse's station around the large Philco radio sitting on the countertop. Ella stopped to listen.

An orderly turned the dial. Through the radio static, the announcer's voice came in one breath:

...unconfirmed by Allied sources, but according to German news sources, heavy fighting is taking place between the Germans and invasion forces on the Normandy Peninsula, about thirty-one miles southwest of La Havre.

The radio announcer seemed winded as he read various wire bulletins being handed to him.

Here's another bulletin, also from Berlin radio, and as yet, still unconfirmed by American sources: it says the British and American landing operation against the western coast of Europe, from the sea and from the air, are stretching out over the entire area, between Cherbourg and LeHavre, a distance of about sixty miles. I repeat, there is no confirmation from Allied sources. And here is another bulletin just in, a German news agency says, again, this is unconfirmed, that the most important airdromes in the area of the Normandy peninsula of France, have been wiped out.

Ella covered her mouth with excitement. "Can you believe it?"

Uh, and now we have just been informed that we can expect, in a few seconds, a very important broadcast from the British capitol.

The announcer paused. Silence followed. The nurses leaned forward, and the whole hospital around them waited as if holding its breath. Ella moved a stack of hospital gowns and clean towels away from the speaker. White noise static filled the radio signal until the telephone connected from New York to London. A monotone voice said:

The text of communiqué number one, will be released to the press and radio of the United Nations in ten seconds. Repeat. Ten seconds from now.

The radio slipped into complete silence. Was the signal broken? Ella exchanged puzzled looks with the others. They clung to each other until an announcer with an American accent read a prepared statement:

This morning, under the command of General Eisenhower, Allied naval forces, supported by strong air forces, began landing on the northern coast of France. This ends communiqué number one, from the Supreme Headquarters Allied Expeditionary Force.

Cheers rang out at the nurse's station. Half a world away, their men—husbands, fathers, brothers—had invaded France. Ella said a silent prayer as she listened to the announcer's frantic descriptions.

The radio announcer's unrestrained excitement kept the graveyard shift alive, infusing it with energy that Ella had never seen before. History was being made, even if it was 1:30 a.m. at a quiet hospital in Utah, and everyone could feel it.

Ladies and Gentlemen this is New York again. This is a momentous hour in world history. This is the invasion of Hitler's Europe. The zero hour of the second front. The men of General Dwight Eisenhower are leaving their landing barges, fighting their way up the beaches, into the fortress of Nazi Europe. They are moving in from the sea to attack the enemy under a mammoth cloud of fighter planes, under a ceiling of screaming shells from Allied warships.

This is the supreme test of Allied spirit and of Allied weapons. Casualties in the subsequent drive inland may reach a dreadful toll. The German war machine is still powerful and is still strongly entrenched. Nazi troops have been ordered to die rather than retreat. However, die or retreat they must. For the Allied command is throwing all the strength they can into this battle on the shores of Europe. The final chapter in the history of the Second World War is finally being written.

A drum roll rumbled through the static like thunder through pattering rain, then the Star-Spangled Banner played. The staff hid their tears from each other.

The call button was flashing, and Ella dragged herself away from radio to tend to her patients.

The charge nurse said, "Ella, Mrs. Wood in room three would like some more help with her bed. Can you please see what she needs?"

"Again?" Ella asked. "I just gave her two more pillows."

"I know she's still a few hours away from delivery, but I think she's quite miserable."

Ella went to Mrs. Wood's room.

"How nice of you to break away from the news to help me," Mrs. Wood said. "Don't let me bother you, but can I get another pillow or two? I'm so uncomfortable."

"I'm sorry, Mrs. Wood. I'll go find you some more pillows."

On the way to the linen closet, Ella paused behind the huddle of staff members near the radio. "What's going on now?" she asked.

"The invasion is definitely in progress right now," a nurse replied. "We're waiting for a statement from General Eisenhower... oh, I think this is it."

...now back to London for a special statement from Allied Supreme Commander, General Eisenhower. Stand by.

Loud static noises erupted from the radio speaker, along with a few bleeps and clicks, then another long pause.

Soldiers, Sailors, and Airmen of the Allied Expeditionary Force!

General Eisenhower spoke with confidence.

You are about to embark upon the Great Crusade toward which we have striven these many months. The eyes of the world are upon you. The hope and prayers of liberty-loving people everywhere march with you. In company with our brave Allies and brothers-in-arms on other fronts, you will bring about the destruction of the German war machine, the elimination of Nazi tyranny over the oppressed peoples of Europe, and security for ourselves in a free world.

Your task will not be an easy one. Your enemy is well-trained, well-equipped, and battle-hardened. He will fight savagely.

But this is the year 1944! Much has happened since the Nazi triumphs of 1940–41. The United Nations have inflicted upon the Germans great defeats in open battle, man to man. Our air offensive has seriously reduced their strength in the air and their capacity to wage war on the ground. Our home fronts have given us an overwhelming superiority in weapons and munitions of war and placed at our disposal great reserves of trained fighting men. The tide has turned! The free men of the world are marching together to victory!

I have full confidence in your courage, devotion to duty, and skill in battle. We will accept nothing less than full victory!

Good luck! And let us beseech the blessing of almighty God upon this great and noble undertaking.

As the radio went silent again, the nurses and attendants scattered like mice to attend to the flashing call lights.

Throughout the night, they gathered to the radio and broke away again, over and over like the tide washing on the shore. World events were unfolding, and no one in the maternity ward wanted to leave the radio, at least not yet.

At the end of her shift, Ella picked up her purse and made her way out the door to punch her time card.

"What a night!" she exhaled. "It's been a while since I've worked labor and delivery. How many babies did we end up with last night?"

"Six deliveries," a fellow nurse replied with a sigh. "Definitely a night for the books."

"I think I'll remember tonight as long as I live."

When Ella arrived at home, she changed into her nightgown. She made herself some toast and sat at the dining room table while the radio droned on with news about the invasion. She moved to the sofa and within minutes, was sound asleep.

Ella's work and study schedule filled so much of her days, she had little time to be worried about the war. Working as a nurse cadet required forty hours a week, Thursday through Monday, as well as studying for her state board exams next week. It took everything she had to stay focused when her feet ached and her head pounded at the end of each shift.

She would often soak her feet in a tub of hot water and Epsom salt at night, giving a loud, exasperated sigh as her feet touched the soothing water. While she soaked her feet, she studied. She'd read until her tired eyes gave in to sleep.

She had heard stories about nurses failing the exam because they were tested on procedures they hadn't practiced, or because they were asked about the administration of medications they hadn't discussed in class. By late Saturday night, she closed her books and went to bed, with calculations of medications still bouncing around in her head. After an hour of tossing, she drifted off to sleep. One day left.

All day Sunday, even at church, she thought about cracking open her books to study. But she had made up her mind not to study on Sunday. It was the Sabbath day, a day to rest rather than study. If she wasn't prepared now, she never would be. She enjoyed a sound sleep that night and rose early to arrive at the school at half past seven for her eight o'clock test.

Seven hours of exams filled the long day, and she went home with a cramp in her hand but with a confident smile. All she could do now was wait until the results came in the mail.

Ella's original Monday shift was scheduled at the enlisted amputee ward. By switching her shift to Tuesday, she was assigned to the officer's ward. She preferred working the amputee ward; the only ward she avoided was the neuropsychiatric ward. She didn't enjoy talking to psychiatric patients because they were so unpredictable. It was hard to muster a way to cheer them up.

She arrived at seven o'clock, feeling relaxed about work for the first time in as long as she could remember.

"What are you doing here?" her charge nurse asked with a surprised look.

"I switched with Dorothy Martinez because I was taking my state exams yesterday."

"Oh, that's right. There you are." She reviewed the duty roster. "How'd the test go?"

"We'll have to wait and see. But it's such a relief to finally be finished with school."

"Enjoy your new-found freedom. The feeling won't last long!"

The charge nurse from the graveyard shift sat at a table with Ella and the other nurses coming on for the day shift. She gave a quick progress report for each patient in the ward. Ella took notes, making sure she was prepared for the day.

As the reports ended and everyone stood, the charge nurse spoke to Ella. "Would you mind taking the first two hours of the receiving bay? I understand we have a new patient coming in this morning. Just do a quick assessment and start the admission packet. You'll have the rest of the day to finish it, as you'll be his nurse for the day. Are you comfortable with that?"

"No problem at all. I've worked the receiving bay before." Ella made her rounds with a bounce in her step. Her exams were finished, the war was finally going well for the Allies. At long last she could feel a sense of peace.

The military ambulance came from Hill Field, about an hour away. Each day it delivered patients at odds time throughout the day, most of the patients coming from overseas. It backed into the receiving bay, the silhouette of a lone patient visible through the small window. At least they hadn't brought a full ambulance. The male attendant next to Ella bobbed back and forth to get a look. "He's got casts on both legs, his right arm, and his neck," he muttered.

The door of the ambulance opened. Ella overheard the patient say, "So glad to get out of here!"

Ella gasped. She knew that voice. The glare of the morning sun hid the man's face. She put up a hand to shield her eyes. Orderlies helped lower him from the ambulance, and as he came into view, Ella's heart jumped, and her throat tightened.

"Tom?"

Chapter 59-Note 1: The events of D-day, June 6, 1944 are well documented and don't need to be retold here. However, the text of the radio program presented here is a close approximation of how it happened and is a composite of the actual broadcasts of NBC, CBS, and pool reports from various international radio networks. All rights belong to their rightful owners, and no copyright infringement is intended. These excerpts are used to help convey the sense of angst and fear Americans faced during this pivotal and historic event.

"The Rachel Maddow Show for Friday, June 6th, 2014" https://www.nbcnews.com/news/world/rachel-maddow-show-friday-june-6th-2014-wbna55367652, Retrieved January 4, 2021.

Chapter 59-Note 2: The account of Mrs. Wood having a baby is a true account, based on Mrs. Lucille Wood, my grandmother. She delivered my Aunt Drew that night, and she complained bitterly that she couldn't get the nurses to pay attention to her, as they were all preoccupied by the news of the invasion on the radio.

Chapter Note 3: Madelyn Cook's account of meeting her husband is the basis for Ella's story of meeting Tom. Madelyn attended nursing school at Weber College from 1941 to 1944. She became a nurse cadet and entered Bushnell Hospital. During a week in September 1944, she had to trade shifts to take her state nursing board exams in Salt Lake City. She arrived at work on her appointed shift and was assigned to the officer's ward and to the receiving bay. She writes,

"I found myself staring at the surprised face of my husband who had been shot down over Austria in May. I had known he would eventually be sent to a military hospital in the states, but had no idea it would be to Bushnell, and certainly not on the day I would be sent to meet the ambulance. I don't know who was the more surprised, me or him. Our story and picture were printed in *Army Life magazine*, (and was) sent to military personnel and recruiting stations all over the world."

Madelyn Cook Harding, *Weber's WWII Memories: Remembering the Events that Defined a Generation.* (Weber State University Alumni Association, 2004): p. 96.

CHAPTER 60

July 5, 1944

Stalag 17-B, Krems-Gneixendorf, Austria

Hank finished writing his fourth postcard to Ella. He was allowed one postage-paid card per month, and this time the short letter he wrote left mostly white space on the card.

Dear Ella,

Why hasn't anyone written to me? Are you okay? It's very lonely here, and I sometimes wonder if God has forsaken me. If I have done something to offend you, please forgive me.

Hank

Maybe she didn't know he was a prisoner. Maybe she thought he was dead. Every other man in his barracks had received a letter or package from home. There had to be a logical explanation.

He addressed the card and crossed the compound to drop it in the mailbox adjacent to Kurtenbach's barrack.

"Hey, *schweinehund.*" Sikkar bellowed in English.

Hank turned to find Sikkar glaring at him, arms crossed.

"My name is Meyer, sir." Even with as much respect as he could muster, he couldn't hide the disdain in his voice.

"You are a *schweinehund.* You'll always be a *schweinehund* to me," Sikkar spat.

Hank stepped around him and kept walking.

"Don't move," Sikkar snarled.

Big Stoop hovered over Hank from behind and said in German "Are you disobeying an order?"

Hank turned around to stare up into Big Stoop's oaf-looking face.

Big Stoop let loose a barrage of German insults and obscenities, his spit flying into Hank's face. Hank wiped his face while Sikkar threw his head back in a cackle.

When Hank turned to walk away, Big Stoop's giant hand smacked him squarely in the temple. Hank dropped to the ground, head bouncing in the dust. Pain pounded through his skull as the daylight turned to black.

Hank could hear Sikkar cackle again as Big Stoop let out a raucous laugh at seeing his accomplishment. Hank lay motionless, still aware that Big Stoop was hovering over him. Through the ground, he felt the patter of footsteps gathering near to see what had happened. Hank's blurry vision turned gray, the shadow of Big Stoop hovering over him like a boulder. Hank tried to roll over, but his head flopped like a rag doll. Two prisoners leaned over him and hefted him to a sitting position, but Hank wobbled. "Let's just let him lay on the ground for a minute."

When Hank stirred, another prisoner asked, "What barracks are you in?"

Hank's head bobbed back and forth as he tried to focus, but he could only mumble.

"What barracks are you in?" the prisoner asked again, pronouncing each word with care. Hank was still too confused to respond.

Sergeant Kurtenbach's voice came through the haze. "Bring him in here for a minute until he recovers."

They lifted Hank and carried him along, his feet dragging on the ground as they lifted him into the barracks. Carefully, they set him on a bunk. Hank sank back into semi-consciousness.

After a few minutes, he lifted himself to his elbows, blinking to focus.

"You got clobbered by Big Stoop," Kurtenbach said. "You alright now?"

Hank squinted and then blinked again.

"Just stay there for a bit until you get your bearings."

"Yes, sir," Hank mumbled.

"We've got to find a way to separate Big Stoop and Sikkar. This is out of hand."

Hank's spinning mind was aware enough to agree with Kurtenbach.

"Big Stoop is too dimwitted to be bribed. He's by-the-book; too dumb to take risks," Kurtenbach explained. "He would just as easily smack you as listen to you try to bribe him."

Hank rubbed his head to feel for a goose egg, but that hurt too much. He shut his eyes and groaned.

"Sikkar will trade for cigarettes and D-bars to get anything we want from outside the camp, if he can, so we know he can be bought, but he'll snitch on you." Kurtenbach smiled grimly, and asked, "Do you need help back to your barracks?"

"No, I'll be okay." Hank fumbled for the right words. "I...I appreciate the use of your bunk."

"Stay out of the way of Big Stoop for a while, okay?"

Don greeted Hank at their bunk.

"I heard you got smacked by Big Stoop."

"Boy, news travels fast."

"They said he knocked you out cold."

"Not quite, but I'm okay."

For nearly an hour, Hank sat on his bunk, fiddling with the empty D-bar wrapper.

Don studied Hank for a moment and said, "What are you thinking about?"

Hank twisted the D-bar wrapper in his fingers.

"I wish you'd open up a bit. I'm beginning to worry about you."

"I don't want to talk about it."

"Why not?"

"It's hard to explain."

"I've got a few minutes before my next appointment, so shoot."

Hank sighed. "There's a lot to it, and I don't think you would understand. I don't really understand it all. I don't know how to explain it."

"Try me." Don settled in to listen.

Hank lowered himself onto his pillow and rested with his hands beneath his head. "Even if I wanted to tell you, it's very complicated and involves some secrets that I can't really talk about."

"Religious secrets?" Don's bushy eyebrows cocked in question

"No," Hank said, "nothing like that. It has to do with my family, and, well, it's just complicated."

"So, your family wants you to be isolated in a prisoner-of-war camp with no outside communication, because of some family secret?"

"No, Don," Hank snapped. "I told you it's complicated..."

"Your family isn't communicating with you in this forsaken war camp in the middle of nowhere..."

"Thanks for reminding me," Hank spat.

"But even if it has nothing to do with that, what do you have to lose by telling me what's troubling you? It might help you deal with this place better. You've lost just about everything you've cherished in this world. Your faith is shaken for some reason, and that faith was your bedrock. We've got nothing here except for a few packs of cigarettes and some rock-hard chocolate bars, and if you don't come to grips with your questions, you will not survive this."

"I'm *fine.*"

"Hank," Don said, "you are my brother. It matters to me that you survive."

Hank took a deep breath. Of course, he wanted to tell him everything, from the day he was shot down, to his grandmother's betrayal to his raging questions about God. But that would mean revealing his German heritage. It would mean explaining a lot things.

Don continued, "Look Hank, the only thing we've got left here is hope. If you've lost your hope in a God, in a heaven, and in getting out of here someday, then as a religious man, you've lost everything."

Hank's throat tightened. *How could he possibly know so much?*

"You may as well cash it in 'cause there's no reason to stay in this bug-infested rat hole another day. Lots of us have given in. But you're hanging on for some reason. There's still a shred of hope in you somewhere."

Sitting up, Hank crossed his feet on the bed. One foot twitched back and forth as he thought.

"You have my solemn promise I won't tell a soul," Don said, "as God is my witness."

Hank took the chance. "Okay," he said. "You're right."

Don sat back to listen.

"My parents were born in Germany. They met in Utah and raised me and my sister there. But my mom always insisted that we only speak German at home, and so my sister and I are really fluent."

"No kidding?" Don asked with amazement.

Hank sighed. "I wish I were, but yes; it's true."

"Why haven't you used it here?"

"Listen, Don. You can't tell a single person about this, okay? You promise?"

"Hank. I promise. But what's the big deal?"

"You don't understand. My German has no American accent. I could hide here in Germany in plain sight, and no one would be any wiser. It means I should have been a spy, not on a B-17 crew."

"Why didn't you want to be a spy? They get paid a lot more."

"My uncle was a spy in the first war, and it ruined him. My dad says that before the war, my Uncle Willy was a lot like me; now he's the town drunk and a laughingstock because the memories haunt him. He's a good man with a big heart but lives a rough and lonely life now. I probably would have been a spy if he hadn't made me promise not to."

"Go on."

"So, here's why it matters. Of all the bombing missions we completed throughout Europe, in France, in Norway, and in Germany, where do I get shot down? Twenty miles from my grandmother's house near Bremen. My sister and I spent a glorious summer there when we were kids. I loved Germany. So, I knew my way around, and thought landing near her house was God's way of protecting me until the end of the war."

Don looked on as he listened to Hank's story.

"Boy, was she shocked to see me. She didn't want me there. Then she calmed down, but after I went to bed, she called her bishop… a Nazi officer, and I was arrested. She snuck away without telling me anything. She didn't even say goodbye. Can you see why I'm a little cynical? My own grandmother betrayed me; the presiding church leader was more loyal to the *Führer* than he was to his promise to 'feed the hungry and liberate the captive'." Hank rocked back and forth, shuddering with anger. "God abandoned me."

"You know that isn't true," Don scolded. "As for your grandmother and the bishop, maybe they had a reason for doing what they did."

"To save their own bacon?"

"Could be. But there's got to be better reason."

"Maybe it's just God punishing me for something?"

"Not likely. We both know He's not like that. There's got to be a logical reason."

"I can't come up with a good reason why she would do that to me. But why didn't God warn me, or stop me from going to her house in the first place?"

"You think God is to blame?"

Hank muttered, "Look where I am now. I'm still here, and I'm not going anywhere."

"Do you really think God would ignore you in the moment of your greatest need, and just not care that you became a prisoner of war? Does that sound right to you?" Don asked.

A mist blurred Hank's vision. Don stood and added, "You know better than this, Hank. God allows bad things to happen to good people to see if they'll stay true to their faith. It's just a test Hank. It's just a test."

As Don walked away, Hank whispered to himself. "It's a pretty cruel test if you ask me."

Chapter 61

August 16, 1944
Bushnell Army Hospital, Brigham City, Utah

Ella's work kept her busy as Bushnell expanded with more patients and employees. She lived in the nearby dorms instead of finding housing in crowded Brigham City. Her sporadic schedule had her working day shifts one week, swing shifts the next, and the occasional graveyard shift.

She visited Tom almost every day. His neck and back injuries brought him the most agony, and doctors could do little to ease the pain. The constant pain took a toll on his patience, and his short temper became known throughout the hospital. Other nurses and staff whispered that he snapped at them when he didn't get his way. Ella had gotten only glimpses of his temper before the war, and now his anger boiled beneath the surface even when he was with her. Still, each time she came to his room, it was with more trepidation and a softer tread than the last.

She came in one morning and stood by his bedside while orderlies helped lift him into his wheelchair. When they accidentally dropped him a few inches into his seat. Tom gasped through his teeth.

"Be a little more careful, will you?" he snarled. "Just because my legs are out of their casts doesn't mean you can throw me around."

"Tom," Ella didn't hide the sternness in her tone, "you could be kinder."

The orderlies ducked out of the room, but not before giving her sympathetic glances. Or perhaps they wondered what she saw in this guy. She wasn't so sure herself anymore. Before he left for the war, they had talked of marriage, children, and of a future together untouched by the fighting in Europe and elsewhere. Now at every turn, she saw glimpses of the war in his eyes, which were battle-hardened and full of a strange, frightening kind of anger she'd not seen in him before.

"They could do their job right, Ella," he muttered. "I'm in so much pain."

She sat next to him. "Did the pain keep you awake again last night?"

"Yeah. Well, that, and some other things."

Frowning, she asked, "Like what?"

He sighed. "Did you know they've got German prisoners here doing laundry? I saw one yesterday, when the door to my room was open. He walked by with a load of linens."

"Yes, I know. They're hard workers. Very helpful."

"But this guy, he stared at me. He stared at this," he gestured to himself, with braces on his legs and the wheelchair. "Looked me right in the eye. I should be the one walking on my own two feet, not him, and he knows it."

"Maybe he was feeling sorry for you?"

"Oh, that makes a lot of sense. A German showing sympathy. What a joke." Tom's anger was escalating. He gripped the arms of his wheelchair. "What are they doing here?"

She kept her voice calm. "There's a shortage of workers. We need the help, and they're willing to do it. They work about ten hours a day for just eighty cents a day."

Tom scowled in disgust. "I saw another one delivering the meal trays yesterday. It's so…"

Ella looked away from his clenched jaw and the angry twitch in his eye. From the way his bitterness and displeasure streamed out of him, he had been troubled by this for some time.

"Why do they have to be *here*?" he asked. "I know we house a lot of German prisoners here in Utah, but why put them around us? Why remind us of all the horrible things they're doing?"

A knot formed in Ella's throat. She swallowed and said, "Horrible things *who* is doing?"

"The Germans. All those hateful Germans," he spat.

"I'm German, Tom. Am I hateful?" She raised her voice, even though it trembled.

"You're as German as I am. You were born here. Real Germans are evil, and I hate them."

Ella stood, her chair scooting back on the floor. "Maybe we need to increase your pain meds."

"I'm fine," he shot back. "I don't need more pain meds."

"I've never heard you talk like this." Ella looked at him with pity.

"You don't know what they're capable of doing. I've sat in on intelligence briefings. I've heard some of the horrible things the Germans have done. It makes my blood boil…"

"Nazis, Tom, Nazis," she cried. "They are the ones doing these things."

"I know they're systematically trying to kill all the Jews. Did you know that?"

"There's been conflicting reports." Ella breathed in deep through her nose.

"Don't be fooled. It's happening. I know it is," he barked. "Ever heard of Lidice?"

"I have not." Ella kept her voice calm, hoping to keep him from growing more agitated.

"It's a town in Nazi-occupied Czechoslovakia. Or it was a town, until the Germans destroyed it. Do you know what they did? They wiped it off the map. I'm not just talking about blowing it up, like they've done to thousands of villages. They executed all the men, one at time; then they sent the women to a forced labor camp. There were a hundred orphans they just left to die, and they bulldozed the village flat. They even dug up the cemetery because Hitler wanted the world to forget this town ever existed. All because of a rumor that some citizens had assassinated a German general."

Ella bit her lip and cried.

"Have you ever heard that?" he asked. "The Germans bragged about it in their newspapers. I could tell you about other horrific and blood-curdling stories, but you wouldn't believe me. You'd think I was making it up."

Breathing heavy, Tom stopped to catch his breath. "A friend of mine from England is here at Bushnell. A week or so ago, he sat in on a debriefing of a B-17 crewman who was shot down in France and he was picked up by the resistance and they snuck him back to England. He described seeing the remains of a village in France where the Germans rounded up all the men, women, and children and shot them all. They crucified a baby and left it hanging for everyone to see."

"Tom, please," Ella whispered. "Stop."

"But that's just the tip of the iceberg."

"I'm going to leave now." Her voice was firm yet calm. "I'll come back later."

Tom looked at the floor. "I'm not going to apologize for telling you this," he said. "I could go on for hours. I know what I'm talking about."

"And I'm not going to apologize for not wanting to be around you. Spewing this much anger and hatred is not how I remember you."

Chapter 61-Note 1: Unlike other brutal massacres the Nazis tried to keep under wraps, the Lidice Massacre was openly and proudly proclaimed by the German propaganda ministry. The Allied response was swift in condemning the attack. Several towns in Mexico, Venezuela, Panama, and Brazil renamed their cities to include the name of Lidice, to spite Hitler's intention of removing the city permanently from the world's memory. The morning of May 27, 1943, the citizens of Lidice were rounded up in retribution for the assassination of SS-*Obergruppenführer* and General of Police, Reinhard Heydrich, under the theory that citizens of Lidice were responsible. All 173 men and 52 women of the town were taken to a wall and summarily executed. The surviving women and all 105 children were separated. The women were sent to Ravensbrück concentration camp. Some women survived the forced labor conditions. As for the children, some were taken into SS families and "Germanized." Eighty-two children were taken to Chelmno and gassed. Only seventeen children survived.

Chapter 61-Note 2: The massacre of 642 residents of the French village Oradour-sur-Glane occurred on June 10, 1944. The incident was incited by false reports that a *Waffen*-SS officer was being held hostage by some residents of the city. 190 men, 247 women and 205 children were executed or burned alive. In late April of 1944, an American shot down over Avord, France was taken in by the French resistance and witnessed the aftermath of the massacre. He was flown to England and debriefed. In his official statement, he said:

"About 3 weeks ago, I saw a town within 4 hours bicycle ride up [sic] the Gerbeau farm [of Resistance leader Camille Gerbeau] where some 500 men, women, and children had been murdered by the Germans. I saw one baby who had been crucified".

After the war, General Charles DeGaulle ordered that the village should never be rebuilt, but the ruins should remain as a memorial to Nazi brutality and cruelty. Today, the town appears much as it did on that fateful day. Wrecked buildings, sewing machines, furniture, assorted hardware and even bicycles are among the remnants that remain to this day, as an eerie memorial to the massacre at Oradour-sur-Glane.

"They Got the Wrong Village: SS Troops Massacred Over 600 French Villagers in Oradour-sur-Glane" Colin Fraser for War History Online; https://www.warhistory-online.com/world-war-ii/they-got-the-wrong-village-ss-troops-massacred-over-600-french-villagers-in-oradour-sur-glane.html; Retrieved January 3, 2021

CHAPTER 62

August 20, 1944

Stalag 17-B, Krems-Gneixendorf, Austria

Hank listened to three guards as they whispered among each other. He who stood in the shade of the barracks overhang, just around the corner and out of their sight. He leaned against the wall with his arms crossed, striking a casual pose.

"My brother was ordered to leave Paris," one guard said. "They're pushing so close; we're probably giving up on it soon."

"It sounds like it won't be long before they take it," another responded.

Take Paris? Hank leaned forward, but as he shifted his weight the boards underneath his feet creaked. Hank's heart pounded. A guard dashed around the corner. Sicko stopped when he saw Hank, putting his hands on his hips.

"*Schweinehund*," Sikkar barked. "Stop listening to our conversation?"

"I'm not listening to you," Hank said. "I'm trying to find some shade."

"You lie, *schweinehund*, you lie."

Hank turned his gaze away.

"Maybe you are the *Kriegie* hiding the radio, huh, *schweinehund*? I think I'll look to make sure." Sikkar turned on his heel and stepped toward the door of Hank's barracks, one hand gripping the strap of the rifle slung over his shoulder. The vengeful look in his eye was one Hank hadn't seen before.

An American on lookout duty saw him coming, and shouted, "Sicko's coming."

Sikkar flung the door open and marched to Hank's bunk. "Show me all that is hidden in your bed," he demanded.

"What have I done? Why only me?"

"Because I don't like you. Because you are a no-good *schweinehund*."

One by one, Sikkar piled up all of Hank's and Don's belongings. A crowd of prisoners gathered to watch

"It looks like you have too many cigarettes," Sikkar said. "I will need to inspect them for contraband. But I will return them if they pass inspection." Sikkar snickered as he shoved a handful of Lucky Strike cigarettes into his tunic.

When Sikkar's back was turned, Hank glanced at the board in the ceiling above their bed. Good. It was still concealed.

"Oh, look at what else I found? Two American candy bars."

Tossing items to the floor, Sikkar stopped only when he could find nothing else to steal. "I think I've found enough today. Maybe next time, *schweinehund,* you won't listen to us talk."

Sikkar smiled like a child clutching a handful of Halloween candy. "As you were," he demanded as he marched out of the barracks.

"What's Sikkar got against you, Hank?" one of the prisoners asked.

Hank picked up his blanket and tossed it up on his bunk. The other prisoners wandered away, but Don stayed.

"What did you overhear that got him so upset?"

"Don't get your hopes up," Hank replied, "but it sounds like the Germans are giving up Paris. They're on the run."

By the end of August, the *Kriegies* sought out any shade they could find outside, rather than endure the stifling heat in the barracks. During the long, slow, summer days, guards and prisoners alike milled about, dabbing sweat off their faces and squinting at the sun.

Hank slouched in the shade, straining to hear something, anything else besides the buzzing flies and stomping footsteps of guards—maybe the drone of a plane's engine or splashing water in a creek back home. Chester's laugh. Billie's giggle. He closed his eyes.

Around the corner, hushed voices mingled together as guards huddled again to talk. Hank sat still and listened. Sometimes he wondered where they got their information, whether it was accurate, and if so, how they could be allowed to chat about it. With a pinch of regret, he realized maybe they wanted him to hear them. Even so, he noted every word shared between them.

"I just heard about Paris."

"The Americans keep sending more troops our way, but I am more worried about the Russians."

"Why?"

Hank imagined the speaker's brow wrinkling in confusion.

"Didn't you hear?" The guard's voice lowered, and the only word Hank caught was "Romania."

"When was that?"

"A few days ago. The king of Romania led a coup, then surrendered to the Allies. The entire Eighth Army fled into Hungary."

"That's not just a rumor? You know for sure it's true?"

"My friend heard it on BBC radio last night."

"If we're going to lose this war, let's hope the Americans make it here first. I would hate to see what the Russians..." Their voices faded as they walked away.

After a moment, Hank yawned, stretched, and got up. He made his way to the White House, ambling through the camp with his hands in his pockets. His heart pounded with excitement. Could it be true, the war was drawing to an end? Could all of this nightmare be put behind him?

Out of nowhere, Billie came to his mind like a light piercing through the fog. He saw Billie's wild, bright smile as he imagined her fiddling with knobs and dials in the cockpit of her plane. She ripped through the sky just like she tore through life. She gave it her all or nothing. He missed that spirit of hers, the way it used to make his blood boil when she mocked him, or how she argued with him just to see if she could make him angry. He laughed to himself as he choked back a cry. It startled him back to the present. He rapped on the White House door.

"Anyone seen Kurtenbach?" Hank called.

"Nope," someone replied. "Not for an hour or so."

Hank looked for the camp commander in all the usual places. He went to the vegetable garden, the main compound, and stopped by other barracks. Finally, he rubbed the sweat off his neck and headed to the camp library.

The library was shared between the Americans and the British. Thousands of books lined the shelves, donated from the YMCA, the

Red Cross, and other organizations. Other books had been left behind by prisoners. Hank poked his head into the library, found it empty, and turned to leave, but several buildings down, Sikkar came around the corner with Big Stoop, laughing his sickly snickering laugh. Before they could glance his way, Hank slipped inside the library and shut the door behind him.

While he waited for them to pass, he browsed the books. He'd been here a few times, but always came away empty-handed. He ran his fingers over the spines of the books, imagining where they had been before they were here. He searched the volumes for something that might pique his interest.

The stomp of Big Stoop's footstep and Sikkar's howling laughter faded, and Hank crept to the door to leave. But something in a far upper corner of the library caught his eye. A splash of reddish brown and gold embossing, something familiar. Could it be? He stepped closer and reached up to grab the book, one so small it fit in his hand, even as thin and frail as they'd become from malnourishment. The small size was designed to fit inside a serviceman's front shirt pocket. He knew the words on the cover before reading them.

He opened the cover of the *Book of Mormon* to find the name of its owner, *Tom Tanner, Gilbert, Arizona*, which was scrawled in the front flap. He fanned the pages, thumbing through the thin, crinkled paper. All the stories found inside that book came back. His old love for God and his church washed over him with that same feeling shivering down his spine that happened when heard a familiar hymn. He'd come to the brink of giving up on God. Now he held religion in his hands, and the weight of it comforted him, even as it pressed on his conscience. How could he have ever thought to abandon this part of his life?

He tucked the book in his front pocket and left the library.

He waved down a couple of *Kriegies* walking by. "Have you seen Kurt around?"

"I saw him about twenty minutes ago, but I don't know where he went."

Sighing, Hank walked back to the White House to wait. He went inside to find Kurtenbach sitting at his desk, chatting, and laughing with one of his security officers.

Hank stepped up. "Have you got a minute?"

"Sure Meyer. Will you excuse us?"

The other man left the room.

After the room emptied, Hank cleared his voice and whispered, "You heard about the fall of Paris?"

Kurtenbach leaned in toward Hank and smiled. "It happened yesterday. Did the guards talk about it?"

"Yes. They seemed pretty concerned. Also, the King of Romania surrendered to the Allies."

Kurtenbach raised his eyebrows. "I have not heard that piece of good news."

"The Russians have them spooked," Hank laughed.

"Who knows? At the rate we're going, some are saying we could be in Berlin by Christmas. Wouldn't that be great?"

"I'm not going to get my hopes up," Hank admitted. "But if I could avoid spending another winter here, I would vote for that."

"I've been here since early '43, so I have been here for most of three winters altogether," Kurtenbach said.

"No thanks." Hank stepped back, as if Kurtenbach's longevity was somehow contagious.

"Just keep it up, Meyer. It all helps us to paint a clearer picture of what's happening. Feel free to spread the word, too. Encouraging news like this can be a real boost to morale."

Hank left the White House, holding back a smile. He walked to his barracks with a lightness in his step.

"*Schweinehund!*" Sikkar bellowed. "Come here."

Hank froze. Behind him, the White House was the closest place to hide. He could make a run for it—

"*Schweinehund!* I said come here."

Hank twisted around to find him. A short distance away, Sikkar stood, alone, under the shade of a barrack's overhang. Hank's shoulders sagged as he approached him.

"You look too happy, so you must be up to no good, *schweinehund.*"

"My name is Meyer."

"What's that in your pocket, *schweinehund?*"

Hank's heart dropped, but he reached into his pocket and pulled out the book. Sikkar snatched it from his hand.

"A Bible?" he sneered. "No—it's a *Book of Mormon?*"

"It's approved. I got it in the camp library."

Sikkar thumbed through the pages and pointed to the numbered verses. "You are a Christian?"

Hank gave a slight nod, his eyes looking away, unable to hold eye contact with Sikkar. His gaze dropped to the ground. Of all people to tell that he had lost faith….When he looked up again, the expression of anguish that crossed Sikkar's face made him stiffen in surprise. But it disappeared, eclipsed by his usual malice. "I guess it makes sense," he said. "You are a sneak and a liar. Now I know why. I'm taking the book, so I can…inspect it."

"Why would you do that?"

"If it's valuable to you, then I don't want you to have it."

"You have no right. The Geneva Convention rules state that religious books cannot be confiscated," Hank said.

"I am not confiscating it. I am only going to inspect it. If it passes inspection, you will get it back." Sikkar cackled with laughter.

"Like you gave back my Lucky Strikes and my D-bars? I've heard that before."

"Well, *schweinehund*. Your little book must mean something to you." Sikkar laughed and gave Hank a go-away gesture with the back of his hand. "Get out of here, *schweinehund*, before I report you for threatening a guard."

Hank stared a moment, his face darkening with a scowl. "What have I ever done to you? Why are you always targeting me?"

Sikkar put his nose inches from Hank's face, then screamed in German. "Because, *schweinehund*, you have lied to me since the day I first met you. You said you didn't speak German, yet you eavesdrop on the guards' conversations. And when I call you *schweinehund*," he lowered his head, as if sharing a secret, "you cringe, and not just because you know what it really means—because you believe it."

Hank's vision swam with red and heat rose up his neck. He lunged closer to Sikkar, who reeled back and stumbled. Hank jabbed a finger in Sikkar's face. German filled his mouth, and he spoke in the language he'd avoided for so long. "Okay Sicko, have it your way. I speak German. So what? How does that change anything? I'm not the only American who does, and guards gossip all the time about meaningless things that don't get any of us out of this rat hole. So why don't you just leave me alone and give me my book back?"

Hank's torrent of words pummeled into Sikkar like fists, and he stood, leaning away from Hank, eyes round with fear. When Hank waited for him to answer, the fear died away and a sneer replaced it. "You are as stupid as I thought you were, *schweinehund*. Blowing your cover for a precious little book."

Hank's throat tightened. "You mean you didn't... you were..."

"Of course, I didn't know. How could I know? You obviously knew enough German to make my bluff worthwhile, but now I know for certain!"

"Will you please," his voice was small, a dry whisper. "Please give the book to me."

"I think I'll hold on to it. If it makes you act so stupidly, maybe it's dangerous. It's messing with your head."

"You can't do that," Hank protested.

But Sikkar was already cramming the book into his pocket. Hank looked around him, as if all of a sudden finding himself or waking up from a dream. He trembled with red hot anger but forced one slow step after another to his barracks. He climbed into his bed, burying his face in his blanket and weeping.

The next morning on his way to roll call, he heard his name called. One of the more friendly guards—if one could call any of them friendly—beckoned him, with a crook of his finger and furtive glances around him, into a doorway.

Hank glanced around for Sicko or Big Stoop, then he drew closer.

The guard waved his hand faster, his face brimming with excitement. "Come here," he said. "I must tell you something you will like to know."

"What's going on?"

"I know what Sikkar did to you yesterday," he admitted with a wry smile. "He was ecstatic about revealing your secret."

Hank wanted to roll his eyes. *Hank's secret.* Giving it such an identity gave it more substance than he wanted it to have, and already men were gossiping about it.

"But last night, the camp *Kommendant* confronted Sikkar about some things he had hidden inside his bed. One of the stolen items belonged to the *Kommendant* himself, though of course Sikkar said he didn't know how it got there."

At this, Hank leaned closer. "You're joking, aren't you?" His eyes were wide with anticipation.

"The *Kommendant* was furious. He told Sikkar if he didn't want to be turned over to the *Gestapo*, he'd have to join an infantry unit."

"Go on." Hank held his breath, even though he didn't need to, because either way it meant Sicko would be gone. Already the very air of the camp felt freer, the skies wider, and the dusty ground less desolate.

"Sikkar chose combat. He left the camp this morning. He's gone forever."

"Please don't joke about something like this," Hank said.

"I'm not joking. And I told the *Kommendant* that this belonged to you." The guard produced a small book. "This is your book, yes?"

"Yes!" Hank took the book, grin widening until he thought he would cry. "I can't thank you enough for the good news and for giving me back my book."

The guard put his finger to his lips. "You had better not say anything to anyone just now. Let it sit for a few days, okay? At least until it's all blown over."

"Promise. But you just made my day. My week. My month! Heck, I don't think I've been this happy since I've been here"

The guard smiled. Suddenly, Hank wondered about these guards forced into this service, if their lives had any ray of hope, or if all hope had been dashed to pieces as his own had. What if this guard had been miserable for as long as Hank, or even longer?

"I have to ask," Hank said. "Why are you doing this for me? What does it matter to you?"

The guard sighed and rubbed his cheek. "I don't believe in God any more than I believe Hitler is good for Germany. But," he gestured to the book that Hank held between them, clasped in both hands. "I had a great aunt who went to your Mormon church. She always was always nice to me."

"She'd be proud of you for this moment." Hank watched the shade of doubt creep into the guard's eyes. "And I thank you from the bottom of my heart."

"You're welcome."

After roll call, Hank raced back to his barracks to slip the book under his bunk. Don was chatting with another prisoner at the other end of the barracks but rushed over when he saw Hank.

"What's got you so happy?" Don asked.

"Promise not to say anything for a couple days?"

"You know I keep secrets."

"Sikkar got sent to an infantry unit last night for stealing something from the *Kommendant*. Can you believe that?"

Don's jaw dropped. "Seriously?"

"Yep! I heard it from one of the guards who didn't like Sicko either," Hank laughed.

"No kidding." Don put his hands on his hips grinning.

"Sicko tried to say he didn't steal the *Kommendant's* things, but that didn't change anything. I wonder if Kurt had anything to do with that?" Hank said.

"I wouldn't be surprised, but it sure is great news," Don said. "Now if they would get rid of Big Stoop and few others, life would be much better around here."

"I also got my book back. Sicko stole it from me yesterday," Hank smiled.

Don held out his hand for it, and Hank gave it to him. Frowning, Don turned it over, then looked inside the cover, rubbing the title page between his thumb and forefinger as he hesitated to turn the page. "A *Book of Mormon*." Curiosity was written all over Don's face. "My pastor always warned me about this book."

"Really? What did he say about it?" Hank asked with a humored smile.

"I can't tell you how many sermons we heard about how evil this book was, and how we should never even touch it because it was poisonous to our souls."

"You're serious?" Hank asked.

"Serious as can be," Don said.

"I've heard a few stories that some religions don't like Mormons," Hank explained, "especially in the South. They've even run the missionaries out of their towns. But I never really knew if those stories were true."

"Oh, it's true," Don sighed. "In Oklahoma, we've run Mormons out of many towns. My pastor taught us how to quote the Bible to trip up the Mormon missionaries."

This didn't make sense. Don had always treated him right. He was as decent a person as anyone he knew, and Don's faith had been a light in this dark prison camp. Surely back home he didn't treat Mormons the way he had described.

So, do you think I'm evil for having this book?" Hank's question was sincere.

Don put his arm on Hank's shoulder and smiled. "The jury's out. I think I'll need to get to know you a little better before I decide," he joked. "I guess what really matters is whether or not you're going to try to convert me." He winked.

Hank didn't try to hide his big sigh, didn't care if Don could see how relieved he was. "Oh, don't worry. I'm still working on my own conversion."

"Then I guess I won't try to run you out of town," Don grinned. "Sound fair?"

"Fair enough."

CHAPTER 63

October 2, 1944
Long Beach, California

Billie stood in front of the Operations Center in Long Beach. She'd retrieve her orders and her mail, then head back to her own place, rest, spend some time alone—no parties this time. She wondered how long she could keep herself out of trouble.

Her hand on the door, she started to push when a familiar voice called her name from behind.

"Billie!"

Billie glanced over her shoulder. "Hey, Dottie! I haven't seen you in months. How've you been?"

"I'm hanging in there. How about you?"

"Busy as ever and loving it," Billie said. "So, where you headed?"

Dottie rolled her eyes and said with some exasperation, "Love Field. Just my fifteenth time in Dallas in the last two months. Where you headed?"

"Don't know. I'm just going in to get my orders."

"You're still ferrying P-51s and P-38s, right?"

"Yep, still quite a few left," Billie beamed. "I can't imagine flying anything else."

"I think I'm gonna regret not going to pursuit school," Dottie said.

"I'm glad Betty and I did it early on. It's harder to get into pursuit school now, from what I hear."

Dottie sighed. "Yeah. So, are you still engaged to that Captain what's-his-name from Vermont?"

"No, we broke that off a few months ago. I've kind of sworn off men for now. They're just not worth the emotional effort."

"Maybe you're just looking in the wrong place."

"I'm not looking anywhere. They find *me*, and then I find out they're all a bunch of horny toads."

"Don't give up on them forever," Dottie said. "I've got a guy who takes great care of me. At least, he does if we're ever in the same city. But it won't be long before we're together once and for all."

Billie gave her a nervous smile. Should she congratulate her? Dottie didn't seem to be bragging, but Billie couldn't imagine herself responding without it sounding like sarcasm. She had narrowly escaped getting tangled up in marriage and didn't know if it was worth congratulating anyway.

She changed the subject. "I'm glad I bumped into you because I've wanted to ask you about Susie Clarke."

Dottie's face darkened. Billie realized all the female pilots Dottie ran into probably wanted to know the details, and she figured she was probably tired of answering questions about it.

"What do you want to know?"

"I heard you were there when it happened."

"I saw it all."

"I've heard," Billie said, "that there are some questions about the final investigation. That they white-washed the whole thing. Is that true? Can you tell me what really happened?"

"Susie was on a cross-country trip to Greenville, North Carolina in a BT-15. Her second-to-last stop was in Atlanta, and some lieutenant begged her to take him back to his base in North Carolina. I had to over-night at Columbia Army Airfield when she stopped in Atlanta to refuel."

"Did you see her or talk to her?"

"No, she wasn't there long enough, and I only found out at the last minute that she was there. When I finally did find her, she was already taxiing into position for takeoff. It was textbook, and then all of a sudden, her plane just died. It peeled to the left and went nose down into the ground. It was horrifying."

From the dry tone Dottie used to tell the story, with a flatness in her voice and sparse details, Billie knew she'd told it enough times to find a way to tell it without making herself cry.

"An investigator speculated that one of the cables was torn; another thought it was an 'air strike' from a flock of birds, or something like that." She pointed her finger to make her point. "But I can promise you there were no birds. The thing is, whatever anyone says about the 'official cause,' every person who knows anything about the investigation also knows it was sabotage. The engine just suddenly died on her initial climb. The guys who tore the engine apart said it was obvious that someone put sand in the carburetor."

"Sand in the carburetor?"

"The recovery crew found it, but I heard that the investigator was ordered not to report it. The official report says the cause of the crash is undetermined."

"Why won't they say it was sabotage?"

"That's the big question, isn't it? I really don't know."

"That's terrifying. You think they still want to cancel the WASP program?"

Dottie's eyes widened. "Didn't you get your letter from the Pentagon last week?"

"I haven't picked up my mail yet."

"They're shutting down the WASPs on December 20."

"You're joking."

"I wish I were. They sent every one of us a letter saying they will no longer need our services because they have enough male pilots now."

Billie shook her head. *It couldn't be true.*

"That's why I said before that it wouldn't be long before I'm always in the same city with my boyfriend. Sorry to bring you the bad news," Dottie said, looking at Billie with sympathy.

Billie craned her neck back, looking all the way to the top of the building. She sighed "I just can't believe it. I thought we were doing a great job, and we were finally gaining some respect. Why all of a sudden shut us down?"

"I've heard some girls speculate that it was because Jackie Cochran wanted to become a general, and since they refused to give her a commission, she decided to shut it all down, but I don't believe that. I think the real issue is that there have been about thirty girls killed in this service. Some in training, which could be understandable, but a lot on active duty. I can see that some are legitimate accidents, but there are more suspicious deaths than anyone is willing to admit. Like Susie's death, for example. So, I think Jackie knows more than she is able to talk about, and she just figured it wasn't worth having us girls killed over a losing battle. You know?"

"It makes me so angry," Billie snapped through clinched teeth. "It's just not fair. Why…"

"Don't get mad at me," Dottie said, "I'm just the messenger."

"I know." Billie glanced at Dottie with a wince. "I'm sorry."

"Looks like we have about two months to find a new job. I hear the CAA is hiring inspectors, and the Army is hiring link trainers."

"I thought I would be doing this forever," Billie muttered.

"They also say you could resign after November twentieth without any penalty."

"I'm not resigning early!" Billie exclaimed. "Heck, I'm going to squeeze every hour of flight time I can out of these planes."

"I'm with you. I'm going to keep flying until they drag me out of here kicking and screaming!" Dottie turned away, heading back the way she'd been going. "So, Billie, it's been great to see you. But I've gotta run. Go get your letter."

Billie smiled, "It was nice talking to you, too. Thanks for telling me about everything."

She watched as Dottie walked with confidence to her plane, knowing it would be the first of many last things she'd see in the next two months.

"Please be safe out there, Dottie!"

"You too, Billie!"

Chapter 63-Note 1: WASP Susan Parke Clarke (44-W-2) was killed on July 4, 1944 when the BT-13 she was ferrying crashed near Columbia, South Carolina. The details surrounding her death in many ways closely matched the events described in this chapter. According to WASP pilot, Joanne Wallace Orr (44-W-2), who was a friend of Suzy's and familiar with the circumstances surrounding her death, "There wasn't a single person (familiar with the investigation) that did not say she wasn't killed because of sabotage."

Joanne Wallace Orr. "An Oral History, Women Airforce Service Pilots Oral History Project," *The Woman's Collection*. (Denton, TX: Texas Woman's University, 2004, p 33).

CHAPTER 64

December 1, 1944

Stalag 17-B, Krems-Gneixendorf, Austria

The *Kriegies* enjoyed a few short, blissful weeks without Sicko. But the day the *Gestapo* came, everything darkened again to the beat of their marching, polished boots and cruel shouts. Hitler blamed the Americans for an assassination attempt and sought revenge by ordering the *Gestapo* and SS to assume control over the prisoner-of-war camps. Since that time, the guards were allowed to supplement their own rations by taking what they wanted from the Americans' Red Cross packages.

Kurtenbach demanded an official meeting with the camp *Kommendant*, *Oberst* Kuhn. When he entered the *Kommendant*'s office, he stood squarely before him and saluted. "Sir," he said. "I respectfully demand that the German guards stop taking contents of the Red Cross parcels intended for prisoners of war."

Oberst Kuhn tilted his head, folding his hands behind his back. "What makes you think the guards are stealing from them? How do you know these items were even included in the parcels?"

"The parcels have empty spaces where cans of meat are missing." Kurtenbach's voice rose as he shook with rising anger. He cleared his throat.

Kuhn looked at Kurtenbach, measuring his response. "You cannot prove the guards are taking anything. They could have been pilfered in shipment."

"When our men are on KP duty, they find empty SPAM and tuna cans in your garbage cans. You know, and I know the guards are stealing from our parcels, and it has to stop."

The *Kommendant* paced closer, leaning into Kurtenbach's face with a sneer. "I will order an investigation and determine what is really happening to the Red Cross parcels. I expect that when our investigation is complete, our guards will be exonerated."

Kurtenbach opened his mouth to speak. "Sir—"

"I give you my personal assurance that your next shipment of parcels will be complete."

Kurtenbach's hands curled into fists as he drew back, restraining the anger in his voice. "Thank you, sir." He saluted and turned to walk out of the *Kommendant*'s office.

The *Kommendant* called after him. "But we must take special measures to ensure that each can will spoil if it isn't eaten."

His back still to the *Kommendant*, Kurtenbach narrowed his eyes and looked over his shoulder. "You want to do *what?*"

"We will make sure that each can of meat is eaten. They cannot be stored. They must not be useful for long journeys."

"Your reason for this, sir?"

"You know exactly what I mean, Kurtenbach. Don't tell me you haven't dreamed of trying it."

Kurtenbach swallowed. "If you mean an escape…"

"I do."

"Well, if someone were to make such an attempt, why would they weigh themselves down with heavy cans?"

The *Kommendant* simply sighed. "That is my final offer. Take it or leave it. I will report to the Red Cross that you are getting your packages in their entirety."

The next Friday, the guards opened nearly a thousand parcels, enough to feed over four thousand prisoners for a week. They lined up every can of meat on row after row of tables, standing neat as soldiers at attention. The bedraggled prisoners hovered near, watching with hungry, confused eyes. The guards pressed the tip of their knives to the lids of each can.

The prisoners lurched forward, arms outstretched in fear, but guards held them back, as small holes were broken through each tin can's seal. Row after row, can after can.

When the guards allowed the prisoners to retrieve the punctured cans, they looked on in astonishment. After they carried the cans back to their barracks, they sealed each bayonet puncture with oleo margarine. No one dared breathe a word to the guards that all this effort was a waste—only a display of control and cruelty, nothing more.

For the next two weeks, most all the *Kriegies* received complete Red Cross parcels. It was the first time in months. But instead of one package per man, it was one for every four men.

The third week in December, *Oberst* Kuhn summoned Kurtenbach again to his office.

"It is my duty to inform you that from now on, your men will no longer receive Red Cross parcels," Kuhn declared with a smirk.

Kurtenbach's jaw dropped, but he recovered and squared his shoulders. "I will be forced to file an official complaint to the Swiss legation about this violation of the Geneva Convention."

"Go ahead," Kuhn shrugged. "I'll give you some paper if you'd like."

"What's your justification for doing this? We depend on those because you don't feed us enough."

"It is out of my hands. You can thank the Allied bombing attacks on our railroads."

"The Allies know not to target trains from Switzerland. You're making excuses."

Kuhn smiled, watching Kurtenbach's face, who did his best to remain tranquil. Seconds that felt like hours passed, and when the *Kommendant* didn't get a rise out of Kurtenbach, he spat, "We have nothing more to discuss. Tell your men that it was not our desire to deny you these parcels, but your country has bombed the trains so these packages can no longer be delivered."

Kurtenbach told each barracks himself, one by one, although from the despair in some of their eyes, word had gotten out ahead of him. His orders to all Americans spread quickly: "Enjoy the last of it while you can."

CHAPTER 65

December 17, 1944
Long Beach, California

Today was Billie's last ferrying assignment, and then she was out of a job. She walked a bit slower than usual, drinking in all the surroundings that had long since become background noise: the buzzing of airplanes as they took off, the smell of high-octane fuel, the ubiquitous drab-colored desks and filing cabinets lining the walls of every building she entered.

She stepped into the Operations Center to receive her final orders. The flight duty officer looked up and his face broke into a smile.

"Hey Billie!" His enthusiasm was so eager they both stood in awkward in silence until he cleared his throat and continued.

"Um… I've got your orders. I think you're going to like where you're going."

"Is that so?"

"How about McDill Field in Tampa, Florida? You can't beat sunny Florida in December. In fact, you're flying the only P-51 I've ever sent to Florida."

His voiced faded to a dull echo in Billie's ears as she quit listening. *Florida*. She just wanted to go somewhere she could call home. If she couldn't fly these planes anymore, why did she care about Florida? "Great," Billie interjected when it seemed he was finished. "You remember I'm going to the final WASP graduation in Texas after that, right? Is that on my orders, too?"

"Yes, ma'am, it is. And your termination point is right back here on Thursday, December 21. Isn't that what you wanted?" His eyebrows raised, uncertain.

"Yes," Billie said. "Thanks for taking care of it. I'm glad I don't have to pay for my way back here from Texas."

"No problem. If you don't mind my asking, why aren't you going back to Nevada for Christmas?"

"Utah."

"Right, Utah."

"I told my parents I couldn't make it."

"How come?"

"I think I'm going to get a job as a link trainer. I'm waiting to hear from them."

"When would that start?"

"If I get it, it'll start in a week or so."

"So, you'll have plenty of time to get back and still see your folks." He tilted his head in a gentle, reprimanding way. "Billie. They haven't seen you in a while."

"Look, I haven't got a whole bunch of reasons to go back to Utah."

"I thought you had a boyfriend there?"

"No. I don't have a boyfriend," she said, her eyes glancing at her feet. "I have a close friend who's somewhere in the Pacific." She paused. "I guess… I guess him not being there is why I don't want to go back. Well, part of it, anyway." She sighed and rubbed her eyes. "Why am I telling this to you?"

"I want you to be all right. If you're avoiding something—"

"I'm not avoiding home." With a tight smile, she said. "Plus, it's none of your business. I've got my last ferrying assignment to finish."

"Maybe I'll see you when you come back on Thursday. If not, it's been great working with you."

Billie felt her mouth quiver as she shook his hand.

She climbed into the shining P-51 and settled into her pre-flight routine that was now second nature, this time lingering at each step. She committed to memory every dial and control, the levers and the canopy.

This flight was just like many others Billie had flown. After refueling at Luke Field in Arizona and Kelly Field in San Antonio, she would overnight at Keesler Field in Biloxi, Mississippi. She could make it to McDill by noon the next day. With the shortened daylight hours, she had to hurry to make it to Biloxi by nightfall.

All went as planned on the first day. She landed her plane in Biloxi and secured it for the night. After a terrible night's sleep, she finished breakfast, yawning and rubbing her tired eyes, before waving down a base taxi driver for a ride to the flight line.

"Which plane are we taking you to?" the driver asked.

"It's the P-51 over by that hangar." Billie pointed to a hangar about a quarter mile away.

"Seriously?" He glanced at her. "You're flying that P-51?"

"Yes, I am."

He said nothing, but his eyes widened as they approached. "We don't see many of these around here. She sure is a beauty."

"And she's a dream to fly," Billie sighed. She looked again at her plane. "It also looks like she's attracted a small audience." A handful of maintenance men had gathered about her plane, but they scattered at the approaching car.

"You can't blame them for wanting to take a peek," the driver said. "This may be the first time they've ever seen a pursuit plane, let alone a P-51."

Billie grinned, counting out the money for the ride. "I don't blame them at all. Let them have one last look."

She gave the plane a final inspection, though everything worked just as she'd left it the night before.

Once airborne, she headed toward Tampa over the Gulf of Mexico. Drifting over the water, she settled back with a sigh. She'd have time to kill. She switched her radio frequency to the Army Airways Communications System for the latest weather updates. Laughter from several pilots cackled over the frequency as soon as she dialed in.

"Okay, I've got one for you. What's the difference between a pursuit pilot and a pig?"

After a pause, another voice said, "I don't know."

"A drunk pig doesn't turn into a pursuit pilot!"

Billie couldn't help but laugh out loud.

Another voice chimed in, "How many pursuit pilots does it take to change a light bulb?" Silence. "Just one. He holds the bulb, and the world revolves around him."

"How would a girl know if she's dating a pursuit pilot?"

"He says, 'Okay, enough about me; let's talk about planes'."

Billie snatched up her pencil and said into her radio, "Go a little slower on these jokes, I'm writing them down."

Only radio static filled the silence that stretched for half a minute.

Finally, one said, "Did I just hear a woman's voice?"

"You sure did," Billie said. "And I love your jokes. Keep them coming."

"Are you one of them WASP pilots we've heard so much about?"

"Yes I am." Billie agreed with pride.. "I'm glad to know you've heard about us. But don't stop the jokes; they're hilarious."

"Okay," another pilot interjected. "I've got another one: What's the difference between a pursuit pilot and God?"

"I give up. What?" Billie said.

"God doesn't think he's a pursuit pilot."

Billie's radio erupted with laughter. "That's the best one yet," she said. "I'm sure glad all your pursuit pilot jokes are about men because I think I'd be a little offended otherwise."

"No kidding? You're a pursuit pilot?"

Billie laughed. "I'm in a P-51 headed to McDill."

"Looks like we just got busted by a lady pursuit pilot, gentlemen."

"Oh, I don't mind," Billie replied. "Most times they bring it on themselves. The jokes wouldn't be funny if there wasn't a bit of truth to them. I don't just fly pursuits; I fly bombers and transports and everything in-between. So, I'm not a true pursuit pilot," she admitted.

Billie cleared her throat after a brief pause. "Sorry fellas. I'd love to chat more, but I've gotta run. Nice talking to you all."

She called the McDill tower to get instructions for her final approach.

As she made her descent, she flipped the switch to lower her landing gear, listening to the hydraulic mechanism. But instead of snapping into place as it should, a muffled thud shook the plane. A warning light on her instrument panel flashed red.

She rocked and rolled the plane to dislodge the landing gear. The light could be malfunctioning. Grunting, she pulled a few other switches and knobs and jerked the plane back and forth—there, did she hear it settle into place? The light blinked steadily, pulsing bright.

"Tower," Billie said, "would you mind taking a look at my landing gear? My light is on, but I heard something that sounded like it was down and locked. Can you confirm?"

"Affirmative. You have clearance to do a fly-by."

Billie leveled off at about three hundred feet as she passed the tower. "So, what's it look like?"

"Your landing gear is definitely not down. Repeat. It is not down. One wheel has partially unfolded, but the other hasn't budged at all."

"I'm going to take her upstairs and see if I can shake her loose."

She climbed to ten thousand feet over the uninhabited swamps of central Florida. She pulled the fairing door emergency release knob before she made a steep dive. Pulling up with a jerk, she guided the plane in a series of snap rolls. More faint thumps rumbled in the landing gear compartment, but the light still glared red.

"Tower, can you take another look at it? My light is still red."

As she made another low-level pass over the tower, the controller said, "It doesn't look like your landing gear has moved at all. I would say to do a belly landing, but the one wheel is down too far. You'd probably end up in a ball of fire. You're just going to have to bail."

411

"Bail?" Billie exclaimed, her white knuckles gripping the throttle. "Don't joke around; I can find some way to land this…"

"No, ma'am," the controller said. "You're going to have to put that pretty 'lil Mustang into the bay."

"On my final ferrying flight, I have to bail?"

"That's the way it happens sometimes, ma'am. I'm sorry."

She had never bailed before. Not once. After hundreds of slippery landings and a flight or two that had brought her within a breath of losing her life, this was how it was to end: with some faulty landing gear and clear, blue Florida skies. "You're going to have to remind me of the bailout procedure. Can you walk me through it?"

"Sure. First, maintain an altitude of about two-thousand feet, then reduce your speed to about one-hundred fifty miles per hour. The slower you go, the easier it is to bail out, but don't go so slow that you stall."

"Alright. Good to know. I think I've just pushed all that training to the back of my head because I never thought I would have to do this."

"You're not the only one," he replied. "Now, when you're ready, lower the seat, pull the lever on the canopy, and duck. If you don't duck, the canopy will knock your head off."

"Okay." A familiar detail, it was coming back now.

"Once the canopy has been jettisoned, disconnect your headset and oxygen hose, and release your safety belt and shoulder harness. Some pilots forget to throw the straps off their shoulders and just loosen them, but it's a lot harder to rise out of the seat with straps hanging on your shoulders."

"Got it."

"Then you pull yourself up onto the seat so you're in a crouching position with your feet on the seat. Make sure you trim the plane and aim it at the bay. Then dive out with your head down toward the trailing edge of the right wing."

"Why the right side?"

"You can go left if you want; but if you go to the right side, the slipstream will help you clear the airplane."

"Is that everything?"

"In a nutshell, that's it. I see you're headed northeast. Just make your turn at Lake Thonotosassa and make your heading two-four-zero. You'll head right over the runway and straight for the bay. We really don't want to pull you out of the bay, so I suggest you bail out just as you cross over the airfield. I'll clear the airspace around you."

Billie breathed in deeply, her chest shuddering. "How can you be so calm at a time like this?"

"This isn't my first bailout. We fly a lot of B-26s out of here."

"Is the runway dangerous?"

"Haven't you heard the saying 'one-a-day-in-Tampa Bay'?"

"Can't say that I have," Billie replied.

"Let's just say we see more than our share of pilots bailing out around here. But you'll be fine. Just remember your training."

"I'm glad I'm in good hands."

Billie circled north to burn off some fuel, the corner of Lake Thonotosassa appearing in her view. She banked right and headed toward the bay. On the ground below, the runway rose up faster than she'd anticipated. Her heart pounded, and her mouth grew dry.

"You can do this," the tower encouraged. "Just stay calm, and remember the steps we discussed. Good luck."

"Thanks." Billie's voice was soft and calm. "I appreciate your help."

She checked and double checked her parachute harness. Below, the runway seemed to rush at her. She gasped in a breath. "God, please help me."

She adjusted the plane's trim and reached forward to the right side of the cockpit where the canopy attached to the fuselage. Wrapping her fingers in a tight grip around the emergency release, she closed her eyes and pulled. Nothing happened. She opened her eyes as she pulled on the lever again. It stuck fast.

With both hands on the lever, she reached forward and pulled with all her might, gritting her teeth. With a jerk, the latch released and the momentum threw Billie back into her seat. The canopy swept backwards from the slipstream. It smashed into the top of her head, and she screamed in pain. The world spun and reeled around, growing blurry, and she reached up a hand to feel for the oxygen hose. As she fitted it to her face, her fingers brushed against a gash where warm blood oozed into her hair.

413

Hands sticky with blood, she found the safety belt release for the shoulder harness. Blood dripped from her hair onto her shoulder. Panic tightened her chest, sending a tingling down her arms. She could lose consciousness, could bleed to death, could crash with the plane tangled in her parachute straps... "Breathe," she said to herself. "Focus."

Crouching, she lifted her feet on the seat. The roaring wind and screaming engines deafened her ears, and the propeller chopped the air with a powerful wallop. The nose of the plane dipped forward, bringing the glistening bay into view.

She hoped its trajectory would still carry it into the bay, but had no time left to make adjustments. She glanced one last time, then leapt head-first toward the right wing. The slipstream pounded her in the chest, whipping her blood-soaked hair into her face and stinging her eyes. She tumbled, flailing her arms, before regaining enough control to fumble for the ripcord. When she gripped it tight with both hands, it came free with one firm tug. The bright white chute flapped like a great bird rising behind her, but in the static electricity around her, the silk stuck together.

Only hundreds of feet from the ground, her chute flapped with a soft swoosh in the violent wind. The ground rushed toward her. She looked up again, willing the parachute to open: pulling on the risers, shaking, jerking. Every ounce of energy she had left, every terrified plea, begged the canopy to open.

She looked down one last time as the ground screamed toward her. Just before she came collapsing onto the runway, something tugged on her shoulder harness, as strong and controlled as a human hand. She looked up, squinting her eyes against the stinging wind. The wad of silk caught the wind and slowed her perceptibly, but her risers were still a tangled mess.

Time slowed, and with it her fall, the rushing wind, and her wild heartbeat. She drifted mid-air. A calm feeling enveloped her, unmistakably warm, serene, magnificent. This peaceful feeling deepened, expanding all around her until, like a stretched rubber band, it snapped. The pavement flashed inches from her face.

Pain exploded through her ankles, knees, ribcage, everything. As her body collided with the ground, her back and shoulder crumpled on the impact with the hard pavement. Her head hit the ground, and she felt every crackle through her skull. All sound, light, and pain ended as her mind plunged into a void.

Billie sprawled out on the edge of the runway, motionless, just a few feet from the drop-off to the rocky shore of Tampa Bay.

The silence in her mind was shattered by a humming noise, at first so distant it could be miles away. Within seconds it grew louder, more frightening, as it howled through the fog in her mind. She didn't recognize the wail of the siren until it stopped a few feet from her head.

The ground vibrated with the pounding of running footsteps.

"Holy moly," someone said. "She's alive."

"She's got a gash on her head. Let's get some pressure on that. She may have a spinal injury, so don't move her."

The voices receded, becoming jumbled and faint, like she was underwater.

Another siren approached in the distance. Billie tried to open her eyes. She let out slight groan. Someone touched her shoulder. A shot of pain blasted from her collarbone, pulling her from the darkness.

"What happened?" she mumbled.

A paramedic stooped down and whispered to her, "You bailed out, and it looked like your chute didn't open."

Billie opened her eyes, just a slit. Two blurry figures huddled over her, talking to each other, but she couldn't understand what they were saying. She lifted her head, but the pain in her collarbone blasted up and down her neck. Her head wobbled, then dropped again to the pavement.

"Just relax, please," the paramedic asked quietly. "We'll take care of you and get you to a hospital, okay?"

Billie awoke again to the sensation of being wheeled on a gurney, with a bright light beaming into her face.

"Can you turn the light off?" Her own voice sounded so loud in her head. "Too bright."

In a graceful southern drawl, a nurse said, "That's the sunlight, honey."

"Can you pull the curtains?"

"How about I move you over here? We need the sunlight, it's pretty dark in here otherwise."

Billie's eyes adjusted as the gurney spun around again. She blinked, looking into the pleasant face of a rotund woman with broad shoulders. A neat bun sat at the crown of her nurse's head, and large-rimmed glasses perched on her nose. She watched Billie with kind, intense eyes.

The rounded ceiling of a Quonset hut domed above them, with one dim light hanging from the apex of the room. Shelves on the walls were strewn with darkened-glass medicine bottles. Medical equipment had been stuffed into the corner where the curved roof met the floor.

The nurse rolled Billie's gurney to a darker corner and placed a large room divider between Billie and the bright window.

"How's that, sugar? Any better?"

"Much better, ma'am. Thanks."

The nurse left her side, and Billie fell into her thoughts. Details of the bail-out rippled the surface of her memory, but some of the story still hid deep below where she couldn't reach it.

The nurse returned. "How are you doing, sweetie?"

Billie glanced up at her. "Why am I so exhausted? I can't wake up."

"Your body has endured quite a shock. Are you in pain?" Her voice was kind and caring.

"My collarbone hurts." Everything hurt, but that pain flared the most intense, at least for now.

"We're taking you down to x-ray in a minute. Is there pain anywhere else?"

Billie moved her toes back and forth, then her feet and her legs. She felt soreness, but no sharp pains. She flexed her hands and lifted her arms.

"Moving my arm hurts my collarbone, and my head is throbbing. I think everything else is okay."

"We're guessing you've probably got a concussion, so I'm going to try to keep you awake. Do you understand? You need to stay awake, okay?"

"Why can't I sleep?"

"You hit your head so hard, we need to be sure you don't slip into a coma. We'll keep an eye on you for a few days."

"A few days? I can't stay. I need to be in Sweetwater, Texas tomorrow. It's a big reunion for all the WASP pilots. I have to be there."

"Honey, that would take a miracle because I don't think you're going anywhere any time soon. But I guess anything's possible with you, the miracle girl who jumped from a plane without a parachute and survived."

"I had a parachute." Trying to smile hurt her head.

"Well, then you're the miracle girl who jumped from a plane with a *bad parachute* and survived," the nurse answered.

"What's your name?"

"Call me anything, girl," she teased. "Just don't call me late for dinner."

"What does your husband call you?"

"I ain't married, honey," she retorted with forced indignation.

Billie giggled. "What does your mother call you?"

"Nothing. She's been dead for ten years."

Billie chuckled again, wincing at the pain in her head. "Okay," she insisted. "What does the doctor call you?"

"Behind my back he calls me 'stupid'…but to my face he calls me Nurse DuPree. Clareese Dupree," she said, smiling at Billie. "It's a pleasure to meet you, Billie."

"How'd you know my name?"

"You're famous, girl! We turned away a couple reporters who wanted to talk to you."

Billie held a disbelieving gaze.

"I'm as serious as a heart attack. They had those big cameras and everything. They wanted to interview the 'miracle girl,' the one who jumped from a plane," she paused for effect, "with a bad parachute and survived!" She winked.

A scoff escaped Billie's lips. "Very funny."

"The last part was a joke, but they were here. The doctor said it would be a couple of days before he'd let them talk to you."

Was it true? Reporters clamoring at the door to speak with her, to get her picture? She shuddered.

417

"I used to think that I'd love to be famous and have reporters want to interview me. Now the thought is terrifying."

"Don't worry about it. You don't have to talk to them if you don't want to."

By nightfall, Billie rested in a hospital room. Her x-ray indicated a broken collarbone and a cracked skull. After giving Billie something for the pain, the nurse left.

A soft knock sounded on her door, and two uniformed men entered the room. One wore a silver cross on his shirt collar and garrison cap, the other, a major's cluster.

"Billie Russell? Do you mind if we come in?"

"Not at all," Billie replied, then cleared her groggy voice.

"I'm Chaplain Donson. This is Major Harrell. We heard about your accident. How're you feeling?"

"I'm doing okay," she replied.

"You're quite the celebrity."

"I'm as surprised about it as anyone," she shrugged.

"Do you feel up to talking for a minute?"

She glanced between them, then to the door. How long would their questions last? Sleep tugged on her eyelids, weighing on her shoulders. But the nurse had told her to stay awake, and as much as the thought of their probing made her squirm, it could help keep her from falling asleep. "Sure."

"I'm the lead investigator for this incident," the major said. "I'd like to ask you a few questions."

Investigation? Billie's heart raced.

"Did you inspect your plane upon taking off in Biloxi?" He pulled up a chair and sat near Billie's bed.

"I did a thorough inspection. Yes, sir."

He scribbled something on his notepad. "Did you notice anyone near or around your plane before you began your inspection?"

"I saw several maintenance men admiring my plane. They don't see many P-51s, so I didn't think anything of it." Narrowing her eyes, she said, "Why do you ask that?"

"Your plane was recovered from the bay, and we discovered your landing gear had been tampered with."

Billie sat up straighter. "How—what? Someone did this to me? On purpose?"

"We're not sure what happened to jam it, but it appears someone did tamper with your landing gear."

"Why would someone do this?"

"You're certain you didn't miss this on your inspection?"

Anger seethed through the numbing fog of pain and exhaustion. Billie leaned into his face. "I'll admit I may have been a little lackadaisical at times about my pre-flight inspections," she snapped. "But not this time. This was my final flight. I wanted it to be perfect." She clenched her jaw, eyes burning. How could he dare ask that?

He didn't flinch at the angry words she thrust at him. Calmly, he continued, "Who else knew this was your final flight?"

"I don't know," she stammered. "I might have said something last night at dinner with some of the maintenance guys in Biloxi. They seemed like good eggs."

"Do you have any reason to believe that anyone would tamper with your parachute?"

"Did somebody get to my parachute?"

"We're not sure yet. We're still looking at it," he said. "Did you talk with anyone, or make anyone upset with you?"

She leaned back, looking at the ceiling. "Honestly, by the end of the night, I was feeling a bit tipsy, so I don't remember all of it."

"Were you alone in your hotel room?"

Billie nodded, "Yes, sir. All night."

"Is there anyone you can remember who you may have angered or rebuffed? I'm sure a fine-looking lady like you gets hit on all the time."

"Not last night. At least, not that I can remember."

Major Harrell narrowed his eyes, brushing his chin with his thumb in contemplation. "We'll get back to you if we have more questions. Where are you based out of? Long Beach?"

"Yes. I hope I'm out of here pretty soon."

"I'm afraid that's not up to me," he smiled. "I think the chaplain here has a few questions as well. Will you excuse me?" He lifted his hand to his garrison cap and stepped out of the room.

The chaplain settled into a chair, resting his elbows on the arms and folding his hands on his lap. Billie clutched the sheets on the hospital bed in her fists, clenching and unclenching the fabric as she grew more and more angry. "Sabotage," she whispered. "They think someone sabotaged my plane?"

"I'm sorry this had to happen to you. You're lucky you weren't killed," the chaplain said. "You must be living right."

Billie laughed out loud, then gasped as a sharp pain burst throughout her head.

"I didn't mean to hurt you. I'm here because we noticed your dog tag has an 'X.' Your religious preference is neither Catholic, Protestant, nor Jew. Who should we get to come visit you if you want a minister?"

"When they issued those dog tags, I was really trying to be a good little Mormon girl, but I've more or less fallen off the wagon. So, don't bother."

"I have a friend who's a Mormon chaplain. Do you mind if I have him come see you?"

"I don't think he's going to want to come see me. Really sir…"

"Honestly, Miss Russell, I wouldn't worry one little bit if you're feeling unworthy of having someone come to visit you. None of us are perfect, and all of us at one time or another need some spiritual support. So, unless you specifically tell me not to call, I'd like to invite him to come see you. Would that be okay?"

"I guess so," Billie sighed. "Go ahead."

"Great. I'd love to hear what happened to you. But maybe I can hear your story some other time."

Billie smiled automatically and thanked him for coming in. As the door closed, a pang of remorse struck her. A Mormon chaplain making a special trip to see her would be for nothing; she didn't want to talk religion, at least not tonight. But it wasn't because she cowered away from it, the way she had for so many years. Something new was blooming inside her, a deep, raw, connection with God she had never felt before today. Right now, she wanted to keep it to herself.

Yet something important had happened, whether it was God or a fantastic stroke of luck, she was alive because of it. She needed to know why, and like everything else in her life, she would make her own path to do it.

CHAPTER 66

December 26, 1944
Stalag 17-B, Krems-Gneixendorf, Austria

Christmas passed, gray and depressing, and Hank and the other *Kriegies* spoke little of it to each other. The day after, Hank stood with the other prisoners waiting for mail call. He had nothing better to do, but he wasn't holding out much hope because he still had yet to receive any mail from home. Bouncing on his toes to keep himself warm, Hank watched his breath dissipate in the air. His thoughts turned to warm Christmas dinners at home, a crackling fireplace, Ella and Billie's laughter filling the house. A voice calling his name jolted him from his memories.

"Hank Meyer?"

"Here." Hank's voice cracked. He pushed his way to the front of the crowd.

The man handed him a letter postmarked "Ogden, Utah, USA," graced with Ella's effortless handwriting. Hank rushed back to his barracks through a group of *Kriegies* that parted to let him pass through. Finding a quiet spot alone, he peeled back the edge of the envelope. His hands were quivering and caused him to slice his thumb on the paper's sharp edge. He laughed at himself—Ella always had paper cuts back home.

Home. Here it was, a piece of it in his hands, something that, not long ago, sat on Ella's desk. He imagined the way she would sit to write, the pen she'd use, and how she drummed her fingers gently on the table as she thought of what to write. Other details emerged around them, like the smell of the fire crackling in the wood stove, branches tapping the frost-covered window, or Papa's slippers by the door. Small glimpses of his home in the winter, memories he had forced himself to suppress, now found their way into his consciousness, and now that home was a palpable thing. His breath caught in his throat as he held back his emotions.

Then, pursing his lips, he gave a quick blow to open the envelope, exposing the contents inside. He pulled out two folded letters.

The first was from Chester.

Dear Hank,

Ella said I should write you a letter, and she would send it to you. If you're reading this, her plan worked.

I'm somewhere in the Pacific training for a big battle. They don't tell us much, and I can't say anything about it, other than it's going to be an important island when we take it. But they've said that about all the other islands we've taken from the Japs.

Ella said you are a prisoner in Germany. I'm very sorry to hear that. I wanted you to know that I'm praying for your safe and speedy return. I'm sure everything will turn out okay. Keep your chin up. See you soon back in Huntsville.

Your friend,
Chester

Hank grinned at Chester's swift penmanship, noting an inky spot here and there—the few words he had scribbled was more than Hank would have expected from Chester. When he opened Ella's letter, her familiar, fastidious cursive filled every possible inch of the page. His heart leapt as he started reading, his hands trembled, and his eyes watered. He forced himself to slow down. He wiped his face and took a deep breath, wanting to drink in every word.

Dearest Hank,

I hope you get this letter. I've tried several times to send letters, but they keep coming back as undeliverable. Apparently, I was given an address that was transposed, so I apologize for taking so long to get anything to you. You probably thought we had forgotten you, but we will never forget you. It's amazing how many people have told me they are praying for you.

I've also sent two packages full of canned meat and chocolate like you asked. Let me know when you receive it.

I'm not sure if you know, but Mama and Papa were released from their detention camp in Texas and involuntarily deported back to Germany. It all happened in late February, about the time you were captured. Anyway, I haven't heard anything from them yet, and the Red Cross isn't very cooperative. I've argued with them until I'm blue in the face, and they won't budge. They simply won't deliver a letter to them in Germany. And since they can't get any letters out of Germany, we can only hope they made it to *Oma*'s house. It has been terribly frustrating. If I hear anything, I'll let you know.

Oh, the irony of them being in Bremen, at *Oma*'s house, where he could be with them now if only she—but he shoved that thought aside before anger overtook him.

Chester is in the Pacific somewhere. I spoke to his family, and he doesn't tell them much about where he is or what he's doing. He wrote to me a while back, and I suggested he send you a letter. I never thought he'd actually follow through, but I got it the other day. I'm sending it along with mine. He's a good guy.

The Army is going to shut down the WASP program in December. After that, Billie won't be flying anymore. The last I heard she was trying to get a job as a link trainer, which I think is like a flight simulation contraption that they use to train new pilots. If she doesn't get that job in Long Beach, maybe we can convince her to move back home. Who knows? She doesn't write very often to me or anyone else in her family.

A censor had painted a big black mark, obscuring a few sentences Ella had written. He squinted to try to decipher the censored words then gave up to finish reading the letter:

My other big news is that one day in March, when I was at work at Bushnell Hospital up in Brigham, I was assigned to admitting new patients. When I opened the door to the ambulance, there sat Tom with casts on both legs. I was so excited and surprised. We both laughed and cried at how amazing it was that I was the one to be his intake nurse. We are still dating every now and then. He wants to get married, but I'm just not ready. I just got my nursing license, and I like being a nurse. Anyway, he's still recuperating and will be for a few more months.

Now you're caught up on all that's happened around here. Keep writing me, and I'll keep writing you. Let me know what you need, and I'll send it as soon as I can.

We love you and pray for you every day.

With love,
Ella

By the time Hank read and re-read the letter over the next hour, he could nearly recite it by heart. He re-folded the letters and tucked the envelope into his thin, tattered coat. Smiling to himself, he stood to stretch the stiffness out of his cold limbs and strolled back to his barracks. Christmas had come after all.

CHAPTER 67
January 3, 1945
Stuhr, Germany

Every day during the spring and early summer, Karl toiled on *Oma*'s land, slipping out into the field an hour before dusk, or in the gray hours of early morning. He had every inch of Hildebrandt soil tilled and sown with potatoes, along with a few turnips, onions, and carrots. He and Marta had built a massive root cellar, and by the end of October, they had almost filled it with their crops. Each day after their work, Karl squeezed Marta's hand in his soil-stained fingers. They laughed at the smudge of dirt on her forehead or in her tousled hair. Before retreating into the house, they would make one last check to make sure the tree stump at the far end of the field was not disturbed.

The root cellar's trap door lay hidden under the old, hollowed-out tree stump, safe from scavengers and animals. By late summer, an increasing number of strangers seemed to be eying their crop; Karl sensed his neighbors were growing agitated. By autumn, all the farmers complained bitterly about refugees pilfering their crops. Food shortages throughout Germany sent the poor and hungry wandering the countryside for food. Karl counted and recounted the yield of his harvest, treasuring every golden potato or purple-topped turnip like the wealth of a dragon's horde. "Church, community members, family, refugees… there should be enough," he added each time he dug a potato from the ground. He was determined to make sure there was plenty for everyone.

By mid-January, Karl and Marta noticed the glow of fires on the horizon. The city of Bremen lay in ruins. Smoke and ash sullied the snowfall. Pieces of broken dwellings spilled into the streets, trampled underfoot as people fled. All commercial enterprises had ground to a halt. Markets and shops were not spared the destruction, so residents streamed out into the rural areas with nothing but hope, desperation, and ash in their lungs.

The first visitor gave a timid knock on the Meyers' door. As time passed, the knocks grew louder with each newcomer.

"I'll get it, Mama." Marta glanced through the window. A man stood on her porch, his tattered coat and woolen scarf covered in dust, and his soiled beret slouched over his head. A woman and two children stood a few steps behind him. Marta opened the door a crack.

"Hello. We understand that we might be able to get some potatoes from you?" His voice rose as he added hopefully, "We have no money, but would be willing to trade my wife's wedding ring for them."

Marta bit back a look of pity. *What was she supposed to say to them?* "Please, come inside."

"Oh, no thank you." He stepped back, his voice raspy, "I wouldn't want to get your floor dirty. My boots are covered in mud and snow."

"Okay. Just wait here." She closed the door behind her to keep the warmth from escaping the living room.

"Who is it?" *Oma* called from the kitchen, then met Marta in the doorway.

"It's another family wanting potatoes. This is the third one today. How do they know that we have them?" Marta asked.

"Word is spreading quickly. Maybe the bishop is telling people? Maybe it's just word of mouth," *Oma* added. At the back door, a small bag of potatoes leaned against the wall, the last of the paper sack Karl had filled that morning. Marta hoisted it into her arms and returned to the front door.

Another man stood at the end of the sidewalk, waiting with a bag slung over his shoulder and bouncing on the balls of his feet, to keep warm or with impatience; she couldn't be sure. She looked at the first man, and whispered, "Here's our last sack of potatoes. Please don't tell anyone where you got them."

He blinked back a stunned look as his wife clasped her hands in relief. "Yes. Of course. Absolutely," he said. "Here's my wife's ring. It's very valuable. Please take it." He held it out to Marta.

"I couldn't take your wife's ring. Please just go your way but keep this a secret."

"I hope someday to repay you."

Marta noticed the second man approach; he waited for the first man and his family to pass. Marta called out, "I'm so sorry, but that's the last of the potatoes for the day."

The man drew his gaze away from the children and dipped his head with a rueful smile. Then he tipped his hat and walked away.

Marta sighed, then bundled up and went outside to the milk shed where Karl was clearing snow and mud. He looked up when she entered. "Another one?"

"Another. With children this time. I'm not sure how long our supplies will last at this rate."

He straightened, folding his hands on the end of his shovel and resting his chin on the back of his hands. "That's what we worked so hard for, to help people." His voice was reassuring and calm.

"Three people already this morning!"

"Then I'll have to go get more." He smiled and bent his back again, shoveling.

"Our supplies won't last forever, Karl. We have to ration it out better."

"Do you really think we're going to run out, or is there another reason?"

She looked at him, following his movements, but he did not look up at her silence. After a moment, she said, "We're not keeping a very low profile with so many people on our doorstep."

"I can't just turn away hungry people, especially those with children."

"I don't want to, either."

"What if we gave away no more than two sacks a day? How about that?" His eyes locked on to hers, his eyebrows raised.

Marta turned away without another word, leaving the musty odor of the milk shed to trudge back to the house. She knew limiting themselves to two sacks a day wouldn't stop people from coming to their door.

On a snowy January morning, *Gestapo* and *Waffen* SS agents surrounded the Hildebrandt home. An SS officer kicked open their door shouting, "Karl Meyer! Marta Meyer! Come here now!"

Marta awoke that instant, listening as shouting soldiers were stomping through the house downstairs, rifling through drawers, cupboards, and desks. She glanced toward her mother's room, hoping she was awake enough to go hide behind a false door in her closet. They had discussed this scenario of a government invasion, and Marta had asked Karl to build an escape room to help keep *Oma* safe.

Two soldiers rushed into Karl and Marta's room and flipped on the light. "Get up! You are coming with us!"

They both shielded their eyes, blinking in the bright light. Marta's heart pounded in her chest. "What have we done? Where are you taking us?"

The soldier jerked her to her feet by her hair. She cried out as he pushed her to the floor and grunted, "Don't move a muscle."

Karl brushed past the other officer, reaching for Marta. The officer rammed the butt of his gun into Karl's ribs. At the sound of cracking ribs, Marta gasped through her teeth. Karl's knees buckled, and he sank to the floor.

"Where are your Jew-loving books? Tell me now, or I'll shoot you here on the spot."

Jew-loving books? Marta stifled a sob, she trembled with renewed fear. *Could this be about more than just giving away potatoes?*

"Your Zionist propaganda!" he spat.

"I don't know what you're talking about."

The other officer had hauled Karl to his feet. He turned to them and said, "Show me where you keep all your Jew-loving books. We know you have them."

Karl looked on in confusion; his chin dropped as he moaned in pain. The soldier snarled and grabbed his collar, shaking Karl. When he still didn't answer, the soldier struck his face with the butt of his rifle. Karl slumped to the floor, blood gushing from his nose.

He lay semi-conscious for several moments, out of Marta's reach. She didn't dare move to help him, but her eyes didn't leave him, watching his chest for breathing. Slow and ragged it came, unheard beneath the sounds of the soldiers rummaging through their bedroom.

One of soldiers slung his gun strap over his shoulder, fumbling through books and pamphlets on the desk, caring little if it was valuable. Karl's eyes fluttered open, and he reached for his nose where warm blood trickled onto the floor. He glanced around, then reached for a dirty sock just under the bed. Marta watched as he pressed it to his nose. Their gazes met, just before a stack of papers thudded to the floor between them. The officer swept pamphlets, books, and magazines off the desk, and loose pages fluttered around the room like feathers blowing in the breeze.

"What are you looking for?" Karl asked, voice small and stuffy through the sock.

The officer curled his lip in disdain, but before he could answer, the other soldier snatched up two books from a drawer, and said, "Are these the ones? *Articles of Faith* and the *Book of Mormon.*"

"It looks like those are the ones." He beamed with a self-satisfied smile. "Take the rest. We'll sort through them later."

Marta's heart pinched with pain. Not again, not this again. Karl's eyes followed the officer as he gathered up their scattered books and papers. The soldiers reached for Karl first, then Marta, grasping their clothes and lifting them toward the door. They were dragged down the stairs where other soldiers were waiting for them.

"There's supposed to be an old woman here too," one of them said.

"I couldn't find her," another complained. "Should I keep looking?"

"She's not worth the bother," the officer replied.

Two black cars idled in the driveway, where another SS soldier sat patiently waiting. The officer holding Marta dragged her, wrists-first, through the open door, then shoved her into one of the cars.

The snow in the yard, the rough hands shoving and harsh voices breaking the morning's quiet, icy darkness...Marta was at her home in Huntsville again, FBI agents crawling everywhere. Memory blurred with reality as she saw her children's faces through the frost-tinged rear view mirror. She muttered a disjointed prayer under her breath for Hank and Ella to stay back, to be safe, until the image of her mother huddled in a closet upstairs snapped her back to the present. Karl caught a glimpse of Marta's frantic eyes before his car door slammed shut.

The lead *Gestapo* officer sat in the front passenger seat of Marta's car. He rested his elbow on the door's window ledge, his cheek leaning on his fist. From her angle and the window's reflections, Marta watched his eyes roam over the landscape, as if forgetting the brutal work he had been doing.

She twisted as far around in her seat as she dared, glancing out the back window. The other car followed behind but had now disappeared.

They drove for what seemed like an hour going southwest from Bremen, as far as she could figure in her mind. They passed a sign welcoming them to the city of Verden as they entered its streets. Making a sharp turn, they headed into a darkened alleyway, stopping at the entrance of a run-down warehouse. The officer in the passenger seat snapped back into focus, striding to the heavy wooden door while the other soldier came around the car to Marta's side. He grabbed her by the shoulders of her pajama top and dragged her inside the building. They pushed her down a long, dark corridor, where the soldier opened the door to a cell.

Small and cramped, her cell had only a small toilet and a straw mattress. She watched the front door, her gaze unbroken from its frame as the minutes passed. She didn't sit down until, at last, it creaked open, a group of *Gestapo* soldiers bursting through with a handcuffed Karl in their grasp. He wrenched away from their clutches, but they shoved him along, jabbing an elbow or rifle into his side. Blood covered his clothes and already, even in the dim light, bruises and wounds discolored his neck and arms. Marta bit her lip, wishing Karl would stop struggling. She sank slowly into a seat on the edge of the mattress, knees trembling, as he disappeared down a darkened staircase.

Karl was pushed inside a fetid-smelling interrogation room. In the top half of the door was a small sliding window, allowing someone to look in without opening the door. With the door closed, no light leaked in from anywhere. Karl pressed his hands along the cold and damp concrete walls, feeling each corner of the room, but finding no window or outlet except for the door. Darkness surrounded him, sinking deep into his eyes. After pacing awhile, he collapsed on the bed.

Hours later, the door opened, and a small overhead lamp flickered to life. Karl squeezed his eyes shut, lifting his hand over his face.

Hobnailed jackboots clacked menacingly on the cement floor. "Welcome back to Germany, Mr. Meyer," the man snarled in a German dialect he couldn't recognize.

Karl's eyes grew stronger, but still he squinted.

"You are a most interesting case, Mr. Meyer, because you present us with a curious situation."

The broad-shouldered outline of a *Gestapo* officer came into focus. He carried something by his side, a briefcase, perhaps?

"Either you are a Jew-lover, or you're an American spy here to help pave the way for the Allies' invasion of the Fatherland. My job is to find out which one you are. You can avoid some of our… shall we say… sharpened interrogation techniques by simply signing one of these confessions."

There came a click of something unfastening, then a rustle of papers. "This one says you admit to aiding and supporting Jewish fugitives, feeding them, and hiding them in your home."

Karl bent his head over the paper, still unable to read the words.

"The other one says you admit to being sent here by the Americans and are operating as a spy and a functionary of the resistance. Which one will you be signing today?"

The words became clearer, the dim light casting the officer's shadow over most of the papers.

"I'm sorry; I didn't hear you. Which confession will you be signing?"

Karl answered, voice dry and small, "Neither."

"You are a fool." The man slammed his hand on the papers, crumpling them into a ball. "Don't make it harder for yourself."

"I am innocent."

"You are a Jew-lover, an accomplice in helping fugitive Jews escape justice. I have evidence taken from your home that proves it."

A sardonic snicker escaped under Karl's breath at the idea of whatever trumped-up evidence they could concoct.

"You seem entertained by all this," the officer said, lifting the corner of his mouth.

Karl shook his head, not the least bit entertained.

"Our investigation found enough evidence to convict you in a tribunal. For example, do you deny having a book of songs in your possession with titles like," the agent lifted his notes to his face, frowning, 'Israel, Israel God is Calling' and 'Hope of Israel'?" He stumbled over the English words.

Karl's eyes widened at the familiar names from his hymn book.

"Do you deny it?" the *Gestapo* officer spat.

"No," Karl admitted.

"You have underlined passages throughout some of other books we confiscated. These, too, are illegal."

Karl felt a rock in his stomach. He hadn't considered that his church books were banned in Germany for the mere mention of the word *Zion*.

"And *Articles of Faith*? It is your book?"

Karl opened his mouth to protest, but then remembered: he had written his name on the inside cover. "Yes, it is my book."

"And you know it has chapters about Jews and the establishment of Zion? Such books are forbidden."

"I brought it with me from America. It was a gift from my daughter. I have not been in Germany for many years. I had no idea these were banned."

"Ah, yes," the officer leaned back with a satisfied smile. "You came from America. When was that exactly?"

Karl shifted his weight, leaning against the wall to reduce the pain in his back. "Last March."

"And you are a citizen of the United States?"

Karl hesitated, contemplating the dilemma of his citizenship.

"Not anymore, I suppose."

The officer paused to look at his notes. "But you have a son serving in the United States Army Air Corps."

The tightness in Karl's stomach moved upward, fear mounting in his chest.

"Yes," he said, adding quickly, "Heinrich," he added hoping his German name would count for something.

"Do your loyalties lie with America because your son is a member of the U.S. Air Corps?"

No answer was better than the wrong answer.

He flipped through more of his notes. "You have been building some kind of bunker in your yard. Tell me about that."

"It's a bomb shelter," Karl lied in a memorized response. "We need to protect ourselves from the American bombers."

The officer sniffed and continued, "You have a lot of visitors. People you don't know. They always leave with a package of some sort."

"I give them potatoes or carrots to feed their families."

"We suspect you are passing messages to our enemies, hidden in that produce."

"I am simply giving a few potatoes to refugees who have nothing to feed their children. I have a little to spare, so I thought I would help. Is there anything wrong with helping others?"

"You are very clever, Mr. Meyer, but your glib responses don't fool me. There is no question you are a spy. Why would anyone leave America to come to Germany unless he was a spy? You would be the perfect operative. You are a German native. You have family here. You speak the language."

"Germany has always been my homeland. I only want to take care of its people and my family."

The officer sneered, "You are still a traitor."

Karl bristled and accused under his breath, "No more than you Nazis betrayed the German people."

Karl's jaw clenched as the officer grabbed his head, slamming his face into his knee. The impact on Karl's already broken nose sent an explosion of pain through his face. The officer lifted him by his hair and shouted in his face.

"How dare you say such a thing," his chin quivered with anger. "You Mormon Jew-lover. You will be sorry. Just you wait."

He dropped Karl to the floor. The officer turned on his heel, thrusting the toe of his steel jackboot into Karl's head. As the door slammed, the dim room began to spin until it darkened. Karl slipped into a deeper blackness.

Marta had spent two days in solitary confinement. At mealtimes, a guard would slip in a tray with a single slice of black bread and a pewter cup filled with water; it had the unmistakable odor of sulfur.

On the third day, the *Gestapo* officer flipped the light on in Marta's cell. "Why did you come back to Germany after living in America for so long?"

She sat up, blinking a few times, trying to comprehend his question. "We were accused of being Nazi spies," she answered.

"Why would they accuse you of that?"

"Because when we visited my mama in 1935, my son brought home his Hitler Youth uniform and other Nazi things."

"You kept them in your home in America?"

"Yes. The government arrested us both. After a while, we ended up here."

"Are you happy you came back to Germany?" He spoke calmly but with a directness that would not allow silence for an answer.

"I have mixed feelings. I am glad to see my mama again, because I didn't think I ever would."

"Why would you want to stay in America?"

"After all this happened, I've wondered the same thing. Why would I want to stay in a country where they imprison people without charge, or don't allow their families to know where they are, and don't allow them to have legal representation?" She leveled her gaze at him, tilting her head and raising an eyebrow in question.

He didn't take the bait. "Why do so many strangers show up at your house?"

"Starving people have heard that we can help them."

"Do you feed Jews?"

"We don't ask people if they're Jewish, or Polish, or anything."

"You must make plenty of money off of these poor people."

"We don't charge them anything."

"Come now; you mustn't lie. Are you telling me you are giving away your food?"

She stopped before she slipped and gave away how much food they really had stored. "We only give a little food to starving families who need it."

"Why would you do such a foolish thing? You are not getting any money?"

"People offer to trade jewelry or family heirlooms, whatever they have of value. But that's not why we do it. We don't take their property."

"So, you are a rich American and have come here to flaunt your wealth and mock these poor refugees by giving them your food?"

"We have a little bit to share, and so we do. But we had no idea that people from all over would show up at our door."

"What if I told you we have evidence that you are communicating with the resistance through your so called, 'food donations,' and are really passing information on to the Allies?"

"I would say it sounds just like America, where people are arrested and held on trumped-up charges."

The man dropped his eyes to notes again to begin a new line of questioning.

"What about your Mormon friends who meet at your home—how long have you been doing that?"

"My mother has invited members of our church to have worship services in her home since before we came here. I don't know how long she has been doing it."

"Do you believe that the Jews are a chosen people?"

"I believe we are all loved by God." She stared at him. "Even you."

He didn't flinch, but spat out, "Are the Jews going to gather in Palestine to rule the world?"

"No. But I believe someday we will all live in peace, and there will be no more wars."

"So, you like the Jews?"

"Jews, Germans, Arabs, Americans. I try to love everyone. Some people are harder to love than others."

He scratched behind his ear distractedly. Perhaps he was nervous. Marta bit back a smile.

"You Christians are so sanctimonious. So smug. You make me want vomit from just being around you."

He looked over his notes, flipping pages back and forth. Without a word, he stood and left the room. Everything went dark as he shut the door behind him.

Early the next morning, the sound of her door unlocking awoke her. An SS guard turned on the light and said, "Get up. You are free to go."

"What about my husband?" Marta asked.

"I know nothing about your husband." His words were void of emotion.

Marta jumped up and hurried from her cell, looking back one last time. Of course, she didn't leave anything, she chided herself. "I need to find out about my husband. Where is he?"

"I have nothing to tell you," he quipped as he opened the door to the outside. A light snow drifted, and in only her thin pajama top, she wrapped her arms around herself.

"How am I supposed to get back to Bremen?" she asked, as much to herself as to the guard holding the door open for her.

"No questions. Just be glad you're leaving." He pulled the door handle back toward him. "Not everyone who comes here is so lucky."

CHAPTER 68

January 26, 1945
Stalag 17-B, Krems-Gneixendorf, Austria

By the end of January, the frigid Austrian winter had taken a toll on the *Kriegies'* collective ability to cope. Overnight temperatures often dipped below zero Fahrenheit and hovered there for days on end. *Kriegies* used what little energy stores they had to try to stay warm. Hank's coat now hung on his shoulders as if he were a child wearing his father's jacket. He figured he had lost at least fifty pounds; he couldn't be sure. He noticed the skin on his stomach and face now sagged.

Voices drifted from around the corner of his barracks. Hank stepped with care over the frost-hardened ground, his footsteps crackling. He peered around the wall. Two guards sat with their heads together, muttering.

"I'm almost as starved as the *Kriegies*," one said, rubbing his arms. His woolen coat fit his square shoulders, and Hank narrowed his eyes. But the guards, though not as haggard as the prisoners, had also become thin.

"Another train just arrived. If we can get a few things before they pass the parcels out, we can help each other. Follow me."

Hank slipped away, but he'd heard enough. He ran to the White House, stopping to catch his breath and clutching his empty stomach more than once.

Kurtenbach had already heard of the train's arrival. "He's already been there and back. There are no Red Cross parcels," an assistant explained with a dejected frown. "The train is full of toilet paper."

News spread quickly, and desperation settled on many faces.

Each day, the distributed food rations dwindled. Bread was heavier, containing almost more ground up wood scraps and rusty nails or screws than actual flour. *Kriegies* sometimes split a single loaf among twenty men. The paper-thin slices all but dissolved on their tongues.

One day, after Hank returned from the latrine, he climbed up to his bunk. His eyes narrowed with anger when he saw that someone had pilfered his food stash. The slats didn't fit into one seamless piece like he left it. Someone had slapped them together in a hurry. He let out a heavy exhale, making sure everyone around him could hear his disgust. He removed one of the slats to peer inside the wall.

Hank stood next to his bed and looked around the barracks at a handful of other prisoners resting in their bunks nearby. "Who took my cigarettes?"

A guilty, complicit silence choked the room. Their shoulders stiffened, but they kept their eyes away.

"You guys were here; who stole my stuff?" he demanded.

He knew from their faces they were listening to him, to each other, holding their breath for someone to break. But who would invite retribution and risk their own stash being pilfered?

"Is this what we've sunk to? Stealing from each other?"

A wince here, a shifted glance there, but still no one spoke.

"I'm missing two full packs. Where are they?" he demanded, his voice growing louder. "Please, somebody. Tell me who did it. I won't turn anyone in. Just give me back my cigarettes," he pleaded.

A few men rolled over, turning their backs on Hank. He climbed up to his bed and collapsed. He rubbed tears out of his eyes and said under his breath, "I can't believe it's come to this. I'm crying over cigarettes."

Three days later at morning roll call, *Oberst* Kuhn announced that a delivery of canned meat would be arriving later that day. Cheers erupted among the *Kriegies*. At noon, a large truck lumbered into camp. *Kriegies* slid open the door to find twenty crates, the wood darkened and splintering with age, and the lids all stamped with the word, *Rinderpökelfleisch*.

Don asked Hank quietly, "What does that word mean?"

"It's some kind of pickled meat, I think. I'm not really sure, but it looks like it's military surplus from somewhere."

The shipment contained five-thousand cans of meat left over from the Great War. Each prisoner stood quietly, saying nothing until it was their turn to be issued a can of meat. Hank's stomach turned, but his mouth watered at the idea of something besides broth in his stomach.

Hank and Don inspected their cans, looking at the stiff, hand-soldered tin cans with a mix of fascination and horror. The labels read "1916."

Don snorted, "Could they actually be giving us thirty-year-old food?"

"I wouldn't be surprised."

When Don peeled off the lid, his eyes widened with disappointment. Blackened mold sat on the top.

"Mine is ruined."

"Maybe it's not all ruined. Dig down a bit and see," Hank said.

Don used his knife to dig into the mold, and about an inch down the meat appeared unspoiled.

"What are you going to do?"

"What should I do?"

"Are you going to eat it?"

"What if I cut off the layer of mold? Do you think it will kill me?" Don lifted it to his nose and sniffed. He shrugged, "Smells okay."

Hank smelled the bottom of his meat but wasn't as confident as Don.

"I'm not so sure mine smells so good."

They traded cans and compared the smells.

"Smells the same as mine," Hank replied with a smile.

"What could happen to us?" Don's casual voice revealed his desperation. "If we die, we die. Then we don't have to deal with this forsaken place anymore. I think it's worth the risk."

Hank cut off a tiny portion and wiped it on this tongue. Don did the same.

"I think it tastes okay," Don said.

"It tastes better than it smells," Hank admitted.

"Did it tingle in your mouth? Like it's spoiled?"

Hank wrinkled his nose. "Nope. I think it's worth a try."

Don cut off a couple inches and put the rest of his unspoiled portion back into the can. Hank spooned out a portion onto his plate and put the remainder of his meat into an old Klim can.

They took their plates over to the fire, where a crowd of prisoners huddled shoulder to shoulder around the small pile of smoldering coals. Hank and Don waited for half an hour before warming their meat and eating it with their fingers. They licked every morsel off their plates, savoring each tiny portion. That night, both enjoyed a deep and sound sleep. It was the first time they'd slept well in weeks.

Chapter 69

February 15, 1945
Kronberg im Taunus, Germany

The day after Marta's release, *Gestapo* agents led Karl out of his dark room and up the stairs. He passed by Marta's cell, and his heart sank at seeing it empty. He twisted around in their grasp, trying to resist as they pushed him forward. He staggered out into the daylight, where a car waited.

They transferred him from the *Waffen* SS to the *Gestapo* headquarters in Kronberg, passing through Frankfurt and the old *Staatspolizeistelle* where *Gestapo* interrogations had once been carried out. It now sat in ruins, a ghost of what it had been before last September.

They pulled up to the Schützenhof Hotel, where they led Karl down into the cold, dank basement. Conditions here were no better than the prison in Verden. Old spills stained the hard cement floor, though Karl sighed with rueful familiarity at the thin blanket and straw mattress. Once a day, he was let out of his room to empty the toilet bucket.

Each day he asked, "Where is my wife?"

"She is being held in another cell," the guard lied.

"Where?"

"That is none of your concern. She is being taken care of because she is cooperating with us."

Karl returned to his cell, and the guard left him alone in the darkness until the next day. He nibbled at the hardened bread they tossed at him, wondering if the *Gestapo* had enough compassion to treat her better than this, even if she were cooperating. But Marta was smarter than that; he was sure of it.

He spent each mindless, dull day in near total darkness, without interaction of any kind. Most mornings he received a thin slice of dark bread and lukewarm ersatz coffee. Some days, he was given nothing at all. On those long, hungry days, he paced his cell, wringing his hands. His scattered nerves sent his mind in all directions. Did he hear distant sounds from the world above, whispers, rumbling motorcars, birds? "No, no. it's not real," he muttered and laid down to sleep. He curled up on his side, hunching over with a painful, empty stomach.

A scream for help jerked him from his sleep. He pounded on the door, calling. "Marta, Marta!" Then the sudden screams—he was sure he'd heard her—were gone, and only the echoes of his own voice answered him.

Days passed, isolation blurring them together in one seamless ocean of darkness, hunger, and silence. Karl began stashing a small portion of the day's bread ration under his mattress, scraping off the bugs and eating it on the days they gave him nothing. The practice of eating something when his captors assumed he was suffering served as a simple act of defiance, helping him cling to his sanity, or what was left of it.

In the silence, the screams began again, sometimes near and sometimes far off. He called out for Marta, pounding on the door. When she didn't answer, he covered his head with his arms. How could he listen to it when he could do nothing for her? But this only made the sound more real in his ears, and he sprang up, anxious and pacing the cell until he sat on the floor. "Marta..." he called out, curling his fist while reaching for hers, squeezing it three times.

In her absence, faint memories of her favorite verses welled up in his throat; poems he used to recite to her leapt onto his tongue again and again. He spoke to the darkness, raising his voice when the screams were the loudest, pouring out hymns, folk songs, and scriptures, their measured cadences and rhythmic shapes bringing his fuzzy mind into focus. He sang to her, soothing the chaos in his mind into symmetry once again.

More time passed. His voice grew hoarse, until he could just mumble the words with a dry tongue.

For three days, they brought only tin mugs with lukewarm coffee. Days might have been weeks or minutes, were it not for the changing of the guard. His stomach tightened in a hungry knot.

One day, they came to his cell, blinding him with light. "An important SS officer is coming to examine you at eleven tonight. You must be awake to speak to him."

Karl kept himself awake, slapping his face and rubbing the sleepiness out of his eyes. He couldn't let himself fall asleep if this was his best chance. Every fifteen minutes, the guard opened the door and shouted. Karl snapped his head up to look—drifting in and out of sleep.

Hours passed until at last, the guard returned. "The examiner will see you tomorrow. You must be ready."

Early the next day, Karl received a meager breakfast, and the guards again warned that the examiner would come soon. They pestered Karl each half hour, and he'd shake his head to wake himself. At noon, they again told Karl the examiner was delayed until eleven that night.

This pattern continued for the next two days. Karl rested in brief catnaps. He scowled at every sound, unsteady on his feet. If they were doing this to Marta, too...she was stronger, but how much could anyone bear?

He didn't remember leaving his cell until they were ascending the soft-carpeted stairs of the hotel. Holding him by the shoulders, they escorted him down a long, beautiful corridor and into a room with large windows.

The examiner wore a dark suit and tie and introduced himself as a State Secret Police officer.

"Why did you come to Germany?" His voice was calm and nonthreatening.

"I was deported from America for being too German," Karl's answer was also calm.

"What do you mean by 'too German'?"

"They found pictures of Adolf Hitler and the National Socialist flag in my home."

"Are you in favor of National Socialism?"

Karl hesitated, "I'm not sure I know enough about it to say."

The interrogator rubbed his chin. Karl's stiff face turned to the nearest window; the yellow sunshine seared bright and hot against his skin. A tree tapped the windowpane, and his heart nearly sank within him. How could it be spring already?

"Did you want to come to Germany?"

Bleary-eyed, Karl replied, "I had a farm and a home in America. I didn't want to lose that."

The interrogator stood and pulled the blind down over the window.

"So, you don't want to be here, but America betrayed you," he said. "Tell me, why didn't you want to come to Germany if you weren't welcome in America?"

"My children grew up there. I belong where they belong."

He grunted, "You admit you like America, even though they hate you and made you leave their country?"

Karl didn't reply. It had to be no later than mid-March. Back home, the snow would be melting; the cow might be calving or plump enough and walking slow. Ella would be watching out for the daffodils to peek through the crusty snow.

"Did you vote?" The interrogation continued.

"Yes."

"Did you consider it your duty to vote?"

"More or less."

"So, it sounds like you were politically active. Did you vote for Roosevelt?"

"We aren't required to disclose who we vote for."

"By *we* do you mean Americans?

"When I was there, it was our right not to divulge who we voted for."

"You are here now, so what's stopping you from telling me whether you voted for Roosevelt?"

Karl tightened his lips into a hard line.

"What have you got to hide? If what you say is true, you are no longer an American."

"How could I be an American if they took away my citizenship and shipped me here?"

"Maybe you are lying about being sent here. Maybe you are a clever spy, here to help the Jews."

"I am a farmer," Karl gestured with his hands. "I am not smart enough to be a spy."

"Your books tell me you are a Jew-lover. Is that true?"

"Is it illegal to not hate Jews?"

"It is illegal to aid them, to support them, or to promote their Zionist causes."

"My only concern for the Jews relates to ancient Biblical prophecy. I have no hidden agenda to aid them."

"But you are a capitalist, are you not? You support capitalism?"

"Is that illegal, too?"

The man sat up straight, rage twisting his face. Karl flinched.

"It was the Jews who made Germany lose the last war. It was the Jews and their greedy capitalism that convinced our government to sign the Treaty of Versailles, and it was because of Jews that millions of Germans suffered and died after the war. We have endured far more than you can imagine, and all because of Jews and their capitalism."

"As long as I've been in Germany, I have never said anything against National Socialism."

"But you are an American, so you must believe in capitalism and democracy."

Karl looked the officer in the eyes. "And look where it's gotten me."

He snarled, "You are a dangerous man, Karl Meyer. We will find out who you are working with. We will expose your little spy ring, and once we do, I will enjoy seeing you executed. Guard!" he shouted, "put this vermin back in his cell."

Karl cringed, waiting for the strike. But the guard grabbed his arm and lifted Karl from his seat. They made their way down the brightly lit corridor trimmed in dark, rich wood. Karl wanted to run his thumb along the smooth workmanship, to find some splinter or fault in the beautiful house where such ugliness lived.

As they approached the basement stairwell, Karl lingered upon each step, savoring each moment of delicious sunlight shining through the large lobby windows of the hotel. It disappeared out of sight, and he was again plunged into the cold darkness of his cell.

Chapter 69-Note 1: According to Yad Vashem (World Holocaust Remembrance Center),

"After *Gestapo* headquarters in Frankfurt were damaged on September 12, 1944 in an Allied air raid, all departments moved to the Schützenhof Hotel in Kronberg. On March 26, 1945, three days before American forces occupied Frankfurt, the *Gestapo* staff abandoned the headquarters and fled from the advancing Allies." *Gestapo* Headquarters; http://db.yadvashem.org/deportatlon/bureaucracyDetails.html?language=en&itemId=8034265, Retrieved May 10, 2018.

Chapter 69-Note 2: In 1934, the Nazis issued a decree that no religious denomination could use Hebrew words such as *Israel*, *Sabbath*, and *Zion*. Popular books by author and church apostle James E. Talmage were often confiscated. Nazi police were known to tear out songs from church hymnals that referenced the forbidden words. For members of the Church of Jesus Christ of Latter-day Saints, these words were used frequently when referring to Biblical prophecy. *"Chapter Forty: The Saints during World War II," Church History in the Fulness of Times Student Manual* (2003), 522–34; https://www.churchofjesuschrist.org/manual/church-history-in-the-fulness-of-times/chapter-forty, Retrieved January 5, 2021.

CHAPTER 70
March 8, 1945
Huntsville, Utah

Chester's parents heard the rumble of a car just after noon one day in March. They peeked through the window as an officer and chaplain approached their front porch. Mrs. Bailey held her handkerchief while her husband answered the door.

"Mr. and Mrs. Richard Bailey?"

"Yes," he whispered.

The chaplain held his hat in both hands. "Would you mind if we came in?"

"Just tell me," Mrs. Bailey demanded.

The officer cleared his throat. "The Secretary of the Navy has entrusted me to inform you that your son, Navy Pharmacist Mate Third Class Chester Bailey, was killed in action on March 1, 1945, during the course of battle on the island of Iwo Jima. On behalf of the Secretary of War, I extend to you and your family my deepest sympathy in your great loss."

Mrs. Bailey sank to her knees. Her husband knelt down, and she buried her face in his shoulder. He held her while her body quivered against him in silent sobs.

Mr. Bailey's lip quivered. "Do you know how he died?"

"I'm sorry sir; we weren't notified of any details, but you can expect to hear from his commanding officer soon. He will send you a letter with more information."

Mr. Bailey thanked him, then guided his wife to a chair, still holding her hand and turning to face the two men.

The chaplain stepped forward and asked, "Do you have a minister or religious advisor you can speak to, or would you feel comfortable speaking with me?"

"No. Thank you," Mr. Bailey replied quietly, "I appreciate your offer, but we'll contact our bishop. He'll make arrangements for the funeral. Do you know when my son's body will be returned?"

"Because of the dangerous conditions that still exist in the Pacific theater and how difficult it is to get to the island of Iwo Jima, his remains will not be repatriated until hostilities have subsided, and we can safely bring him back to America."

"Oh. Do we know how long that will be?"

"The War Department will notify you as soon as possible."

Mr. Bailey looked at his wife, who covered her face with her other hand. His heart shuddered in his chest, seeing her in such anguish.

The chaplain continued, "You can also expect to hear from the War Department about Chester's death benefit. Your son had signed up for the National Service Life Insurance program, and they will discuss the details with you."

"Thank you. That's very helpful."

For almost half an hour, the Baileys talked about Chester, about his good nature, his athletic ability, how he loved to dance with Billie. The chaplain listened. Then the conversation went silent for an uncomfortable minute.

"Um. Would you like us to stay? Will you both be okay, Mr. and Mrs. Bailey?"

She looked up at her husband, and he reached for her other hand to help her to her feet.

The chaplain asked again, "Will you be alright if we leave?"

She wiped her eyes and gave a pained smile.

"I wish we could have met under different circumstances," the officer explained. "We wish you all the best during this very difficult time and hope you will find peace and healing very soon."

Mr. Bailey walked the two officers to the door and watched as they drove away.

The word of Chester's death spread fast throughout the community. The neighbors watched the Army's car, a rare sight in rural Huntsville, following it to the Bailey's driveway. As soon as the officer and chaplain drove away, people from all over the valley came to their door.

"It's not right," they said to each other, shaking their heads. "It's not fair for this to happen to such a happy-go-lucky kid like him." To his parents, they offered smiles and condolences. The entire town walked about with gray faces and slow, forgetful strides, like something was missing from them.

Grandma Russell called Ella, who cried herself to sleep that night. How could she write this news in a letter to Hank? Should she wait to tell him? What about Billie? What should she say to her?

A week after the official visit, the Baileys received a letter postmarked with "Fifth Marine Division Headquarters," from Chester's commanding general, Major General Keller E. Rockey.

Mr. & Mrs. Richard Bailey
Huntsville, Utah

Dear Mr. and Mrs. Bailey.

It is with the greatest regret that I write to confirm the Adjutant General's telegram regarding your son, Pharmacist Mate Third Class Chester Bailey, who died in combat against the enemy at Iwo Jima, Volcano Islands.

The sadness and distress caused by his sacrifice is fully realized here among his brothers-in-arms, and I hope the knowledge that he died in the act of saving another man's life will, in some measure, alleviate your pain at his passing. He died instantly and with minimal suffering.

Eyewitnesses confirm that he and his platoon were attacked by a series of enemy hand grenades. Chester heroically ejected several live grenades that landed near him. When two grenades simultaneously landed near his feet, he threw himself on the grenades in the supreme act of self-sacrifice.

Those whose lives he saved will forever be in Chester's debt. He was a true hero who went above and beyond in the performance of his duty.

His remains rest in the Fifth Marine Division Cemetery, Plot 2, Row 17, Grave 138, on Iwo Jima, Volcano Islands. A burial rite was conducted by the chaplains in charge, in accordance with your son's faith. A formal memorial service was held with full military honors.

As a result of ongoing efforts to defeat Japan within the Pacific theater of operations, along with other circumstances outside the control of the War Department, unfortunately, it is still not known when his remains will be repatriated.

Nonetheless, the unconquerable spirit of your son Chester, his bravery, and indomitable soul, will forever be an inspiration to the men of the Corps. May the courage he demonstrated comfort you in the days ahead.

On behalf of myself and his comrades, I convey my most heartfelt condolences, and wish to extend to you our best wishes for the future.

Major General Keller E. Rockey
Commanding General, 5th Marine Division.

They read the letter in silence. Mrs. Bailey finished and pushed it away from her, taking a slow, deep breath.

Mr. Bailey folded it, like any piece of mail, and said, "I'll tell the bishop not to make any plans for a memorial service."

She went to the window and pulled away the drapes, standing back to look at the red silk banner. The gold star shone with fresh, newly sewn stitches. Mrs. Bailey set to scrubbing the windows inside and out, the better to see the monument to her son's memory in the clear polished glass.

Chapter 70-Note 1: The heroic death of Chester in this chapter is based upon the Medal of Honor citation of Donald J. Ruhl, who died on Iwo Jima on February 21, 1945. It reads in part:

"Ruhl, with his platoon guide, crawled to the top of a Japanese bunker to bring fire to bear on enemy troops located on the far side of the bunker. Suddenly a hostile grenade landed between the two Marines. Calling a warning to his senior non-commissioned officer, Ruhl instantly dove on the grenade and absorbed the full charge of the explosion with his body. His action not only saved his companion but also prevented the grenade fragments from wounding other nearby Marines. Rather than using his position on the edge of the bunker to easily drop down into a more protected spot, he sacrificed his life to save his fellow Marines."

"Private First Class Donald J. Ruhl—Medal of Honor Series." *The National WWII Museum* online. https://www.nationalww2museum.org/war/articles/private-first-class-donald-j-ruhl-medal-of-honor.

CHAPTER 71
March 26, 1945
Kronberg im Taunus, Germany

Karl did not hear from the examiner for days, or could it have been weeks? He wasn't sure. His captors let him out once a day to use the toilet, sometimes supporting him by the elbows when he stumbled from his cell. They spoke only a few words to him, but even in the darkness, he learned to recognize each one by the smallest grunt or the tread of his footsteps. The guards would lead him back to his cell, and that short outing was Karl's only marker to measure the passing of time.

He wasn't sure if he was the lone prisoner in the hotel. In the beginning, he had heard faint stirring in other cells, but as time went on, he called out for anyone to respond and heard only silence in return. He hadn't noticed when they left, wondering if they were ever there at all.

The first explosion sounded to Karl like thunder, a weak, far-away rumbling that caught his ear. They grew louder as the days passed. With each boom, the walls trembled, and dust rested on his head as the ceiling crumbled from overhead. At that moment he realized the truth: The Allies were coming.

For the first time, he bowed his head in thanks that his cell was underground.

The guards' daily visits grew more and more tense, with shoves and barking commands as if the advancing enemy were somehow his fault. One day the guard threw open his cell door. "You will be examined early in the morning. You must be ready." The door slammed shut.

When sleep wore on Karl's mind, and his eyelids drooped, he let himself fall into a light slumber. He wasn't about to exhaust himself again, waiting for an examination that never came. They could wake him up, if they arrived. He let himself fall into a deep sleep.

But in the morning, they did wake him. The guards dragged him from his bed, bringing him, foggy-brained and dizzy, to his feet. He followed them upstairs, passing a window in the hall that showed darkness outside. They left him in a dark room, closing the door behind them. Karl patted the furniture with his hands until he found a chair, the same one he'd sat in before. He sank into its cushioned seat. With the curtains drawn tight over the windows, no reflection or glow from the streetlights filtered into the room. He couldn't be sure he was alone, though after being in solitary confinement for so long, the silence of isolation had heightened his sense of hearing. He steadied his breathing, making it low and quiet beneath any other possible noise.

Between one inhale and exhale, he caught the tread of footsteps. Voices murmured through the walls, from the room next to his. He held his breath. Had they said the word "retreat"? His heart pounded as fast as it dared in his weakened state. There it was. He heard it crisp and harsh in the German tongue, "Americans, British."

The urgency in their voices told him more than the words themselves. The tide of the war was changing, but against whom? Were the Germans retreating or the Allies?

He was listening so intently that the sound of the door opening startled him. The *Gestapo* officer flipped on the light and leveled an annoyed glare at Karl.

"You know why you are still here?"

Karl put his hands on his lap. "Is my wife still here?"

"Your wife is dead. She admitted to being a member of the underground, communicating with the enemy, and passing along coded messages."

Karl didn't hear the rest of what he said. Accusations of Karl's crimes against Germany, feeble attempts to get him to confess to something, anything. Everything faded away as his heart echoed in his ears. How long had she been gone? Had he been singing hymns and reciting verses to a Marta who wasn't there?

He squeezed his curled fist three times, and he knew: Marta would never confess to something untrue, even under such torture as he had endured.

"You're lying," he blurted. "My wife isn't dead."

The officer stopped speaking, the next syllable still on his lips. He raised his hand. In the next moment, pain exploded in Karl's jaw and his eyes smarted.

"Who do you work for?"

"Nobody. I swear." Karl's voice cracked as a sob wrenched all remaining strength away from his words. "I am only trying to help people," he cried. "I just wanted to help."

"Stop your blubbering. You disgust me."

Karl rubbed the side of his head and answered, "People are hungry. We knew they would need food over the winter."

"You are telling me that you planted hundreds of pounds of potatoes, risking that you would draw our attention, because you…"

The floor beneath them rumbled, and the windowpanes rattled. The officer gripped the edge of his seat, tilting his head to listen, eyes turned to the ceiling as dust fell from the light fixture. His gaze darted over the room, no longer seeing Karl.

Three explosions blasted somewhere outside. Karl winced and covered his ears with his palms, certain the bombs fell just outside their room. The officer jumped from his desk and yelled for the guard outside the door. "Take him back to his cell." He darted out of the room. His hurried footsteps could be heard despite the ringing in Karl's ears.

Karl craned his neck to stare at the officer, frowning. The door did not fall shut behind him, and the hushed tones of the guards outside could be heard, although diffused and muffled by the distant explosions.

Minutes later, a guard came in to escort Karl down the stairs.

Before he closed Karl's cell door, he shoved a tin plate of food across the floor. "This is your meal. We are finished with you."

The door slammed with a metallic echo, the lock clicking into place. The weight of the guard's words carried a strange finality, a feeling that sank into Karl's gut. The guard hurried back up the stairs.

Odd, he thought. *They usually remained downstairs to maintain order and keep the prisoners from talking to each other…if there even were other prisoners.* A sense of dread tingled down his limbs, and his hands trembled.

"Hello! Is there anybody in here?"

Silence, yawning out before him in the pitch blackness.

"Please, anybody!" he yelled. "Are you here? Is anyone here?"

Panic rose in his throat. Had he been left alone to die?

From above, a door opened and boots thudded on the stairs.

Karl shouted again, "Help, is anyone——"

"Shut up, or I'll put you out of your misery!"

Relief flooded his chest, and his breathing returned to normal. He curled up on his bed and drifted off to sleep.

He woke again, hours later, by more explosions, even closer than before. But these were different, without the same hiss as they fell from the sky. A flurry of artillery rounds flew, hitting the ground and buildings and everything in between. The entire building trembled.

Karl leaped from his bed and pounded the door with his fist. The iron creaked and groaned, joining in the chorus of rumbles from overhead. "Please help! Anyone!"

For twenty minutes, he screamed for help. Then he stopped. He needed to save his energy. They were gone for good, and now he was alone with little to eat or drink.

Chapter 72

March 15, 1945
Stalag 17-B, Krems-Gneixendorf, Austria

A *Kriegie* spotted the railroad cars full of Red Cross packages, smoke from the engines swirling into the sky. The organized work detail of *Kriegies* unloaded the contents, but as they stood in line watching the guard's rifle through the boxes, their hopeful faces fell.

"What are the chances any of these packages have anything left in them?" Hank was asked by another prisoner.

"Who knows?" Hank was too tired to even look at him.

"Last time our package was filled with garbage. The guards ate the meat and put the empty can back to make it look like it was new."

The prison hospital overflowed with sick, starving men. Hank had heard of a few men who went blind from malnutrition, and others who were so weakened they didn't care whether they lived or died.

Hank continued trying to eavesdrop on conversations between guards. As the threat of German defeat loomed, their care with keeping their conversations quiet soon gave way to indifference. They spoke loudly, the chatter overlapping and bouncing just like any conversation, not the deliberate hushed tones of sharing secrets. He came upon the guards easily, slinking around between barracks and stopping just far enough away not to be seen.

"Will you do it?" one asked.

"If that's the order, I guess I'll have no choice," the other replied, a note of concern in his voice.

"Have you heard an official order?" the first one asked.

"No, just the stuff on the radio from Hitler."

"So, it's coming directly from Hitler?"

"That's what *Oberst* Kuhn said."

The guard paused to contemplate his dilemma. "They'll shoot me if I don't do it."

"I know," the other replied. "But maybe the American Army will be here before they make us do it. We're supposed to kill them all before they get here."

Hank's knees weakened. He ran, legs tired and stumbling, to the White House.

Kurtenbach looked on at Hank in disbelief.

"Are you sure?" he asked.

"Clear as day," Hank replied. "Hitler ordered that all American prisoners had to be shot."

Kurtenbach sent out an order to each barrack to devise a plan to resist. "Figure out what you can do," he said. "Even if it's rushing the gates *en masse*; someone's bound to get through before they can shoot us all," he said.

Ted Ross, the barrack's chief, called all the *Kriegies* from Hank's barracks together. "We're not going to go down without a fight. As soon as we're near any guard who's pointing a rifle at us, we work together to attack and get his weapon," he explained. "We can create a lot of havoc if we can somehow get a weapon."

Conversation erupted among the men. "How are we going to over-take a guard?" someone shouted. "We're too weak. We're too slow."

"We'll gang up on them," another replied. "I say we all just rush them at roll call. They won't know what hit them."

"That's stupid," someone else snapped. "You'll get us all killed."

With men shouting and arguing with each other, Ross called the meeting to a quick end. The *Kriegies'* nerves were on edge, watching the guards' every move. They feared the guards could open fire at any moment.

The days dragged on and nothing happened, but like a finger poised on the trigger, the *Kriegies* tensed more and more with paranoia. Some men cracked under the pressure, kicking and screaming nonsense until they were taken to the hospital.

On March 26, the clandestine crystal radio set picked up a news report. Patton's Third Army had crossed the Rhine River, and the Russians were advancing from the south. The *Kriegies* looked at each other with a fear in their eyes so bright they saw nothing else. Would the Americans arrive at *Stalag* 17 before the Germans began shooting?

CHAPTER 73

March 25, 1945
Kronberg im Taunus, Germany

Karl was left alone in his cell for three days. At least, that's how long he estimated he had been there, since he could only deduce the time of day from the sound of vehicles passing by on the street in front of the hotel.

He had run out of food. What little he had stored under his mattress was gone. The slice of bread he was given just before the *Gestapo* abandoned the hotel was savored to the last morsel. He rationed his ersatz coffee to one sip, twice a day. Each day that passed, the coffee receded, disappearing as fast as his hope of any chance he'd be rescued.

At times he forgot which wall faced the door. He would feel around the cold, concrete walls with the palms of his hand until he felt a hinge or the doorknob. Then he would laugh at himself for caring where the door was. But curling his hand around the doorknob, like he would his own front door at home, brought reality closer when his frayed thoughts tried to push it away.

He still heard someone crying for help; though as the days passed, children's anguished voices replaced Marta's. When they echoed in his ear, he spoke louder to keep them quiet. "How would anyone ever find me? I'm in a hotel that has no military significance. Why on earth would anyone come here?" He paused to think. "Maybe the Americans know this place was being used by *Gestapo*? But then again, how would they know? Maybe some of the locals are curious to see if the *Gestapo* left anything behind? What if the hotel owners decide to come back and retake the property after the war?"

He sang when he could find the strength. Hymns and German patriotic songs resounded off the bare walls. To keep order, he kept the bucket used for his toilet in the corner farthest from the door, as far from his bed as he could put it. In the corner closest to the door, he stored his valuable cup of coffee. It was in the opposite corner of the toilet bucket to keep it from spilling as he paced the short distance from wall to wall.

On his sixth day, Karl woke feeling a new burst of energy. "I've got to keep my blood moving, to stay alert!"

Gripping the edge of his mattress, he lifted it to lean it against the wall. He fumbled, almost dropping it, but pushed it back and slapped the dust off his hands. Such a flimsy thing should never have been a struggle for him to lift. He pushed away the thought and sat in the middle of the floor. Humming the music to the Viennese Waltz, he danced with his arms, gently, as if he held Marta's hand. He laughed. "We learned this as children, Marta," he spoke as if he could feel the warmth of her breath on his neck. He kept his shoulders level and smooth, parallel to the floor. His head turned in the direction of where he intended to lead his partner, always looking over her right shoulder. Gradually, he imagined rising to his toes, then onto the balls of his feet.

With every step, she danced in and out of his vision, keeping a tight hold onto his hand. The dance ended, and he found himself gasping in the dark, alone again. "What has become of you, Marta? Are you okay? Of course, you are. You are the strongest, most courageous woman ever."

He stood, legs wobbling, and leaned against the corner, tilting his head back. When was the last time he'd danced with her? Would it be the last? He wept, shaking with grief.

If she were here, she'd set her firm eyes ahead and give every ounce of energy to help him keep his hope alive. She wouldn't let him sob, and especially not for her.

"I'm sorry, Marta," he cried, covering his eyes. "I'm so sorry you had to see me like this."

He sank to the floor, his back scraping the concrete wall.

His foot slipped, and his toe knocking against something in the dark. The faintest sound of tin clinked against the concrete floor, and something wet seeped into the leg of his trousers.

"Oh, what have I done?" He patted the floor with his hands, snatching up the mug of coffee. But the last sips of the precious liquid were gone.

Perched on the edge of the mattress, Karl listened. His dry tongue swelled in his mouth, and he had no strength to stand anymore. Every breath stalled in his chest and might have been the last, holding each fragile moment together. Sometimes he called for help, but he couldn't hear anything. He hadn't had water for almost two days. His mind was foggy.

The artillery fire raged in the world above him, as if the war had dropped him into the earth and forgotten about him. He laid down, his hands behind his head, listening, holding his breath to hear the smallest of sounds. His eyelids fluttered closed, a somber sleepiness overcoming him. He knew it was more than sleep. If life was to end for him this way, at least he knew the Americans made it this far. He prayed one last time for the Allies to win so the good people of Germany could rebuild his homeland.

A strange noise wavered outside his cell, the warm tones of a human voice, or almost. It was hard to tell. He tilted his head.

"No," he said. "I am hallucinating again."

If he was going to die now, he would do it grounded in reality.

But it came again, unmistakable; this time the soft thud of footsteps on the stairs.

He bolted up. "Help! I'm down here!"

From beyond the door, Karl listened for any movement or echo in the silence.

He shouted again in German, his voice raspy. "They left me here to die! Please help!"

He waited for a reply, wondering if they couldn't hear him.

"Who's there?" A man's voice responded in English.

Karl's heart leapt, and he said in English, "I'm in here." He propped himself up as much as he could. "The *Gestapo*…" he stopped to catch his breath, pain bursting in his side. "Arrested…"

A pounding knock shook the door. "Are you in here?"

"Yes—help me."

"I don't have a key, and I don't have any way to get in. Hang on. I'll be right back."

Receding footsteps carried the man away, but near the top of the stairway, more voices rang out.

"Captain! There's a man locked in a room down here."

Another man bounded down the stairs and knocked on Karl's door. "Who's in here?" he said.

"I am Karl Meyer. I'm a German immigrant. I haf a farm in Huntsville, Utah. My son ees a gunner on a B-17."

"Get this fellow out of here," the captain said. "I don't care if we have to blast this thing open. We've got an American in there."

After a moment, he called out to Karl. "Hold on sir; we'll get you out of here. How long have you been here?"

"Months? Who knows? I don't—I don't know. I must find my dear vife. My vife…" The words stuttered to a halt as he felt the throb of his own pulse in his ears, slow and watery. He was slipping away into an overwhelming fatigue.

"Just hold on, my friend."

A chorus of footsteps pounded down the stairs, and hushed voices conspired for a moment outside his door.

A man said, "Sir, we can't find a key. We have to break the lock by force. Are you ready?"

Karl used every ounce of energy to turn over, his back faced the door, and he pressed his chest against the wall. "Go ahead."

A deafening bang slammed into the door as a gunshot pierced Karl's sound-starved ears. The door slammed open against the wall, shuddering and clanging. Karl felt someone pulling on his shoulder, trying to turn him over without hurting him.

A flashlight beamed into his eyes, so bright it pained him, and he covered his face with his hands.

"He's all right," the man called. "Hold on there, partner. Let me help you."

He took his hand as Karl tried to stand but couldn't.

"Sank you for finding me," Karl whispered. "I vas going to die."

"We're going to help you upstairs. We'll get you something to drink and eat in just a jiffy."

The GIs picked up his thin, frail body. With each step, Karl fought to keep his mind from fading to blackness. He opened his eyes as they lowered him gently into an office chair. They offered Karl a drink from their canteen, and he gulped it, spilling water out of the side of his mouth.

"You are one lucky SOB," the captain said. "I'm with SHAEF, the European Civil Affairs Division, and we're looking for a new head-quarters. We heard about a couple of hotels that were being used as hospitals and escaped our bombs. Yesterday we found a hotel over in Bad Homburg, about ten minutes from here, but someone said we should take a look at this one. When we drove up, we took one look at it and just about turned around because it was too small. Then we thought we might as well take a look while we're here. Good thing we did, eh?"

"I vouldn't have survived much longer." Karl's voice was hoarse and soft. "I owe my life to you."

CHAPTER 74
April 2, 1945
Stalag 17-B, Krems-Gneixendorf, Austria

Word came on April 2 that the Russians had reached the outskirts of Vienna, about an hour away from *Stalag* 17. With every distant explosion the guards grew more anxious. They exchanged glances; fear written on their faces even when *Kriegies* were near.

The *Kriegies* huddled around their crystal radio, listening to reports about the advancing Americans and the Allied bombing campaign in

Europe. Hank spent much of his day with all the other men outside, watching the parade of B-17s and B-24s fly overhead. Every day the air raid siren blared, and explosions could be heard in the distance.

By April 6, a Russian tank was spotted far off on the Danube plains, close enough to be seen with binoculars. That day at roll call, the guards gave orders to be ready to evacuate the camp in the morning.

"All prisoners will be issued new clothing. Your barracks number will be called, and you will report in an orderly fashion to receive your new clothing."

Kurtenbach then sent a message to all barracks warning *Kriegies* that the Germans couldn't get them out by train or vehicle. The entire camp would evacuate on foot. Although he wasn't sure of the destination, he speculated they were going westward, toward the approaching Americans.

Hank and Don were among the first to be given some of the new clothes the Germans had kept "on reserve." The U.S. quartermaster had rejected it all and tagged it as surplus. No one was disappointed to have new "surplus" clothing.

"It looks like everyone is getting a new pair of woolen trousers, socks, and undershorts, and they have a few pairs of boots." Don said, carrying the stack of clothes under his arm and watching the other *Kriegies* walk back to their barracks. Men exchanged articles for better sizes, most clothes being far too large, but everyone smiled in relief when they slipped out of their dirty, thin rags and put on the new clothes. It felt like they were going somewhere special, someone remarked, and not another prison. New canteens were also issued, with one canteen for two or three men.

"Where've they been hiding this stuff?" Hank wondered. "It would have been nice to have had this a few months ago when it was so blasted cold." Those who heard him gave an audible "amen" in agreement.

The Germans called them together again, and the *Kriegies* watched as the guards carried out box after box of unopened Red Cross parcels. They piled up around the prisoners, towering and sprawling around the camp center. The *Kriegies'* mouths dropped open, and they reached out to touch the parcels. When the guards barked, they snatched their hands back and waited. Hank counted several stacks and multiplied in his head. There had to be over four thousand parcels. There were thousands of meals, and after a long winter with no food, a thousand more wouldn't hurt. Hank's coat draped on his bony shoulders, dwarfing his small frame. He tied his trousers with a rope when his belt had run out of room for more holes. The same ghostly, malnourished appearance haunted the rest of the camp, prisoners with protruding ribs, sunken eyes, and gray faces.

At evening roll call, the guards announced that all prisoners, except those bedridden in the hospital, would leave the camp. Kurtenbach volunteered to stay behind with almost a hundred sick and injured prisoners and take his chances with the Russians.

The men fashioned backpacks out of blankets to carry their food parcels and anything else they wanted to keep. Radios and all other contraband items were left behind.

Hank took a pack of cigarettes for trading, but after Don had taken what he wanted, they left several more packs hidden inside the walls of his barracks.

He picked up his *Book of Mormon*, thumbing through the thin pages and feeling each engraved letter on the cover with his finger. As the hard winter had come and gone, he'd cracked the book to find something in its pages to warm him, to help him forget the misery around him. But every time he read from it, he heard his *oma's* voice reading in his head, and he'd slam the book shut in anger. *Look what you've done, Oma. Even my favorite book is repulsive to me because of you.* As long as the book remained closed, it reminded him of home, and that was the closest thing to religion he'd experienced since he arrived.

Maybe this was better left behind, he told himself. He had more than enough to remind him of this place anyway, but a strange impression overcame him. What if he needed it? What if the next place was worse than this? He shook his head. It had provided little value here, but abandoning it felt too final, too faithless. A grunt of frustration escaped him.

Don looked over. "What's the matter with you?"

"Nothing. I'm trying to decide what to take and what to leave behind."

"You're taking *that* I hope." Don's gaze flicked from the book to Hank's darkened eyes.

Hank shot Don a look of apprehension. "I guess so. I'm not sure why. I guess it's the only thing that's worth keeping. I sure don't want anything to remind me of this place."

"It may come in handy," Don said with an encouraging smile. "You never know."

Hank stuffed it inside his Red Cross parcel, content that it looked like an afterthought, wedged between the canned food and the cigarettes. He was ready to leave whenever Kurtenbach gave the order.

At roll call on Sunday, April 8, Hank stood before the prison gates that had remained guarded since his arrival. *Kriegies* gathered around the camp entrance, holding their breath for the guards to give the order. At last, they threw the gates wide, spreading them open on the outside world like the lifting of a veil. The prisoners surged forward, but the guards corralled them into order and herded them through. Hank passed between the prison fences he'd hated for so long, already feeling a bounce in his gait and a freshness in his lungs he hadn't felt all spring. Suppressed cries of joy and bittersweet groans sifted through the lines of men marching out into the world. They allowed themselves, for a moment, to pretend it was freedom.

The first group of five hundred men marched toward Krems. As they approached the town, the SS guards turned the prisoners over to a large group of *Volkssturm* guards, a local militia made up of conscripts, ages sixteen to sixty. These guards looked nothing like their SS counterparts. Some were pudgy, awkward, and gray-haired. A couple had German Shepherds yanking on their leashes, snarling and barking at the *Kriegies*. The dogs escorted the columns of prisoners, baring their teeth at any stray movement or step. Hank watched the guard at the head of his section, a plump man that toddled along, thick lips twisted into a grim sneer. A revolt would be all too easy against these weary old guards, if the prisoners had more strength to avoid recapture. But the dogs kept them in line, and if what was said about the Russians was to be believed... Hank quit trying to plot an escape and focused on the beat of the march.

For the first few hours after leaving camp, the excitement of being outside the wire energized them. But as the day wore on, their lack of strength and malnourished bodies slowed them down. Each man had survived thus far on a poor diet and meager rations; none of them were prepared to climb the looming hills ahead of them.

"How far do you think we'll be going today?" Don stopped to catch his breath.

Hank shrugged, already dizzy from exertion.

After more than fifteen exhausting miles, they approached a large orchard in a thick, forested area. Hank noticed the sign outside of town said Lobendorf. The Germans distributed a cup of thin soup for each man and a loaf of bread to be shared among five *Kriegies*. The prisoners licked every bite off their fingers.

They slept in the cold, under the stars and barren trees with thin coats and blankets. Temperatures dipped below freezing, so the men huddled together to keep warm, taking turns being in the middle.

They nibbled at their meager food rations to keep up their energy for the grueling mountain trek. But as days passed, men collapsed from exhaustion, and the guards would force them to get up and keep marching.

By April 12, they approached the town of Ysper and were led to an abandoned paper factory. It provided the first roof over their heads since they had left the camp five days ago. The guards distributed bread and soup. That night, the men slept well in spite of the cold, concrete factory floor.

The westward march began every morning before sun-up. Most days they marched without much food. At times, prisoners would stray from the group to beg for food from locals, who looked on as the parade of sorry-looking American soldiers passed by. The guards didn't seem to mind the *Kriegies* scrounging for food, as long as they came back. And every *Kriegie* did return, because escape was pointless.

On April 16, the weary prisoners were squeezed into a large cow barn for the night. When the room filled with slumber and deep snores, someone nudged Hank's shoulder. Don cupped his hand over Hank's ear. "How about that milk cow?"

Hank took the drinking cups from their sacks, and as he climbed over the men, a few tugged at his leg. They pressed their cups or empty cans into his hands. He crouched by the cow, patting her side and speaking soft, soothing words. He milked her gently, each stream of milk whispering against the tin sides of the cup, frothing as it filled. He carried a quart back and shared his cup with Don. They drank deeply, the warm, steaming milk coating their throats and tongues.

A few hours before dawn, they were awakened to resume their march.

"*Raus! Raus!*" the guards bellowed. "Get up now because we must be in Linz in time to get food."

They urged the prisoners to pick up the pace, and Hank noted an unusual degree of agitation. They were afraid of something. But the *Kriegies* couldn't walk any faster, even under the torrent of threats and flashing tempers.

When the morning sun peeked over the horizon, the guards pushed them even harder. They glanced toward the road ahead of them, desperation in their eyes.

"Do you think the Russians are coming up on us?" Don looked at Hank for an answer. "Is that why they're so jumpy?"

"We would have heard them fire, don't you think?" Hank answered. "But something's got them wound up pretty tight."

As they passed the small town of Mauthausen, the guards grew quiet and sullen. In the middle of the column, shoulder to shoulder between two other men, Hank lifted his chin to look ahead and watch a few Austrians emerge from their homes. They passed one house where a woman clutched the posts of her gate, crying out to them. Hank frowned, and when she met his gaze, an anxious look entered her eye, and her words tumbled out more fervent and frantic. She was telling them to go back. Hank could only piece together a little of what she was saying, but he turned away before someone could catch him talking to the locals.

At the word *Konzentrationslager*, Hank swiveled back around again. He pushed through to the edge of the marching column.

"What did you say?" He lowered his head toward the woman and spoke in German. She answered with pleading eyes. "A concentration camp. You must turn around and find a different road; you don't want to see what is ahead."

Hank rejoined the column.

Another Austrian woman implored, "Go around to the other way. They are working them to death in the quarry."

The morning had not yet warmed the earth. More people emerged from their homes, even as their breath fogged in the air, warning the prisoners of what lay ahead.

"They are burning the people in large ovens, and the smoke fills the air every day."

Hank's stomach churned. The other prisoners looked at him to translate.

"They said something about a concentration camp where Jews are dying." Hank struggled to translate. "There's a rock quarry of some kind. That's about all I can understand."

As they proceeded up a slight incline, Hank's gut tightened. Something was very wrong. He noticed an oily, pungent smoke wafting through the air. As he walked further, the acrid smell accosted his nostrils. He gagged, and others covered their mouths. As they approached the crest of the incline, a large stone fortress came into view. The gray brick walls loomed more than twenty feet high, with huge circular towers overlooking the sides of the fortress. Cresting a hill, they could look down over the camp's walls where barracks for thousands of prisoners lined the stronghold inside.

About a hundred yards beyond the main compound, they came to the edge of a massive pit. Hank looked down into a large rock quarry, where thousands of emaciated prisoners in striped prison uniforms trudged in a zombie-like shuffle. Armed SS guards stood poised to shoot.

Most prisoners lined up at the bottom of a long stone staircase that stretched to the top of the quarry, curving alongside the quarry wall. Every inch of the staircase was filled with prisoners hefting large cut stones. Hank noticed how each prisoner was bent over from the burden of what he was carrying. He figured each stone must have weighed a hundred pounds or more. Others waited in line for their turn to begin their slow, excruciating climb to the top.

The whole column of *Kriegies* staggered to a halt. The guards screamed at them to keep moving, to go faster.

Don tugged on Hank's coat. "Come on, Hank."

Hank couldn't move. Something rooted him to that spot, his eyes fixated on the scene before him. These prisoners crawled along like insects, mindless and numb. Some lay still, scattered over the ground, as guards and other prisoners stepped over them. Because of the sick feeling in his gut, Hank realized what he was witnessing. Human corpses were strewn on the ground like debris, like filth.

The acrid smell alone was disturbing enough, but how could both guards and prisoners be so casual in the presence of one human corpse, let alone so many? The pungent odor clung to his nose, and deep in the pit, it had to be unbearable.

"Hank! Listen to me right now! You have to keep moving. Do you understand?" Don's voice startled Hank back to himself.

Forcing his eyes away from the quarry, Hank nodded at Don, and took a few more steps. On his right, a plume of smoke billowed from one of the faraway buildings inside the prison compound. The crematorium, he thought, consuming human fuel. How many lives were they breathing in the air now? The idea made him retch.

His eyes were drawn back to the quarry, as prisoners wandered about. One stumbled to the ground in front of an SS guard, and the prisoner struggled to rise. The guard struck the prisoner in the head with his rifle butt, and, as the prisoner's head snapped back, Hank's knees gave out from under him. The prisoner lay still, and the guard kicked him in the head again for good measure before casually walking away.

The fickle wind changed directions and blew smoke toward the *Kriegies*, who coughed and choked from the smell. Hank's eyes and nose burned, and he fought to keep from vomiting what little food he had eaten.

"Let's go Hank; you've seen enough. Come on buddy!" Don pulled the sleeve of Hank's coat. He lifted Hank to his feet. Sluggishly, Hank turned to Don as he beckoned him to follow. His lips moved, shouting silent words at Hank. "Don, didn't you see what happened?" Hank pointed with his weakened finger.

Don yanked him back into the line and shouted in his ear. "Keep moving! The guards are watching you!"

Hank took a step forward but couldn't feel the ground beneath his feet. His head swam.

"That's it, Hank. Just keep walking and forget about that. We're alive, and we're going to be home soon," Don said.

Hank walked slowly, mumbling, "Going home soon."

The guards prodded the *Kriegies* to move faster.

"Keep moving. Ignore what is ahead and keep moving."

"There's more ahead?" Hank gasped. "I can't."

"Yes, you can." Don gripped his arm. "I need you to."

Once the Mauthausen compound was out of view, the marching Americans approached a large field where thousands of men were wandering aimlessly. Some appeared to be sleeping in the open field.

Guards trailed along ahead of them. Men and teenage boys stumbled along, some chained at the ankle. They were little more than skin and bones, walking skeletons hunched over like old men. Further on, guards gathered the dead, lifting the stiff corpses from the ground and tossing them into a truck like cord wood. Hank stopped counting the dead; there were too many.

These men were dressed in dirty and worn civilian clothes. Many were carrying a small suitcase, as if returning from a weekend trip. Looters rifled through the abandoned luggage of the dead. Something snagged on Hank's feet, and he looked down to shake his foot free of discarded clothing. Family photographs, soaked with the morning dew, littered the ground like autumn leaves.

As they walked a little farther down the road, another group of prisoners appeared, many were teenagers. A group was crawling on their hands and knees through the thick grass, bending down like cattle to eat the grass from the ground with their teeth. As the *Kriegies* passed, the boys looked up, grass hanging from their mouths.

Hank knelt to the nearest one and spoke in German. "Where are you from?"

They looked at each other, confused, until one man came closer, heard him, and understood the German. "We are from Hungary," he said in broken German. He searched Hank's face. Hank smiled, then his gaze dropped to the man's coat. A Star of David was stitched onto the lapel.

"They promised us there was a camp just ahead where they would feed us and take care of us, but we are too weak to go much further."

Hank sprang to his feet. "Turn around and go back! They work people to death there!"

Across the field, they stopped crawling, turning to listen, disbelief and stunned silence written on their weary limbs and faces.

Hank locked his gaze with the young man who had answered him. They stood close enough to reach out to each other. "You must believe me. Do not go there. It's the most horrible thing I've seen in my life!"

The man peered deep into Hank's eyes and took several steps backward. "I believe you," he said. "I believe you."

The prisoner turned in a flash and shouted, "They lied to us. They plan to kill us. Run away before it's too late!"

Panic scattered the Jewish prisoners in all directions. Some ran, some stumbled along in their shackles, their ankles raw and bleeding. They tripped, crying, and peeled themselves off the ground. Guards scrambled to regain control. Their orders rang out like gunfire.

Another Jew asked Hank, "Did you see this camp?"

"Yes. And the smell of death is everywhere. You can smell the crematorium from the road."

Screams erupted from the field of prisoners. "They are going to kill us!"

The *Kriegies* kept walking, but Hank caught the seething gaze of a *Wehrmacht* guard just before he turned to a man who was screaming, "It's a death camp!" The guard slammed the butt of his gun into the Jewish man's chest. He sprawled on the ground, unmoving.

Another man cried, "They lied to us…they lied to us!" A *Waffen* SS guard pointed his pistol and shot the screaming man point blank in the head. The man flopped dead on the ground.

The gunshot fueled the panic, as prisoners fled anywhere they could go, their feeble strength and withered legs stumbling in the grass.

The *Volkstrum* guards shouted at the Americans, "Keep going! Faster!"

The *Kriegies* marched, looking over their shoulders. Hank strained his neck to watch the SS guards fire on one Jewish prisoner, then another.

As the Americans continued marching, the road dipped and turned, and the awful scene was blocked from their view. Screams and gunfire rang in their ears. The Americans kept trudging on, one foot after another. Then the roar of machine gun fire broke loose like a storm, thundering out the screams. When it was over, the smell of gunfire replaced the hollow emptiness where the men's cries echoed. A few Americans wept, unashamed.

Hank slumped to the ground "I hate the Germans. I hate them all."

Soil and tears and blood stained his mouth. As Don grabbed Hank's coat and lifted him up, he spat dirt from between his teeth. A sob racked his chest. "Come on Hank, you've got to keep going, or the guards will take it out on you. You've got to get this out of your head."

Hank walked without knowing how, his mind full of the quarry prisoners and the field full of dead men. With each step his mind became a jumble of confusion and fear. As Hank's pace slowed, the other men began stepping around him. Don kept close to Hank. "Come on Hank, we've gotta keep up."

They lagged near the end of the pack when a tall SS guard glowered at Hank and Don for slowing down the column.

Hank drew himself up, thrusting his finger into the guard's face. "I was always proud of my German heritage. My parents were born here. But it is a filthy place. How can you treat people like animals? *Worse* than animals?"

"Hank…" Don's warning came subtle in his ear, but he ignored it.

"It's dirty work." The guard spoke as he stood tall and unapologetic. "But we're making the world a better place without Jews and other *untermenschen.* Someday the world will thank us."

Untermenshcen. It sent a shudder down Hank's spine. He'd heard it before, tossed around in casual conversation between the SS guards and other Nazis when talking about Jews, Poles, Slavs, *sub-humans*. He turned his back to the guard, clenching his fists. "I am ashamed to be German, and you should be, too."

Pain struck in the side of his head, and Hank dropped to the ground. The guard kicked him again in the ribs and spat, "Get up, and shut up."

Don grunted as he helped Hank to a sitting position. Don's arm wrapped around Hank, lifting him to his feet. Hank rubbed his head, stars still spinning in front of his eyes. A fog enveloped his mind, and he couldn't remember where he was. His mind was spinning. He looked at Don for a moment and was confused; then after an instant, he recognized him.

"Come on, Hank. Hup, two, three, four. Hup, two, three, four," Don chanted.

Hank focused on matching his steps to Don's cadence, repeating the chant in his head.

"There you go, Hank. Just keep marching, hup, two, three, four."

Under his breath he mumbled the word *untermenschen*. He took a few steps more and whispered it again. *Untermenschen.* The word sounded silly to Hank's disordered mind. *Untermenschen!*

With every fourth step, he whispered, *"untermenschen."*

He grew louder, until he shouted the word in cadence with Don's voice.

"Hup, two, three, four. *Un-ter-men-schen.*"

"Hup, two, three, four. *Un-ter-men-schen.*"

"Shut up, Meyer!" someone called out.

"Hup, two, three, four. *Un-ter-men-schen.*"

Another man in front of him shouted out, "Hey, Meyer, haven't you killed enough people today? You're going to get us all killed with your stupid chanting."

Guilt surged through Hank, stopping him in his tracks. Don looked around to see if the guards were nearby. The SS guard that had smacked Hank approached, the butt of his gun ready to strike. Don positioned himself between Hank and the guard, forcing the guard to hesitate. Using what little strength he had left, Don pushed Hank forward, clenching his coat as he dragged him along.

"Come on Hank, let's keep moving. We're almost there."

Don's strong will kept Hank moving for a few more kilometers. Hank's feet shuffled along, trance-like. His shoulders drooped, and his arms dangled at his side. He mumbled to himself, drool wetting his chin. Don tugged on Hank's coat to keep him focused on the task of marching. He didn't let him drop to his knees.

The guards stopped without warning and shouted, "This is where we're staying for the night. Prepare to make camp."

They had arrived at a large meadow in a dense forest; the sign outside of town said Abwinden. Hank could see the calm Danube River less than a half-kilometer away. He collapsed in a grassy area, staring ahead of him.

As the *Kriegies* began to settle in for the night, a large truck loaded with several large vats of soup and loaves of bread pulled up. The guards started a fire and warmed the soup for the prisoners, basking in the heat of the flames and rubbing their cold hands together.

Don took Hank's soup cup and stood in line, then returned with Hank's portion. The soup smelled of spoiled vegetables and a few potatoes, but it was warm, and they gnawed the bread between their teeth.

Darkness approached, and Hank's thoughts swirled in his head. He rocked himself back and forth, voices interjecting between the comment that played itself over and over and over in his mind. *Haven't you killed enough people?*

Whispers among the *Kriegies* continued to echo in his mind, and he put his hands over his ears. He bit his lip until it bled, then drew a shuddering breath. "I killed those Jews. I am a Jew killer."

The group of *Kriegies* within earshot of Hank's tearful cry turned away. Everyone was just a shade away from madness, and they knew it. Hank's shoulders curled over his chest as he shook with sobs.

Don rushed to Hank's side to console him.

"You didn't kill anyone," Don insisted.

"But I told them not to go there, and they got shot because of me!"

"You didn't kill anyone, Hank. But I need you to be quiet or you'll wake the guards!"

Hank gasped for breath, sinking further into the earth. "I am just like them."

Don shouted and slapped Hank's face, "What's the matter with you? Get control of yourself. I need your help."

Hank was shocked into silence.

"I need your help," Don demanded again.

"You need my help?"

"Yes, Hank. I need your help to get our beds ready for the night."

Hank picked himself up, but could only wander around, too confused to focus on the task of finding branches or pine boughs for bedding. Hank was too tired to wander any more. Don took Hank's arm and forced him to sit down and rest. Some of the other prisoners settled in beneath the shelter and huddled next to each other to conserve body heat.

As the camp grew silent for the night, Hank's racing mind slowed to a steady chant, throbbing with the Jew's helpless cries. Sounds of machine gun fire and plumes of smoke drifted between echoes of *untermenschen*. Exhaustion at last overcame him, and he drifted off into deep sleep.

Chapter 74-Note 1: According to an account written by Orlo Natvig, witnessing the horrors of the Hungarian Jews was both significant and traumatizing:

"These Jews had been forced to sleep on the concrete streets of this town, and as we were walking by, I can well recall, two big burly German guards in green uniforms wearing rubber gloves, throwing these dead Jews up into two-wheeled wooded wagon boxes, just like they were so much cord wood. These were the ones that had died during the night. The others we met later, and when we saw the condition they were in—including the children who were still alive—it was hard to comprehend what we were seeing, because they were in such dire straits there is no way of describing their condition."

The Memoir of M/Sgt. Orlo Natvig, 324th Bomb Squadron, 91st Bomb Group, Orlo Nativig, Master Sergeant, US Army Air Corps, Traces, https://usgerrelations.traces.org/USPOW.Natvig.html, Retrieved January 5, 2021.

CHAPTER 75
April 20, 1945
Braunau am Inn, Austria

The *Kriegies'* forced march continued for another week. The sounds of artillery and other explosions were getting closer, but how close, no one knew. It all came from the west. Spring rainstorms soaked everyone throughout the day, and they shivered as night came upon them.

Night after night, they slept in fields, barns, or abandoned factories. The German food trucks no longer brought soup and bread. Desperate for food, small groups of *Kriegies* would break off and beg for food at farmhouses. Most returned empty-handed.

On Wednesday, April 25, this rag-tag group of hundreds of Americans approached the city of Braunau am Inn. It was the last city in Austria before crossing into Germany. Hank knew the German border was not the end, but he pushed that thought aside. Some end had to be in sight, even an imaginary one.

By midday, they passed through the city. It rained again; the dripping, cold prisoners left a trail of muddy footprints through the city.

They marched a few kilometers past Braunau, toward the bend in the River Inn, a natural border separating Germany from Austria. In a thicket of trees within the *Weilhart* forest, the Germans announced, "This is our final destination. Make your camp here until further notice."

The weary Americans let out a small cheer and began setting up camp. After they rubbed their blistered, calloused feet, they set out to cut branches from nearby fir trees for makeshift shelters. Groups of prisoners teamed up, using blankets and coats to protect each other from the rain.

Hank kept to himself. He couldn't speak, except in short, broken whispers, and only to Don.

The wet grass and green trees made it difficult to build a fire. Dry kindling wood was almost impossible to find, yet for the *Kriegies'* health, keeping a fire lit and burning was a constant and necessary effort. Don and the other men of their group searched long distances for anything they could burn.

For three days the rain fell. The anxious guards glanced at the thin smoke wafting upward, saying their fires would invite an air attack. But the Americans had not been warm since they left Krems, so they took their chances. Hank wasn't sure how long they camped in this secluded area, but it seemed like a week or more.

On a day like all the others, the sound of a car's engine rumbled toward them from deep within the forest. All heads turned toward the west to listen while it approached.

"What is that?"

Headlights appeared through a grove of trees.

"It sounds like a Jeep!" Don shouted. "It is. It's an American Jeep!"

Someone else said they saw just one man in the driver's seat, but they couldn't tell what kind of uniform he wore.

"Is it an American or is it a Kraut?" Don asked. Hank looked on in curious anticipation, along with a few guards and the other *Kriegies*. Their eyes fixed in the direction of the approaching vehicle. After a long pause a voice shouted, "It's an American!"

Cheers erupted as the Jeep pulled up to the *Kriegies* and stopped, the engine still running. An American Army lieutenant stood on the hood and surveyed the situation. His eyes locked on this group of disheveled Americans, and Hank watched him steady his reaction. The *Kriegies* stood about the camp wrapped in blankets or dressed in tattered clothes that clung to their skeletal frames. Hank knew by the lieutenant's reaction that these men looked like neglected children with the darkened eyes of feeble old men. He didn't see them as American soldiers.

Hank hadn't realized he'd also stopped considering himself to be a soldier a long time ago.

"Hey!" The lieutenant yelled so all could hear him. "All you guys are free. You're officially liberated. But unfortunately, I can't help you right now."

The guards and *Kriegies* looked at one another, surprise mirrored on their faces. Guards glanced around for an escape, but the lieutenant's command halted them in their tracks.

"So, all you Kraut guards? You're still in charge for one more night. I'll be back tomorrow to get the rest of you out of here."

With that, the officer sat again and drove away. No one cheered. No one whooped or celebrated.

"Really? That's it?" Don asked. "We're free?"

"Looks that way," someone replied.

"That's not quite how I envisioned my liberation," Don said, voice dripping with displeasure.

"Yeah," a voice retorted. "I'd always dreamed of tanks rolling in and forcing the Germans to surrender. Maybe killing a few Krauts by…" he emphasized the word "accident," then winked. Some of the men laughed in agreement.

They returned to their camps to fight the wet and cold, battling the rain to keep their fires going. The last night was like every other night had been on their long, desperate, and miserable march.

The next morning, a convoy of American Deuce-and-a-Halfs rolled into their camp. A handful of American soldiers emerged. They were strapping, large, and battle-hardened men. Hank stood with his arms at his sides, watching them bounce around with energy to spare. Hank looked at himself, then looked at them with a tinge of envy.

"We're going to get you out of here as quickly as we can," one of the officers instructed. "We're taking you to a place where you'll be airlifted to France, and there we'll get you plenty of food, a hot shower, and we'll get you back to health."

Hank caught the confused expression on the other *Kriegies'* faces; their weary minds and bodies were slow to comprehend what they had just witnessed. But Hank understood enough. They were going home.

They weren't *Kriegies* anymore.

An Army staff sergeant approached Hank and Don, offering to help them climb up to the bed of the truck. Hank reached out to shake his hand. Tears dripped over his lip, and he wiped his nose.

"Thank you," Hank whispered.

The sergeant looked at Hank in pity, tears welling up in his eyes as he squared himself and saluted. His lip quivered as he whispered in reply, "It's an honor, sir. Welcome home."

CHAPTER 76
May 2, 1945
Pocking, Germany

The convoy of trucks drove west from Braunau about twenty miles across the German border. They arrived at an abandoned *Luftwaffe* airfield filled with German aircraft. The sign on the main hangar read *Flugplatz Pocking*, or Pocking Airfield.

"You're going to have to stay here for a few days until we can get you airlifted out," the captain explained.

Hank grabbed the hand of a soldier who helped him down from the truck. His gaze scanned over the airfield and took in every craft. He knew these by name, ME262, Junkers 88; most of these planes he'd seen in combat or heard about from his initial training. Not far from the trucks, a *Messerschmidt Gigant* cast its massive shadow over the ground. A small smile pulled at his lips. Even for a Nazi plane, this massive empty aircraft held a certain fascination. Something about the smell of grease and the roar of engines brightened Hank's mood. He caught Don looking at him through the corner of his eye, then shrugged at him.

Hank and Don wandered up to the giant plane, inspecting the fuselage, the engines, even a few bullet holes. "Let's see if we can get inside." Don looked at Hank with mischief in his eyes. Hank watched Don scour the area for something that he could use to break into the plane. He returned with a crowbar and pried open the huge bomb bay doors under the fuselage. He waved Hank to come and see.

"Look at how big this thing is, Hank," Don beamed with excitement.

Hank leaned in and turned his head to look up and down the seventy-foot cargo bay. "How about that? They even left us a couple of blankets."

Hank and Don climbed into the plane, arranging some discarded tarpaulins into bedding. Hank stretched out, and although the make-shift bed was not as soft as a mattress, he couldn't complain. Inside the hollow, dark plane, the roof and walls curved around him, warming and enclosing him inside the belly of a great metal whale. Sounds from outside came muffled through the panels, and sleepiness weighed on his eyelids.

"This is a lot better than the cold, wet grass, wouldn't you say, Hank?"

Hank put both hands behind his head, crossed his ankles, and took a deep breath. Even a German plane was like home to him. He smiled at Don.

They made their home inside the plane, and no one seemed to mind. The other Americans created mayhem—tearing up the hangars and offices, destroying German planes and equipment, and making a huge bonfire. They burned anything that looked German. Hank watched from a distance, the smoke rising into the night air, a strange mix of feelings in this throat. Burning German items smelled the same as burning anything else.

Hank and Don slept inside the gigantic plane for three nights. Meals were brought to the base mornings and nights. On the morning of May 6, C-47 transport planes arrived; more than twenty of them lining up to unload fifty-gallon drums of fuel. The prisoners sat on the tarmac, waiting for their turn to board. When the crews called for men with physical or mental injuries to board first, a few prisoners glanced sidelong at Hank, some offering encouraging smiles or extending a hand to help him up. He chose to board when Don did and waited.

Don and Hank boarded the sixth plane taking off from Pocking Field. Once airborne, the pilots announced they were headed to a newly built camp at La Havre, France.

As the prisoners stepped off the plane in France, Red Cross volunteers greeted each man with donuts, peanuts, coffee, and a wool blanket. Don helped himself to a few donuts, peanuts, and the coffee. Hank nibbled a bit of the donut, but even a small bite made his stomach ache. He wrapped the wool blanket around his shoulders as they led him and the others to a reception tent. A group of medics and other officers assessed each former prisoner.

A medic sat in front of Hank, greeting him with a warm but war-weary smile. "So, how are you doing?"

Hank cleared his throat to speak through the fog of nausea. "I've felt better." His eyes ached, and the blistered soles of his feet burned with each step. He stood straight and bit back his grimace.

"Are you in pain?"

Hank gave a blank look and said, "No."

"Do you have diarrhea, dizzy spells, nausea, blurred vision, skin infections, boils?"

"Everything but the last two."

"Are you feeling lethargic? Sad? Do you cry easily? Do you feel like hurting yourself, or do you wish you could die?"

A tear pricked the corner of his eye, and he spoke before the medic could see his lip trembling. "I don't feel like hurting myself. I don't feel much of anything."

"Do you wish your mind could think better? Are you easily confused? Do you see things that aren't there?" His eyes bore down into Hank's eyes.

"I don't see things that aren't there."

"But you are having trouble thinking clearly?"

Hadn't he already asked that? "Yes." Hank frowned.

"We're going to help you. First, we're going to get your weight and take some blood for some tests. Then you'll get rid of the clothes you're wearing now, and you'll be able to take a shower. We've got a care package for you. It has food, toiletries, and other necessities."

After completing his initial medical exam, Hank was sent to the next station, where he was issued a RAMP card, identifying him as a "Recovered Allied Military Personnel."

"Don't lose that card; it's very important," the young nurse instructed. "And here's a pamphlet you need to read. It gives you all the instructions for the next few weeks."

She held out a booklet with bold words across the cover *Glad You're Back Soldier: Important information for all RAMPs*. Hank thumbed through it. The print was just a blur, but he gave her thumbs-up sign to acknowledge he would read it.

His next stop was the Red Cross tent, where each man completed a form so a telegram could be sent to his family.

"Name, rank, and serial number please." The Red Cross lady spoke to Hank in a voice similar to his mother's.

Hank narrowed his eyes and looked at the ground. Numbers came as a jumbled mess into his mind, until he picked out the right ones. It had been so long since he'd thought about it. She waited, tapping the pen against her clipboard until he finished repeating it one number at a time.

She scribbled on her clipboard and didn't look up at him. "Who should we send a telegram to announcing your release?"

"Could you send it to my folks who live in Bremen?"

"And what state is that in, son?"

"Germany."

She lifted her head in surprise.

"Germany?" she said. "I can't send a telegram into Germany."

"But that's where my folks are."

"I'm sorry, but that's not possible. It's a mess in Germany. There's nobody there to accept a telegram, and no one to deliver the message even if we could get through."

Hank rubbed his forehead. "I have my sister listed as my primary contact back in the states."

"What's her name and address?"

"It's..." His voice trailed off, and he let out an exasperated sigh. "I can't think. I'm sorry."

"That's okay," the nurse said. "Take your time."

After an uncomfortable pause, Hank looked up and replied, "Her name is Ella Meyer."

"What's her address?"

"I think she's at Bushnell Army Hospital in Brigham City."

"And that's in what state?" the nurse asked.

"Utah," Hank mumbled.

"Utah? Okay, great. I'll send it to Ella Meyer, and she's in Brigham City, Utah? Is that right?"

Hank whispered, "Yes."

"Thank you. We'll get that telegram out today. I'm sorry we couldn't send it to your parents. Why are they in Germany, if you don't mind my asking?"

"My grandmother lives there, and they are helping take care of her." The truth took too much energy to explain.

She looked at Hank with sympathy, then rubbed her chin in thought. "You know, you can always try calling them. Sometimes you can get through, and sometimes you can't. But since it's not an overseas call, I think we can use a military line to call a civilian operator."

"Hmm," Hank grunted. "How would I do that?"

"I'm happy to help you. First, I've got to take care of something, but if you will go to the next tent, over there," she pointed with a kind smile, "I'll finish up here."

"What happens in the next tent?" Hank asked.

"The quartermaster will give you a portion of the money that you are owed for back-pay, so you can get by while you're here. Once you have that taken care of, come back here, and I will take you to an office where we can try to place a call. Okay?"

Hank blinked a few times, then leaned inward. "Okay."

"Do you know how to reach them, such as their number and city?"

"I think so."

"Great. When you're finished, come and find me. We'll see if we can make a call."

"Thank you."

Hank stood in the military pay line, and at his turn, he signed several forms.

"When did you become a prisoner?" the quartermaster asked.

"I think it was early February of last year."

"Okay," the officer said. "Let's figure it out from February. That makes it fourteen months of accumulated pay. When we consider your base pay, flight pay, and other allowances, that means Uncle Sam owes you somewhere between fifteen hundred to two thousand dollars."

Hank's eyes widened. "Really?"

"Yes, sir. You won't see it all at once. We're allowed to give you thirty dollars right now, but when you get home, they'll get it all figured out and cut you a check."

"They're going to give me fifteen hundred dollars?"

"Yes sir. And maybe more because I don't have access to your pay records."

"That's a lot of money."

"Make sure you don't spend it all at once, okay?" the officer smiled.

"Yes, sir."

The warm smiles and heavy blanket around his shoulders brought a strange feeling that sank deep into Hank's core. American voices resonated as soft and gentle tones in his ears, so different from the year-long grunts and stern faces of his German captors. He looked around at his countrymen, catching both empty gazes and compassionate smiles, and the memory of a day that now seemed centuries ago sprouted on the surface of his mind. He thought back when he and other boys were leaving home for the first time, with something hidden behind their eyes, unspoken. Now, he saw the same thing in these fellow soldiers and airmen around him, full and open, in everything from one prisoner's trembling hands to another's eyes gleaming with a silent prayer of relief. No one ever came back from a war unchanged.

Hank wondered if Ella would see what was wrong with him, the same way they both noticed how Chester wasn't himself when he came to visit.

He returned to the Red Cross tent to find the nurse.

"Welcome back," she said. "Let's go over here, and we'll see if we can make that telephone call for you." She walked briskly, reaching the tent door before he could take a few shaky steps.

She paused to let him catch up. He dragged each step, hurrying himself, but still couldn't move quickly no matter how hard he tried. He winced as pain radiated through his aching feet and legs.

She led him out of the tent and down a short dirt road to a series of permanent buildings. The nurse slowed her steps to match Hank's more deliberate pace. Entering a nondescript office, she asked him to sit and wait while she spoke to the officer in charge. The office hummed with workers scurrying through the room, papers shuffling at each desk and phones ringing. They stole glances at Hank but kept working.

As the nurse explained Hank's circumstance to the officer, he quipped "Okay. No problem," and he motioned toward Hank.

"Jump on over here, young man," he said cheerfully. "Have a seat. I've got to get one of our military operators to get a connection with a civilian operator. It's hit or miss, and sometimes it takes a while, so be patient."

Hank lowered himself into a chair near the officer's desk.

"Do you speak German?" the junior officer asked.

Hank's jaw tensed as he fought back the familiar need to hide this fact. But the word "yes" came easily, with no straining to keep the lie undetected. Another year-long weight fell from his shoulders. "Yes, sir. No problem."

"Okay. I'll let you speak to the German operator once our French operator makes the connection."

He spoke a little French and English with the operator, waited for a moment, then handed the phone to Hank, who put the receiver to his ear. A woman with a strong French accent said, "What city are you calling?"

"Bremen," Hank whispered.

"Excuse me, sir?"

Hank cleared his throat. "Bray-man."

"One moment please." A flurry of French instructions was given to another operator, and after a series of clicks and quick electronic beeps, the woman said, "Go ahead."

Hank stated in German, "I need Stuhr, please. I think the number is 11-42-11, it's the Hildebrandt residence."

"One moment, please."

Hank's breathing quickened, waiting for someone to answer. After a minute, the operator said, "It looks like the phone lines are damaged in that area; I'm not able to make a connect…," she paused. "Oh wait. Never mind. I think we're getting through."

Hank's heart raced in anticipation. Until now, he hadn't thought about what he would say—or who would answer.

"Nope, that didn't work," the operator replied with disappointment. "But let me try something else."

Whispers of static came over the receiver—every second of the long silence stretching his hopes thin.

After a minute, the operator returned to the line. "Hello?"

"I'm here!"

"I didn't think it would take this long, but many of the phone lines are destroyed and getting through is unpredictable."

"Well, thanks for trying." He reached to hand the phone back to the officer, who shrugged.

"Oh, wait!" she shouted. "Don't go. I believe we have a connection. I can hear someone on the line. Go ahead…"

Hank held the phone to his ear.

"Hello, Hildebrandt residence," a familiar voice answered.

Mama. It was her. He couldn't breathe for a moment; every emotion he'd ever felt before was slamming into his chest.

"Hello?" Marta said. "Is there anyone there?"

"Mama?" Hank whispered.

"Hank?" She spoke softly, as if saying the name too loud would make him disappear.

Hank's breathing shuddered as he sobbed.

"Yes, Mama."

The officer put a hand on Hank's shoulder and then moved away. The dull roar of the surrounding office went silent. People wiped tears from their own eyes as they witnessed this dirty, emaciated ex-prisoner sob without shame at hearing his mother's voice.

Hank bit his lip, another cry shuddering in his chest.

Mama's voice soothed in his ear. "That's okay, son. It's okay. Go ahead and cry."

The officer came back from around his desk and bent over to put his arm around Hank's shoulder.

"I'm so glad you are okay," she said. "How are you doing?"

Hank inhaled deeply, pursing his lips as he exhaled.

"I'm…so glad to hear your voice…," he gulped, feeling he had at last gained his composure.

"Where are you, Hank?"

"France. That's all I know."

"France?" she exclaimed. "I thought you were in England."

He rubbed his face. So, *Oma* had told them nothing. There was so much Mama didn't know, and just thinking of telling her everything made him dizzy.

"Didn't *Oma* tell you I was shot down near Bremen?" he asked. "Didn't she tell you I was at her house?"

"You were here?" she said. "You mean in Germany?"

"At *Oma*'s house." Silence.

"No, she didn't say a thing." Mama's voice was shaking. "I'll have to have a word or two with her," she said.

"No, don't tell her I'm calling." Hank clenched his fist, voice shaking. Through the phone, he heard her muffled voice shouting, "Mama? Mama? Come here, please?"

"She's somewhere outside," Marta said with frustration.

"It's really all right," Hank sighed.

"*Mama!*" she shouted again.

Hank winced, pulling his ear away from the phone.

"Why are you in France?" her voice inflecting up as she asked.

"Um…" Hank let out a sigh, his knee bouncing with nervousness. "I've been in a German prisoner-of-war camp."

She listened, letting the words sank in. He sensed the hitch in her breath and the long silence before any words came out. "How long?"

"We were liberated just a few days ago."

"You don't sound well. Have you seen a doctor?"

"Yes," Hank admitted. "But I've lost a lot of weight."

"How much?"

He replied quietly, "I don't know how much, but they told me I weigh ninety-three pounds."

"Hank—that's so…" she stuttered, looking for words.

"I'll be okay, really, Mama."

"What did they do to you?" She started to cry.

Memories intruded of picking up crumbs of bread off the floor, bringing visions of his protruding rib cages and his hollow, aching stomach. He pushed it all aside. "I'm in good hands here, Mama. I'll be fine."

"Please make sure you keep eating, my son, but be careful not to eat too much at once, okay?"

"Yes, Mama. I will."

After a silence, he said, "How are Papa and *Oma*?"

"You're papa is doing much better than he was a few weeks ago."

"What happened?" Hank fiddled with a pen on the desk. More bad news.

"Your father and I were taken by the *Gestapo* in the middle of January."

"What! Why?" Hank caught people looking over and lowered his voice. "Are you all right?"

"They accused us of spying. They released me after a few days, but they kept your father for... I didn't hear anything about him for two months."

Hank swallowed. "How is he now?"

"He has really struggled for the past few weeks. It's a miracle he's alive. If the Americans hadn't rescued him from that jail cell..." her voice fell. "Hank, the *Gestapo* left him behind, underground, starving—he barely knew his own name when they found him."

The father he'd known all his life—broad-shouldered, face tan and weathered from hours of farming in the Utah sun, a loud laugh and quiet, gentle hands—that wasn't what his mother described now. Hank imagined a thin, pale man in *Oma*'s rocking chair, sleeping near the window with a crocheted blanket across his lap. But his mama would have helped him get stronger soon, moving about and laughing, working in the garden. Doing something to keep him busy.

Marta spoke into the silence. "Hank, I'm sorry. That was too much for you right now."

Speaking very hushed into the phone, Hank asked, "Saved by the Americans?"

"I guess that is a bit ironic, isn't it?" Marta laughed a little. "We owe everything that's happened to us to them."

"Can I talk to him?" Hank asked.

"He's out in the barn. Your *oma*'s here. Hold on a second." Marta put her hand over the phone again and Hank heard their overlapping, muffled voices. From the voice nearest the phone came something hot and sharp, and a second later, Marta hissed into the phone "Here. Talk to *Oma*, and I'll go find your papa." The telephone receiver changed hands.

"Hank, is that you?"

"Hi, *Oma*." Hank narrowed his eyes.

"Oh, Hank," *Oma* cried, "you are such a sweet boy. I've wondered if you would ever forgive me for what I did to you."

A new wave of resentment rose from his gut. He had thought about what he would say to her every day for fourteen months. All of it left him now. Everything came tumbling out—not in the eloquent speeches he'd heard in his head, but in something bitter and venomous and anguished. He didn't keep his composure, but he didn't care.

"Why did you do that to me? Why did you leave without telling me? You'll never know how much I have suffered because of you and that so-called bishop of yours."

On the other end of the line, she cried. He heard a sniffle, and a long shuddering breath.

"Why did you do that to me?" Hank was too angry to cry now, although he felt his emotions rising up from within.

Oma cleared her throat.

"Bishop Roterman kept you from being arrested by the *Gestapo*. He pulled some strings and had you taken you to a civilian prison where they wouldn't find you right away. We both knew that if the *Gestapo* caught you, they would have tortured you and killed you."

What difference did that make? Didn't either of them know what the Germans did to soldiers in prison camps?

"Hank?" *Oma* asked. "Are you still there?"

"Why would the *Gestapo* have killed me?"

"Because you were out of uniform, and you had removed your dog tags. When you did that, you became a spy," *Oma* said.

"Really?" he reacted sarcastically in a whisper. "Oh," he stopped. "That's right." His Uncle Willy's warning at Christmas dinner rang in his ears.

"You don't know how close it was. They were on your trail. They came to my house looking for you about two hours after you left," she added. "Bishop Roterman took care of it so they couldn't track you down after that."

"*Oma*, I had no idea." Hank covered his face, breathing deeply, leaning his elbows on the desk.

"We saved your life, Hank," *Oma* said. "Please tell me you understand now."

He let her words sink in, the telephone line hissing with static.

"Is that true?" Part of him wanted it to still be a lie, but a pang of remorse stabbed at his heart. "All this time I thought you were trying to save yourself."

"Hank," she said pointedly, "you should know me better than that. I love you. I would never want to see you hurt. I had to make a decision between the *Gestapo* or a prisoner-of-war camp."

"But why didn't you tell me? Why didn't you let me know what you were doing?"

"Because I knew you would have run away if I had told you." She acknowledged this matter-of-factly, as all grandmothers do when they are right, and they know it.

Hank remembered how he fought the temptation to run when he thought the bishop was knocking on the door, but he stayed because he trusted his *oma*.

"You're right."

"They would have found you, Hank. Nobody gets away from the *Gestapo*," *Oma* said. "They had dogs looking for you. It was only a matter of time."

A rustling noise shook the phone, and his mama's voice exclaimed into the phone breathlessly. "Hello, Hank, I'm back."

"*Oma* and I weren't finished," Hank said.

"I just wanted to tell you that I can't find Papa. I'm so sorry," Mama reported with dejection in her voice. Just then, the military officer tapped Hank on the shoulder and pointed to his watch.

"Mama, I would love to talk to you more," Hank said. "But my time's up."

"I'm sorry that you had to go through everything that you did. I will speak to your *oma*," his mother said.

"Mama, tell *Oma* I forgive her. For everything. Tell her—" Hank stopped and glanced at the officer. "Tell her I'm sorry for everything I said."

In the pause, Hank could imagine his mama's pursed lips, a contemplative frown wrinkling her forehead. "It sounds like I have to hear her story."

"Yeah," Hank sniffed. "Just tell her, please?"

"I'm so happy you called. I'm relieved to hear your voice. I wish your father were here."

"Me too, Mama. Please tell him I love him. I miss you both. I'll write you when I can, okay?"

Hank said goodbye and handed the telephone receiver to the officer. "You'll never know how much I needed that."

The officer smiled with kindness, squeezing Hank's arm with tenderness as he took the receiver from him.

The Red Cross nurse tapped Hank on the shoulder. "Let's get you back to your tent," she said. "You've had a busy day."

Chapter 76-Note 1: The job of processing returning POWs fell upon military personnel and volunteers with little experience in dealing with malnutrition and diseases caused by prolonged exposure. Many POWs were unknowingly risking their lives when they arrived at Camp Lucky Strike, being given hot coffee, donuts, peanuts, and other high-calorie, high-density foods. After a flood of RAMPS were admitted to the hospital for gastro-intestinal distress, significant changes were made to the welcoming process, not the least of which was giving RAMPS a bland diet until it was determined they could tolerate more fat and calories.

"Administrative Repatriation Procedures & Evacuation and Disposition of Recovered Allied Military Personnel." *WW2 US Medical Research Centre* online. https://www.facebook.com/ww2usmrc/. Accessed January 4, 2021

CHAPTER 77

May 9, 1945

Camp Lucky Strike, La Havre, France

The banner hung over the RAMP camp, its name rippling in the wind declaring it "Camp Lucky Strike." Hank passed under the sign on his way to his tent, smiling at the irony.

He and Don were still bunkmates, but this time, they each had their own bed. Hank was given a bland diet to help his body adjust to regular food. After a week, he gained seven pounds, and after two weeks weighed in at just over a hundred pounds. His goal weight of one hundred thirteen pounds would give him clearance to go home. It seemed so far away. With each full swallow of food, he groaned at the thought of eating more.

Don met his goal weight after two weeks. He was lucky because he was able to keep down all the malted milk shakes, eggnog, and cheese sandwiches he could get his hands on. Kiosks were stationed at frequent intervals around the camp, offering free treats to any RAMP who needed to put on weight.

Don received orders to transfer to the "pending shipment" section of the camp. He didn't know how long he would have to wait to board a ship; it could be days or weeks. Those ready to make the trip simply had to wait their turn as ships became available.

Hank had known since they were rescued that he would someday say goodbye to Don. He'd planned to say lots of things, but, of course, nothing Hank had been planning to say had been coming out right these days. He gave Don a hearty slap on the back and started crying.

Don, too, was misty-eyed as he extended his hand to Hank. "I'm going to miss you, Hank Meyer. You were a Godsend. I couldn't have hand picked a better bunkmate and partner. Thank you for your goodness, my friend."

Hank choked up as his vision blurred.

Don smiled. "Let's keep in touch, shall we?"

Hank clenched Don's hand, pulling him near to embrace him warmly. His throat was tight, and it was difficult to speak.

"You saved my life." Hank could only whisper. "You saved me many times. I will always be indebted to you."

Hank could feel Don flinch as his friend's now strong arms embraced his own withered frame. His ribs still stuck out above his stomach, and his thin wrists looked as though they could snap like a pencil. Don's embrace was hesitant, but warm.

"I learned a lot from you," Don said. "You'll never know how much I needed a friend like you…," he stopped to clear his throat. With a quick, broad smile, he quipped, "And maybe you ought to go on a date with that Billie girl you're always talking about in your sleep. She's gotta be quite a girl." He winked at Hank and grinned.

Hank's mouth hung open. "You're—you're joking. I do *not* talk in my sleep."

Don held his arms out. "How else do I know her name?"

A blush crept up Hank's neck.

"Don," Hank stopped him. "Before you go, can I give you something?" He stepped up and held out his small and tattered *Book of Mormon*. "It's truly the only thing I own in the world, and so I want you to have this."

Don took the book and turned it over in his hand. He opened the cover and read a short note Hank had inscribed with his shaky penmanship. Don looked at Hank and smiled. "Thank you, my friend. I'll always cherish it. It will always remind me of my favorite Mormon."

They embraced again, and Hank declared, "God bless you, and have a great life. You deserve it. Thanks for all you've done for me."

"You're welcome Hank. I hope we can get together someday."

"Someday we will, Don. You can count on it." Hank waved at Don as he dipped his head to clear the door of the tent.

CHAPTER 78
May 4, 1945
Long Beach, California

Billie sat alone in her Long Beach apartment. She was waiting for a call from work about a change in her schedule. She answered the phone on the first ring.

"Billie! It's Ella!"

Billie stood up from her seat and inhaled. "Did something happen? Is everything okay?"

"Everything's great!"

Billie sat again and listened. "So, what's got you so excited that you'd spend a fortune to call me?"

"I just got a telegram about Hank, and I had to tell someone."

Billie straightened up, clutching the phone with both hands as if using all her strength would help her hear every word. "Read it to me," she said.

"'The Secretary of War desires to inform you that Sgt. Hank Meyer returned to military control on 2 May 1945.' Billie, Hank's alive!" Ella almost shouted in the phone.

Billie's heart pounded, filling her with relief. The news eased a tenseness in her shoulders she hadn't known she had been carrying. "That is amazing news, Ella! I've been so worried about him. Does it say when he's going to be back?"

"No, but I'm hoping I'll get a letter from him soon."

"Where's he going to live? He can't live in your dorm."

"I don't know, to be honest. I haven't thought about that yet. The house is still boarded up."

"He can stay with my parents in Ogden," Billie said, "or he can live with my grandma if he wants to be in Huntsville."

"But I hate the idea that he'll come back and have to live alone, with no family around. We'll have to see what he wants to do."

"Does he know about Chester?"

"No," Ella sighed. "I couldn't tell him that in a letter. I didn't want to make it rougher on him, you know?"

Billie's voice cracked. "I've felt so guilty for being such a jerk to both Chester and Hank, but I just never imagined something like this would happen."

"Nobody could ever have imagined that this would happen to anyone from our small town, especially to someone like Chester," Ella sniffed, "but it isn't your fault."

"I probably didn't tell you, but Chester wrote me quite a few letters. He was so sweet. He told me that he loved me. I didn't write him back as much as I should have. Maybe a few times. But I could never tell him I loved…" She stopped herself. "I just wish I had a do-over. I'd treat him better. I really would."

"I know you would," Ella said. "We all miss him, Billie. Chester's parents haven't been able to plan his memorial yet. Once they do, I'll let you know, okay? Maybe you could come."

"Maybe," Billie replied, trying not to reveal her true feelings. "So, what's going on with you and Tom?"

"I told you I broke it off, right?"

"You never told me why."

Ella hesitated as Billie waited for her to collect her thoughts.

"He's changed so much, you know? It's really hard to explain," Ella said. "To start with, he's just angry a lot. Then he told me that he thought I had changed since I lost weight."

"He said that?" Billie exclaimed. "What is that supposed to mean?"

"Maybe he means that I'm not fawning over him like I once did, and he misses that," Ella giggled. "And then he said he wanted me to stop being a nurse so we could start a family."

"What did you tell him?"

"I told him I'd think about it. He knew I didn't want to just up and quit after all I'd been through to become a nurse," Ella's voice grew louder with protest. "I've already applied for graduate school. He knows I did, so I couldn't believe he would even say that."

"Okay. Then what did you do?" Billie prompted.

"Uh…" She paused to think. "I stopped seeing him for a few months. I avoided him as best I could. Then I ran into him at the hospital about a month ago," Ella explained.

"How was that?" Billie asked.

"It was awkward," Ella sighed. "Really awkward."

"I'll bet. Did you talk?"

"Yeah, a little. He asked me out."

"And…how did that go?"

"We went out for a milkshake. It was nice. We had a long talk but it…"

"Keep going."

"It's still very awkward," Ella chuckled.

"Are you going to get back together?"

"Not yet," she replied with long, drawn out words. "Maybe not at all. I'm not so sure we're meant for each other anymore."

"You do what's best for you, Ella," Billie advised. "Don't take this wrong, but I'm proud of you for knowing what a catch you are. You didn't know that before I left."

"I know," Ella said. "Tell me about you. You haven't written me in a few months. How are you feeling? What's the latest with your love life now?"

"No comment," Billie shot back.

"Oh, come on. Tell me."

"I'm not dating anyone. Let's just leave it at that, okay?" Billie said.

"Not fair," Ella whined. "But I'll leave that alone because you never told me what happened when you bailed out of that plane. All I know is that you were lucky to survive."

"It's hard to talk about all of that. Besides, I just want to forget it ever happened."

"Forget about it? Why? It sounds like you have an amazing story. Why do you want to forget about it?"

Billie paused, considering. Maybe she didn't want to forget. Maybe talking about it would just commit the experience to memory in an odd way, a way that wasn't all true. How could she explain everything that happened? How would anyone but her understand it?

"Maybe someday you can tell me about it," Ella acquiesced. "It sounds like an incredible story you'll be able to tell your kids someday."

Billie heaved a heavy sigh. Miracles, marriage, kids. That brought the reality of her survival all too close.

"So," Billie asked with an annoyed tone, "is that the only reason you called? Or is there any other big news worth the price of this expensive call?"

Ella was bewildered by the change in Billie's tone. "I also just wanted to hear your voice and see how you were doing, but it sounds like you're really busy so…"

"I don't know what more you want me to say," Billie interrupted. "I really don't know what else to tell you. I'm working. I do the same thing every day. And I'm fine."

"You don't sound fine. You sound angry at the world."

"Maybe I need one of those heart-to-heart church lectures you always give me," Billie retorted, "but I'm not feeling up to it tonight."

"Billie." Ella stopped her sharply. "You've been my best friend since we were little girls. I'm really just interested in catching up. I miss you. I haven't seen you since you left over two years ago." Ella couldn't hide the sadness in her tone.

Billie swallowed back the defensiveness; her voice strained as she lowered her tone to something softer, gentler. "I know. My mom tells me the same thing, but I've been terribly busy, and…" her voice tapered off.

"And, what, Billie. Why are you so afraid to come home?"

"I don't want to come home and have to explain why…" She couldn't finish.

"Why what?"

"Why…Why I," Billie paused again. "I just don't need to hear people talk about me and judge me because of some of the things I've done."

"Who's going to know?" Ella asked. "Have I ever told anyone your secrets?"

"I know how it goes, Ella. I've lived there most of my life. I'm just not cut out to live in Utah anymore."

"Just come home and visit me. I really miss you."

"I miss you, too. I'll think about it," Billie shrugged. "I've gotta run. Say hello to my grandma if you see her, okay?"

"I will, Billie. Hang in there. Please remember, we love you no matter what you think you've done," Ella said.

"Ha, that's a laugh," Billie countered.

"What do you mean by that?"

"I mean that I'm basically a lost cause. Let's be honest." Billie fought her emotions. "But we can talk about it later, okay? I'm sure this call is costing you an arm and a leg."

"I don't care. It's my money…."

"No. Really, Ella," Billie felt heat rising in her throat.

"Alright, Billie. You keep your chin up, won't you?" Ella encouraged. "And I promise, you're not a lost cause."

"Whatever you say," Billie sighed again. "Thanks for calling me. I'm so glad to hear about Hank. Write me a big, long letter and tell me everything that happened and how he's doing, okay? Bye-bye."

"Wait, wait, wait!" Ella shouted as Billie hung up.

CHAPTER 79
May 18, 1945

Camp Lucky Strike, La Havre, France

With the luxurious mattress, clean sheets, and pillow on Hank's cot at Camp Lucky Strike, he was determined to catch up on a year's worth of sleep lost because of conditions at *Stalag* 17.

Dark images continued to fill his dreams at night when depression gripped his soul the hardest, and he would lay in his cot, shaking. As his body healed, the fatigue from these restless nights had him sleeping the day away in his tent.

He wrote to Ella, describing his life at Camp Lucky Strike, and how eager he was to come home. As his strength returned, he ate everything he saw, from cheese sandwiches to ice cream. If the food was high in calories, the RAMPs could eat as much and as often as they liked. Hank tried to eat as often as he dared, but he was slow to put on weight, although he did little more than eat and sleep all day. He still felt small, thin, and fragile.

He watched preparations for the next ship departing for America, the camp bustling with men strong enough to throw a piece of luggage on their shoulders. They announced a departure date of June 4, and Hank's heart sank. It was already May 22. Looking down at his own scrawny arms and bony shoulders, those suitcases and cargo felt heavy just thinking about them.

That evening, he went to the dispensary for his check-in, holding his chin high and cradling a small hope that however small, his progress had been sufficient.

Hank stepped on the scale. The attendant looked at the scale, then back at Hank. "Tell me your goal weight again?"

"One hundred and thirteen pounds," Hank replied hopefully.

"It's looking good," the attendant murmured as he moved the slider on the scale.

Hank held back a disappointed sigh. But he squared his shoulders and stood straight.

In small increments, the attendant moved the indicator as it rocked before being balanced. He watched it, eyes narrowed in focused expectation. He sat up, slapping his knee and exclaiming, "Congratulations, Meyer, One hundred thirteen and a quarter pounds. You have a quarter of pound to spare!"

Hank raised his arms in victory. "Thank you, sir. I appreciate your encouragement." The two shook hands, and Hank hurried back to his tent. He packed his small collection of new clothes into a newly issued duffel bag.

His bunkmates turned to watch, observing an energy they'd never seen in him.

"It's been nice to meet you guys, but I'm going home!" Hank exclaimed.

"Good to see you're going home, Meyer," one announced as he shook Hank's hand.

"You've been here longer than most of us, my friend, and it's about time," another commented.

Across the room in the corner, one voice shouted, "Yeah, and now we can finally sleep at night!"

The group laughed as Hank gave the man a puzzled look. "What do you mean?"

"Let's just say you have a lot of nightmares," he replied. "It gets pretty loud!"

"Oh," Hank felt warmth penetrate his cheeks. "You should have told me."

"Don't worry about it," the man replied. "We understand. You just go get in line for that big ship headed home."

After waiting almost two weeks, Hank boarded the *USS Moore Mac*, destined for Newport News, Virginia. He settled into his bunk, relaxed, and let the ship carry him home. He arrived in Virginia just after three in the morning of June 4.

As the ship neared the port, lights swinging in the dark appeared, and a dull roar of voices and strange sounds drifted through the morning fog. Hank watched from the deck as everything came into focus, the faces in the crowd becoming distinct from the darkness around them. A marching band played patriotic songs, their brass notes straining above the sound of the ship's engine and the stiff breeze. The solemn, patient figures on the shore, some wrapped in blankets or holding their hats in their hands, created a strange sensation in Hank's chest. He was home. Yet it was a different place now, as he could never look at it the same way he did before he left. None of these people had seen what he'd seen or done what he'd done.

The gangway wobbled as he took slow, deliberate steps, clinging to the rails with both hands to steady himself. Other soldiers sank to their knees and bent down, kissing the ground. When Hank stepped off and his feet pressed into American soil—not German, Austrian, French, or British—the very breath in his lungs changed, and he was on his hands and knees, crying into the dirt.

The RAMPs marched from the dock at Hampton Roads Port of Embarkation to a nearby railroad station. The POWs who were still too weak to walk long distances were helped into waiting trucks. One young soldier stepped up to Hank.

"Would it be all right if I helped you into this truck?" he asked. "It's a long jaunt over to the train station, and this truck can take you straight there and drop you off at the front door."

Hank didn't argue and reached out his arm for the man to help him up. While they drove in the truck, the soldier started to yawn, but clamped his mouth shut. Hank asked, "So how did you get stuck with this late-night duty?"

Anxious, the soldier drummed his fingers against his leg. "Oh, I volunteered, sir. I wanted to be here to welcome all you boys home," admitted the soldier.

Hank turned to look at his face, the light from the train station highlighting the young man's profile. "Thank you for giving us such a warm welcome home. I appreciate your kindness."

"It's an honor, sir."

Hank wondered how old he was. He looked so young. But Hank figured he shouldn't ask, as he would turn just twenty-one in September. Somehow, he felt twice his age.

After driving past at least a half-mile of soldiers making the long trek to the railroad station, Hank was glad he didn't walk it. Another man helped him step down from the truck and pointed him to a sign that read "For RAMPs Only." Hank turned to say goodbye to the young soldier, but he was already helping another RAMP. He caught Hank's eye and snapped to attention, giving Hank a quick salute and a smile. Hank swallowed hard, his lips quivering. "Thank you," Hank whispered, trying to speak normally.

He followed in the direction indicated, stopping in the large entryway into a room with a cavernous ceiling.

"Come on in!"

The voice belonged to a shapely USO volunteer. Hank returned her smile.

"Over there you can take a hot shower. In that area, we're offering a steak dinner." She pointed next to row after row of phone booths. "You can make a collect call to your parents or girlfriend over there."

Just a few RAMPs had arrived with him on the truck, so Hank could be first in line for whatever he wanted first. He headed straight for the hot shower. He had enjoyed only one hot shower during his entire time at Camp Lucky Strike. This was a real shower, not in a tent, but with tile and plumbing. For fifteen minutes Hank stood and let the steaming water massage his back.

He stepped out, invigorated, rubbing water from his hair and ambling over to the telephone line. The large, circular clock hanging high on the granite walls read 4:35 in the morning.

It would be two-thirty in the morning in Utah. Should he wake her?

He picked up the phone and heard a woman's voice on the other end. "Who are you calling please?"

"Bushnell Army Hospital dorms in Brigham City, Utah. I'm trying to get in touch with Ella Meyer."

"Please hold."

The telephone rang, and an operator answered. "Bushnell Hospital."

Hank was about to talk, but the local operator said, "We're calling from Hampton Roads, Virginia. I am helping a recovered Allied military personnel who just returned from Europe speak to his family. Can you help me locate a Miss Ella Meyer? I understand she's in the dorms."

"Yes, we'll find her. One moment please," the operator responded with eagerness. The familiar buzzing rang several times in his earpiece, then the rustling of the phone as someone put it to their ear.

"Hello?" Ella spoke as if in a daze.

"Will you accept a call from Hank Meyer?"

"Hank! Yes!" she cried.

"Go ahead."

"Hank, where are you?" Ella asked.

"Hi, Ella. I'm in Virginia. I just arrived a few hours ago. Sorry to wake you," Hank replied, happy to hear her voice.

"It's okay. I'm so thrilled that you called," Ella said. "How are you doing?"

"I'm doing much better after spending the last month eating and sleeping all day." Hank laughed at himself.

"Oh, Hank, I've missed you so much. When are you coming home?"

"They told me I have to be rehabilitated at a hospital of my choosing, and I chose Bushnell."

"That's wonderful! When will you get here?" Ella was delighted.

"I'm not sure. I'm getting a first-class ticket for the train home. At least that's what they told me."

"So, if you leave today, that means you'll arrive here on Wednesday or Thursday. I'll keep an eye out for you and have a big welcome-home party at the Ogden train station."

"Oh, please don't do that," Hank said. "The Army said they would take me up to Bushnell. I don't want a bunch of people there to pity me."

"They won't pity you, Hank. They'll be happy to see you."

"You don't understand, Ella. I look and feel like an old man. I'm not steady on my feet, and my clothes just hang on me. When I left France, I weighed about a hundred and fifteen pounds. I doubt I'm much more than that now."

He could hear the sharp inhale as well as the muffling of her gasp, her hand covering her mouth. He knew she hadn't wanted him to hear the shock in her voice. "Of course, Hank. It's completely up to you," she said. "But there are many, many people who would love to see you and thank you."

"Please don't," Hank implored. "I'm not ready to face many people right now. I hope you'll understand."

"Don't worry, Hank. I'm eager to see you no matter what you look like."

"Thanks, Ella."

"By the way," Ella said, "I got the letter you sent me about two weeks ago. How many letters did you end up sending?"

"I don't know," Hank shrugged. "Probably a few, but I can't remember. I told you I spoke to Mama and *Oma*, right?"

"Yes! I haven't been able to talk to them at all. Maybe now we can send letters back and forth."

"It would do them good to hear from you," Hank said.

"Did... did you ever get my letter about Chester?"

Something was wrong with her tone. He frowned.

"No," Hank said. "What's he doing?" Somehow, he knew her real news was more serious, but he posed a lighthearted question. A last chance to speak about his friend this way, the way they did before all of this happened, as if he was just catching up on the events of a weekend or making plans to go dancing at White City Ballroom. A last hope that everything would be all right.

"Oh, Hank. I didn't want you to learn this way. But Chester..."

"Please, Ella—"

"He died heroically, saving the life of another man. He threw himself onto a grenade."

Hank took a deep breath.

"I'm sorry, Hank."

"I was really looking forward to seeing him. I needed to talk to him."

Then the line went silent for a minute.

"How was his funeral?"

"Chester's parents still haven't been able to figure out when they will have it. The Navy hasn't been able to send his body back. Chester is buried on the island right now."

Hank cringed at the word "body."

"I'm so sorry, Hank," Ella said. "I wish I didn't have to be the one to tell you, but you needed to know."

Hank didn't want to talk about it anymore. "What do you hear from Billie and her family?"

"I called her a few weeks ago when I got the telegram about you! I was so excited, I had to tell someone. She's still working in Southern California."

"Is she still flying?"

"No," Ella replied. "But she's an instructor on a link trainer, if you know what that is."

"That's a perfect job for her. Well, other than flying planes, but that's pretty good. If you talk to her, tell her hello from me," Hank said.

As the conversation lagged, the USO volunteer warned Hank his time was up. They said their goodbyes.

Home would not be the same, and Hank knew that. Things change. People change. But he grew more anxious as he prepared for the journey home to accept what he might and might not see.

On the train ride home, he shared a seat with a young mother and her infant son headed to Logan, thirty miles north of Ogden. They talked about their families, living in Utah with its quirks and benefits, and their shared faith. Hank asked her about her experiences during the war. As she talked, she looked out the window a lot, as if seeing the faces of lost friends in the window reflections or passing scenery. Her baby seemed content, bouncing on her knee.

She tilted her head, looking at Hank with a sharp kind of compassion. "Do you mind my asking... what did you do during the war? It seems like you've been through a lot."

Her kind, inviting manner set him at ease, and he found himself saying, "I was a prisoner of war in Germany."

He felt her warm hand take his as she replied, "I'm so sorry to hear that."

He'd only said those words to family, and he felt that, although coming from his mouth, the words belonged to someone else. Someone much older.

"I spent about fourteen months in the camp." He looked away. "I'm glad to be out of there," he said, voice softened. He watched the reflections in the window, and for an instant, saw Utah, home, the way she saw it.

As the miles passed, the woman listened to his story, sometimes seeing it only through his eyes when he struggled to order the words. She waited with patience through Hank's brief bouts of confusion or a sudden onset of anxiety. At times he'd stop talking mid-sentence and stare blankly out the window. As the journey tired him, his sentences fell apart, and he rubbed his hands together in a nervous response. Despite his somewhat disheveled state of mind, she wasn't afraid of him. She listened, letting him say as much or as little as he wanted.

At about nine at night, they approached Ogden. The twilight illuminated the majestic mountain range in a soft orange and purple hue.

"I never thought I'd miss those mountains so much," Hank said. "Aren't they grand?"

"We take such beautiful things for granted." Her eyes beamed as she scanned the towering mountains. "We have to leave for a while to truly appreciate them."

Hank thanked the woman for her kindness and shook hands with her. As he stepped off the train, anxiety gripped his chest, and he wobbled. Another man reached out to steady him, but Hank waved him away.

Hank entered the giant lobby inside the Union Station. Returning servicemen were greeted with cheers and "welcome home" signs. Strangers grabbed Hank's hand to shake it, but he shrank away from the noise and chaos.

He looked around. Where was Ella? Had she not listened to him and sent a big greeting party to make a fuss over him? He clenched and unclenched his fists, turning to look over one shoulder, then the other.

At last, he saw two muscular orderlies in white uniforms approaching, pushing a wheelchair.

"Are you Sergeant Meyer?" one asked.

"How do you know me?"

"We were waiting for you. We're from Bushnell Hospital."

Hank grinned in relief and reached out to shake their hands.

They rolled the chair forward, gesturing for him to sit. "Just sit here until we can get your luggage."

"I don't have luggage," Hank confessed as he lowered himself in the seat. "Just this small duffel bag."

They wheeled him through the din of screams and cheers. He ducked his chin, trying to avoid each tearful reunion. That was the right thing for soldiers coming home who filled their uniforms, but not for him. The orderlies stopped at the curb where an ambulance waited for them.

"I have to go in an ambulance?"

"I'm afraid so," the orderly said. "It's the only transportation we have."

They strapped him to a gurney, and the orderlies lifted the head of his bed a few inches so he could see out the back window. They sped down Washington Avenue, northbound on Highway 89, familiar landmarks passing by. He didn't notice the tears running down his cheeks until the orderly sitting with him handed him a tissue.

After the twenty-five-minute ride, the ambulance backed in carefully to the double doors of the hospital receiving area. The orderlies opened the doors and gently pulled Hank's gurney out from the ambulance.

A nurse approached. "Please tell me you're Sergeant Meyer."

"Yes," he replied. "Why?"

"Your sister has called me every half hour for the last five hours asking if you've arrived yet." She gave a tight smile.

Hank laughed, even more thankful that, in all her excitement, Ella had honored his wishes and hadn't made a big scene.

The double doors of the hospital flung open. "Hank! Hank, you're here!" Ella cried, pushing aside an orderly and running to Hank's side.

She threw herself into Hanks outstretched arms.

"I'm so thankful you're finally home," she whispered.

Hank hugged her, then held her back at arm's length to look at her. "Wow!" he beamed. "You look fantastic. You're a shadow of what I remember."

Everything would be a shadow of what he remembered, but some would be like this. Some would be good.

"So are you," she teased. "Between the two of us we've lost the equivalent of the sibling we never had!"

They laughed as he squeezed her with as much strength as he could manage.

"I've dreamed of this very moment for more than a year," he said, choking back tears. "I can't tell you how wonderful it is to be home."

Ella wiped at her eyes. "Let's get you admitted and settled in. We have a lot of catching up to do, but I'm sure the doctors will have a ton of questions for you first. Did you talk with a psychologist when you were in France?"

He chuckled, watching her shift from sister to nurse and back again. "Not really."

"All RAMPs have to go have a psychiatric evaluation, but that can wait until tomorrow."

CHAPTER 80

June 8, 1945
Bushnell Army Hospital, Brigham City, Utah

Hank spent his first night at the hospital in the medical ward; twenty beds lined up on each side of a long, narrow room, with patients resting in each bed. A nauseating smell permeated the ward, a combination of Merthiolate, rubbing alcohol, and urine from the pans beneath the beds. Hank learned early not to breathe too deeply.

The man next to Hank had no left leg. Another man was being treated for malaria and had an intravenous line stuck in his arm. He lay unconscious, but during the night, he startled Hank awake with a fierce shaking and bouncing in his bed. When it ended, Hank struggled to fall back to sleep.

In the morning, the doctor appeared at Hank's bedside. "I'm Doctor Layton." He extended his hand to Hank.

"Pleasure to meet you, sir," Hank replied.

"How was your night last night?"

"I think the guy next to me had a seizure or something. He was shaking and bouncing around, but other than that, I think I slept about as well as I usually do."

"Do you remember a nurse coming to your bedside last night?"

"No sir." Something about the tone of the doctor's question made Hank glance around the room. The other patients looked directly at him, ears straining to pick up every word of their conversation.

"Do you remember some orderlies coming to your bedside?" Dr. Layton asked.

"No..." Hank replied in a long, drawn out voice. "Are you joking or just testing my memory?"

"You don't remember any of that?"

"No sir, I don't," Hank snapped. "Should I have?"

Dr. Layton gave a quick, nervous smile. "Last night, you punched an orderly and woke up screaming."

"I did that?" Hank drew back in surprise. The other patients were nodding.

"Yes, I'm afraid you did, son."

"I'm terribly sorry. I...I..." Hank stuttered. "I'm very sorry."

"It's okay," the doctor explained. "You're not in trouble."

Hank stared at a loose asbestos tile on the ceiling for a moment. "My bunkmates in France told me I talked in my sleep a lot."

The doctor laughed softly, "You did more than talk. You were in all-out combat, and it was hard for the other patients to sleep."

He sat up in his bed to look around the room. "I'm so sorry. I had no idea." But they all waved it off with a smile.

"I think it's in your best interest that we move you to another floor," Doctor Layton said. "I think we would be able to observe you more closely there, and there are fewer people in the ward."

"Okay..." Hank scratched the back of his head, uncertain.

Dr. Layton pursed his lips, thinking, then drew a deep breath. "You know about a special floor we have to help veterans who need help with their thoughts and emotions, right?"

"Oh. You mean the psycho ward."

"It's called the neuropsychiatric ward. The one thing it does offer is a private room for you, which is especially nice because we have only a handful of private rooms in the entire hospital."

"You're giving me a private room in the psycho ward?" Inside, he chided himself for sounding like Billie.

"Yes, Sergeant. I think we can manage your physical health there just fine, but the most pressing concern I have is for your mental health. If you're having these screaming episodes, and you don't remember them, then we need to get to the root of it. You don't need to be lying in bed all day, either. We need to get you up and about, going outside, and building up your stamina."

"So, I don't have to be locked up with all the crazy people?"

"It is a locked ward, and you'll have to be escorted by a nurse or a visitor, but unless you're with a doctor or in group therapy, you can go out and walk around the grounds any time. The more you get outside, the better."

Hank shrugged. "I'll go where you want me to go, doc," he said, shooting a sly smile as he mused if the doctor would understand his reference. The doctor raised his eyebrow and smiled in recognition.

That morning, Hank was escorted by his orderlies up two flights of stairs to the fourth floor. As they approached the two locked double doors of the neuropsychiatric ward, one of the orderlies reached up and pushed a big, black button. He peeked inside the small window and stepped back. Seconds later, the lock blasted with a menacing buzz, and the other orderly yanked the heavy wooden door open.

"This is Sergeant Hank Meyer," he told the duty nurse at the desk.

"Yes, sir. We've been waiting for you." She stood, walked around the counter, and escorted Hank to a private room at the end of a long hallway, behind another set of double doors.

"This is your room," the nurse said.

Glaring white walls boxed in the room, windowless and sterile. Aside from a metal bed and a small dresser, the room was bare and plain. A gray water pipe stretched the length of the room and disappeared into the adjacent wall.

Hank thanked the nurse and sat on his bed with his head in his hands. Here he was, among the crazy, scary, unpredictable people. He laughed a little, realizing that he, too, was unpredictable and perhaps scary. He coughed, the sound echoing inside his room.

Hank tried to rest on his bed but couldn't get comfortable. Noises came from outside his room, unfamiliar and distracting. He stood and with a gentle pull, opened his door to look at the people milling about in the hallways and common rooms. The door creaked as he stepped out, moving with deliberate steps, as though escaping. He kept his eyes to the ground to avoid eye contact, especially with those that seemed agitated by deeper disturbances than his. Some patients paced the hallways. Others sat with blank stares, looking out windows. Some looked like normal, everyday people, and Hank wondered if they looked at him the same way. Or would they see the deep, dark suffering in his eyes?

Hank returned to his room.

A few minutes later, he heard a knock on his door. A nurse with a sing-song voice and a big toothy grin approached Hank. "Sergeant Meyer?"

Hank tipped his head. "That's me."

"We're ready for group therapy. Can you join us in the community room?"

"I guess so. Is it mandatory?"

"You should attend," the nurse stated, "but I'm not going to force you, if that's what you're asking."

He sat on his bed, but she lingered at the door, watching him. "Okay," he sighed. "I guess I've got nothing better to do."

He followed her to a large room filled with folding chairs. The tables were pushed to the edges of the room, with a few chairs organized in a circle in the middle. Hank selected a seat with empty chairs on either side of him. But soon every seat was filled, and Hank's stomach tied in knots. His heart raced, and his right knee quaked.

He stared at the tiles in the floor, following every slight crack and stain until the nurse started talking.

"Okay, for anyone new, here are our rules: First, everything we talk about is confidential and stays here. Second, be courteous. Third, we cannot talk about people who are not present to defend themselves. Fourth, everyone is encouraged to participate. Any questions?" She scanned the room and saw no hands. "So, today's question is: when in your life were you the happiest?"

One by one, each patient spent a few minutes talking about a time in their life when they were happy. Many spoke very little. Some men's troubles lurked close to the surface. Others had buried it deep, and Hank watched as the nurse was patient, giving each one a chance to try. None, he felt, were like him. From small behaviors, like the way they were startled by sudden noises, Hank could tell which ones were there because of combat trauma or some other soul-staining mark of war.

Hank found himself leaning forward in his seat, listening to the intelligence coming from the mouths of the most disheveled men. Some blinked wildly or sat muttering to themselves. But anyone who spoke held Hank's fascination.

Hank was the last to speak.

"Everyone, this is Hank Meyer. He's new here. So, Hank, when were you the happiest?"

"I think..." his voice wavered. "I think the happiest time of my life is when me, my sister, and my parents, sat around the dinner table on Sunday, and ate a simple meal we made with our own hands. We'd just talk and laugh, about what? I don't even remember." He sighed. "I will miss those days."

"What about those times made you happy?"

"I guess because we were together as a family; we felt safe. And now that won't happen again anytime..."

"Did something change?" she asked. "Can you tell us about it?"

Emotions rumbled deep in his gut, and he preferred to leave them there. But in a near whisper he explained, "My parents were deported to Germany against their will, and we don't know if they'll ever get to come back to America." Tears choked his words, and he wiped his face with the back of his hand.

The man sitting next to him put a hand on Hank's knee.

"I'm sorry," Hank said. "I'm very sorry."

"You don't have to apologize for being sad," the man said.

"Thank you, Edward, for giving Hank those words of encouragement," the nurse said. "You are very right."

After making a few announcements about the rest of the day's events, she dismissed the group, but asked Hank to stay after for a moment.

"Are you okay now? I'm sorry to hear about your parents."

"It just caught me off guard a little. I haven't talked about them at all since I got back."

The nurse put a gentle hand on his shoulder.

"Don't ever be ashamed of having emotions," she said. "Letting ourselves feel them, even when it is uncomfortable, helps us process and let go of whatever is still affecting us. That's what we're here to help you with, okay?"

"Yeah," he shrugged. "I understand."

"My name is Charlene, by the way. I'm a friend of Ella's."

Hank forced a smile. "Ella already told you about me?"

She ducked her head as she laughed. "She adores you, and it means everything to her that you're back."

After chatting for a while, Charlene helped Hank feel more at ease with the whole situation. She was attractive, but not in a vain or fussy way. Her dark eyes sparkled with her easy smile. The kindness and confidence she exuded reminded him of Ella.

After she explained the ward's daily routine, he felt a sense of ease build inside him, and he asked, "How long am I likely to stay here?"

"It really depends on your progress," she said. "You're not here to just get physically rehabilitated, but to get your head straight, too. War is hard on people, physically and emotionally, and you've had to deal with trauma that most of us will never experience. You have to be patient as you heal. I think it always takes longer than you want it to, so it's hard to predict, and I don't want to set you up with any expectations that aren't realistic."

"How long do most men stay?"

"Again, it depends," she said. "Sometimes a month, sometimes much more. But we haven't had any war prisoners in here yet, just men coming from combat. Unfortunately, we won't know how long it will take before you're ready. Our goal is to get you back to fighting condition. There's still a big job to do in the Pacific, and no one knows how long that will take. The good news is, you're still getting paid to be here."

"Yeah, I guess that's some consolation," Hank said. "And it's not as though I have a place to live right now anyway, so I guess I may as well just relax and take it easy."

Charlene lifted her chin and smiled. "That's a great plan."

She walked him back to his room. Despite her encouraging smile, the feeling of hopelessness had returned. He was determined to do everything he could do to get out of this place, and as soon as possible.

CHAPTER 81
June 9, 1945
Huntsville, Utah

Ella was carefree as she drove up Ogden Canyon, anticipating each familiar turn and bend in the road. Pineview Reservoir came into view, its waters reflecting the bright afternoon sun, the light dancing and shimmering off the surface. She rolled down the window of her car and felt the breeze on her face, drinking it all in.

She pulled into her driveway, and heaved a quick exhale at the familiar sight of her home. It sat boarded up and very lonely looking, with dust in the windows and dead leaves littering the porch. But it seemed to hold itself up like a resolute monument to everything her family had been through.

She had a lot of work to do.

As Ella turned off her engine and stepped out of the car, Grandma Russell's door flew open, clanging against the side of her house.

"Ella! Is that you?" She wiped her hands on her apron before hurrying to meet her. Ella opened her arms and embraced her. "It's been far too long," she said.

Ella looked at her house, both hopeful and frightened memories dancing in her dark eyes, her jaw set in determination. Grandma asked, "Have you come back to live here?"

"Probably in about a month. My commitment at Bushnell ends on July 13, and then they are kicking me out of the dorms."

"And Hank?"

"I think he doing well. It's the best place for him."

"How's he doing, anyway?"

"He's..." Ella bit her lip.

Grandma took her arm and guided her to the Russell's house, where they sat on the steps.

Fumbling with her hands in her lap, Ella sighed. "The poor guy is just a mess." Embarrassment crept up her neck just for saying that much, but at Grandma's reassuring, expectant eyes, she continued. "He saw so many awful things over there, and what he went through..." she shrugged. "He won't tell me very much."

"Something told me he was unwell," Grandma said. "I pray for him every day. Make sure you send him my love when you see him."

Ella beamed. "Hearing about you should cheer him up."

They went into Grandma's house and sat at her kitchen table. The sun streamed golden and bright through the windows, and they talked for close to an hour.

"And how's your mama and papa? What do you hear from them?"

"I received my very first letter from them about two weeks ago. They didn't say anything I didn't already know. Hank talked to them on the telephone when he was in France. It sounds like Papa's helping people fix their homes, plant their gardens, and just rebuild their lives. Everything is destroyed, and people everywhere are really suffering. Mama wondered, if she and Papa had not gone to Germany, how many more people would be suffering." Ella rambled on, playing with the hem of her skirt. A troubled frown crossed her face, and she looked up at Grandma Russell.

Grandma looked at Ella and asked, "You miss them, don't you?"

Tears clouded Ella's eyes. "Mama says they're doing what they were put there to do. There's a purpose for everything that's happened to them."

"Really? So, you think they won't come back?"

"They'll have to apply for reentry, and who knows what obstacles and red tape they'll face, or how long that will take?" Ella said. "But I think they want to stay where they are, at least for now."

"It's awfully lonely looking out my window and seeing your house the way it is." Grandma stood to make sure Ella wasn't looking at her as she peered out her window. When Ella did look at her, she reached for her cookie jar and offered one to Ella.

"That's why I'm here," Ella said. "To see what we need to do to get this house whipped back into shape. The garden needs a lot of work, and the flowerbeds are really overgrown. But all in all, it shouldn't take us too long. I wish we had the time to plant a garden, but by July it will be too late. I've got some friends from work who offered to come help me move all our stuff back from the bishop's barn, but I'm more worried about what has happened inside the house while we were gone."

"I've been over there once or twice since you've been away. It'll need a vigorous cleaning, but we can make it a home again."

They waded through the thick grass in the Meyer's yard, Ella walking just behind Grandma Russell, hovering a hand to steady her if she stumbled. On the porch, she unlocked the front door and surveyed the scene.

"It doesn't look like wild critters have ransacked the place," Ella observed with a giggle. "So far, so good."

They crept from room to room, as if too heavy a tread would wake the sleeping house and stir up old trouble. Ella opened each door with hesitation, expecting scenes of chaos or decay, remembering everything that had been ripped from the soul of their home. Since her parents' arrest and Hank's departure, the house had scarcely been lived in when she was there, let alone the months she'd been gone. It could have changed in her long absence, she'd told herself. How could it not?

But every surface, every knob and hole and corner waited just the same as it had been. A coating of dust discolored the curtains hanging against the windows and the rugs covering the floor, but the same sense of home that had always been there knit the house together in a way Ella hadn't noticed before. Through a parting of the drapes, a shaft of sunlight shined on the dust, drifting like fireflies in the air.

Ella stood in the doorway of her parents' room when Grandma asked from behind her, "Do you mind if I talk to Bishop Renstrom? He'll want to know you're coming back."

"We'll have to get our stuff from his barn."

"When do you think you'll be up?"

Ella was slow to close the door behind her, scratching her nose as she thought. "Next week, I hope."

Grandma gave a reassuring smile. "I'll bet there are quite a few people from church waiting to help you move it all back in."

"It's not necessary…" Ella started.

"Give me a call anyway when you'll be up, if you don't mind," Grandma stated with finality. "We'll be waiting for the word."

Ella just nodded.

"People will also want to find a way to honor Hank. Do you think he'll be here for the Fourth of July?"

A nervous sigh escaped Ella's lips. "He's not really... he doesn't want..."

"He'll have had time to get his strength back up, and we'll do something small," Grandma prattled on, leading the way down the stairs. "Something to show him how proud we are."

"Grandma," Ella said, her mouth a firm line of determination. "Hank is in the neuropsychiatric ward."

The sudden stillness as Grandma halted with her hand on the end of the stair rail, the impact of it on the old woman's ears drove the reality of Hank's situation deeper into Ella's chest. "I had no idea." At the sound of Grandma's faltering voice, Ella wanted to sit down and cry.

"That's why I'm afraid to make any big plans right now. Please don't tell anyone." Her hands shook, and she realized how much she was concerned that he might never be normal again.

"Dear, you should have told me." Grandma turned to look at her as Ella reached the bottom of the stairs. "There's nothing to be ashamed of."

Ella gripped the stair rail until her knuckles turned white, her face flushing with indignation. "I'm not ashamed of him." The defensiveness in her voice surprised her. More softly, she added. "I'm worried about him. He's not okay." A cry tightened the words in her throat.

Grandma wrapped her arms around her, and Ella buried her head in her shoulder. "They may not let him go for a long time. I don't know what to do."

Stroking Ella's hair, Grandma Russell hushed her cries and held her.

CHAPTER 82

June 29, 1945

Bushnell Army Hospital, Brigham City, Utah

Hank had settled into a routine at the neuropsychiatric ward. Daytime wasn't so difficult for him, as group activities and therapy sessions kept him occupied, even though the weeks dragged on.

"When will I be well enough to go home?" he asked the nurse out of curiosity, forgetting he had asked her a few days earlier. The question hung in his thoughts, no one offering an answer.

But he knew why. Every night he woke up screaming or crying, his pajamas often dripping with sweat. He dreaded going to bed, each night filled with new, more terrifying dreams of the massacre of Jews near Mauthausen or Big Stoop or the smell of burning human flesh. He wondered if he would ever escape these memories.

Despite the nightmares, he had become stronger physically. After three weeks, he weighed a hundred thirty pounds and felt a bit more like himself...on the outside.

Ella visited each day, either before or after her shift. She would take him out for some fresh air. The Utah sun was comforting on his skin. Those were the moments that *Stalag* 17 was most remote. When Ella couldn't come, Hank looked forward to taking walks with Charlene.

On the last day of June, the stifling heat inside the hospital became unbearable. Hank wandered the common areas, wiping sweat off his forehead. He stood at the window, drinking in any fresh air he could get. Other patients slumped on their chairs, miserable and hot. Few were willing to speak.

Charlene came to find him. "Are you up for a walk? It's gorgeous out there, and I have an early lunch. Want some fresh air?"

"I'd like that very much," Hank replied.

Charlene seemed to find the good in almost every situation, and Hank was drawn to her incessant optimism. At first, her cheerful smile was annoying, but now it chased away some of the shadows shrouding his mind.

She escorted Hank through the locked double doors, down three flights of stairs, and out into the wide-open lawn of the hospital campus.

They strolled along the sidewalk, and Hank enjoyed the warmth on his skin, stealing glances at Charlene. They talked, awkward at first, but before he knew it, Hank found himself telling Charlene his stories.

A figure approached from the dorms across the campus. Charlene shielded her eyes, then shouted in excitement. "Ella! Over here!" She waved her arms.

Ella hurried over and said, "I was just coming to see if you'd walk with me." She looked at Hank. Then she glanced between them, an uncertain look crossing her brow. "I can come back later."

"No way!" Charlene said. "Join us."

Hank continued his stories, watching Charlene's eyes dance with surprise at every twist and turn. Ella smiled to herself at the details he left out.

"Then my own grandmother turned me in to the Nazis," he admitted with a half-laugh.

Charlene gasped. "You're kidding me!"

"I hated her for it. *Stalag* 17 was a living nightmare." He rubbed the back of his neck, exhaling a nervous sigh. "But she did the right thing." Only when the words hit his own ears did he realize the truth of it. "She'd have made a good spy," he added with a chuckle.

Up ahead, a group of groundskeepers tilled a flowerbed in the hospital gardens. Another group prepared a bed for flowers, and further, still another dug in the dirt. In this most distant group, one of the workers had a certain posture about him, something familiar that twisted Hank's gut. The three strolled past, and bits of the workers' soft conversation drifted to his ears.

He stopped. "They're Germans?"

The girls turned, sharing a quick glance. Hank swallowed back the fear in his voice, but they'd already seen enough, and he knew it. "Why are there Germans here?"

"They're prisoners of war," Charlene explained. "They volunteered to be groundskeepers, or work in the laundry room. They're everywhere, and they're hard workers, too."

Hank's heart pounded. Everywhere?

He turned to Ella in disbelief. "You never told me they were here."

Ella shrugged. "Do you want to go back inside?"

"No," he frowned. "I'm fine."

But he lingered near the workers, listening with an alertness. He translated for Charlene. "One of them says he's a master gardener, and he's trying to tell them how far apart to plant the flowers."

Charlene turned a bright smile on Hank, asking him about what flowers they were planting and how to say them in German. After a moment, the jittery expression faded from Hank's eyes, and he relaxed his shoulders. Charlene led him by the arm, and he followed.

"These guys are bickering about the flowers," Hank observed as they passed another group.

They turned the corner of the sidewalk, and Hank waited as Charlene pointed to a flower then repeated the German name back to him. Then a man shouted to them from a distance behind them, and the hair on the back of Hank's neck stood up.

The strange voice pricked every wound in his soul, even before he could make sense of what they were saying. Hank turned slowly, facing the sun, where a silhouette ran toward him shouting in German. "Is that really you?" he called out, breathless from running. The man emerged from the sun's glare and lowered the shovel from his shoulders, dropping it to the ground with a clang. Hank staggered back in horror at the tall figure with a thin, broad smile approaching him with open arms.

"*Schweinehund.* It *is* you."

CHAPTER 83
June 29, 1945
Stuhr, Germany

Marta thumbed through pages of paperwork, applications, letters, and envelopes spread around her at the kitchen table. Her mother watched in silence as she opened the largest envelope, the *United States Immigration and Naturalization Service* emblazoned on the front in large letters.

She read for a moment, her eyes scanning, searching for bad news, but hoping for good.

"Oh good," Marta exclaimed, and *Oma* jumped. "Our application has been processed and provisionally approved."

"That's nice." *Oma* fumbled with the tablecloth as Marta continued reading.

"You've got to be joking," Marta glowered, throwing down a piece of paperwork and rubbing her forehead in frustration. "We have to sign a paper agreeing not to talk about our experiences. It's required for our application to be approved."

"Like a contract or something?" *Oma* asked.

Marta nodded, then thumbed through the packet. "Here," she said, pulling out a sheet with "Confidentiality Agreement" across the title. She blinked in astonishment.

"What does it say?"

"Karl's not going to like this," Marta said as she read further down the page. "It says we must agree to never talk about our experience in Crystal City, or our deportation, or any event or circumstance surrounding our arrest and detention. If we do, we will be immediately deported and permanently barred from ever returning to the United States again."

"That's a pretty serious threat."

"I know," Marta exhaled as she ran her fingers through her hair. "It also says if we are deported, we must agree to forfeit all our property and our rights to appeal their decision." Marta slumped in her chair and dropped the paperwork on the table. "Can you believe that? Our application is approved, as long as we sign this promise not to say a word about where we were for the past three years. All we have to do is lie about what we've been through and deny that we've been mistreated by the government."

"Does that include telling your children?" *Oma* asked.

"I don't know. I would think so. I wouldn't dare say a thing to anyone for fear of it getting back to the INS," Marta said. "We would lose everything."

At lunchtime, *Oma* stood at the counter preparing sandwiches, while Marta explained the details of the INS letter to Karl. He rubbed his chin thoughtfully, but distress lurked behind his composed exterior. "I wonder if they're doing this to everyone who came from Crystal City who wants to return, or if it's everyone still being held at Ellis Island, too? Maybe it applies just to those of us who were deported? And what about the Japanese? Do they have to sign this secrecy oath too?"

"Your guess is as good as mine."

Karl scratched his head.

"Marta, you know how much I want to go back home. Especially to see Ella and Hank. I miss them as much as you do," he began. "But I don't trust the government to keep their word. This could be just another excuse to scoop up our assets, and we'd have absolutely no recourse."

Marta looked over her shoulder at her mother, then turned back to Karl and whispered. "I can't leave my mother here alone. I simply can't do it. And what if we went back to America and took her with us, and then we got deported? She would be left alone with Ella and Hank," Marta said. "That's quite a burden to put on them."

"But how will we ever see our children again?" Karl whispered back.

"She can't take care of herself forever," Marta argued. "And at least Hank and Ella can retain the rights to our home there. Then maybe someday, we can apply for reentry. Maybe things will be different."

Karl gave a big sigh. "You always have enough hope for all of us. I don't know how you do it."

"What are you two whispering about?" *Oma* set a plate of sandwiches between them.

Marta looked up. "They don't make it easy for us, do they?" she replied with exasperation. "I don't think we have much of a choice. It looks like we're staying here, at least for the foreseeable future."

Chapter 83-Note 1: In late 1947, the last German internee family was released from Crystal City, Texas and transferred to Ellis Island. Virtually all internees held there were of German ancestry. That same year, Senator William Langer (N.D.) sponsored a bill to release all persons still detained as enemy aliens, but the bill failed. The INS warned that releasing enemy aliens was a threat to national security. Yet, despite the warning, no German internee was ever convicted of a war-related crime against the United States. Some Germans were paroled; others were deported. While languishing at Ellis Island, these internees pooled their limited resources to finance legal appeals. In August 1948, the final German internee was released from Ellis Island almost three and a half years after hostilities ended in Europe. To bring this episode to an end, most German internees signed secrecy oaths as terms of their release; many were threatened with deportation with no prospect of return if they uttered a word about their ordeal. Camp employees at various internment camps were likewise subject to oaths of secrecy, all of which accounts for the relative obscurity of German internment during World War II.

"History of Wartime Treatment of Germans from the United States and Latin America." German American Internee Coalition online, accessed January 4, 2021, http://gaic.info/history/timeline-of-related-events/.

CHAPTER 84

June 29, 1945

Bushnell Army Hospital, Brigham City, Utah

Hank took a few steps back, looking on in stunned silence at Sikkar.

Ella had been reaching out to steady Hank, when the word *schweine-hund* fell like a joke from the strange man's mouth. She turned to him in disgust. "Don't you dare call my brother that!"

Charlene caught Hank as he stumbled. "Do you know this man?"

"Yes," Hank seethed through clenched teeth.

Sikkar explained in broken English, "I was a guard at *Stalag* 17."

Hank's heart pounded in his ears. "This man was the most disturbing, ruthless, and conniving..." He caught his breath. "He made me suffer more than anyone else. Out of thousands of other prisoners to torment, he targeted me." Hank started to tremble, and Ella held his arm to steady him.

Charlene stepped in front of Hank.

"You need to leave," she demanded. Sikkar poked his head around her, pushing her aside.

Hank spat in his face, and Ella pulled him back. "Hank!"

He turned to his sister. "His name is Sikkar, but we called him 'Sicko' because of the sick ways he invented to hurt us." Loathing dripped from every word, but Ella heard between the bitterness and anger, notes of pain. A deep-seated anguish.

"How dare you stand there smiling, acting like you're my friend!"

Sikkar stepped back, holding his hands up. "May I speak in German? I understand you, but my English is..." He looked at them, questioning.

Hank clenched his fists.

Ella said, "Go ahead, but be quick."

Sikkar peered deep into Hank's face, but Hank steeled his eyes and avoided the gaze. "I'm sorry, but I can't remember your name," he said. "I know it's not *schweinehund*..."

Ella cringed again. "Stop calling him that!" she said, her voice low and angry.

"I'm sorry. Please forgive me. I just can't remember his name."

"You need to go. Now. And leave Hank alone!" she demanded.

"Hank!" Sikkar cried. "Hank Meyer, right?" He smiled again at Hank. A cloud of rage blurred Hank's vision, fury boiling up his neck.

"It's a miracle I found you, Mr. Meyer, sir," Sikkar continued. "I was hoping that somehow you would return to my life so I could apologize to you."

He straightened up, bowed his head in humility, and said, "I need to tell you, Mr. Meyer, sir, that I'm very sorry for all I put you through. I was brutal and wrong to be so harsh. Can you please forgive me?"

If Sikkar could become even more of a monster, Hank would never have imagined his pleading forgiveness would be the reason why. As if it could be that easy. Did this man even remember the thousands of acts of cruelty he'd committed? "Why are you even here? I thought I was never going to see you again."

"After I left the camp at Krems, I was assigned to an infantry unit in France," Sikkar explained. "But the day after I arrived, my entire unit was captured by the Americans. We had always been told that if we were captured, the Americans would torture and kill us. I've never been so afraid," he glanced at Ella, then Charlene, then back to Hank again. "But they were not evil. They were... unbelievably kind."

He looked down at his feet, and Ella softened her grip on Hank's arm. Something about him, his plainness and simple awe from the way the Americans had dealt with him, struck her.

"The difference tormented me. About a month later, I ended up here in Utah." He gestured toward the mountains nearby. "Not long after Germany surrendered, they made all of the German prisoners of war watch a newsreel about the concentration camps. For the first time, I saw how my country had killed so many innocent people, the children, the women," Sikkar said, tears welling up in his eyes. "People I knew. People I grew up with died in those camps. I had been proud to be a Nazi, hoping for a new and beautiful Germany, but this was too much. I told the Americans I want to give up my German citizenship. I don't want to be a German citizen anymore. They denied my request, but the more I thought about my actions during the war, the more I was tormented by all the people I hurt. I promised myself that somehow, I would make up for all the terrible things I did."

Charlene said, "What is he saying, and why do you keep listening to him?"

She put her hand on Hank's shoulder. "Are you okay?"

Hank didn't respond.

Charlene asked Ella again, "Please tell me what's going on here."

Ella whispered in English, "He is trying to apologize to Hank for how he treated him at the prison camp."

That opened the floodgates of Hank's anger. Sikkar already had his claws in his sister, twisting her against him. "You are evil. You are vile!" He choked up as the words left his lips. "I suffered like you will never know! Because of you! Because of you!" His hands shook; his lungs heaved. Everything was falling apart, all the walls keeping in the memories crumbled away, exposing him to the world. Ella put her arms around him, and he flinched. She wasn't supposed to see him like this.

"I was cruel," Sikkar confessed to Hank. "I knew what I was doing to you, and I made you suffer more than most prisoners. I thought I was doing my job. I was trying to be a good Nazi. But that's just an excuse now." His voice was soft and low. "I hope, someday, you can forgive me, but I understand if you can't."

Hank's body quaked with rage, and he looked at the ground, thinking of all the ways he could make Sikkar disappear. Sikkar waited, hands folded submissively in front of him. That instant, Hank was still. "No," he said. "I don't forgive you. And I will never forgive you, so don't even ask. Don't ever talk to me again. Don't look at me. Don't even think about me. Just go away." Hank shook off Ella, turning his back on them and walking away with even, controlled strides, still pulsating with anger.

Sikkar's face twisted, fighting back tears. His sad eyes watched Hank with pity and sorrow. "I understand." He frowned and turned to Ella, adding, "A few of us are leaving tomorrow to work in a small town somewhere called Salina."

Ella dipped her head in recognition. Hank had turned his back, but overheard Sikkar talking to Ella.

"After that, they are sending me back to Germany. I must go to try to help people there. It is my penance. If I never see Mr. Hank Meyer again, and if you think it is okay, please remind him that I am very, very sorry, and I hope someday he will forgive me." He turned and walked away, then both women ran to catch up with Hank.

"Are you okay?" Charlene asked.

"I don't know how you can even ask me that," Hank spat. He didn't see Charlene flinch. "I need to go back now, please."

In his room, Hank collapsed onto his bed, put his hands under his head, and stared at the light fixture on his ceiling, a maelstrom of emotions in his mind.

"Are you going to be okay?" Ella asked, perching on the side of his bed.

Hank was shaking with rage. He focused on controlling his breathing, hoping he could settle down.

"Give yourself some time. Be patient with yourself," she said. "I don't know, but I can imagine how overwhelming this must be."

The whitewashed ceiling faded in and out of focus as Hank stared.

"Do you mind?" Ella hesitated, "Could you try to explain this all to me? I'm not sure I understand."

Hank breathed in deep through his nose. "At the time, nobody knew I spoke German. I hid it because the German guards were known to treat German Americans harsher than others. But this guy had the sickest sense of humor. He thrived on our suffering and thought it was all just a game. He tormented us, played mind games, and made sure we were afraid of him. He suspected I spoke German, and that started the whole thing. He was always around; he would sneak up on me any time he could. He took my food, my supplies, things I had struggled to save, and these were all I had. They were my anchor, the only things I had any control over, and he took them." He lowered his gaze from the ceiling, settling into Ella's eyes. "He took that away from me and relished my despair."

"Did he... hurt you?" she asked with a tentative voice.

"He had someone else for that, someone bigger. That guy had these huge hands." Hank gestured with his own. "And he'd haul off out of nowhere, and smack a prisoner, for no reason."

"Hank," Ella said, "you never told me all this."

"Sicko would egg him on. One day I was out walking, and the next thing I remember I was on the ground. My head was pounding, and all I could hear was the sound of this guy's creepy cackle."

"Why didn't you make a formal protest or something?"

Hank shook his head, "It's not like here. Things didn't work that way. The Nazis starved us for fun," Hank snorted.

He explained how he found a copy of the *Book of Mormon*, how Sikkar took it from him, then how Sikkar was caught stealing from the *Kommendant* and was suddenly transferred to the Western front.

"Everybody was thrilled to get rid of him, especially me. I thought that this horrible man was out of my life forever. Now all of a sudden, he reappears, calling me *schweinehund*," Hank trembled, "again!"

Hank spat the words out, and Ella winced.

"Hank," Ella spoke slow and deliberate. "Don't you think it's too incredible to be a coincidence that he ended up in Brigham City, Utah? Of all places? And while you're in a hospital, no less?"

Hank's feet twitched as he contemplated her words.

"There's something more that you're not telling me."

"What do you mean?" he said.

"I understand he tormented you, singling you out for some reason. That part I get. But I heard his apology. I understand that you're repulsed by him, but at some point, don't you think you may want to take him at his word that he's changed?"

Hank bolted up in bed, and Ella flinched. "At some point? I doubt it. In fact, I'll never forgive him. He's manipulative and corrupt. Wouldn't he know how to make it sound convincing? I'm not stupid enough to fall for his tricks."

"Is that really it, Hank?" Ella said, a bite in her voice. "Or are you afraid to forgive him because of everything he represents?"

"What are you talking about?"

"Forgiving one Nazi doesn't let all the other bad people off the hook, you know."

A little calmer, Hank answered, "No, I just know he's terribly smart. He's evil and he's cruel. People like that don't change, and not in a matter of months. It just doesn't happen."

"What if he hasn't changed? Is that truly any concern of yours? What if he is up to something conniving and mischievous—why should that stop you from forgiving him?"

"He's gotten away with too much already, and he doesn't deserve my forgiveness."

I've never known you to hold a grudge, Hank. I know this is not like having your feelings hurt, but is forgiveness in this case any different?"

"Yes! It's completely different," Hank burst out. "I was starving, freezing, and Sikkar…"

"I know I have no room to talk because I'll never understand what you went through. But what I'm asking is a serious question."

Hank's foot stopped twitching as he listened to Ella.

"Why would you not forgive in this situation, yet forgive in another?" Ella pressed.

"He's learned to say all the right words, but his nature is to deceive," Hank said.

"This man was deceitful and cruel. But I need you to hear me again: what do you gain by not forgiving him?" She dipped her head forward, boring her gaze straight into him.

Hank boiled inside. "Listen Ella, you can lecture me all you want. You don't know what Sikkar is capable of doing. He doesn't deserve my forgiveness, or anyone's for that matter."

"You don't forgive someone because they deserve it. You forgive because it heals *you!*"

"You don't know anything about this man. Forgiving him gives him what he wants. It's all about him and his power and control. I will never, ever give him that satisfaction."

"You're telling me you're going to let this man *continue* to control your emotions, your attitudes, your peace of mind, your *life*, simply because you think his apology is hollow?" Ella said. "If you get some kind of pleasure out of hating him, you're no better than he is."

Hank's jaw quivered, "How dare you! How dare you compare me to that person? You think I get some type of enjoyment out of this?"

"Are you so conceited and self-righteous that your sins are above comparison with everyone else?" Ella sat on the edge of her chair staring at Hank. "You're not incorruptible just because you think he's done worse."

"I've done some pretty horrible things too, Ella," he admitted through clenched teeth. "I don't expect mercy from anyone."

Hank could see Ella's countenance fall. "Do you really want to make yourself suffer? You're only hurting yourself, not him. Your nightmares and horrible memories will always live in your mind because you can't let go of your resentment for him or yourself."

"Just get out," Hank demanded.

Ella sat back in her chair, gritting her teeth in frustration. "Fine. I'll go." Ella stood and stared at him. "Think about it, Hank." She stormed from his room.

Hank simmered in silence while his thoughts churned in his head, a raging storm of conflicted emotions.

After a few hours, Ella returned to check on Hank. She peeked her head around the door frame.

"Can I come in?" she asked. "Are you okay?"

He waved her in but said nothing.

"So, I spoke to your doctor." Ella's eyebrows raised, waiting for Hank to protest.

"You what?" He shot a look at her.

"Yes." She put her finger up, warning him to let her finish. "I asked him if I could take you up to Huntsville for the Fourth of July celebration on Tuesday."

The subtlest movement in Hank's posture changed, and a brightness came into his eyes. He seemed to subdue it though, turning a wary eye on her.

"He told me you could go, if you feel you're up to it. He'll give you a six-hour pass. We could go up to look at the house, see what needs to be done, and watch that cute parade. It'll be fun."

"Six whole hours," he mused, rubbing his chin. "I'd like that. Are you off that day?"

"All day. If you want to keep it to six hours, we can do that, or I can see if we can stretch it out longer. It's up to you."

A smile tugged at his lips, growing into a wide grin. His shoulders dipped, and he let out a soft moan.

"What?" Ella looked puzzled.

"They told me I can't leave the hospital out of uniform."

"Why is that?"

"I still belong to Uncle Sam. As long I'm on his payroll, I have to be in uniform."

"Oh," she laughed at herself. "You don't have a uniform."

Hank nodded.

"I'll take care of it." Her head rocked back and forth as she thought.

"Great," Hank responded with a concerned frown. "I think."

Ella put her hand on Hank's arm. "It will be just fine. And if it all goes well, the doctor is thinking he may discharge you the week of July 16. That's the Monday after I move out of the dorms. I'll have time that weekend to get the house cleaned up and all our stuff moved back in. So, what do you say to that, Hank?"

"Let's just take it one thing at a time." He drummed his fingers on his leg.

"I'll plan on being here at nine a.m. sharp on the fourth. The parade starts at eleven, so that should give us plenty of time to get there, find a seat in the shade, then run over to the house for a few minutes to take a look around."

Hank scooted to the edge of his bed, stood, and hugged Ella.

"I'm sorry I yelled at you."

Ella gave him a squeeze. As she left, she gave him a playful wink, walking out with a bounce in her step, but she knew his troubles would not be kept at bay for long.

Chapter 84-Note 1: Labor shortages led to many German POWs working at Bushnell Army Hospital. "POWs worked around the hospital grounds, in the kitchens, laundry, and hospital wards; they also picked fruit in the orchards in and around Brigham City. Language was not a big problem because many POWs spoke some English. At Bushnell, the POWs slept in barracks similar to those used by the GIs; however, a wire fence surrounded the POW encampment. ... Because there was little security, (often only one guard with a shotgun) the prisoners could probably have escaped, but (witnesses) never recalled anyone doing so."

Andrea Kaye Carter. *Bushnell General Military Hospital and the Community of Brigham City, Utah During World War* II. Master's Thesis. (Logan, UT: Utah State University, 2008): 162.

CHAPTER 85
July 4, 1945
Bushnell Army Hospital, Brigham City, Utah

Ella held up the new Army uniform, pressed crisp, with shiny buttons down the front.

"That's a Class A uniform," Hank said. "Is that what I'm supposed to wear?"

"I asked a friend who was in the Army Air Corp. He said you needed this."

"Really?" Hank took the uniform from her, holding it gingerly by the hanger.

"If I'm wrong, we can get whatever you need later. For today, this is all we've got."

"Who is this friend?" Hank raised an eyebrow.

"No one you would know," Ella said.

"Maybe this will lead to romance," he poked her in the ribs. Ella rolled her eyes.

Hank inspected the ribbons on the uniform, spotting a few he didn't recognize.

"We checked with the people down at Fort Douglas and told them about what you've done," Ella said. "Where you trained, and where you served. They told me what you should wear, including your aerial gunner wings."

Hank gave her a warm smile as he remembered the day he'd first pinned them on his uniform. It seemed so long ago.

"Okay. I hope I don't get arrested for wearing the wrong ribbons and medals."

Hank was slow to get dressed. With every clasp and button, he hesitated. He'd be unprotected out there, outside of the safety and security of the hospital. The uniform was the least of his worries; anything could go wrong.

"Come on Hank, let's move it. We're late, and I don't want all the good spots to be taken."

"I'm hurrying as fast as I can. I've almost forgotten how to put it on."

"Pants first. Then your shirt. It's pretty basic. Come on!"

The drive through Ogden Canyon mirrored everything he'd dreamed of at *Stalag* 17. He had seared every turn, every corner into his memory. The kiln; the mountains; the remains of the old Hermitage Hotel. All there, like he'd never left it.

As Ella drove, she kept checking her watch.

"We'll be fine," Hank said. "We'll have plenty of time to get a seat. What's got your feathers in a ruffle?"

Ella drove faster.

As they drove around the reservoir and into Huntsville, she blurted, "Let's just skip setting up our chairs for now. It doesn't look so busy that we can't find a seat."

Hank frowned. "What's gotten into you?"

They turned the corner onto their street, where a large group of cars and trucks waited, obscuring the view of their house.

"What's happening?" Hank asked.

"Oh," Ella's voice trailed off. "Probably just staging for the parade." She pulled into an empty space.

Hank stared. His house gleamed with a fresh coat of paint. Patriotic red, white, and blue banners hung from the porch railing. A large sign hung across the porch saying, "Welcome Home, Hank!"

A knot formed in his throat, and his eyes filled with tears. "What have you done?"

"It wasn't my idea. Grandma Russell told Bishop Renstrom you were coming for the Fourth, and the whole town wanted to welcome you home. I promise I had nothing to do with it."

As he opened his car door, slipping his feet to the ground, the townspeople cheered.

"Look at all these people," Ella said. "I've never seen anything like it."

Bishop Renstrom approached, hand outstretched. Hank gave it a firm clasp as the bishop said, "Welcome home, Hank. We've been praying for this day."

Hank took off his hat and scratched his head in amazement, looking around. "Holy cow! This place looks brand new!"

"Come and take a tour. This has been a community project. Everyone wanted to help. So many people have wanted to help, we almost had to turn some away."

The bishop gestured for Hank to go ahead of him, and he walked up to the front porch. All the wooden slats had been sanded and the railing posts polished with new paint.

Inside the house, the ceilings bore a new coat of paint, and new wallpaper hung in every room. New sofas and chairs replaced the old, tired ones.

Upstairs, Hank's room had a new bed and a dresser, the old quilt his mother had made spread with great care over the mattress. Ella's room also had a new, soft bed and bedroom furniture, new curtains, and bedsheets. She squealed with delight.

"This is just amazing!" she said to Hank.

Taking his hand, Ella led Hank and followed the bishop through the kitchen and out the back door. As they stepped outside, a branch brushed Ella's hair, petals falling to her feet. The flowerbeds burst with color, and the garden teemed with new tomatoes, pepper plants bursting with flower buds, and carrot tops high and healthy. The corn stood almost four feet high, destined to rise high above their heads by summer's end.

"Who planted my garden?" Ella reached out to touch a leafy vine trailing the fence.

"That would be your Uncle Willy," the bishop said. "He got the whole project organized in early June and has been taking care of it ever since."

"But Grandma Russell..." Ella started.

"She had to keep you from seeing it when came up a few weeks ago. You were this close to finding out the whole thing," the bishop said. "Your Uncle Willy hid in the back until you left. Every day he came over to water or pull weeds. I've never seen him so happy."

"Where is Willy?" Hank asked. "I'd love to see him."

Bishop Renstrom pointed to Willy, hiding near the edge of the house.

"Willy, come on over," he shouted. Willy looked on in trepidation, hoping to disappear.

Hank recognized Willy's hesitation and walked toward him, extending his hand. Willy stepped back, but Hank was undaunted, grabbed Willy's hand, and gave it a vigorous shake.

"How are you Uncle Willy," Hank asked in German, smiling with sincere eyes.

Willy shrugged and gave Hank an anxious smile, tears dripping down his cheek as he looked for something to say.

"You are very thin." Willy looked at Hank up and down.

"Yes, that's true." Hank tried to be reassuring. "But I'm doing much better now."

Willy hesitated and asked, "They said you were in a war prisoner camp. Is that why you're so skinny?"

"Yes," Hank gave a kind smile.

"I'm sorry you had to go through that." Willy wiped a tear from his cheek with his forefinger.

Hank changed the subject. "I really appreciate all you've done to plant my garden. It's amazing. Thank you."

Willy's expression brightened. "I couldn't have you and Ella come back home and not have a garden."

Hank's voice choked up at seeing Willy not only clean and sober, but clearly focused on a project that he cared about.

"It means a lot. I hope we can share in a big harvest meal together when they release me. Maybe we can enjoy a great big bacon, lettuce, and tomato sandwich from one of those tomato plants you planted for us."

"I'd like that," Willy chuckled. "I'd really like that."

Just then, Ella came over and hugged Willy. He turned one shoulder to her and wrapped one arm loose around her waist. "Thanks Uncle Willy." She smiled at him, and he pulled away.

Hank felt Ella tug his arm. "Look at our trees, Hank." He glanced to where she pointed, to the fruit trees hedging in the garden. Their pruned branches dipped and swayed in the slight breeze, cherries and plums dancing like crimson and indigo ornaments.

"Hank," the bishop said. "Come out front again."

He escorted them back to their front porch. The crowd assembled in their yard now hushed as they reappeared. A man stood at the railing, turning to greet Hank and Ella.

"Oh, Mayor Allen!" Hank announced in surprise.

The mayor was a balding man with red cheeks and a ready smile. He looked at the assembled crowd and called for their attention with a booming voice. "Can I get your attention?" The crowd went silent.

"We'd like to welcome Hank Meyer back home to America and to his hometown of Huntsville. We honor him, along with all the other soldiers who have served our country well. We especially honor the young men like Hank who suffered at the hands of our enemies in prison camps." He reached for Hank's hand, clasping it in both of his hands. "Hank, you're a real hero to all of us here in this community, and we're so proud of you."

The crowd cheered. Hank smiled nervously, and Ella put her arm around him.

"In honor of your sacrifice and your service to our country, and as mayor of Huntsville, on this wonderful day where we celebrate our nation's freedom, I hereby proclaim today 'Sergeant Hank Meyer Day' in Huntsville, and I proclaim you our honorary leader for our annual Fourth of July parade!"

He leaned over and whispered into Hank's ear. "Would you say a few words? Please?"

Hank's hands were wet with sweat, and he closed them into fists, but agreed.

As the crowd noise died down, Hank cleared his throat to speak. With a murmur here and there, people hushed one another and turned their expectant faces on him. The words halted every time he opened his mouth, but Ella put her hand on his back, a firm but gentle encouragement.

Hank looked over the sea of friends and neighbors, then stated quietly, "I am overwhelmed at your generosity and kindness to me and my family. I'm sure Ella would agree that we are both proud to call Huntsville our hometown. It is so wonderful to come home to you generous, kind, and charitable people. I am honored to be your friend. Thank you again."

The audience applauded, and Hank felt anxious as he waved to the crowd. The mayor shouted to the crowd about the upcoming events of the day. While he spoke, Bishop Renstrom took Hank's hand and then reached for Ella's hand. He leaned in to say quietly, "Before they take you for a few more surprises, I wanted to let both of you know that many in our ward feel they owe you an apology. I knew how you were treated, and I was saddened by it. But almost everyone has played a part in this whole celebration to welcome you back. Some may never be able to say they are sorry, but in their own way, I hope you'll be able to accept this as a peace offering."

Ella grasped the bishop's hand with her other hand and looked directly at his eyes. "The things that happened to our family over the past few years have eaten at me every time I thought about it." Ella's face flushed. "The things people did to us... I didn't think it would ever be the same."

The bishop was surprised by her assertiveness. "I hope you can forgive them."

"It still hurts a lot," Ella stated not wanting to hide her pained emotion.

Hank watched his sister, understanding the feelings reflected in her hard blue eyes.

"It hurt. And I hope they know it," she said.

The bishop could only nod with acknowledgment.

"I didn't realize how much you'd been through," Hank whispered in her ear.

Ella rolled her eyes, saying aloud, "Didn't it bother you?"

"Yes. But I wasn't here for most of it. I just figured people were afraid of the unknown."

"I feared for my life." Ella's voice was adamant. "It's sad, but I just hoped my fellow Christians would act a bit more, well, Christian."

Bishop Renstrom said, "You're right. I'm sorry that you were treated so poorly, and I'm sorry it happened the way it did."

Ella embraced the bishop. "Thanks for apologizing on behalf of everyone else. It's time to put it all behind us now, right?"

The bishop patted Ella and Hank on the shoulder. "I sure hope it never happens again."

Hank looked at Ella with admiration. How did she do it? He noticed her strong smile as she looked out over the crowd. How could she speak so boldly about her grievances and yet forgive in the same breath?

A clatter of hooves and squeaking of wheels parted the crowd as the people stepped aside for a two-seat, horse-drawn surrey. Painted black with gold flourishes and gold fringe hanging from the roof of the cab, it pulled up to the front of the house. A single horse swatted flies with its long black tail, while its driver flicking the reins. A sign was attached to the cab, gold and black letters spelling out "Former POW Sgt. Hank Meyer. Huntsville's Hometown Hero."

"That's for you," the mayor said.

"I get to ride in that?"

"Come on over and climb in. We'll take you down to the staging area, because the parade can't start until you get there."

"Ella," Hank called. "Will you ride with me?"

She followed Hank and Mayor Allen to the surrey. After both had stepped up and settled in, Ella slapped Hank's knee. "Well how do you like them apples, Hank? Can you believe this?"

"You sure you didn't know anything about any of this?" he asked.

"I knew Grandma Russell was up to something, and all she said was she had a few people meeting us at ten and don't be late." Ella eyes twinkled.

"I guess people are trying to make up for how they treated us," Hank said. Ella nodded and smiled.

The surrey started forward, moving with the slow clip-clop of the horse's hooves on the pavement. "I guess the question is," Hank glanced around, "do we just let it go?"

Ella didn't hesitate. "I've been so torn apart inside since all this happened, but I knew I had to let it go months ago. The apology is a bonus."

Hank gazed past Ella, staring at the towering mountains. The seeming ease at which she forgave felt like a thousand bee stings. He knew how much she hurt, yet she figured out a way to let it all go. *Why did it seem so impossible for him?*

Hank forced a smile and changed the subject. "Isn't it amazing what they've done to the house?"

Ella beamed. "Yes, it's amazing. And we have the whole day to celebrate your return. What an honor."

"I'm just…" he hesitated. "I'm overwhelmed." Hank tried to smile, but it felt strained.

Hank felt Ella reach over and hug him with one arm. "This is going to be fun." She was trying to comfort Hank. "Don't forget, they start with the cannon. Plug your ears if you have to."

"Thanks, nurse," he said, and she laughed.

As the surrey took its place in the parade line, the loud cannon erupted from the town square. The sound pounded down into Hank's chest, and he drew in a sharp breath. "Easy," Ella murmured. "It's okay."

The driver flicked the reins and clicked his tongue, urging the horse forward.

Hundreds of people lined the streets of Huntsville to celebrate. Most came from Ogden or the surrounding areas, enjoying a small-town celebration for Independence Day.

As Hank and Ella's surrey proceeded along the parade route, onlookers jumped to their feet to honor Hank with standing ovations. Hank gave a nervous smile and waved. The parade lasted all of thirty minutes, ending at the town park, where Hank and Ella stepped down and thanked the driver. Well-wishers approached and shook Hank's hand.

They were escorted to a shady patch near the large pine trees in the park. Spreading a blanket over the ground, they watched the three-legged foot races and potato sack races, plates of barbeque chicken and cornbread on their laps.

The day wore on, and the midday sun beat so heavy on Hank, he removed his jacket. With every friend dropping by to chat, his smile grew wearier.

By two that afternoon, Ella looked at Hank and tilted her head in recognition. "Are you ready to go Hank?" she asked.

"Do you think it would offend them if I left? I'm running out of gas," he replied.

"I don't think they would mind one bit. They brought our car and parked it just over there," she pointed. "It's not far to walk."

At the car, Ella helped Hank get inside. He rolled down the windows to help cool the scorching interior. She slowed to drive through crowds of people walking in the streets surrounding the area, Hank waving until they left the crowds. Then he leaned his head against the window and fell asleep.

Hank snored gently, and though Ella eased the car over every bump, his head bounced helplessly against the door frame. She sighed a little, sad at how his thin, tired body looked so wilted from the heat and excitement of the day

But on the quiet ride back to Bushnell Hospital forty miles away, the ghost of a smile danced at his lips. For the first time in a long time, Ella knew he was sleeping peacefully.

CHAPTER 86
July 5, 1945
Long Beach, California

Early the next day, Ella rose, showered, and dressed, ready for work. She had slipped her purse strap over her shoulders, and had her hand on the doorknob, when the phone rang, its sound clanging in the darkness, making her jump.

It was too early for good news. She answered with apprehension.

"Hello? This is Ella Meyer."

"Ella, it's me."

"Billie!" she exclaimed. "What happened? How are you?"

"I'm fine! How'd it go yesterday? With Hank?"

"With Hank?" Ella rubbed the bridge of her nose in relief. "How did you know?"

"Oh, a little bird told me," Billie giggled.

"Did you have something to do with it?"

"Grandma Russell told me all about it," Billie said. "I heard the house looks—"

"You *did* have something to do with it! You little sneak," Ella laughed.

"Um, I can't talk long, I'm on a long-distance call," she countered.

"Well it's too bad, because I would have told you that it was magical. I have never seen Hank so happy. It was just what he needed."

"Oh good," Billie said. "My grandma did most of the work, but I donated to the cause so you guys could have new furniture."

"I'll tell Hank how you helped."

"Don't you dare tell him a thing!" Billie cried. "Please!"

"Why?" Ella laughed, but concern creased her brow. "He'd get a kick out of it."

"Please. Please, don't say a word."

"Okay. I won't."

"Thank you." Billie let out an audible sigh of relief. "How is Hank?" Billie asked.

"Did I tell you he met one of the guards from his prison camp the other day?" Ella asked.

Ella described Sikkar and the confrontation between him and Hank.

"And this guard was apparently pretty mean and nasty, especially to Hank. But when they met, he asked Hank to forgive him. That's all he asked of him. Hank was livid. He spit in his face."

"Hank? Mild-mannered Hank?"

"But I don't think that's all. He won't talk about it, but I think he's struggling with his faith. I mention God's name and he looks away."

"What is Hank saying about that German guy?" Billie asked.

"He says he will never forgive him. I keep telling Hank that hanging on to the hate is only hurting himself, but he just can't see it that way," Ella said.

"Hank has always done the right thing, was always telling others to do the right thing," Billie said. "He was a rock. He was *my* rock sometimes." Her voice broke.

"Hank has changed a lot," Ella said. "He's human just like the rest of us. War changes people."

"Yes, but Hank?" Billie said. "He was superhuman. You know. The guy that had it all together."

He hasn't told me what is really eating him, but it must be something awful. Something he saw I assume."

Ella gave a quick glance at her watch. "Shoot! Billie, I've got to go, or I'll be late. Write me a letter; tell me how the sabotage investigation into your plane crash is going."

"Nothing to tell," Billie sighed. "It's all going to be swept under the rug. Just like all the other 'accidents.' Don't get me started, or I'll spend an hour telling you how much I hate men."

"You don't hate men," Ella protested.

"Yes, I do. I hate 'em all," Billie joked.

"Don't hate my papa. He's an angel."

"And mine. They're off the list. But everyone else."

CHAPTER 87

July 9, 1945

Bushnell Army Hospital, Brigham City, Utah

Following the Independence Day celebration in Huntsville, Hank's higher spirits put a bounce in his step. A few days later, Hank whistled as he walked to his group therapy session. He entered the circle of patients and sat in his chair with his legs crossed, eager to hear the others tell their stories.

Typically, the ward nurse conducted this session, but today, a woman in a white lab coat joined them. She carried a copy of the local newspaper, the *Ogden Standard Examiner*.

"My name is Lieutenant Hilde Koppell," she introduced herself with hint of a German accent. "I'm a physician in the United States Army Medical Corp, and a resident physician on the neuropsychiatric floor here at Bushnell. I'm joining you today because we have some..." she swallowed. "We've heard some sobering news."

The patients came into the circle of chairs, settling on the edge of their seats with uncertainty. Doctor Koppell held up the local newspaper and read the headline.

"G.I. Machine Guns Germans in Utah POW Camp."

Hank swallowed back a lump in his throat. Koppell's stern features and accent imparted a tone of German seriousness and no-nonsense all too familiar to Hank.

A G.I. stationed in Salina, Utah opened fire on German war prisoners last night, killing six and injuring twenty-two. Private First-Class Clarence Bertucci climbed up to a guard tower in a German prisoner-of-war camp, opening fire with a regulation .30-caliber machine gun. Bertucci was forcefully disarmed by fellow G.I.s, but not before he had fired a full belt of cartridges, hitting thirty of the forty-three tents in his fifteen-second rampage. Bertucci was taken into custody but admitted to a reporter he wished he had time to reload, claiming he was justified because his targets were German.

Doctor Koppell folded the newspaper, creasing it slowly before she set it down. The patients drank in the news in silence. "This is national news. You're sure to hear about it from family and friends, so I wanted us to talk about it."

No one spoke for a long awkward moment. Finally, one guy stirred in his chair and said, "Sounds like that guy was crazy, and believe me, I know crazy." A chorus of subdued chuckles answered him.

"I think your assessment is right," the doctor added. "I don't think anyone in their right mind could do such a thing."

"Why did he do it?" a patient asked.

"All it says is that he hated Germans."

The man crossed his arms, his eyes downcast. "I'll be honest with you, doc," he said, "I kinda hate Germans, too. I've seen some pretty bad things, and I've learned to hate them."

The doctor tilted her head, drawing a deep, careful breath before saying, "Okay."

Hank leaned forward in surprise. He didn't know what else he expected from a professional, but didn't this news and the patient's words cut pretty deep?

She didn't flinch. "That's an honest statement, and I'll bet there's many of you here who feel the same way," she stated without emotion. "It's my heritage, and when I see what the Nazis have done, I'd be lying if I said I didn't feel anger toward them myself."

Hank cleared his throat. "I'm from a German family. I speak German," he began, "but after what I saw when I was there, I'm ashamed of my heritage. I can see why people hate all Germans. Sometimes I hate myself for being German."

Doctor Koppell gave a subtle nod to herself, as if acknowledging she'd been right about some silent conjecture she'd made about Hank. "What bothers you about some of the Germans you met?"

"They are cruel, arrogant…and they torture and kill without remorse." Anxiety trembled through him, his knees bouncing.

"Are all Germans cruel and arrogant?"

"Most of them," Hank said.

"How do you know?"

"Just look at what Germany has done to the world. To the Jews. To the Poles. I'm ashamed to be German. Aren't you?"

"No," she said. "I was born in Germany. But I didn't do anything to the Jews or the Poles, or anyone else for that matter. I'm not responsible for the actions of the Third Reich, or any other person. I hold myself responsible for my own actions and beliefs."

"But the Germans allowed it to happen. They elected Hitler, for heaven's sake," Hank protested. Some members of the group nodding in agreement.

"Do you think the Germans would have voted for him if they knew how things would turn out?"

"I don't know. Probably not," Hank confessed as he concentrated on the dilemma.

"Why not?"

"Because he turned out to be a monster." Hank wondered if the confusion in his head was showing on his face. "But there were plenty of Nazis who did unspeakable things. Hitler wasn't there, twisting their arms to kill all those people, the women and children. There are some Nazis still out there who believe in what he wanted to achieve: the German domination of Europe and of the world."

"That is not who you are, is it?" Her pointed question prompted her patients to think.

"No."

Dr. Koppell looked around the room, "I need you all to listen to me, because this is important. When you look at your experiences with Germany closely, you realize it was only a small minority of men who are ultimately responsible for all of the horror, right? Those who seized power and used brute force to intimidate their way into ruling the country. It was this small group of evil, powerful men who influenced the nation to hate their enemies. This small group excelled at the art of propaganda, persuading the masses to hate Jews for being so-called subhuman, and then killing them. They took a little mistrust, a little prejudice, and twisted it to convince everyone that the Jews were an enemy."

Hank glanced at the sober eyes of his fellow patients, some of their eyes were fixed on the doctor, others glancing around the room unable to meet her direct gaze.

"What is it called when you hate a group of people and judge them all the same?" Their gazes fell. Even the first man who spoke about hatred for Germans shifted awkwardly in his chair. Doctor Koppell said, "Isn't it called bigotry?"

The guilt written on their faces etched Hank's heart, twisting into his conscience.

"A little prejudice turns into a lot of mistrust, then hatred, then violence. That's why just a little bigotry can be dangerous if it's allowed to fester. Guilt-by-association is often the first step to embracing full-blown bigotry," she said. "This madman killed six people because of this. To him all Germans were guilty—by virtue of just being German. But aren't you doing the same thing, Hank, when you say you're ashamed of being German? Isn't that making yourself guilty by association? Are you responsible for the Nazis' crimes?"

Hank slouched in his chair slightly, his arms folded over his thin frame. He covered his face with his hands, taking in deep, slow breaths between his fingers. For the first time in months, he prayed, without any words, and he didn't know what he was asking for. Something inside him just reached out for help, for something. Was he ready to call it asking for forgiveness? For himself? He wasn't sure.

The discussion continued for an hour, then dismissed at the usual time. Hank lingered after the meeting to thank Dr. Koppell. As he walked back to his room, he remained deep in thought until he fell asleep.

Later that day, Ella came to visit Hank. He lay on his side, propping his head on his arm as he read a book. "Hi Ella. Are you off your shift?"

He looked up when she didn't answer. A look of concern wore heavy on her face.

"What's going on?" Hank asked. "You look upset."

"It was just a long day at work, and, uh, I've got only a week left to work here and…," she trailed off, rubbing her arm.

"And what?" Hank sat up, dog-earring the page and closing his book.

"I don't know how much you hear about the news in here."

"Not much. We're pretty isolated."

"Did you hear about that crazy guy who fired a machine gun on a camp full of German prisoners?"

"Oh, yeah. We talked about it in our current affairs group today," Hank said.

"You know it happened here in Utah, right?" She looked in his eyes.

"In Salina, down by Richfield was what I heard. So, what's the latest?" Hank asked gently, his eyebrows raised.

"Some of the more seriously wounded Germans were taken to hospitals in Salt Lake, but one of them came here because he needed an amputation."

"That makes sense, since they specialize in caring for amputees here. Go on," Hank said. Why was she so hesitant to talk?

"He was on my ward today," she said, wincing as if expecting an explosion.

"Ella, spit it out. I can't read your mind."

"It was…it was him."

Hank blinked, giving his head a small shake as he leaned forward. "Sikkar? You're not serious."

"I was his nurse because I speak German."

"And?" Hank demanded.

"He… he wants." She straightened her back, arms at her sides as she lifted her chin, assuming a confidence. Hank wilted a little, ashamed she had to speak to him about this. "He's hoping you'd be willing to visit him."

"No. Absolutely not. You let him demand such things?"

"He said only if you're willing. He wasn't demanding anything. He wasn't being unkind or annoying. He simply asked if you had a few minutes, if you wouldn't mind stopping by his bed before you leave."

Hank combed his fingers through his hair.

"I promised him I would tell you, but I didn't promise that you'd come," Ella explained with as little emotion as possible.

"How bad is he? Maybe he'll die?" Hank smiled with menace.

"No. He was hit above the elbow and the bullets destroyed much of his arm." Her clinical voice listed the details, and Hank looked away. "They had to amputate it as soon as he got here. He also got hit in the hip, but that one was a pretty clean wound."

"How long will he be here?"

"Longer than you, that's for sure, but I don't know," Ella replied. "I hope you will go see him."

Hank stared at the floor, rubbing his chin.

"I don't know Ella," Hank said. "I don't know if I can stand to look at his face one more time."

Ella's eyebrow raised and she shrugged. "It's your decision, Hank. Just make sure it's the right one."

"What's that supposed to mean?" he snapped.

"You know darn well what I mean," Ella said. "You don't find it the least bit mind-blowing that out of five hundred prisoner-of-war camps all over the country with hundreds of thousands of German prisoners in nearly every state, this one man shows up here in Brigham City, Utah?"

His heart pounded against his ribcage.

"This man asks you for forgiveness that you don't grant, then leaves for what we think is forever, and then boom, he lands back here *again?*" Her voice grew more emphatic. "They could have taken him to a hospital in Salt Lake just as easily, but somehow, he comes back here. How on earth can you not see it? If you can't see a little divine intervention going on here, then you really are worse off than I imagined."

He straightened his back, sitting up. "Is that what you think? That I've gone off the deep end because I can't face the guy who made my life a living hell? Because I can't just say 'It's okay?'" Hank stared her down. "All's fair in love and war."

"Don't you get it Hank?" Ella burst into tears. "You are my little brother, and right now you are my only family." She grabbed his hands. "It's not about him. This is about you. You need to forgive him because it will save *you*." Tears stained her face. "Your mind can't wait until it's more convenient or the hurt has faded, because it will never fade unless you can let go. You need this now."

"I need this, or you need this?" Hank stared at Ella.

"I don't like it any better than you do," Ella whispered. "I hate that you suffered. I hate to see you suffering still. But I can't help but see that the stars have align for you, just so you can get this behind you. I think Werner represents everything and everyone that has caused you to suffer."

"Wait. Who's Werner?" Hank pulled his hands out of hers.

"That's his name, Hank. Werner Sikkar. He's from a little town just north of Hannover."

"How do you know all this?"

"We talked for a while today," Ella said.

"So now you two are buddies, are you?"

"That's not fair Hank. Just stop it. I talked to him like I would any other patient."

"But you sure know a lot about him. Where's he from again?" Hank asked, not really wanting to know the answer.

"You ever heard of Linsburg?"

"No, it doesn't sound familiar. But I saw all sorts of places when I *walked* from where I got shot down to *Oma*'s house, so who knows, maybe I've seen it," Hank barked.

He opened his mouth to say more, but she put up her hand. "We're done talking about him." She dug into her purse and pulled out an envelope. "This is for you. I've got to go," she threw the envelope at Hank.

Hank watched his sister storm out of the room before turning over the letter to find his father's unmistakable German handwriting on the cover. He opened it, scanning the German characters as he unfolded it; he sat back on his bed and inhaled through his nose as he read.

My Dearest Son,

I'm sorry I wasn't able to talk to you on the telephone when you called. I'm sorry to hear how much you suffered as a war prisoner. We worried about you and prayed for you daily, and somehow, we knew you would be protected.

While your emotional struggles are persistent and painful, please don't think you have to suffer with the effects of your experiences the rest of your life. I assure you that you can overcome all your problems when you simply do what we've taught you to do. To "choose the right." I have every confidence that you are able to do this, my son. You have never faltered, and I know your faith. I ask you to remember, Hank. Remember what you knew before doubting became easy. Before it became hard to see the good in humanity.

Your mama and I both want to see you and Ella. We miss you so much. We submitted an application to return to the United States, but they required us to sign an oath of secrecy that we would never tell anyone about what we went through. If we say something accidentally to you or anyone else, they could take everything we own and deport us again, permanently. Please forgive us for not returning to you. We believe our purpose is here, at least for the foreseeable future. We're feeding people and teaching them how to plant gardens and provide for themselves. If we didn't do this, I think many more people would suffer or die. We think we are here because God needed us here right now.

I could never have imagined that being forced to live in an internment camp and then being deported could lead to anything good, but that's exactly what we found here in Germany. We will stay in touch with you and would love to have you come and visit us someday. Until then, always remember that Mama and I are so incredibly proud of you and love you more than you will ever know.

Love, Papa

Hank folded the letter, stuffing it back in the envelope. A piercing headache erupted from behind his eyes as he weighed the conflicts in his mind.

Chapter 87-Note 1: The incident relating to Werner Sikkar's injuries is based on a true account of a horrific massacre of German POWs on July 8, 1945 in Salina Utah. Private Clarence Bertucci, a troubled soldier with an avowed dislike for Germans, opened fire with a .30 caliber machine gun, aiming at German POWs sleeping in their tents. He instantly killed six POWs and injured another twenty-two. Three of those injured would later die of their wounds, making nine Germans killed. Bertucci was starting his night shift as a guard over the POWs. He had been drinking prior to arriving for his midnight shift. Later reports indicated he was "of low mental capacity." He was also known as a frequent troublemaker, unable to increase in rank, despite years in the Army, and having multiple disciplinary problems. He was quoted as being disappointed that he didn't have a chance to go overseas to "kill Germans." When the war in Europe ended May 7, 1945, he felt "cheated," but stated later, 'I'll get my Germans.'" It remains the worst massacre at a POW camp in U.S. history. His victims were buried at Utah's Fort Douglas cemetery with full military honors.

Chapter Note 2: Dr. Hilde G. Koppell was born in Germany and emigrated to the United States prior to the war. She joined the Army Medical Corp as a physician the day after she received her United States citizenship. She joined the staff at Bushnell just one year after joining the army, at a time when female physicians were quite rare.

Andrea Kaye Carter. *Bushnell General Military Hospital and the Community of Brigham City, Utah During World War* II. Master's Thesis. (Logan, UT: Utah State University, 2008).

CHAPTER 88

July 12, 1945

Bushnell Army Hospital, Brigham City, Utah

The next day, Hank asked for leave from the neuropsychiatric ward to visit an amputee.

"Your sister told me you might come," the nurse said. "Here. Just sign here."

In the amputee ward, Hank asked where to find Sikkar. The nurse pointed Hank to his bed.

Sikkar lay quietly, his eyes closed, his bandaged stump was crimson red with new blood. As Hank's shadow crossed his face, he stirred, opening his eyelids.

"It's Werner, right?" Hank asked in German as he extended his hand.

Sikkar sat up, happy tears springing to his eyes.

"Mr. Meyer. How nice to see you."

"I hear you're pretty lucky to be alive," Hank said.

"Yes," he said, "very lucky."

"Do you mind if I sit?" Hank inquired gently.

"No, no. Please do. I am honored," Werner said.

A chair faced the adjacent bed. Hank grabbed it, tipping his head to acknowledge the GI in the bed opposite, reading a comic book. The man's head was propped up on a pillow, and his left leg was elevated in traction. As Hank spun the chair around and sat, he was sure the man was listening while he spoke to Werner in German.

"Tell me what happened," Hank asked with sincere interest.

"We had spent the day in the beet fields. At five, we stopped to go back to camp for dinner, and then we went to bed. Shortly after midnight, bullets were ripping through our tents from machine gun fire. I was in the tent closest to him. My head was facing toward him, and two bullets went through the top of my arm, right here." He pointed to his stump wrapped in gauze, his arm only a few inches long below his left shoulder. "I also got hit in the hip."

"That's amazing you didn't get hit in the head," Hank said.

"I've thought about that quite a few times. I could easily have been killed," Werner said. "I should have been killed."

"I heard he's crazy. And I know I don't have a lot of room to talk." Hank ran a hand through his hair with a rueful smile.

Werner laughed.

"They said he was not remorseful. He wished he had more ammunition to finish the job," Werner sighed.

"I hope they've got him locked up for a long, long time," Hank said. He leaned forward with his forearms on his lap, steepling his fingers. He had surprised himself by saying that and meaning it. "Did I hear correctly that you're from Hannover?"

"I tell people I'm from Hannover because that's a city most are familiar with. I'm actually from a town about forty kilometers northwest of Hannover. Have you ever heard of Linsburg?"

"I can't recall it off the top of my head," Hank replied. "But our *oma* lives near Bremen, in Stuhr."

"I know where Stuhr is. That's very interesting. Is that why you speak German so well?"

"My parents are both from Germany. Actually, they are living there now to help take care of my *oma*. My mama always insisted that we speak German at home, and when I was about nine-years-old, we spent a summer in Bremen."

"Well, your German is great," Werner acknowledged. "I cannot hear any American accent at all. In fact, I wondered about it," he caught himself, looking away nervously, but finished anyway, "back in *Stalag* 17."

Hank cleared his throat, and behind him, the GI next to him shifted in his bed. Hank could just picture him trying to listen in on their conversation but hearing just awkward silence.

Hank said, "I just wanted…"

At the same time, Werner started, "I appreciate…"

They laughed as they stumbled over each other.

"Go ahead, Mr. Meyer."

"Please, call me Hank."

"Okay. Go ahead…Hank."

"I've had… my sister has brought to my attention that the odds of you and I meeting each other are rather astronomical and that it hasn't happened only once, but twice. She and my father tried to make me understand the importance of forgiving you," he exhaled. "That's why I'm here."

Werner gave a sincere smile, and sat up in his bed, as if to listen closer.

"I want to forgive you," he said. The words came, without ornament or passion. When they left his mouth, he could see them strike Sikkar in the chest.

Sikkar looked down, he held out his hand to Hank. Their hands grasped. "I am grateful. I don't deserve it but thank you."

Hank's throat felt tight.

"I will never forget this." Sikkar cleared his throat.

"I won't forget it either," Hank replied as he stood to leave.

"Um, if it's appropriate, I'd like to keep in touch with you, please?"

Hank paused as he thought. "I'll tell you what. You give me your address in Germany, and I'll have my mama and papa contact you. Or I can give you their address and you can go see them in Stuhr. They're staying with my *Oma* Hildebrandt. Their names are Karl and Marta Meyer."

"It is a miracle that your parents are there. I would like to meet them," Werner said.

"If that's what you'd like," Hank said, "I'll write them and tell them."

"And you have no other siblings?"

"It's just me and Ella."

"Okay." He looked at the ceiling trying to find his words. "You are a good man, Hank Meyer."

Hank extended his hand to Werner. "If I don't see you again, I wish you only the best in your life."

"I wish the same to you Hank. Thank you for coming to see me. It means the world to me."

Hank gave an awkward nod, waved at Werner then walked off the medical floor. As he climbed the stairs toward his room, something changed. At first it was imperceptible. As he sat on his bed, it dawned on him. For the first time since he had been at Bushnell, the constant knot in his stomach was missing. When he breathed in deeply, he didn't feel his heart hammering in his chest. Anxiety melted off his tense shoulders, leaving an unmistakable feeling of peace, and he couldn't help but smile. The feeling lingered through the rest of the evening.

When he woke the next morning, the nurse came to his room.

"How was your night?" she asked.

"Pretty good, I think. I must have been very tired, because don't recall waking up."

"You didn't," she smiled.

Chapter 88-Note 1: It may seem unrealistic that a single event could lead to an immediate end of night terrors, but this happened to Medal of Honor recipient George E. Wahlen. He earned America's highest award for valor at one of the bloodiest battles of World War II, the battle for Iwo Jima. Recieving multiple injuries and witnessing the horrific death of many of his closest friends, Wahlen was similarly hospitalized and placed in a private room while he recovered from physical and emotional wounds. Many nights he would wake up in full combat mode, screaming and hollering. The night terrors continued for years after the war, until the day he was married. "Since the day I was married, I've never suffered from night terrors again."

Gary W. Toyn. *The Quiet Hero: The Untold Medal of Honor Story of George E. Wahlen at the Battle for Iwo Jima.* (American Legacy Media, 2007).

CHAPTER 89

July 29, 1945
Huntsville, Utah

The last two weeks of July dragged on, long and tiresome. Hank was released from Bushnell Hospital and given thirty days furlough before having to report for duty. Ella returned to her job at Dee Hospital.

Ella and Hank moved into their new home, and Hank spent his afternoons in the garden. He looked at his dirt-stained knees and hands raw with callouses from the shovels and rakes. Sometimes, he thought he was looking at his father's hands. Ella served breakfasts and suppers on the kitchen table, and as she plated up the food, she sometimes heard her mother's voice in the soft humming of the stove, or the tablecloth that swished like her mother's skirts.

The Baileys announced Chester's memorial for August 15, but as the day of the memorial drew closer, events in Japan dominated world headlines. Huntsville people held the memorial in the back of their minds, but they knew without saying anything to one another, that it looked like more delays.

On August 6, the Americans dropped the atomic bomb on Hiroshima. It destroyed the city and killed seventy-five thousand in an instant. The Japanese government was defiant. August 10, the day after the Americans dropped a second atomic bomb on Nagasaki, Japan asked for peace on the condition that Emperor Hirohito retain his throne.

The Allies agreed. The American people heard about the deal on August 14. On that day, Japan announced its unconditional surrender. From coast to coast, the country erupted with the celebration of VJ Day.

Hank and Ella both went to Ogden to celebrate. Washington Avenue teemed with people and flags and banners. The raw emotion was splashing and dancing and waving in the streets. Years of pent-up anxiety and sorrow released, spilling jubilance into every corner of the city. Some families celebrated in a more subdued ways, like opening their curtains a bit more so their blue or gold stars could be seen from the streets.

The morning of Chester's memorial, Ella washed the dishes, looking out her kitchen window. Hank sat at the kitchen table, poring over the newspaper. A dish clattered to the floor, and Ella's gasp made him jump.

"What?" he said.

"It's Billie! She came!" Ella's voice brimming with elation.

Hank's hands started shaking. He smoothed his hair back, but Ella was already gone.

She ran out the back door to meet the taxicab as it pulled up to Grandma Russell's driveway. Hank followed a few steps behind. Before the car even came to a halt, Ella ripped open the door and reached in to hug Billie.

"You did come! I'm so excited you are here!"

Billie beamed as she stood to get out of the car, and Hank's heart skipped a beat. Her thick blonde hair fell over her shoulders, and her deep blue eyes glinted with tears as she wrapped her arms around Ella. Every night in *Stalag* 17 he had dreamed of her, but it was nothing compared to this. He couldn't breathe.

"You look amazing, Billie," Ella said, and she hugged Billie again.

"And look at you!" Billie said. "You petite little thing, you! You're stunning."

The cab driver unloaded Billie's luggage. Hank was careful to step around Billie to grab it, hoping she wouldn't notice him, but she took a step back and stumbled into him.

She turned around. "Hank?"

"Hey there, Billie. Nice to see you," he said. He embraced her clumsily, then picked up her luggage and carried it to Grandma's porch.

Ella could see Billie staring at Hank with a puzzled look. She turned to Ella, "Hank looks so different."

"What do you mean?"

"Well it's obvious he's a lot skinnier, but he also seems to be a lot less uptight. Maybe he's more at ease with himself?"

Ella thought for a moment. "I guess you're right. He does seem at ease, doesn't he?"

"He sure does," Billie added, then remembered she had to pay the cab driver. "Here." She reached into her pocket and handed over some cash. "There's a little bit more for going so far out of your way." The driver thanked her and put the car in gear to drive away. Billie rushed back to the porch where Hank and Ella waited.

Suddenly, the cab screeched to a stop, then backed up. All heads were turned, watching the cab driver get out of his car and rush toward Billie. "Ma'am, you forgot these." He handed Billie her pack of cigarettes and matches.

Billie's face flushed; she swallowed hard and looked away.

Ella stared at her then coughed in her hand before shouting back at the driver, "Thank you sir. You're very kind."

Ella brushed it all aside, declaring, "I'm so glad you came. You don't know how much this will mean to the Baileys."

"I wouldn't miss it for the world," Billie added, still red-faced as she fumbled to stuff her cigarettes in the front pocket of her slacks.

"How long are you here?"

"A couple days at least. They said they were giving all federal workers the next two days off to celebrate VJ day. The instant I heard that bit of good news, I told my boss I was leaving. He said okay, and ten minutes later, I was gone. They've since changed the holiday, but I was already on my way. So here I am," Billie grinned.

"Smart girl," Ella added. "She who hesitates is lost, right? But how'd you make it here so fast? It's only been a few hours."

"I was lucky. I had a friend who was shuttling a B-17 up here to Hill Field, and I hitched a ride."

Ella put her arm around her friend's shoulder. "We have so much to catch up on, but I don't want to take time from you and your grandma. Can we talk tonight after everything has settled down?"

Billie gave a real smile. "You'll have to tell me the latest gossip."

"You do remember we live in Huntsville, right? Nothing as exciting as *your* life!"

"We'll see about that," Billie said, as Hank stood back and watched her slip through her grandma's screen door.

Fifteen minutes before the memorial was to begin, the Huntsville chapel filled with a hushed, solemn crowd. As they filled the adjoining overflow room, people set up folding chairs wherever they could find a space.

Bishop Renstrom stood to conduct the meeting, welcoming the burgeoning crowd. After a prayer from one of Chester's cousins, the congregation joined in a few verses of "God Bless America," their voices swelling and ringing through the chapel.

Hank read the obituary in his Class A uniform, taking a deep breath and gripping the sides of the podium before beginning.

Chester Bailey was born November 11, 1923. He is the son of Mr. and Mrs. Robert Bailey, formerly of Logan, but now living in Huntsville, Utah.

Chester was educated in Weber County schools, graduating from Weber High School. He was an outstanding athlete, lettering in football, baseball, and track. He enjoyed dancing with his friend Billie Russell, and the two were known to have cut a few rugs.

Hank looked up at the audience's laughter and smiled. "My sister wrote that," he blushed. They laughed even louder.

Chester joined the United States Navy, trained as a corpsman, and served with the United States Marines. He was first assigned to Carlson's Raiders before it was incorporated into the Fifth Marine Division. He participated in several important campaigns in the Pacific. Chester was involved in the battle for Iwo Jima. He died heroically…

Hank paused to regain his voice.

…on February 27, 1945. In brutal combat, he threw himself on a grenade to save the lives of his friends. Chester is interred in the Fifth Marine Division Cemetery on Iwo Jima where he was accorded full military honors.

Repatriation of Chester's remains is pending notification from the War Department.

Hank tapped his notes against the podium to straighten them, before clearing his throat. "Chester was one of the best people I've ever known. He was so proud to be serving his country, and I know that what he did to save his comrades in arms was who he was all the time. He was always kind, to a fault. To his family, I say, I miss him. I love him. I will always remember him."

The mayor stood to give a brief tribute to Chester; then Bishop Renstrom gave his remarks. As he finished, the bishop watched a figure enter the chapel and find his way to a seat in the wings.

"President McKay, I see you back there hiding." The crowd snickered. "Would you mind sharing a few words?"

McKay was Huntsville's favorite son. He was an accomplished educator and scholar but was known by members around the world as second counselor in the First Presidency of the Church of Jesus

Christ of Latter-day Saints. At seventy-two-years of age, his step was slower than many had remembered it. He took hesitant steps up to the podium, his thick white hair gleaming like soft snow, his warm smile looking over the crowd before speaking.

"I am honored to pay tribute to this fine young man, Chester Bailey," he began. "While I've only known the Baileys for a brief time, I know of their goodness. That's why I am not surprised to learn how Chester died, sacrificing himself to save the life of another. He did as we are admonished to do: *For greater love hath no man than this, that a man lay down his life for his friends.* We're sad for his family, and for the future he will not have here on this earth. I'm sure he would have spent his life doing good, just like his parents."

"Yet, despite the circumstance of our being here today, and the sadness we feel for losing this fine young man, I can't help but point out that it is a wonderful day. It's wonderful because we know and have sure hope that we will see Chester again and that he is still busy helping others on the other side of the veil. It's wonderful that we have the freedom to join together and worship, as we are doing here today for Chester, as well as for the hundreds of thousands of other young men and women who have paid the ultimate price to protect this great privilege. This privilege we do not, and should not, take lightly. It is one that our forefathers also paid a great price to protect.

"Today is a historic day. We celebrate the end of hostilities between Japan and the Allied forces. Chester Bailey would want us to cherish that peace and hold to the joy of it close. I hope it's a lasting peace. May the good Lord bless us that we will never have to face such a crisis again."

CHAPTER 90
August 15, 1945
Hunstville, Utah

After the memorial service, Billie sat and talked at Ella's kitchen table, just the two of them, for the first time in years. Hours passed, then Ella looked out the window for Hank. "Where has Hank been this whole time?" Ella frowned, her palms resting on the table as she looked around for him.

"He's over at my grandma's, of course," Billie laughed. "She made him a fresh gooseberry pie. He said he's been craving that for a long time, and Grandma is happy to cook for someone."

"I'm sure Hank is happy to have someone cook for him," Ella added.

"I think he's looking pretty good," Billie said. "You said he was super skinny?"

"Oh Billie. He was *really* bad when he first got home. He put on weight in the hospital, but being home has made all the difference. He's always outside working on some project or another, which has helped his stamina, and he's always eating," Ella said.

"How's he doing otherwise?"

"He keeps to himself, but most days he does okay. At first, I wondered if they discharged him too soon, but he seems to be doing better now."

"What he saw... tell me again, the name of that concentration camp? Has he talked much about it?"

"It's called Mauthausen. He's mentioned it only once."

"That had to be terrifying."

"Sometimes you can just look at him, and you know his mind is somewhere else."

"He won't even tell you?" Billie scolded herself for the way her heart fluttered, and a knot clenched her stomach at the idea of how lost Hank was, how he may never be the same again.

"I get little glimpses here or there, but mostly he keeps it all to himself." Ella looked down.

"I could not believe it when you told me about what happened with his former guard. What an outrageous thing to happen to the poor guy."

"Billie, I've never seen Hank so angry. I had to stop him from tearing the man apart," Ella said.

Billie winced. She knew what anger was. Maybe now, after all these years, he'd finally understand her. A hot tear burned in the corner of her eye, and she flicked it away before Ella noticed.

"I was terrified just standing there, watching it all unfold," Ella said. "I'll never know what he went through, but the suffering it caused him just to see Werner's face again, well..."

"Werner? That was his name?" Billie asked.

"Yeah."

"How would you know that?"

"He was my patient on the amputee ward," Ella lifted her hands and shrugged.

"Why didn't you ask to be reassigned or something?"

"I could have, but I'm glad I didn't," Ella replied. "He's actually a very interesting man."

"Ella Meyer, do you realize what you're saying?"

"I know, I know. It looks bad; but he is a fascinating man, and it was so interesting to find out about what happened in Germany from his perspective," Ella said.

"Does Hank know that you find him to be a 'fascinating man'?" Billie snorted, raising an eyebrow.

"No. And if Hank ever found out, he would lose his mind, so please don't say anything. Promise me?"

"Why on earth would you make friends with this guy?"

"He's not the enemy, and…" Ella looked for the right words. "…I was just curious. He spoke German; I speak German. I was really the only nurse who could help him. But by the end of the shift, it seemed like we were destined to talk to each other."

"And it doesn't bother you that he treated Hank so badly?"

"Of course it does. He never denied he was cruel to Hank. But honestly, I think he's a changed man. I really can't see him doing anything like that now."

"He admitted he was cruel?" Billie tilted her head, narrowing her eyes in doubt.

"Oh, yes," Ella said. "He was cruel to Hank. No way to deny it."

Billie gave a puzzled look as she listened to Ella.

"After they forced all the POWs at Bushnell to watch the concentration camp footage, he wanted to give up his German citizenship. He had met many of the locals up in Brigham City, and he was amazed at how kind they were. At first, he thought they were acting or faking it somehow. Eventually, something just changed in him, especially after all he had read about what the Nazis did. He was sickened by it. That's why it's so incredible these two crossed paths like they did, and that they talked it out."

Billie watched her friend, the passion for this story a subtle storm beneath her eyes and jaw.

"It kills me to think, Billie," Ella said, "that if Werner hadn't stumbled upon Hank, how much torment both of them would have endured, probably for their entire lives."

"What about Hank? Was he okay with talking to this guy?" Billie asked.

"We argued a lot about it." Ella giggled. "He wouldn't listen to me. He's so stubborn!"

"Not like you," Billie replied, just loud enough for Ella to hear. Ella ignored her.

"But after a letter from Papa, Hank thought about it, then went down to the amputee ward and sat and talked with him."

"I could never do that." Billie rubbed her temples, a tension headache blooming in her skull at the mere thought of letting go of a perfectly justifiable grudge. "Grudges are for life!"

"So maybe that's good, and maybe it isn't," Ella said. "But remember the nightmares I told you about?"

"Yeah. What about them?"

"They stopped," Ella leaned forward, "that very night after he talked to Werner."

Pursing her lips, Billie sighed. "That's a little far-fetched. He just forgives the guy, and his nightmares suddenly go away? Something else had to have happened."

"Is it any more unbelievable than anything else that's happened? I guess it doesn't matter what we think. Hank believes that's why they stopped."

Billie rolled her eyes. "Well, of course he does."

"He doubted worse than you did at first."

"So, Ella, tell me honestly. Do you like this Werner guy? Are you thinking this may lead to something?"

Ella turned a sharp look on her friend. "Like what?"

"Are you attracted to him? Do you want to get to know him better?"

"No! Billie," Ella laughed. "He's at least fifteen years older than I am. It's not that at all."

But Billie blurted out, "What is it that you see in this guy?"

"He makes homesick for Germany. I really want to go back. I think, most of all, I need to go to see my parents, and…" Ella's voice trailed off.

"Go to Germany? Be honest with me. Is the real reason you want to go to Germany so you can see this guy?"

"Absolutely not. You're starting to sound like me," Ella said.

"Sorry."

"That's not really why," Ella leaned her head on her fist, propping her elbow on the table. "I know it sounds childish but I just…" Ella wiped a hand over her face. "I need to be with my mama. At least for a little while."

Billie reached across the table for her hand. "That's a good enough reason."

"They won't let my parents come home unless they sign some stupid secrecy oath," Ella said, clearing her throat. "So, they may never come back. Billie, what if they get too old before I see them again? What about *Oma*? I haven't seen them for years."

"What about leaving Hank here all by himself?" Billie asked, then thought to herself, *What about leaving me?*

"He'll be fine. He's going to school at Weber College in the fall; that will keep him busy and his mind occupied. He has no interest in going back to Germany, even to see our parents, and I can't say I blame him," Ella explained.

"I can't blame him either," Billie added.

Ella stared at the floor, then looked right in Billie's eyes. "So, what about you, Billie? How's your love life? Why haven't you dated anyone for a while?"

"I'm just tired of being lied to. I don't trust men anymore."

"How so? Tell me what happened."

Billie sighed. "You've heard it before. Just when I think things are going well, they break up with me. Or they cheat. Or they just leave."

"Maybe you're choosing the wrong type of guy. You get what you settle for, you know?"

"Maybe I'm just too hard to live with." Billie bit her lip. "Yeah, I'm pretty sure I'd be a nightmare sometimes."

"You know, I think we're all difficult in some way or another, but you deserve better."

"There was this one pilot…" she paused. "I thought we were going to get married. He liked the same things I did. But I found out he was seeing two other girls on the side. I'm telling you, the guys who fly airplanes are jerks. Worse than women who fly airplanes," she laughed. "And they're nothing like the type of guys we grew up with. Nothing at all."

"Do you think any of the guys you dated actually respected you?"

"Ah… I don't know. Probably not. I just never thought about it at the time. It didn't matter that much."

"Guys take one look at you, and they're smitten," Ella said. "You have that effect on them, you know."

Rubbing the back of her neck, Billie stared past Ella out the window. "That's why I don't trust them anymore. That's all they ever want from me." she said. "I guess I'll have to find a guy who's willing to take on a project!" Billie gave a quick exhale and a half-hearted smile.

"We're all projects," Ella laughed.

"I have a ton of baggage. But take you, for instance. You seem to have a lot more guys paying attention to you, and I can't imagine you're carrying much on your conscience," Billie said, teasing.

Ella laughed. "Oh, please."

"But seriously, since you've lost all that weight, aren't you a little more selective? I mean, don't you feel like you don't have to settle anymore?" Billie asked.

Ella's back stiffened, and she laughed in disbelief, "I never felt like Tom was settling with me, and I never thought I was settling with him."

Billie looked at Ella, her eyebrows raised. "I'm sorry, I didn't mean to imply you were settling…"

"You've never had to deal with it, Billie; you've always been thin. But I'm the same person no matter what size I am."

Billie looked away a little frustrated with herself for getting Ella riled up.

"And once I lost the weight," Ella explained in exasperation, "it never crossed my mind that I should put myself out there to see if I could do better."

Billie tilted her head, her eyes squinting as she tried to understand. The silence lingered for a moment.

"I didn't break it off with Tom because I was shopping around. It's because Tom and I have both changed."

Billie saw a side to Ella she remembered but hadn't seen in a while. She'd forgotten how outspoken she could be. Billie thought it might be better to just listen.

"Since before Tom left, and while he was overseas, I always assumed we'd end up getting married. I loved him. Dearly. But once he got back, everything changed between us. I know I had changed. For one thing, I love being a nurse, and I'm a darned good nurse, too. I fell in love with nursing long before I lost weight. Now I want to teach nursing, if I can. But if I get accepted, then going to school means it'll be a while before I settle down. That wasn't the case when I first met Tom, and now he's not happy with how much I've changed."

Billie smiled at Ella, seeming to enjoy her new confidence and poise.

"There's also no doubt that Tom has changed. Aside from giving me ultimatums about my career, he's always so angry and cynical. That's not the guy I fell in love with."

Billie looked at her feet and suggested, "Aren't you glad you figured it out before you got married?"

Tears welled up in Ella's eyes. "He was my first love, Billie. I'll always cherish the good times we had together." She cleared her throat and whispered. "I miss the Tom I once knew."

Their conversation lagged for an awkward moment.

Feeling the tension, Ella changed topics and blurted, "Did I tell you Hank went on a date?"

Billie opened her eyes wide, wider than she would have if she weren't hiding disappointment. "Oh, is that right? Was it his first date since he's been back? What do you know about the girl?"

"Well," Ella smiled with mischief in her eyes. "She's a nurse; her name is Charlene. We graduated together," Ella said. "I don't think it went very well. When Hank was a patient, they would go on long walks around the hospital grounds, and he seemed to be happy being with her, but she couldn't actually date him until he was discharged. Then the other day, right out of the blue, he said he was going out with her."

"He asked her out?"

Ella cocked her head. "I'm not sure. I know her pretty well from school, so I wouldn't be surprised if she asked him."

Billie breathed a sigh of relief, then straightened herself. "What happened? Do you think he likes her?"

"He talks so little about what he's really thinking..." Ella said. "I think it would take someone else besides me to pry open that brain of his and get him to talk openly about anything that's personal."

"It sounds like he just wants some pretty little Mormon girl to make him happy, give him ten kids, and live happily ever after."

Ella gave her sidelong glance through suspicious eyes. "Hank won't get married any time soon. At least not until he gets over his crush on you."

Billie's jaw dropped. "He's never shown even the slightest bit of interest in me," Billie protested, "and he's never said a word to me."

"He's never said a thing," Ella said, "because you've always been with someone else. Like Chester. But believe me, he's had a schoolboy crush on you forever. I've known it for a long time. It took a few years and a brutal war for him to admit it to himself."

"Oh, come off it," Billie said, "even after how I've treated him for all these years?"

"He's always thought it was just good-natured ribbing, coming from you. He also has a pretty forgiving heart, if you haven't noticed."

"He's like a brother to me, and let's face it, I'm not his type anyway."

Ella sat up straight. "What makes you say that?"

Billie looked away. "All he's ever wanted was a straight-laced girl."

"How do you know what he's always wanted?"

"Look who he's dating. Isn't that Charlotte person a good little Mormon girl?"

"Charlene? No. That's a pretty big assumption you're making. I said she was a nice girl. I never said a word about whether she was Mormon or not."

"Well, is she, or isn't she?" Billie demanded.

"I honestly don't know," Ella countered. "Don't assume that's the only type of girl Hank is looking for."

Billie shot back, "So you think Hank will accept a girl who's a little... on the wild side? I don't believe that for a second."

"You believe what you want," Ella said. "I'm telling you he's had a crush on you since he was ten years old. Haven't you ever wondered why he never went on many dates, or why he never asked a girl to the senior cotillion?"

"I just thought he was shy," Billie said.

"He's definitely shy, but that's not the only reason," Ella admitted. "He's always compared every other girl to you. And they never measure up."

Billie's heart leapt. "If it's true, why hasn't he ever said anything? It doesn't make sense."

"Do you think he was ever going to butt in on you and Chester, his best friend?" Ella argued. "You were never available, nor did you ever show any interest in him. You were barely civil to him."

"I know," Billie choked up. "I teased him because he was always your 'holier than thou' little brother. I hated it. He stopped being like that when we worked together at the airport, but by that time, I never thought of him as anything but your brother. Not to mention he was two years younger, and well, wasn't my type." She shivered. "Back then, I was too caught up in flying and having a career and finding someone I felt comfortable with. I never believed I was a good enough girl for a guy like Hank. I thought I wanted a different kind of life than he wanted, and when my life kept spiraling out of control, I convinced myself it was the price I had to pay for freedom."

"Just ask him who he dreamed of the most when he was a prisoner."

"I think you're crazy," she said. "He would never have good memories of me. I was always making fun of him or trying to humiliate him."

Ella raised her eyebrows. "Believe whatever you want to believe. Honestly, if I didn't believe in who I think you really are, I would tell Hank to move on. But I think he still wants you, and I want what he wants. You need to decide if you want him."

Billie opened her mouth but shut it again.

A few minutes later, the doorbell rang. Ella hurried to the front door to answer it just as Hank came in the back door, startling Billie, who was still at the kitchen table.

"Hey, Billie," Hank said with a smile.

Billie's jumped and twisted around to see Hank. He closed the back door and asked, "Didn't mean to scare you. Is it okay to sit here?"

Billie smiled and motioned to him to take a seat.

"How's it going with you?" Hank asked with curiosity.

"I'm doing okay. How about you?"

"I can't complain," he admitted. "Ella tells me you were able to fly all sorts of nifty planes. How was it?"

"I loved it," Billie answered. "I'd do it again in a heartbeat."

"So, how many kinds of planes did you fly?"

"Oh, let's see," Billie paused, not wanting to appear too eager, though she knew the exact number right off the top of her head. "I think it was thirty-three, or something like that."

"What kind of planes are you talking about?"

"From bombers to pursuit planes. You name it, I flew it."

Hank grinned at her. "Which plane was your favorite?" He knew the answer but wanted to hear her say it.

"Oh, definitely the P-51!" she said. "But don't get me started; I won't shut up."

"We sure loved seeing P-51s escort us on our way out on a bomb run," Hank explained, "or on our way back in. But I only saw them once or twice." Billie watched as Hank's wry smile disappeared. He seemed to have flashes of haunted memories lurking behind his eyes.

"When did you go down?" she asked.

"Early February of last year."

"Yeah, we hadn't delivered enough planes to make much difference for the bombers until about March or April," Billie said. "February of last year. That's an awful long time."

Hank watched as Ella passed through the kitchen again. She raised her eyebrows and smiled, "I'll leave you two alone to talk shop." She winked at Hank and dashed up the stairs to her room. He gave Ella a slight, thankful nod.

Hank felt his cheeks blush, the heat creeping up his face. Turning to Billie admitted, "I'm completely jealous. We all dreamed of being in a Mustang, but you got to fly them. Are there many other women who could fly them?"

"A handful of us could, and they were all just swell pilots, every one of them," Billie beamed.

"Too bad you had to put one in the drink. That had to be scary."

"How did you know about that?" Billie exclaimed. "Did Ella tell you what happened?"

"All she said was you couldn't get the landing gear down, and you had to bail out, then your parachute didn't open."

"Yeah. That's what happened," Billie narrowed her eyes.

"Do you think it was sabotage?"

"I know it was sabotage. The lead investigator told me someone tampered with the landing gear. But the final report says nothing about it. It'll go down in the books as another plane lost due to pilot error."

"What do you mean, *another*?"

"There were a number of girls who had sand or sugar put in their fuel tanks. Some even had their cables cut," she explained. "I know one girl who was on her final approach. She had clearance to land, but a guy came out of nowhere, right on top of her, and killed them both. I watched it happen. Officially, it went down as half her fault."

"Wow!" Hank's eyes bulged. "So if you knew there were saboteurs trying to kill you, why did you keep flying?"

Billie didn't hesitate. "You knew you could be shot down at any time. Why did you keep flying?"

Hank tipped his head and raised his eyebrows in recognition. Both understood without saying one more word.

"Tell me about when you bailed out. What happened?"

"It was the scariest thing I've ever done, Hank. It was a miracle I survived. I shouldn't have."

"You didn't get hurt at all?"

"I broke my collarbone and had a pretty bad concussion, but other than a few bumps and bruises, nothing much else." She lifted both hands and shrugged.

Hank felt his heart flutter. "I'm sure glad you're okay. I can't imagine what I'd do if I lost you and Chester."

Billie blushed.

Hank cleared his throat quickly, then pointed to the front pocket of Billie's slacks. "Can I see those?"

"See what?"

"Your smokes," he said.

She hesitated; her neck flushed.

"Please. I want to show you something. I won't embarrass you."

She reached in her front pocket and pulled out her pack of Lucky Strikes. "Oh Hank, I didn't mean to get hooked on these. I thought I could quit. I just…"

"You'd probably be surprised if I told you I owe my life to Lucky Strikes."

She stopped, her hand in mid-slide across the table, the pack of cigarettes under her palm. "You…you what?"

"Years ago, when I was a lot younger, I hated cigarettes because of what it did to my Uncle Willy. He hated that he could never quit. So, I hated to be around people who smoked. But Don, my best friend at the prison camp, gave me a new appreciation for them. One day he wrote to the…" Hank flipped the pack of cigarettes to read the fine print, "the Lorillard Tobacco Company to ask for some free cigarettes. By some miracle, he got an entire box of Lucky Strikes at mail call one day. Ten whole cartons of them. Nobody inspected it; it just came unopened. In the prison camp, cigarettes were our currency, and Lucky Strikes were like gold, you understand? We traded cigarettes for food. So, when I see somebody light up a Lucky Strike, I smile and think, *they're smoking my brand*."

Billie smiled back.

Hank inspected the pack of cigarettes again before giving them back to Billie, then watched as she stuffed them back into her pocket.

"And while I'm feeling brave, I hope Ella didn't say anything to you about this, because she's the only one I told. A while back, I found out what triggered everything that led to my parents being arrested. So, if she told you, and you somehow think I'm bitter or angry with you in any way, it's not true," Hank said, then took a deep breath and let it out.

Adrenaline surged through Billie's body. "Hank, I'm so sorry. I've hated myself ever since I talked to that FBI guy." Her throat constricted, squeezing her voice, a flood of emotions bursting to the surface. "I didn't know...how could I tell either of you that it was me who betrayed you?" She leaned into her hands and sobbed.

He'd never seen her cry this hard. He reached out a hand to stroke hers but he drew it back.

"Honest, Hank. I didn't mean to say anything. I'm so sorry."

Footsteps treaded softly on the stairs.

Hank caught Ella's eye, and he gestured that everything was fine. She tiptoed back to her room, closing the door. Hank took Billie's hand and led her into the living where they sat on the sofa together.

Billie's voice quivered as she tried to catch her breath and explain. "I just wasn't thinking. They asked if I had ever seen any souvenirs you brought back from Germany. They knew you had been there. And it just came out. I told them I saw your little Hitler Youth uniform and the Nazi flag." Hank reached around her as she sobbed.

"I knew it was a mistake the instant I said it, and it's been eating at me ever since...after they arrested..." she sobbed. "I'm so sorry!"

"I told you, Billie, I'm not angry. How could you know what they would do with that information?"

Hank reached for his handkerchief from his pocket, but she waved him off and pulled out her own.

"It's pretty clear now. They were looking for any excuse to round up Germans, and as many as they could. You have to believe me, Billie. You couldn't have known. I promise I'm not the least bit resentful."

"Really? You don't hate me?"

"Not in the least," Hank said. "I promise."

"What about Ella?" she asked fighting the hiccups. "Will she hate me?"

"Oh, well, yeah. I think Ella will hate you for the rest of your life."

Billie laughed, wiping her nose with her handkerchief.

Hank had never been this close to Billie. He breathed in deeply to take in her scent, her perfume, her skin, her hair.

As they held each other's gazes, something shifted between them.

"Billie, did Ella tell you about what that happened at the hospital up on Brigham City? About the former guard at my prison camp?"

Billie gave a wistful smile, still wiping her nose.

"I've had to muster the courage lately to say things that I never thought I'd have the guts to say, but I'm not going to miss the opportunity right now to tell you this: I have literally dreamt about this moment since the day I arrived at the prison camp. I've dreamt that you and I could be alone together, just talking and enjoying each other. In fact, I saw you and me, right now, in a vision way back at the prison camp. I kept that memory in a special place so I could play it over and over again in my head. And when everything was so miserable... I want you to know that you helped get through it. More than you'll ever know."

Hank noticed tears leaking from the corners of her eyes, and she dabbed them away with the back of her finger.

"In my darkest days, all I had to cling to," Hank said, "...was a tiny, glimmer of hope that I would see you and my family again. When I dared to think of the future, never once did I envision it without you in my life."

Billie leaned in closer and touched his hand. Hank closed his eyes, took her hand in both of his, and brought it to his lips. A new surge of energy burst inside him. His hands and feet tingled, and exhilaration shot through every nerve in his body.

"My most precious memories were of you." He blinked several times, surprised at himself for letting the words come out of his mouth.

He watched as Billie fingered her necklace, then she gave his hands a squeeze. "I think you're the most amazing guy I have ever known. And I've met plenty of men, believe me. But none of them are as kind and funny and patient as you are. I think that's why I've always resented you, because..." she stopped to think of her words. "To be absolutely honest, it's because I've always been envious of you. I've always assumed I wasn't good enough for you. And I guess I'm a little competitive..." She tilted her head and smiled, somewhat embarrassed. "I just wanted to shut you out before you had a chance to prove I wasn't in your league."

Hank chuckled but disagreed. "Not true. You are out of *my* league."

"I honestly don't know why I was always so rough on you, but every time you were nice, or did something kind, I hated you more. Then

I hated myself because I never felt good enough for a good guy like you. When I survived bailing out of a plane and my parachute failed, I realized there had to be a reason I survived. But I hated that too; I had gone too far down this other path and didn't feel like I could ever get my life straightened out." She lowered her head. "I never knew why I survived until this very moment."

Hank took her other hand in his. "You know what? Despite how you've treated me, I've had a crush on you ever since…" Hank tried to stifle a laugh. "Remember that time we were playing baseball? You were playing catcher?" Hank chuckled even louder. "You stood there and guarded home plate with your life, and I mean that literally." They both giggled out loud.

"And that big, fat kid plowed you over and sent you flying?" Hank hooted and stopped to catch his breath. "I think it knocked you silly, but you got up and threw the ball in his face. I thought to myself, 'That's the kind of girl I want. Someone tough like Billie. Someone who would plant her feet and tell the world, I'm tougher than anyone!'"

Billie laughed, "I can't believe you still remember that."

"If you only knew… You eclipse everyone else for me. No one is as smart and determined and as stunningly beautiful as you are to me."

Her face flushed, but she breathed slow and steady. Here, in this small farm home in Utah where she had started, was a love she'd never allowed herself to dream about, a love she thought was always out of her reach. She had only to reach out and take it. Hank shifted his body to sit even closer to her. He whispered, "Will you give me a chance?"

Billie gave him quick grin, looking at him warmly.

Hank caressed her hands. "Will you give me a chance to prove that I'm not that annoying, self-righteous kid I was a few years ago?

She wiped a tear from her cheek and beamed.

"I'd love to spend some time together," Hank said. "Just you and me. Maybe go dancing or something?"

"Hank Meyer. I must be mistaken, but it sounds like you just asked me out on a date."

"I believe I did," he said. His posture straightened, and he tucked a strand of hair over her ear. Her warm blue eyes glowed.

"I always thought you hated to go dancing," she argued with a tease in her voice.

"I've never said I don't like to dance," he said. "I was always jealous that you wanted to go dancing with someone else other than me. And frankly, since you and I have never danced together, I think it's finally my turn."

"Touché," she nodded.

"So, tomorrow night, or the next night. Or any other night. How about we go to the White City Ballroom? Just you and me. Are you willing?"

She reached to embrace him. Hank leaned into her, savoring the warmth of her body as they touched. His heart raced as her arms wrapped around his neck, and she clutched him in a tight embrace.

A chill shot up his neck as her lips touched his ear and the warmth of her breath caressed his neck. She whispered, "I'd be honored to go absolutely anywhere with you, Hank Meyer."

EPILOGUE

In December 1945, Ella quit her job at the Dee Hospital and moved to Germany to be with her parents. The day after she arrived, Werner Sikkar came to visit. Ella introduced Werner to her parents. The meeting was full of stiff, awkward glances. He explained his encounter with Hank at the Bushnell hospital, and after a while, they warmed up to him.

Much to Werner's disappointment, Ella was true to her word to Billie. She had no romantic interest in him at all. She only found him interesting because of his ties to Germany, and although he was disappointed, he wanted to remain friends with his American nurse. Werner often visited the farm Karl had built from the ground up at *Oma*'s house. Karl and Marta even grew to like him.

Unemployment and food shortages ran rampant in postwar Germany, and as an amputee, few employers were willing to hire a man like Werner with his limited physical abilities. Karl taught Werner some of his tricks for planting a successful garden; how to achieve the biggest yield and how to preserve his crop for the winter. But it was too hard for Werner to manage on his own. Without the help of others, Werner was likely to starve if he stayed in Germany.

Werner applied to immigrate to the United States in the spring of 1946, citing his status as a victim of the Salina massacre. His application was approved as long he had a sponsor who was willing to assume financial responsibility for him.

Ella wrote a letter to Hank, explaining Werner's situation and of his need for a sponsor. Karl and Marta both wrote a letter endorsing Ella's idea, and offered to send enough money to support Werner; however, they said they would understand if Hank didn't feel comfortable with the responsibility of being the sponsor.

When Hank received both letters, he immediately replied.

Dear Mama, Papa, and Ella,

    I received your letters regarding your request that I sponsor Werner Sikkar to become a United States citizen and I am willing to help. However, Billie's dad has agreed to sign the sponsorship papers because he is in a much better financial situation than we are. With a baby on the way and me going to school full time, this is the best solution for everyone.

Billie wanted me to point out the irony of this situation. Both of you own property here in the states. You have never been convicted of any crime, and don't need a sponsor to come here. You would think the government would consider you ideal candidates for immigration. Instead, they are fast-tracking the application of a former Nazi!

Don't misunderstand, we know what you've told us about Werner, and we believe you that he has changed. But I guess it just goes to show you there's still no reason to assume the government will always act logically. We both got a kick out of the whole situation. We will welcome Werner and will do whatever we can to make sure he is successful.

Billie is feeling great. She is due in January; we'll send you a telegram when the baby comes and tell you if you are grandparents to a boy or a girl.

Love, Hank & Billie

For many years after the war Hank made numerous attempts to locate any surviving crew members of *"Plano's Pride."* A former POW held at Stalag Luft III reported he was aware of a B-17 pilot named Sterner, but he never met him. Hank wrote letters to the War Department, contacted groups representing former POWs, even contacted his congressman, but all attempts to find Sterner–or anyone else–had failed. Hank eventually abandoned his search, assuming all members of his crew didn't survive.

AUTHOR'S NOTE

The prospect of writing a novel never occupied my thoughts much, nor was it ever a significant goal or aspiration. I've always thought of myself as a non-fiction writer, and I was perfectly content with that. All of that changed when I was sitting in a quiet, contemplative and sacred space, minding my own business. In what could only be described as a revelation, the entire storyline of this book came to my mind. It was startling, as it came in a very clear and personal way. It was a remarkable experience.

When this book landed in my lap, I felt a torrent of emotions. Excitement. Fear. Anticipation. Exasperation. Humility. I couldn't ignore the fact that I was being given something that matched my passions. I love World War II history. This story was daring me to write it. So, I had to make a choice then and there. Write it or let it die. I had to commit to act on this prompting, or else the story would have left me. If I allowed it to die, I would regret it forever.

And here we are.

As with any other book I've written, I started with the research. I'm like many authors who love the research as much or more than the process of writing a book. This is my fifth book, and you'd think by now I would hire a research assistant, but that would spoil the fun, which is probably why it has taken me more than four years to research, write, and edit this book.

While I love making new discoveries, too much research can be a huge distraction. The challenge is to curate my research, and include only the most compelling, yet relevant discoveries. As with any book, most of my research has been excluded and put away for another day. Still, I tried to include as many of the intriguing bits of history as I could reasonably weave into the narrative of this book.

When I first started writing, I had in my mind a basic idea of Hank's character, and whose wartime experience I would use as a jumping off point.

Hank's character was inspired by my friend and *Stalag* 17-B survivor, Ray Matheny. He was born in 1925 and wrote about his experiences as a B-17 crewman and eventual POW in his book *Rite of Passage: A Teenager's Chronicle of Combat and Captivity in Nazi Germany* (of which I had a part in helping him get it published).

Several of Ray's experiences are depicted in the book. His combat training, his trans-Atlantic voyage, his miraculous survival after his plane was shot down, his interrogation, and the incredibly good fortune of being sent a case of Lucky Strikes. Some of Hank's experiences are not based on Ray's experiences. Hank's psychosis and PTSD are just a few of the differences, among many.

I've enjoyed many opportunities to talk to Ray. I will never forget the look on his face or the tears in his eyes each time he described his life inside *Stalag* 17-B: the hunger and deprivation; the eighteen-day, two-hundred forty-one-mile death march; his encounter with the rock quarry at Mauthausen and witnessing the massacre of Jews outside of Mauthausen. What Ray had to endure is beyond my capacity to comprehend.

But research can only help so much. To get a better insight into what Ray and all the other POWs experienced, I set out to follow Ray's path, from England to Germany and then Austria.

I wandered the rolling hills of East Anglia where remnants of RAF Thurleigh were among more than seven hundred operational airfields throughout the United Kingdom. I visited the lush farmlands near Stuhr, Germany. Based on a WWII survival map issued to bomber crews that indicated a black dot for each dwelling, I visited the very house I believed *Oma* Hildebrandt would have lived in.

I visited Austria to find the remains of *Stalag* 17-B deep within a densely wooded area near Gneixendorf. After a bit of searching, I located the concrete ruins of the decades-old prison camp. Today, the overgrown trees and moss-covered cement walls are all that physically remain. But there's more to this place than just concrete relics. I was surprised by the impression I felt that this was hallowed ground. It was a solemn experience that helped me better understand, if only to a small degree, the size and scope of the suffering in this camp. It was here that over sixty-six thousand humans—forty-two hundred of whom were Americans—were held against their will and suffered unnecessarily at the hands of *Kommendant Oberst* Kuhn. He cared little about what the prisoners were forced to endure, or that more than seventeen hundred men died there.

To try to come to grips with the distance of the death march, I traveled across Austria to see what it took for an emaciated POW to walk from Krems to Braunau. I also spent a day at the notorious Mauthausen Concentration Camp near Linz. I strolled through the prisoner barracks, the execution room, and crematoria, where each day fresh flowers and candles are placed inside the cremation ovens. Tens of thousands of prisoners were cremated here; worked to death according to the Nazi's systematic and premeditated plan.

Nearby is the rock quarry mentioned in the book and the one hundred eighty-six "stairs of death." Prisoners were forced to carry hewn rocks up these stairs until they collapsed from exhaustion. It was horrifying as I stood at the foot of this steep stairway, imagining how daunting it would be to carry a hundred-pound load to the top. If someone slipped or fell, it would cause a domino effect of bodies tumbling down the stairs. I could see why so many men jumped to their death, rather than endure one more trip up the stairs.

As for Billie, Karl, and Marta, I assumed I would need to create characters who would fit the narrative I had in my mind. But as I wrote and continued digging through journals and other sources, I was amazed to find the historical records of real people whose lives and experiences were incredibly similar to the characters I had envisioned.

The story of Karl and Marta Meyer is inspired by many families who suffered because of mistreatment from officials of the U.S. government. These were real people, like Arthur Jacobs, the Eiserloh family, Gunther Graber, Doris Berg Nye, and Peter and Franziska Greis. Their stories have been mostly ignored by historians, and I believe they deserve greater exposure.

Most Americans know of the shameful treatment and internment of Japanese Americans during WWII. In 1988, the federal government issued a formal apology, along with a check for $20,000 to all known survivors.

Few Americans, however, are aware that nearly eleven-thousand ethnic Germans were likewise sent to internment camps like Crystal City. Many were naturalized American citizens who were unjustifiably stripped of their constitutional rights. To this day, the government has refused to acknowledge responsibility for this incident, and no apology or compensation has been given, despite numerous failed attempts in Congress.

Sharing many of the same experiences as Karl and Marta is the tragic story of Mathias and Johanna Eiserloh. They were born in Germany and emigrated to the United States in 1922. They built a home in Ohio, and in 1929, went to Germany to visit their families. After returning to America, they joined a German social club. It was not a political club, but was more focused on German culture, food, and sociality. Two days after Pearl Harbor, Mathias was arrested at his work, his assets were frozen, and he was questioned about his membership in the German club and about his trip to Germany. After his arrest, their friends and neighbors treated them with "astonishing coldness." After two years of confinement, Mathias was reunited with his wife and three children at the Crystal City Internment Facility. Later, the Eiserlohs were deported back to Germany. Within weeks of their arrival, Mathias was beaten severely by the SS in their home in full view of his terrified wife and children. The *Gestapo* then arrested Mathias, and he was interrogated and detained as an undercover spy for the advancing U.S. military. His wife did not learn of his survival until months after the war, when he was discovered by the occupying U.S. Army.

As it relates to the oath of secrecy, hundreds of ethnic Germans were still being held at Crystal City and Ellis Island until 1948, three years after the war. Congressional legislation was proposed to allow all the enemy aliens to be released, but it failed. The internees pooled their money, and their lawyers forced the government to negotiate their release. As a condition, many were forced to sign an oath of secrecy, promising not to discuss their arrest, internment, and deportation. This secret oath is a big reason why many WWII historians are unaware of the German side of the internment story.

I would highly recommend Jan Jarboe Russell's book *The Train to Crystal City*. Her work inspired me to dig further into this incredible story and discover the original documents revealing German internment, and the secret prisoner exchange authorized by FDR. Mounds of documentation exist on this matter, and rather than cite every detailed reference, you can learn more from the German American Internee Coalition at GAIC.info.

The character of Billie Russell is a composite of multiple WASP pilots, like Byrd Howell Granger, Dorothy Scott, and Nancy Love, among many others. However, Billie's closest comparison to a real WASP would be with Betty Tackaberry "Tack" Blake. In a 2004 interview for the Veteran's History Project. She admits she was a "tomboy" who played baseball with the local boys. While Billie's character differs from "Tack" in many important ways, I hope those who knew Betty would appreciate Billie's grit, determination, and many other unintentional similarities. Betty died in 2015, just a couple of years before I started this book. I would love to have met her.

I've included many citations of the remarkable courage and bravery of WASP pilots in the historical notes that follow many chapters. However, I wanted to draw special attention to the incidences of sabotage that plagued these women flyers. While historical references about widespread sabotage is sparse, it was indeed a problem that caused these women pilots great anxiety and fear. I appreciate Ann Haub, the curator of the WASP museum in Sweetwater, for helping me with my research on the matter.

From the official record, we learn that WASP pilots logged over sixty million miles. We know of four hundred thirty-three accidents involving WASP pilots. Thirty-eight women were killed, seven suffered serious injury, and twenty-eight suffered minor injuries. Another three hundred sixty women suffered accidents without injury, but their aircrafts were somehow damaged. The number of incidences are statistically the same as those of their male counterparts, yet they were not under constant threat of sabotage.

In the historical notes after many chapters, you see some of the most compelling evidence that exists relating to sabotage, and how fear and intimidation resulted in many incidences of sabotage not being reported. We don't know why we are only learning about the extent of sabotage so many years later.

When the WASPs were disbanded in December 1944, the women were forbidden to talk about their contribution to the war, fearing that the Germans would exploit the "desperation of Americans having to use women" as pilots. Throughout the war, WASPs were never accorded military status.

After the war, the WASPs faded into history until 1977, when an Air Force press release announced that "women will be flying military aircraft for the first time." Many former WASPs spoke out to contradict the Air Force's own historical record. Senator Barry Goldwater led congressional efforts to retroactively give the WASPs military status. Opposition came from all corners, including the VFW and other veterans' groups, who claimed the WASP pilots weren't veterans because they couldn't be court-martialed. Fortunately, when the WASP records were released, historians could finally give these women the honor they deserved. By 2009, the WASP pilots had been awarded a Congressional Gold Medal for their service and had been accorded full veteran status.

As most WASP pilots are no longer with us, their journals and personal stories are coming to light, giving us new insights into what they endured. But for many WASPs, talking about sabotage was a distraction from what they accomplished. They were proud of their service, and who could blame them for not wanting the issue of sabotage to overshadow their historic contributions.

ACKNOWLEDGMENTS

I want to recognize Arthur D. Jacobs, Major, USAF (retired) and researcher into the internment of ethnic Germans during World War II. His website FOItimes.com first alerted me to the issue of German Americans being interred and deported to Germany against their will. His monumental efforts to set the public record straight deserve continued support and publicity.

I was fortunate to find the works of author Sarah Byrn Rickman, whose books tell the story of the WASP, WAFS, WFTD, and notable pilots like Nancy Love, Dorothy Scott, and B.J. Erickson. Her books are well-researched and highly recommended. I have cited her extensively in many historical notes and want to recognize her for the significant contribution she has made to the body of knowledge about these remarkable women.

I would like to express my gratitude to the late Ray Matheny and his wife, Deanne, for their kindness and patience. Ray has willingly given his time to share his incredible story with me. Many of those painful memories weren't dimmed one bit after seventy plus years. Yet he was always ready and willing to stand as a personal witness of Nazi brutality and the reality of the Holocaust. His real-life experiences and achievements—not just as a WWII veteran, but academically and professionally as well—far exceed any small honor I've tried to pay him here. I was able to discuss this book, and even give him this manuscript, before his passing on July 1, 2020. I'm confident his legacy will endure long after I am gone.

It would be careless if I didn't thank my wonderful editors, Dayna Shoell, Christina Perkins, Brooke Fenton, Kendra Lusty, and Elizabeth Wehman. Each has contributed their vast talents to help improve some element of this manuscript and get it ready for publication. I'm especially grateful for Abigail Swanson whose monumental efforts as a line editor truly brought this manuscript to life.

I am also forever grateful to my parents for being my first-hand sources. My father, Robert E. Toyn, was born in 1927 and served in the Navy during WWII. My mother, Joy W. Toyn, was born in 1929. They both remember well many of the historical events described herein. Both have been invaluable in helping me describe the setting and atmosphere of Ogden, Utah during WWII because they were there. They danced to many of the big bands at the White City Ballroom. They went to *Ross and Jack's* for a burger and spuds, *Farr's Ice Cream* for a large cone, and both were students at Weber College. While they were crucial technical advisors and proofreaders, I am most grateful to be their son, and to have been taught at their feet. I thank them both for their love and support.

Finally, this book would never exist were it not for the encouragement, patience, and long-suffering of my wonderful wife Danita. She read every word of the book aloud, adding another level of proofing to help improve the overall readability. Her love of reading inspired me to become an author. She is my eternal best friend and companion. I'm blessed to have her by my side.

BIBLIOGRAPHY

Printed Sources

Boots, Bikes and Bombers, Karen Brewster (ed.), (University of Alaska Press, 2012).

Carter, Andrea Kay. "Bushnell General Military Hospital and the Community of Brigham City, Utah During World War II." (Master's thesis, Utah State University, 2008).

Carter, Steve. "Patriotism and Resistance, Brotherhood and Bombs: The Experience of the German Saints and World War II." *International Journal of Mormon Studies*, 5 (2012): 6–28. http://ijmsonline.org/wp-content/uploads/IJMS/2012-5/2012-5-FULL.pdf;

Glass, Charles. *Americans in Paris: Life and Death Under Nazi Occupation*. (Penguin Press HC, 2010): 350–1.

Harding, Madelyn Cook. *Weber's WWII Memories: Remembering the Events that Defined a Generation* (Weber State University Alumni Association, 2004).

Jacobs, Arthur D. *Freedom of Information Times, WWII Internment of German American Civilians* online. https://foitimes.com/.

Matheny, Ray. Rite of Passage: *A Teenager's Chronicle of Combat and Captivity in Nazi Germany* (American Legacy Media, 2012).

Merry, Lois K. *Women Military Pilots of World War II: A History with Biographies of American, British, Russian and German Aviators* (McFarland, 2010).

Nichol, John and Tony Rennell. *The Last Escape: The Untold Story of Allied Prisoners of War in Germany 1944-1945* (Penguin, 2003).

O'Rourke, J.L. "Historical Narrative of the Crystal City Internment Camp, September 9, 1945." Record Group No. 85, *Immigration and Naturalization Service Crystal City Internment Camp*, File 217/021, pp. 14–15.

Orr, Joanne Wallace. "An Oral History, Women Airforce Service Pilots." *Oral History Project, The Woman's Collection*, (Denton, TX: Texas Woman's University, 2004).

Report of Aircraft Accident Accident No. 44-12-3-7, December 20, 1943, War Department, 21st Ferrying Group, Palm Springs, California.

RG-59 General Records of the State Department, Special War Problems Division, Subject Files, 1939-1955, Second Gripsholm, Spanish Photostat List to Instructions to Agents, Box 176 – ARC2173219 Entry A1 1357. Declassified NND917307.

Rickman, Sarah Byrn. *Finding Dorothy Scott: Letters of a WASP* (Texas Tech University Press, 2016).

Rickman, Sarah Byrn. *Nancy Love and the WASP Ferry Pilots of World War II* (University of North Texas Press, 2012).

Rickman, Sarah Byrn. *WASP of the Ferry Command* (University of North Texas Press, 2016).

Russell, Jan Jarboe. *The Train to Crystal City* (Simon & Schuster, 2015).

Schrader, Helena Page. *Sisters in Arms: The Women Who Flew in World War II* (Pen and Sword, 2006).

"Vittel." *The Holocaust Encyclopedia*; United States Holocaust Memorial Museum, Washington, DC. https://encyclopedia.ushmm.org/content/en/article/vittel

"War Crimes Testimony of Dr. Leslie Caplan, The Evacuation of Luft IV, 31 December 1947." http://www.stalagluft4.org/Testimony%20of%20Dr.htm

Digital Sources

"Administrative Repatriation Procedures & Evacuation and Disposition of Recovered Allied Military Personnel." *WW2 US Medical Research Centre* online, accessed January 3, 2021, https://www.med-dept.com/articles/r-a-m-p/.

"Betty Tackaberry Guild Blake Collection" (AFC/2001/001/47086), Veterans History Project, American Folklife Center, Library of Congress

"Capture and incarceration—Dulag Luft." *Ken Fenton's War* online, accessed January 3, 2021, https://kenfentonswar.com/dulag-luft/.

"Clarke, Susan P., 2nd Lt" *Together We Served* online, accessed January 3, 2021. https://airforce.togetherweserved.com/usaf/servlet/tws.webapp.WebApp?cmd=ShadowBox-Profile&type=Person&ID=153063.

"D-day broadcast." *"The Rachel Maddow Show for Friday, June 6th, 2014"* https://www.nbc-news.com/news/world/rachel-maddow-show-friday-june-6th-2014-wbna55367652, accessed January 4, 2021.

"Establishment of the Eighth Air Force in the United Kingdom." *The Army Air Forces in WWII* online, accessed January 5 2021, https://www.ibiblio.org/hyperwar/AAF/I/AAF-I-17.html#page645.

"Gestapo Methods of Interrogation Used in Norway." *British National Archives* online, accessed January 5, 2021, http://www.nationalarchives.gov.uk/education/worldwar2/the-atres-of-war/western-europe/investigation/occupation/sources/docs/3/transcript.htm, Catalogue ref: HS 8/852.

"History of Wartime Treatment of German from the United States and Latin America." *German American Internee Coalition* online, accessed January 3, 2021, http://gaic.info/history/timeline-of-related-events.

"Intelligence Report for 13 December 1943." *306th Bomb Group Mission Reports* online, accessed January 3, 2021. http://www.306bg.us/MISSION_REPORTS/13dec43_v2.pdf.

Oradour-sur-Glane massacre. *"They Got the Wrong Village: SS Troops Massacred Over 600 French Villagers in Oradour-sur-Glane"* Colin

Fraser for War History Online; https://www.warhistoryonline.com/world-war-ii/they-got-the-wrong-village-ss-troops-massacred-over-600-french-villagers-in-oradour-sur-glane.html; accessed January 3, 2021

"The Eiserloh Story," by Jacobs, Arthur D.; https://www.foitimes.com/internment/Ei-serloh.htm, accessed January 3, 2021

"The Forced March." *Stalag XVII-B* online, accessed January 3, 2021, http://www.sta-lag17b.com/forced_march.html.

"The Grabers." *German American Internee Coalition* online, accessed January 3, 2021, https://gaic.info/the-grabers/.

"Timeline of Related Events" *German American Internee Coalition* online, accessed January 3, 2021, http://gaic.info/history/timeline-of-related-events.

"Ulio, James Alexander, 1882-1958 Person Authority Record." *National Archives Catalog* online, accessed January 3, 2021, https://catalog.archives.gov/id/10573587.

"Utah Prisoner of War Massacre." *Wikipedia* online, accessed May 16, 2020, https://en.wikipedia.org/wiki/Utah_prisoner_of_war_massacre.

"World War II—Prisoners of War—Stalag Luft I." *Stalag Luft* online, accessed May 16, 2020, http://www.merkki.com/chumleyperk.htm